PRAISE FOR THE INSPECTOR DAVID GRAHAM MYSTERY SERIES

"Bravo! Engrossing!"
"I'm in love with him and his colleagues."
"A terrific mystery."
"These books certainly have the potential to become a PBS series with the likeable character of Inspector Graham and his fellow officers."
"Delightful writing that keeps moving, never a dull moment."
"This book is a MUST to read."
"I know I have a winner of a book when I toss and turn at night worrying about how the characters are doing."
"Totally great read!!!"
"Refreshingly unique and so well written."
"Alison outdid herself in this wonderfully engaging mystery, with no graphic violence or sex."
"This series just gets better and better."
"DI Graham is wonderful and his old school way of doing things, charming."
"Great character development."
"Kept me entertained all day."
"Wow! The newest Inspector Graham book is outstanding."
"Great characters and fast paced."
"Fabulous main character, D.I. Graham."
"The scenery description, characterisation, and fabulous portrayal of the hotel on the hill are all layered into a great English trifle."
"Inspector Graham is right up there with some of the icons of British mysteries."
"This is her best book, so far. I literally could not put this book down."
"Character development was superb."
"Please never end the series."

THE INSPECTOR GRAHAM MYSTERIES

BOOKS IN THE INSPECTOR DAVID GRAHAM MYSTERY SERIES

The Case of the Screaming Beauty (Prequel)
The Case of the Hidden Flame
The Case of the Fallen Hero
The Case of the Broken Doll
The Case of the Missing Letter
The Case of the Pretty Lady
The Case of the Forsaken Child
The Case of Sampson's Leap
The Case of the Uncommon Witness
The Case of the Body in the Block

COLLECTIONS

Books 1-4
The Case of the Screaming Beauty
The Case of the Hidden Flame
The Case of the Fallen Hero
The Case of the Broken Doll

Books 5-7
The Case of the Missing Letter
The Case of the Pretty Lady
The Case of the Forsaken Child

Books 8-10
The Case of the Missing Letter
The Case of the Pretty Lady
The Case of the Forsaken Child

THE INSPECTOR GRAHAM MYSTERIES

BOOKS 8-10

ALISON GOLDEN

GRACE DAGNALL

The characters and events portrayed in this book are fictitious. Any similarity to real persons, living or dead is coincidental and not intended by the author.
Text copyright © 2025 Alison Golden
All rights reserved.

No part of this book may be reproduced, stored in a retrieval system, or transmitted in any form or by any means, electronic, mechanical, photocopying, recording, or otherwise, without express written permission of the publisher.

Cover Illustration: Richard Eijkenbroek

Published by Mesa Verde Publishing
P.O. Box 1002
San Carlos, CA 94070

ISBN: 979-8313723365

"Books break the shackles of time - proof that humans can work magic."

∼ *Carl Sagan* ∼

"Your emails seem to come on days when I need to read them because they are so upbeat."
- Linda W -

For a limited time, you can get the prequels for each of my series - *Chaos in Cambridge, Buckeye Breakout, Hunted* (exclusively for subscribers - not available anywhere else), and *The Case of the Screaming Beauty* - plus updates about new releases, promotions, and other Insider exclusives, by signing up for my mailing list at:

https://www.alisongolden.com/graham

ALISON GOLDEN
Grace Dagnall

USA Today Bestselling Author

AN INSPECTOR DAVID GRAHAM MYSTERY

The Case of
Sampson's Leap

The characters and events portrayed in this book are fictitious. Any similarity to real persons, living or dead is coincidental and not intended by the author.
Text copyright © 2021 Alison Golden
All rights reserved.

No part of this book may be reproduced, stored in a retrieval system, or transmitted in any form or by any means, electronic, mechanical, photocopying, recording, or otherwise, without express written permission of the publisher.

Cover Illustration: Richard Eijkenbroek

Published by Mesa Verde Publishing
P.O. Box 1002
San Carlos, CA 94070

ISBN: 979-8752690754

CHAPTER ONE

UNDER A THREATENING sky the colour of burnished lead, Freddie Solomon urged his group of half a dozen tourists along the rough seashore path, toward the beach at the foot of the cliff. They chattered with expectation, excited that Freddie had secured "special permission" for them to be there. Only now, at low tide, was the beach even visible, and in just a few hours it would be claimed again by the same foam-topped waves that had battered the cliffs for millennia.

"Watch your feet, please," Freddie said, pointing out jagged crevices and patches of slippery rock. "I've never lost anyone on a tour, and I don't intend to start today." The group followed his steps, pausing on the higher rocks to let waves advance, then recede, before moving on again. At low tide, there was no real danger, except for the indignity of having to walk back to Gorey in trousers the lower legs of which had been soaked by the cold Channel, but Freddie wasn't averse to manufacturing a little faux danger to add to the frisson of the experience. So far, the group had faithfully obeyed his safety briefing.

Freddie turned and gestured for the group to assemble on a flat stretch of rock that emerged above the waves for only a handful of hours each day. Behind him was the equally temporary sandy beach, entirely dwarfed by its surroundings. For, looming above them like some misshapen, haphazard cathedral was the great cliff face known as Sampson's Leap.

"You've all heard the legend," Freddie began. "But hardly anyone gets to see exactly where it happened." Phones and cameras punctuated his presentation with a combination of old-fashioned clicks and soft digital beeps. "One hundred seventy-five years ago, almost to the day"—Freddie glanced at his watch for emphasis—"a man stood on that cliff top facing the most terrible moment of his life." He watched his audience, their gazes swinging up to take in the immense sweep of rock that filled the gloomy sky. Like a great tower at risk of losing its battle with gravity, the cliff leant toward the Channel so that a vertiginous awning of ancient stone hid its grassy crest from onlookers. Professional rock climbers rated it an eleven out of ten. A gut-curdling prospect, it had never been scaled in its entirety. The journey around the overhang to the top placed an intolerable strain on the human body and proved terrifying for the mind, such that it had never been ventured.

Once six pairs of eyes again fixed on him, Freddie continued. "It's a fate too terrible to imagine," he warned, "but let's try. There you are, running a moderately successful business as an apothecary, travelling between the islands, selling medicines, or"—he smirked—"a range of tinctures and potions of *supposed* benefit to one's health, you've had no trouble with the law, and many of your customers return again and again. So why on earth, on a day probably much similar to this one, in the mid-1800s, could you have found yourself accosted by an angry mob, dragged to the top of the cliff and, with a pistol pressed into your back, *ordered to jump?*"

To Freddie's quiet delight, one of the women in the group visibly shuddered. He enjoyed creating these tense moments of drama, although it was equally likely the woman's hiking boots had just filled with water and she was simply miserably cold. Behind her stretched the dark-green sea, moody beneath the gloomy sky which seemed ready to enclose them like the lid of a coffin. *How perfect.*

Flicking his gaze up to the sky, Freddie noted he needed to get a move on. "Had this poor man, whom we know as one Charles Villiers Sampson, committed an atrocious crime? Something *unspeakable*? Something truly *ghastly*?" The tourists imagined for a half-moment, then Freddie pressed on. "Could he have slain a clergyman, or locked his unfaithful wife in a burning house? Or worse still, betrayed state secrets to the beastly French?" His group enjoyed the barb, one he included only when he'd confirmed everyone's origin, lest he inadvertently put a Gallic nose out of joint.

"I'm afraid to say," Freddie said, drawing his audience in as though sharing a long-kept secret with the group, though there wasn't another soul for at least a mile, "that Mr. Sampson had to defend himself against accusations of the most heinous crimes, the kind that can stain the soul of a place." His audience leant in, listening for Freddie's thin voice as he laboured to make himself heard over the noise of the waves that beat at the rocks behind him. "You see, friends, Mr. Sampson was accused that day of *murder*.

"The magistrate informed a large crowd, gathered to watch the punishment, that Sampson was not just once a killer, or twice, but *thrice*." Appalled now at his own story, Freddie stumbled over the definitive fact: "Charles Sampson was convicted of the murder"—he almost choked—"of *women*." Even their phones were still as the six tourists huddled together, rapt and silent.

"The evidence was damning. The three young women were," Freddie continued, scanning the group before alighting on the youngest, a gleaming-eyed, blonde teenager, "well, no older than you are now. The townsfolk quickly established that Sampson was a deranged serial killer, bent on revenge." The group trembled at Freddie's use of the word "serial," deliberately chosen to evoke the psychotic, the unreasoning, the demented.

"Those poor, poor girls," someone muttered, only to receive quick, silencing glances from the others.

"On Sampson's final, fateful visit to Gorey," Freddie said, "he administered to them a special potion of his own devising. But this was neither a harmless skin lotion, nor a hearty expectorant. It was a deadly *poison*."

CHAPTER TWO

"IN THE MOST dreadful pain, the three teenagers were carried off in a matter of days. The last to expire, Susan St. Edmund, was the youngest and strongest, but her fortitude only redoubled her agony and delayed the blessed mercy of death." Freddie spoke sombrely, so that they might feel the tragedy of a sickly girl's final, miserable days, even now, generations later. "A whole week, ladies and gentlemen, of the most horrible pain and torture, and then came the end. Word was the women had rejected Sampson's advances."

Freddie led the group further along the beach, careful to keep them together whilst monitoring the time. Still smarting from his last run-in with the Gorey constabulary, he couldn't allow anything to go wrong. This recent side-hustle, giving tours and talks to visitors to Jersey, had been lucrative. Business had been brisk as Freddie's talent for embellishment and hyperbole had found eager ears. But the ever inventive and resourceful blogger, or "citizen journalist" as he liked to style himself, knew he had to stay vigilant. It didn't take an expert to see that in addition to the gloomy sky, he had to keep an eye on the tide. Indeed, only recently, a tourist who had attempted a similar close inspection of the beach had erred in his timing and had to be winched off.

"I mean, what would *you* do?" Freddie asked. "A quack, nothing more than a charlatan according to accounts at the time, stood accused of callously murdering three young women from respected families whose only sin was to have apparently preferred the hand of another man, or at least not that of the accused. Any of us would demand punishment, but remember, in those days, 'punishment' was swift and harsh, and the mob itched to exact vengeance upon him." Freddie rubbed his hands like a torturer welcoming his victim to the chamber. "Back then, they'd plan a public hanging perhaps, the centrepiece of a grand day out. There'd be music," he couldn't help adding, "a pie seller, and jugglers. Fun for the whole family." Freddie wasn't at all sure of the accuracy of this, but it suited his narrative, so he said it anyway.

A woman walked off to his left. Freddie feared losing the rest of his group. He picked up the pace. "But hanging was considered too good for Charles Sampson, a man once trusted by the town but now condemned as a multiple murderous misogynist. The magistrate agreed that Sampson was responsible and that the mob should have the outcome they most desired: swift and final justice."

Another shiver, Freddie was glad to see. An amenable bunch, the tourists raptly listened to his narration—nodding and holding eye contact, though he did wish the distracted woman would regain some focus. She peered at something, having taken a couple of steps off to the side, threatening the cohesiveness of the group as she did so. With dark, looming clouds and thundering waves, the surroundings were enigmatic and fascinating, to be sure, but Freddie had worked hard to develop an engaging style, and the guide/blogger/local historian was disappointed to see her attention wandering.

"And so, Sampson was seized by a braying crowd and frog-marched up to the clifftop we now call Sampson's Leap. The magistrate gave him the choice: admit responsibility for his crimes and jump, or face the rude justice of the mob, with much the same result."

"Is that what those kids were doing up on the cliff yesterday? Reenacting the scene?"

Freddie nodded. "Portsmouth University students, filming a project to commemorate the anniversary of Sampson's death. And no doubt earn some good grades in the process." He'd already interviewed the ambitious young director and a striking, gifted actress who would play one of the doomed women. "Very dedicated bunch. Really immersed themselves in the history."

"But why are they filming *now*, when it looks like it's going to pour with rain?" The woman who had wandered off returned to the group.

Confused, Freddie replied, "They aren't. There are five of them. I don't see anyone."

"But, over there," the woman insisted, pointing. The whole group strained to see what she was pointing at. "By those rocks. Someone in period costume . . . Or am I seeing things?"

"Could be a ghost," suggested another of the guests. "Haunting the site of the tragedy."

"Well, there have been sightings . . ." Freddie began, unwilling to pass up an opportunity. "But it's probably just flotsam. The students aren't filming down here anyhow, just on the cliff top."

"No, look. Someone's lying there, on the ground." The words halted the group, chilling them as surely as the knifing wind that had picked up and was beginning to slice through them. Certain now of what she'd seen and spurred on by Freddie's scepticism, the tourist began clambering ill-advisedly over the slippery rocks.

"Please stay with the group!" Freddie called, but he was ignored. He moved off after her. "Won't you please *wait?*" he cried more loudly, trying to catch up whilst he might still salvage control of the situation. A flash of brown fabric could be seen between the rocks, billowed by the wind. "It's just an old jacket or something," he called to her. "Things wash up here all the time."

Moving faster than was safe, the tourist could barely keep her footing, scrabbling along jagged rocks until she reached what looked like a collection of abandoned clothing. Then, her hands flew to her face, and she turned away with a scream, utterly horrified.

"Freddie!" shouted the oldest of the group, a German professor travelling alone. "Look at this." The zoomed-in image on his camera's display left no doubt. "You have to call the police, man. Right now."

CHAPTER THREE

"NO THANKS. I'VE got a wedding to organise." Janice waved away the form Roach wafted under her nose. "There's no way I can take on anything else. What about you? Just your thing I should have thought."

"Gosh, no. I'm studying for my exams," Roach said. "Haven't you heard?"

Janice smiled. She'd heard of nothing but, for weeks. Roach's preparation for his Detective Sergeant exams had become a team effort. If he were to pass, it would largely be because the entire Gorey constabulary had pitched in, Roach's role in the process being only a relatively minor one. Janice had been testing him during her breaks, repeatedly going over the questions Roach was likely to get on his paper. Detective Inspector Graham had worked with him on some of the more detailed investigative set pieces, whilst Dr. Marcus Tomlinson had been posing complicated forensic scenarios for Roach to assess. Barnwell had held the fort when necessary. If Roach didn't pass, it wouldn't be for the want of the team trying.

"Shall I give it to the boss?" Roach said, flapping the piece of paper in his hand. Janice paused what she was doing and looked sceptically at him over the top of her computer screen. "No? No, I suppose not." Roach dropped the form and watched as it floated onto a desk. "Tea? Coffee?"

"Coffee please."

Roach disappeared to the break room and Janice shuffled some papers. Since her engagement to Jack, she had had a hard time concentrating on her work. Her mother, who loved Jack almost as much as Janice did, was bothering her, not understanding why they weren't married already. "If you'd got yourself organised, you'd be done and dusted by now," she'd complained.

"I want to get it right, Mum. There's no rush," Janice had said to her over the phone that weekend. "I'm not going anywhere."

"No, but Jack might if you don't get a move on." Janice sighed at the memory and refocused on the crime returns she was submitting to HQ. Suddenly, bells went off.

"Red phone!" Roach yelled from the break room, quite unnecessarily. Janice pressed a button and picked up. Roach brought her coffee and stood by as he attempted to interpret the nature of the emergency call from her expression.

"Right . . . right . . . gotcha." Janice wasn't giving anything away. Roach drummed his fingers on the desktop, eager for news. "Okay, Sampson's Leap. Yep, I'll get a unit on it right away. Tell everyone to stay put until we get there." She paused. "Okay, you have their contact details? Get yourself out of there and we'll follow up." She put the phone down. "That was Freddie."

Roach's shoulders slumped and he rolled his eyes to the ceiling. "Uh, and there was me thinking it was something important."

"It is. Body on the beach under Sampson's Leap. A young woman. One for the boss." Janice picked up her cellphone.

"A jumper?" Roach wondered. Janice shrugged. "Bit of a coincidence with the anniversary coming up, wouldn't you say?"

"I would. What a great way to start the week," Janice replied. She called Graham's number.

"It's what we live for, though, isn't it? The unknowable, the surprise, the rush."

"Maybe you do, sonny, but I like my Monday mornings nice and peaceful."

"Filling in crime returns? Come on, Janice, you can do better than that. We've got a puzzle to solve, a detecting wizard to watch. The game is on!"

"Are you ever less than totally enthusiastic?"

"Almost never. Haven't you noticed?"

Graham picked up. "What can I do you for, Harding?"

Janice straightened as she prepared to give him the news. "Body, sir. Bottom of Sampson's Leap. Thought you'd want to know. What would you like me to do?"

CHAPTER FOUR

THE OUTBOARD MOTOR of the Zodiac thrummed as Barnwell inched it closer to the rocks. "Steady, lad," Graham said. "It's all of five degrees Celsius in that water, and I'm buggered if I'm going swimming this early in the day." Barnwell throttled down and watched the waves carefully.

"Little closer, almost there," Graham shouted. He was perched daringly at the front of the boat. "Angle into that gap, and I'll see if I can jump off." A steady rain had begun, the exhausting kind which took its time but eventually seeped through every piece of clothing until fabric slipped across slick skin, feeling as cold as snow. Ahead of them, amidst rocks, was the unmistakable shape of a prone human lodged between two outcrops. "Alright . . . One, two . . . *three*."

The detective inspector heaved himself ashore, landing awkwardly on one foot, then finding the other refused to grip anything at all. "Oh, hell," he groaned as he slid backward. Just in time, he reached out and grabbed a lance of rock that spared him the ignominy of an instant soaking. Clutching at gnarls of rock, he pulled himself hand-over-hand until his heavy boots met an easier, flatter plane that didn't slip beneath him. Regaining his balance, Graham stood up carefully and found himself just short of an area where rock pools formed during low tide, but which would soon be submerged by the rising swell. "Oh, hell," he repeated.

A young woman, alabaster white and morbidly still, lay on her back, her head turned to face the rock as though she might kiss it. Blonde hair was plastered to her head.

"Barnwell?" Graham was shouting. The sounds of the boat, the sea, and the acoustics of the cove combined to make it almost impossible for him to be heard.

"Boss?" Barnwell called back after a delay. He held the Zodiac in place, treading water whilst he waited for instruction.

"It's a girl. Twenties, I'd say!"

Barnwell blew out his cheeks. "What do you think?" he shouted.

"Got to be a fall," the DI said quietly to himself, glancing up to judge the physics of the incident. "Recent," he shouted back. "Get on over here."

Barnwell anchored the boat and waded through ankle-deep seawater to reach him. "Shall I call Tomlinson? Get a SOCO team out here?"

"Marcus might be ready to go the extra mile, and I mean that literally," Graham said as he considered the overland journey necessary to get to the spot where he and Barnwell stood, "but he's going to be outfaced by the conditions. We're pressed for time. These bloody waves are going to be a real problem very soon. Most of this rock and the beach will be submerged at high tide."

"How did she end up here?" Barnwell looked up at the cliff face that towered over them. It seemed to cradle the body, protecting it. "If she jumped off the cliff, she'd have been much further out, washed away even."

Graham looked around him. To his left, lay the beach; to his right, rock and the freezing water of the Channel. "My bet is she fell on the sand and was washed here. Look, there's no blood to speak of. But we've no time for a recce. We need to get her out of here, pronto. We've got less than half an hour before the tide'll be in. It'll take us with it if we're not careful."

But Barnwell was still focused on the body at his feet. "Why on earth is she dressed like that?"

The woman wore formal period costume. The front of her brown, ankle-length dress was buttoned to her throat and cinched in tightly at the waist before ballooning out in a voluminous skirt. The seawater had disturbed the patterned fabric to reveal a sodden mess of grey crinoline beneath it. The petticoats, normally stiff and bell-shaped, now lay across her legs like pale dead fish. Her fair hair was messy and strewn with dark blood but was still gathered in the remnants of a bun. On one of her feet, she wore a modern flat Chelsea boot, the other bare except for a wrinkled sock.

"Dressed up for a date?" Graham speculated, turning to Barnwell, who grunted as he recorded the details. "Some jewellery, not removed. Obvious signs of trauma . . ." Graham said, peering more closely. "But no major amounts of blood." Graham brought out his phone and quickly took photos.

A large wave approached, whipped up by the increasing wind. Barnwell had time only to call out, "*Mind*—!"

Graham shoved the phone in his pocket just as the charging sea swallowed him. He re-emerged, utterly soaked but still on his feet, and gave Barnwell a thumbs-up.

Barnwell, equally wet, returned the gesture before stating the obvious. "Okay, time to go."

Another large wave came in to batter them—a dozen buckets of ice at once, making them gasp. When Graham opened his eyes again, the woman's body was floating in shallow water. She had begun to drift away from him. He silently cursed conditions that seemed intent on consummately destroying any evidence. "Have you got the stretcher?"

"No time for that," Barnwell said as he grabbed the woman's ankles. "We're going to have to do this the old-fashioned way. This tide's in a hell of a hurry."

"Poor lass. What happened to you, eh?" Graham muttered before picking her up by the shoulders and carrying her to the boat.

CHAPTER FIVE

"MORNING, MR. COURTHOULD-BRYANT," Laura said cheerfully as she opened the library. "You're early."

The old man raised his flat cap in greeting and leant a little more heavily on his walking stick. "Got to get ready for the weekend, you know?" Laura looked at him quizzically. "The anniversary of Sampson's Leap! Got people coming from all over," the elderly man explained. His grey raincoat unbuttoned, Laura could see that, as usual, Courthould-Bryant wore a shirt and tie under a navy-blue cardigan, the buttons of which were covered with leather. Courthould-Bryant was a long-time Jersey resident, long since retired from his job as curator of the Jersey Heritage Museum. His interest in local history was undiminished, however, and he now sat on the board, often agitating against proposals for new developments in Gorey. "Change," he was fond of saying, "isn't necessarily *progress*."

"I want to be fully up on the whole story, and at my age I need to refresh my memory now and again. Do you know about it?"

"Local man killed three women, I believe," Laura replied. She walked around, turning on lights, powering up the computers. Courthould-Bryant trotted behind her like a little dog.

"Accused. He was *accused* of murdering them. But the details are a little . . . shall we say, *vague*. Things ran a bit hot, and although he was definitely killed, there was feeling in some quarters that he never got a good hearing."

"Different times, hey?" Laura said.

"Well yes, of course. There was virtually no public record of the case, and so a game of Chinese whispers got up, and now we have very little to go on other than hearsay."

Laura raised her eyebrows. "Are you suggesting a cover-up, nineteenth-century style?"

"I'm honestly not sure. But I do want to be well versed in the matter in time for the weekend. I'm scouring all the books in the local history section for . . . what do the kids call it? Ah yes, *intel*." Courthould-Bryant beamed, pleased with himself for successfully using the word.

Laura made to extricate herself from the conversation. "Well, I'll leave you to it."

"Ah, before you go. I've got some more of those—"

"Boxes," Laura finished for him. She suppressed a wince. Courthould-Bryant had been clearing out the basement of the museum and for months had been bringing her piles of documents to sort through, ostensibly to record on microfilm anything of importance. But most of it was random, undefinable, and unsourced. The contents of these boxes were interesting, possibly valuable, but when you've filed the tenth bill of purchase for a cow bought in 1870 for two shillings, it did become a teeny bit boring, even for a keen librarian such as Laura.

But Laura was a public servant. And a very polite one. "Sure," she said, plastering on a smile. "Bring them along, and I'll take a look."

"Marvellous," Courthould-Bryant said. "You're simply marvellous." He beamed again and, evidently forgetting the expressed reason for his visit, walked over to the library's magazine section to pick up that morning's copy of the *Racing Post*.

CHAPTER SIX

HIS FACE WREATHED by fragrant steam, Graham stood in the constabulary's reception area, still with a silver thermal blanket around his shoulders. "Another?" asked Janice. It had required four big mugs of tea before Graham felt his core temperature return to normal.

"Thanks, but I'd better not. Even for me, this is a caffeine binge. I know I need to be up for hours yet, but still."

"By all the saints, if this job puts me in that sodding Channel *one more time*," Barnwell complained, his damp hair sticking up in spikes, "I'll give up and join the bleedin' Navy."

"They'd be lucky to have you," said his boss. It had been another stout, exemplary showing from Barnwell, despite the enormous difficulties of carrying the young woman's body across the rocks and into the boat, then through what seemed like endless, pummelling waves as they brought her safely back to shore. Graham had been forced to cling onto the woman whilst Barnwell navigated the querulous water. "She'd have pitched into the sea without some quick thinking from you, no doubt about it."

"A mispers report came in whilst you were out," Janice said. "Guest at Bonner's hostel. Someone by the name of Jacqueline Prentiss claims she last saw her friend Mia Thorne at about six o'clock last night. Mia hasn't shown up to an arranged meeting. The description matches the one you gave us of your girl. I sent Roach over to the hostel as soon as I heard, sir."

"If she was staying at Bonner's, she's unlikely to be local," Graham said. "A tourist? Or from one of the other islands?"

Janice quickly told him about the film project, news she'd gleaned from Freddie Solomon, much to her chagrin. She didn't like learning *anything* from him. "The five students have made the hostel their base. Mia Thorne is one of them," said Janice. "Part of LeapFest."

"Part of what-fest?" Graham asked.

"You know, the anniversary thing of Sampson's Leap."

"The anniversary of what?"

"Um," Janice said, "the *leap*."

"Leap?" A memory flared in Graham's brain. It was extremely rare that he genuinely forgot anything, but there were many facts that didn't rise to the level of importance necessary to justify a stake at the front of his mind. Sometimes he had to dig a bit. "Ah. Yeah, Laura mentioned something. It might explain the dress," he said. "The victim was in Victorian clothing. Not the kind of thing you usually see women of her age wearing outside of a festival. But it doesn't explain how she came to be at the bottom of the cliff. Not unless she took method acting to a whole new level." Graham took another gulp of hot tea, relishing the heat as it hit the back of his tongue and his throat. "Right, Sergeant. Get yourself over to the hostel, pronto, and take the lay of the land. Report back. I'll talk to Tomlinson, see what he can tell us and prepare him for an identification. Barnwell, SOCO on site?"

"Yes, sir. They're combing the cliff top as we speak, but the rain is being a bother. Be a few hours before we hear, I reckon. I've also got the details of the tourists with Freddie at the time the body was discovered."

"Okay, contact the tourists, see if they have anything to add. And let me know if SOCO finds anything— signs of slippage, a struggle, anything we can use to determine the manner of death."

"You don't think it was suicide, sir?"

"I think we don't know what it is, Constable. And therefore, we need evidence." Something in Barnwell's subsequent nod caught Graham's attention. "You don't agree?"

"Well, no, sir. I mean yes, sir. I mean, I was taught that in police college, but in reality, things are different, aren't they?"

"Ah, the old 'if it looks like a suicide, treat it like a suicide' method of detecting?"

"Yes, sir."

"Lazy police work. Understandable when you are harried and pressured to investigate too many serious cases, but this is a big one for us. We must be seen to do our job thoroughly in order to protect the island's reputation and economy. Besides, I take pride in my work and absolutely refuse to do a half-arsed job. That young woman and her family deserve an investigation into her death that is detailed, respectful, and conclusive. If it does turn out that she took her own life, or there was an accident, then so be it, but if that isn't the case and she met her end in a more nefarious fashion, the culprit needs to be apprehended, the local community needs to feel safe in their homes, and her family deserves justice as some order of recompense for their loss. If we don't do a good job, we will deservedly find ourselves in hot water."

"And Freddie Solomon will be the one to turn on the hot tap, no doubt."

"Quite."

"What about Freddie Solomon, sir? Want me to speak to him as well?" Barnwell asked.

Graham's shoulders sagged as he let out a long sigh. "It *had* to be Freddie Solomon that called this in, didn't it? No, I'll deal with Freddy *bloody* Solomon. But I'll do it in my own good time. I'm going home for a change of clothes. Man the fort here, would you?"

"Will do, sir." Barnwell was more than grateful for some quiet desk work. He'd found the boat ride back to the harbour harrowing. Graham had covered the woman's face and held on tight to her body, but inevitably, the combination of rough waves and size of the small Zodiac had caused them all to be thrown around. Barnwell had found himself steadfastly focusing on the horizon, especially when the young woman's sock-clad foot determinedly kept tapping his own. The whole experience had been nauseating, and he was grateful for a breather to get his emotions under control.

As he walked to his car, Graham scrolled through his contact list. "Marcus, are you there?"

"To my infinite regret," Dr. Tomlinson replied as he paused mid-examination. "I had other plans for the afternoon, you know. Much more pleasant ones." The pathologist had been finishing an agreeable brunch with a friendly female companion when warned to expect that the rest of his Monday would be spent examining a body.

Graham waited patiently whilst Tomlinson had his customary moan before launching into the reason for his call. "What can you tell me so far?"

"Not much. Young woman, early twenties I'd say. This'll take a few hours more, but I'll tell you now, we're looking at fractures literally from head to toe. Consistent with a fall from a great height, and perhaps further injuries from secondary impacts."

"How's that?"

In the examination suite, Tomlinson screwed up his face and peered at the pictures Graham had sent him. "She might have rebounded off the rocks and landed again. Maybe several times."

"Oh." The ugly image of a woman's ragdoll-floppy body flying through the air, bouncing off rocks before landing in a broken heap, was an upsetting one.

There was a pause. "It's a shame you had to move the body so quickly. We've lost a lot," Tomlinson grumbled.

"We'd have lost even more if we'd waited. The tide was coming in. She'd have been washed away, possibly lost forever."

"Understood. But anything else you can get me would help."

"SOCO is on site."

"Right you are." Another pause.

"I suppose I should leave you to it, then." Graham hesitated. He almost ended the call, but couldn't help asking, "What's your gut reaction?"

"That you're right. You should leave me to it," Tomlinson replied. "I've got your number."

CHAPTER SEVEN

JANICE CALLED GRAHAM on her way back from the mortuary. "Yeah, it's her." She was returning to Bonner's hostel on the outskirts of Gorey, an old boarding school converted into a mix of dormitories and private rooms for the budget traveller. "Twenty-one-year-old Mia Alexandra Thorne. Blonde with blue eyes, a hundred and sixty-three centimetres. What's that, about five foot five in old money?"

Graham gave the sensation a moment to pass, that sharp and all-too-familiar pain with its sorrowful downward pull on his soul: the regret that a promising life would now go unlived.

"I've confirmed she was here filming with a group of four others from Portsmouth Uni. Two of them came to identify her," Janice added.

"Thanks for accompanying them, Janice. It's the second-to-worst job I can give you." He left the rest unsaid. The worst job—the death notification visit—was, in his experience, infinitely worse. "Who identified her?" He was lying on the sofa at Laura's, having just woken from a fitful nap, but Janice didn't need to know that. He stretched and yawned silently whilst she answered.

"Noah Stimms, one of the film students. I get the impression he and Mia were together. He's shaken, barely able to talk. The other was the film's director, Jacqueline Prentiss, also a student. She called Mia in as missing."

Graham jotted down the names and particulars in his notebook. "Who else is there?"

"The director's younger sister, Fawn Prentiss—she wrote the music and also acts—and Clinton Wells," Janice said. "'Clint' to his friends, apparently. He's the cameraman and sometime actor."

"No sound engineer? The bloke with the furry grey thing?" Only a month before, an episode of the crime drama *Unmasked* had been filmed just outside

Gorey. An exciting cross-country chase had to be expensively reshot because the furry microphone muff used to absorb the sound of wind had repeatedly trespassed into the frame, bringing the director and sound engineer almost to blows. The local Gorey constabulary had got involved, cordoning off streets and redirecting traffic, causing them all to grumble whilst secretly enjoying the excitement and a light break from their regular duties.

"Couldn't afford one, I suppose," Janice guessed. "The hostel manager said they used every discount and coupon they could. Tight budget, I expect."

"I can imagine. Alright, what state are they in? We need to question them."

"I'd give them until tonight, at least," Janice said. "They're super close. Mia and the Prentiss girls were friends even before college."

"We can't wait, I'm afraid. We have to press now whilst the iron's hot. There was a romance going on, you said?"

"Hard to be sure, but Stimms is in pieces. Collapsed sobbing when he identified her."

"Poor sod. What about the others?"

"Various. Fawn is staring into space," Janice reported. "The other guy said he's so angry he doesn't know what he'll do. Seems stable enough, though. The director is the one to start with, I think. Calm, together."

"Right. Thanks, Harding. I'll come down to interview them. Be there shortly." Graham sat up and brushed his shirt down, smoothing the crinkles and straightening his tie. "Any sign of her phone? There was none in her personal effects." Graham had been forced to perform the unfortunate task of rummaging through Mia Thorne's clothing whilst she lay in the Zodiac. Her phone would form the crux of any investigation.

"I'll look over her room, make a few inquiries. Jim's talking to the other guests. Everyone's staying put until we're done."

"Good. Anyone pushing back on that?"

"One or two people's plans got messed up. There was some aggro in reception earlier, a couple of Australian surfer types making a fuss, but Roachie handled it."

"Pay some attention to them. There might be a good reason why they're arguing. I'll see you soon."

CHAPTER EIGHT

JANICE SURVEYED THE common room that had been given over to the four remaining students of the film team. It was a gloomy scene. Noah Stimms, tall with twig-like limbs, slumped with his back against the common room wall. His hands raked his mousey hair, a small passport-size photograph of a couple mugging for the camera slotted between his index and middle fingers.

Next to him, his bulk splayed out on a thinly padded sofa, Clinton Wells—the blond highlights in his curly brown hair catching the afternoon light, his ample bearded chin propped up by his hand—had the big-eyed, motionless look of a man traumatised by events. He stared ahead at the flickering images of a wall-mounted television, the sound on mute. He was as still and sullen as a gargoyle, or perhaps a contemplative Buddha.

In the middle of the room, Jackie Prentiss, the film's director, sat in a wide lime-green minimalist chair that reminded Janice of the IKEA catalogue she'd recently been flipping through looking for items with which to furnish her future marital home. Jackie typed ferociously on her phone, her thumbs flying, whilst Fawn, her younger sister, sat at her feet staring into the distance, dazed and heedless, like a soldier after a terrible defeat.

"Fawn?" said Janice quietly. It took a long moment before the ashen-faced girl would even look up.

"No questions. No questions, please. I can't," was all the young woman said, waving her hand in front of her face, her dark, heavy curtain of straight black hair swaying whilst merging with her sister's clothing—Jackie was clad entirely in black—so that it was difficult to make out the end of one sister and the beginning of the other.

"Okay, no questions for now, but soon, we'll need to talk to all of you. Try to drink this, okay?" Janice handed Fawn a mug of tea. The student wouldn't take it, so Janice set the mug on a side table.

With the others equally unresponsive, their worlds shattered by grief, Janice was relieved to see the face of Jim Roach at the common room's windows. "Absolutely shell-shocked," Janice told him quietly after she'd closed the door behind her. "The youngest is only eighteen."

"Worst day of their lives by a mile, I should think," Roach said.

"The boss is coming down to interview them. Did those Australians calm themselves down?" Janice accompanied Roach through to the hostel's reception area. A world map dominated one wall. It was festooned with coloured pins representing the hometowns of a thousand or more visitors.

"They just got a bit upset being stuck inside, that's all. When I explained we weren't going to cancel a long-standing surfing plan of theirs, just delay it a bit, they were fine," Roach said.

"*Really*," Janice countered. "Can't they see that investigating the death of a young woman is more important than 'going tubular,' or 'getting barrelled,' or whatever it is they call it?"

"These guys are serious. See for yourself," Roach said, bringing up a website on his tablet. "Apparently, it's possible to make money from being a surfer, enough to get you through an around-the-world trip if you can get some online buzz going." Janice and Roach read the webpage together, finding that the pair of twenty-something Aussies—blond, tall, and provocatively handsome—had plans to commemorate the 175th anniversary of Sampson's Leap in their own unique way.

"You're kidding," Janice said, reading the blurb underneath a video. "Go ahead, play it."

Sitting astride their boards, out on the water just off Sampson's Cove, the two young men animatedly told the original story of Sampson's Leap, exclaiming at the remarkable choice Charles Sampson was given: jump to his death, or be thrown. The title of the video was "Righteous Waves at the Cliffs of Justice."

"When did they post this?" Janice asked.

"Two days ago. Look at the weather. Saturday was the only sunny day all week," Roach pointed out. "But they were planning to go out again today, and then on the anniversary at the weekend."

"Antipodean surfers with an interest in history? Seriously?" Janice remarked.

Roach laughed. "You sound like the boss. Personally, I think it was less about celebrating history than for the 'lulz.'"

"The what?" Janice asked.

"The laughs, you know."

"Try laughing after an ice-cold wave has smacked you in the gob and dragged you straight onto jagged rocks," Janice muttered. "Wait, what're they on about now?"

CHAPTER NINE

IN AN ACCENT that trod a fine line between the adorable and the incomprehensible, the tanned surfers reached the climax of their tale. "So, they marched him to the cliff face, yeah? And he's going, 'I'm not gonna jump! That's crazy. I'll die for sure!' But the crowd was like 'You got to, or else we'll kick you off!' So Sampson says a prayer"—the surfer paused for effect—"and he jumps!"

The video cut to a slow-motion shot taken as their camera fell through space. A blurry film clip of rock interspersed with blue sky and darker green water ensued.

"How'd they do that?" Janice wondered.

"Probably tossed it off the cliff on the end a rope," Roach replied.

The video abruptly cut back to the surfers slapping the water with their hands in amazement. Or appreciation, it wasn't clear which. "The dude survived!" they exclaimed together.

One of them continued. "Fell nearly five hundred feet, but he swam back to shore and says to the crowd, 'Haha! Whaddaya think about that, eh? God is on my side, and he doesn't want me to die! 'Cuz maybe I didn't poison those women like you all said I did!'"

"Wait," said Janice, frowning. "Is any of that remotely true?"

"Sampson did survive the first time," Roach said. "Look, they explain it further."

The video continued. "So, they grab him again, and the crowd's all mixed up, can't figure out what to think. People are on their knees, crying out, 'It's a miracle, a miracle!' Others are shrugging their shoulders, like 'Some buggers get all the luck.' But there's another part of the mob who aren't happy at all."

The other, almost identical surfer took over from his friend. "They're angry because they want justice, but this guy's still alive. They feel cheated. So, some bright spark has an idea and says, 'We need a do-over!'"

"No *way*," Janice exclaimed.

"They grab him, dripping wet, and march him right back to the same spot, but Sampson's feeling all cocky by this stage, so he says"—the Australian put on an attempt at a posh British accent before lapsing into his slow native drawl—"'I'll jump of my own free will, and if I survive, don'cha agree that'd be fair dinkum? It'd be natural justice—God saying I'm innocent.'"

"So see, Sampson's got his chest all puffed out, like, 'I'm gonna be fine, and then you'll have to let me go, no drama, no questions asked. Justice served, everybody goes home, end of story, yeah?' And the mob puts their heads together, and they agree!"

"He jumped a *second* time?" Janice found the story hard to believe, the Australian accents in the telling of it making it even more so.

"So, they all back off, and Sampson says his prayer again, takes a deep breath, and jumps . . ." The shot of the camera falling in slow motion through the air returned, but this time it carried on. Seconds passed before the screen abruptly cut to black. "And he smacks into the rocks like a ton of bricks!

"Silly bugger, talk about pushing your luck. Maybe the tide had gone out, or maybe he went off at a different angle, or whatever, but he's not so lucky this time. The mob starts cheering and yelling, and it's all a big party, and they're like, 'The first one was just a false start, that's all. Everything came out right in the end.'"

The second tanned, blue-eyed, shaggy blond took the story to its climax. "That Sampson fella lost out eventually, but you gotta give it to him, he was a lion. And so, on Leap Day, we're gonna do like him: we're gonna test our luck, like Sampson did. No, we're not gonna throw ourselves off the cliff, we're not crazy, but we *are* gonna ride Sampson's Curve! One of the biggest rides in Europe, and we're gonna take it all the way in! Here's to Charles Sampson, who went epic!" The video ended in a curtain of gleeful splashing.

"He still ended up dead as a doornail, you numpties," muttered Roach, pausing the video before it assailed him with ads.

"They can't back out now," Janice said. "They've got *two million followers*."

Roach peered at the tiny number on the screen. "The DI will be jealous. His new #GoreyConstab account only has six."

"Seven. I got my mum to join. I told her there'd be nothing on there about my wedding, but she still joined."

"Your mum's a brick." Roach put the tablet away. He nodded toward the common room. "Whilst we're waiting for that lot to thaw out, let's see if Crocodile Dundee's two idiot grandsons are in the mood to talk, shall we? They might have something to tell us. They seem to have a lot to say about a lot of things."

CHAPTER TEN

CONFINED TO THEIR room by the hostel manager after their earlier outbursts, the disappointed Aussies were still pacing around, bemoaning their lot, when the two officers arrived. "Oh, here we go," said one. "It's the boys in blue. We're in trouble now, mate."

"Not yet, but try calling me a boy again," Janice growled, "and see what happens."

The surfer peered. "Sorry, didn't know one of you was a girl."

"Here, it's pronounced 'Sergeant'," Roach said. "Do you two want to get in a better frame of mind, or should we have this conversation somewhere less comfortable?"

"Oh, it's all apples," the surfer announced. "Sweet as."

"Names?" Roach fired up his tablet.

"I'm Nozz, he's Zink."

The two police officers stared at them. It was hard to tell the two men apart. Wiry veins protruded along their forearms; there wasn't an ounce of fat on them. Below their board shorts, their blond leg hair bleached by hours in the sun curled to form a frenzied, furry covering. Both were tanned and barefoot.

"*Full* names, please," Roach said.

One of the men folded his arms, the other looked at the ceiling. He mumbled something as he studied a crack in the plaster.

"What was that?" Another mumbling. Roach put his finger behind his ear. "What was that?" he said louder, slower.

"Regis Nosworthy."

"Middle name?"

The surfer sighed. "Regis Viscount Nosworthy, 'kay?"

"Regis Viscount Nosworthy." Roach spoke slowly as he laboriously tapped out the surfer's name. "And you?" He pointed at the other surfer.

"Vladimir Anatolyevich Zynkovlev."

Roach stared at him, challenging, but Zink gazed directly back, relaxed, neutral. "Spell that for me." The surfer complied, taking as long about it as Roach had over his friend's name. *Touché*. Roach let it go.

"Tell us your movements from yesterday to eight a.m. this morning," Roach said.

"What for?" Nozz asked.

His companion tugged on his elbow. "Nozz, remember, mate, if we can't get out of here, we won't be able to try our luck before the water gets messy. Just do as they ask, alright?"

"Yeah," Nozz said warily. "Fair doos."

"We were on the boards in the morning, but then all that wind came up. It got epic," Zink said.

"I remember saying 'one epic per trip,' you know?" Nozz cut in. "It's our mantra."

"But it was too soon. Surf's all about timing," said Zink.

"Wouldn't want to go *epic* at the wrong moment, I guess," Janice added.

"Too right. So, we skedaddled. Hung about in the afternoon, fixed some dings in our boards, had a nap. Planned a few cold ones in the evening, but then Nozz meets this girl. She's a knockout, so I'm like, 'Fair dinkum, best give him some space.'" Zink grinned lasciviously at Janice.

"Who was the girl?" Janice asked, ignoring him. "Someone staying here?"

"Yeah. Classy chick," Nozz replied.

"What was her name?"

"Mia. English girl. She was here with some friends."

"Ah, yeah," Zink replied for his friend. "He told me *aaaaaaaalll* about her. They say a gentleman never tells, but that's not your style, Nozz, is it, mate?"

But Nozz had seen Janice's face fall. "Hey, what's wrong? I didn't mean nothing."

"Guys," Janice said, sitting on one of the bunk beds and gesturing at the one on the other side of the room. "Why don't you sit down."

The surfers accepted her invitation and sunk onto the bottom bunk next to one another. Roach remained standing, his tablet at the ready.

Janice looked at Zink. "So tell me more about yesterday evening."

Zink shifted uncomfortably on the blanket covering the thin, cheap mattress. "Like I said, we had come back after a day hanging out. There's not much to do here except eat and drink, so that's what we'd planned. But Nozz got off with this girl, right, and I just hung out here until he came back."

"What did you do whilst he was gone?"

"Just chatted to a few peeps. Listened to some music."

"Tell me about the woman. Did you know her?"

"Nah, just seen her around. Blonde, pretty." He looked at his friend, then back at Janice. "Just his type."

Janice turned her attention to Nozz, who was looking down between his knees at the ground, his elbows on his thighs as he listened. "So, tell me about the girl."

"Ah, yeah, she was grand. I saw her in the kitchen. Suggested we go for something to eat. She was an actress." Nozz paused. Janice lifted her eyebrows and he continued. "Ah, yeah, well, she was still wearing her costume, so I suggested she change first, but she said she liked to stay in character. Bit weird, but okay. We went out, got something to eat, and she showed me where they filmed. It was just casual, like."

The quiet was interrupted by a snigger. Zink wiped his top lip.

"Got something to say, Mr"—Janice leant over as Roach showed her his notes—"Zynkovlev?"

Zink continued to grin. "Nah, not me." Janice lifted her chin and half-lowered her eyelids. Zink's leer vanished. He cleared his throat. "Ahem, no, nope. Nothing." Janice turned her attention back to Nozz when the sound of smothered laughter bubbled up from his friend. She immediately shot a frigid glance back at the brawny Australian. Zink's shoulders were shaking, his eyes squeezed shut. "What's so funny?"

"Nothing. I'm just nervous, that's all."

"About what?"

"Well, it's just the idea of Nozz and that dress. I mean, how could he manage it?"

"Zink." His friend banged his fist on Zink's furry knee.

"I mean he must have the skills of Houdini to get past that lot!" Zink burst out laughing now. "All those petticoats! Least spicy outfit I've ever seen!"

Janice decided further questioning of this man-child in front of her was beneath her. She focused on Nozz. "What's he on about?"

"Ah, yeah, well, you know, me and Mia, we were alone, and I thought I'd chance my arm. I mean, you got to, haven't you?" He shrugged.

"I see. And what was her reaction to you *chancing your arm*?"

"You know how it is. We both had a good time, and I came back to the hostel. Zink and I had a few drinks before turning in." He turned to his friend, who slapped him on the back, sniggering.

"Mia didn't come back with you?"

"No, she wanted to stay. Something about practicing her lines . . . or something. I wasn't that clear."

"I see, so you went out to the cliff, had *a good time*, and then came back to the hostel by yourself."

"Yeah, that's about it. Got back at eight."

"And was that before or after she fell nearly five hundred feet to her death?"

CHAPTER ELEVEN

AS GRAHAM PREPARED to leave Laura's, his phone rang. It was in his jacket pocket, buzzing with violence against his chest. Laura had made him install a vibrating alert that would wake an elephant, given his tendency to just ignore the thing. "Sergeant Harding?"

"Hello, boss."

"What's up?"

"Sir . . ." Janice said, slightly uncertain. "Um, I don't want you to think we're getting ahead of ourselves, but . . ."

"Yes?"

"We might have got something . . . or someone. We're at the station."

Graham shrugged his jacket over his shoulders. "Save it 'til I get there. I'm on my way, Sergeant."

Janice nervously awaited Graham's arrival. She was caught between a giddy delight in progressing the case so early and a lingering uncertainty she might have made a fool of herself. But she didn't have long to wait. Gorey wasn't a big place, and she soon saw the detective inspector's car pull up outside.

"What have you got for me?" Graham was on tenterhooks, thrilled at catching an early break.

"It's one of the Australian surfer blokes at the hostel, sir," she reported. "Regis Nosworthy."

"You think he's sketchy?"

"'As a pencil drawing' was Sergeant Roach's opinion. And mine, sir," she hurriedly added in case she appeared subordinate and uncertain compared with her younger colleague.

"I need a little more than that. What did he say?"

"He was with Mia at Sampson's Cove last night. Says she was alive when he left her," explained Janice. "But he told his friend, or let him believe, that Mia and he were . . . intimate."

Graham rocked back on his heels. "Aha."

"Now he's being vague, so we brought him in. We reckoned," she added, "you were best placed to establish the actual facts, using, you know . . ."

"My famed abilities for extracting information from reluctant people?"

"I was going to say something about 'scaring the pants off him', but yeah."

"Alright, let's get to the hostel to build a picture of the victim before we speak to him, though. Barnwell can look after him here for a bit."

"What? You mean lock him up?"

"No, just let him sweat it out over a long cuppa. It'll save us time in the long run. Any sign of her phone at the hostel?"

"No, sir. I bagged up her effects and brought them back, but there was no phone or computer."

"Hmm, alright. Let's hope SOCO comes up with something."

CHAPTER TWELVE

GRAHAM WATCHED THE four-person group for a few seconds before stepping into the hostel's common room. "They've barely moved since this morning," Janice said.

"You lead," Graham directed her. "Your light touch might be helpful in the circumstances."

"What did he do to her?" Noah Stimms fired at the detective inspector as soon as he walked in the room, instantly intuiting Graham's greater authority and senior rank.

Graham looked at this rangy, agitated, tufty-haired young man with cool eyes. "And you are?"

"This is Noah Stimms, sir," Janice intervened. "He identified . . ." Noah placed his hands over his ears and Janice let her words fall.

Stimms continued to prowl the common room like a caged hyena, snarling questions at the two police officers. "Did he try to . . ." His hands returned to his face over and over, wiping away tears or hiding from the sequence of awful truths he was creating for himself, moment by moment. "Oh, God, don't answer that." His fists balled, then he banged them together in front of his chest. "No, *do* answer that. I want to know everything."

"Mr. Stimms, I'm afraid that we don't know everything, or even very much, yet. It's early days, and this kind of evidence isn't easy to collect. We were unable to retrieve much from the scene, so we are very much relying on statements from people like you. Our current focus is to understand Mia's background in order to build a picture of what might have happened." In the silence that followed Graham's words, Fawn let out a small moan.

"You should speak to those Australians. I mean, you only need to look at them," Noah continued. "Reprobates. Nobodies," the young man muttered.

"Noah, do you mind if I give you some advice?" Janice said softly.

"Yes, I do mind," he said. He threw himself into one of the armchairs, hiding his face once more behind white-knuckled fists.

At that moment, Jackie Prentiss pushed herself out of her chair with a heave and approached Janice. "I need to get out of here." Piercings through her eyebrow and nose jiggled as she spoke. "I need to walk, and breathe, and . . ."

"Forget?" said Noah sarcastically. "Is that what you want to do?" he demanded. "How fortunate you are to be able to . . . *forget*."

Jackie turned to him. Shorter by at least six inches, she confronted Noah with poise. After a decade spent amidst theatrical productions, mostly children's and high school theatre it later turned out, Jackie was used to the vital drama of a play, and the wholly unnecessary drama of people who couldn't control their emotions. "My heart," she said, clutching at it, "is *shattered*, Noah. I loved her like the rest of you." She gestured around the room. "And I can't believe she's gone. It's going to hurt, deep down, for a long, long time. I know that for certain." She turned to Graham. "I'm Jacqueline Prentiss, Jackie. I'm the director of this film. It is . . . was . . . is . . . oh, I don't know, a uni group project for the four of us. Fawn, my sister, was helping out for fun."

"But we're just sitting here, doing *nothing* . . ." Noah continued to complain. "That's all we have done, all day."

"*They*," Jackie said, gesturing to Sergeant Harding's uniform with an air of authority, "are doing *everything* they can. You heard the pathologist earlier."

"Doddery old man," Noah said dismissively.

You should see him power through two bottles of claret, then give a boss lecture on anticoagulants . . .

"He's an expert, and he's got other experts helping him," Jackie said. "He told you that Mia died from massive injuries following a fall. Now *they*"—she nodded over to Graham and Harding again—"are investigating what made her fall. They'll figure it out, but they need time. Bawling and complaining isn't going to help, Noah."

"Look, sit down, you two, and tell us about the movie you were making," Janice said. "Were you interested in Jersey, or the story of Mr. Sampson, or . . ."

"Jackie's fascinated with him," said Clint, the heavy chap sitting on his own on the sofa. "We all are." He lifted a hand. "Clinton Wells, sound engineer and bit-part person," he said to Graham.

"It's a crazy story, like nothing else we found," Jackie agreed, retaking her seat. "The fact that it's a true story only makes it more compelling." Jackie quickly moved on from her angry silencing of Noah, glad to focus on her art instead of his pain. "Mob justice intrigues me—the way rumours spread and become *facts* in the public's mind, so very fast. Despite it happening one hundred and seventy-five years ago, there are parallels with what we see today in terms of how narratives propagate and their potential for manipulation."

"Nobody knew a thing about Sampson one day, but the next, he was somehow identified as this vicious, misogynistic serial killer," Clint added.

"Turns out that Jersey has history when it comes to harbouring men who like to murder women," Noah spat. "Maybe there's another one around." He collapsed in on himself as he sunk to the floor and began shredding his fingernails with his teeth.

Everyone glared at him except for Fawn, who still had the look of someone who'd rather be alone at the bottom of the sea, or adrift in space, than witness the unfolding of this emotional cataclysm.

"Noah, I swear to God . . ." Clint growled, long since exhausted by his friend's voluble distress.

"What?" Noah said. "I have to bottle everything up or you'll push *me* off a cliff? How can you be so relaxed?" he demanded. "At least back in those days, they *caught* the guy and meted out proper justice! They didn't mess around, those early Victorians. It's high time *we* got our own mob together. Let's light the torches, dragoon him, whoever he is, to Sampson's Leap ourselves!"

Jackie rolled her eyes, whilst Clint looked up as if he would find the strength to endure Noah's barrage amidst the stippled, swirling Artex on the ceiling.

Leaning over Noah's shoulder, the quietly authoritative voice of Sergeant Harding brought him up short. "Steady, love. I doubt you'd feel better with a charge of incitement to violence on your record."

"Eh?" Noah said, spinning his head around. The look in Janice Harding's eyes halted the tirade he was close to emitting.

"Everyone's tired, and upset, and this isn't going to get easier for a long time," Janice told them. "But one way you can help, right now, is to share every little detail. Do you think you can put aside your grief for a few minutes and do that for me, for Mia?"

Fawn spoke. "Yes," she said simply. Her voice was tiny, like that of a frightened child who didn't trust the world around her to be good, or bright, or happy ever again.

"Yes, of course we will," Jackie said briskly. "Everything. We'll tell you *everything*."

CHAPTER THIRTEEN

"WE'VE KNOWN MIA for years," Jackie started. "She'd dealt with a lot in her life. Her father is a big-time classical musician. He travelled constantly, but when Mia's mother died, he put his career on hold to take care of her. He'd always expected Mia to follow in his footsteps; she was an excellent musician. When Mia decided to study drama instead, he went ballistic. Didn't calm down for months. I mean, Mia was a *natural* actor, she could do it all—take the lead, comedy . . . Fawn and I were at school with her, and she was known throughout the county for her talent. Everyone wanted to be her friend."

"More than that," said Clint. "Much more. A future star. She could work a room, get everyone laughing, charm the clouds out of the sky."

"Someone special," Noah added, rocking slowly and crying again. "Beautiful, inside and out."

"Mia and her father didn't talk for a long while," Jackie said, "but then he relented and came to see our production of *The Cherry Orchard*. Mia played Madame Ranevsky. And he was, like, *wow*. Finally, he could see her potential."

Clint recalled the evening, his heart heavy with memories of their success. "He was overcome."

"He'd been so hurt and angry," Jackie added, "at the direction Mia had chosen to take."

"But he was there, in front of everyone, praising her to the skies, announcing how proud he was, and . . ." Noah couldn't get to the end without welling up. "Oh, my God, somebody had to *tell* him, didn't they?"

"We have officers with special training for that kind of thing. I know some of them, best people in the world," Janice said. "If you have to receive that kind of news, it's the least awful way, I promise." This seemed to help, if only slightly. "What about her mother?"

"Died," Fawn said softly, "when Mia was ten. Cancer, I expect."

"They sent her to the loony bin before that," announced Noah. "She tried to top herself. Mia told me."

"Her father didn't like Mia to talk about her mother," Jackie explained. "Toby Thorne didn't have any truck with 'namby-pamby rubbish' like, you know, depression," she added. "Which was unusual for a musician. Thankfully for him, Mia's mother died of an obvious, physical illness as far as we could gather, but it was after a long struggle with mental health."

"Did Mia have similar struggles?" Janice asked.

The four looked at each other. "Not really. I mean, she was a bit highly strung, but that's so common in acting, it passes for normal," Jackie said.

"But she *might* have been a bit crazy. That's what you mean, isn't it?" Noah said, boosting his own anger as he found yet another source of outrage. "Much easier for *them*"—he pointed at Janice and Graham—"if she was just depressed and threw herself off the cliff."

Clint moved quickly, but Graham read the signs and got there first. He put himself between the two young men.

"You can't *say* things like that!" With Graham in between them, Clint railed at Noah. "You *mustn't*!"

"Put the brakes on, son," Graham said, squaring up to the big guy.

Noah shouted, "People kill themselves all the time!"

"No," Clint said, very decisively. "Mia wouldn't. She wouldn't kill herself."

"But she *was* exhausted by *you*," Jackie spat at Noah, her composure suddenly evaporating. "*Fed up* with you and your childishness, she was."

Noah opened his mouth to argue, but then a realisation hit him. "You think . . . I drove her to it?"

"Of course, she doesn't," Clint said, calming down. "Look, stop arguing. We're all on the same side. We want justice for Mia. We want to know what happened to her."

"Oh, that's great! That's just perfect!" Noah cried.

"Noah, please, calm down," Janice said. Suppressing this emotional maelstrom felt increasingly futile.

"No, I appreciate it being made so simple. We can lay her death at *my* feet, apparently," Noah roared. "I may as well throw myself off a cliff, too, like Mia, like Sampson! That way, everyone can feel *so* much better!" He clattered out of the room, knocking over a chair and slamming the common room door so hard the walls shook.

"Infant," Jackie said once the reverberations stopped. "I can't understand what I ever saw in him."

"The tortured artist within," Fawn said. "That's what you saw."

"We all make mistakes; crashing, monumental ones at times," her sister said.

As he quietly walked back to the corner, although reluctant to make an overt scene of taking notes during a meeting so raw, Graham felt the need to produce a diagram. He wanted to keep things straight. As he did so, Janice shifted focus. She found out what the group needed—food, time alone, rest. She and Graham worked as a slick one-two: one providing distraction and nurture, the other focused and clinical until it was time to leave.

"I think we've done all we can here tonight," Janice finally whispered to her boss.

"Agreed. Let them have a good night's sleep and we'll come back tomorrow after we've spoken to the surfer."

As they left, Graham had a quick word with Roach, who stood outside the room. He nodded over to Noah, who sat alone in the lobby, ignoring the knots of happy travellers coming and going, oblivious to his endless, waking nightmare. "I wonder what's going on there."

"No idea, sir. He's a strange one, that's for sure."

Graham's phone rang. It vibrated in his pocket so loudly it would have travelled several inches if not constrained by 100 percent cotton. "Yes, Barnwell." Roach waited as Graham listened. "Right, thanks for letting me know."

"Anything useful, sir?"

"No, unfortunately. Nothing of interest from the tourists who found her, nor SOCO. They got nothing on the cliff top that could relate to a fall, or a fight. Nor did they find her phone."

CHAPTER FOURTEEN

"HE'S IN THE interview room?" Graham asked Harding. The sound of knuckles crisply rapping the top of a table could be heard in the distance. "Right. What do I need to know?" He readied his notebook.

"Regis Viscount Nosworthy," Janice said, consulting her tablet and ignoring Graham's raised eyebrows at the sound of a name which wouldn't suggest "Australian surfer dude" to anyone. "Age twenty-two, from Wollongong, New South Wales. Been backpacking for six months with his friend Vladimir Anatolyevich Zynkovlev. They landed on these shores last Tuesday and have been staying at Bonner's since then. Nosworthy says that he first met Mia Thorne on Friday night and walked out to the cliff above Sampson's Cove around seven p.m. yesterday evening. Says he left her on the clifftop at seven forty-five and arrived back at the hostel at eight o'clock."

"You should also see this, sir." Janice turned the tablet to Graham and ran the video of the Aussie pair telling the story of Sampson's Leap. By the end of it, Graham's eyebrows had disappeared into his hair.

"Right then," was all he said.

It had been a few hours since Nozz accompanied Harding to the station. Although he had been planning to surf waves out at sea earlier, he was now surfing waves of panic and nausea instead. "You the bloke in charge?" he asked Graham, tracking the detective inspector with big eyes from the moment he came into the room.

Graham sat down across the table from the Australian. "That's right. Did someone get you some water?"

"Yeah, but what I really want," Nozz said urgently, "is to call the high commission. Someone's really made a mistake here, mate. Things went and got *completely* bent out of shape."

"We haven't arrested you—yet—so there's no official requirement to alert your government, but we can notify them if you wish."

"Yeah, I wish," the tanned Aussie said.

Graham pulled out his phone and sent a text. "My officer will contact their twenty-four-hour hotline. I'll let you know what they say. In the meantime, my colleagues said you consented to an interview without the presence of a lawyer."

"Yeah," Nozz replied, his voice rising quickly, "but I thought I was just being helpful. Turns out they were trying to stitch me up!"

"No one's doing anything of the sort, Mr. Nosworthy. My officers are professionals."

"But I didn't do nothing, alright?" Nozz clenched his fists. "Just hung around with the girl for a bit. Had some dinner. I didn't push her off any bloody cliff, I swear blind I didn't!"

Hands open in an appeal for calm, Graham said, "I know you're a long way from home . . ."

"Too bloody right I am!"

". . . so this is a scary time for you, but Jersey isn't some banana republic. You have rights, and nothing fishy will happen. You just need to tell us the truth."

"You ask it, I'll answer it. Whatever you want," the red-eyed surfer promised. He rubbed his face with calloused hands, nails bitten to the quick, a plaster crossing the back of his hand. "But then, once we're all straightened out, you got to let me go, okay?"

Scanning his notebook quickly, Graham said, "You've made some ambitious surfing plans for LeapFest, I'm told."

"Yeah, that's one way to put it. And if I'd done something bad to that girl, I wouldn't be, you know, returning to the scene of the crime, would I? Why the hell would I go back to Sampson's Cove if I'd done anything to her? I'd be on the run! Do I look like a guilty man?"

"Her name was Mia," Graham enunciated carefully, slowing the panicked Australian down.

"Yeah. Mia. Sorry."

"Just tell me what happened," Graham said, starting a new section of notes. "Then we can move on. My officers tell me you spent time with Mia on the night she died."

"Yeah."

"And you met her at the hostel?"

"Yeah, three nights ago. She was there with some guy, so I thought 'fair doos', but after he wandered off, me and the girl—Mia—got chatting."

"About what?"

"This and that."

CHAPTER FIFTEEN

"SHE TOLD ME about the Sampson thing. That was why me 'n' Zink made our video and plans for surfing the cove. It's just a lark, you know, nothing serious. She—Mia—mostly talked about the project she was doing. She *loves* movies." Nozz caught himself. "*Loved*, I suppose I mean. Bloody hell, it's a bit much, isn't it?"

"Very difficult," Graham agreed. He took a different direction. "What movies did she enjoy most?"

As Nozz paused and thought back, Graham observed the man. "'Film nwah,' she called it. Didn't even know what she was on about. Anyhow, turned out it was old detective movies, crime dramas, black 'n' white, that kind of thing. I let her do the talking. I don't have much conversation, more an action man, me."

"I'm sure that was wise," Graham said. "And you had dinner together on Sunday?"

"Yeah, we hadn't planned anything, and, I mean, me and Zink, we're on a tight budget, like, but when Mia said she was hungry, I took her for a hot dog."

"Romance is alive and well, I see." Graham smiled genially.

Nozz smiled broadly back. "Yeah . . ." When the young man didn't continue, Graham raised his eyebrows. "Oh, right. Yeah, I wanted to show her the curve we're gonna surf," Nozz said. He began to draw circles on the tabletop with his forefinger. "Turned out it was right where they'd been filming their show, you know, for college. So we went there. She was wearing her costume. I thought that was a bit weird. Old-fashioned. All those frills, like she was in one of those fancy TV dramas or something. Lots of petticoats and stuff."

"Uh-huh," Graham said. "And then what?"

"We ate our hot dogs and talked about surfing and movies. Then she said she was tired, and it was getting cold . . . It's always bloody cold in England, isn't it?"

"We're more northern Europe here, but I won't argue with you."

"So, I left."

"You didn't walk her back?"

Nozz shrugged and shook his head. "She wanted to stay a bit longer. Something to do with preparing for final filming. You know, now I come to think about it, she was a bit funny. One minute, she'd be talking a hind leg off a donkey, then she'd go as silent as a mouse. It was weird. The dress, all of it."

"So, she goes walking off along the cliff top, alone, in one direction, and what did you do?"

"Went back to the hostel in the other. It was bloody *freezing*."

"That's about what . . . two miles, maybe a little more?"

"I dunno. I ran the coastline path back. Couldn't wait to get there. Had a few tinnies, slept in the dorm, got up this morning ready to go out on our boards. That is, until you guys turned up. Zink'll tell you."

"I see. Except," Graham said, "that's *not* the story you told earlier. To your friend."

"Eh?" Nozz started.

"He—your friend, Zink—indicated that you told him you'd been intimate with Ms. Thorne."

Nozz shifted in his seat. "Well, yeah, um, I didn't *tell* him as such, not in so many words."

"But you implied it."

"Eh?"

Graham sighed. "You let him *think* that you'd had relations with Ms. Thorne."

"Relations?" Pink spots appeared on Nozz's cheeks. "What, you mean a bit of naughty?" Then, to Graham's visceral distaste, he started to laugh. "You got to understand. That was just for Zink's benefit. I mean, she was *beautiful*, like an actress . . ."

"She *was* an actress," Graham pointed out, his temper coming to a simmer.

"Well, exactly, I reckoned it'd be fun if Zink thought I'd, you know . . ." Nozz trailed off, sensing that something was wrong but not quite understanding what it was. "I had to hold my end up, didn't I? It's what we guys do . . ." He started to stumble. "Don't we?"

Graham stared at him.

"If I made Zink think I was some kinda Casanova . . ." Nozz's face bloomed then. He finally understood that he was digging himself a very deep hole and that he should stop before it collapsed in on top of him. He trailed off. "Ah, yeah . . . I see what you mean."

CHAPTER SIXTEEN

GRAHAM PUSHED AWAY his notepad. "You misled a pair of experienced officers who were investigating an unexplained death so that you'd look like The Big Man in front of your friend?"

"I'm a bloody idiot," Nozz said. He looked down at his hands and picked at the Band-Aid.

"No further evidence required on that score."

"But I didn't lie. I didn't."

"Semantics," Graham grunted.

"Seman—what?"

"Never mind."

"And I didn't know she was dead."

"And that makes it alright, does it?" Graham leant forward, his forearms on the table. He scrutinised the young, wide-eyed, tanned visage in front of him. "So, what *actually* did happen?"

"Bit of this, bit of that," Nozz said, not daring to smile. "But it didn't get heavy. Nothing her dad would throw *me* off a cliff for. She had that beast of a dress on for starters. And it was too cold. Look, it was no big deal, just some fooling around." A remote spot, Sampson's Leap was ideal for youthful shenanigans. "I saw her later, back at the hostel," Nozz finished. "She'd changed her clothes by then. Can't blame her, right? Must be difficult to move around in those things."

"Say I believe you . . ."

"I believe you," Nozz said at once.

"What I mean is *if* I believe you. Assuming I do, tell me when you saw Mia back at the hostel," Graham said. There were no reports of Mia being seen in the hostel later than early evening.

Nozz looked around the room as though the information he was scouring his memory for might be found in the corners. "I saw her . . ." Nozz began, but then found he doubted himself. "Wait, *did* I see her again?" Unwittingly, he brought Graham's simmer close to a boil again.

"Think carefully, now," the DI recommended, his patience already drained by this inept, bumbling, not-very-bright Lothario. "Take your time."

"Zink scored some Brisbane Bitter, you see. Christ knows where from; he's like a wizard sometimes, finding things from back home that we miss, like his favourite biscuits, and . . ."

"Mr. Nosworthy," Graham said, "get to the point, and stay there."

Nozz coughed. "We had a couple of cold ones before turning in."

"A couple?" Graham said, making the inevitable note.

Another cough.

"How many?" Graham probed.

"Six," Nozz mumbled. "Each."

"So, you had an impromptu hot dog with an attractive woman," Graham summed up, "enjoyed some of Jersey's fetching scenery, left her to walk two miles home alone at dusk"—Nozz opened his mouth to object, but Graham didn't pause —"then got pie-eyed on your favourite swill."

"Not a bad way to spend an evening. Apart from, you know," Nozz conceded, his face falling, "everything."

"'Everything' being the unexplained death of your dinner companion at or around the time you spent together, the content of which you lied about. You know what that makes you?"

"I already said I was a bloody idiot," Nozz conceded.

"You're also a *person of interest.*"

"I *can't* be!" the Australian cried. "It must have been an accident, or perhaps she topped herself. You can't believe I *pushed* her. Why would I do that?"

"You wouldn't be the first man to react badly to being turned down."

Nozz half rose from his chair. "Now listen, mate."

"Sit down. *Sit.*" Graham spoke to the Aussie like he was a disobedient dog.

Nozz did as he was told, repeating, "But I can't be a suspect, mate."

"I disagree," Graham told him, looking around. "Hence, your current accommodations."

CHAPTER SEVENTEEN

NOZZ PLACED HIS hands over his eyes, then waved his arms in the air as though dissuading a jumbo jet from landing on the wrong runway. "No, no, no, you've got it all wrong, mate. She was off doing her own thing. I dunno, for the life of me, how she ended up falling like that. I mean, she wasn't drunk, far as I could tell. And girls like her, well, they're not really into drugs, are they?"

In truth, most of the details surrounding the circumstances of Mia's fall were still unclear, as was the involvement of the hapless Nozz. Graham asked wearily, "Is there anything else you can tell me about your time together? What did you talk about? Was she upset about anything? Angry with anyone?"

Besides being something of a cad, Nozz appeared to be not much of a sparkling conversationalist either. Apart from scattered pieces of their conversation, there was nothing useful in what he related. "She was excited about the movie, but said she wanted to do bigger things."

"Like what?"

The limited well of Nozz's memory, indeed his entire cranium, was running dry. "She talked about an audition—whether or not to do it, like. I wasn't really listening, to be fair."

"Alright," Graham said, tossing his pen on the tabletop. "So, you got back when?"

"'Bout eight, bit after p'raps. Like I said, I ran. Didn't take long."

"Then came your demolition of the twelve-pack with Zink, right?"

"Too right," Nozz said, caught halfway between regret at the resulting hangover and pride in his drinking skills.

"And I'll ask one more time: Did you see Mia Thorne again at the hostel that night?"

Nozz went through a wide range of expressions, screwing his eyes closed, blinking tremulously, muttering to himself. Then came, "I dunno. I thought I did, but it could have been some other good-looking girl. There are some stunners staying there." He looked up pleadingly. "Aw, they all look pretty much the same when you've got your beer goggles on, you know?"

"Steamed up, were they?" Nozz looked at Graham blankly. "How many of those young women were wearing formal nineteenth-century garb? Petticoats and *stuff*."

Arms aloft again, helpless as a newborn, Nozz said, "I had my wobbly boots on, mate. Wish I could say for sure, but I can't. I'm not gonna risk lying to you."

"You lied to Sergeant Harding," Graham shot back.

Nozz flashed an angry look now, the whites of his eyes showing. "I didn't lie," he said through gritted teeth.

"You implied an untruth; same difference. Look, sit tight," Graham said, standing and tossing the young man a notepad. "Write down literally everything that comes into your head. You can write, can't you?" Nozz nodded. "Once you've got things straight, we'll take a formal statement."

"When?"

"Tomorrow."

Nozz looked crestfallen. "What happens until then? I mean," he said, trying to brighten, "we're good, you and me, right?" Nozz regarded the detective inspector hopefully. "I told you everything, and I'll write down the rest, everything I can remember."

"You do that," Graham said.

"So, I can go back to the hostel? Zink's still there. He's got no idea what's going on."

"I'm pretty sure that's more or less a permanent state of affairs, Mr. Nosworthy. We're going to take a DNA swab and I've made arrangements for you to stay in the most comfortable room at the Constabulary Guest House."

"Where's that?" Nozz asked.

"You're sitting in it. One night here should be enough. Maybe two."

The howls of complaint, including some inventive turns of phrase, could be heard outside in the reception area. They ended when Graham sent Barnwell in for a chat, the detective inspector confident that, with his singular powers of persuasion, the burly constable would quickly prevail upon the young man to desist with his invective for the duration of his stay at their establishment. His confidence was well-placed. Regis Viscount Nosworthy immediately quietened his noise and prepared to wait out his incarceration in virtual silence.

CHAPTER EIGHTEEN

"WHAT DO YOU think, boss? Have we got a result, or did I leave the blocks before the starter's pistol went off?" Janice nervously watched her boss return from the holding cells.

"Mr. Nosworthy is not the cleverest creature in the ocean by a long shot, and his story is not an honourable one. It certainly bears more scrutiny, and that's enough to put him in the clink for a few hours. Whether he had anything to do with Mia Thorne's death is another question."

Satisfied she hadn't made a complete fool of herself, Janice relaxed. "So, what did he say?"

Graham walked through to his office and put the kettle on. He took a seat. Janice followed him and stood, waiting.

"We've got a young man who's expressed a romantic interest in the victim. He was, by his own admission, inebriated during part of Sunday evening, though he claims this was *after* his liaison with Ms. Thorne."

"Hmph."

"Mia told him the story of Sampson's Leap on Friday night apparently. It was after talking to her that he and his mate visited the cove to make that silly video. So, it's no secret that he's a fame hound and a mysterious death would do nothing to harm his viewership statistics, I suppose, especially one that echoes a strange and unique historical event. The parallels with Freddie Solomon in that regard are frightening, come to think of it," he added.

"I know we would all love to pin *something* on Freddie," Janice said, "but he has a solid alibi for Sunday night. I already checked."

"Poor woman," Graham muttered.

"Our victim, or Freddie's date?"

"Take your pick," Graham answered. "Anyway, where our antipodean friend comes closest to hanging himself is by altering his story, having first claimed 'familiarity' with the victim and now by denying it. The question is, is he covering up malevolent activity, or is he blindingly, inexorably stupid and as lightweight and dumb as the lump of polystyrene and plexiglass he surfs on?"

"The hostel manager said he and his friend were drunk and obnoxious last night. Singing loudly in the lobby, being a nuisance to the women. Did he mention that?"

Graham looked up, even as he resumed his note-taking. "Not exactly, but it fits a pattern." Janice leant over to see what her boss was writing; she thought she made out the word 'obnoxious,' but equally, the notes could have been those of a myopic alien. The page was decorated with a tangle of absurd squiggles and condensed abbreviations, an entirely personal script. "If I'd just been slapped with a heartbreaking refusal by the girl of my dreams," he said, "I might turn to drink, too, but I suspect this bout of heavy drinking was more habitual."

"Or maybe," Janice suggested darkly, "he was drinking to forget."

"Hmm. All it takes," Graham said, "is one burst of anger, one sharp shove in the back, maybe when she was already off-balance, or looking the other way, and—"

"Over she goes," said Janice.

"I find it hard to believe, though. He lacks the . . ." Graham wagged his finger in the air. "Killer instinct? He's a dimwit, Janice." He rose to pour his tea. It was eight p.m. "I don't know why I don't just hook myself up to this teapot intravenously and be done with it. I could stay up all night." He sat down again and returned to the subject of Nozz. "I thought he was as daft as a brush, if I'm honest. I'm struggling to believe a well-educated, beautiful young woman, talented, with a bright future, would decide to chance it with a ruffian like him."

"Not at all," Janice disagreed. "It may seem illogical to you, but the lure of the 'dangerously inappropriate boyfriend' is fascinating to some women." Graham looked at her. "So I'm told," she added.

"Well, she changed her mind, then," Graham pointed out. "He claims he didn't get past the barrier, despite buying a ticket." He squinted at his own choice of metaphor. It was something Barnwell might say. "He bought her a hot dog."

"Not exactly 'wining and dining,' is it?" Janice said. "More a ticket to see stand-up in a grimy working men's club than a flashy concert at Wembley Stadium."

Graham held up his hand. "This conjecture is nice, but it doesn't prove a thing. If Tomlinson finds his DNA in a defensive wound, we might be onto something. In the meantime, we'll hold Mr. Nosworthy pending a better alternative. We'll charge him with affray. Honestly, Harding, if it weren't for alcohol, the volume of reliable evidence conveyed to the police would probably double. How many serious crimes have gone unsolved because crucial witnesses were too blotto to remember the details? How many major crimes are committed because the perpetrators are drunk? If alcohol were banned, half the police force in Britain would be out of a job."

"You're not wrong, sir."

CHAPTER NINETEEN

"HERE HE COMES," Graham announced as he saw Freddie Solomon walk through the doors of the reception area. "Looking sheepish as usual." The DI was leaning against the doorframe of his office, mug of tea in hand.

"That'd be because I don't love being summoned to the police station," Freddie said. "I told Sergeant Harding everything I knew when I called in the sighting of the body yesterday."

"Yes, but my name's Detective Inspector Graham, and you haven't explained yourself to *me* yet."

"'Explained myself'? I've done nothing wrong."

"You say that so often, you should stencil it on your forehead; save yourself some time." Graham ushered Freddie into his office and closed the door. "Tea?" he said, lifting the lid of the steaming pot.

"Very kind."

Graham dropped the lid in place. "Actually, it would be a waste. You're going to be too busy getting told off."

"Told off for what?" Freddie cried. Stumbling across Mia Thorne's body yesterday had shaken him. He hadn't slept well and could have used a caffeine hit. He set down his satchel and flopped uninvited into the chair in front of Graham's desk.

"For taking a bunch of tourists to Sampson's Cove, near high tide, in threatening weather, against posted advice, without telling anyone."

"You'd only have stopped us," Freddie replied. "Besides, they weren't in any danger."

After giving him a sceptical look, Graham brought Freddie's attention to his wall map by tapping Sampson's Cove with a meter ruler. "Observe, Solomon.

The cove is at the bottom of a five-hundred-foot cliff, surrounded by treacherous rocks," he said, pointing out a blizzard of red crosses intended to warn people away.

"The tides are predictable . . ."

"But the *waves* are *not*," Graham retorted. "Barnwell and I almost got swept away when recovering the body."

"That was over an hour later when the tide was higher. I know how to do my homework, you know."

Graham snorted. "You know how to rake in money from naïve idiots. What did they pay you, anyway?"

"That's between me and them," Freddie tried. The exasperated scowl on the DI's face showed him the error of being opaque. "Alright. Eighty quid apiece."

"Good," said Graham. "That helps me set the level of the fine."

"*Fine?*" Freddie wailed.

"Civil trespass with reckless endangerment of some hoodwinked tourists. And all just to line your pocket."

"But . . . you'd still be searching for that poor girl if it weren't for us!"

"True. And you did keep the tourists away from the body."

"Yes, I did," Freddie said, proud to have done the right thing.

"And organised copies of the photographs they took."

"You're welcome." Feeling emboldened, Freddie asked, "So, no fine, then?"

"Four hundred. Payable immediately."

"*What?*"

"You're lucky it's not a thousand," Graham explained.

"A *thousand?*"

"Your stupidity put six people's lives in danger, you cloud-brained pillock. And your own, for what little that matters."

"Boss?" Barnwell knocked tentatively at the door. He always enjoyed listening in on the DI's lectures, but Graham was due at the hostel and Janice was waiting.

"Yes, yes, I know, hostel. On my way. Solomon, settle up with the constable, then go and be a nuisance somewhere else. And you're not to approach anyone about this case, got it?"

Freddie harrumphed indignantly, but after catching Graham's glare, picked up his satchel and shuffled from the room.

CHAPTER TWENTY

JACKIE PRENTISS WAS prickly from the outset. With her arms and legs crossed, her lips pursed impatiently, she was unyielding. Graham might have been arguing with a forbidding landlady (Mrs. Taylor of the White House Inn came to mind) rather than interviewing one of the victim's grieving friends.

"We just came here to make a movie. Everything that's going on, it's just . . . Well, it's turned into the worst week of my life, I can tell you."

"I don't doubt that for a moment," Graham said, keeping his tone level and conciliatory. "But let's go back. How did you come across the Sampson legend?"

Jackie regarded the investigating officer with puzzlement. "That's what you want to talk about? Nineteenth-century history? The film we're making? Not Mia?"

Something told Graham that his notebook would play a useful role, and so he scribbled as he spoke. "It helps to have context when I talk to someone new."

"It was mentioned in a book I read, and then I met someone from Jersey who knew about it. Once I saw the possibilities, I couldn't resist."

"Did you consider Mia for a leading role right from the start?"

"Not really," Jackie said. Graham listened carefully. Based upon what he'd heard, he'd thought Mia to have been an obvious choice. "There are a lot of talented theatre people on the course at Portsmouth. A dozen women auditioned. I gave them all a chance, but Mia is—was—simply the best. She was being considered for a West End play."

"But you condensed the three murdered women into a single role? Am I understanding that right?"

"That was for budget reasons."

"But you're not paying the actors, surely?"

"No, but more actors mean more filming, more time, more expenses. It all adds up," Jackie answered simply. "Also, the three women aren't very differentiated in the story. Mia was playing Alice Pritchard. We refer to the others for authenticity, but Sampson could have killed just one of them and the result would have been the same." Jackie uncrossed her legs. She was wearing all black again. Thick eyeliner ran across her upper lids, sweeping out in wings far beyond the corner of her eyes, the piercings that were threaded through her eyebrows glinting in the morning sunlight. Chunky, clunky industrial-style Doc Martens completed her rather threatening appearance. Next to them, on the ground, was a tan leather tote bag bulging with the detritus of her important director's life. A script, a blister pack, and scarf were among the many items that caused the expensive bag to morph into a misshapen mass.

"Tell me about Mia and Noah."

Jackie straightened abruptly. "You too?"

"Hmm?"

"You think he had something to do with Mia's death, don't you?" Jackie's posture relaxed. She planted her feet apart and sat forward. "Noah's not a very good actor, you know. I mean, he's the right height and build for Sampson, based on the newspaper sketch, and in the audition he—"

"Slow down, Jackie," said Graham.

"Eh?"

"The cause of Mia's death isn't even clear yet. Noah isn't a suspect."

"But . . . he *has* to be!"

"And why's that?"

Jackie began to check off reasons on her fingers, as though lecturing a forgetful child. "He and Mia were all over the place, he was *crazy* jealous of that Australian guy, he's been very worried he might not graduate, then, he turns on the waterworks for your sergeant at the hospital and since." Jackie rolled her eyes. "It's been like watching a B-movie or a daytime soap opera. You should look into him. I mean, seriously."

"Tell you what, Jackie, I won't advise you where to point your camera and you stop telling me how to investigate Mia's death, okay?"

Jackie blinked. "But I'm—"

"Go back and tell me about Mia and Noah. What do you mean they were all over the place?"

Jackie made a show of collecting herself. She sat back, crossing her legs again and brushing an imaginary speck from her jeans before continuing in a more moderate tone. "I don't know why, or how, but he persuaded himself they were a match made in heaven. Talked about settling down with her, the whole nine yards. But then," she added, "he was the same with me."

"You?"

"Yes, we went out together for a time." Jackie folded her arms and pursed her lips again, clearly unwilling to say more.

"And what happened?"

"Why is that relevant?"

"Because we're investigating an unexplained death and we need to know as much as possible about the circumstances that led up to Mia's death." Graham held Jackie's gaze and let his words hang.

"He left me for Mia. As you no doubt saw, he's no loss. You saw how he opened the valve to his emotions, turning the tap on full bore, flooding the group like an oilfield mishap? I had a lucky escape."

Graham let Jackie talk. He wondered if she would play the role of leader, if she'd try hard to hold her team together, but she seemed keener to diss her ex-boyfriend.

"So, was it a serious relationship? Mia and Noah?"

Jackie gave a harsh laugh, laced with judgment. "Seriously? When it came to *men*? Not Mia."

"She preferred things casual, then?"

"You could say that," Jackie said, stone-faced. "Hasn't anyone told you?"

"Told me?" Graham raised an eyebrow.

CHAPTER TWENTY-ONE

JACKIE BEGAN TO walk around the room. Graham squinted in distaste, but he didn't stop her. "Mia was a very up and down sort of person. Happy as anything one day, angry and miserable another. She could be lovely, but at other times she could be a right so-and-so. You just never knew which Mia would show up. And things had been worse recently for whatever reason—Noah's influence, probably. He could make anyone erupt like a volcano after years of dormancy." Graham remained silent, allowing Jackie to get wherever she was going. "But Mia was also fragile. Despite her beauty and magnetism, she was very insecure. A Marilyn Monroe-type figure, you know? She reached out to other people, clingy, needed their approval, liked to gather an audience around her. It made her feel better. I think it's why she loved performing."

Jackie paused for a few seconds as if checking to make sure that Graham was the right calibre of person to hear what she was about to tell him. "And she was like that with men. Blew hot and cold. Boys were like a drug to her, and she to them. She needed the attention, the conquest, the high. Then, when she had them caught, she ghosted them and went out on the hunt again. If they didn't come chasing after her, which they usually did but occasionally didn't, she'd start the process with them all over again. Does that give you an idea about Mia and Noah's relationship? So much wasted energy. It was exhausting to be around." Jackie's eyes flashed with righteousness, her jaw set, her lips thin.

"And what about you, Jackie?" Graham glanced at the packet of pills in her bag. "Do you blow hot and cold with people? Or do you take a more medicinal route to managing your emotions." It was an impertinent question, but Jackie's reaction showed Graham his instincts had been correct.

She scowled in surprise. "Who said I—?" Still on her feet, she placed her hands on her hips. "You went through my things! How dare . . ." She bent down and pressed shut the top edges of her bag. Anger quickly turned to indignation. "Don't you need a warrant or something?"

"We did no such thing," Graham said. "Merely an educated guess." He pointed at the bottom bunk. "Would you please sit down?" For a moment, he thought Jackie might tell him where to stick his instruction, but she kept her cool and sat back down on the soft mattress covered by a blanket made from what in times past might have been dubbed "horsehair," but was in reality dour, scratchy, and almost indestructible.

"All I know is she didn't show up for her seven o'clock morning call. We were going to walk over and make a start on her monologues before Noah came over to do his Sampson bit. I don't know what she did on Sunday night. Noah was ranting about Mia going off with one of those Aussie surfer guys. Anyhow, I couldn't stand to hear it, so I went to my room, where I stayed all night."

"What did you do there?"

"Went over my notes, planned the shots for the next day. Made a couple of cups of tea in the kitchen. Brought them back to my room to drink. Had an early night. That was it." Jackie shrugged.

"You didn't see anyone?" Jackie shook her head. "Your sister?"

"She came to collect her stuff for a shower, but that was it. I share a room with her, but I'm not her keeper. I was asleep when she came to bed." Jackie sighed heavily. "Look," she said. "I know she's my sister, but before you speak to her, you should know she's a complete mess." Whether Jackie meant recently, today, or generally was unclear. "I'll ask her to pull herself together, but she can be very obtuse at times."

"What about Clint?"

Jackie shrugged. "Not much to say. He's steady, quiet, sensible. No one pays him much attention. Acting types usually get turned on by chaos, personal drama, but he takes his work seriously, shows up on time, does an adequate if not stellar job. Bit of a blank, really."

"But in the grand scheme of things, as the director, didn't you appreciate having at least one person like that, someone you could rely on?"

Jackie smiled gently at a memory, the only time she softened throughout the angsty interview. "Yeah, yeah, I did. Clint's alright, really."

"Did he have feelings for Mia too?"

Jackie's mood changed again. She began to laugh, the only audience to a private, dark comedy that played out in her mind. "I don't think so, not really. They seemed to be just friends. Perhaps the only genuine friendship I ever saw her have. And he wasn't her type, nor she his. He's a real steady Eddie, and whilst she claimed to have dated half the hot young actors on the south coast, he's not hot, so . . . ."

CHAPTER TWENTY-TWO

IN A MOMENT of generosity, or because he'd realised that keeping on the right side of the local constabulary was a smart move, the hostel manager upgraded the police team to his office. Harding and Graham sat nursing weak tea in polystyrene cups as they considered their next move.

"Let's try the sister next," Graham said. "Check her movements and see if she can confirm anything Jackie said."

Graham finished a text exchange with Laura and looked up just as Fawn Prentiss slouched her way into the hostel office, her hands deep in her longline cardigan's pockets, her head still down, her long black hair acting as protective cover. She slumped into the chair Janice showed her to and tipped her head to one side, tucking one of her curtains of hair behind her ear.

Graham leant forward. Yesterday, Fawn had appeared almost catatonic. Even now, she seemed vague and unfocused. Graham stared at her pupils. She didn't show signs of drug use, but her energy was dull and her reactions slow. "Fawn, tell me what you were doing on Sunday night."

Fawn opened her mouth to speak but croaked. She cleared her throat and tried again. "Um, I-I w-watched the rushes with the others. We had, um, pizza. I'm a vegetarian, so I had a slice of Margherita." Fawn spoke robotically. She was painfully thin, and Janice wondered if she'd eaten that day.

"And after that?"

Fawn gazed at Graham as if not comprehending what he was asking her. Janice leant forward and lightly touched her arm. "Fawn?"

"Um, I just hung around here. Went to the pub later with some others."

"Who did you go with?"

"Just some random girls passing through." Fawn let out a long sigh as if she'd just exerted herself beyond her limits. "Like we all are."

"What time did you leave to go there?"

"Hmm?" Fawn squinted as if in pain.

Graham repeated himself. "What time did you go to the pub?" Fawn still looked at him blankly, so Graham decided to prompt her further. "Did you see Mia that evening?" At the sound of Mia's name, Fawn flinched.

"Don't say that," she said. "Don't say her name!" Fawn lifted her heels onto the chair and reverted to the position she'd sat in on the common room floor, her hands wrapped around her shins, her head dropped over her knees. Janice touched Fawn's arm again, but this time the young woman turned her head and lay her cheek on her knees, facing away from the two officers.

Janice looked up at Graham and shook her head. Graham, exasperated, sat back and put his hands on top of his head, interlacing his fingers as he looked at the young woman turned from him. He glanced at his watch.

"Okay, Fawn, you can go back to your friends. We'll catch up with you later if we need to." The young woman stood and, like a crab, shuffled sideways out of the room, her face pale, almost ghostlike.

"What was all that about?" Janice wondered out loud.

"I don't know. Grief? Confusion? Shock?"

CHAPTER TWENTY-THREE

FREDDIE SOLOMON LEANT on the dark wood of the distribution desk, once again expressing his gratitude for what he called Laura's "best idea in ages." He'd hurried to the library as soon as he'd received her call.

"I'd have had to borrow that four hundred if the DI had insisted," the blogger said. "Either that, or I'd've defaulted and given him yet another reason to put me in jail, like he needs any more." Freddie mimed handcuffs and being dragged off to a cell, glad to see that Laura found the humour to smile even whilst busily sifting through books waiting to be reshelved.

"Twenty hours of community service beats a night in the constabulary guesthouse certainly. I'm as surprised as you that he changed his mind, actually," Laura admitted. Seeing Laura and Freddie in the same room generally irritated Graham beyond reason, but since Freddie had been on a couple of dates with a local primary school teacher, it seemed Graham's jealous impulse was starting to soften.

"So, you said you were going to 'put me to work,'" Freddie said. Of all the outcomes that "community service" could mean, working in the library was one of the best, but he was yet to learn what drudgery Laura Beecham had in store for him. He looked around. As usual, the place was busy with local readers searching for their next book, students staring at laptops, as well as the usual crop of folks who simply preferred quiet surroundings to do the crossword, catch up on news, or read a magazine without the expense of their own subscription.

"Oh, there's plenty to do," Laura said, eyeing the pile of books waiting in the library's drop-off box. "With all the hullaballoo about the one hundred seventy-fifth anniversary of Charles Sampson and his 'leap,'" she said, "I thought we'd put together a display board, maybe scan some documents from that decade, put them online, perhaps print them too. Probably the less tech-savvy would prefer them that way."

"With that," Freddie said, proud of his credentials as a researcher, "I can definitely help. Where should I begin?"

"I thought we'd go with these." Laura led Freddie to a worktable at the back of the library, where he found three battered crates packed with documents.

"Wow, how long have these been collecting dust?" Freddie asked, setting down his satchel.

Laura nudged her blonde hair behind her ears, then handed Freddie a pair of white fabric gloves. "Long enough that they might be fragile." She lifted the lid of the topmost crate, moving slowly to avoid both splinters and smudging her white blouse. "In fact, these *should* originate from around Sampson's time, 1830 to 1860."

The crate was a filing clerk's nightmare, jammed with rolled-up, bound, or loose papers of every kind. "Where did they come from?" Freddie asked.

"The cellar of the museum. Percival Courthould-Bryant's been having a clear out. The papers need to be sorted and documented, then stored safely."

"What do you think is in there?"

"The answer to that question awaits the attentions of a kind and patient soul such as yourself," Laura said, coughing slightly at the dust that hung around the box like a veil.

Freddie lifted the first collection of papers, bound in faded red cord. "How did old Courthould-Bryant get them?"

"Oh, you know, someone passes away and their family can't figure out what to do with their things. Or there's a fire, and the items that survive are never claimed. This one," she said, patting a crate, "was found, just like this, in the back of a broom closet in St. Michael's Church. Things like this get handed in to the museum all the time. Now they've been handed over to us for cataloguing."

Laura gave Freddie strict but simple instructions: read and catalogue everything in the box and flag for review anything that mentioned Charles Sampson or his three victims: Alice Pritchard, Penelope Levin, and Susan St. Edmund. "And look out for Sir Jeremiah Creaveley too. He was the magistrate at the time, and probably decided Sampson's fate. I'll check in with you in a couple of hours."

CHAPTER TWENTY-FOUR

GRAHAM PRESSED A button on his phone. "Marcus? What's the word?" He stood in the hostel driveway to take the call.

"Bloody tragic," the pathologist said immediately. "Somebody needs to say it. I mean, she was twenty-one, for heaven's sake, in the bloom of youth."

"Seconded," Graham said rather stiffly, unwilling to linger on the extent of Mia Thorne's loss. "But what can we say about the nature of her death?"

"Quite a bit. Could you come down? These things are easier in person."

"Er, yeah. Alright. Give me an hour?"

Reluctant for a reason he had never shared with Marcus, Graham planned to conduct two more interviews before he drove the station's unmarked car to the fancy new pathology and forensics lab in St. Helier. There was no use in allowing his feelings to take hold, but every time a young person met a terrible fate on his patch, the reminder came, swift and deep as a stab wound: *they were someone's child.* An unfortunate officer in Mia Thorne's hometown would have made the notification visit within hours, maybe minutes, of her body being identified, faced then with the unrestrained despair of a parent permanently separated from their greatest love. That he had once been the recipient of just such a visit was never lost on him.

Despite his resolution to share his tragic past with those that were close to him, Graham still had not done so. He had planned to tell Laura about his daughter during a quiet evening at home but found himself unable to spoil the atmosphere. Then he tried as they enjoyed an afternoon stroll one Sunday afternoon but changed the subject at the last second. His most recent attempt came during a dinner for two at The Bangkok Palace, but just as he worked himself up to say something, the waiter had interrupted them with the drinks' menu. He was frustrated with the situation and with himself for not being able to scale this particularly treacherous mountain. Laura deserved better.

Katie would have been seven and a half if she'd lived. She'd have been skipping to school, learning to read. Perhaps he'd be taking her to martial arts classes, ballet, or watching her as she fearlessly clambered up play structures in the park. The thoughts wouldn't stay away, wouldn't leave him in peace. He had become a pressure cooker of pent-up emotion, and he knew he had to release the valve. Perhaps soon, he could try again. Laura, completely unaware of what consumed him, had never questioned his past or his occasional evasiveness, but now, as he faced the prospect of confronting someone else's dead daughter, his experience as a father seemed too big a part of himself to keep from her.

It was almost ten minutes before the shaking stopped and he could breathe normally once more. "Come on, Dave," he said, tidying his rumpled appearance. He patted his hair and wiped his face. "Get a grip."

"Ready, sir?"

Graham turned to see Janice waiting for him further up the driveway. He took a step toward her. "Ready, Sergeant."

CHAPTER TWENTY-FIVE

"O**KAY,**" HARDING SAID. "Who're we talking to next?"

"Let's deal with 'the angry one.'" Graham idly spun left and right on his office chair. "Wouldn't it be marvellous if we could bottle anger and let it ferment?" he wondered out loud.

"You mean like some kind of emotional kombucha, sir?" Jack had recently introduced Janice to the fermented tea. She was willing to try new things, especially for Jack, and had tried hard to like it, but eventually tipped it down the sink when he wasn't looking.

"Kombucha?" Graham considered this. "Quite so, Sergeant. That'd be a blessing for so many, don't you think? Bottle the bad stuff and put it to one side until it's fizzing with positive purpose and possibilities, instead of it eating away at us from the inside."

"I think the whole of mankind would benefit from that, sir. But I think talking things out is better. And sooner rather than later. If you leave it too long, kombucha turns to vinegar. Turns nasty." She stood to get Noah Stimms. A minute later, he appeared in the doorway, Janice behind him.

"This won't take long," Graham said to the young man, who still seemed infused with the essence of a big cat caged against his will.

"Have you found something?" Noah asked, throwing himself into the chair earlier occupied by Janice. Graham stood and let Janice take his seat whilst he carried another chair over. He brought out his notebook. "Early days," he said simply. "Let's talk about Mia."

"It's that Australian bloke, isn't it?" Noah said. His lip curled and his nostrils twitched as he said the word "Australian."

"What makes you say that?"

"The two of them were chasing girls around the place on Sunday night, sloppy with booze, and noisy as hell. 'Nozz' had been trying to get Mia into his room for days; it was obvious. I mean, *that* kind of guy . . . she'd never usually give him the time of day. Never mind, you know, show *interest*."

"But she did?" asked Graham.

"She flirted with him a bit."

"So, you saw the two of them together?" Graham saw the exhaustion in the young man's face, the physical costs of this whirling gale of emotions.

"On Friday, yeah, then again on Saturday. The two guys had been out surfing, making a video. I heard them boasting about it. But I saw her talking to him during the evening. I could tell from his body language that he was trying to impress her."

"And then what happened?"

Noah sighed, and Graham saw a flicker of reluctance. "It's alright, Noah. The more you tell me, the faster we can—"

"We argued." Noah's fatigue was right on the surface—the pale skin, the purple bruising under his eyes revealing his tiredness.

"This was Saturday?"

Noah nodded. "She said to me, 'You don't know how to be in the world.' She had a big future ahead of her. I wasn't good enough: not to act opposite her, not to help her, not to be her friend . . . not to make her happy." Out with the truth came a torrent of sadness, and Graham waited whilst the worst of it passed.

"Tell me how to help you," Noah said eventually. His eyes—ringed by red and pierced with despair—focused on Graham. He pleaded, "Tell me what I need to do to help you find out what happened."

CHAPTER TWENTY-SIX

AS HE BEGAN the long swim upward out of his well of despair, Noah became more helpful. "We finished rehearsing at three; it was too windy on the cliff to continue. We'd been there since nine." Graham wrote everything down, his hand almost vibrating as he rushed to get down his notes whilst behind him, Harding steadily tapped away at her tablet. "After the rushes, I wanted to talk to Mia, try to get back in her good books, but she dodged me. She went out with that Australian guy."

"Did you see her leave?"

Noah shrugged. "No, but Clint mentioned it later. He'd seen them go."

"How did you spend the evening?"

"Hung out around the hostel. I had a drink with Clint later, just the one," he said. "We went to the pub."

"People will have seen you in there?"

"Yeah, loads. Fawn joined us for a bit, but she was being a complete . . ." He was embarrassed, but Graham waved it away. "She poked fun at me. Said something like, 'Crocodile Dundee came along and snapped up your girlfriend.' Typical of her, really. She can be mean. I didn't want to be around her, so I came back here and went to bed, listened to an audio book with my earbuds in. I probably fell asleep about half eleven. I didn't hear Clint come back."

"What about Jackie?"

"After we looked at the rushes, I didn't see Jackie again until the next morning. Then, well . . ." Another wave of pain slammed into him. Noah blew air forcefully through tight lips that formed an O. "Jackie was sitting there in reception, nervous, tapping her feet together the way she does before a show when she's anxious to get on with things. And Fawn was hanging around; she had ants in her pants too. I was just going to get some breakfast in the common room, but they both insisted something was wrong, that Mia hadn't shown up, and I should help them look for her."

"What time was that?"

"Eight. They'd been due to leave at seven to catch the light, and then me and Clint were coming at nine to do our bit. I mean, this is Mia we're talking about. She was *never* late. A real professional. Despite what was going on with her, she'd always be on time. Learnt it from her dad, I guess. 'Be on time, the rest'll be fine,' she'd say."

"And did you? Look for her, I mean?" Graham asked, inscribing the quote in his book along with everything else.

"I didn't see the point. I figured she was with the surfer guy. I may be daft about many things, but I know enough not to poke a bruise."

Graham stared at Noah hard, assessing.

"Look, I didn't hurt her. You're wasting your time if you're looking for a confession from me." Noah wasn't angry or defiant. He was completely certain. "There's nothing else I can tell you. I didn't see her again after the rushes."

"Okay." The camera in Graham's head shut off, but his calculating mind was abuzz. "Is there anything else you can tell us?"

Noah managed a tight smile. "She was auditioning for a play, you know. Some scouts came down from the West End and selected her. She mentioned getting some weird messages after that."

"Do you know what type of weird messages?"

"Not exactly. She didn't seem too concerned. Difficult to tell with her, though. She was very . . . What's the word? Mercurial."

Graham nodded. "I understand that you used to go out with Jackie."

"Yes, that's right. We broke up."

"And you started going out with Mia immediately afterward."

"Uh-huh."

"There were no bad feelings?"

"Not really. We're adults. Jackie could be a bit of a taskmaster sometimes, which I put down to jealousy, but, you know, you win some, you lose some. I think I was the winner out of the pair of us, so I just rolled with it." Noah took in a huge gulp of air and let it out in a big whoosh.

"Thanks, Noah. I think that's enough for one day. We're done. Go and get something to eat and try to relax a little."

With the interview over, his shoulders slumped and barely able to walk in a straight line, Noah accompanied Janice back down the hallway with the haunted look of a man whose home had vanished in an earthquake. Graham watched him go. To a woman like Mia Thorne, Noah Stimms was merely a toy, a dim foil, a moth to a flame, fluttering pointlessly but eternally hopeful around it until, eventually, he got zapped in a flash of scorching heat and acrid smoke. Mightier men had met similar fates with much the same outcome.

CHAPTER TWENTY-SEVEN

IT WAS BECOMING a habit that he despised, but there just wasn't time for Graham to call Laura between interviews. "We had arranged to meet for lunch," he said to Janice, "but I've got to get these kids on the record before too much time passes."

"And you'll be distracted until you've talked to them all," Janice said. "I get it, boss. Jack's going to think I've taken a second job or something. When we're on a big case, I mutter things at breakfast, and that's all he hears from me until bedtime. We've all got something, or someone, but it's the job. The people in our lives understand. Text her, though, would be my advice. Just a note. Thirty seconds is all it takes, and it makes all the difference."

Graham did as she suggested, tapping out a quick note of explanation, suggesting Laura carry on without him. He'd catch up with her later. "How are the others doing?" Graham liked to keep his personal and work lives separate, but he knew the members of his team weren't so compartmentalised.

"Jim's doing okay. He's still blasting about on that motorbike, and he's renting a flat in the same building as Bazza. I think he's glad to be out of his mum's. Don't think he has a girlfriend at the mo, though." Janice held open one of the hostel's doors for Graham to walk through. "But right now, he's so deep in his textbooks and quizzes for his exams, he needs a periscope just to talk to us."

"What about Barnwell?" Graham asked. "Who or what does he have outside the job?"

"No particular person; a committed bachelor, I think. Likes to do what he wants, when he wants. He's done the early shifts for three years now, and he's become quite the morning man since he joined 'Fortytude.'"

Graham stopped short of the hostel's reception desk, hovering between the giant wall map with its coloured pins and a huge eight-person couch that seemed permanently occupied with young people, their heads tilted at precisely the same angle as they stared at their phones. "Since he joined *what*?"

"'Fortytude,' sir. It's a morning exercise group. Bunch of fellas, all in their forties."

"Really? Is he forty then?"

"Not quite, but he liked the sound of the program, so they let him in. Easier to turn over a new leaf and drop a few more pounds if you've got some mates doing the same. Especially at five a.m. in January. So he said, anyway."

They passed the front desk, the hostel manager looking far from impressed to see them again. "You still here?" he complained. "You're freaking out my guests."

Janice gave Graham an "I've-got-this" glance and leant over the counter. "Let's see what kind of reviews you get on social media," she muttered to the irritated man, "when someone lets it out that your CCTV was broken for weeks on end."

"I was waiting for the engineer . . ."

"I can see it now. 'One star,'" Janice threatened. "'A rat in the shower, a weird smell in the hallways, and a *murderer* in the next room.' We'll be here for the duration, and won't be leaving until we're finished, however long it takes, got it?" She stalked away, seeming to gather energy and focus with each step, leaving the manager staring after her, blinking rapidly. Graham glanced at the scowling man before quickly trotting after her. It seemed the wisest thing to do.

They found their next interviewee, Clint Wells, the curly-haired, husky cameraman, still in the now-empty common room. He watched the news on the big-screen TV, distractedly chewing his fingernails. "Mr. Wells," Graham said politely, extending a hand, "thank you so much for waiting."

Clint stood quickly, wiping his hand on his grey T-shirt before offering it to the detective inspector. "No problem. I've got nothing *but* time."

"Well, thanks anyway. Now," Graham asked affably, "do you prefer Clinton, or just Clint?"

"Clint's fine." The young man looked anxiously from one officer to the other. "How can I help?" Graham took a seat opposite the sofa Clint was sitting on.

"Would you like a cup of tea?" Clint asked.

"I'm fine, thanks," Graham said. The efforts to produce a mug of tea that resembled something stronger than used dishwater from the hostel's supplies had been heroic but ultimately futile. He'd wait until he got home.

Clint flicked a glance at Janice and raised his eyebrows. "No, thanks," she replied.

Graham kicked things off. "We're in the process of nailing down what happened on Sunday night, but before we get to that, tell us about the . . . well, I suppose I'd better call it the 'love triangle' for want of a better phrase, that developed among your friends."

Clint rolled his eyes with unforced theatricality. "Oh, jeez, I wouldn't call it that exactly, but those three . . ."

Graham produced his notepad seemingly out of nowhere and clicked the end of his mechanical pencil.

"You still use one of those?" Clint observed.

"Of course," the DI said proudly.

"I just thought, with all the technology these days . . ."

"I leave that to my sergeant here. I tried an iPad once," Graham said, as though recounting the unfortunate purchase of a second-hand car. "One day, it decided to crash, and I lost all my notes from a three-hour interview. That was the end of that. Never again."

Clint made a face. "I hope it wasn't anything important given that it's gone for good when that happens."

"Gone?" Graham tapped his temple. "Not at all. Now, this 'triangle' . . .?"

Beginning his statement with a long, exasperated groan, Clint did his best to lay out the group's romantic entanglements. "I'm sure you've heard it all from the others. This is how it goes with the 'beautiful people.' They can never make up their minds which other beautiful person to be with. They say they want excitement, or something new, but then after a while, things change and all they want is stability, someone dependable. They get that, and five minutes later, they're craving more spontaneity. Next thing I'm hearing," he says, reciting the ceaseless pattern, "is 'they're too difficult, they're too flighty, I can't deal with them, we're fighting,' so they argue, break up, look for the opposite type of person to the one they're with, and so it goes, on and on in perpetuity." Clint's hands circled each other whilst he shook his head, despairing of his friend's antics.

"Jackie and Noah were together for a while. Then Mia made a play for Noah, who immediately obliged, dumping Jackie, and there ensued an on-again, off-again relationship between the two of them, punctuated with bursts of euphoria and rivers of grief. To be fair, Jackie stayed above it all, took her rejection on the chin, and didn't harbour grudges. I mean, she made Mia the star of her production. Not many women would do that after what Mia did to her. And, if she sat back suppressing a smirk as she watched Mia and Noah combust on a several times a week basis, who could blame her?"

"And what about you, Clint? Where do you fit in to all this?"

"Well," he said, reddening a little, "I'm not one of the 'beautiful people,' am I?" Graham was halfway through writing "jealousy" in his notebook when Clint unexpectedly added, "Besides, I've been with Kirsty since high school."

CHAPTER TWENTY-EIGHT

CLINT BROUGHT OUT an old-fashioned wallet photo of a beaming, bespectacled redhead. She was leaning on a mobile camera rig, where she seemed entirely at home. "Haven't so much as looked at another girl in six years."

"Fair enough," said Janice.

"The way those two carried on, Mia and Noah," he said. His voice wobbled as he pronounced Mia's name.

"Like what?" asked Janice.

"'You never listen!'" Clint said, affecting a creditable impersonation of Noah's thin, whiny voice before launching into a higher pitch that Janice and Graham assumed represented Mia. "'You're too jealous . . .'" Back and forth Clint went, mimicking the pair. "Don't be so possessive . . . You're not attentive enough . . . You're too controlling . . . You're a big sissy . . . Get lost . . . Some friend you are . . . I'm doing you a favour . . .'" He gestured again with whirling hands. "They wouldn't know a good relationship if it slapped them across the face. They just wanted the other person to be what they needed at all times, like they were ordering an expensive coffee. No compromise, no give-and-take, no considered responses. Just reaction, emotion, and chaos." Now his hands circled his head like tweeting birds around a stunned victim. "The whole thing was *crazy*."

"But you stuck with them through this whole project."

"Longer. Mia and I have been good friends the whole time we've been at uni. She was kind to me when I got bullied," he recalled. "Nothing too serious, just a bit of ribbing about my weight, you know, but she yelled at the idiots, made them think twice. We've been friends ever since. She was kind, generous. I like to think I provided her with a safe space whilst the rest of her life shifted from one real-life drama to another. She gave me some street cred and a bit of glamour and was a real sweetheart underneath it all. So many people didn't see that side of her, though."

"But no romantic relationship."

Clint gave a small smile. "No, like I said, Kirsty's the only girl for me. Hardworking, solid, dependable. Just like yours truly."

"So, what happens now, with the project?" Janice asked.

Clint puffed out his cheeks. "Jackie's in a hole. I don't think she's ready to make any decisions. I have," he admitted, "*literally* no idea if we'll ever see a single scene of this Sampson thing. Twelve minutes of film it was going to be—that's all—but we hadn't filmed every scene, and with Mia . . . Her father's feelings need to be taken into consideration too."

"Will you be able to graduate without it?" Janice had a younger sister at uni. All Christina seemed to talk about was her timetable.

Clint blinked. "Not sure. I haven't thought about that; other concerns have taken priority. If I can't, it'll cost me thousands. Probably have to take out a loan to afford the extra classes I'll need."

"Bring us back to Mia and Noah," Graham said. "They were arguing a lot this past week, right?"

"Oh, yeah." Clint's eyebrows illustrated that the arguments were difficult and incendiary. "Things had got really tough between them these past few days. Things were coming to an end. I've seen Mia go through this cycle with guys a number of times. She creates a drama and moves on."

"Noah says he had a drink with you on Sunday night."

"Yeah, about nine. We went to the local, not sure what it's called. The closest one to here, anyway. Just a few drinks. We couldn't have more, not on a school night, at least we shouldn't. Noah was stuck in a cycle of sending drunken texts to Mia, half out of his mind, though. They were either 'I'll love you forever!' or the opposite, 'Why do you torture me?!' That kind of thing. Never heard back, of course. Presumably because . . . Oh God . . ." Clint wiped his face with his hand.

There was a pause as Graham tapped his pencil against the surface of his notebook, apparently thinking to himself. Then, a new tenor of question emerged. "Clint, we've heard that Mia mentioned receiving some unwelcome messages. Did she say anything to you about them?"

Clint pursed his lips and frowned. "She may have mentioned something, but she didn't make anything of it. Women like her are bound to get a few like that. Goes with the territory these days, especially for beauties like her. Not that it should, of course."

"Can you give us your movements for the rest of Sunday night?"

"Absolutely. After the rushes, I played Dungeons and Dragons with some others until around nine, when Noah texted me and suggested we go for a drink. We'd finished with our D and D session, so I jumped at the chance."

"Dungeons and what?"

"Dungeons and Dragons. It's tabletop role-playing game." Graham opened his hands and shook his head. "It's kind of like a board game where we play characters. We played over there." Clint nodded at the big dining table at the end of the room. "There were six of us."

"And you went straight from here to the pub?"

"Yes."

"Where was Noah when he texted you?"

"I don't know. We went straight out, within fifteen minutes anyway, so I assume he was here somewhere. He'd been in the room earlier, but you've seen how he is. He was in and out, pacing about. It's exhausting. Sucks a room of oxygen."

"So where were Mia and Noah in their cycle, given the on-again, off-again nature of their relationship?"

"Off I'd say, or close to it," Clint said. "She called him a 'horrid little termite, forever in search of a queen' earlier in the day. I won't forget that one! Very creative. No," he said, waving away the idea, "it was all but over. And she went out with that Australian in the evening. I saw them leave."

"Last question, Mr. Wells. Mia's phone. Can you tell me what it looked like?"

"Pink," Clint said. "It was a pale, dusty pink. She was never without it."

"Alright, thank for your time, Mr. Wells. We'll be in touch." Graham rose and held out his hand. Clint took it, and as Graham turned to leave, he gave Janice a little wave.

CHAPTER TWENTY-NINE

SLIDING GLASS DOORS and modern, open-plan workspaces were the hallmarks of Tomlinson's new digs. Graham found the pathologist at his desk facing three huge flat-panel monitors. "You could have some first-rate movie nights down here," Graham said as he came in. "All you need is the popcorn."

"Levity, really?" Tomlinson said, turning with a frown.

"Sorry." Graham had the grace to look abashed. "Why don't you show me what you've found?"

"Time was," Tomlinson remarked, "when these briefings began with someone opening a cold-storage cabinet and lifting a white cloth. I'll spare you that," he said. "And show you these instead. Mia's fractures." Tomlinson pointed at the centre screen with his mouse. A dozen X-ray images overlaid with other visual data—the type of bone, nature of the fracture—filled the three monitors alongside Tomlinson's own notes in a small, red font. "See anything?"

"Isn't that your job?"

"Thought you might want to have a crack at it." Tomlinson coughed. "If you'll pardon the pun."

"Levity?" Graham said, feigning his own frown. "Really?"

Over half of Mia Thorne's bones had been distorted and shattered into spider-web patterns, held together only by the body's own structure. "You could take a hammer to a skeleton and scarcely hope to create damage like this. It's not a surprise," Tomlinson said. "Remember the DS that was killed in that hit-and-run a few months back?"

Graham grunted. How could he forget?

"She had Messerer type fractures, breaks caused by one or a very few impacts." Tomlinson pointed at the screen. "These are different; they are diffuse and widespread. Mia certainly died from massive blunt force trauma to her head, but any number of these secondaries could have caused death." Graham nodded.

"But the essence of what you are trying to determine is not so much what killed her—that much is obvious—but was she pushed, did she jump of her own accord, or did she slip, yes?"

"Go on."

"Look at this." Tomlinson brought up another image, a photograph. "Her left hand."

Graham copied the position, bringing his fingertips tight to his palm. "A panic gesture?"

"It's what's called a 'cadaveric spasm.' It's caused by intense physical activity in the moments immediately before death. If we're not careful, we can overlook a feature like this and chalk it up to regular old rigor mortis. But this is different. Her fingers can't be uncurled. Believe me, I tried. With rigor mortis it would have been possible."

"'Intense activity?'" Graham queried, his mind already racing off in this new, interesting direction. "You think she was fighting with someone?"

"No evidence of that yet; the stress of falling through the air could equally have caused this. But the DNA tests might prove helpful and guide us. We're waiting for them to come back. I've found no evidence that another person was a factor in her injuries—no fingermarks in the bruising pattern for example—but we might find something under her nails or from her clothing. If the water hasn't washed it all away, we may get a hit."

Graham blew out his cheeks. They weren't getting very far. He began to wonder why Tomlinson had called him in.

"But I found something else. Look closely."

Magnifying the image on the screen, Tomlinson showed Graham tiny strings of green grassy material on a background that took some moments for Graham to decipher. It was the dead woman's hand enlarged twenty times. Several of the strands seemed to have been compressed between Mia's fingertips and her palm, but the amount was tiny.

Graham looked again at the image on the screen and took the mouse so that he could zoom in on each individual fingertip. "I'm guessing you think she reached out to grab for something in the moments before she went over the top."

"Reached, grabbed, tried to hang on tight," said Tomlinson. "We'll need to take a look at these, and the saltwater won't have helped in the slightest . . ."

"We moved her as fast as we could," Graham assured him. "But what does this tell us exactly?"

"It's too early to say. A slip, a push, a change of heart following a jump—all are possibilities."

"Ugh, what a thought."

CHAPTER THIRTY

"MANY WHO ATTEMPT suicide regret their actions as soon as they take them, especially jumpers. On its own, a sign that she tried to prevent her fall doesn't necessarily point us in any one direction. But in combination with other evidence, it could push our conclusion one way or another. These data points start to build a picture, but it's imperative we get further evidence, David. I really can't stress this too much. I'm unable to make a judgment at this point."

"What about where she landed? Does that give us anything to work with?"

Tomlinson shook his head as he jiggled his mouse. He clicked on the left-hand screen and it sprung into life, beaming out a 3D mathematical model of the cliff on a dark background. "As for the 'geography' of her fall, we may never gain any clarity. It would have been impossible for her to land directly where her body was found under the cliff's overhang. I've checked with the coastguard, the meteorologist, even a few fishermen, and they all agree that the tide would have washed her to the spot where you found her. She had to have fallen onto the beach and from there, high tide washed her northeast to her resting spot."

"When was high tide?"

"Just past midnight."

"So, time of death was sometime before that?"

"Yes, I'm afraid I can't be more accurate. Seawater does terrible things to the integrity of a body."

"Quite right. What else?"

Tomlinson sat back. "I offer an all-singing, all-dancing, full-colour presentation like this," he said haughtily, "and you have the gall to ask 'What else?'"

"Sorry, it's just that all we know is that she was smashed to pieces. I didn't need you to tell me that."

"And that perhaps she tried to stop her fall."

"But even that doesn't help much. I still don't know if she jumped, fell, or was pushed. Suicide, accident, or murder."

"You need more evidence. We need to build out the picture," Tomlinson said testily. "What about her phone? That's all we really need these days."

"We haven't found it. All we know is that it's pink." Tomlinson opened his mouth, but Graham raised his palms and added, "And I'm aware that we need it, but the thing is, if it was washed away, we may never see it." Tomlinson conceded the point. "Anyhow, I better get back to the investigation. Thanks for the information."

"How's Roach getting on? I haven't seen him much lately."

"He's been interviewing hotel guests and truculent surfers."

"And studying for his exams."

"Yes. Between you and me, I'm a little worried that he'll—"

"Leave Jersey for a more high-profile posting?"

Graham gave a crooked smile in acceptance of what he considered inevitable. "Wouldn't you, at his age?"

"Probably," Tomlinson answered honestly. "Not that Gorey has been short on excitement in the last few years." The pathologist turned back to his screens, but then asked quietly, "Want me to try to persuade him to stay?"

"Not a bit of it," said Graham decisively. "An officer's career decisions should be their own. It's been my job to make sure he's happy and fulfilled whilst he's here, and all evidence points to success. We mustn't box him in. If he keeps on the way he's going, he'll move eventually. In fact, if he decides he wants to try life in the Met, I'll put a word in for him."

Tomlinson straightened. He clasped Graham's hand in his. "You're a good man, Detective Inspector Graham. Your team is fortunate to have you." The elderly pathologist's gaze bored into Graham as though seeing something Graham would rather he didn't. "Listen, I'm sorry I don't have anything concrete for you yet. I'll call when we get more. There's toxicology, DNA, and the analysis of the grassy remnants still to come. They might tell us something."

"Thanks, Marcus. I'll await your call."

Marcus flicked the air with the back of his hand. "Now be off with you. Get back to investigating. No point hanging around here."

CHAPTER THIRTY-ONE

LAURA WAS FILLING Graham in, a babbling brook of words and energy and ideas, all whilst he was still blurry and insufficiently caffeinated. "Those three boxes are amazing! He found this set of architect's drawings for a town hall that was never built, and others for a huge, charitable hospital up where the White House Inn stands today." Laura was a study in efficiency and balance, still in her pyjamas. She tipped granola into her breakfast bowl and raised her voice over the clatter as toasted grains and nuts, honey, and raisins hit the shiny ceramic with a stream of *tings*. "I was thinking of doing an exhibit called 'Gorey That Never Was.' You know, show people the 'what-if' moments, get them to imagine what the place would—"

"Love?" Graham interrupted, leaning against the kitchen doorway, mug in hand and a plaintive expression on his unshaven face. "I may not have told you this before, but I've got an unyielding policy never to discuss Freddie Solomon until I'm at least partly dressed."

"Fair enough." Laura took the mug out of his hand and refilled it from the cozy-covered teapot. "But next time he causes a mess that blights your workday, send him for another twenty hours' library service, alright? He's a keeper."

"That'll depend on whether there's an empty cell with his name on it at the constabulary," Graham said, unwilling to automatically grant such leniency to the man he considered The World's Most Annoying Person. "But," he added, mug back in his hand as he pottered his way to the bathroom (in Laura's tiny cottage, it was only a few feet away from the kitchen), "I'm glad he's helpful. I was beginning to give up hope."

Laura spooned granola into her mouth impatiently. "Shame he hasn't found anything about Sampson. What with all the carry-on at the cliff this weekend, it would be great to unearth something new. What's on your schedule today?"

"The Australian consul is showing up, so I'll have to either charge that dimwit surfer or let him go."

"I thought you'd already charged him?" Laura said. "He's in one of your cells, isn't he?"

"Yeah, but we still don't know what type of death we're investigating! Janice and I wrote him up for drunken affray after his antics on Sunday night. Gave us a couple of days to question him whilst ensuring he couldn't skip the country."

"Tricky of you," Laura said, wagging a finger. She put down her cereal and moved on to assembling her packed lunch—last night's leftover chicken, a salad, and some fruit.

"Not a bit of it. Half the women in the place said he was a noisy, offensive prat. It'd serve him right if we hung onto him for a week."

"What about his billions of followers?" Laura asked. "Isn't he supposed to do some stunt on his surfboard at the weekend?" She smartly snapped shut the locks on her lunch container.

Towelling his face, Graham's reply was intermittently muffled. "They're calling it 'LeapFest.' Apparently, re-enactors are showing up en masse in period costume. About a dozen food trucks have applied to sell food. Barnwell's going up the wall about public safety. People are even applying for climbing permits. He's refusing them, obviously."

"Blimey," Laura said. "I thought it'd be a history lecture and maybe a memorial wreath."

"Oh, people have gone to *town*. Social media is catalysing everything, aided by your mate, Freddie Solomon, who's spreading the word via his blog. Sampson's Leap is going to be jam-packed with onlookers, tourists, musicians, vendors and, in all likelihood, drunk youngsters urging each other to replicate Sampson's miraculous feat. We're going to need to be out in full force. I've asked for reinforcements from St. Helier. Stunt monkeys like those two surfers are the last thing we need."

Laura tossed him a fresh button-down shirt.

"Thanks, but I won't be needing this first thing. Me 'n' Bazza have got some action ahead of us." Graham pushed his arms into a T-shirt. "Actually, once I'm done with the consul, can you do me a favour and lend us one of your nice, quiet research rooms?"

"The new ones in the basement?"

"Say, eleven, just for an hour?"

"No problem," she said. "Why?"

"Janice and I need to have a conversation with someone. The hostel didn't work out, and the interview room seems like the wrong venue. I'd like to try somewhere else."

Laura knew enough of the Mia Thorne case to be able to guess. "One of the film students?"

"Yeah. With your help," he said, kissing her cheek on the way out, "we might actually get somewhere."

CHAPTER THIRTY-TWO

FEELING AS EXPOSED and windswept as the rock face itself, Barry Barnwell glanced over to his boss and asked, "You sure this is *entirely* necessary, sir?"

The DI was already in his harness, grinning from under a red hard hat, quite comfortable among the array of ropes and clips. "Where's your sense of adventure, Barnwell?"

"Really thought I'd already proved myself on that score," the constable muttered. "At least it's stopped raining," he said more loudly. He nodded uncertainly to Melanie Howes, the Gorey fire crew manager in charge of their safety. He could hear music—opera— blasting out from her 4X4. "Is that supposed to calm me down?" he grumbled.

"You know they say 'Don't look down'?" Melanie said to them both. "Well, that's rubbish. Look *everywhere*. You'll touch down about seventy-five feet south of the overhang. You've got four hours to high tide, so you've got plenty of time."

"Shouldn't need nearly that long. I've got the Australian consul coming in at ten," Graham informed her.

"Go *slowly*. Keep communicating, and don't get too far ahead of each other."

"Righto," said Graham. He let out the rope and slid down the cliff face in a smooth arc as though he did it every morning before breakfast, which, indeed, this morning he had. Coming behind him, Barnwell let out some slack, jarred to a stop, let out a little more, and progressed down the side of the cliff in a series of inelegant fits and starts.

"Whee," he said flatly.

"Come on, Bazza. Just relax and let the ropes do the work," Graham shouted.

"Easy for you to say," the constable shouted back. "Didn't you used to do this all the time?"

"No," Graham replied, watching Barnwell begin to get the hang of it despite having his feet too far apart as he bounced gingerly off the cliff face. Graham landed on the small beach as gracefully as if he'd jumped off his own desk, and then watched Barnwell come in slightly less skilfully. "I just skydived a few times back when I was younger. Not the same at all. You wouldn't believe how fast the ground comes up right at the end. At least this way, we arrive lightly on our toes—or at least some of us do," he said as Barnwell crash-landed a short distance away. "And it beats sploshing around in the surf trying not to sink the Zodiac, doesn't it?"

Relieved to be on solid ground, the constable agreed. "Waves are too high today. We could have hiked in, though, sir. Like Freddie and his mates did."

"I wanted to take the direct route. It helps us get a feel for the case, and besides, it's much quicker. It was scour down the cliff face in a minute or hike in for over half an hour. This way we have the time we need."

Barnwell looked around, noting the small beach they had landed on and the jagged rock that surrounded it. To his left and right were raised beds of rock interspersed with pools of seawater. "Sir, do you really think we'll find anything among this lot?"

"Unlikely," Graham admitted, unclipping himself from the rope system. "But I noticed that some of the bigger rocks actually stay above the waterline, even at high tide." The brutality of some of the waves would have thinned even this slender hope, but still, it seemed worth the effort. "Let's start there, eh? We need to find that phone."

Graham waded over the rocks without complaint until he reached the rock pool where Mia's body had been found. "Tomlinson believes she fell over there"—he pointed to the beach—"and was washed into this pool by the tide. We're not going to be able to do any complicated calculations . . ."

"That's a relief," muttered Barnwell.

". . . to work out whether she was shoved, slipped, thrown, or took a run-up."

"A 'run-up'?"

"When people jump to their deaths, you'd be surprised how many people take a run at it."

"You're really thinking suicide? A lovely young woman with everything to live for?"

"It would be unusual, but we can't rule it out. Four percent of people who attempt suicide choose this method"—Graham looked up at the cliff top—"and half of them die."

"But we've found no note, sir."

"People don't leave notes on the mantelpiece any longer, Barnwell. They send them electronically."

"But no one's reported receiving anything."

"True, but over five thousand Britons end their lives every year, and fewer than half leave notes. We have to consider it," Graham said. He bent down to rummage in a rock pool. "And we have to find her phone."

"Alright, I'm off to search the beach."

For the next hour and a half, the two men worked in a grid, minutely examining the crevices, cracks, and flat surfaces of the beach. Apart from an old towel, a drink container, and a tangle of plastic sheeting and seaweed, they found nothing.

"I think we're drawing a blank, sir."

Graham pursed his lips. He hated to admit defeat, but he had to agree. "I haven't examined that crop of rock over there," he said, unwilling to give up. "Let me check that out and then we'll go." He jogged over to take a look.

Barnwell was quiet and still for twenty seconds. "Sir?"

"Hang on," Graham called back as he clambered over the rock. It was wet and slippery.

"Sir!"

"Constable, *please*," Graham said. "Climbing over this rock is hard enough without . . ." But Barnwell wasn't paying attention. He pulled his iPad from inside his jacket and held it up to the cliff face.

Graham slithered his way down the outcrop and meandered over. "What is it, lad?"

"See that stunted tree growing out of the cliff face about"—Barnwell used his thumb-length to multiply the distance—"a hundred feet from the top?"

The detective inspector looked where Barnwell was pointing. "No."

"Exactly."

CHAPTER THIRTY-THREE

BARNWELL TURNED THE iPad to show Graham a still shot from Nozz and Zink's video. "It was there on Saturday, and it's not there now." Heads bent together, they stared at the unmistakable outline of a small, puny conifer—an arboreal triumph of hope and courage—protruding stubbornly from the cliff face in the background of the video shot by the two surfers.

"Bloody hell, boss. Now you see it, now you don't."

"Well done, Constable." Graham looked at the screen and checked the cliff face once more. "No sign of the tree on the beach; must have been washed away. We need to take a closer look. Call Melanie. Tell her where we're aiming for, and that we need to come up that way."

"Okay, but who are *you* calling?" Barnwell asked his boss as Graham tapped buttons on his phone.

"Tomlinson. If I'm right, he'll give me a little speech about how clairvoyant I am, or some such."

Using the mechanical winch on the back of Melanie's vehicle and a couple of metal belays that Graham hastily banged into the rock, the pair made their way back up the cliff face and traversed across to where the tree had been. Tomlinson came to the phone just as Graham reached the spot, surprised to hear that he was apparently in a wind tunnel.

"Marcus?"

"You know, I was just about to call you..."

"The Mia Thorne case," Graham said impatiently. "Tell me you've found something about the grassy material between her fingers."

"Funny you should ask. I just got the results. Where are you?" Tomlinson said, confused by all the noise.

"On a search with Barnwell," Graham said hurriedly. "What's the story?"

The wind was whipping his words away almost before Tomlinson could hear them.

"Ah. Well, it's bad news, I'm afraid," the pathologist said.

"How do you mean?" Graham replied, his optimism quickly dimming.

"She didn't grab grass at the top of the cliff to stop herself falling. It's not a match."

"Yeah, alright, but let me guess," Graham said, relieved. "You found resin from the crushed needles of an evergreen conifer on her hands."

There was the sound of Tomlinson exhaling as he puffed out his cheeks. "Even for you, David, that's quite something. How did you . . .?"

"I think you'll find it's an especially hardy Scots pine."

Tomlinson checked the lab results, then blinked in amazement. Finally, he said, "You know, back in the fifteenth century, they'd have paraded you through the town before burning you as a witch."

"I didn't have a prophetic vision, Marcus. I'm trussed up on a rope with Barnwell, dangling over Sampson's Cove, holding on to the *stump* of the blessed thing. I think Mia tried to grab it on the way down and yanked most of it right out of the cliff face."

Tomlinson made a note, then tried to imagine the event.

"Do suicidal people keep their eyes open and look for opportunities to arrest their fall?" said Graham, looking down the cliff face to see where, he now felt sure, Mia Thorne had met her end.

"Not normally," agreed Tomlinson. "But remember what I told you yesterday. We know that jumpers often change their minds mid-flight. This tree is an interesting find, but it doesn't tell us anything concrete about the manner of her death."

Disappointed, Graham had to agree with the pathologist. "At least we solved the mystery of what was in her hand. And we now know the approximate point of her fall."

In his office, Tomlinson consulted tidal charts. "It does confirm what I said yesterday. The tide would have come in around midnight. If we presume that she'd have been washed out to sea had she fallen at high tide . . . When was she last seen?"

"The Australian says he left her at seven forty-five, *if* he's telling the truth. We've no corroboration yet."

"That puts her death at sometime between then and midnight. Narrows the window. Does that help?"

"I'm not sure, honestly, but even if we're not making great progress, we are plugging some holes. We can at least eliminate some possibilities and not waste time worrying about them."

A gust of wind caught hold of Graham, sending a rush of adrenaline through his body. He quickly pulled his line taut. "Alright, thanks for that. Look, I'm going to get out of here. Speak to you when I'm on solid ground."

Melanie, the fire captain, winched them up. "What does it all mean, sir?"

Barnwell asked him as they unclipped themselves and stepped out of their harnesses.

"It means," the DI said, cursing quietly as one of the ropes tightened somewhere he'd rather it hadn't, "that we have another piece of the puzzle, maybe two, but we don't know where they fit, or even if they're meant to."

CHAPTER THIRTY-FOUR

"CONGRATULATIONS, MR. NOSWORTHY!" the Australian consul announced as she strode into the holding area outside Nozz's cell. "You've become the one millionth Australian to be arrested for drunkenness in the United Kingdom! Let's show the people at home what you've won..."

Graham left the two to talk and brought Sergeant Harding to his office for some preinterview planning. They were going to try again with Fawn. "She's the youngest of the group, by a couple of years, right?"

"Three. She turned eighteen last month. I think it's a good idea to interview her at the library. Neutral ground."

"Think she knows anything?"

"I'm hoping she can expand on Mia's state of mind or give us more insight into the other students. A solid timeline of her evening would help too."

"You have more faith in her than her sister," Graham warned. "Jackie was pretty negative about her."

"She was."

"Were you surprised?"

"I was a bit. In the first moments after the identification, I saw Jackie calm Noah down, or she tried to. When we got back to the hostel, she showed some mature leadership, but then in that interview, she showed a side of herself I wasn't expecting."

"Odd," the DI agreed, spotting the consul passing his open door as she returned from the cells to the reception area. "How are we doing?" he called out.

An experienced diplomatic officer, Arlene Loomis could claim to have seen nearly everything. "He'll cough for the affray if you'll do me a favour and fine him, rather than something more."

"Maybe," said Graham cautiously.

"Ah, yes. You're keeping him around because someone's trying to pin a suspicious death on him. Does he seem like a callous, devious, psychopathic murderer to you?" Loomis looked at Graham incredulously.

Graham explained the case with his usual efficiency. "An unexplained death," he corrected. "Mr. Nosworthy is not a suspect, merely a witness at this point, and I'm not in the habit of bringing a murder charge, if that's what it proves to be, and then dropping it. He won't be spuriously charged."

"What evidence have you got?" Loomis asked. Without waiting for an answer, she listed the shortcomings of the case against Nozz as though counselling a novice against sailing the Atlantic solo. "No DNA evidence. No forensics."

"Yet, Ms. Loomis, yet," Graham said unwilling to let the woman win every argument.

Arlene Loomis checked her notes. "His friend can alibi him for a good chunk of the night..."

"They were both drinking heavily," Harding pointed out. "And he was the last person to report seeing her alive."

"What about CCTV from the hostel? Does that give us anything concrete?"

Layers of frustration had to remain hidden whilst Graham lamented the latest chapter in Gorey's growing saga of digital incompetence. "Camera system was on the blink."

"So, you have no evidence to connect Mr. Nosworthy and Ms. Thorne beyond sights of him leaving with her and returning without her. Sights that he has readily admitted to. That isn't good enough, as you well know. He has cooperated with you. He admits to seeing her on the cliff. And there's no suggestion that she wasn't alive at the time he left her. He has no discernible motive over what we can imagine but not prove. You have nothing hard," said the consul. She sounded increasingly confident she'd be walking out with her compatriot.

Graham coughed. "Our investigation isn't complete."

"Oh, come on!" Loomis insisted. "I need more than that, or I'll have the high commission request his immediate release."

"Six more hours," Graham said. "We're still interviewing. If we find nothing to implicate Mr. Nosworthy in Ms. Thorne's death, we'll drop the affray charge and he'll be out in time to get back on his board and pull whatever ridiculous stunt he had in mind in the water."

"Alright," the consul said after a moment's thought. "Four thirty this afternoon, and not a minute later." She flicked her card onto Graham's desk before Harding escorted her out. "I expect to see him at four thirty-one."

"Even if those two muppets were harassing half the women in Gorey?" Graham muttered. He looked out the window to see Roach lifting his motorbike helmet from his head. "Ready to spend some time with Fawn Prentiss?" he said more loudly to Harding as she came back into the room.

"I'll get my tablet."

"I'd like a lot more from her this time. I know we'll be in a library, but let's hope she ignores the signs about being silent."

CHAPTER THIRTY-FIVE

"READY FOR ANOTHER day of servitude?" Laura smiled. She'd been neatening tourist brochures that sat in rows on a new wall-mounted display, and to Freddie's eyes, she looked even more elegant than usual.

"A lady as beautiful and accomplished as you"—he grinned, doffing a flat cap he'd chosen mostly to look dashing and hip—"could put me in a harness all day."

Laura's rolling eyes caught sight of his drink. "You're not planning to bring liquids in here, are you, Mr. Smooth Talker?" Laura gestured to the poster of prohibitions on the wall by the main entrance.

Freddie quickly sealed his empty to-go cup and stashed it in his satchel. "All done. But after that much coffee, I hope you've something exciting for me to get stuck into."

"You're righter than you know," she said, leading him back to the research table. "Percival Courthould-Bryant showed up a minute after we opened, asking about you."

"I saw Philomena here yesterday. We had a little chat. She asked me what I was doing."

"That's how he got wind of your charitable research efforts," she said. "You'll be delighted to learn he brought in a new crate of papers for you to look at. He claims they are from the early- to mid-nineteenth century." She gestured over to the crate as though introducing an honoured guest.

There was a handwritten label on the side of the crate that said "God Knows What." Freddie laughed. "I guess the archivist had the day off?"

"Have a ball," Laura said. "I'm heading off to lead a 'Book Baby' group for new parents."

"Thanks," Freddie muttered. He leant over the crate. "Alright, what have we got?"

There were letters from members of the clergy requesting money for church repairs, then begging for an extra pair of hands during the Christmas season. Someone had produced two lengthy, handwritten monographs—one about oyster farming, and the other providing advice for raising grouse in advance of the "Glorious Twelfth,"—both almost crumbling and amateurishly bound. Beneath those were more yellowing, brittle letters, some from a local headmaster and others, almost indecipherable, regarding the sale of a dozen horses. There was an unpublished book, *Jurisprudence and Matrimony*. More muttering from Freddie. "Sounds like a right page-turner."

The next document was entitled, simply, *Arguing in Court*. It was in the same neat hand, and beneath that were dozens more pages, apparently an early draft of a novel. "A real Renaissance man, this one," Freddie said as he waded through what was now obviously a musty pile of the man's personal papers. "I wonder who the author was?"

🌍

"Fawn, this is our librarian, Laura Beecham." The two women shook hands whilst Janice arranged three chairs around the table in the small research room. Graham closed the blinds. Laura had been diverted from her "Book Baby" mission to escort the visiting trio to the basement.

"I've got six adults, seven babies, and all seventeen pages of *Persephone the Pig* waiting for me"—Laura smiled—"so I hope you'll excuse me. Shout if you need anything, alright?" She gave the two officers what she hoped was an encouraging look and headed out.

Once Laura had left the research room, Fawn said, "You didn't need to go to any trouble. We could have talked at the hostel. I mean, I'm not, you know . . . a mental case, or anything."

"Absolutely not," said Graham.

Janice added, "Nothing was further from our minds."

"Okay," Fawn said. "Although if I was a bit loopy the other day, I had good reason." She sighed and repeated her mannerism, a hasty sweeping away of strands of hair from her face. The long, black, absolutely straight hair was as thick as a carpet. Janice, who possessed ultra-fine, wispy waves, wondered how many hours it took to dry after she'd washed it.

"We just thought," Graham began, "a change of scenery might help."

"Yes," Fawn said, then added more tentatively, "maybe without Noah screaming at people, or Jackie alternating between being snappy, bossy, or acting as though nothing happened. Clint sitting staring at some screen or other for hours on end didn't help either."

Fawn's youth wasn't the only difference between her and the others. She seemed slightly more together than earlier in the week when Graham had wondered if she was drugged. She still had a misted, faraway expression—quite unlike the fury of Noah's accusatory tirades or Clint's vacant but clear-eyed stare, or Jackie's jabs of criticism that emitted from her like the punches of a featherweight boxer—but her movements were sharper, her voice clear. She seemed quite unworldly, naïve, her light not yet dimmed by the harsh demands of adult life.

"Fawn, we're trying to understand Mia's state of mind," Graham said. "If someone was angry with her, or jealous, or bullying her. Can you help us understand what was going on?"

CHAPTER THIRTY-SIX

FAWN'S HANDS IMITATED those of an unsteady, novice juggler throwing balls with their hands too far apart. "Her feelings went this way and that. She was *awful* to Noah, but then, I think she treated most of her boyfriends badly." Her gaze fell to the floor, and she stared at the hard-wearing, commercial-grade, institutional-grey carpet. Her piercing blue eyes were hard and fierce. She was suddenly angry with herself. "I shouldn't have said that."

Janice asked, "What do you mean?"

"She's *dead*, and I'm here, all but calling her a . . ."

"Your honesty," Graham reminded Fawn, "is the most helpful thing you can offer Mia."

The stare melted steadily, and Fawn closed her eyes. "I kind of idolised her. People who didn't know Mia saw this confident, life and soul of the party, an extrovert character. But I saw her differently. It was like . . . she didn't rate herself highly, didn't think she deserved praise from critics, or attention from boys. So, when someone obviously liked her, or praised her, she thought *less* of them, as though they'd let themselves be duped by her. She was complicated. The only person I think she felt truly comfortable with was Clint. She wasted perfectly good friendships for what? Nothing."

"Was she like that with you?"

"Oh no. I don't think she saw me as a threat, or even noticed me much. She was nice enough to me."

"But your sister became an 'enemy' of Mia's?"

"Well . . ." Fawn explained, "Jackie wasn't serious about Noah. She just didn't like Mia stealing him from her. *He,* on the other hand, was very strange. Got serious way too quickly. Plain creepy, if you ask me. He was just the same with Jackie before he glommed on to Mia."

"So why did Noah end things with Jackie?" Janice asked. She was intrigued by the intense young man. She never met any like him when she was his age. Players, commitment-phobes, and unreliables had been her experience.

"Better offer, I suppose. On the face of it, Mia was much more of a prize. Noah was flattered she was interested in him. Thought she was genuine, which, of course, she wasn't."

"So how was Jackie toward Mia after Noah went off with her?"

"Angry at first. Noah was no great loss, but Mia made her look a fool. It definitely strained their relationship, but Jackie's a professional. She wouldn't let personal issues cloud her work. She's much too ambitious for that." Amidst the crowd of hieroglyphics on a new page of Graham's notepad, words emerged. *Revenge?*

"Did you see Mia with the Australian fella, Regis?" Janice asked.

"Regis?" Fawn almost laughed. "Is *that* his real name? Only a little bit. I think Mia was nervous about the film, maybe she just wanted a fun distraction. She kept in character virtually the whole time. She was big into method acting. And she wouldn't change out of her costume! Goodness knows why. Wearing one of those dresses was like walking around with a tank strapped to your waist. Jackie spoke to her about it several times. The dresses would get muddy and damaged." Graham wrote again. *Trip?*

"But we were all on edge about the shoot. I mean, Jackie's spent a year planning everything, writing the script, auditioning people, raising money . . . She sold some jewellery she inherited from our grandmother to pay for the travel down here."

"How did you feel about that?" Janice asked moments before Graham could.

"I was fine with it. Gran would have been happy to help Jackie pursue her dreams. Would probably have sold the jewellery herself if she'd still been alive," Fawn said simply. "I like to go permanent, if you see what I mean." The young woman lifted her cuff to show them a fabulously ornate dragon tattoo, in seven different colours, snaking up her inner forearm, its tail forming a golden S-shape just inside her elbow.

"Wow," was all Janice could manage.

Fawn smiled as she looked down at the fearsome creature whose spiky, scale-covered body and snarling, bared fangs could be considered a work of fine art. "I have another on this arm." She pulled back her sleeve to show the same dragon, this time asleep.

"Tell us about Nozz," Janice prompted.

"I thought Mia just fancied a fling. I knew she'd gone out with Nozz, but I saw him later in the lobby with his friend . . . what's his name?"

"Zink," Graham reminded her.

"Yeah. Anyway, they were both hammered. The night manager threatened to throw them out. I was on my way to the pub. Everyone saw them. Or heard them. There was no sign of Mia." Fawn pressed her teeth into her top lip.

"Did you see Jackie after the rushes on Sunday night?" asked Graham.

"I went to get some clothes from our room. I needed a shower..."

"No other time?"

Fawn glared at him. "Stop it."

Graham feigned innocence. "I haven't started anything."

"You're implying that my sister had something to do with Mia's death and you're asking me to incriminate her."

"I'm doing no such thing. Facts have to speak for themselves. That means I need all of them, without bias or selectivity."

"I didn't see Jackie again until I went to bed. She was already asleep when I got back."

"And what about you? What did you do Sunday evening before you went to the pub?"

"Hung about. There's not much to do here, is there? I sat in the common room working on the music for the film. I had my head down, my headphones on. Moved around a bit. I didn't notice much at all."

"And the others? Noah and Clint?" Janice asked.

"They were doing their own thing. I saw both of them at the pub, but I didn't spend the evening with them."

"And you didn't spend any time with your sister," Graham intervened again, "on the night before a most important filming day of a crucial project? Didn't you have things to talk about?"

"Like what?" Fawn snapped, her anger suddenly eclipsing all other emotions. "I'm just doing the music and the odd acting thing, aren't I? Even Jackie said I was just helping out *for fun*." Fawn widened her eyes and jiggled her head in irritation. "We'd spent all day together, met for the rushes, discussed what we planned to do the next day. Everything that needed saying had been said."

"She didn't need to run things past someone she trusted? Or complain about one of the others?" Graham asked. "Or think out loud? I do, all the time, when there's something important going on."

"No!" Fawn said, standing and clasping her hands. "Look, I don't have to be here, I know that. We're finished. I want to go back to the hostel." Fawn began to roughly rub her tattoo, the fiery one, her eyes darting anxiously between the two police officers.

Balancing on a thin edge between two choices, Graham chose to take one more risk. "Are you sure you didn't go out anywhere other than the pub that night? It'll make things easier if you tell us everything now," he warned.

"I am!" Fawn cried. "Why are you doing this? Saying these things? I can't..." She dissolved into sobbing.

Direct and unmistakable eye movements told Graham that Janice needed him gone. More questions were bubbling up, but the DI thought better of it and left Janice to deal with the distraught young woman on her own.

CHAPTER THIRTY-SEVEN

OUTSIDE IN THE hallway, in the subterranean quiet of the library basement, regret bored a hole in Graham's chest. "Too harsh, too fast, Dave," he growled. He strode down the hallway, grunting with dismay. From behind him, he heard the sounds of Laura's "Book Baby" session finishing up—doors opening, chattering mothers with squirming infants, scraping chairs. A painful vision of a memory flashed in his mind for a split second before he pushed it away as fast as it had come. A few moments later, he felt a hand on his.

"Hey," Laura said softly, peering into his stricken face. She cradled a stack of children's books in the crook of her arm. "How did it go?"

Harding chose that moment to lead Fawn Prentiss from the interview room, her arm around Fawn's shoulder as the teenager sobbed. They pointedly headed the other way down the corridor.

"Oh," said Laura, her eyebrows knitted with concern.

"As my old boss, Nigel Needham, used to say," Graham recalled, "I was 'using concrete when the occasion called for Lego.'"

Laura watched Harding shepherd Fawn to the stairs. "Janice is going to be mad at you."

"And she'll be within her rights. I saw something," he explained with a shrug. "I can't even explain it, a gap in the defence, and went for it."

"And your opponent ended up with a broken leg and you the red card?"

"Something like that."

"If you want to let off some steam, you can come upstairs and be horrible to Freddie for a minute," she said.

"That sounds like fun, but no thanks. Talk later?"

"Any time," she assured him, squeezing his hand. "You know that. I'll walk out with you."

Graham waited as Laura deposited her pile of books on the table behind the distribution desk. She was fetchingly backlit by the library's front windows, her blonde hair shining gold at the edges. "You shouldn't do this to me," he said as she returned to him.

Laura kissed Graham's cheek, then took his hand before heading for the doors. "What now?"

"I mean," he said as they left the building, finding the afternoon warmer than expected, "you have to stop looking so unbearably attractive when we're in public. It puts me in a difficult position."

Laura smiled and squeezed his hand. Graham wasn't a man easily given to displays of emotion, so watching him open up gave her a glow of pleasure. He'd always been so *shy*, so protective of his privacy. Barnwell once claimed that he could write everything he knew about the detective inspector on a single sheet of paper and still have room for an amusing sketch.

Laura suspected that David was someone in recovery from something, slowly regaining the use of faculties long left on the sidelines—his willingness to laugh, his sense of fun, and yes, his readiness to talk about himself. And for someone who struggled to shed his police persona and be himself, to be genuine and vulnerable, she knew that each inventive little kindness from her was a lifeline. She knew she meant the whole world to him. Even if, at times, it felt that she was grappling in the dark for something to cling on to.

CHAPTER THIRTY-EIGHT

CONCERNED ABOUT GRAHAM but with a full afternoon ahead of her, Laura almost walked right into an excited Freddie Solomon.

"Is it Sampson?" she asked at once. Since Freddie had been working on the boxes, Laura had been forced to acknowledge something she hadn't been prepared to say out loud before. Deep down, she was hoping for a breakthrough—something new and significant the library could contribute to LeapFest. Glory, fame, and public recognition weren't values she espoused or considered in concert with the publicly funded library, but she found herself eager for reports of Freddie's progress and having to concentrate unusually hard on her work lest she broke off from it to help him.

"Er, not exactly. But I've found another very, *very* interesting bloke." Freddie launched into a brief history of the anonymous author whose papers he was examining. "He's a credentialed lawyer, a gentleman farmer, someone with an interest in natural history . . . Sounds like he read everything and was interested in most of it."

"What's his name?"

"That's the thing. It might be down at the bottom somewhere, under all these informative little books and essays, but it's almost as though he's keeping his name off his work."

"Why?"

A shrug. "Because they're unfinished?" Freddie guessed. "Or just hobby projects? Maybe he wasn't looking for fame."

Laura raised her eyebrows. "Something you'd find impossible to understand," she said, smiling. In general, Freddie took a joke pretty well, and she rarely passed up the chance to needle him, but this time he didn't react even a little.

"Hey, um," he said, following her, "what's going on downstairs?"

"Hmm? *Persephone the Pig* was a huge hit, thank you for asking," she said, picking up a pile of books left on a table in the corner. Each batch of books represented a line on her to-do list, whether it was cataloguing, reshelving, or even making the occasional repair.

"No, I mean . . . an unmarked police car was parked outside."

"It was?"

"Is David here?"

"He'll slap you with another twenty hours of servitude just for using his first name if you're not careful," she warned. "And you're not allowed anywhere near his case after that foolishness at the cliff."

She showed Freddie a photo on her phone. About to remove his rappelling harness, the DI stood next to Melanie Howes and her red 4x4 emblazoned with emergency stripes and the insignia of Jersey Fire Service. Graham's hair was plastered to his head with sweat. "And you assumed he just sat in his office and thought *big thoughts*, didn't you?"

Seeing the image irked Freddie, though he didn't show it. He would rather have been covering the investigation, speaking to Mia Thorne's friends, and piecing together her final movements. But Graham had laid down the law. He'd have been truly stupid to test this proscription; one night in the cells would be one night too many.

"Go on, throw me a bone," Freddie pleaded, leaning in close.

"Not a chance."

"Was he interviewing one of the film students?"

Laura picked up a massive, hardcover reference copy of *Jane's All the World's Aircraft*. "Don't push your luck. And can't you see I'm busy?" The book landed on the distribution desk with an intimidating thud. "I'll end up doing community service *myself* if he thinks I've tipped you off. Back to your table. And find out who that polymath of an anonymous author might be," she said, waving him away. "That'd at least be useful."

Laura wandered back to the distribution desk as Freddie began trawling through the papers again. Most were bills of sale, contracts for legal or actuarial work, insurance policies, and the like. There was a notice announcing a meeting to protest parliament's passage of The Factory Act that proposed limiting the workdays of women and children under eighteen to ten hours. "What will they ask for next?" Freddie murmured. Another notice vigorously rejected the notion of a new income tax on wealthy landowners. "Times change," he noted, "but people don't."

After an hour spent carefully cataloguing, he found a hand-annotated program for a concert celebrating Queen Victoria's twenty-fifth birthday. He brought it to Laura's attention during one of her patrols. "Charming," she agreed. "We'll include it in the display."

"Shame that Old Vic didn't 'leap' anywhere, though." Freddie returned to the slow process of reading and taking notes, enlivened only by Laura's periodic visits, but the time passed quickly enough.

CHAPTER THIRTY-NINE

"I WAS A bit harsh with her. Sorry," Graham said when he and Janice got back to the station. The journey there from the library had been quiet. Although he outranked her, Janice's combination of moral rectitude, friendly compassion that bordered on the maternal, and ever-immaculate uniform lent her a natural authority that could, at times and with certain people, outperform his. "Tea? I've got some of those fruity ones you like."

"Have you the 'Apricot Blush'?"

He checked his lower desk drawer and gave her a thumbs-up.

"Sir, I've seen you come down like a ton of bricks on all kinds of people."

"Yes," he agreed, still embarrassed.

"Is there any chance," Janice continued, trying to tread carefully, "that this is personal for you?" Before he could shut her down, she added, "It's just . . . you get very wrapped up in cases, particularly those involving a young victim. Very emotionally invested."

She was right, but the timing wasn't. "I caught sight of something that led me astray," he chose to say. "She was being evasive," he added. *As am I.*

"You felt that Fawn was protecting Jackie?" Janice said.

"That, or not being quite truthful about her own movements."

"But I mean, if one of them did do something she shouldn't, wouldn't they have conspired to alibi each other?"

Graham shook his head, ignoring his tea now. "Only if they confessed to one another. If Fawn realised during the interview that Jackie *did* have something to do with Mia's death, she had to improvise."

"Like what?"

"I feel awful for saying it, but like . . . an angry rebuttal, with lots of tears, ending the interview early before she said something that might contradict her sister's story."

"You think I'm falling into a trap?"

"I'm saying that Ms. Prentiss, the younger, might not be as squeaky clean as she appears." After a very long, very deep sigh, Janice silently took a string of sips. "Just . . ." she said, "let me know next time we're doing 'good cop, bad cop.'"

"I think I was just being 'dumb cop,'" Graham admitted. "I could have been more . . . nuanced." He put more tea on to steep, letting the fragrance of an apricot orchard calm them both.

"Alright, what are we going to do with that noisy prat in the cell?" Janice asked.

"How's he been doing?" Graham said, pouring himself yet more tea. The apricot wasn't his favourite, but it carried a freight train's worth of caffeine, and he needed it.

"Bazza said he was entertaining himself singing a song of his own composition called 'Banged up in Jersey' to the tune of 'Waltzing Matilda.'"

"A man of the arts," Graham noted. "I underestimated him."

"You really, *really* didn't," Janice said. "Anyway, what are we going to do? The consul will be ticked off if we keep him."

"What's she going to do?" Graham asked. "Sentence me to transportation?"

"Is that, like, being stuck directing traffic for six months, or something?"

For the first time in what felt like many days, Graham let himself laugh, probably loud enough to be heard by the incarcerated Nozz. "No, back in the day, they'd send you to colonial Australia with little chance of ever returning. It was a punishment for murder, and a host of other things, many of them quite petty."

"Nozz would accept that in a flash."

"Let's have one more chat with him, shall we?"

On hearing footsteps approaching his cell, the surfer struck up another tune. "Alright, that's enough for one day," said Graham, coming to a halt with his hands deep in his pockets. The hallway had always reminded him more of a 1970s high school than a jail, managing to look institutional without being intimidating—until one saw the metal bars, of course. "I don't suppose anything has occurred to you that might assist us in our inquiries?" he said as he opened the cell door.

Nozz stood up from his grey-blanketed bench. He was unshaven and looked weary. "It's occurred to me," he said, "that I'll probably have solid grounds for suing you lot once I get out of here. That lady said so."

"Really?" said Graham, as if notified by a five-year-old that they were running away from home.

"Wrongful arrest. Or wrongful imprisonment. I can't remember what she said."

"Well, a razor-sharp legal mind like yours should make short work of it." Graham came closer. "Nozz, seriously, lad," he said. "Talk to us."

CHAPTER FORTY

"I TOLD YOU the truth!" Nozz insisted yet again. "The whole truth, the whole-grain mustard truth, the hole-in-one-on-a-par-three truth . . ."

"Except the bit about you being a jack-the-lad," Janice pointed out.

"Yeah, but after, I told you truthfully that I lied about it!"

"Big of you," said Graham. "One more time. Why did you leave Mia Thorne on the cliff top, all by herself?"

"Because she *told me to*," Nozz enunciated slowly. "Wanted to walk around. 'Take the air,' I think she said."

"Why do you think she wanted to do that?"

"I *dunno*! I told you, maybe something to do with her play or whatever; she didn't say. For all her being something of a chick, she was a bit cuckoo."

"Is it just possible," Janice asked him, "that as she was giving you the elbow, she was trying not to hurt your feelings? Didn't want to walk back with you? That she was going to wait a bit, then follow?"

Nozz's pride was already severely dented, and this didn't help. He considered Janice's idea. "Ah yeah, I mean, maybe." He frowned. "It's not the usual way of things, but yeah, it's possible. But she was so *keen*, earlier."

"Girl's entitled to change her mind," Janice said, "however Brad Pitt-esque you might appear at first glance."

Nozz looked over to Graham, just as confused as ever. "Is she serious?"

"The Brad Pitt bit or the being-given-the-elbow bit?"

"Search me, mate," Nozz said, throwing up his hands. "Who says she wasn't shooing me away 'cos she didn't want an audience for her jump, eh? I've been sitting here, starting to reckon with it all, and I'm thinking she had some bad wiring"—he tapped his temple—"up here. On the fritz."

Narrowly resisting the urge to douse Nozz with pepper spray until he apologised, Janice said, "Is it also possible that she intended to meet someone else that night?"

This stung, and Nozz didn't mind showing it. "What, like I was the first course," he asked huffily, "and some other bloke was the entrée? Bit much, isn't it?"

"No need to take it personally."

"It got bloody personal when you stuck me in jail!"

"I stuck you in jail,'" Graham reminded him darkly, "because of your harassing and abusive behaviour at the hostel."

"Then why isn't Zink in here too?" Nozz cried. "You picked on *me* because you think I'm some evil bastard, that I'd push Mia off a cliff! Nobody ever spent two days behind bars just for asking some Scandinavian girl, a bit too loud, whether she'd like to—"

"That's enough," Graham and Janice said together. Graham continued, "Listen, I'm letting you out because I *have* to. I can't legally order you to leave Jersey, but I'd like to. I also can't stop you from surfing, as long as you do it in permitted areas. You're pretty much free to leave and do as you please, much as it pains me to say so."

"Too right," said Nozz, eyeing the bunch of keys in Graham's hand optimistically.

"But Noah Stimms wants to tear your head off, there's a posse of Northern European women who would gladly mace you into oblivion, and an Australian consul who would yank you by your didgeridoos if you make her come all the way down here again. So, keep your head down and your nose clean. Got it?"

"Loud and clear," said Nozz, gulping. "I'll be good as gold, promise."

"We'll see."

"Where's Zink?" Nozz asked as Graham stepped aside.

"Waiting for you at the hostel, I expect."

"And where's this Noah bloke? The one who wants me dead?"

"Waiting for you at the hostel, I expect."

"Right," Nozz said, gulping again. "Reckon I'll be off then."

Graham stopped him, a cautionary hand on his shoulder. "*Don't* make me regret this, you hear?"

CHAPTER FORTY-ONE

HAVING SEEN NOZZ off the premises, Graham saw he'd missed a call from Tomlinson. "News?" he barked when Tomlinson picked up. Graham paced the constabulary car park despite the falling temperature. After the day's activities, he was ready for some air. And some good news.

"I have DNA and toxicology results," Tomlinson reported. "And one is a bit complicated."

Graham took a deep breath. "Okay, let's have it."

"She'd had a drink, but not more than one. Beer."

"Probably an Australian brand, but let's not assume."

"Let's not," Tomlinson agreed. "Seems the last thing she ate was a hot dog. Mustard, but no pickles," he added.

The detective inspector whistled. "That new lab of yours is sending back some cracking stuff."

"It's like working with Dr. McCoy aboard the *Starship Enterprise*," Tomlinson said. "If you'd told me back when I left medical school in nineteen-never-you-mind..."

"Anything under her fingernails?"

"Just a trace of the aforementioned mustard," Tomlinson reported. "No sign of any foreign DNA, either defensively or intimately."

"Interesting," Graham said thoughtfully, "but not exactly helpful."

"The lack of clear evidence with respect to defence wounds—remember most of her injuries would have been caused by her fall—*and* the lack of DNA means we still have to keep an open mind as to the reason for her fall. There's nothing to point conclusively to another party being involved *or* to her being alone. I'm sorry I can't be more helpful. No sign of her phone, I suppose?"

Graham sighed and looked up at the sky in disappointment. "No, not yet." He rocked back on his heels. "I thought you said something was complicated."

"We found trace amounts of anti-depressants in her body."

"Her friends did say she was prone to mood changes. They'd become worse recently. Her mother had a history of mental illness."

"Thing is, you see, I made some calls to her university doctor and hometown GP. Neither was particularly candid, patient confidentiality and all that, but I got the impression that she wasn't being prescribed anything."

"Hmm, so what do you think? She was buying them? Or someone was sharing theirs with her?"

"Yes, that's exactly what I think. One of those two things. It's not uncommon among young people, especially at university. It's illegal, and potentially very problematic," said Tomlinson.

"But what does it mean that there were only traces?"

"It means she hadn't taken any for several days, a very dangerous thing to do if she was taking high doses and stopped them suddenly."

"How would she have been feeling?"

"Well, if she had stopped a high dose abruptly, she'd have gone downhill, fast," the medical examiner said. "She'd have gone into withdrawal—listless, low on energy, anxious. If she was depressed before she started taking them, she'd have felt worse,; if she wasn't, she soon would be."

"Enough to feel suicidal?"

"Possibly."

"Hmm." Graham's mind started doing somersaults as he sought to think through the implications. "This is the first break in the case. Thanks, Marcus!"

"Make sure you make the most of it, young man. Right, I'm done for the day. What's next for you?" Tomlinson said. It was past time to pack up, and he had a superb 2011 Grenache from California sitting patiently on his kitchen counter. Better still, a good friend of his had promised to share it with him once she'd closed her law office for the day.

"I'm going to do some thinking. And perhaps there'll be a warm dinner waiting for me, if I'm luckier than I deserve," Graham said.

CHAPTER FORTY-TWO

WITH HIS EYELIDS starting to droop, Freddie lamented yet again the library's prohibition on coffee. He'd learnt more than enough already about the ins and outs of horse breeding in the 1800s and the migration patterns of a dozen species of birds. Completing his cataloguing of the current set of documents, he pulled yet another collection of pages bound by red fabric from the bottom of the box. "Oh, goody," he muttered to himself. He opened up to the first page, expecting another stodgy screed on the efficient use of pastureland or advice on gathering local fungi.

But the words on this page indicated something quite different, and far more personal than earlier papers. Rather than advice on husbandry and horticulture, Freddie found that he'd stumbled on a journal. It was identifiably in the same hand as other papers in the crate he was working through, but written with a more relaxed penmanship, as though the author were certain it would not be read. "Maybe he was tired?" Freddie asked the lines of text that slanted slightly to the right. "Or a bit drunk?" One of the smaller books of advice he had uncovered had concerned "the fermentation of diverse liquors," though Freddie had learnt enough about the author to believe that he was too high-minded and serious for frequent excesses.

"Wait . . . what's he saying here?" It was a full minute before Freddie realised he'd inadvertently stood up from his seat and was reading with both hands pressed to the desk. "'*A most terrible incident, a plague of miserable deaths fit to be visited upon damnable sinners, but scarce ever sent to poison the happiness of good, God-fearing folk.*'" Not every word was immediately clear, and Freddie found he had to guess the odd one. "*For the last week, I have been assailed by the . . .*' Demands? Yes, '*the demands of Mister . . .*' can't-read-his-name," Freddie said. He pushed on. "'*And his Masonic brethren, who are most fiercely and . . .*' Stubbornly? Maybe. Anyway, '*determined that the aforementioned . . .*'"

The next word completely stumped him. "'*Ap . . .*'?" He peered closer. "Apostasy? Or . . . apoplexy?"

"Who's in apoplexy?" asked Laura. She had stopped during her final round of the day to peer over Freddie's shoulder as he read to himself.

"I think it's a journal," Freddie told her. "But"—he turned to catch her eye—"look at this, would you?" Laura grumbled but set down the books she was carrying. "I mean, what in the name of Pete . . ." he asked, his finger hovering over the misshapen word.

"Apothecary," said Laura at once. "Like a pharmacist."

"Oh, right, '*determined that the aforementioned apothecary should suffer punishment befitting the horror of his deeds.*' Wow, someone's in trouble!"

But Laura had jumped ahead of him. "When was this written?" she asked, finding suddenly that the document had her complete attention.

"The year is 1846," Freddie replied, pointing to the date at the top of the page.

"Freddie . . . don't you see?" Laura said, breathlessly. "He's talking about Charles Sampson!"

CHAPTER FORTY-THREE

NUDGING THE THROTTLE forward, Barnwell brought the Zodiac to thirty-five knots, perhaps a little quicker than strictly necessary. He enjoyed the sensation of wind on his face. The small powerboat skimmed across waves that were mercifully calm. Close to the marina, he'd not have dared shoot out of the harbour so fast—that kind of thing was frowned upon, especially when most of Gorey hadn't yet woken—but he was pushed for time. He wanted to carry out his plan before anyone back at the constabulary noticed that he was missing. The ever-reluctant manager at Bonner's hostel informed him that Nozz and Zink had left with their surfboards before six. "I don't know how they manage it, the way they drink."

And so, following in the wake of Gorey's fishing fleet that had headed out earlier to catch lobster and crab, Barnwell hung on tight, kept his knees bent, and scanned the horizon in search of the two reckless Australians.

It didn't take him long to find them. "There you are," Barnwell muttered. The two men straddled their boards, one green, the other orange, as they bobbed around in the swell about 100 yards offshore, waiting for the waves to build. Sampson's Cove was away in the distance, but out at sea, patterns were already emerging. A sequence of crests grew by degrees, offering early hope that in half an hour or so, Nozz and Zink would be riding the inner walls of some impressive waves. Barnwell could tell by the Aussies' languid ease that they knew their surfing stuff.

Barnwell's air horn was hardly necessary—the Zodiac's engine was the only sound on the water—but he enjoyed blasting it. "Morning, fellas!" he called over the loud-hailer. "You look a bit cold out there. I thought I'd bring you some breakfast."

"Yeah?" Zink asked. "Bacon and eggs?" He slapped his belly through his wetsuit. "Haha, get it? Bacon! Cos, he's, you know, a—"

"Law enforcement official with the powers of arrest," Barnwell reminded them. "Actually, I've got a question for you, Nozz, before the waves get up and you risk your necks."

"It's not that dangerous!" Nozz informed him. "I mean, look!" He spread his arms out at the gently rolling, wet surface.

"We're a few hours from high tide," Barnwell said. "And at this time of year, with some brisk weather further to the east, Sampson's Cove can become one of the most dangerous areas of water in the Channel. You didn't come out here to bob like a duck on its flat surface, now did you?"

"No, and it totally rocks!" Zink insisted. Then his face fell. "You're not really here to drag us back to shore, are you? We've been waiting *days* for this."

As Barnwell came closer, he noticed that both men wore headsets that combined a microphone and a camera. "Forcing you to disappoint two million fans? I don't think I'd be able to sleep at night."

"Right!" Nozz cried. "Then come along and help. Film us! That would be awesome! We'll make you famous too!"

Barnwell let the comment pass; they'd have been nonplussed by his tales of past nautical achievements and visits to the Palace. "Just clip on for a minute and answer a couple of questions. Then you can pointlessly imperil yourselves to your hearts' content."

"Is this about that posh middle-class girl again?" Zink asked.

"Come a bit closer," Barnwell said. He gave Zink such a hard stare that the surfer shrank. The thought of being alone with the constable inside a locked cell did not appeal.

"No thanks."

"To answer your question, yes, it is. Mia Thorne's death remains unexplained, and my boss isn't going to give me a second's peace until that situation changes."

"I'm not gonna give you a different answer, sitting here on my board, than I gave you in that freakin' jail of yours," Nozz said. "Like getting thrown into Guan—" He stumbled over the name. "G-Guantanamo, that was."

"Why didn't I bring the water cannon?" Barnwell asked the developing waves before addressing the two men. "You two were 'sinking some cold ones,' or whatever, in the lobby on Sunday night. Here's what I want to know: Would you recognise the guys from the film crew if you saw them?"

Nozz thought. "Ah yeah, two fellas, right? Were they both actors, or . . .?"

"No, one of them has a body for behind the camera," said Zink, sniggering, "Don't reckon he'll be landing any leading roles in Hollywood unless he loses that spare tyre, you know?"

Barnwell muttered to himself, "The water cannon, or . . ." He slapped his forehead. "The taser! Why on earth didn't I bring that?"

"So, yeah. I guess I'd know them if I saw them," Nozz decided. "Why?"

"I've read your statement and in it you said you saw someone when you were coming back from the cliff top."

A memory swam up and words came straight out of Zink's mouth without connecting with the wiser part of his brain. "Was it the annoying bugger who kept telling us to keep it down?"

"Nah, that guy was German," said Nozz. "Like, really, *really* German."

"Oh, yeah," Zink remembered. "'Die guests cannot zleep vit all diss noise!'" he said in a remarkably unsuccessful accent.

"Keep thinking," Barnwell said encouragingly. His patience was wearing thin. "This is important. What did he look like, this person you passed?"

Another memory of Zink's made its presence known. "Did he have a permanent scowl? Like"—he tried—"like someone just told him they'd accidentally scraped his jeep?"

"Shut up, Zink. I'm thinking." Nozz reprimanded his friend. Barnwell hid a smile and waited for Nozz's brain to kick into gear.

"Yeah!" Nozz exploded. "Yeah, I saw him! I passed him as I ran back." He let out a whoop. "Six foot-ish, good hair, you know, like he went to an English boarding school early last century. That was him, one of the acting guys!"

"It's amazing to see," Barnwell noted, "that the possibility of your memory matching up with reality is rare enough to warrant a celebration. Now," he said, bringing out his iPad from its waterproof case, "tell me exactly what you saw of him, and *when*."

CHAPTER FORTY-FOUR

"**H**E WAS WALKING along the cliff path about five minutes out from the hostel. I took a shortcut through the bush for the last few and saw him."

"Did he see you?"

"Dunno. Nah, don't think so."

"What time would that be?"

"Well, let's see. I got back at eight, so just before that, I reckon."

"And you're sure it was Noah?"

"Ah yeah. Sure thing. He's a right dag."

"You weren't drunk? Didn't have your beer goggles on?"

"Nah, I'd only had one at that point. Who do you take me for?" Nozz rolled his eyes.

"Yeah, mate," Zink said. He pointed at his friend with his thumb. "His beer drinking is legendary back home in Wollongong. I've seen him get barrelled after a crateful. He's the man." The pair high-fived.

Barnwell looked between them to check they were serious. They were. Drunk in charge of a surfboard. There was probably a law against it. He shook his head and tapped out a text to Graham. "Right, next thing. You have the wonderful opportunity to redeem yourselves after that mess-up the other day."

"Oh, how's that then?" Nozz said.

"I want you to paddle in and help me with something on the beach."

"Like what?"

"We need to look for the victim's phone."

"That'd be washed out to sea days ago."

"Maybe, but we're going to have another go at finding it. Things'll go a lot quicker and a lot smoother if you help, so come on, lead the way."

The two Aussies, judging rightly for once that compliance over resistance was the better option, started to paddle in. Barnwell fell in behind them, shepherding them like they were sheep he would shear when they landed.

"Right, you start in that corner," Barnwell said to Zink. "You in that corner," he said to Nozz. "Go up and down from cliff to sea edge and back again. Eventually, you'll cross over and do the same all the way across the width of the beach."

Zink opened his mouth to complain. Barnwell interrupted him. "You'll be checking each other's work that way and with you two, that's absolutely necessary. I'm gonna take the rocks."

For forty minutes, the men scoured the cove. For Barnwell it involved a good deal of clambering and panting as he pushed his fingers into crevices and swished them through the sandy waters of rock pools. He wanted a result, and if he didn't get one, he wanted to be absolutely sure he'd done his best.

Barnwell and Zink met up at the edge of the cove. "Anything?" Zink asked.

Barnwell puffed out his cheeks and let out a long breath. "Nope, nothing. I think we'll be going back empty-handed. Damn." He took a swig of water from a bottle and offered it to Zink. Over Zink's shoulder, he saw Nozz. "What's he doing?" Nozz was climbing up the cliff face. He'd gone a few feet and was looking for a new foothold.

"He likes to climb sheer cliff faces when he's not surfing the sickest waves," Zink replied. "He's always frothing for something."

Barnwell nodded. "Ah, right."

Nozz found the foothold he was looking for and lifted himself a foot higher. He let out a shout. "Hey!"

Barnwell saw something flicker close to Nozz's right hand as the sun caught it. "Don't touch it!" Barnwell raced over, stumbling over the wet, heavy sand. He pulled out his phone and started taking pictures. Zooming in, he saw it, tucked in a crevice between two rocks, twenty feet up the face of the cliff.

Wedged in a crack lay a beige, crocheted lace shawl, and caught in it, nestled between rows of intricately ordered stitches, lay Mia Thorne's pink mobile phone.

Roach had his eyes closed when he heard the bang of the front doors. He was testing himself on stop and search powers under the PACE Codes of Practice when Graham blasted into the station like a tornado.

"Roach! Go and get me Noah Stimms from the hostel. Don't tell him you're coming, and don't take any monkey business. If I'm busy when you get back, stick him in the interview room and leave him there." Graham disappeared into the break room.

"Erm, yes, sir!" Roach scrambled to close his book and shuffle his papers. The DI wasn't messing around, he could tell. "Can I tell him what it's in connection with?" he called.

Graham walked back into reception. He was out of breath. "Mia Thorne's death obviously. But other than that, no." Graham was wielding the office kettle like it was a lethal weapon. "Just go and get him."

Roach grabbed his jacket and the car keys and raced to the door. He passed Janice on her way in.

"Watch out, Inspector's on the warpath," he hissed at her.

"What's going on?" Janice called as her eyes followed Roach to the car. Roach shrugged. "I've been ordered to pick up Noah Stimms from the hostel. That's all I know," he yelled back.

"Huh. Well, good luck," Janice muttered as she turned to enter the station building.

"Harding!" Graham barked as soon as she made it through the doors. "Get me Jack on standby. Barnwell's on his way in. He found Mia Thorne's phone at the beach."

Janice's eyes widened. "You're joking! I thought you looked there." She began sending a text to her fiancé.

"Yeah, well, Barnwell brought in reinforcements. It was found partway up the cliff wedged in a gap in the rocks."

"Hallelujah. Jack's on his way, sir."

CHAPTER FORTY-FIVE

"IT'S NOT IN the greatest of shape, but I'll see what I can do." Jack Wentworth, the constabulary's technical consultant, turned over Mia's phone in his hands. It was wrapped in an evidence bag and dusty with fingerprint powder. Roach, back from the hostel with Noah Stimms, had already performed external forensics on it, uncovering nothing but the owner's fingerprints. Now the entire Gorey constabulary stood awaiting Jack's appraisal.

Graham took a sip of his tea, confident that what Jack really meant was that mining the innards of the phone for data which might blow his case open would prove to be a piece of cake. In the background, Barnwell whistled, euphoric that his early morning boat ride and improvised requisitioning of the surfer bros had turned up not one but two pieces of pivotal case evidence.

"Alright," Graham said. "We'll leave you to it. Let me know as soon as you get something."

"Are you going to interview Noah Stimms now, sir?" Roach asked.

"No, I'm going to let him stew for a bit and wait to see if Jack here can get us an early result. Give me a shout in an hour, alright?"

"Thanks for everything," Freddie said as Laura handed him back his phone. The hurriedly staged but flatteringly lit photo managed to make Freddie look almost professorial. For that, Laura deserved all the credit. "It's not every day I get to keep my audience happy, contribute to a case, *and* enrich our understanding of Gorey's history!"

"But it certainly *is* every day that you get completely carried away," Laura said. "Remember, those women were murdered, so a certain person might believe that those documents fall under *his* jurisdiction."

Letting out a groan, Freddie asked, "What, he's going to bang me up for interfering with an investigation he hasn't yet started into murders that happened almost two *centuries* ago?"

"The least, tiniest excuse is all he'll need, mark my words," Laura warned, smiling. "And Freddie?"

"Yeah?" He looked up.

"Well done finding that journal. I mean it. We'd never have got to it on our own, short-staffed as we are." At the very bottom of the opening page of a paper that lay next to Freddie's keyboard, a cluster of initials could just be discerned: *JBMcCAC*. Freddie had come upon them some ten minutes earlier. Moments later, Laura had agreed that there was only one man to whom they could have conceivably belonged.

"Let's just hope," Freddie said, returning to typing, "these things I've found are genuine, and meaningful."

"Funny," Laura couldn't help muttering, "that's never stopped you before."

"Jack's got something, sir. Texts between Mia and Noah. They're time-stamped Sunday evening at seven forty-five."

"That's after Nozz says he left her." Graham quickly weaved his way between the desks in the open-plan office to look over Janice's shoulder at her computer screen. Jack had sent her screenshots.

```
I'm at the cliff. Meet me?
When?
Now
KK
```

"Not exactly Barrett and Browning were they?" Graham muttered.

"Who?"

"Elizabeth Barrett and Robert Browning. They were poets, mid-1850s. They . . ." Graham glimpsed Janice's blank expression. "Never mind."

"This proves that Noah was with Mia on the night that she died."

"It also takes that Aussie bro out of the frame."

"And puts Noah in it."

"Yes, it most surely does."

"Something else, sir. There was another text that arrived after that."

"What did it say?"

"'I think you should do it.' Jack's traced it to Clint Wells. Arrived at eight forty-three."

"Huh. I wonder what that was about? He never mentioned it."

"After that, there was also a whole heap of texts from Noah declaring his undying love. You're the only woman for me, blah, blah, blah."

"No surprise there. Ask Jack to dig around a bit more, would you? See if he can find any trace of those abusive messages she was getting."

"Will do, sir."

"And Janice, get one of the others to find out from Clint what that text was about."

CHAPTER FORTY-SIX

"HE'S READY, BOSS," Roach said after knocking at Graham's office door. "The lad's not in the best of moods, I should warn you." Roach had roused Noah from a lie-in, giving him very little time before hauling him to the marked car. The student had blinked himself awake in the sunshine, complaining bitterly and loudly about this impertinent and aggressive wake-up call. He'd then sat in the interview room with only a cup of tea for company for over an hour.

"Oh, I'm not going to worry about that," Graham said, rising from his desk chair cheerfully.

In the same red-and-green striped rugby shirt he'd slept in, Noah sat hunched over the table. He cut a forlorn, moody figure. He'd been crying, and his hair was sticking up on end again in the way that seemed to be normal for him. As Graham came into the interview room, notepad ready, Harding followed him in. The twenty-one-year-old stood. "This is all wrong, all *wrong!*" he wailed.

"Have a seat, please," said Graham. He made sure to behave like a bank manager about to assess a new loan applicant. Laura would be pleased. And Janice.

"A lawyer," Noah said breathlessly. "Don't I get a lawyer?"

"If you'd like one, of course," Graham replied, "but this is just a friendly chat, and we're hoping that won't be necessary. We just need to clear a few things up." *Like why you lied about being at the hostel all Sunday evening.*

"So, I haven't been arrested?"

"No." *Not yet.*

"Then . . ." Noah asked, his emotions swinging between despair, confusion, and anger, "why did you pull me out of bed and drag me down here?"

"Some information has come to our attention," Graham said. "Everyone's stories must be checked and checked again until we can conclude with sufficient certainty what happened on the cliff prior to Mia's fall."

Noah folded his arms. "You're trying to scare me into confessing to something I didn't do!"

"Of course not," Graham said. "But I'd be very grateful if you confessed to what you actually *did*. Because it seems that so far you haven't done that."

"What? *What* did I do?" Noah demanded.

"You lied to a police officer about your movements on Sunday evening."

"No, I didn't!" Noah insisted.

"And that makes twice," Graham observed. "You told us that you didn't return to Sampson's Leap on Sunday night after you'd finished filming for the day." He made a show of checking his notebook. "That you hung around the hostel until you went to the pub with Clint at nine. That wasn't true, was it?"

"I don't know what you—"

"We have a witness who saw you five minutes away from the hostel prior to eight p.m. on Sunday night. We also have phone records that show Mia asked you to meet her at the cliff top. And you complied. Not only did you make a false statement—*two* false statements—to a police officer, you are now the last known person to have seen her alive."

"But it's not—"

"The Perjury Act of 1911 begs to differ, I'm afraid. You should know that the Crown Prosecution Service recommends a minimum sentence of four months."

Noah stammered. "It's not that I meant to perjure myself, or anything like that. It's . . . it's because we were only at the cliff for a few—"

"Stop obfuscating, Noah," the DI said. "It doesn't matter in the slightest how long you were there."

Graham spotted the beginnings of an angry retort on Noah's lips, but it melted away, and instead he saw the blankness of a mind faced with an unyielding brick wall of reality.

"We only . . . we only talked, for like, ten minutes," Noah said. "She texted me that night, told me to come back out to the cliff and meet her."

"And did you do as she asked?"

"Of course, I did. I always did what Mia asked." Noah spoke bitterly. Graham wondered if there were any negative feelings that Noah hadn't yet pulled from his emotional range. He seemed to exercise them broadly and often.

"And what time would you say you arrived at the cliff top to meet her?"

"Oh, I don't know. I walked, so around eight fifteen, I think."

"How was the conversation?" asked Graham. "Did it go as you expected?"

Like a diplomat exhausted after too many hours' fruitless attempts at a compromise, Noah puffed out his cheeks. "Should have seen it coming, I suppose."

"It was a 'Dear John,' only done face-to-face, was it?" Harding guessed.

"Yeah, but more like a 'Dear Noah, please sod off.'" Bitterness and anger gave the joke a sombre hue. "I was too much 'drama' for her." Now Noah actually laughed, hollow and resentful. "Two theatre students, one too *dramatic* for the other. Can you imagine?"

"We're both trying," said Graham. "Mia told you the relationship was over, did she?"

"Yeah." Noah ground his teeth and looked away. "She said it was better not to spend weeks and months, when there were . . . other people who might make us both *happier*. Words to that effect. She was rambling a bit. Didn't always make much sense."

"And did that concern you?"

"Not really. I just thought she was struggling to find the words."

"And how did you react, Noah?" Graham asked. "To being dumped."

CHAPTER FORTY-SEVEN

GRAHAM TOOK A hard look at Stimms but didn't see anything devious in his manner. Noah seemed simply a frightened, trembling kid blinking back at him.

"It's important to remember," Harding said, "that we're investigating someone's death. I'm sure," she added with a quick but meaningful glance at Graham, "that you want to be as helpful as you can. But you weren't honest about your movements on Sunday night, and we need to clear that up. Take a couple of deep breaths and just let it all out. I promise you'll feel better."

As afraid of the intimidating detective as he was keen to help the friendly, approachable sergeant, Noah did as he'd been advised. "Alright, I didn't know for sure what Mia was going to say, but she'd been dropping hints. We were all super stressed," he explained. "Short on money, going into our final year . . . and, you know, after we were finished with college, what next? There aren't any jobs for decent money; we're not looking at a bright and breezy future. I know I can be an emotional pile of rubbish, but she wasn't exactly a walk in the park either. But she *did* have a future, a bright one, one that didn't include me."

"She dumped you, pulled the rug from under you," Graham said curtly. "Not nice."

"The worst," reinforced Harding. "Disorientating, and a big wound to your ego."

"But not unusual," Graham added.

Noah squinted. "You think I pushed her," he said, staring back at them both. "That's what you think. I loved her, and she ended it, and I pushed her. That's your big theory."

Setting down his pen with care, Graham said, "Is that what happened, Noah?"

"No! And look, 'innocent until proven guilty,' isn't that how it goes? And it's *you* who has to do the proving." Noah let his boiling emotions take over, his fear and confusion mixing to generate an ambitious level of sarcasm and impertinence. "It's *your* job to prove things, mister . . ."

"It's Detective Inspector Graham to you." Graham fixed Noah with a look that would have dented body armour. "Why did you lie to us? About seeing Mia that evening?"

"I was embarrassed. And in love. For me, this . . . *thing* with Mia was a relationship with real potential, well worth trying to save, and not a *fling*." He spat the word out before slumping over the table. "I'm not very experienced, you see, with . . . relationships," he said, his voice thick with ill luck and failure. "After she died, I just wanted to remember the happy times. Be the boyfriend she had at her end. I wanted to block out our final conversation, pretend it never happened."

"You mean, you used her death to acquire some status for yourself? The bereaved boyfriend? You sure you didn't push her off and pretend her rejection of you hadn't happened at all? Have you ever seen the inside of a prison cell, Noah?"

"*Prison?*" he bleated.

"I've put young men like you in cold little cells, saddled with sentences so long that their friends completely forget about them."

"Boss?" Harding tried, aware of the need to slow the accelerating train of Graham's anger.

"Some of them," Graham continued as his suspect paled before him, "won't even *recognise* the world they walk out into."

Harding gave it another try. "Why don't we . . . ?"

"There'll be lanes in the sky for flying cars," Graham carried on, painting the picture with his hands, "and cities on the *moon*, by the time some of them get out."

Janice closed the lid of her iPad with three times her usual conviction.

"Or you can tell us *everything*, Noah," the DI insisted, oblivious to his sergeant's protests.

"We talked about our relationship, how it wasn't working out," Noah said, his tone deliberately level. "It was all very quick. Then she said she wanted some time alone, because it'd been a crazy week."

"And?"

"And," Noah parroted, "I gathered what pride I had left and walked to the bus stop. She texted me, after."

"When?" the DI demanded.

"Not long after I left the cliff. She sent me a big hug emoji, said she'd never wanted to hurt me, all that stuff."

"Where were you when you received the last text?"

"I was on the bus back to the hostel, I think." Noah thought back. "Yes, because I was getting on the bus when I received it and stood in the aisle to read it. The driver asked me to sit down so he could move off."

"What happened when you got back?" asked Harding.

"I told you. Clint and I went for a few drinks."

"You're changing your mind again," Harding said whilst Graham sat, breathing slowly, gathering his thoughts. "You said earlier you only had one drink."

"Look, I don't remember exactly. I do remember that Clint was drinking heavily. Totally irresponsible seeing as we were filming the next day. I just wanted to de-stress a bit, not to get blackout drunk. One? Two? Three? What does it matter? It was no big deal."

"We have reports that you were drunk. You were sending texts to Mia begging to get back with her." Noah was silent. They could hear his heel tapping against the floor.

"Noah, listen, lad. It's really difficult," Harding warned him, "to take you seriously when you keep contradicting things you said earlier."

"I didn't contradict—"

"Oh, for heaven's sake." Graham dropped his pen, snatched up his notebook, and stood abruptly. He headed for the door. "They're not even *good* lies, Noah," he said.

CHAPTER FORTY-EIGHT

BARNWELL FINISHED FILLING in a form left on his desk just as Graham stormed into the main office. Janice followed him, flustered, her tablet clutched to her chest. There was a gust of heated conversation.

"I know, I know. But he says he got the bus back," Janice said. "And look, he's telling the truth about the texts she sent him. The phone records prove it."

"We've only got his word for it that she sent them. He could have grabbed her phone, pushed her off, sent himself a text, tossed the phone over, *then* caught the bus." Janice paused, frozen by the logic of Graham's theory. "When was the last text sent from her phone?"

Janice consulted her tablet. "Eight thirty-three."

Graham rubbed his hair. "This case is damnable. If we can prove that her text was sent to him after he left her, he's in the clear."

"How are we going to do that, sir?"

"I'm not sure at the moment. Let's think."

"Are we going to let him go?"

"No, not yet, but we may have to. He's not been truthful, but really, we've got nothing. Let's just hang on to him for a bit; maybe Jack can come up with more. If nothing else, we'll give Mr. Stimms a scare so he doesn't pull a stunt like this in the future."

Barnwell stood and stretched as he looked at his watch. "Anyone want a coffee? I'm going to do a bit of community policing down at Ethel's." The other two, only just realising he was there, shook their heads.

"See ya later, then." Barnwell picked up his police cap, strode through the doors and, turning right, walked down the hill to the shops in the centre of Gorey, glad to be out in the open air, free of the frustrated atmosphere at the station.

"Afternoon, Ethel,"

"Afternoon, love. The usual?"

"Yes, please."

There was a shudder behind Barnwell, followed by a wheeze as a bus pulled up outside the coffee shop. The bell above the door tinkled as it opened.

"Afternoon, Bill," Barnwell said without turning.

"Afternoon, Bill. The usual?" Ethel repeated. Barnwell guessed that Ethel probably said those words thirty or more times a day.

"Thanks, duckie." Bill, the bus driver, nodded at Barnwell. "Bazza."

"Alright? How's things down at the depot?"

"Pretty good, mate. Tourist season's slowing down; kids'll be back at school next week. Different faces, same problems."

"How's that then?"

"Ah, you know. They all need to be told where to get off. Tourists obviously, but they're grateful and well-behaved for the most part. The kids?" Bill let out a whistle. "They wouldn't know I existed unless the bus stopped moving and even then, only when they got hungry. And as for being grateful and well-behaved? I had one try to wrap himself round my wing mirror the other day!" Bill shook his head. "They really need to be told where to get off, I can tell you. The kids are why I still do Sunday nights. Means I can avoid Monday mornings."

Barnwell murmured in sympathy. "Still doing the cliffside route?"

"Yep. Pickups at the car parks and through to St. Helier and back."

"How many years has it been now?"

Bill sucked air through his teeth. "Ooh, at least seven."

Ethel put their orders on the counter. A decaf almond milk latte and a chocolate croissant in a paper bag for Barnwell. Tea the colour of rust and an egg and cress sandwich for Bill.

"I'll get these," Barnwell said, handing over a note.

"Thank you kindly, sir." Bill picked up his order, balancing the pack of sandwiches on top of his tea.

"So, you were working last Sunday?" Barnwell asked him.

"Yeah, but I didn't see anything to do with that girl's fall if that's what you're asking. I had a think, but I never saw her, or I would've said."

"Did a lad get on your bus? About eight thirty. Tall, skinny, sticky-up hair. I could get you a photo if you needed."

Bill pursed his lips and looked up at the ceiling. "Was he early twenties? There weren't much business on Sunday, so I do remember one lad. He was the only person on the bus. Seemed a bit upset. Kept sniffing and pulling at his hair. I picked him up at the number two car park and dropped him off at Bonner's. That the lad you mean?"

Barnwell snapped on the lid of his coffee with a sharp click. "Sounds like it."

"Yeah, I had to yell at him to sit down because he was standing in the aisle looking at his phone. I was running behind and needed to pick up the pace. Didn't want him crashing to the floor when I drove off and doing himself an injury."

"So, what time would that have been? Can you tell me, roughly?"

"I can tell you exactly: eight thirty-three."

CHAPTER FORTY-NINE

"THE BUS LEAVES that stop at eight thirty-two and I was a minute late. You know what I'm like, Bazza. Punctual as. My supervisor expects it."

"Could you pick him out in a lineup, d'you think?"

"Yeah, I reckon I could."

"Thanks, mate. If I need you to, I'll be in touch."

"Anytime, Bazza. Cheers for the drink. D'you want a lift anywhere?"

"Could you take me back to the station? My boss is going to want to hear about this pronto."

"Yep, if you don't mind telling a few tourists where to get off." The bus driver cackled at his own joke as he pressed the button on the outside of his bus. The doors opened with a hiss, and the two men climbed aboard.

Harding and Graham were still discussing the case when the door burst open and in blasted Barnwell like he was blundering about on a rugby pitch. There was a slight sheen to his hairline. He wiped his upper lip. "Sir, I've got more intel about the case."

"Intel? Constable, have you been watching *CSI Jersey*?"

"What? No, sir. I prefer *RHOJ*."

Graham's eyes widened.

"*Real Housewives of Jersey*, sir," Janice explained. "It's a reality show about the rich wives of the island."

"Doing what?"

"My thoughts exactly, sir."

"I watch it for intel," Barnwell said. "You never know what they might say. There could be evidence, sir."

Graham burst out laughing. "Good man, Barnwell. What did you come in to say?"

"Noah Stimms was on the bus like he said, at the time he said. Bill, the bus driver, confirmed it. Says he'll pick out Stimms in a lineup if we need him to."

"Aaargh." Graham flung his pen onto his desk. "So, what you're telling me is that we're back to square one."

"'Fraid so, sir."

"Perhaps I should start watching *RHOJ* for *intel*. I might make more progress."

It was painstaking and dusty work, but later that day, fully ten of Freddie's twenty hours had passed in reasonable contentment. The draft of a codicil that disinherited a landowner's eldest son in favour of his "cherished and unblemished" younger brother and an elaborate bill of sale for 160 sheep from "fine, broad-shouldered stock of surpassing excellence" were among his recent discoveries. "Their farmers wrote better than most of today's journalists," Freddie told Laura. But it was his finds relating to Charles Villiers Sampson that most held his interest.

In a blur of excitement and despite his growing fatigue after a hard day bent over centuries-old documents, Freddie punched out the first draft of a blog post entitled, "The Sampson Case: A Cry from the Past." Rereading it and deciding that much of it was a bit too "purple," as his creative writing teacher used to say, Freddie tried again with a more level, professional tone until, minutes before nine o'clock, he was ready to publish.

CHAPTER FIFTY

The Gorey Gossip
Thursday, September 1st

I have in my hand a document that has likely not seen the light of day in over a century, written by a man whose name will soon be as famous as that of Charles Sampson. He was the magistrate of Gorey, an unelected official who worked alongside the mayor, somewhat like an attorney general. On that fateful night in 1846, he was faced with a terrible and complex legal matter, one that quickly spun out of his control.

Sir Jeremiah Blackstone McCannish Arthur Creaveley, much like his gorgeously absurd name, was very much a man of his time. Highly educated in the law and broadly read, Creaveley was an avid student of the natural world, both as a professional farmer and as a hobbyist. Among his papers are more than a dozen concise booklets on birds, fish, husbandry, and the gentle art of brewing. This latter interest apparently collided not at all with his strict religious beliefs, expressed in his role as a lay preacher.

His chief occupation, though, was the law. Creaveley observed how vital it was to survey evidence "with coolness of mind, and a heart that knows only dispassionate calm." He'd have made a very fitting conversational partner for a certain detective of our own time. Later, he wrote that "A judge may be admired only when he undertakes to consider neither the profession nor the social station of the accused" when making his decision. As you can see, Creaveley's pen dripped with honey. And so, it is all the more frustrating that key pages of his journal remain unavailable to us.

Let me explain. Deep in the collection, beneath a treatise that could have been entitled *How to Be a Decent Husband in the Nineteenth Century*, I found thirteen loose pages that comprise a journal that Creaveley kept during the time of Sampson's famous "leap." Only three pages are so far legible to me; the rest will take longer due to some damage—most likely spilled droplets of red wine—as well as the highly individual nature of the magistrate's handwriting.

So, I won't delay. Straight from his pen, through mine, to my readership, Jeremiah Creaveley finally speaks about the Sampson case:

> *Poison was the method of these deaths in the assessment of our physician, Dr. Barclay, a finding with which I could not disagree. First showing a pallor, and a sudden weakness of the stomach, all three afflicted women convulsed at great and terrible length, as though the Devil had made of them his own hapless marionettes. They could not eat or drink without violently returning every morsel in an instant. Trembling as though frozen, poor Alice Pritchard was gathered unto Jesus before Dr. Barclay could exsanguinate, as was his intent, and then a day later, Penelope Levin fell silent after a bout of pain the doctor likened to a fatally difficult childbirth. God's will kept my dear friend's daughter, Susan St. Edmund, with us a day longer still, but such was her suffering that all around her wished the end would come, and prayed together without pause until dawn, when God finally called her home.*
>
> *And then, as a wistful breeze becomes a furious storm, the good people of Gorey sought the truth, or failing that, whatever scrap of revenge could be found. As sure as the turning tide, notions of the case were begotten by drinkers in the taverns, and by chatterers at the docks; they were exchanged across neighbours' fences and passed along church pews, speeded by that*

most effective agent: prejudice. Strangers to science, and with their backs turned against Lady Justice, the public quickly sealed their own certainty that the apothecary was to blame.

He was a jealous lover, claimed one rumour, his infatuation unreturned by women already promised to more suitable men. Another claimed he'd attempted the recourse of those who cannot woo but possess great strength, but yet found the women his equal, with scratches and bruises the result. Some told me that Sampson was "demented," suffering perhaps from a long-dormant natural disposition to murder, or from some mental derangement arising from his work with exotic plants. I even heard a speculation that the killings were a desperate bid to vouchsafe against accusations of quackery, as the women planned to unmask him unless he furnished them with expensive potions, free of charge.

The extremities of speculation are a territory apt to bring despair to men of learning and science, but there resided some crackpot notions: that he had been conducting some despicable, underhand experiment that had achieved only death; that some new concoction, intended as a love potion, had gone terribly awry; even that Sampson was a cursed warlock or a hell-spawned demon under Satan's command, avenging the women's imagined sinful conduct on behalf of the Horned One.

One may pity these credulous simpletons, but the air never refused words to be spoken, neither can the human ear reject entirely their sound, no matter its folly.

Me, Freddie, again. I'm afraid that's all I can determine at present. It seems that Creaveley chose to pour himself a fortifying beverage and did so haphazardly. It is also late on this evening, and so I won't risk a spill of my own before publishing.
   There will be more, we can be certain, just as soon as the condition of the document permits. I will update you as soon as I am able.

CHAPTER FIFTY-ONE

THE GAGGLE OF ten men that made up Fortytude huffed and puffed their way along the cliff path. The early morning sun was just appearing on the horizon, the sky brightening behind the clouds. It was chilly, but none of the men noticed, their shoulders rolling in unison. They were warm, having already run two miles; another three to go.

Barnwell brought up the rear of the pack. He was the youngest of the group, but the newest, and happy simply to keep up. There was a hierarchy to these things—level of fitness, age, toughness—and he wasn't there to disturb the established, unspoken rules. He stayed at the back, knowing his place, focusing on the rhythmic pounding of the feet belonging to the runner in front of him, matching him stride for stride, his breath freezing around him as the cold morning air heralded the changing of the season from summer to autumn.

Bash Bingham, a former SAS major and "world adventurer," led the group of men. He was well-known on the island. Jersey folk regarded him as a local celebrity, someone they were proud to know, and on being invited to join Fortytude, Barnwell had shivered with a frisson of pride and excitement that was largely due to Bash's reputation. Tales of the ex-military man's derring-do abounded, some of them likely talked up but never shot down.

Bash was a man of few words. He let his achievements speak for themselves. At the age of forty-seven, and after a twenty-year career, he had climbed Everest, crossed the Himalayas on a motorbike, and walked the length of Great Britain carrying the weight of a small child in his backpack—barefoot—for charity. But this morning as he led his men along the cliff path, Bash carried nothing but his phone and a headlamp. The lamp was becoming increasingly unnecessary as the sun came up, but at this time of year it played an essential part at the start of their morning runs.

As they ran along the narrow track worn into the grass by animals, hikers, and sightseers over eons, Barnwell glimpsed the flapping yellow tape he'd used to fence off the spot from which Mia Thorne had fallen to her death four days before. The group slowed. Bash had noticed the cordon and turned around. To keep his place at the back of the pack, Barnwell jogged in place, but as Bash came toward him, he signalled Barnwell to run alongside.

"That where that girl fell, Bazza?" Bash had a neat, clipped English accent that belied his rugged appearance, and which instead pointed to an expensive private school education. "I saw it on the local news."

"Yeah, f-found her body f-four d-days ago," Barnwell stuttered. He wasn't experienced enough to run at this speed *and* hold a conversation. Bash was as fit and ripped as it was possible for a human to be, though. This five a.m. run was merely a warm-up for the series of activities he planned for the rest of the day, which probably counted flipping tractor tires and wrestling a bear at the zoo among them. Only Barnwell's pride forced him on.

"Rough," Bash replied. "Did she jump?"

"We're not s-sure, still trying to work things out. Usually, if things look like a s-suicide, we treat them as such, but the boss is a st-stickler. He wants evidence to point the way." Barnwell took a gulp of air. He was beginning to struggle.

"Would you like me to take a look?"

Barnwell glanced over at Bash. He had sandy hair and freckles. Laughter lines fanned outward from the corners of his eyes. Bizarrely, it occurred to Barnwell that such a fair complexion would be a hindrance in the hottest climes of the world, climes in which Bash had no doubt operated. The constable imagined Bash slathering on the SPF 100 before he embarked on some kind of covert op. But perhaps he'd done most of his work under the cover of darkness.

Bash sensed Barnwell's hesitancy. "I'm a man tracker, remember. The ground gives up a lot of secrets if you know what to look for."

The possibilities dawned on Barnwell. "W-would you?"

"Absolutely. Let's get the men back and we'll head out again. That okay with you?"

Barnwell's thighs felt leaden, his stride becoming uneven. "Er, yeah. Thanks, that would be great."

CHAPTER FIFTY-TWO

TWENTY-FIVE MINUTES LATER, the former SAS soldier came to a halt at the edge of the cordon. He turned around, hands on hips, waiting for Barnwell to reach him. The constable staggered up, thighs mottled, sweat pouring down his neck. He lifted the hem of his T-shirt to wipe his face.

"Need a breather?" Bash asked unnecessarily. Barnwell put his hands on his knees and leant over to catch his breath. There was no one around at this time of morning, but they could hear the waves below and the occasional seagull overhead. It was low tide; there were a few hours yet before the sea met the cliff face. Bash leant over to check out the view. "So, you think she fell here?"

Barnwell straightened. Still unable to speak, he shrugged. A few more breaths. "Pretty much. We think she fell here on Sunday evening and the tide washed her overnight to a rock pool under the cliff. We fingertip searched this area but didn't find anything." With a weak, shaking hand, Barnwell indicated a thirty-yard stretch of the cliff.

"So, people have been inside this tape?" Bash asked.

"Yeah, me, SOCOs, the boss, and the fire captain. It was already pretty churned up due to activity here before she fell. She was working on a film with some other students."

Bash made a face. "Hmm, the area's contaminated, but let's take a look, shall we?" He walked around the perimeter, his eyes firmly fixed on the ground. "She fell on Sunday, you say?" Barnwell nodded, still winded.

"It was a clear night, nothing special in terms of weather," Bash murmured as he continued his thoughtful check of the area. When he got to the point where the cordon crossed the track, he bent down. "Nothing to be learnt here. Too many have walked this path since." He stood. "Alright, I'm going in. You stay here." Bash switched on his headlamp and swung himself low under the plastic tape. He walked slowly up and down the area whilst Barnwell valiantly remained upright for a few moments before dropping to the grass to rest and watch.

"She was staying at the hostel, wasn't she?" Bash called.

"Yeah, that's right," Barnwell shouted back.

As he walked, Bash occasionally crouched and looked at the ground more closely, shining his lamp onto the matted, coarse grass. He walked perilously close to the cliff's edge, alarming Barnwell, who stood ready to intervene although he was too far to be of any help if Bash slipped. The SAS man pulled out his phone, took some pictures with it, then held it up, twisting it this way and that. The sea and sky stretched out behind him like a massive, boundless canvas.

"What're you doing?" Barnwell walked over to where Bash was working, keeping outside the perimeter of the fenced-off area.

"I'm measuring. These apps aren't perfect, but I wasn't expecting to track anything when I left home this morning." Bash moved over a few feet, stared at the ground, and then up across the scrub that lay inland. He ducked under the tape again and took a couple of steps. He pointed. "What's over there?" A group of trees huddled together.

"Trees?" Barnwell said.

"No, beyond that?"

"The St. Helier road."

"Yeah, and what's close by?"

Barnwell thought. "Bonner's hostel!"

"Right."

"What've you seen?"

"Hmm, not sure. There's flattened grass and a partial track here. It's small." Bash took a couple more paces, crouched, and measured again. "But there's something here. Starts just inside the cordon. See this print?" Bash pointed to the ground. "And this one here? They're distinctive."

Barnwell knelt down. He couldn't make out anything other than some blades of grass lying on its side.

"Here." Bash moved on and pointed to some dirt. This time, Barnwell could make out a partial footprint. "This person's a woman, she's running, fit, she's about five foot seven, and slight."

Barnwell gazed at Bash in awe. "You can tell all that from"—he pointed to the marks in the dirt—"that?"

"Yup, come on." Bash took off at a march. Barnwell trailed behind him, trying hard to keep up but tired from his earlier exertions. Every few yards, Bash pointed out another print and took a photo. Eventually, they reached the trees.

"How do we know this isn't a wild goose chase? They could be anybody's footprints," Barnwell said when he caught up.

"They could, but does the description match anyone connected to your case?"

Barnwell thought for a moment. Bash took off again. Barnwell trotted after him. "Now what?" Bash was staring at a bush.

"She came this way. Look, here's a broken twig. And see those stingers?" A patch of stinging nettles had been trampled through. "Would you run through nettles?"

Barnwell thought back to an experience he'd had as a child. Growing up in London, he hadn't had much experience of the countryside until he went on a school field trip to a farm. He'd been around seven. As the kids jostled to get on the coach home, he'd slipped and fallen on his knees into a patch just like the one he was looking at. Of course, he'd worn shorts. His legs itched and hurt all the way home, leading him to cry to his mum when she met the bus that he never wanted to go to the country again. "No, I would not."

"Aha! Look at that!" Bash pointed to the ground. There, half in and half out of a puddle, was a perfectly formed footprint. A foot ahead, there was another, slightly less clear.

"Okay," Barnwell said. "What are you going to tell me now? Her hair colour, whether she's a cat or a dog person, and that she prefers Marmite to jam?"

"Nope," Bash replied. "But I am going to tell you how to positively identify this person."

"How?"

"See the tread marks? This is a running shoe. That's not terribly helpful on its own, but see this?" Bash pointed to a mark in the tread on the outside edge of the print. "This is the left shoe, and this represents a nick in the sole that is unique to it. Find this shoe, and you'll find the person who ran away from where your girl fell. And in the direction of the hostel."

CHAPTER FIFTY-THREE

"THAT BLOOMIN' HOSTEL manager is going to breach the peace if we don't solve this case soon," Barnwell hissed at Roach as he strode into the hostel's lobby. It was quiet. There were only a couple of backpackers who stood flicking through tourist guides, ready for a day's exploring.

"What're we here for, Bazz?" Roach smoothed his hair. "I was just in the middle of testing myself on the Road Traffic Act."

"Well, consider yourself lucky then, boyo. Boss wants me to follow up on something. Then I've got a thing of my own to check out. I want backup."

"Sounds mysterious. Not dangerous, is it?"

"Follow me." Barnwell walked up to the reception desk. "Are either of the Ms. Prentisses in?" Barnwell asked the pretty blonde woman on duty. As if on cue, the hostel manager emerged from the office to retrieve a set of keys.

"No, they both went out earlier," the manager said, interrupting the woman who had opened her mouth to speak before shutting it like a trap.

"Any idea when they might be back?" Barnwell gave the man a forced smile.

"No."

Undeterred, Barnwell tried again. "Okay then, what about Mr. Wells?"

"In the common room," the manager said, frowning. "And when—?"

"Thank you, sir," Barnwell cut in courteously. The manager glared at them. Neither Roach nor Barnwell reacted to his hostility or his question as they wandered off down the hallway to find Wells.

They found Clint sitting in his preferred spot on the sofa. He was watching the wall-mounted television. Barnwell winced at the sound of the TV anchor shouting over a politician who was attempting to get his point across. He wasn't making any sense judging by the derision with which the anchor addressed him.

Barnwell quickly found the remote control and pressed mute. "I don't know how you can bear to listen to that ruckus at this time of day," he said.

"Nothing like a bit of outrage to get the brain going in the morning." Clint spooned a mouthful of cereal into his mouth before placing the bowl on the table next to him. He wiped his beard and fingers with a napkin. "Works better than caffeine. How can I help you, officers?"

Roach stayed by the door as Barnwell moved aside some magazines and perched on the low coffee table. "Just a routine inquiry, sir, won't take long. It has come to our attention that you sent Mia a text at around a quarter to nine . . ."

"Eight forty-three, to be precise," Roach added helpfully.

"Eight forty-three on Sunday evening," Barnwell finished. "You didn't mention it earlier. Can you explain what that was about?" Barnwell sat forward, his elbows on his knees, scrutinising Clint's face.

Clint's eyes glazed over briefly, but he held Barnwell's gaze and gave a slight nod. "Of course, let me check." He pulled out his phone and scrolled. "Ah yes, it was about the audition. Scouts had come down to the uni and wanted Mia to try out for this show in the West End. It would mean recognition, stardom, and would have been a great add to her portfolio, but it also meant her having to leave the course if she got the part. She'd asked me earlier what I thought about it. I was unsure at the time. I didn't want to lose my only friend at uni, and she was in her final year, so close to getting her degree. I was . . . hmm . . . ambivalent shall we say? Not entirely positive, anyhow. But after thinking about it, I changed my mind. It was too good an opportunity to miss, and there was no saying if she'd get the part. Of course, she never wrote back." The rims of Clint's eyes reddened as he blinked back tears.

"Did it not occur to you to tell us about it?"

Clint's eyes widened. "No. I honestly forgot all about it until just now. It had no bearing on anything, and in the shock of it all, I just clean . . . forgot." Clint shrugged, his midriff rippling as his shoulders came to rest. "Is there anything else I can help you with?"

"No, that'll—" Roach replied.

"Yes," Barnwell said firmly. "You can show us to Fawn Prentiss's room."

"No problem," Clint said, heaving himself out of his chair. Roach frowned. Barnwell ignored him and pushed Roach ahead as they followed Wells down the corridor.

CHAPTER FIFTY-FOUR

"WHY ARE WE here?" Roach hissed when Clint left them.

"I'm looking for something," Barnwell replied. He tried the door; it was locked. "I wonder if we could get that lass on the desk to give us the keys."

"We need a search warrant, Bazz."

"We *need* to find those shoes, that's what we need," Barnwell argued.

"What shoes?"

"Bash Bingham said that someone ran from the site where Mia Thorne fell, through those trees by the St. Helier road, in the direction of the hostel. He showed me a footprint of a shoe that had a nick in the outside of the left sole. We need to find that shoe's owner. We need to find that shoe."

"Then we *need* to get a *search warrant*. I can't risk this. Not now, Bazz."

Roach stomped off. Barnwell swung around and followed him like a child dragged away from his toys to visit a great aunt.

"Why do you think it's one of the Prentisses anyway?" Roach asked.

"I've read their statements. They're the right height. Fawn's the right height *and* size. It was amazing what Bash could tell from that print. What if one of them pushed Mia or saw her fall and ran away in terror or something?"

"But we're days away now; it's Friday. Mia died on Sunday. Anyone could have run through that copse since then."

"Have you ever run through a patch of stinging nettles?" Roach had to agree he hadn't. "No, and you wouldn't, right? Not if you could help it. A person who runs through stinging nettles has her mind on other things, very important things, maybe very scary things. I want to know what those very important, very scary things were. And for that we need to find the owner of the shoe. Let's start with those two."

"Alright, but we need to go talk to the boss. He can apply for the warrant. It's way above my pay grade, Bazz."

"Okay, okay, but let's see what we can find out."

Barnwell walked to the reception desk again. "Do you know where Jackie or Fawn Prentiss might have gone?" he asked the young woman behind the counter. In the office, the lobby manager, hearing Barnwell's voice, wheeled his chair into view with his heels, leaning back to stare at the policemen.

The woman pressed her lips together and shook her head slowly from side to side. "Sorry."

Barnwell rapped the reception desk once with his knuckles and turned to face Roach, finally defeated. "Okay, let's get back. I need a shower anyway."

"Yes, you do," Roach said, wrinkling his nose.

Barnwell was still in his shirt and shorts from earlier. At least his thighs had stopped shaking. "Ah, mate! You didn't bring the car?" Parked outside the hostel was Roach's motorbike.

"No, but I can give you a lift. I brought a spare helmet."

Barnwell growled. "Kind of you, but I don't want a lift on *that* thing."

Roach held out a helmet. "Come on, it's not far."

"It doesn't have to be far to be gobsmackingly rubbish," Barnwell growled.

"Well, it's that or walk."

Barnwell swiped the helmet from Roach's grasp and rammed it on his head, the visor preventing Roach from hearing the stream of invective that Barnwell emitted as he contemplated four minutes of terror as Roach's pillion passenger.

Roach laughed. "Get on." He revved the throttle as Barnwell stepped up and threw a weary leg over the seat. "Off we gooooooo!!" Barnwell grabbed Roach's waist just in time.

Roach sped down the St. Helier road for half a mile before stopping at a red light. Barnwell, who had experimented with keeping his eyes shut only to find that it made his pillion experience even worse, looked around him. Walking across a field to his left he saw two women. He squinted, then tapped Roach on the shoulder. "Over there." His voice was muffled.

"What?" Roach shouted.

"Over there!" Barnwell pointed. Chatting animatedly as they crossed the field using a public footpath were Fawn and Jackie Prentiss.

"We don't need a search warrant to see what they have on their feet in the middle of a field!" Barnwell shouted. Roach turned the bike to the right and spun it around in an impossibly tight turn.

To Barnwell's great relief, Roach quickly pulled up to where the footpath met the road, and they both dismounted to wait for the women at the gate.

"Hello, ladies!" Roach called to them. "How are you doing this fine morning?" Jackie and Fawn slowed. They were both carrying coffee cups; Fawn was carrying two. "Clint" was scrawled on the side of one of them. Roach leant on the wooden gate, effectively barring their way.

"This fine morning? You sound like a perv, Roachie," Barnwell muttered under his breath.

"Shut up. I'll keep them talking. You take a look," Roach said quietly. Then, louder to the women, "Nice day for it, wouldn't you say?" Jackie and Fawn looked at him suspiciously. Fawn's phone tinged. She glanced at it as Roach asked, "Been anywhere nice?" Barnwell rolled his eyes at the banality as he stared at the ground.

"We went to get coffee. Why?" Jackie said.

"Bringing one back for someone?"

"Just Clint."

"Nice of you. Hope you went to Ethel's. She does the best coffee in town."

"Look, Sergeant, is there something you wanted?" Jackie asked.

"Just saw you and wanted to let you know that the investigation is continuing."

"But you're no closer to finding out what happened to Mia?"

"Like I said, the investigation is continuing."

Barnwell looked up and gave the two women a big smile. "We'll let you know when we've concluded things. Now, we'll get out of your way and let you get on." He stepped aside as Roach opened the gate to allow the women through. They crossed the road, and as Jackie and Fawn disappeared from view, Roach held up his hand. Barnwell high-fived him and then performed a little jig. There was no doubt. In the side of Fawn Prentiss's left running shoe was a deep gouge, just as Bash described.

"Let's go see the boss, Roachie! But don't kill me first on that mean machine of yours."

CHAPTER FIFTY-FIVE

FOUR HOURS' SLEEP would have to suffice, Freddie told himself as he sat down at the research table he now considered his own. He rubbed his tired eyes before returning to the challenge of Creaveley's near-indecipherable handwriting. Freddie had put on a chequered button-down shirt that morning. It was less formal than his usual look, but it was fresh, which was more than he felt.

"What on earth," he asked the page, "are you *on* about?" Time and again, a single obstinate word, often one rarely seen in the twenty-first century, obscured the meaning of the most critical sentence in each paragraph. "English, Mr. Creaveley. Please use plain *English*."

"That's just the thing, isn't it?" said Laura, floating quietly past. She was on her rounds once more, shelving, shushing, and shaking awake those who were snoring too loudly. "He's using the English of his time. And, to be sure, of his social class."

"If you mean," Freddie said, setting the page aside for a moment, "that he never uses three syllables when he can use five, then yes."

"That's always been a mystery of nineteenth-century literature," Laura agreed. "Why spend twenty words when forty are only twice the price?"

"Spot-on."

"But this is Creaveley's personal journal," she reminded him. "He has latitude to sound exactly how he *wants* to sound."

Freddie rubbed his eyes again. "Latitude to completely confuse a researcher like me, more like." He stretched his fingers, the sound of his joints cracking testament to long hours of intense literary examination.

"Fancy a break?" asked Laura.

"Yeah," Freddie said, brightening.

"Well, tough," she said, a firm hand on his shoulder preventing him from standing. "You're on the clock, m'lad. Three more hours of community service still to go."

Freddie slumped, but in truth, this time at the library had been some of the most exciting of his career. "How about this? I need to make a phone call, directly connected," he emphasised, "to the Sampson research."

"By all means step outside," Laura said, moving on. "No mobile phone use in the library; you know that." It was a kindly reminder rather than an admonishment. Freddie's detective work was proving to be historically valuable and a potential boon for the library and its reputation, something that would come in useful when the library applied for its next round of council funding. Whilst David's opinion of the journalist didn't stop at bordering on contempt but went way further, Laura found she held Freddie in a steadily rising regard.

Freddie scurried outside the library to stand on the steps. A small square of lawn, the middle of which was dominated by a lone apple tree, spread out next to him. Unusually nervous about the call he was about to make, Freddie prepared himself. He suspected it was likely to be brief and to end in a dismissive harrumph. But before he could look up the number, a familiar face greeted him cheerfully.

"Mr. Solomon! All hail the Discoverer! All honour to the Seeker of the Truth!" cried a beaming Percival Courthould-Bryant. The councillor, the person who deposited the crate of documents that Freddie was currently wading through, gave him some fatherly applause as he walked over from his cream Saab. "I read your blog. You've got a feather in your cap this morning, I'd say! Maybe several."

"Too kind," said Freddie, distracted from his purpose, but always happy to hear from a reader. "The credit should go," he added with uncharacteristic modesty, "to whoever had enough foresight to keep those documents rather than toss them away."

"They were waiting for you!" Courthould-Bryant said, joining Freddie on the stone steps. "Any more revelations from the pen of Sir Jeremiah Blackstone McCannish Arthur Creaveley?"

"One or two," Freddie promised, tapping the side of his nose. "You'll have to wait for my special report."

"We have some of his personal effects in the museum, you know," Courthould-Bryant said. "Nothing, I think, that would shed any more light on the Sampson case, but . . ." Percival finally noted that Freddie had his phone out ready to make a call. He thanked Freddie again and headed inside, still rubbing his hands with excitement.

Able to focus again, Freddie quickly looked up the number he needed and dialled.

"Tomlinson," a man answered.

"Um, Dr. Tomlinson, my name's Freddie Solomon. I'm a local journalist and I've been researching the—"

"I know precisely who you are, young man. You-know-who will lecture me about 'wasting police time' just for taking your call," Tomlinson said at once. There was a pause that neither man filled. "But I've done it now, I suppose. In for a penny, in for a pound." Freddie could hear spectacles being dropped on a stack of paper. "Out with it, young blogger. I believe that's the correct term for you."

"I prefer online investigative reporter . . ."

"Yes, wonderful, whatever," Tomlinson said. "What have you got?"

Freddie crisply laid out what he'd found about the deaths of the three women that Sampson was accused of murdering. "The women suffered the same symptoms: stomach pain, vomiting, then convulsions that came and went for several days. I wanted to check whether you agreed with the original pathology analysis that the women were poisoned."

"Sounds like it," Tomlinson said, sounding slightly less irritated. "But I'll need more than that. What else have you got?"

"Well, there's a lot of damage to the documents, but I'm steadily clearing—"

Tomlinson interrupted him. "Get back to me if there's more."

As though illuminated from within, Freddie gushed with relief. "I'm glad you —" The line clicked.

"Alright, Dr. Tomlinson," said Freddie, taking deep breaths of Gorey's fresh air. "I'll get more."

CHAPTER FIFTY-SIX

"DETECTIVE INSPECTOR," FAWN said as Graham sat down at the table in the interview room. "I heard you've found Mia's phone."

"We're working on unlocking its secrets," Graham confirmed. "Not personally, of course; we have experts for that. Given its condition, it requires a constellation of tenacity and inspiration combined with some covert stellar engineering skills known only to those that have them."

"We have a highly gifted engineer on our team," Janice couldn't help adding.

"So, how are you?" Graham asked Fawn.

"I want to go home. You've already interviewed all of us. Me in particular. What is it, three times now?"

"The earlier interviews," Janice reminded her, "were incomplete. But we're sorting that out right now, aren't we?"

"Sure," said Fawn, uncertain. "I suppose I should apologise for getting upset."

"No need," said Graham. "Just be completely honest today, alright?"

"I *was* being honest . . ." she began to protest. Fawn looked around her. "We have to be here, at the station, I suppose? Somewhere formal, I mean, when doing a notification like this?" She motioned to the ceiling-mounted video camera.

"Notification?" asked Janice. "How do you mean?"

"You found something, I assume, that was sufficient to bring me in. A clue on Mia's phone that confirmed that her death was . . ." Fawn began, but her face fell within seconds. "Suicide." She seemed on the verge of a sob that she held back only narrowly. "That Mia took her own . . ."

"Let's say there are good reasons to talk here rather than at the library or the hostel," Graham said, flipping through his notepad as smoothly as a dealer shuffling a deck of cards.

Janice showed Fawn her running shoes, now encased in a plastic evidence bag. When the young woman did nothing but stare back at Janice, the DI stepped in. "We have evidence, Ms. Prentiss, that you ran from the cliff top where Mia fell to the hostel."

"Yes, I do that sometimes."

"Did you do that on Sunday night?"

"No, I was where I said I was."

"So, you didn't run away from the spot at which Mia fell, run through a copse, through a patch of painful stinging nettles, to the hostel and tell us otherwise?"

"No." Fawn shook her head.

"If we get our highly gifted engineer to examine your phone and laptop, we won't find any periods of inactivity on Sunday evening, perhaps between the period of eight thirty and nine, will we? You know, perhaps the period during which you were running on the cliff top?"

Fawn stared at him. She lifted her curtain of hair and pressed it against the lower part of her face.

"Because, you see, Ms. Prentiss, I don't think you've been entirely honest with us." Graham leant forward now. "I think you saw something. Something that scared you so much that you ran back to the hostel in a flap. And then you lied about it the next morning. What do you have to say about that?"

Fawn didn't refute him but gazed back at Graham blankly. He tried again. "Would you care to explain why you were in the vicinity when your friend fell to her death and why you didn't care to tell us about it?"

After three long, deep breaths, Fawn said, "Alright, I went out for a run. And yes, I ran along the cliff top. On my way out, I saw Mia and Noah. She was in her costume for the film." Another two breaths, and then, "I thought she was practicing her lines at first, but then I realised she wasn't. Mia played her character very prim and proper. Very restrained. She said high-class Victorian ladies never showed that they were sick, or in love, or tired of the world."

"Is that so?" asked Janice.

"She would improvise a bit, it's true." Fawn shifted in her seat. "Jackie didn't like that. Told her to stick to her direction. And there, on the cliff, she was clearly impassioned. I could tell from her body language. And Noah's. She was giving him the heave-ho." Fawn grasped for the edge of the table, her eyes squeezed shut, pained as though electrocuted by her own memories.

"Fawn?" said Janice very softly. Fawn's eyes flew open. She stared at the far wall, just over Graham's shoulder.

"Oh, God." She began to cry. "Neither of them were there when I ran back. I thought at the time they'd gone to the hostel, but now I know she must have been lying at the foot of the cliff, battered to pieces." Fawn's hands curled inward, arms across her chest, protecting herself from the sudden assault of memories, uncaged now and pitiless.

Her fingers scampering over the surface of her iPad, Janice wrote all this down. But Graham wouldn't take his eyes off the woman in front of him, an act penetrating and comprehensive. Each of Fawn's tears was logged in his databanks; every sob carried subtle meaning that others might have missed.

"Why didn't you tell us this in the first place?"

"I was in shock, I suppose. After she was found dead, I didn't want to believe what must have happened. That perhaps if I'd run back earlier, I might have prevented her from going over the edge. The thought that she had been lying there as I ran past just . . ." Fawn shuddered.

"But you can't have known that at the time. Anyone would have reasonably assumed that she'd gone back to the hostel. So why, Ms. Prentiss, did you run across the scrub, through trees, through stinging nettles, back to the hostel?"

Fawn blinked and sat up in her chair, sober and calm. "Because I was late. I had a date. I told you, I was meeting some girls from the hostel in the pub. I don't like being late, Inspector. Jackie taught me that."

CHAPTER FIFTY-SEVEN

JANICE ESCORTED FAWN off the station premises and watched her as she walked away. She turned when Fawn hurried across the road and down a footpath. The sergeant had expected to hear the slam of Graham's office door, but it remained open. She shot a worried glance at Roach.

"Trouble?" he asked, looking up from yet another criminology textbook.

"Not sure." Janice cleared her throat and walked over to Graham's office. "Boss?" she said, knocking on the door.

"It's okay, Janice." There was the sound of the kettle being clicked on. "I'm not going to explode."

"All evidence to the contrary," she said, stepping in and closing the door. If Graham was wrong about his disposition, it'd be unfair for Roach's exam preparation to suffer the noisy ramifications.

"What do you think?" Graham said, pointing.

Janice took a look at the whiteboard, crowded with textual and graphical representations of the available evidence. "Seriously? It's my turn to play detective?"

"You understand the case, Janice. I need to step back a bit. I'd genuinely like to hear your thoughts. Go on, review the case."

Janice stared at him, seeing only an inscrutable, sometimes plainly incomprehensible copper who right now didn't show any signs of stress except perhaps some slightly elevated breathing. She picked up a black marker pen.

"Okay," she said, still wary of possible mines dotting the field across which she was about to walk. "Let's do a timeline. We know the film crew wrapped at three p.m. due to wind. Weather confirmed. They watched the day's film clips over pizza until six."

"Yes."

"About seven on that same Sunday night, Mia walked out with Regis Nosworthy and was treated to a five-star dinner of hot dogs and lager. But then she left him disappointed by declining to . . . you know."

"Play with his boomerang. Go on."

"He returns to the hostel at eight and proceeds to spend the evening drinking with his long-standing surfing buddy."

"Mr. Vladimir Anatolyevich Zynkovlev."

"I'm impressed."

"What?"

"The name, sir. That you remembered."

"Oh, right. Well you know, wasn't that difficult. It's in the notes." Graham coughed. "Anyway, back at the hostel, Aussie drinking rules . . ."

"Whereupon a fine and boisterous time was had by all."

"Except for the Nordic women."

"And the Germans," Janice added. "Now, thanks to Jack and the texts, and finally confirmed by Mr. Stimms, we now know that shortly after Nozz departed the cliff, Noah shows up, summoned for a meeting by Mia." Janice took another marker pen and put a red X next to Nozz's name.

"Hmm, what time was the text from Mia to Noah?"

"Time stamp was"—Janice checked her tablet—"seven forty-five."

"And he told us that he arrived at the cliff half an hour later, having walked from the hostel."

"Correct."

"Mia and Noah talk for a bit. Noah's protestations of love notwithstanding, Mia dumps him, and he catches the bus back to the hostel, also with his heart broken, though rather more seriously than our Australian friend."

"His alibi is confirmed by the bus driver, and Noah is out of the picture at eight thirty-three p.m." Janice put another big red cross next to Noah's name.

She watched the DI pour a mug of tea and, in resolute silence, thoughtfully stir it for a full thirty seconds. She decided she needed reinforcements. Opening the door, she called over to the reception desk, "Jim? Would you mind stepping in? I think the DI's having a funny turn."

Roach reluctantly closed a thick textbook, sighed heavily, and said, "*Another* one?"

"Hello, Jim," said Graham, pouring second and third mugs of tea from the pot. "Milk?"

"What's going on?" Roach said, eyeing them both suspiciously.

"We're reviewing the case. We've eliminated the Australian and Noah Stimms so far. Now, moving on . . ."

"What about Clint? What can we conclude about him?" Graham asked.

"Seems a pretty straight up guy. Nothing obvious against him, anyhow. Big though, could easily knock her off a cliff, but can't imagine what his motive might be," Janice said.

"He did 'forget' about that text though," Graham reminded them.

"Explanation was plausible enough. He has a cast iron alibi, too. He was with multiple people all evening. I did the checks myself," Roach said. "I can't see how he could have been involved."

"Agreed," Janice said. She circled Clint's name in green. "So, let's move on to Jackie. What do we think about her?"

CHAPTER FIFTY-EIGHT

JANICE TOOK A deep breath in through her nose and leant back to survey the board, her arms folded as she considered. "Jackie has motive. If someone poached Jack from me, you'd better believe I'd toss them off a cliff." She narrowed her eyes. "Noah isn't the world's finest catch, but Jackie could have been downplaying her feelings for him, overstating his shortcomings, or both."

"Or she might just have been angry as hell," Roach said.

"Yep," Janice agreed.

"Mia held some good cards when it came to this little movie of theirs," Graham added. "She was also their big draw and essential to the plot. She was a main character. If she'd threatened to withdraw, to go back to Portsmouth without shooting her scenes, Jackie could have exploded."

"Maybe," allowed Janice. "A lot depended on getting everything filmed on time and within budget, for sure. But there's no evidence they had a row, or Mia threatened to do that."

"Quite right, Sergeant. Let's not speculate, eh? What about her alibi?" Graham turned to Roach.

"She was in her room for chunks of the evening but was seen occasionally. That's backed up by her sister."

"Whose reliability is now in total question, of course," Janice said.

"Hmmm." Graham leant forward over his desk, steepled his fingers, and rested his chin on top of them. Janice put a red question mark by Jackie's name.

"And now we have a new suspect, Fawn Prentiss, who admits to being at the cliff top on the evening in question and who failed to tell us about it until we copped her for it," Janice said.

"What could be her motive?" Graham wondered. "You think she was in love with Mia?"

"Oh, I don't know, but she seemed a little more favourably disposed toward her than her sister, don't you think? It might be just a girl crush, the intense admiration of a younger, less worldly person."

"Intense enough to do her harm?"

"I wouldn't have thought so, but you never know. Mia was breaking hearts left and right. Sooner or later, *someone* with questionable control over their emotions was going to confront her. She might have led Fawn on, then turned on her or snubbed her in some way. Or perhaps Fawn was upset about how Mia treated her sister."

"But what about her running across the scrub? That was dead suss," Roach said.

"She said she was meeting some friends and was late. That's why she ran from the cliff top in such a hurry." Graham roughly rubbed his face, leaving white streaks that quickly turned pink.

"Sounds like a load of cobblers to me, sir," Roach said.

"She's definitely in the frame." Janice drew a red ring around Fawn's name, followed by an exclamation mark. "But we've no evidence, and if we assume that Fawn is telling the truth, and in the absence of any other suspect, we have to conclude that Mia took a tumble off the cliff as a result of an accident or by personal choice sometime after that, falling fatally to the ground."

"The fall wasn't fatal," Graham said.

"Eh?"

"The impact of landing among sharp, jagged rocks after falling five hundred feet. *That's* what was fatal."

"Pedantic," Janice objected before noticing Graham's sharp look. "But absolutely correct, sir."

In one breath, Graham summarised. "In the absence of a suspect, we can conclude Mia took a tumble off the cliff as a result of an accident or by personal choice and died as a result of the impact of landing on rocks, after which she was left in a seawater pool by the cruel, unrelenting attention of the tide. Alright, let's look at the possibilities of accident or suicide." He stood. Janice handed him the pens before sitting down.

CHAPTER FIFTY-NINE

THE DI WROTE "Suicide" at the centre of a circle. "Mia in and out of relationships," he muttered. "Lost her mother early. Family history of serious mental health issues. Volatile personality, especially recently. Reports of receiving abusive messages." Harding and Roach watched the DI inscribe small representations of each finding on the board. He leant in close, as though short-sighted, but proximity was merely an aid to accuracy; each mark was neat and precise.

Graham continued. "But . . . she was close to graduating. Her father had just made things right after a difficult time." More information went onto the board.

"She was admired as an actress . . . Considered to have a bright future ahead of her. Talent scouts had come knocking."

"No one reports that she signalled her intention to harm herself either, sir," Roach added.

"Happiness on the outside can mask sadness on the inside though, sir," warned Janice.

Graham concurred. "'Successful' people choose to check out early surprisingly often. Any word on those messages yet, Janice?"

"Not yet, sir."

"Okay, no sign of any note, either?"

"No, sir."

"Hmm, let's move on." On the bottom left of the board, Graham wrote "Accident."

Janice referred to her notes. "We've done a check of the ground at the cliff. It was muddy where they had been filming. We've reviewed the weather report—no rain, fog, wind. She wasn't drunk. The light was fading—sunset was eight fifty-three on Sunday—but still, there's nothing to suggest she slipped, fell, or was accidentally blown off the cliff."

"She was wearing that ridiculous dress though." Roach frowned and shook his head in disbelief.

"Fawn said it was like wearing a tank. Perhaps she just tripped?"

Graham stood back to review the board. "It's possible."

Janice pursed her lips but nodded. "It's still in play?"

"Absolutely. I mean, anything about this case is still in play."

Graham threw the marker pens into a box and flopped down in his chair. "This is a confounding case. I mean, they've *all* lied, directly or by omission, except perhaps Jackie, but we can't prove the lies were meaningful to the case. The death of a beautiful woman," he commented, "seldom brings out the best in people." He turned to the whiteboard, now a strange mosaic of interconnections and drawings.

"Isn't this where you neatly summarise the case, come to a brilliant conclusion, and tell us who to arrest?" Janice said.

"I wish, Sergeant. I wish. If we can't come up with something soon, we'll have to posit an open verdict to the coroner." An open verdict was as close as medical and police professionals ever came to throwing up their hands and saying, "We just don't know," a state of affairs Graham detested. "Or, worse, we'll have to confront the possibility that she was shoved off by a random stranger. What a fiasco."

CHAPTER SIXTY

"IT'S A FABULOUS building, the conference centre. Nice and old on the outside; light, bright, and modern on the inside. Nigel Needham said so when he was here for the conference." Laura was chattering away to Graham as they cleaned up after dinner in her small kitchen. It was so small that it was a squish with them both in there. They bumped into each other and were forced to dance around in order to put the plates in the cupboards and the cutlery in the drawers. It worked best when one of them stood stock-still, elbows in, as they washed up—there was no room for a dishwasher—and the other did the drying. Usually after that was done, one of them left the room so the other could put the things away. "I think he was rather fond of Gorey."

It was Graham's turn to do the washing up, but he was only half listening, his mind still on the case. Even over dinner, it niggled at the edges of his brain. His thoughts prevented him from truly focusing on what Laura was saying about his former superintendent.

"He said something, actually, just as he was leaving, that's been bothering me. I wanted to ask you about it."

"Hmm?"

"Who's Katie?"

The sound of his daughter's name shot through Graham like a bullet, the stab of adrenaline almost incapacitating him. He sloshed soapy water over himself as the saucepan in his hands slipped. "Nigel said to give her his love. Do you remember?"

"Of course I remember," Graham said rapidly, both hands now tightly gripping the handle of the saucepan. He deliberately took deeper breaths. "Yes, that's what he said."

Laura brightened her tone as she turned to place a dish on the worktop. "Is she someone you worked with?"

"No, it's nothing like that," Graham said, struggling to keep his voice even. "Nigel made a mistake."

"Really?" Laura asked.

"You remember how he was, so forgetful and everything . . ."

"He said the wrong name?"

"No, it's not . . ." The heaving emotional weight of his daughter's passing hit him anew. Whenever it came, after a sudden reminder or simply out of nowhere, a little more of that pain was relived. He struggled even to guess how he might convey the torture, the endless weight, to Laura. Now might be a good time to tell her, but he'd been caught by surprise. His instinct was to evade, however unfair that might be. "Nigel didn't mean what he said. Got himself mixed up. Alright?"

It was only when Laura's arms wrapped around him that Graham realised he was still holding the saucepan in a double-handed grip, almost as though it were a life raft. He set it down and rinsed his hands.

"I believe you," she said. "Nigel was very mixed up. But you're upset right now by that name. And if it's okay with you, I'd like to ask if Katie is someone I need to know about?"

"No," he said, shaking his head and turning to face her. "No, you don't. It's not like that at all." He made sure they had eye contact. "Seriously. It's *not* like that."

"We have a deal," she reminded him. "The Bangkok Palace Agreement." After dinner one night, on perhaps their seventh or eighth date, they'd ruminated on how complex their lives were. Problems from the past and the trial Laura was a key and protected witness for. Problems of management and qualification and career progression.

And so, to help navigate the parallel challenges brought by London's underworld, Gorey's murderous responsibilities, and the sheer newness of their relationship, Laura proposed an agreement.

"We always disclose anything which might negatively affect the other," Graham recited from memory.

"Is this one of those times?" Laura asked. "Please think carefully, David, because I want that agreement to mean something."

"This is not," he assured her, "one of those times."

"Are you sure?"

"Yes. I promise. Laura, love," he said, taking her hands in his, "if it's okay, I'd like to talk about something else."

A distraction was already available. "Duck-billed platypuses," she proposed, leading him back into her small living room. "No one's negatively affected by those, right?"

They curled up and caught the last twenty minutes of a documentary. Laura seemed calm, content just to watch the film, but Graham was in turmoil. *It's not the right time. I'm not ready. I can't talk about it yet. Pleeease don't make me tell you about her.*

But still, the memories came, and he was back in their home in Chiddlinghurst, in that country kitchen with his grandmother's dining table at the centre. There was the fridge, covered with reminders and artwork and photos. He found himself focusing on one tiny aspect of the memory, like a camera zooming in on a long shot: a half-square of brown among other drawings on the fridge. Katie had drawn an animal gliding through the water, its wide webbed feet expertly powering its awkward, unbalanced body—a very neat, precise drawing of a duck-billed platypus.

CHAPTER SIXTY-ONE

AT HOME THAT night, Graham dreamed fitfully of duck-billed platypuses gliding and twisting through the water, the strange-looking bird-mammal that defied classification. Katie had taught him that they were shy animals, gentle with their young, highly adapted to their watery environment with a flattened head for graceful swimming and dark, thick, brown fur that repelled water to keep them warm and dry even after hours in rivers, streams, or lakes. But these apparently harmless animals had a dark side—stingers on their heels that produced venom so toxic it was like being attacked by hundreds of wasps.

In the morning, Graham sat down at his kitchen table and knocked his fingernails rhythmically against his mug of Tetley tea, his current favoured first brew of the day. It was at moments like this, when he was alone, that he wished he had a dog. Or a cat. Someone, some*thing* to talk to. After the documentary the previous evening, he'd made his excuses and left Laura's, desperate to be on his own with his thoughts.

The case was at a stalemate; *he* was at a stalemate. He needed to break the case into little pieces and rearrange them into a coherent order. Himself, too, he thought ruefully. What had he overlooked? Graham thought again of the duck-billed platypus, the timid, cuddly looking animal whose sting could take a victim down for weeks.

Katie had had one as a stuffed toy. She couldn't sleep without it. It had become raggedy, matted, and stained. His ex-wife had washed it repeatedly, but it only seemed to come out looking worse. Still, Katie loved it. Then one day, a seam split and out poured white, clumped stuffing, spewing all over her bed. The sight of it had made Katie scream, and she never wanted her beloved soft toy again.

There began nights of constant wakings, nightmares, and not enough sleep for her parents until she settled again. *Focus, man; the case.*

Graham drained his cup. The tea was doing its job. He thought of the platypus again—endearing, innocuous, but under certain conditions, terrifying. Graham stood suddenly. He tossed the dregs of his tea and clumsily left the unwashed mug in the sink. He threw on his jacket and pulled out his phone.

"Harding? Get Roach and Barnwell to the station. I'll meet you there in ten minutes."

Janice's phone tinged as she, Roach, and Barnwell stood in Graham's office, awaiting their instructions. They were as still as rocks, concentrating, whilst Graham picked up the kettle that had recently boiled. Janice's eyes widened. "Jack's found them, sir! The messages."

Graham banged down the kettle. "Now you're talking, Sergeant!"

Janice scanned the message from Jack. "They were left for her on various social media accounts. A variety of them, all to do with death. Death threats, sir, telling her to die, that she should kill herself. Nasty stuff. There's a whole stream of them sent every day over the past three weeks. Would scare the life out of anyone. The most recent was Sunday evening. And there's something else, sir."

"Give. What?"

"A sum of £9,543 was withdrawn from Mia's account just a few days ago."

Graham looked at his three officers. All stood at attention, alert and eager to get on with the job. He considered how far they'd come in the past few years. Janice was assertive, compassionate, no longer the harried hen trying to hold them all together. Barnwell was fitter, stronger, keen to make a good impression, willing to go beyond what was asked of him. Roach's energy was honed and focused. "Right. Listen up. We've got a lot to do to bring this case home. Roach, Harding, you'll be based here, working with people on the mainland. Absolute secrecy is required. I don't want anyone on the island to get wind of what's going on. Any authority you need, you come to me. Got it?"

The trio in front of him nodded. "Sir."

"Harding, I need you to keep on Jack. I need him to prioritise finding the IP addresses of those messages. We need to locate where they came from, and I need you on top of that. Feed the information to me as it comes in. Don't wait, you understand; *as* they come in.

"Roach, I want you to trace Clint Wells's girlfriend. Interview her, check his story. Find out when she last saw him, how long they've been together, and if he had any money problems.

"Barnwell, I want you to go to the hostel and bring back Jackie Prentiss. Just tell her you need to ask her a few questions. Then when she's here, get her to tell you what type of anti-depressants she's taking. I saw a packet of them in her bag when I interviewed her. She got defensive . . ."

"What if she won't tell me?"

"Tell her if she doesn't cooperate, you'll get a search warrant. When you've got the name of the drug, I want you to contact Tomlinson and check it against the trace amounts found in Mia's body, see if they are a match. Keep Jackie here until I decide we can let her go. I don't want her releasing any information to her friends. Let's keep them in the dark.

"Off you go, all of you, skedaddle. Keep me informed!" he shouted as the trio scurried for the door.

CHAPTER SIXTY-TWO

TWO HOURS LATER, Graham tried not to pace around his office. He'd toyed with bringing the young people in for yet another interview but had satisfied himself with a coffee run as his officers worked the phones and scoured the police databases. Jackie Prentiss was in the interview room. Barnwell was speaking to Tomlinson. Finally, Janice came to his door.

"Do you have an update for me?"

"I've got good news and bad news, sir."

"Hit me."

"The good news is that Jack's found twenty-five messages, and so far he's traced eighteen of them."

"And the bad news?" Graham winced.

"They were all sent from coffee shops along the south coast. We can't trace them back to one individual."

"Damn!"

"But the final one was sent from the hostel."

Graham pumped his fist into the air as he jumped up from his chair. "Bingo!"

"Sir?"

"Well don't you see, Sergeant? This means that one of the students must have been responsible for the messages. They're the link between the south coast and the hostel. Tell Jack great work, but don't let him slack. We need as much information about those messages as we can get. Anything he can supply us will help."

Barnwell appeared in the doorway. "Jackie Prentiss's medication doesn't match that found in Mia Thorne's body. Dr. Tomlinson just confirmed it." Graham puffed out his cheeks. He looked up at the sky to see if it was about to fall in on him. "It's not a match, sir."

Roach strode in. "But Kirsty Machin's medication is!" His cheeks were flushed with excitement. "And there's more. Seems like Mr. Wells has been lying to us, sir. Kirsty isn't his girlfriend. They were mates in school, but the relationship was platonic. They like gaming, the same TV shows, music, and such, but that's about it. They communicate mostly online these days. I've spent the morning on the phone with the local force. They sent two officers to interview her. She's a film student living in Huddersfield.

"When was the last time she saw him?"

"Three months ago. Which is when, surprise, surprise, her prescription for anxiety and depression went missing. Says she goes mental without it; they're really strong. She had to practically beg her doctor for another prescription to cover the missing one."

Graham sat back in his chair to absorb this information, weirdly calm now. "Janice, get Jack to trace where that money withdrawn from Mia's bank account went to, stat. Barnwell, get the details of those coffee shops. Roach, find out where that prescription was filled."

CHAPTER SIXTY-THREE

"I'VE FOUND OUT who the money went to, sir." Graham was now manning the office phones as Harding, Roach, and Barnwell sat at their desks, progressing the action items he'd given them. He'd taken three 999 calls: one about an attempted theft of school supplies from St. Andrews primary, another concerning a missing parrot, and a third to do with a boisterous Jersey cow chasing an inquisitive tourist who wanted a photo.

"Who, Janice? Who?"

"Clint Wells. The amount of £9,543 was transferred directly into his account from Mia's bank by direct debit."

"Good, now we need to find out who sent those threatening messages to Mia." Graham stood and finally succumbed to his need to pace the office. "We have the time and dates the messages were sent, and we need to link one of the students to them. Any ideas how we do that?"

Barnwell, Roach, and Harding focused on their detective inspector. They were all buzzing with the adrenaline of a case suddenly blown open.

"We could go coffee shop to coffee shop with photos, see if the staff remember any of them?" Roach suggested.

Graham nodded. "Not bad. That will connect them with the coffee shop but not necessarily the time and dates we're seeking. Plus, the chances of them being remembered over twenty or so instances is iffy at best."

Janice had a go. "CCTV?"

"In every coffee shop?"

"No, you're right. Probably not."

"Credit card payment?" Roach tried again.

"What if they paid in cash?"

"Bazza, you got anything?" Roach deflected.

Barnwell was staring at the floor. He seemed to be examining his regulation boots. They were gleaming. He scrunched up his eyes. They waited in silence, all out of ideas.

Suddenly, Barnwell burst into life. "Yes!" He punched the air with his fist. His eyes shone as brightly as his shoes.

"What is it?"

"Wait, here. I'll be back in a jiffy."

A cry came up from reception. It was Roach.

"They're all in, sir," Janice cried.

The three officers crowded around Roach, who had been so absorbed he'd forgotten all about his exams for the first time in weeks.

"Twenty-five results, sir."

"And?"

"Twenty-three matches."

Graham's eyes lit up. "We've got them."

"Well done, everyone. You've worked extremely hard and I'm proud of you. Are you ready?"

Harding, Roach, and Barnwell were lined up in full uniform, awaiting their inspection. Graham looked them over. He adjusted Barnwell's tie. "Great work, Barnwell. A stroke of genius at the end there," he murmured. He flicked a speck from Roach's jacket. "Good luck in your exams, Roach. Any force would be lucky to have you." He could find nothing on Janice; she was perfect. "Couldn't run this station without you, Sergeant."

Graham stood back to address his team. "I've called the hostel manager and they'll be waiting for us in the common room. I want you, Harding, in the room with me, observing. Roach, you know what to do."

Harding and Roach acknowledged their orders. "Sir."

"Barnwell, I want you to stand by the door, in case anyone makes a run for it."

"Yes, sir. Should we take the taser?"

"I don't think that'll be necessary, Constable, but we will take both cars."

CHAPTER SIXTY-FOUR

THE COMMON ROOM was quiet. Each of the assembled students showed their anxiety differently. Fawn sat on the floor, her head tipped forward. She played with her hair whilst her sister leant back in her chair, her arms folded across the front of her black jacket, apparently impatient for the proceedings to begin.

Noah and Clint were a study in contrasts. Picking at a loose bit of rubber on the sole of his shoe, his lips in a thin line, Noah was pale, as though the evening air chilled him. Ruddy, bearded Clint's demeanour was calm and attentive as he awaited answers, the only sign of his nervousness a gentle tapping of the soles of his Converse shoes on the floor.

Nozz and Zink, invited because of their involvement at the periphery of the case, sat on stools with their feet firmly planted on the floor. Leaning over their knees, their hands clasped in front of them, they looked uneasily at the stressed-out souls around them.

Barnwell guarded the door as instructed. Harding stood against the wall opposite Graham, leaving the detective inspector to host this unorthodox gathering.

"We've concluded our investigation, and I'm going to tell you what happened to Mia," Graham announced. "But there's a rule: if you interrupt me, it must be to correct a factual error. If your statement is irrelevant, I'll have no patience. If it's untrue, I'll arrest you for perjury and stick you in a cell. Agreed?"

There were nods, but only Clint spoke. "Of course."

"Firstly, I want to tell you how sorry I am about Mia." Graham chose a sympathetic tone to begin. "I know you were close, and that she was integral to your film, which was a huge deal for you all." He nodded first to Jackie, who was sullen but nodded back, and then to Noah, a jangling bag of nerves, now drumming his fingers incessantly on his knees. "Next, you need to know that there's a special place in hell reserved for people who lie or mislead investigators during inquiries." Nozz looked down at the floor, Noah's eyelashes flickered, Fawn brought up the end of her curtain of hair to cover the lower part of her face.

"We all know the evening's timeline by now, don't we? First, you gathered to look at the day's rushes, eating pizza—a large Margherita and a pepperoni." Graham looked around for nods of assent. "Then you split up to spend your evenings independently. Mia went with Nozz to the cliff. Once he had left, she texted Noah to invite him to join her. He arrived half an hour later. During this meeting, Mia tells Noah their relationship is over and, after speaking for ten minutes or so, he leaves in a very bad mood, running to catch the bus back to the hostel. At eight thirty-three, having just got on the bus, Noah receives a text from Mia. We've confirmed this with the bus driver, so we can conclude that she was still alive at this point. Subsequently, Noah and Nozz pair up with their respective friends, Clint and Zink, and drink the rest of the evening away. Am I right so far?"

"Yeah," said Clint, still the most verbal of the group. "No problems from me." Noah acknowledged Graham's version of the evening's events with the merest lift of his chin. Zink and Nozz nodded their heads vigorously like headbangers, eager to agree and be cleared of any involvement in this most unlikely Pommie drama.

"As we investigated Mia's death, everyone in this room, with the exception of Mr. Zynkovlev, came under suspicion. Film director Jackie was the most reliable of you all. She worked hard, entirely committed to making her film a success, putting her own, strong, negative feelings aside for the sake of the project." Jackie narrowed her eyes, unsure where this speech was heading. "But you had a complicated relationship with Mia, didn't you, Jackie? At once jealous of her *and* dependent on her. She had wronged you, but you needed her. You had to stuff down those hateful feelings whilst pandering to her in order to get your film the most attention. Because you are ambitious, are you not, Jackie? You want to make it in the film world and not as the assistant to the assistant director's assistant, either."

"I had nothing to do with her death."

"That's right, Jackie, you didn't."

CHAPTER SIXTY-FIVE

"ULTIMATELY, I DISCOUNTED you. You want to be a top dog. And Mia was pivotal to that. You needed your film finished with her in it," Graham said.

Clint shifted his heavy body in his seat, making it creak. Noah rubbed his hands through his hair, making even more of it stand on end. Fawn flicked her hair back.

"I should add that neither Mr. Nosworthy nor Mr. Stimms were entirely truthful in their recounting of Sunday evening's events. One could go so far as to say that they lied. They certainly omitted sharing details that would have made our jobs as investigators much easier and should be ashamed of their roles in this regard." Nozz looked down at the floor, accepting the reprimand. Noah was more of a holdout, directly gazing at Graham until the last moment, when his nerve failed him. He blinked and looked away.

"But they weren't the only ones." Graham moved over to stand by Jackie and Fawn. "The inability to be frank about her Sunday evening also befell the younger Ms. Prentiss, who only confirmed her movements after we uncovered evidence thanks to some extraordinary sleuthing on the part of my officers. In her latest telling of the evening, Ms. Prentiss maintains she saw Noah and Mia on the cliff top. When she returned from her run, both had disappeared, and apparently late for a date, she ran back to the hostel where, unconcerned, she changed clothing and went to the pub. That she didn't tell us about this excursion until forced to caused us to look closely at her behaviour."

Nonplussed at this revelation, Jackie stared at her sister, Noah's head whipped around to see if Graham was joking, and Clint glanced at everyone in sequence, one to the other, waiting for a refutation. Instead of contradicting

Graham, Fawn stared angrily back at him, her face hidden from her sister by the broad arc of her hair.

"My sergeant and I spent time with Fawn, trawling through her version of that evening's events. Most interesting, to say the least," he said with a glance at Harding.

Fawn maintained her cold stare, but still, she didn't speak. She drummed her fingers against her shins. "I was traumatised. When I heard that Mia was missing, then dead, I realised that she must have been lying at the bottom of the cliff as I ran past." Fawn closed her eyes. "I just wanted the memory to go away, so I acted like it never happened." She crossed her arms in mute echo of her sister; the two even held their heads at the same curious angle, projecting a mixture of defiance and vulnerability.

"You liked Mia, didn't you?"

Fawn nodded, her hair swaying, one hundred thousand strands moving in unison. "I thought she was so cool. Mean, but edgy. I wanted to be her friend. I wanted to be in her orbit. I know she could be difficult, but the world is duller without her in it." This outburst seemed to drain Fawn of all energy, and she slumped.

Graham began to step slowly around the common room. "But let us turn our attention to Clint—faithful, dependable Clint. Friends, Clint was the only person for whom Mia seemed to have kind actions. Clint was the only person who did the very best for her, stuck up for her, supported her, worked on her lines with her; the one who encouraged her to follow her star to the West End. But let's not go overboard." Graham leant against the wall next to Clint. "Because Clint had his own beef with Mia, didn't you, Clint?"

Clint shuffled in his seat. "Look here, what are you saying? I had nothing to do with her death. I was nowhere near the cliff that night. I have plenty of alibis—in the hostel, and the pub."

"That's right. Rock-solid alibis. You're telling the truth, Clint. The rest of you, let me be categorical about this: Clint did not push Mia off the cliff. Neither did Fawn. Or any of you. Mia did, in fact, kill herself."

CHAPTER SIXTY-SIX

GRAHAM PAUSED TO let his statement sink in. Noah closed his eyes. Jackie lifted her bottom lip over her upper lip, blinking rapidly. Fawn's chin wobbled, tears welling in her eyes. She leant into her sister's legs. Jackie put a comforting hand on her hair. Nozz and Zink looked over at the door, then at each other.

"No one was directly involved in the act of Mia's death. She wasn't murdered. But she was driven to distraction and despair by a campaign designed to destabilise her. And you were at the heart of it, weren't you, Clint?"

"Don't be so ridiculous! I would never do such a thing. Mia was my friend!"

"So, you hadn't been encouraging her thoughts of suicide with messages of your own? Her death would solve a big problem for you."

"What problem?" Clint sighed. He tilted his head back and lifted his ankle onto his opposite knee. "This is insane."

"Not insane. I will grant your plan was rather clever, except you made a mistake, several actually. You see, Mia received a final text from you on Sunday evening. One you didn't mention until we raised it. 'I think you should do it,' you texted her. Imagine how Mia must have felt when the final message urging her to end her life arrived. The final treachery from her supposed friend. Was it a mistake that it came from your personal texting account, Clint? Or did you mean to turn the screw like that at the very end?" There was silence in the room, except for Jackie's long exhale. Nozz and Zink stared, now dumbstruck.

Clint's face flushed. "That was nothing. I told you. I was encouraging her to attend the audition. Getting that part could have kick-started her career. Given her an unassailable lead over her contemporaries."

Graham weighed this explanation. "Plausible, I suppose. But we have only your word for it, and when considered alongside the rest of the evidence against you, your word isn't terribly valuable." Beads of perspiration had formed on Clint's brow. He rubbed the back of his neck before folding his arms across his chest. The people in the room were riveted. All eyes were on Clint.

"You see, once I realised there could be another meaning to your text, we started to dig around. And we found other lies and omissions.

"First, there was the case of your mysterious girlfriend. Except she's not your girlfriend at all, is she, Clint? According to her, Kirsty was never more than a mate!" Graham waved a piece of paper in front of him. "Lo, a copy of a prescription made out to your friend. Filled by a chemist in Southampton, only a thirty-minute drive from Portsmouth University. Kirsty lives in Huddersfield, hours away. A mere coincidence?"

"Kirsty must have filled it when she visited me."

"Kirsty hasn't seen you for three months when, it should be noted, her prescription for a drug to treat anxiety and depression, traces of which were found in Mia's body, went missing! Kirsty has never visited you in Portsmouth."

Graham circled Clint, like a shark intimidating its prey, waiting to pounce. "Come, come now, Clint. You underestimated us. They don't call us detectives without reason."

Clint didn't reply. Noah leant in. Jackie and Fawn were frozen like ice statues.

"Then we looked at Mia's bank records. Yours too. She lent you nine thousand pounds for your final year, didn't she? There was a transaction from her account to yours a few weeks back just in time to meet the tuition deadline. What was the problem, Clint? Was she asking for it back, or did you want to default on the payment?"

"This is all lies. Mia was my friend!"

"But your biggest mistake was in relation to the messages. Week after week you sent these hateful, angry missives from coffee shops in or around Portsmouth. Dropping them in Mia's direct messages so that she saw them when she least expected them. Criticising her, frightening her, encouraging her to take her own life. Twenty-five were sent in all. One was sent from the hostel, probably whilst you were playing that role-playing game with other backpackers."

"You can't prove those messages were from me."

"Oh, but we can. Because *I*, unlike Jackie here, have a *great* team of people working for me."

CHAPTER SIXTY-SEVEN

"YOU SENT THESE twenty-five messages from coffee shops over a period of three weeks. You thought you were being clever, using different IP addresses, sending them from public places, thinking that they couldn't be traced back to you, but you forgot something." Clint glared at Graham.

"Can you imagine what kind of mistake that might be, ladies and gentlemen?" Graham looked around, his arms out. "No? Well, I'll tell you. Mr. Wells here is a creature of habit. At every coffee shop, he bought a cup of coffee, the same cup of coffee, and as we do nowadays, he enjoyed an uncommon preference for a certain *type* of coffee.

"Ladies and gentlemen, this afternoon a team of local officers fanned out across the south coast, visiting all the coffee shops identified by our crack technical team. They were armed with a picture of your friend here and details of his chosen coffee order. How many of those coffee shops, do you think, produced till receipts with time stamps for a purchase of a particular type of uncommon coffee that matched the time stamps on the menacing messages?"

"That doesn't prove anything!" Clint jumped up. He could move quickly for a big guy. Barnwell took a step forward, but Graham squared up to him, two inches taller. With a fingertip, he pushed Clint back down onto the sofa and put his face in his.

"Oh, but it does. You paid in cash every time and used a false name, but your drink of choice is so novel"—Graham pulled a piece of paper from his pocket—"it is memorable." Graham read from the list that Barnwell had given him following a conversation with Ethel earlier. "'Oat milk mocha, extra shot, extra foam, four shots of cherry syrup.' Very fancy. We got an eighty percent hit rate matching the time stamps of the till receipts with those of the abusive messages. That's more than enough to convince a jury."

Clint went silent. The others stared at him, their understanding of their friend completely shattered by the unveiling of his deceit.

"Clinton Wells, motivated by your unwillingness to pay back the loan of nine thousand pounds, you embarked on a campaign of menaces and drug withdrawal designed to destabilise the mental health of a young woman, an only child, such that she was driven to suicide. You never physically laid a hand on her, but your efforts to prompt her death were calculating, evil, and as effective as if you had killed her with your own hands."

Graham stepped back and looked around the room. "People, I hope you never do, but if you ever choose to commit crimes, let me give you a hint; it might save you doing time. Don't establish any kind of pattern. If you do, we will find you, we will arrest you, and we *will* imprison you."

The crowd in the room shuffled, stunned. Deep breaths were inhaled, joints were cracked. "But before you leave," Graham quickly announced, "there is one more thing. The campaign against Mia was all Clint except for one *teeny*-tiny thing." Nine pairs of eyes searched Graham's face. Everyone in the room, even his officers, waited for his next words, unsure of what was to come.

"Crucial to the successful execution of this plan was Mia's use of anti-depressants. She stopped taking them suddenly. Do you know what happens when someone does that?" Graham looked around. No one stirred.

"Listlessness, disorientation, insomnia, extreme anxiety—all can occur. In fact, I suspect that was what accounted for her capricious moods—a supply that was stopped and started. An actress like Mia can hide things up to a point, but inside she was most likely in turmoil.

"Now, Clint's pretty small-time. In fact, this all started out as a little bit of drug pushing, a favour for a friend. Only later did it turn into a deadly game of cat and mouse, and Clint isn't nearly ruthless or clever enough to have come up with that. Believe me when I say this plan required someone with nerves of steel, cunning, *and* smarts.

"Clint needed someone else. He did just as he was asked. He sent the messages and he supplied the drugs, but not to Mia, he supplied them to someone else and *that* person shared them with Mia, didn't you"—Graham spun around, his eyes alighting momentarily on everyone in the room—"Fawn?"

CHAPTER SIXTY-EIGHT

FAWN'S CLOUDY EYES struggled to focus. "Um, what? Wait, are you accusing me of having something to do with Mia's death?"

"Are you denying that you took stolen prescription medication supplied to you by Mr. Wells and gave them to Mia? Did you not supply her sporadically thereby leaving her in an unstable mental state? You toyed with your friend like she was a puppet on a string, a dog on a lead, a vulnerable woman in the thrall of vindictive, malevolent people."

"Of course, I didn't! I would never do such a thing! Besides, she could have got her own prescription. She didn't need me or Clint."

"But you were so much more convenient, weren't you? Mia complains of difficult people, and there you are with a pill in your pocket. Perfect. No popping to the doctor to justify herself. No prescription to refill, no picking it up from the chemist, no piffling around. At other times, you could just as easily deny her. *Oh, I'm out, sorry.*"

"Why would I . . .? I told you, I liked her," Fawn growled.

"But there were many points of contention, were there not? Mia had treated your sister badly, stealing her boyfriend away. She could also be difficult to work with, behaving in direct opposition to Jackie's wishes. Or," Graham said, stopping by Fawn's chair and leaning close, "was it something to do with how much energy this film demanded, depriving you of your sister's attention, your family's money, your precious time, your status? You were, after all, only here *for fun.*"

"*Tell* him," Jackie insisted. "You had nothing to do with her death, right?"

"That run you went on but didn't tell us about, that was to check that your little plan had succeeded and *that* was why you ran like a maniac back to the hostel."

"Fawn, tell us you didn't . . ." Jackie repeated, beginning to cry.

"I didn't," Fawn said clearly. "She was alive when I last saw her!"

"Technically, you are correct. You knew she was at the edge, literally *and* figuratively. Clint was playing his part with searing precision. But you both knew that it was time. Just one last message. A quick text to Clint was all it took. And when you ran back, past the point where you'd seen her last, she'd gone. Then, you ran as straight as the crow flies, through the copse to the hostel, too exhilarated or appalled by what you'd done to be bothered with a few stinging nettles." Instinctively, Fawn smoothed her jeans that covered the scratches the nettles had left on her shins.

"It's an extraordinary place, Sampson's Leap. So high up, and it juts out so very far," said Graham. "You could look out there and think there's no beach below, not even the sea. Just endless sky." He sounded calm, his voice soothing. "Mia fell five hundred feet. Imagine her terror as she flew through the air, grabbing on to a pathetic tiny tree as she regretted her action and tried to save herself. Charles Villiers Sampson survived his first fall, but Mia didn't have the same luck. What started as a little supply and drug using turned into a deadly game, one you played almost to perfection."

Fawn flicked back her hair and left it curling against her shoulder like a swathe of rich, glossy fabric, her eyes glittering, as, now exposed, she shed her mantle of victimhood. She looked defiantly at her sister, who turned away in disgust.

Graham continued. "Mia Thorne was a promising, vital young woman. A soul who deserved all the opportunities that life could offer. And you threw her away like she was nothing, a piece of litter in the wind. And for what? Your own amusement and a few pounds.

"The injustice that you are alive and she is not, is not lost on us. And we will do our ultimate best to ensure that you receive punishment that will in small part make that imbalance slightly more just."

Graham raised his voice. "If anyone wants to say anything, now's the time. When next you see them, Mr. Wells and Ms. Prentiss will be in court."

Noah stood, quaking with anger. "DI Graham," he said, his actor's voice rising above the turmoil of hurt, "I want something on the record. I loved Mia Thorne. And these *monsters*," he said, fists balled, face contorted as though ready to spit at Clint and Fawn, "had *me* halfway to jail when *they* took Mia from me. From us all." There was a lot more to say, but Noah gathered himself just enough to hold back. "In court, yes," he said. "Depend on me to be there." Shaking his head, he stumbled on his way to the door, closely followed by Nozz and Zink, who looked like they badly needed a drink. Harding escorted a sobbing Jackie from the room, leaving her in the care of a bewildered hostel manager.

Back in the room, on Graham's command, a small wag of the finger, Barnwell moved to arrest the two young people left behind.

CHAPTER SIXTY-NINE

A MAD FLURRY of phone calls and emails had achieved something Graham would have thought impossible a day before. Preparations for the LeapFest celebrations had accelerated with real enthusiasm from several quarters. Jersey Heritage Museum board members had helped put the word out through Gorey's tourism websites, the LeapFest organisers proved nimbler than expected, and Freddie Solomon had connected efficiently with his readers. After groups of tourists had enjoyed Gorey Castle's own small Sampson exhibit and the highly rated art exhibition in the basement, staff gently urged people in the direction of the conference centre in time for seven o'clock.

"On a weekend, of all the awkward times," Laura said to Graham as they prepared for an evening that promised to be fascinating. "We managed to get everyone talking and figuring things out. My staff at the library, officials at the town council, the medical examiner..."

"The police, too, and they're notoriously stubborn," Graham intoned.

"*And* Percival Courthould-Bryant, all happily sharing information in aid of the public good."

"It certainly won't be in aid of the *original* story of Charles Sampson," said Graham, tying his tie in a Windsor knot. "We've probably heard the last of that."

"Hardly seems fair," said Laura. She was wearing a shimmering emerald-green cocktail dress. "Hundreds of people were gearing up for LeapFest, ready to decry Sampson all over again as a murderous fool who agreed to jump to his own death. Turns out," she said, "it wasn't as simple as that."

"Never is, once all the evidence is available."

Laura turned and said, "Speaking of evidence, did Percival come to the station?"

"Yes, he did. He was reluctant to let the artefact fly anywhere, but future DS Roach persuaded him that a police officer was an adequate courier. It's due back in Gorey"—Graham instinctively checked the kitchen wall clock—"right about now."

"That was solid of him to do that."

"Yeah, he was sorry to miss the denouement of the Mia Thorne case, but he loves going over to the mainland now he's been on that fear of flying course, and especially when Dr. Weiss lets him play with the high-end scanners. Plus, I don't think he's done this particular kind of analysis before. Good string to his bow."

Laura kissed him on the cheek. "Gorey Constabulary is lucky to have a leader who never passes up a chance to help his team learn something."

"Believe me, that cuts both ways." Graham folded a handkerchief for his top pocket. "And with a bit of luck, he'll be able to escort Noah Stimms off the island tomorrow. I'll be happy when that stick of dynamite's no longer our problem. And hopefully, he'll not be someone else's either."

"What about the sister?"

"Jackie insisted on staying, at least for a while. Fawn will be kept on remand and perhaps transferred to the mainland whilst awaiting trial. I'm sure Jackie will go home as soon as she realises this isn't all a dream."

"What will happen to them? Noah and Jackie?" Laura leant toward the mirror to put her earrings on.

"Noah will disappear back to university, no doubt. If the acting doesn't pan out, he might possibly wail and rend his way through life. Heaven help those who find themselves around him. Jackie, who knows? This kind of thing will destroy a career before it's even started."

"I'm glad you got it sorted." Laura turned her back to Graham and held up her necklace for him to fasten.

"Me too. There was a real chance the coroner might have been forced to record a verdict of misadventure, or worse, an open verdict. *That*," he emphasised, leaning in slightly to inhale the fragrance of Laura's skin, "would have been *highly* unsatisfactory."

"It's a shame about the film," said Laura. "I mean, it's terrible for Mia's family, first and foremost. But Jackie and her crew planned to hold open rehearsals and rope in some of the cosplay people as extras. It would have been fun to see it through."

"What might have been," lamented Graham. "But all is not lost. Now, instead of roping people in, we've roped the place off. No one's going to get close to that deathtrap."

"Very droll," she said, swatting him with the gold wrap she was planning to wear with her sparkly dress.

"There's no *way* I'd allow people to gather in numbers at Sampson's Leap. I thought it was a pretty macabre idea *before*, but now . . ."

"Right thing to do," Laura told him. "And the surfers are still doing their thing, so the cliff itself will be . . . what's the right word? Celebrated?"

"I think it's their viewer statistics they'll be celebrating," said Graham sceptically. "Provided they don't drown."

CHAPTER SEVENTY

THERE WAS A pleasing buzz of anticipation and a crowd that grew into the hundreds until it was clear even the spacious conference centre would be crammed. It offered a splendid venue for the evening's main event: an open, public meeting to air the new findings in the Sampson case. All those participating hoped to enthral the public whilst laying to rest some tattered myths.

The biggest challenge had been to persuade Freddie not to publish the final section of his research in advance of the meeting. It would have spoiled the surprise.

"But . . . it's the scoop of the century!" Freddie told Laura over the phone earlier in the afternoon. "All I need is for Sergeant Roach to confirm the scientific stuff, and, well . . ." he said breathlessly, "I'm tempted not even to wait for that."

"Only a hack," Graham moaned when Laura told him, "would claim to have an ironclad case before all the evidence was in. Tell him to be patient."

"He said he's already waited twenty-four hours . . ."

"When putting on a fireworks display, it's best if everything goes off in the right order, isn't it? We don't want an errant rocket distracting everyone from the central feature. That would be," he added heavily, "extremely annoying. Tell him he'll get his scoop. He can let everyone know his role in all this later. I'm sure he won't be slow to tell everyone. For once, could he just put the public interest first?"

Freddie's excitement was close to bubbling over. "Yes, but . . ." he told Laura.

"Pinkie promise, Freddie," Laura warned. "You'll hold your tongue. Don't spoil it for everyone. There's a lot more boxes from where that last one came from." She glanced at Graham. "And we have the means to make you be the person to go through every last one."

Obliged to give the couple his word, Freddie spent time mingling with the crowd, touting his proposed subscription-only blog to see if there might be interest and nervously awaiting Roach's return with the crucial data.

Jack Wentworth checked, double-checked, and triple-checked the conference centre's PA system for any sign of an electrical fault. "I don't think anyone's used this since . . . well, you know, last time," he said. No one had been keen to use the equipment since an electrocution death on stage during a police conference. To calm everyone's nerves (except Janice's), Jack personally tested all the microphones to show they were absolutely safe, and then entertained the burgeoning audience with some gentle, classical music.

"Classing up the joint, Jack?" the detective inspector asked him, walking in with Laura to find the clamorous hall in festive mood.

"All written in the few years before 1846," Jack explained of the music selections from Verdi and Donizetti operas. "If there'd been radio back then, these arias would have been on *Top of the Pops*."

"Nice way to augment the atmosphere," Graham agreed, humming along. Many in the audience were in period costume, venturing fulsomely into the weekend event that included a nineteenth-century fair, games, music, and food of the period. Percival Courthould-Bryant had also given a local history lecture. Sometime the next day, waves permitting, the Australian surfers would be showing off their moves in Sampson's Cove. The festivities would end the following evening with a concert.

All of this had got the approval of the local police force, but after the unexpected revelations in Creaveley's journal, Graham found general agreement that a proper, public mulling of the evidence was in order. Roach's arrival with the precious artefact he had been entrusted with and the results of his high-tech investigations in hand only reinforced the wisdom of that choice.

"There's no doubt, then?" Graham asked the sergeant as soon as Roach arrived in the hall, having sped back from the airport on his motorbike.

"Dr. Weiss is certain," Roach said, even before he'd set down his helmet. "Marcus signed off in a half-minute, and for what it matters, I'm convinced too."

"Brilliant," said Graham, genuinely thrilled. "This is going to stir things up, and no mistake. But first, tell Freddie before he springs a leak."

The blogger's reaction was closer to relief. "Thank science for that," Freddie heaved. "I've already written it up."

"Of course you have." Roach chuckled, leaving him a copy of the findings. "Good luck with the session," he said, noting that it was minutes away.

Marcus Tomlinson arrived just then. "Sorry to cut it so fine, David. We were having an early dinner at the Foc's'le, and it was packed, small wonder." On Tomlinson's arm, much to Graham's surprise and delight, was an elegant lady dressed in the same nineteenth-century fashions that were currently all the rage in the hall. "May I introduce Francine Delafort?" As the two shook hands, Tomlinson said to his friend, "My dear, Detective Inspector Graham and I have been working closely together these last few years. And I've been providing an education in forensic pathology to one of the constabulary's bright, young sergeants."

Graham smiled broadly. "It's a pleasure to meet you. Has the good doctor told you anything about what's going on tonight?"

"Not yet," Francine said, obviously as excited as the rest of the audience. She was dressed in a rich ruby-red dress with full skirts and a bodice that pulled everything in so tightly that her body escaped from wherever there was an outlet. "I think Marcus enjoys a mystery almost as much as you do."

"We enjoy *solving* them, my dear," Marcus told her, patting her arm that was linked through his. "But . . . all in good time. Given the circumstances, I saw no harm in agreeing to participate in this evening's spectacle." Tomlinson guided Francine to a reserved seat before taking his own place on the stage alongside Freddie Solomon, whose bodily energy was also barely contained, but in a different manner to that of Marcus's lady friend.

"Like I said on the phone," Tomlinson said with a smile at the near-vibrating blogger, "it's an interesting case."

"There's a book in this," Freddie proposed. "Maybe even a TV special." He'd already pictured himself being acknowledged as the local expert on the case, hosting or narrating a show that might air on Channel 4 or BBC 2. "My ticket to the big time."

"Good luck," said Tomlinson. "Everyone ready?"

The lights dimmed and, striding to the front of the stage, Freddie was captured by a spotlight. Nervous enough that his knees trembled, but as fascinated by the attentive crowd as they were by this local, ancient mystery, he began to read aloud.

CHAPTER SEVENTY-ONE

"'HEAVY IS THE *heart, and reluctant the pen, that transcribes my own perspective of a most terrible incident, a plague of miserable deaths fit to be visited upon damnable sinners, but scarce ever sent to poison the happiness of God-fearing folk.'"*

Freddie's voice was steadier than expected as he read from Jeremiah Creaveley's journal. Despite the capacity crowd, there was rapt silence.

"*'For the last week, I have been assailed by the demands of Mr. Clarembaux and his Masonic brethren, who are most fiercely and stubbornly determined that Charles Villiers Sampson, an apothecary lately of this parish, should suffer punishment befitting the horror of his deeds.'*" Freddie followed this opening with a newly revealed section of Creaveley's journal.

"*'I must commit to paper a private duplication of my formal report, submitted today, that it might ease my troubled mind, and unburden me of the worrisome fear that I have disgraced myself by an insufficiency of legal prudence.'*" Behind Freddie, Percival Courthould-Bryant rubbed his hands in excitement.

"*'Charles Sampson, may Almighty God rest a sinner like he, stood accused of instigating a most appalling incident. I can scarce write their names, so vexed is my heart at their passing, but Sampson was generally felt to be guilty of three most callous murders: Alice Pritchard, daughter to a Jersey family of five generations; Penelope Levin, only four years since arrived on Jersey with her parents; and, bless her memory, Susan, youngest daughter of my friend and client, William St. Edmund. We are a stoical brotherhood in this town that faces the oft-enraged English Channel, but we have wept,'*" Freddie intoned, fist clenched to his sternum, "*oh wept as like to create another sea, here ashore.*"

Laura walked slowly into the spotlight as Freddie withdrew. "*'The good people of Gorey sought the truth,'* wrote Jeremiah Creaveley. But what they actually got was hearsay. Thanks to many hours of scholarly work by a friend of the community, we now know the depths of Gorey's ignorance during that fateful time. Simply: people *made things up*. They promised that lies were true. They egged each other on, and as the days passed, they found less and less fault in crackpot theories that deserved only to be debunked and discarded. The sad, humiliating result was that a mob of people, among them some of your great-great-grandparents," she said, raising some eyebrows in the audience, "hauled Charles Sampson to a cliff top and said, 'Jump, or we'll push you off.' Or, as Jeremiah Creaveley put it, *'Thy shalt meet thine Maker, by your hand or by ours, for thou art a foul murderer, as sure as daylight.'*" Laura stepped back as Freddie cleared his throat and once more took his place in the spotlight.

"Their sense of certainty was an illusion, ladies and gentlemen," Freddie told his audience. "Charles Sampson was irresponsible, certainly, but innocent. It was the mob's stupidity that cost him his life, not even at their first attempt, but at their second. Sampson sent himself, as Creaveley wrote in amazement, *'Splashing into the shallow waves at just such an angle as to dispel the energy of his fall. He gesticulated from the beach as though cast upon it by a sea only too willing to rebirth him into a second incarnation.'*" Projected onto the wall behind the speakers, images of the cliff and the wave-lashed cove appeared and dissolved, one after another. "The execution was botched, as is well-known. But that's hardly a surprise, when there had already been so many other failures in this particular lamentable case."

Freddie stepped back, receiving a discreet pat on the back from the advancing DI Graham, whose arrival in the spotlight generated a warm undercurrent of applause. He read from Creaveley's journal.

CHAPTER SEVENTY-TWO

"'S AMPSON WAS A *jealous lover, claimed one rumour, his infatuation unreturned by women already promised to more suitable men.*'

"But Creaveley leaves no evidence that Sampson knew these women well. He was of relatively modest station, and though he'd have had cause to interact with Gorey's high-society figures, we can assume these were very brief encounters. A suggestion that he became hopelessly, dangerously infatuated with not one, or two, but *three* different women was mere guesswork.

"There were claims that Sampson carried out physical assaults." Graham began to walk slowly across the stage, the spotlight following him. "But these must be supported by evidence in order to carry weight." Graham paused and looked out into the audience, fixing his gaze on one spot despite the bright stage lights preventing him from seeing anything in the blackness. "If Sampson were such a serial offender, there'd be police reports, salacious warnings published in Jersey's newspapers, constables going door-to-door warning residents, especially young women. Police work then wasn't so very different from basic policing today.

"Then, there was a popular idea that this case involved a perpetrator who housed a so-called 'long-dormant natural disposition to murder.' Important exceptions notwithstanding," Graham said, "most murders—nineteen of every twenty, in fact—are improvised, opportunistic. They're not planned, premeditated, or otherwise anticipated."

Surprised by this, the crowd buzzed with interest. It struck Graham that some nearly three hundred were now completely absorbed by his interpretation of crime in times past. "Poisonings such as the Sampson case are in a special category. They require a great deal of preparation, require access, and as such are rare. If Sampson was a committed serial killer, as Creaveley suggested, then we'd surely have evidence of other mysterious deaths in the preceding years and in the same manner. Sampson had been an apothecary for decades prior, but no such records exist. Neither is there proof that contact with 'exotic plants' as Sampson may have had are likely to generate murderous impulses as was also suggested at the time."

Mutters of agreement were overlapped by more applause as DI Graham took a few steps back, his place taken by the dapper Tomlinson, his red plaid bowtie offsetting the earthy colour of his tweed suit. "A 'quack', they said. For a medical man, it's a serious charge. But Charles Sampson never claimed to be a qualified physician, nor did anyone formally prove the method of murder. Perhaps," Tomlinson mused, "the townsfolk of Gorey, way back then, were not nearly as informed and curious as those of today?" No audience ever objected to flattery, and most of the crowd decided at once that they were going to like Dr. Marcus Tomlinson.

"We rely instead on Creaveley's formal report. It provides sufficient details for a diagnosis to be attempted, even one hundred seventy-five years later. Now," he cautioned, "I will not act as coroner in these cases. No death certificates will be issued, neither are exhumations nor postmortems possible," he said. "Instead, we must compensate for another failure: a deficiency in the forensic findings. And in this, I will invite your assistance."

He brought out his cellphone and held it aloft. "If you possess one of these, please bring it out. We'll forgive the anachronism of men and women, dressed as many of you are for church on a Sunday in the 1840s, avidly searching the internet," he said, smiling at the incongruity, "but crowdsourcing our medical findings is surely no more irresponsible than the fact-free, ignorant 'mob science' that convicted Sampson.

"Creaveley noted the women's symptoms in two sections of his journal. Mr. Solomon has already made the first available, and it tells of pale skin, vomiting, bodily pain, and convulsions. Whilst you search for ailments, diseases, or poisons that might provoke such symptoms, I invite Freddie to read from the latter part of the journal."

In a much darker tone fit for the horrid details of the case, Freddie stepped forward and read, "'*By the sixth day of the crisis, the exhalations of all three women presented a noxious scent, as though they had recently eaten garlic. Their bedsheets were spoiled, and the women copiously perspired, though their attendants cooled them as best could be managed. One by one, they doubled over and brought their knees to their breasts as though pained by womanly afflictions, miscarriage, or childbirth. Their fingernails became discoloured and strange, and by degrees they seemed to lose their senses, forgetting their whereabouts and even their own names.*'"

Freddie paused and looked up to find that fully a third of the audience was searching on a device or peering over the shoulders of those who were, their faces glowing in front of the brightly lit screens.

"'*In poor Susan's final days, her attendant was shocked to find, when soothing her head with a kind hand, that the girl's hair came loose and fell out. In the final hours, she seemed asleep but had no response whatever, even to a stout slap across the face. The attending physician, Dr. Barclay, could only assume her body's grievous failures had sapped her to unconsciousness.'"*

"I believe this last piece of evidence," Tomlinson told the audience, "indicates coma." He withdrew and gave the audience several moments to mine the internet, and those of a medical bent time to hone their own suppositions, whilst Jack resumed the quiet, heartfelt operatic chorus over the PA system.

"They're loving it," Laura whispered to Graham. "Whose idea was the 'crowdsourced forensics'?"

"Jim's," he answered softly. "We gave him everything from Creaveley's journal, and he admitted all he could realistically do was check online. Figured we may as well all look together."

"But *you* know for sure, right?" she asked.

"I didn't, until Jim came back from Portsmouth. And even then, it's a tiny bit of a stretch. But it makes sense. Let's see how they do."

CHAPTER SEVENTY-THREE

RESUMING HIS POSITION centre stage, Tomlinson asked, "Well, friends? What illness carried off these poor women all those years ago? Who has a suggestion?"

Various hands were raised, and Tomlinson picked a woman toward the front. "It says here that radiation poisoning can cause some of those things," she said.

"What, like after a nuclear weapons test?" someone asked sceptically. "This was a hundred years before the first bomb."

"It's possible," Tomlinson said, "for radioactive elements to exist in concentrations that can harm a human. A swimming hole, for example, surrounded by soil with peculiarly high levels of pitchblende. But I'm afraid no such radioactive rocks exist on Jersey, nor anywhere the women are likely to have travelled. Alright, what else?" Tomlinson said invitingly.

"Liver disease!" shouted a man from the back.

"Ah! Interesting!" Tomlinson replied. "It would explain the garlicky breath, at least. But there are only two potential causes: three simultaneous infections of hepatitis—highly unlikely—or years of heavy alcohol consumption. Neither seems likely. Also, if it were liver disease, Creaveley would have noted jaundice, a yellowing of the skin."

A teenager called out, "They were throwing up and doubled over in pain. What about food poisoning?"

"Another good idea," Tomlinson allowed. "But most such toxins leave the body, especially young bodies, on their own eventually. Alice, Penelope, and Susan were young, fit women well able to contend with a bout of food poisoning, unless," he added, glancing at Graham standing in the wings, "the noxious substance is repeatedly administered. More generalised food poisoning would also have been easy to track down with other people reporting similar symptoms. Doesn't explain the convulsions or hair loss, either."

A raised hand belonged to Lewis Hurd, barman at the Foc's'le and Ferret. "We're thinking it's chemical poisoning, then?"

"I'd stake my house on it," Tomlinson said. "There's nothing naturally occurring, nor anything that comes from sheer bad luck, that explains such a collection of symptoms."

"Something called 'thallium' fits the bill pretty well, according to this," Lewis said, raising his phone.

"Yes, yes," Tomlinson said thoughtfully. "Another radioactive element sometimes used as a poison. It would produce most of these symptoms, but Creaveley didn't note any pain in the extremities or effects on the women's vision, which is what you'd expect. I can't imagine thallium was available to Sampson either in 1846. Might there be a simpler explanation, Detective Inspector?"

Graham strode to the front of the stage. The audience settled down immediately. "Inheritor's powder," he said. "A metalloid poison, notoriously difficult for pathologists to discern. Made famous in the nineteenth century before being banned in 1851, just five years after the Sampson case." Graham resumed his gentle pacing as he explained. "So-called because following administration, the *pater familias* of a wealthy household would unexpectedly keel over, often just after dinner, leaving a vast fortune to his lucky but evil heirs. You won't be surprised to learn there'd usually be evidence of a family feud or dispute, some source of bad blood that preempted the death."

"Who of you has already caught up with Jersey's finest detective?" asked Tomlinson.

"Arsenic!" said a dozen people at once.

"Precisely!" said Roach, accepting Tomlinson's encouraging gesture and taking his own place on the stage. "The symptoms are all a perfect match for massive, sudden arsenicosis."

"So, Sampson poisoned them with arsenic!" a person in the audience declared. "It *was* him!"

"Yes," Roach said, letting the word linger as the crowd buzzed, "*and no.*" There were grumbles of confusion until Roach held up his hands for quiet. "Firstly, know this: a large dose of arsenic was always going to result in death for these women. No cure was available in 1846, and so, they were doomed. But *who* was it that doomed them?"

Freddie, by now considering the spotlight his natural habitat, returned to the stage carrying Creaveley's journal to round out the tale. "Gorey's public made its fateful verdict," he said, "based upon a single strand of evidence, a murmured accusation from Alice Pritchard as she lay dying. She had taken a draught of Sampson's Beauty Cordial, she told those lingering around her deathbed. This, it turned out, was something shared by all three of the afflicted women. The apothecary was immediately blamed. But we are fortunate that another, more dependable source of evidence is included in the journal: Mrs. Katherine Creaveley, by that time Jeremiah's wife of sixteen years. Through her husband, she tells us in his journal that Sampson's Beauty Cordial was 'as safe as any such product' and that she'd taken a teaspoonful each morning, as directed by Mr. Sampson, for at least ten months, without any ill effect.'"

"They overdosed!" concluded several people at once.

"It might seem so," said Tomlinson, stepping forward. "But the journal is our starting place, not a collection of conclusive facts. The symptoms provide clues, but not proof. We need to know," he explained, "whether the cordial truly contained arsenic. This requires a testing of blood, urine, hair, or fingernails.

"I could propose an exhumation so that we may analyse the remains of the women. Some nail fragment or strand of hair may remain." The audience met this idea with wrinkled noses, frowns, and downturned mouths. "But don't worry, I'm not about to send you to the cemetery with picks and shovels! Instead, we have taken a different course."

Percival Courthould-Bryant stepped forward.

CHAPTER SEVENTY-FOUR

"WHEN SOMEONE DIED back in Victorian times, it was fashionable to commemorate them in ways that might seem . . . well, a little macabre today. Eight years after the Sampson case, Katherine Creaveley's time came, and her husband wrote of his terrible grief."

It fell to Freddie to utter some final lines. "'*We laid to rest our Katherine today. She is ascended into sunlit perfection, but she leaves here on Earth a man bereft, a ship without its anchor. I stand as confused as the sea suddenly without any sky above it, without any shore upon that to rest, a dawn unkindly denied its sunrise. What can I do but cling to what remains, and weep for all that has gone forever.*'"

"He was true to his word," Courthould-Bryant said, "and employed a jeweller so that he might never be parted from a little of 'what remains' by wearing this remarkable piece." On the screen appeared a picture of a man's gold ring, fronted by the initials KJC. Around its circumference was wrapped a tight braid of slightly faded, dark hair. "We are indebted to Jeremiah Creaveley in many ways, not just for his recording of the events surrounding this case, but for having preserved the only forensic evidence. Isn't that correct, Sergeant?" Courthould-Bryant asked, turning to Roach.

"Quite right," Roach confirmed. "We were able to analyse a sample of Katherine's hair. Everyone has a tiny amount of arsenic in their bodies. Don't worry, it's less than one-tenth of a microgram for each gram of your body mass, an insignificant amount. Mrs. Creaveley's hair, on the other hand, was almost weighed down by it—3.9 grams, nearly forty times the natural amount. This suggests that Sampson's Beauty Cordial contained measurable amounts of arsenic. That Katherine Creaveley took the cordial regularly without ill effects strongly suggests that the three women who died did so because they swallowed *hundreds of times* the recommended amount, all at once."

Graham appeared on stage again. "Charles Sampson was an ignorant fool, and these days, he'd have been sentenced for manslaughter, but he was not guilty of premeditated murder as the Gorey mob insisted. He sold a dangerous substance, and may have included more arsenic than intended, batch by batch, but at least he was sensible enough to give his customers fair warning: take a teaspoonful, at most. It was a warning the three women ignored, young and vain as they were. It cost them their lives."

Freddie joined Graham. "The rest came from assumptions, spread and warped into 'facts' by the mob. It's not a long distance from 'Sampson gave them a tonic that they abused' to 'Sampson poisoned them.' Nothing Katherine Creaveley said at the time would have changed the outcome. As her husband wrote in *Arguing in Court*, '*Anger is poisonous to reason, and prejudice obscures facts better than a thick winter fog.*'"

Graham delivered the final word on the verdict. "This, ladies and gentlemen, was a failure of medicine, honesty, *and* investigative rigour. Let us not forget the lessons of this miscarriage of justice."

Seeing the long-established myth crumble in front of them, the audience broke out into applause. "We leave you," Freddie said, even as applause continued to erupt, "with a final reminder from Jersey's senior legal mind. '*We cannot rush Lady Justice to present a finding, not until we have informed her through apt questions and honest answers. Only then, with the truth laid out before her, plain and majestic as the myriad stars of the firmament, can we ask that she render a perfect judgment.*'"

Graham and Laura walked back to her cottage slowly, quietly basking in the success of the evening's event. There had been many handshakes and pats on the back after the presentation. Tomlinson had charmed, Roach had glowed, Freddie was positively energised.

"Well done, young men!" Courthould-Bryant had said to them. "Not you, Marcus. You're an old man like me. Time we stepped back, don't you think? Let the young 'uns take over?"

"I'm doing my best, Percival," Tomlinson had said. "Doing my best."

It had taken a long time for the hall to clear, and eventually Laura decided she'd take down the small exhibition she'd put together the next morning. She and Graham walked out into the clear, brisk night, the air silent as it stung their cheeks.

"I realised something tonight," Graham said as they walked away from the bustle of the conference centre and down the meandering side streets to Laura's cottage. A cat walked across their path, pausing before skittering off.

"Oh?"

"That when there is insufficient explanation, the imagination runs riot, filling in holes and gaps where explanations are lacking. I realise that I've not been fully honest with you and that you are probably imagining things, wild things, because of that. I'm sorry."

Laura remained silent, allowing David room to speak. This time he didn't hesitate and stepped into the opening.

"Her name was Katie. My daughter. She was seven when she died. The car she was travelling in was in a collision with one driven by a drunk driver. My marriage broke up—we were unable to comprehend Katie's loss together—and I moved down here to get away from my memories.

"But you can never get away from them, not really. You can only put them away for a while. And eventually, you can't avoid them any longer. Like boxes, they demand to be unpacked. It's time for me to do that, and I'm starting by telling you. There is nothing for you to be afraid of; it is I who is afraid. But I am determined to face this, I hope with your help. Bear with me, my progress will be slow, and I will no doubt be clumsy. I ask for your patience, your tolerance, and" —he looked down at her—"your love."

Laura gazed up at Graham and smiled. She stood on tiptoes to kiss him, then simply put her warm, slight hand into his cooler, meatier one, and they carried on up the road.

CHAPTER SEVENTY-FIVE

"A WOMAN IS *walking along the street one morning when she is approached from behind by two men. One of them demands she hands over her bag. She refuses.*" Janice was reading off her computer screen. "*The other man attempts to take it from her, but she fights him and runs away. As the men chase her, she trips, hits her head and later dies from head trauma. Which of the following options is correct? One . . .*"

Roach closed his eyes and screwed up his face as he answered what felt like the 1,000th test question Janice had posed him. As he listened to the possible answers, Graham appeared in his office doorway. He leant on the doorframe, sipping tea and listening. The sound of Janice carefully reciting the four answers for Roach to choose from, her voice soft and mellow, reminded him of the clergy who said prayers on the radio, subject matter notwithstanding. The sight of Roach intent on answering her question like a young boy wanting to please his teacher made him smile. His eyes softened and his breathing slowed as he watched them.

"Answer three, the men could be liable for her death."

"*KER*-rect!" Janice replied. Roach let out a big sigh and slumped.

"How are you feeling, Jim? About the exam, I mean," Graham asked him.

"Ah, you know. I don't like to get too confident, sir. I'd much prefer to be on edge. Don't want to get too cocky. Everyone's been so kind to help out, though. Dr. Tomlinson had me over for dinner last night. Had me dissecting a chicken whilst testing me on forensic evidence collection and analysis."

"He's a good man, Tomlinson. Good teacher too."

"I'll say, but I'll never look at roast chicken in quite the same way again."

"He's worked hard, sir. He deserves to pass," Janice said.

Graham turned to her. "And you, sergeant, how are things going for you?"

"Ah, same old, same old." Janice smiled ruefully, raising her eyebrows and pressing her lips together.

"Do you need more action, more spice to your duties?"

"Definitely not, sir. My mother is salty enough for me."

"She's giving Janice a hard time over her wedding," Roach said. He put an arm around Harding's shoulders and pulled her into him before releasing her and patting her shoulder in solidarity.

"She thinks we should get a move on. That Jack might do a runner if I don't lock him up sharpish."

Graham nodded. "That you need to nail him to a fifty-year stretch."

"Yeah, and she wants the supreme court, not some minor county court affair."

"Ah, I can see why that would be bothersome. Well, if I can be any help, I could offer to keep him on remand for an extended period."

"She'd like that, sir. Might make up for her lackadaisical daughter pussy-footing around. To her, Jack's an open and shut case."

"Sir, changing the subject, how was it that the other day, you twigged on to Fawn being involved in the Mia Thorne case?" Roach asked.

"Good question. It was speculative to be honest. I just couldn't see good old Clint being the mastermind. It made a lot more sense that he'd have an accomplice. This was a particularly nasty crime, and he didn't seem the hard, cold, pathological type. She, on the other hand, seemed far more devious, and an actress with skills as worthy as the victim. And then there were those two tattoos . . . I was spinning my wheels a bit to see if I could get any traction, and ultimately, she coughed, didn't she?"

There was a bang, and they all looked up to see Barnwell coming in through the doors backwards. He was wearing his civvies. It was his day off. As the doors swung closed behind him, he turned around. For a moment, for Graham, Harding, and Roach, nothing else mattered—not the case, Janice's wedding, Roach's exams.

In unison, their eyes widened, the conversation stopped, their movements froze. Big, burly Barnwell was cradling a small, brown-black-and-white bundle of fur in his arms as gently as if it were an infant. The puppy wriggled and licked Barnwell's neck with a tongue so pink it was like a scoop of strawberry ice cream on top of a scoop of chocolate and vanilla, streaked through with caramel sauce.

"What?" Barnwell said as he looked at them staring at him.

Above the station, seagulls cawed. "What?" Barnwell repeated.

"Y-you filled in the form?" Roach croaked.

"Yeah, I thought I was supposed to. It was left on my desk." Barnwell looked down at the puppy who, emboldened, had now embarked on a thorough licking of Barnwell's jaw and cheek. He half-heartedly wrestled his face away. "I've just picked her up from St. Helier. She flew in this morning; she's a Beagle. They're sniffer dogs. Drugs. We start training tomorrow." He looked down at the puppy and scratched her between her ears. "I'm going to call her Carmen." He gently dropped the puppy to the floor and pushed his way back through the doors. Carmen trotted after him, leaving Barnwell's stunned fellow officers silent in his wake.

EPILOGUE

After an extended debate involving Gorey Constabulary and the Crown Prosecution Service, **Fawn Prentiss** and **Clinton Wells** were tried for voluntary manslaughter for their role in Mia Thorne's death. The basis of the case centred on Fawn as the author of the plan to incite Mia's suicide, with Clint acting as her co-conspirator.

Fawn's family engaged four experienced defence lawyers who worked to undermine the evidence against her, claiming diminished responsibility. After three weeks of deliberations, the jury were unable to come to a unanimous verdict, and despite the judge declaring that a majority verdict would suffice, the jury was eventually dismissed.

However, after a high-profile newspaper campaign and at a retrial, both defendants were swiftly convicted, the jury accepting that the intent of Prentiss's and Wells's actions were to drive Mia to the point of suicide and encourage her to take her own life. They were both sentenced to fourteen years imprisonment.

Fawn's sister, **Jackie Prentiss,** didn't complete her degree and returned home to live with her parents. She works in a clothing shop. The film of Charles Villiers Sampson was never completed.

Noah Stimms abandoned his dreams of acting and is training to be a dentist.

Regis Nosworthy and **Vladimir Zynkovlev** became successful surfing influencers, boasting some six million followers. They chase the world's best surfing conditions, making remarkable video clips using the latest wearable camera and drone technology.

Sergeant Jim Roach aced his exams and is in discussions with DI Graham about his future.

Sergeant Janice Harding and **Jack Wentworth** gave up on hipster living after her favourite plant died and he admitted he'd tipped his kombucha into the plant pot. Her mother is still giving Janice grief about the wedding; Janice and Jack are thinking of eloping.

Constable Barnwell and **Carmen** can frequently be seen exploring the open spaces of Jersey, occasionally with their best friends, firefighter Melanie Howes and her pitbull, Vixen. After training, Carmen will specialise in drug searches and smuggling crime.

On a visit to meet her parents, **David** showed **Laura** around Chiddlinghurst, the village in which he had lived. Whilst there, they visited Katie's grave in the church cemetery. Laura left flowers, and after reading to the Year 3s, she donated books to the village primary school library in Katie's name.

Two months after the 175th anniversary of his death, **Charles Villiers Sampson's** grave was finally marked in a ceremony attended by the local vicar, dignitaries, Freddie Solomon, Dr. Marcus Tomlinson, and Inspector David Graham. A year later, a memorial service was held in Sampson's name and attended by several hundred Gorey locals.

ALISON GOLDEN
Grace Dagnall

USA Today Bestselling Author

AN INSPECTOR DAVID GRAHAM MYSTERY

The Case of the
Uncommon Witness

The characters and events portrayed in this book are fictitious. Any similarity to real persons, living or dead is coincidental and not intended by the author.
Text copyright © 2022 Alison Golden
All rights reserved.

No part of this book may be reproduced, stored in a retrieval system, or transmitted in any form or by any means, electronic, mechanical, photocopying, recording, or otherwise, without express written permission of the publisher.

Cover Illustration: Richard Eijkenbroek

Published by Mesa Verde Publishing
P.O. Box 1002
San Carlos, CA 94070

ISBN: 979-8361674671

CHAPTER ONE

THE GROUP OF four women and one man stood in a loose row. Captivated by the scene before them, hands holding paintbrushes raised expectantly, they stared out over a calm, sun-washed bay. They were on a cliff top, the sky a deep sapphire-blue streaked with only the odd wispy cloud. Below, the waves of the English Channel lapped gently.

"Breathe the scene in, my friends," Peregrine Wordsworth began. He paced slowly behind the row of students, his hands behind his back like an amiable, encouraging professor dispensing wisdom and guidance. "Feel its shapes, its subtleties."

In front of each student stood an easel and a canvas on which was painted a seemingly random arrangement of colourful splodges. Almost an hour into their first session, none had yet begun to represent Crescent Bay that lay below them or the bluffs that surrounded it, on top of which a stylish, modern home was built. First, Wordsworth insisted, they would collaborate to "achieve the conceptual origin" of the painting.

"Breathe with the waves," Wordsworth continued. "Let the light of the bay *speak* to you."

"Talking light?" scoffed the lone male. "Really?"

"Mr. Barr, *everything* is talking to you," the veteran artist assured him. "It is we who fail to listen." Peregrine Wordsworth was sixty-seven but seemed almost immune to aging. He could pass for forty-five. His was a slender frame, topped with a mop of white, corkscrew curls. The loose, black shirt and charcoal jeans he wore made him seem lithe and nimble one moment and strangely statuesque the next.

"Ridiculous," Fergus Barr muttered. He was a tall and skinny Scot with wavy, brown hair. He was constantly moving, exhibiting a series of tics—twitching, scratching, jiggling, brushing his hair off his face. In contrast to the smooth, graceful movements of his mentor, he was a distracted, agitated figure.

"Talking to us, yes!" the woman next to the Scot exclaimed. "Every scene, every blade of grass." She glanced appreciatively at the sky. "Even the clouds. Like waves of energy." Dr. Hiruni Ramachandran was a pleasantly plump woman wearing a long, flowing maxi dress and sandals which showed off toes dusted with long, dark hair and un-manicured toenails. She was the very opposite of her neighbour—calm, still, softly spoken. She had big, brown eyes with long, thick eyelashes and full lips that sprung readily into a wide smile, displaying perfectly straight, white teeth. "Sound, magnetism, kinetics—they all use the same base substance."

"The very same elemental energy, Dr. Hiruni!" Wordsworth agreed, happy to find a kindred spirit. Peregrine Wordsworth had been considered a voice in the art world for over three decades. He'd lectured all over the world, gaining as much fame from his outlandish attire that often involved wearing makeup and the odd item of women's clothing as he had from his art. He'd even hosted a reality show in which a group of non-artistic celebrities came together at a retreat. He taught them how to paint. He set them challenges. Each week, based on the strength of their work, they were voted in or out by the public.

But then, in books and interviews, Wordsworth hypothesised the existence of a world *behind* the one we see, claiming that very few people had "the gifts" to access it. He appeared rarefied and out of touch with the audience he had courted with his earlier, more accessible endeavours. Subsequently, he was pilloried in the British media, and his work dried up. After a drink or three, Wordsworth would devolve into complaints about being "cancelled." These days, his teaching engagements existed to pay the bills.

"Crescent Bay vibrates with that same energy, don't you think?" Wordsworth turned to look out at the horizon and admired the play of light on water and the stubborn jut of the cliff standing defiant against the sea. "A place of oppositions, each one crackling with something we can barely perceive. It is these contrasts," he added, "that make this place special."

Dr. Hiruni, as the group had agreed to call the Sri Lankan-born physician, opened her mouth to answer, but Fergus cut her off. "So, what you're saying," he said, visibly tiring of Wordsworth's esoteric and often verbose viewpoints, "is I should learn how to paint better by using 'the force'?"

Fergus's quip sent Belinda Dunn, a local teenager whom even Wordsworth had to admit possessed an uncommon talent, into a fit of giggles. While the usually taciturn young woman recovered, Dr. Hiruni refocused the group. "The contrasts create the character of the bay, you mean."

"We could say 'character' or 'spirit', I suppose," Wordsworth said, "but think of it as layer upon layer of wave forms. The water," he said, his gestures fluid, "is the fastest, the most obvious, but above all, is not the atmosphere obeying the same rules? Being pushed and pulled?" His hands embodied the tension, locked together but tussling for control. "Not by gravity, but by heat and moisture. And beneath," he continued, completing the metaphor which appeared in one of his books, "there are waves of geological activity, each millions of years long. Everything is *energy*, after all."

"Interesting idea." Dr. Hiruni nodded. "I don't know if I can *paint* it," she qualified with a smile, "but I think I see what you're saying."

Peregrine Wordsworth meandered around the group, peering over his students' shoulders as they attempted to represent the scene as he described it on their canvases. The beautiful weather allowed them to work outside today, but behind them stood the grounds of a private school. The artistic hub of their retreat was the former headmaster's cottage. It offered them a large sunroom to paint in when they needed it and remarkable views over the bay.

Wordsworth approached the artists one by one, delivering sage advice to each. "There can be beauty in every single brushstroke if we pay attention and bring our *unfiltered* selves to our work."

One of his students, Magda Padalka-Lyons, was a solid, affluent woman in her mid-forties, dressed today in a tight, pink velour sweatsuit and accompanied as usual by her Pomeranian, Pom-Pom, who sat by her feet asleep. Magda had made a start by sketching the outline of the cliff that stood on the other side of the bay and then shifted her focus to the house that stood on top of it. "The owner is friend of mine," Magda told Fergus in broken English. She remained indivisible from her East European accent despite twelve years of marriage to a Jerseyman and an even longer time spent on the British mainland. "Katerina Granby. She's a lovely person. Such nice parties. Dog lover."

The new, custom-built Granby residence seemed precarious atop the cliff. Perfectly private, divorced from neighbours by swathes of green, the house was surrounded by manicured lawns. A long driveway that ran from a road the artists couldn't see highlighted its isolation. The house was a modern fusion of glass and white concrete that, despite the suggestion, integrated with the landscape by appearing to emerge from it. It was one of those rare cases where the form and function of a home matched the ambition of the architect's rendering. The tasteful lawns and the occasional flowerbed were given height and interest by hard landscaping that comprised walls, walkways, and platforms of wood, rock, and more concrete. There were sun-traps, sculptures, and shady spots. At night, a constellation of low-level lights lit up the features. There was even a swimming pool. Magda would have been jealous, but her pool was bigger.

On Magda's right was a refined woman in her seventies. She'd found a stool on which to perch. Wordsworth found her first efforts—bold, geometric outlines—a little too confined. "Imagine, perhaps, that the cliffs are made not of rock, but of something alive and breathing." Mrs. Courthould-Bryant glanced between Wordsworth and her sketch a few times before saying simply, "Lovely," and carrying on precisely as before.

Fergus continued his monologue of quiet scoffing. "First, light that can talk. Now, cliffs that can breathe. What's next?" he wondered, gesturing to Magda's Pomeranian. "Dogs that can write poetry?"

"Pom-Pom *very* expressive," his owner said.

"Look, why did you even come if all you're going to do is criticise?" Belinda, the talented teenager said to Fergus. "You knew what you were in for." She jabbed the end of her brush at Wordsworth, who was quietly talking to Magda over the woman's shoulder. Belinda exhaled and shook her head as she refocused her attention on her painting.

The artists continued to apply paint to canvas, working over the pencil sketches they had started with. Wordsworth monitored his time carefully so that his attention was evenly divided between his students. He had an excellent memory for what he'd already observed, a skill honed during dozens of these small, three-day workshops. "Remember," he said, speaking quietly as he patrolled the group, "your plan reflects your intentions, but we also make second-to-second decisions *within* the plan." He stopped and posed a question. "Ultimately, can we even say which is in control: the plan, or the artist?"

"But . . . the artist makes the plan!" Fergus responded, unable to restrain himself despite Belinda's remonstrations.

"You know, I sometimes wonder if it's the other way around," Wordsworth said, his mind momentarily carried away by the idea. "I really do. I sit in my bathtub, and I ponder that *very* question." The group fell quiet for a while. There was silence except for brushstrokes and the mixing of paint.

Wordsworth resumed his patrol. His look—pale and tall, black-clad and elegant—made him at once invisible and, somehow, omnipresent. "Miss Dunn," he said quietly to Belinda, "what has Crescent Bay said to *you* today?"

Belinda spoke quickly, in anxious, truncated bursts, as though afraid of being interrupted or causing offence. "Contrasts and layers of waves. Like you said. They're everywhere." She looked up and found the edge of the cliff with her fingertip. "A precipice, but also a home." She spread her hands, trying to encapsulate the tension through her gesture as Wordsworth had earlier. "Safe, but also in peril." She turned to face the sea. "Shallows and depths, starlight and sunlight," she said, realising the possibilities. "Ancient chalk and yesterday's dust."

The group hadn't quite known what to make of Belinda, but mostly they were relieved that she seemed to be on Wordsworth's wavelength from the outset. At breaks, he had monopolised her, leaving the rest of them to relax. "Yes, the contrasts, those collisions and agreements between elements," he trilled. "Now, what *is* the house, from the cliff's point of view?" The veteran artist's workshops were full of open, intriguing questions like this.

"Impostor. Invader. Tyrant," Belinda replied.

"But never a partner?"

"There's no contrast in partnership," she pointed out.

Wordsworth smiled. "You're not married, I can tell. What about parent and child? Cliff and house? A symbiotic relationship rife with tension as one pulls away and the other clings, or maybe turns away. Do you see anything there?"

Belinda dropped her brush and stared at him. "No," she said bluntly.

"Spontaneity, within a good design, should never find itself confined,"

Wordsworth said to the sea air before moving on to ponder the achievements of the others.

After lunch, they would imagine the bay anew with a different affect. It was about capturing the basics and then bringing imagination to complete the details. As far as Wordsworth was concerned, the more varieties of execution on display at their final exhibition in a few days' time, the better.

CHAPTER TWO

AS COUNCILLOR ZARA Hyde had hoped, Peregrine Wordsworth's name ensured a steady stream of visitors throughout the three days of the exhibition held in the lobby of the Gorey council offices. At the opening reception on Wednesday evening, those with business there paused for a moment, joining the tourists and locals to peruse the display of workshop paintings in the lobby. Their reactions were as varied as the styles of the paintings.

"It was a *deeply* difficult selection process," Wordsworth was saying to Freddie Solomon. "Each of the artists is naturally talented, and at my workshop, they are guided to depict the view, of Crescent Bay in this case, not as they ordinarily would, but as *someone else* might. Happily, there was time enough to make several interpretations, not just one. In this way," he told Freddie, who transcribed these grade-A, highbrow quotes into his phone with flying thumbs, "we enter undiscovered territory. Our thousandth view of a place becomes our first. All it takes is a simple change of perspective."

An excited cluster of exhibition visitors lined up to take photos with Wordsworth, a task he was more than happy to undertake while adopting just the right air of resignation to communicate he was above the trappings of celebrity, more interested in answering questions and interpreting the artists' works. "You find it confusing?" Wordsworth was asking a visitor whose expression gave him away.

"Why . . . I mean, all these funny blocks and what have you," the man said, unimpressed. "What's wrong with painting it as it is?"

While Belinda joined Wordsworth in a combined explanatory offensive, Freddie took notes on the discussion. "Solid gold," he whispered to himself, finding that Wordsworth was compelling enough that even the arrival of Laura

Beecham didn't distract him too much. She was flanked by Janice Harding and her fiancé, Jack Wentworth.

"I see they've tidied the place up nicely," said Janice as she entered the lobby.

As part of a renovation of the council offices, wood panelling had been painstakingly stripped away from around the lobby walls. Without their severe, almost ecclesiastical influence, the council office's lobby seemed brighter than before, and more spacious. "The whole place looks great," Laura said, tucking blonde strands behind her ear.

"*And* they approved the budget for some of the new cameras we wanted. Only six, when the DI wanted nine, but it's a start. Amazing what they can do when they try," added Janice. "A new broom on the council, apparently. Ambitious. Boss told me about her." The newly appointed Councillor Hyde was determined to adopt the constabulary's recommendations on the cameras and had hit the ground running. In his first meeting with her, Detective Inspector Graham had been cautiously impressed. Promises were made. So far, they had mostly been kept.

Two war memorial plaques were displayed on the newly whitewashed walls, and Councillor Hyde had also installed a suite of enlarged, century-old photographs of Gorey, showing the town as it had been for so long: a quiet fishing village. But Laura, Janice, and Jack hadn't come to see them.

"Right, where's this art, then?" Janice wondered aloud. The display occupied one half of the lobby, but the cluster of people around Peregrine Wordsworth was holding up those interested in seeing it. "Might have to do some traffic duty in a minute."

"The more *avant garde* pieces are at the end. So, we'll see the students' progression," Jack told her.

Since they'd been together, Jack had introduced Janice to all sorts of new cultural phenomena. To her surprise, Janice had found she loved learning new things, and was proud of her intelligent and sophisticated fiancé, even if she didn't always appreciate what he introduced her to. She'd never been to an art exhibition before and wasn't sure it was her thing, but she was willing to give it a try.

If she was honest, despite their best intentions, both she and Jack mostly reverted to type after a period of experimentation. They'd made a decent attempt at installing a varied and eclectic tea habit similar to Graham's but had eventually given up and returned to their favourite Yorkshire brew, a type they could readily get just about anywhere. They enjoyed their experiments, even if most of the time they found they preferred what they'd been doing all along. It was a good way to learn what the other liked and to bond as a couple, which Janice deeply appreciated.

She turned to Laura. "It's becoming a habit, this is. He watches a documentary and suddenly he's an expert."

"I only said, if you remember," Jack responded innocently, "that I think I've got a more sensitive eye for artistic merit."

Janice made things crystal clear. "More sensitive *than me* is what he's saying." She winked at Laura.

"That's quite a claim," her friend replied, returning Freddie's wave from across the room. He seemed caught between wanting to say hello to her and his need not to miss any juicy quotes from Peregrine Wordsworth.

"Just making an observation," Jack said with a little shrug. "Art is everywhere if you care to look. There's artistry to the way you solve a crime, wouldn't you say? The way you work as a team, pooling intel, navigating evidence, compiling theories. It starts out as a random series of datapoints which eventually merge into a cohesive form that identifies the perpetrator of a crime. That's pretty much what's going on here." Some space opened up amidst the crowd, and Jack peered closer to take a look at one of the paintings. "Except perhaps they haven't *quite* come to a conclusive resolution."

The idea of policing as an art form struck Janice as profound. She went quiet. "Yeah, maybe. I hadn't thought of it quite like that. Hmm."

Jack wrapped an arm affectionately around her waist. The crowd was beginning to move through. They joined a loose, rightward-drifting gaggle of visitors.

About a dozen people still wanted to get a moment with Peregrine Wordsworth. They eyed him expectantly or stood patiently in short lines. This was Wordsworth's chance to drum up business for a second annual workshop in the early spring, or maybe a commission from the well-heeled, of which there were many on Jersey. He was always at his most engaging when potential customers came along.

Some of the visitors looked at the artwork and, apparently feeling nothing, moved straight through as if browsing a shelf in a bookshop. Others took more time, trying to puzzle out the artist's intent or reading the short description by each canvas. A dapper man in his fifties seemed to be comparing two or three of the paintings, peering closely at each as though judging them in some way. One or two visitors were dismissive, their criticisms muted only by the presence of the artists themselves. Laura heard one observer, a craggy curmudgeon with a West country accent, telling his wife, "Bloody rubbish." He finished up with the inevitable "I could do better than that."

Laura was drinking in the details the way David would, more interested in her surroundings than merely the art on the walls. His habit of cataloguing people had rubbed off on her. She could hold more in her mind now, her memory more accurate. Clothes, shoes, hair colours . . . She had yet to graduate on to gestures and facial expressions; that was "people *reading*," she'd told Graham, not "people watching," and for her, this habit was recreational, not professional. But David's mind never stopped, and some days, she found herself struck dumb at the sheer level of detail he was able to soak up. For Graham, casing this lobby would have been child's play.

"Don't tell me you're starstruck too?"

Caught unawares, Laura turned to find Freddie Solomon, his keys clicking in his busy hands. "Oh, hey, Freddie." Since the triumphant evening as part of the team involved in the public solving of a 200-year-old cold case, the "citizen journalist" had heeded Laura's plea to give Graham some space. He had downgraded his former habit of haranguing the local police to mild chiding. Such cooperation, quite out of character for Freddie, earned him a friendly smile.

"Not starstruck at all," she said. Like Graham, Laura was not at all affected by the common markers of celebrity. The pub she'd worked at in London had been frequented by a slew of them, and there was nothing like seeing people "off the telly" under the influence of alcohol to correct the impression that they were anything but utterly ordinary. "Just intrigued," Laura added, "at how others are reacting to the paintings."

"Did you have any idea that Gorey was harbouring half a dozen Picassos?" Freddie asked.

"Sounds like you've been impressed by the art."

Laura glanced across the room. Standing next to her paintings, Philomena Courthould-Bryant discussed her artistic choices with some visitors. A few yards away, her husband, Percival Courthould-Bryant, long-time Jersey resident and former curator of the Jersey Heritage Museum, indulged in his usual brand of unconfined snobbery, mansplaining his wife's work to a few others, and leaving Laura sympathetic toward his wife.

Freddie qualified his enthusiasm. "Some of it, sure." In a rare show of self-deprecation, he added, "I can paint with the enthusiasm of a five-year-old and with about the same level of skill. Some of us paint with brushes and colours," he said. "Others use words."

Notwithstanding Jack's contention that art was everywhere, including down at the local police station, Laura found the idea that Freddie's "scribblings," as Graham referred to them, be considered "art" a bit of a stretch. That said, she wasn't about to burst his bubble. In the last few months, whether Freddie recognised it or not, she'd found that his writing had indeed changed. Although still entitled the *Gorey Gossip* and still targeted at the prurient, Freddie had recently taken to using titillating (and often unfounded) material to draw in his target audience before socking them over the head with more complex subjects. Topics such as the local economy, social issues, and the development and future of Gorey were a move away from his earlier, exclusively crowd-pleasing efforts. He could still toss in the occasional firework, and his manner toward Graham remained judgmental, but his attitude had moderated to one of cautious and watchful deference.

"Well, then, did you get some nice, big scoop from the great man himself?" Laura nodded over to Peregrine Wordsworth.

"That man," Freddie said, "is *unbelievable*. Never interviewed anyone who—"

"Thought so much of himself? Produced so much rubbish?" Appearing out of apparently nowhere, Mrs. Taylor, proprietor of the White House Inn, was evidently unimpressed with the exhibition. She folded her arms. "My six-year-old granddaughter could do better than that."

"Not a fan, then, Mrs. Taylor?" Freddie said, hoping for a juicy, slightly controversial quote which would guarantee her an appearance in his blog.

"A fan?" A couple of minutes had been enough to persuade Mrs. Taylor that her evening would be better spent elsewhere. "Not my cup of tea. And that 'artist,' Mr. Wordsworth . . ." She tutted dramatically. "Well." She left her thoughts unsaid but effectively communicated. Regarding Wordsworth with visible scepticism, Marjorie Taylor patted her recently wavy-permed hair and strode out.

CHAPTER THREE

"THEY SHOULD HAVE skipped that house and painted the White House Inn instead," Jack said, overhearing Marjorie Taylor's words. "Mrs. Taylor would have been thrilled in that case."

"Not if they'd transformed her hotel into some impressionist monstrosity," Janice said. "Some of these are a bit . . . 'out there.'"

"They're just experimenting," Jack said. "Doing Wordsworth's 'contrasts' thing, I suppose. At least he didn't bring his loony friends with him and make Crescent Bay vibrate." It had been ten months since the incident in the Lake District. The artistic event which had been billed as "an opportunity to generate abundance, trust, and connection through a meeting of minds, hearts, and vibration" had consisted of a group of people descending on Lake Windermere who, at Wordsworth's urging, hummed without interruption for twenty-four hours. It had been innocent enough, but wilfully and hilariously misinterpreted by the media. A visitor to the local youth hostel was quoted as saying it was like "living in the middle of a beehive without the benefit of honey."

Jack, Janice, and Laura slowly walked past interpretations of the bay, some of which were comprised of unidentifiable swishes of simple, swooping lines, while others were dioramas, exquisitely detailed and precise. By the end, the artists' efforts defied description; in one of them, even the fastidious realist, grouchy Fergus Barr, had let his guard down and interpreted the scene more freely. The house atop the bluff, sheets of glass held together by columns of white pebbled concrete, became a reflective surface for clouds and sunshine, a huge mirror on the cliff top.

"Well, I think I've done my bit for the creative arts today," Janice decided, waiting for Jack to finish his viewing. "How are you doing?" she asked Laura. "Generally, I mean. I haven't seen you in a week or so."

"Oh, you know. Juggling as usual, trying not to drop anything."

"The library was jam-packed last Saturday," Janice said. "I only went in to return a book. Crossed my mind that I might need to do some crowd control."

"The Early Reading Festival," Laura said proudly. "It went better than we could ever have expected. Since we worked on the Sampson case last year, ideas for new literary and historical educational projects have piled up. Councillor Hyde has lobbied the mayor, who seems ready to support a few of our more ambitious plans. It's just been so much fun." Laura's excitement was never far from the surface. "Helping children to read, people of all ages, really, and being able to help them find what they need has never felt more gratifying."

"And didn't I hear that you're head librarian now?" Janice flicked a glance over at Jack. He seemed to have caught the celebrity bug and couldn't resist loitering within a few feet of Peregrine Wordsworth.

"*Acting* head," Laura said. "Nat is due in about three weeks, and she'll have another three months' maternity leave after that."

"Those are big shoes to fill, but you'll do great."

They stepped away from the crowd. "What about you? How are your plans for the big day coming along?" Laura observed her friend carefully. She knew Janice to be stressed.

The bride-to-be heaved a sigh. "Can I plan another police conference instead?" she joked, then made an awkward face. "Maybe *without* two really awful murders."

"Nobody's fault except the killer's, remember," Laura reminded her. It was the kind of thing she regularly said to David.

"Right now, Jack and I are just trying to successfully get married without killing *anyone*."

"Is it the choice of venue again?"

"No, that's all sorted," Janice said. "St. Andrew's on Princess Road. This is different. Family stuff."

"Ugh."

"Jack's got a crazy, belligerent aunt..."

Laura snapped her fingers. "We'll sit her next to David," she suggested at once.

"Wow, that doesn't seem very fair. What kind of girlfriend are you exactly?" Janice laughed.

"One who knows that a word from David will shut your aunt down and we'll all have a great time, including her." Laura winked at her friend.

"And I've got this cousin," Janice whispered, raising an eyebrow, "with an alcoholic husband." She paused, then clarified. "I'm not talking about a few drinks and some silly dancing. This man has a tendency to spontaneously give long, morose speeches."

"Maybe make it a cash bar?"

"Not the worst idea," Janice said. "There's lots of other stuff to sort out. It's getting out of hand. We wanted to keep it small but then we'd exclude the people we do want to enjoy our day with. And the church will be rather empty. Plus, it's getting expensive, especially for my family, who'll be travelling. Jack's family is being great, offering to put my side up, and we're trying a few less expensive options." Janice blew out her cheeks. "It'll work out. Jack's helping out where he can. Just listening to me blow off steam is a great help."

"A man who can provide tech support for complex police investigations," Laura marvelled, "*and* contribute helpfully to a wedding? Definitely a keeper, Janice."

Jack walked up, and Janice pulled her fiancé to her. "He's so shy about how brilliant he is sometimes. Only I know how truly incredible he is. And how helpful to Gorey police." Janice smiled. "Did you know he once thought about being a lawyer? He finished the first half of a law degree."

"Really?" Laura was surprised.

Jack gave her the short version. "Got myself recruited by a tech company in London midway and kinda fell in love with encryption and firewalls. But I still love the chase, so what I do for the police is just up my street."

"Jack, a frustrated lawyer?" Laura laughed. "Will wonders never cease? What else have you been hiding?" She let out a deep breath. "Are we done here? I think I've had my fill."

"I think so," Janice replied. Jack nodded. Janice linked arms with Laura, leaving Jack to bring up the rear. Feeling dispensed with, he good-humouredly pursed his lips. At least he wasn't facing the complete destruction of his masculinity and carrying Janice's handbag. Ahead of them, fingers still jangling his keys, Freddie Solomon pushed through the council building's wide glass doors and meandered slowly down the steps.

Janice called to him. "How did you like the exhibition, Freddie? Did Wordsworth say anything worth your readership's time?"

"Yes," Freddie said, brightening and leaning in close when they caught up with him. "But I'm debating whether or not to use the best bit. It's a little scandalous."

"Doesn't sound like you, Freddie," Laura said. "What did he say?"

"He said," Freddie confided, suppressing his own laughter, "'I'm profoundly uncomfortable watching the public consume art. It's like feeding time at the zoo, only less dignified.' Amazing," the blogger added as he absentmindedly wandered off, his thumbs still flying as he composed the first draft of his next missive.

"Wordsworth's a snob," Janice said, sniffing. "And his paintings are weird."

"Now who's the art critic?" Jack said.

"I know what I like," Janice replied.

"You know, they might just be amateurs trying out different styles, but it was kind of fascinating to . . ." Jack stumbled. A man barged past an elderly couple walking behind Jack, knocking one of them into him. Surprised, Janice and Laura both moved to steady the pensioners as the man stormed down the steps.

"Ack, sorry!" he cried without stopping.

"Hey!" Jack called, ready to reprimand him, but the man was away, jogging across the high street and merging with a crowd of shoppers.

"An unsatisfied customer?" Laura wondered. "Or maybe he's just not a Peregrine Wordsworth fan."

"Well, all I can say is he's doesn't look very happy," Janice said. "Are you alright, Jack?" She looked at him with concern.

"Yeah, I'm fine, fine," Jack said, brushing himself down. "By the way, where's Detective Inspector Graham this evening?"

Laura pulled a face. "I'm a bit worried, actually. Jim Roach normally coaches the kids' football, you know, the under-twelves, under-fourteens, and such. For the older ones, he acts as referee on game nights. But with Jim away in London, he asked David to . . ."

"Oh, no," Janice muttered. "What's tonight?"

"A game night." Janice pulled a face. "Yeah," Laura said, clearing her throat. "David's refereeing the game." She checked her watch. "Started half an hour ago."

"Well, let's hope it all goes off smoothly. I'm sure it will." Janice turned around to pull a face at Jack, one Laura couldn't see.

"I hope so," Laura said. "It's like the start of a bad joke. 'What do you get if you cross a rabble of muddy teenagers, lots of competitive parents, and the single most unyielding referee in the history of football?' I'm going to make my way there now to see what's what."

Janice enjoyed the mental image. "I'd line up for days to buy tickets to *that*." She grabbed Jack's arm. "I think that's enough experimental art for one day. What do you say, oh future husband of mine? Ready to try another cake place?"

"Is this going to be the one with gluten-free almond flour?" If so, Jack's tone implied there would be rebellion.

Checking the list on her phone, one of many in a large folder labelled ∼Wedding!∼, Janice had good news. "No, this is the place with the mind-blowing Swiss chocolate, French buttercream, pâte à bombe icing. We have half an hour until closing. It's only a five-minute walk."

"Well, there are worse ways to end an evening. Laura, always a pleasure," said Jack, clicking his heels and giving her a slight bow. He'd daydreamed about this particular cake from the moment Janice had suggested it. He knew already that it would get his vote over the eight other cakes they'd already tried. "Say hello to David for us."

"I will," Laura chuckled, "once I've pulled him out from under a pile of squabbling parents." There was time for Janice to wish Laura luck, and with a quick wave, they were off.

"Right, then," Laura said to herself. "Time to rescue the under-fourteens."

CHAPTER FOUR

The Gorey Gossip
Saturday, April 9th

It's been another week of opposites in Gorey. Maybe you were woken by the loudest thunder in years last night—I certainly was—but this morning, only a few hours later, the sky is an outstanding springtime blue and families will be back to sunbathing on the beach by lunchtime. These strange swerves in the weather help us remember to cherish the sunniest days and not waste them. Me, I've been growing vegetables. For the record, it's murdering my back, but I *can* see why people like it, and the sense of teamwork at the allotment is a tonic for any writer, normally such loners.

Last week, I was fortunate to interview the controversial and irrepressible artist of TV reality show *Art Lover's Island* fame, Peregrine Wordsworth. He presided over an exhibition of his students' paintings from his most recent retreat. Peregrine and five artistic visionaries spent three days painting their impressions of Crescent Bay before their works were exhibited at the council offices. I have to say, the refurbishment has gone very well, and it was the ideal space to show off the town's talents.

Dressed in his trademark black, Wordsworth was in an affable mood, sharing with me, "I like the rhythm of returning to Gorey. Consistency is hard to find in a life like mine. Annual fixtures help keep me settled." When I spoke to him, he quickly meandered into the poetic style with which he has become synonymous. "The waves provide one rhythm, the turning of the world provides the other. It is the ideal period of rest from my other work."

Like most people, I was curious how his "other work" contributes to these more conventional workshops. "There's real permeability there," Wordsworth said, apparently in answer to my question. "It's not that one informs the other," he (sort of) clarified. "They share a stage but have different drummers." Those who understand this answer might find they enjoy one of Wordsworth's (many) books; if you get through one, you'll have done better than I.

Wordsworth must be used to an uneven public reception by now. After all, when it comes to modern art, the occasional outburst is to be expected, particularly in Gorey, where affluence has encouraged a new wave of interest in art collecting among would-be connoisseurs. Not everyone appreciates these modern interpretations, however. Wordsworth would probably be appalled if they did. Perhaps the only real *faux pas* is to storm out angrily, refusing any debate with the artist. An open mind is necessary, but not always afforded.

CHAPTER FIVE

"CHEERS, MIKE!"

BARNWELL held the door open for the man coming toward him, who nodded as he passed the constable. Outside, a woman on a bench lifted her face to the sun. She rose as the man walked up, and hand in hand, they wandered off in the direction of town. Barnwell's eyes tracked them for a few seconds, then he bundled through the doors of the police station. His dog, Carmen, trotted by his side.

Barnwell had had Carmen for a while now. They'd got into a smooth routine of walks at the weekend with Melanie Howes, the ultra-efficient Gorey fire crew manager, and her pit bull Vixen. He'd also taken Carmen on early morning runs, sometimes with Fortytude, the group of forty-something men led by adventurer and local celebrity Bash Bingham. An animal lover, Bash encouraged doggie participation in the runs once a week on Saturdays.

During the workday, caring for Carmen had required some creativity. Barnwell had held some concerns about how he would handle her while on shift, but Detective Inspector Graham had come through for him. Graham was partial to a good dog and had quickly recognised Carmen's community building advantages. He'd granted permission for her to come into the office, where she was cared for by the police team during Barnwell's shifts, and he had suggested that the constable take Carmen with him when he was patrolling low-risk daytime beats.

While it was helpful to Barnwell to structure his day like this, it made operational sense too. The benefits that ensued from the opportunities a beagle puppy provided when out in the community far outweighed the small risk that she hindered Barnwell's work or distracted him. Far from it; it was amazing how the barriers between the force and the public dropped away when Carmen was "on patrol."

Barnwell had also added a new duty to his role as community police officer. Carmen regularly accompanied him on school visits, a new program he'd devised. He called it "Dog and Doughnuts." Carmen was very popular. Barnwell's schedule was booked up. The doughnuts didn't hurt either.

Barnwell was Carmen's official "puppy walker." Under the police dog training scheme, she would stay with him until she was a year old. After that, if she passed her assessment, she'd leave to move onto formal training. And a new handler. Carmen was coming up on twelve months, and Barnwell had ringed her assessment date on his calendar. A small knot of dread was making a permanent home in his stomach.

"Morning, sir."

Graham's eyes flicked up. He stood at the reception desk sifting through some post. "Morning, Barnwell. Good weekend?"

"Not bad. You?"

"Pretty good." Barnwell cocked his head in the direction of the station's doors. "Who was that?" he asked.

"Hmm? Oh, an inspector from Truro. Came in to file a report. He's on his honeymoon and needed to wrap up some unfinished business to do with a case. I had a chat with him, let him use our computers. Good guy."

Barnwell unclipped Carmen's lead from her collar before walking into the break room. "Tea?" he called out as he flicked the kettle on and prepared to finish getting dressed. He pulled his tie and uniform jacket from his locker and looked at himself in the mirror.

"No thanks," Graham called back. The inspector, while not averse to a cup of generic tea prepared by someone else, vastly preferred his own, brewed in his own teapot, to his own specifications. Could he be a tea snob? Probably.

Barnwell returned, steaming mug in hand. He sat at his desk and prepared to review his to-do list. He'd started to make one ever since he'd taken an online course suggested to him by Melanie Howes. Carmen, as was her habit, sniffed around the office, proceeding to check into all the nooks and crannies that the tables, chairs, filing cabinets, and masses of cables offered her. Satisfied, she curled up at Barnwell's feet for a snooze.

Graham eyed his constable from the reception desk. There was churn in the lives of his officers. Janice's wedding date was getting closer, and Roach was off in London with the Met on a week's assessment. In the last few months, Barnwell had lost both his parents, and while he seemed to cope admirably, Graham had observed the constable getting noticeably gruffer as the days to Carmen's first birthday drew close. He wondered where the team would be in a year. Still together—a tight-knit bunch, an effective operational unit in touch with the hard and soft policing needs of the island? Or would they face change, fresh blood, a new team for him to forge in the burning fires of the Gorey community?

"Your brother's in town, isn't that right?" Graham said.

"End of the week he arrives, sir."

"Will it be his first time?"

"Yeah, it'll be good for him to get away after the events of the past few months. I've promised him a different pub each night. But my guess is he'll settle in on the Foc's'le as his favourite. He's something of a whisky connoisseur, and they have the best range."

"Are you the eldest?"

"By a few years, but we're quite different. He's a bit of a scally, unlike me." Barnwell grinned. "Likes the ladies, bit of a drinker, although he keeps it in check. Works in marketing. I looked out for him a lot when we were younger, but he seems to be managing on his own now."

"What's he going to do while you're working?"

"Ah, he'll go for walks, visit the beach, see the sights I expect."

"He might like the war tunnels. I went there this weekend. Not sure why it took me so long. Fascinating insight into life during the Nazi occupation. What do you have on your plan today?"

"I'm taking Carmen to Brickhill Primary for a Dog and Doughnuts lesson, Year Ones. Carmen's a great help breaking the ice between the kids and the uniform. I want to teach them that, you know, we're friendly faces, you can trust us. Get 'em early kind of thing. I'm trying something new today. I've thought up some tales about Carmen, about road and stranger safety and such. I typed them up, and today I'll try one of them out. Miss Edwards, she's one of the teachers, says she's going to develop a curriculum around them, whatever that means."

"I think it means that you are doing a very impressive job, Constable. Is that what's in the box?" A cube of blue cardboard wrapped with a white ribbon, the words "Ethel's" in a flowery script written across the top, lay next to Barnwell's to-do list. "Doughnuts?"

"Yeah. I got all glazed today. I've learned a box of mixed doughnuts and twenty five-year-olds don't go well together. Last time, everyone wanted the iced ones with sprinkles on top and I only had two. There were tears."

Graham laughed. "Never get between a five-year-old and an iced doughnut with sprinkles, I always say."

Barnwell smiled. These easy morning conversations were a welcome change from the awkward "all-business" ones he and Graham used to have. The detective inspector was never going to be an open book, but he was smiling more these days and even joined them for a drink on the regular. That could only be a good thing for a station as small as theirs. Strained relationships, a bad mood, or even just a hangover had a disproportionately greater impact when the team comprised only four people, five if you included Dr. Tomlinson.

"Can you put the careers open day at Gorey Grammar in your calendar for the eighteenth? I need a wingman. St. Helier told me it's time I showed my face at a few more community events."

"No problem, sir. I can bring Carmen along if you like. She's always a hit. Takes me ages just to get to the shops when she's with me."

"You know, I wasn't sure when I saw you come in with her that first day, but she's been a great addition to the team. Good for the community. I'm excited to see what she does next."

At Graham's words, ice crept across Barnwell's heart. When he'd signed up, he'd considered the finite puppy walking period a plus. Full-on commitment wasn't his style. But now, he found himself getting more and more anxious. He wanted Carmen to pass her assessment, to move onto the next stage of her training as a police sniffer dog. She'd be used at the ports and airport to search for drugs and explosives. It was what she deserved. She'd been the best dog. But he would be very sad to see her go. Very sad.

"Roach is back in today, isn't he?" Graham said.

"He is, sir. Do you reckon he'll have some news for us?"

"You mean about transferring to the Met? I don't know. Maybe. Depends on how he found it. It's a big change from Gorey, the biggest. Might be overwhelming for him. But he's a big lad; I'm sure he'll know if it's right for him. We'll see. I suspect we'll be able to tell the moment he comes through the door."

Roach had been away for a week on a "Meet the Met" trial. Ostensibly it was to introduce officers from other forces to the work and practices of the Metropolitan Police in London, but in reality, it was an opportunity for the Met to identify high potential recruits and for those officers to see if life in the Met was for them. Graham had suggested Roach attend. It was an efficient way for Roach, a local boy, to test the waters of police life beyond those of the Channel Islands. Like a father duck guiding his young, Graham had unselfishly prodded Roach into rougher waters, hoping he'd take to it despite the unavoidable chore of replacing him if he swam away.

"Where's Janice? She should be here by now," Graham said, checking his watch.

"Hmm, not sure," Barnwell responded. "She hasn't left a message. Not like her to be late." Barnwell's phone rang. "Speak of the devil." He accepted the call. "Hey, Jan, whassup? . . . Uh-huh. Is it bad? . . . Uh-huh. Need back up? . . . Okay, on my way." He hung up, gathering his papers. "RTA, sir. On the corner of Park and Bolton. Elderly woman hit while crossing the road. Janice was on her way in when it happened. She needs help directing traffic. Paramedics are en route."

"Okay, I'll hold the fort here. Off you go. Car's two spots down. When's your appointment with the children?"

"Eleven forty. I'm sure I'll be back before then." Barnwell slapped on his cap, Graham threw him the car keys, and the constable rushed out the door.

CHAPTER SIX

"WHAT SHALL I do with you?" Graham gazed into Carmen's big, brown eyes. The dog looked up at him expectantly now that her master had gone. "Want to join me for a cup of tea?" Graham went into his office and turned on the kettle, Carmen padding after him. As the water spluttered and bubbled, Graham stared out the window at the long grass that led down to the beach and the sea in the distance. Carmen curled up under his desk. Graham's thoughts turned to a holiday. He was due a break.

He thought back to a recent visit he and Laura had made to her parents, his first. As they had prepared to leave, Graham peered at a picture on the wall in their hallway. It was a pen and ink drawing of women racing around a track, long skirts flying. It was labelled *Women Racing Aquarium, London. 1896.* "Six-day racing, eh?" he'd said.

"Yes!" both Sandy and Meryl Beecham cried together.

"Have you heard of it?" Laura's mum asked, quickly coming over to stand next to him and showing a level of gumption Graham hadn't thus far credited her with. Her husband was the dominant one of the pair.

"Started in 1878, endurance cyclists would race for as long as possible each day for six days. I've read the use of amphetamines was rife, but those Victorians did love their extreme sports.

"That's right," Meryl said, astonished.

"It faded in popularity, in Britain at least, around the turn of the last century. European cyclists went to America where the sport was taking off and offering more prize money."

"Gosh, I . . . I've almost never met anyone who knew anything about it, let alone the history. My great-great-great grandfather was one of the first ever six-day cyclists," Laura's mum said. "I've always had a fascination for it. In fact, it was at a meet-up for a few enthusiasts in Ghent that Sandy and I first met."

"Really?" Graham looked between them, trying hard to imagine this conventional couple's interest in a sport most people had never heard of. The big events had been hugely popular. In the Victorian era, six-day cycle racing had been accompanied by dancing elephants, acrobats, and carnival games.

"Next time you come, we'll get out our photo albums," Sandy said, rubbing his hands at the prospect.

"Just for a few minutes," Meryl said, wrinkling her nose. She reached up to kiss Graham's cheek, a gesture he found surprisingly touching.

"Look after my girl there," Sandy called over Meryl's shoulder as she ushered Laura and David to the front door.

"Speak to you on Tuesday as usual, Mum," Laura said.

"Yes, dear. Drive carefully. Text me when you get home, so I know you've arrived safely."

Laura and Graham walked to their car and got in. They banged their doors shut and Graham turned on the engine. He smiled at Mr. and Mrs. Beecham through the windscreen. They waved at him.

"Well?"

"Well, what?"

"Did I pass?"

"I think you did." Laura reached behind her to pull on her seat belt. She looked out of the window and waved back at her parents standing on the steps of their home. "They're going to show you their photo albums. *Next time.*"

A clunk from reception jolted Graham from his reverie and Carmen from her snooze. "Anybody home?" Graham heard Roach's voice call out, followed by another bang and more voices. Barnwell and Janice had returned. Carmen's ears pricked up and she raised her head, alert to the sound of her owner's voice. The dog scurried into the main office and ran over to Barnwell, who knelt down to give her a good scrub with his knuckles, owner and dog equally delighted to see each other.

"How was the RTA?"

"All sorted, sir," Janice responded. The phone rang. She picked it up.

"Nothing serious?" Graham asked Barnwell.

"No, victim was taken to hospital, but she'll be fine. Driver was a bit shaken. Both were elderly. Combined age of one hundred seventy-eight. Six of one and half a dozen of the other it seems. She was slow to cross, he panicked in the middle of a junction. It'll all be in our report."

Roach had gone to change out of his motorbike leathers and now came back in his good weather uniform—open-necked white shirt, black trousers, and boots. He straightened the epaulettes on his shoulders that indicated his rank. The transformation from leather-clad biker to uniformed officer took only moments, but it was stunning.

"Morning, Jim. Good to have you back."

"Thank you, sir. Good to be here." Graham and Barnwell eyed the younger officer carefully. Seeing nothing that would clue them into the sergeant's state of mind, Graham turned to his other sergeant.

Janice was still on the phone. She gave Graham a patient glance as if to say, "Want to trade?" when suddenly, the call was over. She gratefully put down the receiver.

"Do you think we can solve a computer problem for the ever-patient DI Graham?" he asked her. "I'm in a bare-knuckle fight with my laptop. Can Jack do it ASAP?"

"I'll make sure of it, sir." Janice promptly called her fiancé, who fixed the problem over the phone in five minutes flat.

"Magnificent," Graham said, putting down the receiver. "He's one of a kind, your Jack. I thought we could rely on the coastguard to protect us from illegal fishing, but apparently Jack's got responsibility for that too."

Genuinely unsure as to whether her boss was being funny or shockingly behind the times, Janice felt it best to say carefully, "That's 'fish' with a *ph*, sir. Not an *f*."

Graham's eyebrows shot up. "Crikey, these cyber-criminals are terrible at spelling, aren't they?" He gave Janice a reassuring look and a wink. "Anyway, according to Jack, I'm now *slightly* less likely to get hacked by Freddie Solomon. Or the Russians." He reflected on his words, eyebrows still aloft. "Hard to say which would be worse." His eyes roamed the office and settled on Roach. "So, good week was it, Sergeant?"

"Er, yeah, sir. Great, thanks."

"Right. Good." Graham paused. Roach looked back at him evenly. "Well, I've got some phone calls to make," the inspector said.

Graham returned to his office. After what sounded to the others like a sequence of platitudes, some mild-mannered defence, and finally some laughter, he emerged looking as though he'd been bamboozled by a prank. "One parent tells me off, then another gives me a pat on the back." He shrugged. "I don't know which way's up."

Harding had heard some rumours about Graham's brand of "proactive refereeing" but chose to play it safe. "Still refereeing, sir?"

"Yeah, I quite like it, actually. Thinking of making it a regular thing." Behind him, Janice saw Roach frantically shake his head and draw his finger back and forth across his throat. "Parents can be a bit of a trial though. It was all I could do to keep my temper with them. If they think refereeing's that easy, they should get off their backsides and try running around for an hour with their eyes in the backs of their heads."

"Parents these days . . ." Janice sympathised.

Behind Graham's back, Roach rolled his eyes. "Was that Mr. Allsop on the phone? He called me too. Said something about his grandson being given a red card."

Graham began to explain just as Barnwell appeared from the break room.

"Wait, wait, I don't want to miss any of this," the constable said with a grin. "Alan Allsop's red card, yes? Quite the controversy. Even been grumbling about it down the pub, his father has."

"The *red* card doesn't seem to have been the problem," Graham explained. "Mr. Allsop accepted that jumping into a tackle with both feet constitutes dangerous play. He'll be speaking to Alan."

"From what I heard," Roach said, "you had words with Alan before sending him off. What did you call him?"

"I called him a *troglodyte*," Graham announced. "It only means 'cave dweller.'"

Roach scratched his neck and winced. "What happened with Vinny Weston, then? I got two calls from his mother, one more upset than the other."

"Ah, you see, Master Weston was genuinely caught by Master Allsop's challenge, but his injury wasn't nearly as serious as he made out. Surprisingly," Graham deadpanned, "young Weston was able to continue. And so I gave him a yellow card for simulation, as the rules insist."

This was perhaps unorthodox, but at this level, not the strangest choice. "So, alright, that's one," Roach said. "Where did the second yellow card come from?"

"Once Mr. Weston learned that Mr. Allsop had received the red card," Graham explained as though in court before a jury, "he started laughing hysterically, and then did a *backflip*. So, I gave him a second yellow for excessive celebration."

"You sent off one player for a bad foul," Roach said, piecing things together, "then you *also* sent off the player he fouled?"

"Unsportsmanlike conduct," Graham confirmed. "Two separate incidents. Two yellows still make a red, don't they? I was well within my rights."

Sergeant Harding cleared her throat. "If I may quote the great Mrs. Hetherington, 'It's tasteless to gloat when others are punished. And they'll laugh all the harder when your turn comes.' I hope both boys learned their lessons."

Roach would have applied the rulebook a little less stringently in support of community relations, but he had to concede Graham's correct interpretation. Even if his decisions had been overly fastidious, he wasn't short of a strong rationale for each one. A bit like his investigations.

"How did your week at the Met go, Jim?" Janice asked. She, at least, wouldn't beat around the bush.

Roach scanned his emails. He didn't raise his eyes. Distractedly, he said. "Wha—? Yeah, yeah, good. Learned lots, you know. London was a bit overwhelming. Phew."

Janice, Barnwell, and Graham stared at him. Roach picked up a pen and wrote a note on a pad.

"So did you meet anyone interesting?" Barnwell asked. Roach leant his elbows on his desk and looked at him squarely. "Yeah, loads. Good lads."

"And what did you think? About the Met, I mean?" Graham added.

"I thought it was very interesting. Big. They do important work." Roach's phone pinged. He glanced down. The other three stood like statues, waiting for more. "It's Dr. Tomlinson. He wants me down at the lab. Okay if I go, sir?"

"Erm, yes. That's fine." Graham, Harding, and Barnwell watched Roach disappear into the break room and come out again in his leathers. He'd threaded his arm through his helmet. "Right, I'll see you lovelies in a bit, no doubt. Ciao!" Roach stuck his helmet over his head and pushed through the doors.

"Ciao?" Barnwell repeated.

"Do you think he was evading our questions?" Janice added.

"If he was, based on that performance, we all need an interview techniques refresher. That was pathetic," Graham said.

CHAPTER SEVEN

THE TWO MEN dashed through the rain—one large and muscular, the other shorter, slighter, and leaner. They headed toward the big awning of the Foc's'le and Ferret, side by side, close enough to touch. With its lights on and laughter just audible from outside, the old pub was a welcome sight on such a stormy evening.

"Where d'ya think this little lot came from?" the younger, smaller one asked, breathing hard while shaking rain from his dark hair. It had been unseasonably warm, and the pair had decided against bringing jackets. Inevitably, they were caught out by a "low pressure area" which was yielding short, sudden squalls. Steve Barnwell's jeans had taken a soaking, but he laughed it off. "I suppose I've come far enough south," he said, "that I've found a place where the rain's nearly warm! I mean, it's like taking a shower."

His brother, on the other hand, had begun to rue his wardrobe decisions. "The people who invented 'summer' shirts," he said, pulling navy fabric away from his body, "have yet to encounter *British* weather."

"Don't you worry, mate! Nice, warm pub like this, you'll dry off in no time." Steve grabbed the door handle with an expectant flourish and flashed him a winning smile. "Besides, you never know who we'll meet. No harm showing the girls how you've tightened things up, eh?" He patted his brother's stomach—a gesture that Barnwell silently prayed Steve wouldn't repeat in public ever again. He gave his brother a steady push in the back. "Go on, it's your round."

Striding in, they walked up to the bar. Steve set a black satchel down by his feet. The pair waited for Lewis Hurd to finish pouring pints for a large group who'd pushed together some tables on the far side of the pub lounge. "Kids," Steve noted. "It's never just two or three, is it? Always ten or twelve. Clogging up the place."

"They might look like kids to you, Stevie, lad. But they're customers to people like Lewis here. And later tonight, they might end up mine and all. An important boost to the local economy," Barnwell said. "Or so the boss says."

"Are we, you know, sure they're all legal?"

Barnwell's inner policeman was never far from the surface, but there was no need to intervene. "Lewis is scrupulous about proof of age. Speak of the devil . . ."

"Evening, gents." Lewis looked a bit harried. "Scrupulous is, in fact, my middle name," he said, wiping his hands on a towel.

"Especially when it comes to underage drinking, am I right, Lewis?" Barnwell added.

"Very important responsibility," the barman said gravely. "One of the most important. Now, what can I get you?"

Steve was extremely interested in Lewis's top shelf. "I count sixteen whisky bottles up there in a long and glorious row. They aren't there just for decoration, so I'll have one of those, please."

"All ready to pour. Which'll it be?"

"One can't be hasty about a decision like this," Steve said, stroking his chin.

"You'd get along well with Dr. Tomlinson," Barnwell said as his brother hemmed and hawed. Steve was very particular about his libations.

"Oh?" Steve's eyes never left the row of scotches; each was equally tempting. "Is he also a cultured, well-educated man of the world with a refined nose and sophisticated tastes who enjoys the company of attractive, stylish women?"

"Yes, he is, actually."

After contemplating the matter for as long as Lewis could stand, Steve decided on his perfect tipple, a peaty Highland malt. He then insisted on opening the bottle and taking a dramatic whiff of the whisky's long-restrained aroma.

"Ah, lovely," Steve said, closing his eyes briefly.

Barnwell wasn't impressed. "Smells like a can of paint thinner, if you ask me."

Steve perused the bottle's label, paying it his gleeful respects. "It's enough to keep my nose happy for a week." The distillery boasted an agreeably Scottish, and therefore wholly unpronounceable, name.

"Steve, mate, are you sure, like?" Barnwell said, his brow creasing. "The hard stuff?"

"Just one. I've transformed, you see."

"Ah." In the thirty-odd years of Steve's ups and downs, he'd promised Barnwell a good number of "transformations." Many of them hadn't led to much. But after spending his twenties building a reputation as a "jack-the-lad," getting drunk on stag-dos and pub crawls, going from job to job so often that it made his work history as jumpy as a jack-in-the-box, Steve Barnwell had settled down. A bit. He'd been working for the same company for two years now, a record, and the pub crawls were only once a week nowadays.

"It used to be about quantity, didn't it, lad?" Steve went to tap his brother's flat stomach again, but Barnwell was on to him this time and dodged out the way. "Bit too much, on occasion, back in the day. Eh, Bazz?"

Pulling himself up to his full height, Barnwell found his patience stretching thin. "You *are* aware that I have powers of arrest?"

"Alright, alright," Steve replied, backing up theatrically, palms up. "Just striking a contrast, one Barry Barnwell with the other. You're barely recognisable." Steve swept his wet hair back. Soaked, slightly crumpled, and sporting a two-day beard, he looked part budget traveller, part unconventional lothario. What he lacked in height, he made up for in chat, especially with women. "It's like night and day," Steve was saying. "Like a before-and-after picture. You could be on one of those dieting adverts on TV."

"Same person underneath, though," his brother said.

"I know! That's why I'm trying to congratulate you, big fella. No need to douse me with tear gas." Despite how it might appear to a casual observer, Steve was tremendously proud and fond of his older brother. He tutted and rolled his eyes. "Come on, let's sit down. Nice talking to you, Lewis." Steve would have been more than happy to chin-wag with the staff and other customers, but he steered Barnwell away from the bar, toward the largest empty table. "I've got something to show you," he said.

"Why didn't you show me at the restaurant?" Barnwell sat down on an upholstered bench against the wall. Steve pulled a heavy volume from his bag and slapped it on the table.

"Maybe I thought," Steve said, "we'd both be better off with a drink in hand, you know?" Barnwell eyed the thick, padded photo album carefully. The gold lettering on the front was ornate, almost funereal. "Reckon this was the fashion in 1996 or whenever it was."

"Likely as not," Barnwell guessed, "these were on special offer, two for one. You know what Mum and Dad were like, always up for a bargain." He recognised the album that chronicled their parents' married lives, and the first years of their new arrivals—Barnwell first, and then Steve four years later. "Blimey, you could have warned me you were bringing out the baby pictures. Making fun of my physique not enough for you?"

"Well, if your unbuttoned shirt and your new physique don't do the trick with the ladies . . ."

"It's for *work*," Barnwell reminded him.

"'For work,' sure. That's why your biceps are yelling 'Hey, girls! Get a load of *this*!'" Steve laughed loudly at his own joke. "But that's not all," he said as if advertising heavy discounts. "Just wait until Jersey's fine womenfolk see what a cute baby you were!"

"Pipe down, will you?" Barnwell shrunk a little. The photos had come out of nowhere, a complete surprise, leaving him more than a little off-balance. "Do we *have* to do this in public?"

"Well, there's a reason for that."

"Hmm?"

"This way," Steve confessed, "I could be sure you'd not be losing your temper."

Steve opened the photo album to the first page. It was filled with pictures of Barnwell as a baby. He'd been a rosy-cheeked, chubby cherub, smiley with a shock of dark hair. "Takes you back, doesn't it?" Neither Steve nor Barnwell had looked at these pictures in years. The selection of photos carried a weight, and not just literally. "In our school uniforms, you remember?" The two were pictured, grinning excitedly, getting ready to walk to school through the streets and alleyways of the East End. By Steve's side was Mopsy, their long-lived and faithful greyhound/pointer mix. "Feels like a thousand years ago. A different planet, even."

"Lot of water's gone under the bridge since then," Barnwell agreed. He was skipping through the pages, uncomfortable and still unsure as to his brother's intent. It had been eight months since their father's funeral, and only three since their mother's. It was a lot to lose both parents inside a year. Each photo dredged up strong memories, some welcome, others not. "They went through some tough times together," he said admiringly. "And they worked so *very* hard."

In the Barnwell household of the 1980s and 90s, the greatest sin had been indolence. Leslie Barnwell hated inefficiency, waste, and what he considered laziness. A Tory voter who had come to fatherhood later in life, Barnwell senior had no patience with the "something for nothing" crowd he termed scroungers. And relaxation, fun even, was strictly rationed to holidays and Christmas. His sons knew to knuckle down when he was around and to get their kicks when they were out of his sight. He was fond of saying that a reluctance to get up early, an untidy bedroom, or watching too much TV were certain and direct routes to "the criminal lifestyle." The Barnwell boys certainly knew, or found out quickly enough, how to behave in public and what to keep hidden from his view.

The photos brought back memories. Barnwell's teenage arguments with his father had gone badly, never really resolved, leading to their distant relationship as adults. "Crime isn't like a choice of haircut, Dad. And it doesn't define the person either," he'd said during one of their hot debates, a rather enlightened, philosophical thought for a sixteen-year-old who rarely read a newspaper beyond the sports pages and never a book if he could help it. After that, for a long time, Barnwell had refused to refer to people as "criminals." "Most crimes sort of happen *to* the people who commit them," he remembered saying, a thought his father called "muddled." Twenty or so years later, Barnwell found it harder to disagree with him.

"'Restraint and discipline,'" Steve remembered. "Those were his words for life. And did he walk the talk. Guess I didn't inherit either of those genes. He got most of his personality from the army, Mum used to say."

One of the last photos in the album was of a family gathering to celebrate their parents' wedding anniversary. Even sitting among his family, raising a glass to the camera, Mr. Barnwell had a steely, stubborn air. He had a wide moustache and a full head of dark hair, hair that both sons had inherited. In the photograph, Leslie Barnwell (he insisted on being called by his full name rather than the more common "Les") wore his button-down shirt, sleeves rolled up to his elbows, his tie tucked in between his third and fourth buttons. He looked every inch the factory floor foreman he was. He was no union man though, something that gained him approval from his superiors and suspicion from the shop floor workers during the union weakened nineties.

"Given the chance, Dad would have run our family like a platoon," Barnwell said. "Glad he stopped short of that—just."

"Amazing how Mum and he stayed together when you think about it."

"Yeah, she was more alive when he wasn't around."

"Don't think I got that gene either. Can you imagine me in a forty-year marriage?" Steve said with a wink.

"Nope," Barnwell confirmed. "Wait, is that what this is about?"

"Eh?"

"Are you getting married? Or have you met someone?" Steve laughed uproariously, taking just enough care not to spill the scotch that had been halfway to his lips.

"Alright, alright, then what is it?" Barnwell said, feeling a little played by his brother. "Some other kind of announcement? Are you going off the booze again? Got some woman up the duff? Turning vegetarian?"

Steve took a lengthy, theatrical pull on his whisky before answering. "I'll go off the booze," he said, "when the booze goes off me. And no, and no."

Barnwell didn't particularly love secrets or being kept in the dark. It felt too much like work. "Then what's going on, mate?"

"Like I said, I wanted to show you the photo album. Notice anything odd about it while you were flicking through?"

Barnwell sighed. "Are we playing detective now? I get quizzed enough at the station, thanks. Some days, it feels as though I'm being groomed to infiltrate MENSA. The boss's got this game where you put a dozen objects under a blanket, and then—"

Steve interrupted him. "Did you notice anything *missing*, I mean?" When his brother remained nonplussed, Steve turned to a page halfway through the album.

Staring, Barnwell's mind raced to figure out what Steve meant. "I don't get it, mate. What are you on ab—?"

Shouts travelled from the other side of the pub. A woman screamed. His senses on high alert, Barnwell was on his tiptoes even before the bloodcurdling sound ended.

"Just kids mucking around, isn't it?" Steve said.

"That wasn't kids just mucking around, bro," Barnwell said. Like a mother interpreting her infant's cries, he began to move toward the source of the noise.

CHAPTER EIGHT

"**H**ELP!"

BARNWELL RAN, pushing people out of his way. A man leant against the wall near the pub's back door. He was bleeding heavily, his neck and shirt bright red. The back of his head was matted with blood, the wound feeding rivers of red that trickled down his face like tributaries of the Amazon.

Barnwell tried to hold the man upright, but he was slipping sideways, his eyeballs rolling upward. "Lewis, nine-nine-nine!" The barman was on it.

"Sir, can you hear me?" Pub patrons cleared a space, and two other men helped Barnwell bring the man safely to the floor. "Bar towels," Barnwell ordered the men. He pressed his hands to the injured man's head to stem the bleeding. Immediately, trails of blood appeared between Barnwell's fingers and ran down the backs of his hands. The guy was barely conscious. He gasped for breath. Blood dribbled from both ears.

"Stay with me, mate," Barnwell urged. The man's eyes focused for a second, then drifted upward again. Barnwell was losing the battle. He quickly grabbed the bar towels that were waved in his face and placed one around the man's head. Within seconds, he added another. And then another.

Steve jostled his way through the small crowd that had assembled. He held his arms out to keep the onlookers at a distance. He watched his brother work, as amazed by how fast he'd moved as by his calm, competent first aid.

"Ambulance on its way." Lewis Hurd appeared at Barnwell's elbow. "How bad is it?"

"Very bad. He's out," Barnwell said. "Unconscious but breathing. We've got to stop the bleeding, but the injury's gushing like a geyser." Barnwell's navy shirt, just about dried out from the rain, was drenched again. He doubled up two fresh bar towels and added them to the sodden ones that covered the man's wound.

His phone in one hand, Lewis described the man's injuries to the emergency services dispatcher. "Yes, from the back of his head. It looks serious. He's pouring blood."

"Make sure the ambulance team can get through this lot, will ya?" Barnwell told Steve. Steve switched places with another pub customer, a big, beefy man whose exposed skin was covered with thick hair and tattoos. Barnwell's brother went outside to await the paramedics. Barnwell looked down at the stricken man. His breathing was becoming laboured. "Come on, man, *come on*! Ergghh!" The man vomited.

As news of the incident and its gravity spread, two-thirds of the Foc's'le's customers left. "What's the status, Lewis?" Barnwell said, trying to ignore all the reasons why his soaking clothes stuck to him.

"Police on the way," Lewis reported. "I can hear the sirens."

Barnwell nodded. "Janice is on duty." He frowned again. "Can you check his pockets?"

Lewis Hurd gingerly felt around the man's clothing and pulled out a weathered, black leather wallet. "Flip it open, see if you can get a name. I can't move." Barnwell added another towel to the wad he was pressing against the man's head. "He's very pale." He felt the man's neck. "His pulse is weak. That ambulance better get here quickly."

He gazed into the faces of the surrounding crowd, almost all of them teenagers, their heads tilted down as they furiously worked their phones. "Did anyone hear him say anything? See where he came from?"

The young people who heard Barnwell shook their heads. Those who didn't ignored him. They continued to film or text. No matter, Janice would make more rigorous enquiries. Speak of the devil; the wooden doors to the pub opened, and Sergeants Harding and Roach strolled in. They immediately got to work pushing back the crowd. Arms outstretched, Janice shouted, "Okay, back please! *Back!*" The room around Barnwell cleared out.

Six minutes after they were called, the ambulance team made their way through the crowd. They were brisk and efficient, making their initial assessment mostly by sight. There seemed little need for anything else. "He needs the trauma centre," senior paramedic Sue Armitage said. "More options in St. Helier. And he's going to *need* some options," she added in a low voice. Sue was no-nonsense. She'd seen a lot, even on an island the size of Jersey. With the help of her partner, Alan, they quickly loaded the injured man into the ambulance.

With a medley of lights rhythmically pulsing but no siren, the ambulance carefully drove off, watched by the Barnwell brothers as it headed for St Helier and the island's largest medical facility. The rain had started again, although mercifully, not as heavy as before.

Janice walked up, her nose wrinkling. "How are you doing?" She carefully avoided mentioning the meaty, acrid stench coming off her fellow officer.

"He's in bad shape," Barnwell replied. "Not sure he's going to make it." He roused himself. "But no point standing here doing nothing."

"Give yourself a cleanup and go home," Janice advised. "Jim 'n' me'll take it from here."

"You sure? You don't want me to question anyone? Give you a statement?"

"Nah, I know where to find you. Lewis said he just staggered in, all bleeding like."

"Yeah, I heard the shouts and went over to see what was what. Did Lewis give you his wallet?"

"Yeah, his name's James Reeves. Ever heard of him? I haven't."

"I think I've seen him a few times in here. Never spoke to him, though."

They walked back inside, and Barnwell spent a few minutes in the pub's bathroom attending to his appearance. Wetting paper towels, he fruitlessly tried to clean away the blood and vomit that had soaked into his trousers and down the front of his shirt. Lewis Hurd and Steve joined him. The barman wordlessly handed Barnwell a fresh T-shirt and a pair of jeans.

"Thanks, mate. That's more like it." Barnwell's hands were bright red. When he stripped off his shirt, so was his chest.

"Abs!" Steve hissed.

"What?"

"Abs! You've got a six pack. If I squint a bit."

"Barely."

"But still—"

"Look, shut it, mate, alright? I've had enough. This isn't the time."

Steve sobered. "Yeah, fair enough. I just can't get over the change in you, though. Out there . . . you were the dogs—"

"Yeah, yeah, alright," Barnwell cut in, always uncomfortable with compliments. "Rubbish thing to happen while you're visiting, though. I'm sorry, mate."

Steve saw it differently. "Not a bit of it. I'm sorry I missed your escapade in the speedboat with the Royal Marines. And that other crazy thing with the helicopter in the middle of the night? No wonder they gave you a couple of medals."

Barnwell texted Janice. She was methodically taking statements from the pub goers still left in the bar. She texted back to say that Roach had left for the hospital to follow up there.

"Tonight," Steve said, proud of his brother as never before, "I got to see you in action. Doing what you do."

"Doing what anyone would."

"Don't sell yourself short. Helping others," Steve insisted, "is our highest calling."

"*Trying* to help. That chap was in grim shape when they took him away."

"You did your best. No one else even stepped forward. You notice that?"

"Well, I mean, it's quite a challenging situation. And I did take over. Someone else would have stepped in if I hadn't."

"I'm not so sure. All those kids were interested in was content for their social media. You were out of your seat and around the bar like a rocket, Bazz!"

"Of course, yeah, of course," Barnwell said vaguely. He'd lost his enthusiasm for light-hearted banter. The evening was over for him.

Steve caught his mood. "Look, I'm here for two whole weeks, so let's say this. I'll take myself back to the Black Horse Hotel or whatever it's called . . ."

"The White House Inn," Barnwell said, finding he could still laugh. He wondered if Steve's mistake was deliberate to lighten things up.

"Yeah, yeah. You go home, rest up, have a shower, and get those bloodstains out so you're not mistaken for a serial killer. Toss your clothes in the rubbish too. You stink."

"Definitely."

"And tomorrow we'll have breakfast at . . . what's that place called?"

"Ethel's."

"Right. At what, eight thirty?"

"Seven," Barnwell said. "I'll have to go into work if they don't catch who did this tonight." He felt self-conscious now in his borrowed clothes, with his bloodstained hands. His chest felt a little crispy. Blood residue. "Yeah, I'd best be off."

"Okay, chief," Steve said, a little pale at the idea of such an early start but keen to appear supportive. "See you at Ethel's at seven."

Half an hour later, Barnwell's hands finally stopped shaking. Five times a minute, he felt the impulse to call St. Helier General and get a read on the injured man, but the hospital staff would have their hands full, and Roach had promised to text him if there was anything to report. If the man remained unconscious but stable, there wouldn't be any news until tomorrow.

Bazza paced around his flat. He showered, letting steaming water drain the evening's tensions from his system just a little. When he flicked on the kettle to make himself a hot drink, Carmen, sensing his mood, whined and looked up at him. She tilted her head, her big, brown eyes pleading. Padding over to the bench by the door where Barnwell kept her lead, the young beagle took it between her teeth and padded back to him, dropping it at his feet.

"Good girl. You know what's best for me even more than I do, don't 'cha?" Barnwell bent down and scratched between her ears. "Hang on."

He had an idea, one which sounded better the more he thought about it, and better still when he saw the rain had stopped. "Time for a breather after a complicated night." He pulled on a football jersey and his trainers. He attached Carmen's lead to her collar. Opening the front door, he saw the sky was black, starless. The air, silent and cool. Barnwell opened the wrought iron gate on to the street. It creaked noisily. He tugged on Carmen's lead, and with a little skip to push off, they went for a run.

CHAPTER NINE

The Gorey Gossip
Saturday, April 16th

It is my sad duty to report that Gorey has been the scene of another explosion of violence and grief. Some of my readers were in the Foc's'le and Ferret last night when local man, Jamie Reeves, stumbled in, blood gushing from the back of his head. He attempted to ask for help before collapsing.

Our grateful thanks—yet again—to Constable Barnwell from our local police force for administering first aid, keeping poor Mr. Reeves alive until the paramedics arrived, and to the staff at St. Helier General, where Jamie currently lies in critical condition. In true Gorey style, well-wishers have reached out to Jamie's family.

But what has Gorey come to when someone can't be sure of making it back home without being viciously attacked after a night out? According to local sources, there was no sign of robbery, so what are we to assume? That it was a simple mugging that went wrong? Or something more darkly sinister? Time for our boys (and one girl) in blue to step up! I'm talking to you, Detective Inspector Graham.

As a sudden storm consigns the beauty of a sunny day to a memory in the blink of an eye, last night's barbaric violence reminds us to be vigilant. In Gorey, we are grateful for our small and capable police force. Their recent performance continues an upward trajectory. I'm certain DI Graham's team remains committed to our safety and their own improvement, and sources have promised plenty of old-fashioned "knocking-on-doors" policing to bring the attacker to justice.

I encourage you to tell the police everything you can, even if it's background or peripheral information. And please keep Jamie in your thoughts as doctors work to restore him to rude health.

CHAPTER TEN

"MORNING, JIM," GRAHAM said. "Nice and cool in there, is it?"
Roach gratefully swept off his helmet in a smooth move and quickly shook out his hair, not unlike a dog that had just climbed out of a river. "Not really," he said. The sergeant was uncomfortably hot. He flattened his matted hair with one hand, spiked it up with the other, then used both to give it some semblance of formality. "Great ride, mind. Day after a big rainstorm," he said, taking an exaggerated deep breath. "Fresh as a daisy. Like the place has just been hosed down."

The phone rang. Janice answered. She soon hung up. "That was Barnwell, sir. He's going to pop in for the meeting."

"On his day off?" Roach said. He considered the constable's efforts the previous evening. "Yeah, I suppose he would. Asked me to text him if anything happened. Must've really shook him up. One minute you're having a lazy end-of-the-week drink, the next you're covered in blood, trying to keep some poor bloke alive."

"We've got no evidence," Harding said. "Not a thing. Nobody saw or heard anything outside or inside the pub, no forensics. And the lad's probably going to—"

"Medical science is capable of wonders beyond our imagining, Sergeant," interrupted Graham. "Let's not write him off yet." Privately, he was surprised Jamie Reeves was still alive given his injuries, and it gave their investigation a sliver of hope. What Graham wanted most was a phone call from the hospital to say Reeves was awake and ready to talk.

There was a clatter from the back. Barnwell came through into the reception area. He must have come in the rear door. "Morning, Barnwell. Thanks for coming in on your day off," Graham greeted him. "Get yourselves some tea and meet in my office in five."

"Yes, sir," the trio said in unison.

Five minutes later, they crowded into Graham's office, Janice at the rear so she could keep an eye on reception and an ear listening for the desk phone. "The other stuff can wait," Graham began. "This case is our priority. Right, we've got a twenty-eight-year-old male, a James Reeves, in St. Helier General with serious head injuries. He was attacked just a few yards from his home. His life is hanging by a thread, so I'm told, and this case could turn into a murder investigation at any minute."

"Terrible," Roach said. "I played five-a-side against him a couple of times. Marcus said he hired him to do some gardening for him."

"I've seen him in the Foc's'le," Barnwell added.

"Jack told me he fixed his computer once," Janice said.

"Sounds like he was well ensconced in the community. Tell me everything we've got," Graham said.

Roach took the lead. "Right, sir. Well, he's lucky to be alive. Someone gave him a *ferocious* whack over the head."

"He didn't say anything? Identify his attacker?"

"All he could do was ask for help when he came into the pub," Barnwell said. "Nothing else. Someone really did a number on him. By the time he got to the Fo'c'sle, he'd lost a good deal of blood."

Roach spoke up. "The attacker inflicted a single wound. Dr. Tomlinson says that the margins weren't uniform as you would expect with a tool, but not as irregular as something natural. While we can't run a formal examination, analysis of the bar towels Barnwell used in the pub and bandaging at the hospital didn't reveal any residue. With the rain and everything, we haven't got much, but if it had been a brick or a rock, we'd have found red brick dust or particles of organic matter on them."

Harding reflexively cradled the back of her neck. "Ouch."

"So, he was subject to the classic anonymous 'frenzied' attack, as no doubt Mr. Freddie Solomon will tell everyone when he finds out." Graham was making notes. "Who is this chap? Local lad?"

"Yeah, he's Gorey, born and raised," Roach confirmed. "Works for Sanderson Landscaping. Started out doing what they call 'hardscaping'—putting in driveways, patios, pools, that kind of thing. Plus, a bit of planting too. But now he does some of the design work."

"Okay, what else do we have? No one saw anything, Sergeant Harding? I mean nothing?"

"No, sir. We interviewed the people in the pub and neighbouring houses. They don't report hearing or seeing anything. There was a trail of blood, which suggests he was attacked just a few feet from the pub, so he must have been hit over the head and dragged himself there to get help. He lives alone in a flat close by, but it isn't clear where he'd been beforehand or where he was going. It's all a bit of mystery, really."

"Well, that's our speciality. Mysteries." Graham made a face. "Any sign of the weapon?"

None of them spoke. "No, sir," Roach finally said.

"We haven't been able to do a thorough search of the area yet, but if I can have some help from St. Helier, I can arrange one," Janice offered.

"Not sure I'll get that today, Sergeant. The Bulls are playing the Green Lions this afternoon. Everyone will be drafted to that." Rivals Jersey and Guernsey football clubs were playing a local derby. They were always fiercely contested and well attended. The streets of St. Helier were likely to be quiet, but the football ground would be heaving. "We'll have to do it ourselves. I'll leave organisation of the search to you."

"Yes, sir."

Barnwell was keen to get his boss's first impression. "What do you reckon, sir?"

"Not much to go on, is there? Unusual for the area." Gorey was not known for random, nasty crimes like this. There were incidents of violent conduct when the acutely boisterous met the overly intoxicated, often in the same physical body, but they were extremely rare. "A street mugging gone wrong, maybe?"

"My first thought too. But he had his wallet on him," Barnwell reported.

"And his phone, sir. Jack worked on it last night. Nothing," Janice said.

"There's been no activity on his cards," Roach piped up. "No useful camera footage either."

Graham sighed. He finished his notes and laid out his plan for the day. "Alright, Roach, I want you to go to St. Helier. Check on the victim, then get with Tomlinson. Butter him up a bit. Get him talking about wine and California again. Whatever it takes, I want him to give us something more." Graham looked back at his notes, which were depressingly scant.

"But the victim's not dead, sir. It's not his case."

"He can liaise with the treating doctors, talk their language, leverage the relationships, and perhaps get us some more info. If we can't talk to Jamie Reeves, *anything* will help, Jim, seriously."

"Righto, boss."

"Barnwell," Graham continued, "well done again with providing prompt and professional first aid at the Foc's'le last night. Mr. Reeves certainly owes the fact he has a fighting chance to you . . ."

Barnwell attempted to deflect the compliment. "I was only there for a quiet drink with my brother. I never know what kind of trouble he's going to get me into."

"Nevertheless, you're a credit to us, Barnwell," Graham said. It was perhaps his highest praise, and this time there was no deflecting.

"Thank you, sir," Barnwell said humbly. "Lewis Hurd, the barman at the Foc's'le, texted me about a trio of young lads he calls DKN . . ."

It took only two seconds. "Drunken, kleptomaniac, and nefarious?" Graham tried.

Eyebrows bunched, Roach whispered to Harding, "Remind me never to play Scrabble with him."

"I don't think you're being complimentary, sir, and as character assessments go, I'd say you're on the money. Names are Duncan, Kevin, and Neil."

"Neil Lightfoot?" Roach said.

"The very same," Barnwell confirmed.

"Your very first collar, wasn't he, Jim?" Harding recalled.

"Nah, my first one was that fence-line dispute up on the Longueville Road near Banbury Meadow. Remember? That drunken idiot of a homeowner who brought out his chainsaw and started waving it around, terrorising his neighbours? That was a satisfying nick." Roach laughed. "Neil Lightfoot was my *second* arrest. I found him trying his hand at a new profession. In fact, during his first spell of on-the-job training, he was kind enough . . ."

"Dim-witted enough," Barnwell tossed in.

". . . to let me watch for three whole minutes while he completely failed to break into a new Audi four-by-four on Lyme Avenue."

"It does make things easier," Graham agreed, "when our would-be criminals prove to be gratuitously stupid."

"Anyhow, Lewis thought they might be worth a chat," Barnwell summed up. "I thought I'd go and see them.

"Alright, track these three lads down. If they don't know anything, they might know someone who does. But it's just a chat, mind. Make sure they know that. Janice, you hold the fort down here. Work your magic with the databases. Find out what you can about our Mr. Reeves and his associates."

"Yes, sir."

"I'll go to Sanderson's to speak to his colleagues. Let me know what you get when you get it. Okay, off you go."

The officers, their tasks allotted, smartly walked out of Graham's office. He watched them go, but after they left, he turned to gaze out of the window. They had nothing to go on. But they'd had nothing before and had turned things around with hard graft, teamwork . . . and tea. Graham strode over to his filing cabinet and flipped the switch on the kettle. He'd make himself a pot of Assam before he did anything else.

CHAPTER ELEVEN

"THEY TOOK HIM into surgery in the early hours." Tomlinson led Roach from the hospital's covered entrance and down a long hallway with countless doors leading off to departments of every type. "There was evidence that things were getting worse. He has a brain bleed. They'll decide whether to airlift him to the mainland in a few hours. Tricky decision though; he might not survive the journey."

They washed their hands and walked into the blue-floored, medical quiet of the intensive care unit. Jamie had his own small room, though someone was constantly monitoring him from a nurses' station that looked more like NASA mission control than Roach remembered. Two computer monitors displayed real-time information from eight rooms, including Jamie's.

"Have a seat for a minute," Tomlinson said. "He's got visitors. Besides, all the interesting stuff is here," he added, pointing to the screen. There were a range of scans available, and with a moment's help from one of the ICU nurses, Tomlinson found a CT scan of Jamie Reeves's skull. "There's intracranial bleeding." He called up another high-resolution picture. "It's not looking good, Jim."

"Oh."

"But even depressing, avoidable tragedies can be moments for learning," Tomlinson told his protégé. "Why don't you tell me everything you know about" —he turned from the screen and gave the request a little theatre, performing a quiet drum roll on the desktop before cuing the sergeant with a director's finger— "brain stem herniation!"

Jim collected his thoughts and attempted to sound confident. "When someone takes a traumatic hit to the head . . ."

"Not unlike the one you're in for if you've skipped your anatomy reading," warned Tomlinson with a wink.

". . . a bleed can begin. The buildup of blood puts pressure on the brain stem, resulting in unconsciousness." Roach thought back to his textbook reading. "Then, there's cessation of the breathing reflexes, which leads to asphyxia. Oh, and finally, death."

"Even in the ICU," Tomlinson lamented, "we struggle to successfully treat *that*."

"So, what happened during his surgery?" asked Roach.

"They drilled a hole in his skull to relieve the pressure. He held on," Marcus said, sounding grim. "But barely. I wasn't there, but from what I heard, it was complicated."

Roach frowned. "So . . . what can I tell the boss?"

Tomlinson closed his eyes for a second. "In the first place, Sergeant," he said, irritation creeping into his voice, "you can tell him the patient is stable, gravely ill, and the next few hours will be critical. And second, I can't rightly give you an post-mortem report because he's not actually dead, you see."

"Got it."

"I've said all along that the assailant hit Jamie with a weight of some kind, but I'm going to add a detail. They hit him like they *really* meant it. Caused the kind of damage you might see from a hammer blow."

"No wonder his brain decided to call it quits for a while," Roach said. "How long do coma patients stay asleep for?"

"It's not *sleep*, for heaven's sake, boy," Tomlinson wailed, throwing up his hands. "It's . . ."

"Just a slip, Doc. No need to go ballistic. I know it's not technically sleep. It's like, well, the brain's emergency mode. His brain has shut down."

Placated, Tomlinson said, "About two weeks, typically. By that point, the coma tends to resolve, one way or the other."

"As in, he will either . . ."

"Yes, young man."

"Do *they* know that?" Roach wondered, nodding at the window of Jamie's room through which they could see a small, slight woman sitting anxiously by his bed, her hands clasped in front of her. The woman's face was fixed on Jamie's figure lying quite still in the bed, his arms by his sides. Next to him, machines beeped, administered, and monitored. A man stood behind her, his arms tightly crossed. Every aspect of the woman's body language spoke of concern for the stricken patient, while her companion seemed defensive, even angry. Him being a foot taller and a hundred pounds heavier than the young woman boosted this impression.

"Not sure. The nurse told me they got here an hour or so ago, and the girl was in a terrible state, bawling when she saw him." Tomlinson hadn't taken his eyes off the screens and clicked to another view, a cross section that showed Jamie's brain in remarkable detail. "Just *extraordinary* what we can do these days."

"I'm going to say hello to them," Roach said.

Marcus Tomlinson checked his watch and closed the folder of images. "I'll stay here. They'll only pester me for news, and I don't have any. He's not even my responsibility. Yet."

"Cheery thought. Thanks, Dr. T." Roach left the nurses' station and crossed the corridor. He knocked on the door and went in. The room was a place of intense, worried quiet, except for a susurrus of background hums and clicks and hisses. Aware of the effect his uniform would have—it communicated there was trouble—Roach spoke immediately. "Just a courtesy visit from the Gorey police. We're investigating the attack on Mr. Reeves," he began. He glanced at the patient.

A respiratory tube had been fitted in case Jamie's ability to breathe became compromised. A cluster of IV attachments at each wrist led to two drips. Pads adhered to his skin fed data to a rack of medical machines. The skin around his closed eyes was bruised, his lips parched and swollen.

"He's just . . ." said the woman, her knuckles whitening as she spoke, "so . . . *absent*." She glanced at Roach and her companion, as though hoping for a more positive interpretation, her teary, blue eyes sheltered by bleached-blonde hair.

"He'll be back in no time," said the man who accompanied her. He seemed in his early thirties and possibly the woman's boyfriend. He had curly, brown hair and the generous frame of a heavyweight boxer but with none of the grace. He wore a stern, uncomfortable expression like he would prefer to be anywhere but at Jamie Reeves's bedside. "They can do miracles these days, love," he said, trying to sound reassuring. "Absolute miracles."

"Are you members of the family?" Roach asked. He was confused by this couple. Was she a sister? A girlfriend? An ex-wife?

"Old friends," the young woman said. "From Les Quennier school in St. Helier. We were," she stumbled to add, not sure what word to use, "well, we were *together* until a year ago. I'm Paula Lascelles. This is my new boyfriend, Matthew Walker," she said, nodding at the big man.

"Missed his chance," Matthew added tactlessly.

"I left Jersey," explained Paula a little more sensitively, "but Jamie absolutely loved it here. Refused to move. That's why we broke up. I'm just taking over for a bit while his mum and dad go for something to eat. That was kind of them, wasn't it? To let me in. I'm sure I'm not their favourite person." Paula looked up at Roach forlornly, her eyes wide with anxiety.

Roach made quiet notes on his tablet, angling it into his chest. "Can you tell me anything about who might have done this? Anyone who might have held a grudge against him?" Paula shook her head. "Any other ex-girlfriends?"

"No," Paula shot back angrily. "Only me. There was *only* me."

"Take it easy, babe," Matthew told her. "The sergeant 'ere is just askin' questions."

Paula closed her eyes and took a deep breath. "Yes, yes, sorry."

"Nobody saw anyfin', right?" said Matthew. "So, how're you gonna arrest the person who did it?"

"Examination of the evidence, investigation, and deduction," replied Roach crisply. He had taken an instinctive dislike to this brittle couple. "Honed techniques aided by some of the most amazing technology you've never heard of." He thought he sounded like Graham as he listened to himself and wondered if that was a good thing.

Matthew seemed entirely nonplussed. "And maybe someone just whacked him, random-like. I mean, it 'appens."

"It's possible. But even if they weren't seen doing it, we have ways to discover who it was."

"Some people . . ." Matthew began, but Paula had apparently had enough. She pulled him to her side, and they turned away from Roach, returning to their morose, silent vigil over the motionless Jamie. Roach got the hint and left, but not without leaving them both his card with a reminder to stay in touch. "My detective inspector," he muttered to himself on the way out, "is *definitely* going to want to talk to you two weirdos."

CHAPTER TWELVE

ROACH WANDERED DOWN to the hospital canteen. His eyes roved over the diners, searching for a couple who might be Jamie Reeves's parents. In the corner next to the windows, he spied a pair—mid-fifties, weary. The man had ordered a full English. He chewed thoughtfully. The woman next to him ignored her toast and was sipping tea. She stared ahead, her hands wrapped around her mug, clasping it tightly as though its warmth was life-sustaining.

"Mr. and Mrs. Reeves?" The couple looked up. "I'm Sergeant Roach, Gorey Police. I'm investigating your son's case. May I ask you a few questions?"

Phil Reeves nodded at the empty chair at their table. "We were expecting you last night. Isn't this a bit late? Whoever did this could be miles away by now. Off the island, even."

"I tried to speak to you, but you were in distress and the doctors advised that we wait." Roach's voice was gentle, courteous, respectful.

"Hmph, okay then. What do you want to know?" Reeves senior put his knife and fork down and sat back in his chair. Mrs. Reeves's knuckles whitened as she gripped her mug even tighter.

"Could you give me your full names, please?"

"Phil, Philip Reeves, and this is my wife, Christine."

"May I say that I'm very sorry for your situation, and we're doing everything we can to find Jamie's attacker. Can you tell me when you last saw him?"

"Last night. He was walking back to his flat from our house when that person hit him. He left us around ten p.m. He'd come for dinner and a beer, a bit of a chat."

"He often did that," Christine Reeves said in a whisper. She peeled a hand from her mug and rubbed it across her face. Like her voice, her hand shook.

"Was there anything about his visit that concerned you? Did he seem agitated or worried?" Phil Reeves shook his head. Roach looked at his wife for confirmation.

"No, nothing. Everything seemed perfectly normal," she said.

"We had a couple of beers like we normally do, got fish and chips, watched a bit of TV. Then he left to walk home. Just like many other Friday nights we've had over the years."

"Are you aware of any disputes he's involved in, anything that might get him the attention of someone who might have done this?"

Phil Reeves sat forward now. He glared at Roach. "What are you trying to say? That Jamie was involved in something criminal? Like this was some kind of payback or warning or something?"

"I'm just trying to ascertain the facts, Mr. Reeves. I'm not suggesting that Jamie had anything to do with anything illegal. This might end up being a random street mugging, but I have to ask the questions so we can do our best to see that justice is served on Jamie's behalf."

Mrs. Reeves let go of her mug long enough to put her hand on her husband's arm to placate him. Phil Reeves sat back at his wife's behest. "It's alright, Sergeant. Ask away," she said. "But please be quick. I want to get back to his bedside. I am not aware of anything that might have led to this attack. Jamie is a good boy, not in debt, no troubling friends. He was well-liked, enjoyed his beer like they all do at his age, but nothing to excess, had a few girlfriends, but no one serious at the moment."

"What about Ms"—Roach checked his notes—"Lascelles? I met her in Jamie's room. And her friend."

Christine Reeves and her husband exchanged glances. Mrs. Reeves let go of her mug. "Paula is Jamie's ex-girlfriend. They went to the same school but got together afterwards. They went out for nearly a decade—"

"On and off," Phil Reeves interrupted. "Mostly off."

"Until about a year ago, when she went to the mainland."

"Best day of my life," her husband said. He folded his arms again. Now he pursed his lips. "I wasn't a fan."

"Paula's a very attractive girl, but she had Jamie wrapped around her little finger. He'd do anything she asked, and then she'd tell him to get lost. Just like that. Always picking him up and dropping him again, she was," Christine Reeves said.

"You should have seen the fights they had. Embarrassing. Slamming doors, screaming at each other. Did my head in. I kept telling him to dump her, but she'd call and off he'd trot like he was her dog or something." Phil Reeves tutted and shook his head.

"Eventually she went a step too far. She wanted to leave the island, and Jamie loves it here. He wouldn't leave."

"Oh, she tried to get him to. Wheedling, crying, threatening. But this time he called her bluff. She'd have left him the moment she found someone better anyhow. Someone with more money, status. Girls like her are always like that." Jamie's father stabbed a bite of sausage and munched on it aggressively.

"We were relieved to see her go, to be honest. So much drama." Mrs. Reeves gave Roach a wan smile.

"And we weren't happy to see her turn up this morning when she heard the news," her husband added.

"Apparently, she's visiting her family for a few days. Brought her new boyfriend with her. She offered to give us a break, which is why we're down here . . ." Mrs. Reeves trailed off. "Anyhow, is there anything else you need to know?"

Roach's mind worked furiously. "Wha— er, no. I think that will be all for now. Do you have a photo of Jamie that we can circulate? It will help us with our enquiries."

Christine Reeves seemed grateful for something to do. She rapidly swiped through the photos on her phone, finally settling on one that showed Jamie, bottle of beer in his hand, smiling broadly. "I like that one. It was his birthday. We had a good time. He was happy." Her voice broke, and she handed her phone to Roach so that he could send the image to his email address, the process beyond her.

"Thank you. I'll leave you in peace. We'll be in touch if there are any developments." Roach left his card on the table. Neither of them paid it any attention, and Christine Reeves picked up her mug again, unaware or not caring that her tea was now stone cold.

Alone at the station, Janice banged away at her keyboard with her fingertips. She was the station's police database expert. Training her had been one of DI Graham's first directives, and it was a role for which she was grateful. It had afforded her a small increase in pay, status, and possibilities for advancement should she seek them. But today as she searched, cross-referenced, and categorised, she felt resentful, restless, sidelined.

She wasn't sure why. She didn't normally feel like this. Maybe the wedding was getting to her. She punched another query into the search bar. Nothing. Jamie was as clean as her kitchen at home. Carmen sniffed at Janice's feet and gave a little whine.

"Yeah, me too, doggie." Janice let out a sigh. "I know we shouldn't, but . . ." She punched some numbers into the reception phone. Taking Carmen's lead off a hook in the breakroom, the sergeant clipped it onto her collar. "Come on, let's get out of here. Let's give you some sniffing practice."

CHAPTER THIRTEEN

LOOKING DECIDEDLY HARASSED, his thick, grey-flecked hair in disarray, Lewis Hurd finally stood up and stretched just as Barnwell appeared in the pub's doorway. "We don't open until eleven thirty," Lewis said, tossing down a sodden rag. "Oh, it's you, Bazza. Provided you're not here for a pint, come on in."

It was strange to see the place empty, so orderly, clean, and neat instead of packed with diners and drinkers laughing and talking. Chairs and barstools were stacked neatly upside down on the tabletops. The bar gleamed. Most importantly, though, Lewis had finished soaking and cleaning a patch of carpet near the bar, exactly where Jamie Reeves had come to a bloodied halt.

"Just saying hello, Lewis," Barnwell said. "Seeing if there's anything new. The place scrubs up nicely, doesn't it?" he added, looking around.

"Rumours spread quickly," the experienced barman told him. Hurd walked over to the heavy wooden door and locked it. "I've had a hell of a time trying to persuade people a fight didn't happen *inside* the pub. If we don't clear that story up sharpish, the Foc's'le will get a reputation. And no one wants to come in to the sight and smell of blood, do they? Best if we look shipshape." This had been his morning message to his two junior staff, teenagers who had laboured all morning to give the pub a thorough clean. "We had to get the carpet seen to, in any case. Figured we might as well tidy the place up a bit while we were at it." Lewis cleared his throat. "Got to say, the presence of a uniformed constable won't be a welcome sight once we open."

"I won't harm your bottom line or your reputation, I promise," Barnwell said, keeping an eye on the time. "Your staff did well."

"Thanks, mate," Lewis managed. "Well, like I say, it's busy around here, so if there's nothing else . . ." He said it not impolitely but with genuine enthusiasm to get the Foc's'le back on its feet with a positive Saturday lunchtime crowd. It was one of the busiest times of the week. "I've got a big screen out back so people can watch the game." He raised his eyebrows. "Can I help you with anything?"

Barnwell brought out his tablet and found his notes on the Jamie Reeves case. "Obviously, I'm checking if you've heard anything more about the attack."

"Not a sausage," Lewis replied. His ever-busy hands slid from glass to glass, polishing them quickly with a new, white cloth. "People are shocked; they want to know what happened. But nobody's paraded around the pub claiming responsibility if that's what you mean. And if they do know something, no one's talking." A loud series of thumps on the outside door made both men jump. "We're not open yet!" Lewis bellowed. "That'll be DKN. They always try to get me to open up early. And I always say no. Don't know why they bother, but they're not the smartest."

"I'd like to talk to them actually, but I can do that outside, leave you in peace," Barnwell said, making for the door.

"Hang on," Lewis said. "That would look bad. And I don't want that after all our efforts. I'll let them in. Your presence should keep them from hassling me to open the bar out of hours." Lewis checked his watch, set down a glass, and marched to the pub door. He slid back the bolt. "Come on in, lads. There's someone here to see you."

"'Bout time, Lewis!" said one of the three young men dressed in track suits who had been standing outside.

"We're not open for drinking. Constable Barnwell wants to talk to you. Though Lord knows why he wants to look at your ugly mushes any more than he has to. I certainly don't." This apparently insulting invective from Lewis passed for banter between the barman and the three men that passed through the doors. None of them batted an eyelid.

"What's all this, then?" Kevin Croft, twenty-three, a bit full of himself, and usually affable enough until he'd had a skinful—after that, all bets were off— strode confidently into the pub. He pulled at the crotch of his low-slung trackie while loudly chewing gum. Barnwell considered it extraordinary that he managed to achieve both tasks at the same time, a feat that, had he not seen it for himself, he would have considered Croft to be incapable of.

The tallest of the three copped an eyeful of Barnwell. "What's he doin' 'ere?" Duncan Rayner appeared to be their leader, after a fashion. He hitched up the tracksuit bottoms that hung off his nonexistent backside. His features were sharp and unattractive, like a rodent's, a comparison not aided by hair that was suffering from a clearly recent and ill-advised shaving incident.

"Me?" Barnwell asked. "Oh, I'm just here to gaze into the crystal ball." He hovered around the skinny lad's oddly shaved head. "You know, the Victorians put a lot of store by phrenology." The three men held Barnwell with a steady gaze but said nothing.

"Reading the bumps on your head," Barnwell explained.

"'Ow the bleedin' 'ell did you know that?" Duncan, the leader-after-a-fashion, exclaimed. He squinted.

Barnwell shrugged. "Monday is trivia night down at the Pig and Whistle. I learn all sorts. In olden times, they reckoned they could tell if you were a criminal or not just from looking at your bonce. Absolute codswallop, of course," he scoffed. "But that's what they believed. Interesting people, the Victorians. Really into body snatching . . ." Barnwell trailed off, staring into space. The lads were now gawping at him like he was an alien. "Anyhow," Barnwell said suddenly, snapping back into character, "I've learned to be open-minded about where leads might come from."

"Funny that," Kevin said, poking a thumb at his mate. "Because Duncan here comes from Leeds!"

"Ah, you're the comedian of the group, are you?" Barnwell said. "Listen, why don't we sit down for a chat? We can work on your material, maybe get you a slot at the London Palladium."

The last of the trio was Neil Lightfoot—the twenty-two-year-old whose car-thieving skills had so disappointed Sergeant Roach a few years prior. "Wotcha wanna talk to us for?" Neil asked. He had the most reason to resent Barnwell's uniform, being unique in the group for having served a custodial sentence. He was also chewing gum, and he looked Barnwell up and down while masticating forcefully. He leered, the gum clenched between his top and bottom teeth. Barnwell felt the urge to prize them open and grab Lightfoot's tonsils. Neil called out to Lewis, "Three pints of your best, mate. Chop, chop."

"I already said we're not open," Lewis called back. "Sit down and answer the officer's questions or you'll find yourself outside again looking at the pub sign."

"Why don't we have a quick chat over there, eh?" Barnwell said, guiding the three men to the table by the window. It was the brightest part of the pub. The lads were a little nervous as they sat down, eyeing Barnwell as though he might slap cuffs on them at any moment.

"I'm making enquiries about Jamie Reeves, the lad who was beaten up around the corner last night. About ten thirty."

"Yeah, so what? Did he die or something?" Duncan wondered as if he were asking the time.

"Your concern for Mr. Reeves's well-being is moving, Mr. Raynor," Barnwell said. He made a creditable attempt to focus on the young man's face rather than his odd haircut. "But no, he's still hanging on in intensive care."

"No list of suspects, then?" Kevin said.

"Probably just a mugging," Neil, the inept car thief, added. "Things go wrong, someone gets hit with a brick, and here we are."

"I don't know why I'm bothering!" Barnwell said. "Detective Chief Inspector Lightfoot seems to have solved this one all by himself!"

"Just saying, like," Neil said.

"First things first, lads. Where were you all last night?"

"Playing X-Box at mine," Kevin replied. "*Ring of Fire*."

"*Awesome* game," Neil said.

"Imagine kung fu, but with magic," said Kevin.

"And swords," Duncan added.

"Fantastic, I'm sure. Did you go out at all?"

"Nah," Kevin said, "what with the rain. We were gonnu, but it was coming down straight."

Barnwell remembered his brother's rain-soaked laughter, his willingness to find fun in difficult circumstances. "And did anyone else join you at home playing *Ring of Fire*? Anyone who can vouch for you?"

Three different facial expressions communicated belligerence, indifference, and intransigence. "Nah, it was just us," Neil said.

"So, no one else? You realise that's what we call an 'alibi,' right?" said Barnwell. "Someone who can prove you were where you said you were."

"But we was all together, the three of us," Duncan complained. "I can alibi Kevin, then he can alibi Neil, then Neil can –"

"Sorry, DCI Raynor, it doesn't work like that. You can't alibi each other."

Ratty-looking Kevin sat up straight. "Look, are you dobbing us for this? We had nuthin' to do wiv it." He thrust out his chin.

Barnwell put his hands up. "Just routine, getting that bit out of the way. Keep your shirts on."

Kevin was incensed. "This is police harassment, this is!"

"Stick to comedy, Mr. Croft," Barnwell said. "Alright, look. Tell me what's been going on lately? On the streets, like."

"Oh, so now you want us to grass, is that it? Do your dirty work for you?"

"Not at all. I'm investigating the brutal attack on an innocent victim not much older than you. His attacker is at large. No one wants that. You lot keep your ear to the ground; you know what's going on. This is your chance to do your bit for the Gorey community." The lads stared back at Barnwell, mute.

"Look, did you hear anything, any news on the streets? You're well-connected lads. You see things, hear things. Did you see or hear anything about this beating?"

Apparently Duncan couldn't think of anything pithy to say, so he said, "I never, ever hit anyone. Scout's honour."

Kevin picked at his tracksuit top. He had the air of someone who'd seen the inside of too many pubs during long days without work. "If we do hear or see anyfin', I'm sure we can make an arrangement where it falls into yours, pronto-like, if ya know wha' I mean?"

Neil agreed. "We'll do anything for the filth." He grinned sarcastically.

Barnwell glared at him. "You can start by never calling us that again." He stood and left each of them his card. "Don't be strangers. And stay out of bleedin' trouble, the three of you." He headed back to the bar, leaving the three men in a morose, seething huddle around their table. "Lewis, a word if you don't mind."

"Yes, Bazza," Lewis said.

Barnwell leant over the bar. "Any drug business going on? Anyone dealing in the toilets out the back that you know of?"

Lewis rolled his eyes. "Not that I know about. If I did, I'd have told you. That kind of thing's not going on in my pub. We're the most popular in Gorey because we're clean, we're family-friendly, and we've got great local beers. The tourists love us, you know that. They're spilling out onto the pavement in the summer. That doesn't happen if there's a drug problem."

Drugs being the motive for the attack on Jamie Reeves would make more sense than anything else they had, but Barnwell had to admit that Lewis was right. This was his beat, and the Fo'c'sle was not in the middle of a turf war or anything remotely like it. Gorey was remarkably drug-free, just a little bit here and there. Teenagers mostly, making a day trip to St. Helier to source a stash for the weekend. Confiscation and a chat with the parents was as much action as he'd ever had to take. But this case was unusual enough for Gorey that Barnwell was prepared to entertain the idea that the situation might have changed. "You'll let me know if you hear anything?"

"The very second," Lewis said. He dropped a shoulder and whispered, "Now skedaddle, would you?" It was past opening time, and the pub was filling up fast now with couples and families rushing to grab an early lunch.

As he left, Barnwell noticed that the three young men were sitting not in dejected silence but had begun an animated discussion. Duncan, in particular, seemed angry and frustrated. "Are you teed off about the state of the world, Duncan?" Barnwell asked the afternoon air as he walked back to the police station. "Or are you afraid I'm onto you?"

🌀

While Barnwell had been inside the pub, unbeknownst to him, Janice had peered into the front gardens of the houses on the street that led to it. Bloodstains on the pavement signposted where Jamie Reeves had met his attacker. At intervals, she pulled Carmen back to her. The young dog was finding all kinds of enticing smells but hadn't found anything that interested the sergeant.

Calling the few square feet of ground in front of the terraced houses "gardens" was a bit of an exaggeration. They were more like small, walled flower beds, many left to nature or the less desirable habits of man. On windy and wet nights like the one they'd had previously, these small, boxed areas transformed into traps for leaves and discarded takeaway boxes.

Janice poked around, looking for something that might prove to be the weapon that had assailed Jamie Reeves. She did find a pile of house bricks, but Tomlinson had rejected those. Another house seemed to be storing the contents of a repair shop outside their front window, but none of the items were of sufficient weight to inflict deadly force.

With a sigh, and mindful of the time, Janice turned back. She didn't want to be caught deserting her post.

CHAPTER FOURTEEN

THE DAY WAS becoming warmer and more pleasant, so Graham chose to walk into town, carrying his jacket as he went. It would be healthier, he told himself, and a chance to get some sunshine. He followed some of the smaller roads, preferring residential streets to the main route into Gorey. The last of these, a street where the driveways with hybrid cars parked in them outnumbered those without, boasted a former residential property that had been converted into business premises.

The frontage was now all glass, through which could be seen two sleek, pale wooden desks topped with large screens and laptops. Chairs, presumably for clients, sat on one side of the desks, and set against the wall was a white leather sofa. A purple van sat outside on what had formerly been the front lawn and was now a tarmacked forecourt, the van's purple doors emblazoned with a big, yellow S intertwined with a similarly coloured L: the logo of Sanderson Landscaping.

Graham opened the door and walked inside to find himself immediately greeted by a disembodied but cheery "Good morning!" The voice came from the back of the room. Graham turned in its direction to see a petite, attractive woman with auburn hair walking toward him. Her hair was pulled back into a ponytail which swished from side to side as she walked. She looked in her mid-twenties. A sprinkle of freckles dusted her nose and cheeks.

"Sorry to keep you waiting. We're digitising our records, and all the machines are in the back." The woman stuck out her hand. "Molly Duckworth, how can I help?" Molly struck Graham as bright and confident, if a little tired. There were dark circles under her red-rimmed eyes. He brought out his identification and explained the reason for his visit.

Molly's face dropped. "Oh!" Her open, welcoming expression turned to one of fear. "Is there any news?" Graham saw trepidation in her eyes.

"No change, I'm afraid. I'm here to ask you some questions."

Molly's face fell. "No change isn't bad news, I suppose, but it isn't good either."

"Jamie's being looked after by the best," Graham assured her. "One of my officers is there now, liaising with the medical staff and his family."

"Oh, okay," she said, relieved but obviously hoping for better news. "Should I call Mr. Sanderson?" she asked, still nervous. "He's with a client in St. Helier, but I don't think he'll be long."

"I'll wait. It's fine," Graham said. "We can talk for a bit, if that's alright." There was something about her demeanour, the way Molly's face had shown sudden pain when Graham mentioned Jamie's name. Perhaps it was concern for a friend or a much-valued colleague, though Graham sensed there was more to it. "You see, I don't know Jamie, and the more we know, the more it helps to get to the bottom of things," he said, keeping things simple. "Maybe you could help me?"

Molly pondered for a moment, then made a decision and went to lock the front door. Using a remote control, she activated blinds which quietly sank to cover the windows. "Let's sit down," she said, gesturing to the white leather sofa. "Can I get you some tea? Some water?"

"Some water would be nice, thank you." Graham was warm from his walk. As Molly left to get his drink, he found his trusty notebook and pen and looked around the room. It was tidy and neat. The desks were cleared of papers. A few brochures were displayed in a wall rack. It was unnaturally free of signs of human activity. Graham wondered if anyone actually worked there.

"You don't ever expect that something like this will happen to someone you know. It's just terrible. I've been so upset," Molly said as she returned with Graham's water. She seemed relieved to be unburdening herself to someone, *anyone*. "I mean, one minute he's just walking along, showing up at work with a smile on his face, and the next . . ." Molly handed Graham his water. She caught his eye and her poised exterior suddenly crumpled into tears of anguish.

Embarrassed, she tugged a tissue from a box on a nearby desk and, composing herself again, sat on the sofa. Graham reminded himself that Molly was a *colleague* of Jamie's, and not a sister or girlfriend. But there seemed to be more to the situation, and he gave Molly time to collect herself. "Why didn't this happen to one of those awful people out there? Why did it have to be Jamie?" she cried, getting herself a new tissue and flapping it in front of her face.

His years in the force had never afforded David Graham a satisfactory answer to questions like this. Why did it rain one day and not another? Why did *this* plane hit a mountain and not *that* one? Weren't these events just random? Well, perhaps. Or perhaps not. And it was his job to find out which.

"Molly, what is it that you do here?" he began kindly.

"We're a landscaping business, specialising in hardscaping and native planting. The size of our projects can be quite large, and we work across all the islands, mostly with clients at the wealthier end of the spectrum. We also have corporate clients. About sixty percent of our revenue comes from projects, the other forty percent from ongoing maintenance contracts."

"And what do you do here?"

"I manage the office, making appointments, liaising with suppliers, that kind of thing. Mr. Sanderson does the designing and project management work, but Jamie . . ." Mollie's voice cracked. After a short pause, she recovered. "Jamie was starting to take some of that off him, lighten his load."

"I see," Graham said. "So, a trusted member of the team." Molly nodded. "How long had Jamie worked here?"

"He started as a labourer about ten years ago but worked his way up from there and was learning the software, doing classes online. He wanted to take over the business or start his own."

"Can you tell me when you last saw him? We're trying to understand his movements before the attack."

"He came in to get his things yesterday around three p.m. He'd wrapped his job for the week, but we didn't talk much. Just 'have a good weekend' as he left"—Molly's voice broke again—"and I suppose he walked home. He lives in a flat near the high street, near the Foc's'le and Ferret."

"And after Jamie finished work yesterday, what then? Did he say anything about his evening plans?"

Molly shook her head. "I asked him, as you do, but he just said he was planning to hang out at home, perhaps pop round to his parents—they're close—nothing special. He wasn't—isn't—a wild lad, not much of a drinker. The girls like him, though. They often do—landscape gardener, good shape, tanned, good-looking." Molly's voice hardened. "Once that old girlfriend of his was off the scene, they started buzzing around. But he was pretty easy come, easy go. No one in particular. Hard worker. When he took a break, he often simply sat and read seed catalogues."

"Does he own a car?" Graham knew that Jamie did not, but it often amazed him what information was shared following a seemingly innocuous question.

"No, he has a licence so he can drive the firm's vehicles, but no car of his own."

"So, his job would bring him into direct contact with your clients and he'd travel all over the islands, is that right?"

"Oh, yes," Molly said. "He was well-liked; our clients would request him specifically. That's partly why Mr. Sanderson gave him more responsibility."

"And what had he been working on most recently?"

Molly straightened her green skirt and took a deep breath. "He finished the job up at the Granby place recently . . . That's the modern, custom-architected home up on the bluff. Do you know it? Above Crescent Bay?" Graham nodded. "They've recently renovated it, practically rebuilding it from scratch. The landscaping was the final part of the project. The place was worth millions *before*, but Mr. Sanderson designed them a fantastic garden and pool. Who knows how much it's worth now. Jamie was proud of the work they'd done. But once it was finished, he was straight onto another job just outside St. Helier. We're very busy right now. With the weather as it is, we have to make hay while the sun shines."

Graham's pen never stopped. "Now, I know this is difficult, but can you think of anyone who might have . . ."

Molly stopped him. "I haven't thought about anything else, not since I got the news. I was up all night thinking about it. I figured, maybe the same as you . . . that it could have been an old client who was unhappy with our work, or someone who'd felt Mr. Sanderson had ripped them off. I even called up five or six recent clients when I got in this morning just to hear their reaction to the news, to see if I could hear guilt in their voice."

"That's fine detective work," Graham said warmly, although he didn't approve. "Did anything come of it?"

"No, and I decided not to continue down the list I'd made."

"Why?"

Folded in her lap, apparently peacefully, Molly's hands suddenly clenched. They turned white. "I popped into the hospital. Shut up here and took off. Couldn't help myself, even if I couldn't get in to see him, which I knew I probably wouldn't. I mean, why would I? I'm not family." Graham raised his eyebrows, prompting Molly to get back on track. "But then neither was she." Molly closed her eyes and breathed in through her nose, pressing her lips together so fiercely they also turned white. "Anyhow, I didn't get any further than the ICU reception because I saw her . . . *She* was there. With that man of hers."

"Wh—" Graham heard a key in the front door. They both rose to meet Adrian Sanderson, proprietor of Sanderson Landscaping.

CHAPTER FIFTEEN

ADRIAN SANDERSON WAS a powerful man with a heavy build. Bulging forearms, the result of years wielding a shovel, protruded from his purple polo shirt emblazoned with the business's logo stitched neatly in gold.

"Adrian, this is . . ." Molly paused, having forgotten Graham's name.

"Detective Inspector Graham, Gorey Constabulary."

"Adrian Sanderson," the man said gruffly. He shook Graham's hand. The inspector suppressed a wince. Sanderson pulled up a chair and sat, his feet apart, elbows resting on his thighs, ready to hear what Graham had to say.

"Do they think Jamie'll . . . you know . . . wake up?" he asked, his brow knotted with concern. "We're all worried. My wife's in tears."

"I would be guessing, I'm afraid," Graham said. "And that's no use to anyone. I wish I had better news. They're doing everything they can," he added. "I'm down here making a few enquiries. We don't have any witnesses or motive as yet."

Sanderson nodded. "Fire away. Happy to do anything that might help."

"Can you tell me how you found Jamie as an employee? Miss Duckworth here has told me he was taking on more responsibility."

"He was a great guy, well liked. Never late, did everything he was asked to a high standard. He's been with us for ten years, practically since he left school. He was like family really. The business has thrived, in good part thanks to his hard work, so it only seemed fair to involve him more in the running of the business. He was a young, fit, strong man who wanted to go places. He was even studying for his landscaping exams. Terrible he should end up like this."

"Have there been any arguments with clients? Any complaints?" Sanderson shook his head. "He's been leading the team on the Granby place most recently, but they were overjoyed with his work. Mrs. Granby couldn't stop going on about it."

"Anyone been enquiring after him?" Graham tried. Another shake. "And you've never had a need to reprimand him or drug test him?"

"Not at all. He was always as fresh as a daisy when he arrived for work. Can't say that for everyone in our business. It's one reason why we don't work Saturdays as a rule. Too many hangovers from the night before. But Jamie was never any trouble. A model employee." Sanderson sat back in his chair. He glanced at his watch and jumped. "Look, if that's all, I'm late for a meeting with a fella at the lumber yard."

"One more thing, Mr. Sanderson. Can you tell me what you were doing last night?"

"Sure, I was at home with my wife. We watched the *MasterChef* semifinal. She likes that."

"Thank you." Graham made no move to leave. He offered his card to Sanderson who, with a jangle of his keys, made his way out. But before he left, Sanderson turned and said, his expression sincere, "You know this already, but I'll say it again: everyone's with you, Mr. Graham. The whole town. We want to nail whoever did this to Jamie. Anything you need, even if it's a potted geranium to help you get your thinking caps on, just ask."

The detective inspector nodded. "Thanks, Mr. Sanderson. We'll do everything in our power to resolve this."

Sanderson closed the door behind him, and they heard an engine start. "That wasn't all quite true. He was angry with Jamie," Molly said in a low voice. "A few weeks ago."

"Angry? About what?" Graham said, making more notes.

"The job at the Granby place. They worked together on the final costings. Mr. Sanderson wanted to charge a much higher rate, thousands more, but Jamie argued against it."

"Why so?"

Molly sighed. She split her ponytail in two and pulled to tighten it. "They talked about this all the time. Or should I say argued about it." She seemed embarrassed. "'Class warfare,' Adrian called it. Mr. Sanderson has . . . what shall we call it? An *elastic* approach to pricing. Says the richest people on Jersey should pay more than the others. You know, clients like the Granbys or that woman with the ridiculous dog, Mrs. Padalka-Lyons, or whatever she calls herself. They can afford it, Adrian says. Jamie didn't agree, said it was unfair, that everyone should pay the same. He said Adrian was punishing people for being successful. Adrian argued he was just levelling things up, Robin Hood-like, standing up for the little people.

"It was a bone of contention between them. When Jamie was ready, I reckon this would have been the reason more than any that he'd leave and start up his own business. That way, he could have run things the way he wanted. And if he did that, set up in competition with Sanderson Landscaping, things would get tricky for Adrian. The people are the business really. It isn't a lot different from hairdressing in that respect."

Graham made notes, giving Molly time to provide details. "Their arguments were brief and noisy," she said. "And once they had their say, they each seemed to forget about it until the next time. They would get on perfectly fine in between. Of course, Adrian won. It's his business. He can do as he likes. But there were tensions. It was the only thing they didn't agree on."

"Was there ever any violence?"

"No, none. Adrian might look like he could flatten an entire rugby team, but I've never seen or even *heard* of him throwing his weight around. Jamie neither."

Where have I heard that *before?* Some of the most memorable moments in Graham's career involved people finally realising the truth when some utterly trustworthy soul who "was devoted to his friends and family," the same decent, upstanding citizen who "wouldn't harm a fly," was arrested for having bludgeoned someone to death or something equally heinous. It was always "absolutely unthinkable," right up until it wasn't.

"Tell me about your hospital visit, Molly." Graham was beginning to wish he'd brought Harding with him. She would have done well with Molly.

"The ICU was so scary," Molly said candidly. "I was terrified there'd be an emergency while I was there, that someone would die. They all seemed *so* ill in their glass bubbles, strung up to machines and medicines."

"What about Jamie's visitors, the ones that bothered you?"

"Her name," Molly said, "is Paula Lascelles. She and Jamie were a couple for a long time, until about a year ago. I could never see what he saw in her. I thought she was toxic. Spiteful, manipulative."

"What happened between them?" Graham asked, keeping his tone low. "A fight?"

"Not just one," Molly recalled. "Plenty of them, for weeks and weeks. He'd come into work looking so depressed, wouldn't talk to anyone about it at first. But I've been through my share of relationship ups and downs, so I told him I might be able to help."

"Sounds like you were a good friend."

Molly glanced first at the front door, then at the back. Looking down, she stared hard at the carpet. "No," she confessed. "I was selfish."

"Selfish? How?"

"Paula wanted to leave Jersey. She said it was too small. People get all excited about big city life, but when they get there, it's not what they expect. That's what I told Jamie. He had a good job that he enjoyed, there was enough money. People liked him. He had lots of friends here. I told him, 'Making a change like that is risky, expensive in lots of ways you don't expect'. You know what I mean?"

"I do," Graham said honestly. He remembered his first move to the city as a younger man. It had been intimidating. His mind wandered to Roach. He wondered what the young sergeant had really made of his week in London with the Met.

"So, we talked it over, and I suppose I encouraged him to let her go. I mean, if she really wanted to be in London, paying those prices, with all that pollution . . ."

"You discouraged Jamie from leaving," Graham concluded. "But how was that selfish of you?"

Molly looked at the floor again. It was covered in the type of durable carpet tile that could withstand a nuclear holocaust. "I . . . wanted him to . . . stay." She quickly lifted her head, fire in her eyes. "I might as well tell you. I was—am—in love with him."

"Ah."

"Yes," Molly admitted, pain and regret overwhelming her. Her chin wobbled. "And if I hadn't persuaded him to stay, he wouldn't be lying in that hospital bed." Tears cascaded down her sweet, pretty, freckled face. "Now, *all* because of me, he's . . ." She sniffed. "Besides, he never even noticed me. I was just the 'girl in the office.' Just a mate. A helpful one, but a mate nonetheless."

"Molly, I'd like you to listen to me," Graham said. Her bright, tear-gleaming gaze rose to meet his. Behind the upset, he could see her hopes for some form of redemption. "The only person responsible for Jamie's situation is the person who attacked him. And we're going to find out whoever that was. You are not to blame, okay?" Molly gulped, her eyes still on his, her eyelids twitching. "One final thing. Where were you yesterday evening?"

"I was at my friend's house. Catherine Marsh. She was throwing a dinner party. There were six of us. You can confirm with her. I was there till gone midnight. I helped her clear up."

"Thank you. You've been very helpful, Molly. Stay in touch. Call me straight away, day or night," Graham said, "if you think of anything else, or if Mr. Sanderson says something I might need to know about."

Tears forming again, Molly nodded. "Okay." She quickly dabbed at her eyes with her tissue. "The new boyfriend, you should talk to him. Big guy. Very strong, like Adrian, but young and . . . well, Jamie told me about him. That he had been inside for something. Said he was a bit dense."

"Easily manipulated, you mean?"

"Hmph, he must be. Paula wouldn't be with him otherwise. She homes in on the easily manipulated like a heat-seeking missile. If Paula told him that Jamie was still holding a torch for her," Molly said, developing her theory out loud, "he might have done something, mightn't he?"

"And would there have been any truth in that?"

"What do you mean?" she asked.

"That the new boyfriend had reason to feel jealous?"

"I don't think so. But there wouldn't have needed to be any truth behind it for Paula to suggest something. I've known her for years, since school. She was nasty even then. Beautiful, but nasty."

"I can tell you're very fond of Jamie," Graham said. "I know this must be very difficult."

Molly blew her nose. "I won't deny it's been terrible since I heard the news."

Graham stood to leave. "Have I helped?" she asked, her hands folded, tight and anxious. "All I want to do is help. I want to catch who did this."

"Yes, you've helped very much."

Graham left her to make his way back to the station. He decided to take a detour that took him through fields. An ascending, bright yellow sun was painting them brilliant colours, and for half a mile, he chose to enjoy the play of light on the grasses of the meadow he walked through.

His phone rang. "Sir?" said Roach at the other end.

Graham knew from his tone that Roach felt he had something. "What have you got, Sergeant?"

"I'm still at the hospital, sir. Been keeping an eye on two of Jamie's visitors. Something just doesn't seem right."

Graham stopped amidst the quiet of the lane he was walking along and took a moment to be grateful for the instincts of his officers. "Don't tell me. Paula Lascelles and her simple bruiser of a new boyfriend."

Roach was silent for five seconds. When he spoke, he sounded indignant. "Well, sir, I have to say, that's hardly fair."

"Eh?"

"It's no fun playing 'cops and robbers' with you, boss. Not when you're bloomin' *clairvoyant*."

CHAPTER SIXTEEN

WHEN HE GOT back to the station, Graham found Barnwell manning the reception desk. "Did you find those lads?"

"Yeah, I did, sir. They weren't of any immediate help. But I've got my eye on them, and they're looking out for us. I'll follow up with them in a day or so if we need them."

"Fancy doing a bit of interviewing with me?"

It had taken three phone calls and eventually a threat to use his powers of arrest before the haughty and uncooperative Miss Lascelles agreed to attend the police station and speak to Graham on his patch. "Couldn't we have done it down at the hospital, sir?" Barnwell said.

"Wrong atmosphere." The efforts Paula had made to avoid coming to the station hadn't endeared Graham to her or her boyfriend. "I don't need them surrounded by compassionate people in blue scrubs making me look like a monster next to a barely alive victim. I want them staring down the barrel of my fully loaded interview technique."

"Going to go hard on them?" Barnwell asked. "Roach said we'd be right to. Reckons he's got a funny feeling."

"He's developing instincts," said Graham. "So, let's respect them. This couple dragging their heels doesn't look good either."

"Right, boss," Barnwell said. The constable, initially very reluctant to get involved in formal interviews, had become sanguine about them. Sometimes he even looked forward to their unpredictability. He didn't consider thinking on his feet a strength of his, but with practice, it was becoming easier to formulate a line of questioning on the fly when presented with new information from an interviewee. He was getting nimbler, but no one would be asking him to perform the police equivalent of the quick step anytime soon.

"This is very inconvenient," Paula grumbled to DI Graham as soon as she saw him. "We had to take a taxi."

"We were expecting you half an hour ago, Miss Lascelles."

"We got lost."

"I find that hard to believe. Every taxi driver on the island knows where we are. Follow me, please."

Graham led Paula and Matthew to the interview room, and the couple sat down at the table. Once they were settled, he closed the door and had a final word with Barnwell. "How many times," he wondered, "have suspects come in, all teed off and indignant, only for us to find . . ."

"That they're the guilty party?" Barnwell said. "I've lost count, boss."

Summoning a smorgasbord of wisdom, Graham said, "Remember, beer before whisky, horse before cart, and thought before speech. Alright?"

"Whatever you say, sir."

"Capital."

Graham swung open the door and found a study in human opposites. One was an attractive woman, sunglasses tucked into her blonde hair. She wore a white A-line dress printed with red tulips, belted at the waist. Around her neck was tied an expensive, bright-red scarf. Before she sat down, Graham had noticed Paula Lascelles wore scarlet shoes. He wondered how she walked in them. They had vertiginous heels. Under the table, Paula crossed her legs, a foot bearing one of the aforementioned heels jiggling furiously. Above the table, she rubbed the fingers of her right hand with the thumb of her left. She looked down at them, her lips pushed together in a pout. She seemed deep in thought.

Next to her was the muscle-bound six-footer with huge hands and a vacant expression who was her boyfriend. Graham had learned that his name was Matthew Walker. He wore a T-shirt with a brewery logo plastered across it and baggy shorts with pockets on the sides. He was as still as a statue as he stared straight ahead at the blank wall.

"Thank you for coming in. As mentioned to you earlier, this is not a formal interview. It will not be taped, and you are free to leave at any time. Now," Graham said, moving on quickly in case Paula felt like another round of complaining, "Sergeant Roach has given me the basics, so I won't keep you long. You are not under arrest—"

"I should think not," Paula interrupted.

"You are here voluntarily, helping us with our enquiries as we fill in some details around the attack on Mr. Reeves."

"Good," Matthew said. He pulled at the neck of his T-shirt. "Kinda clusterphobic in here."

Ah, excellent, we've identified the brains of the outfit. "I'd like to better understand your relationship with Jamie," Graham began. "And learn where you were last night."

"Why?" Paula asked at once.

"When investigating violent incidents, these kinds of things tend to interest me," Graham replied evenly.

"Wait . . ." Paula said, her jaw dropping, "you think *I* had something to do with the attack on Jamie?"

"I don't think anything, Miss Lascelles. I am simply making enquiries. Can you both account for your whereabouts yesterday evening when Mr. Reeves was attacked? Around ten, ten thirty p.m."

Matthew shifted in his seat, suddenly concerned. "I never even seen the guy before I saw him lying in that 'ospital bed all beat up. What's it gotta do wi' me?"

Barnwell was taking notes on his iPad, but he stopped and squared with Matthew. "Big lads like you and me," he said encouragingly, "get a bad reputation. Isn't that right, mate?"

"Yeah, I s'pose."

"People are always assuming we're brawlers, or rugby players, or the kind of bloke who'll sink nine pints on a night out."

Matthew smirked. "My record's sixteen."

"So, it's best if you remove any reputation you might have, however inaccurate, by answering our questions quickly and honestly."

Graham intervened. "Let's return to the evening in question. Where were you both?"

"At my mum and dad's place in St. Helier. Two thirty-two Trent Road," Paula replied. "We flew down from London for my nan's ninetieth birthday."

"What do you do in London?" Barnwell asked her.

"I'm assistant to the deputy head of European sales' executive secretary."

Barnwell was more concise in his notes: *Photocopying*. "And was Nana's party still raging on Friday evening?"

"It's tonight," Paula said. "I'm supposed to be helping set up, but I've spent the morning at the hospital and now here. My mum will *not* be happy. We were planning to go out last night, but I was tired, had a headache. So, we stayed in, watched some telly."

"What was on?" Graham asked. He was writing continuously.

"*MasterChef*. Semifinal round," Paula said.

"It was really good," opined Matthew.

"Who went through to the final?"

The big lad shrugged. "I went to the fridge a lot. Can't really remember. Not my thing, you know? But Paula's mum loves it."

"It was that woman with the red glasses," Paula said. "The one with the teeth. I forget her name."

"Yeah, her," Matthew agreed.

Paula gave a quick shrug and a small smile. "All those desserts make me want to eat for miles."

"What time did you turn in?" Graham asked, making very deliberate eye contact with them both. It was one of his oldest tricks, and it nearly always worked.

"Before midnight," Paula said.

"After twelve," Matthew said at the same time.

A raised eyebrow. "Could we perhaps reach an agreement?" asked Graham.

"Mum and I were going to take Nana shopping this morning," Paula reminded Matthew, her eyes narrowing, "and we had to do all the party prep, if you remember. It was going to be a busy day. So, I made sure to get to bed before twelve."

"Whatever you say, Paulie." Matthew shrugged.

"*Don't* call me that," she rasped.

"Can anyone verify your movements?"

"Mum and Dad could, but they went to bed at ten." *So, no one then.*

Graham moved on. "Tell us a little about how your relationship with Jamie came to an end."

The two policemen soon learned this was by far Paula's favourite subject. "I applied to colleges only on Jersey because of him. I limited my career choices, turned down interviews in London and Southampton, all for him. I *sacrificed* for Jamie Reeves, and when the time finally came, he just couldn't find it in himself to commit to me. Jersey always came first for him." The bitterness was right there on the surface. "I couldn't stand it anymore."

"So, you left?" Barnwell said.

"We took 'a break,' but I knew I had to move on. Nine years together . . ." she said. Each of those years now seemed to weigh on her, the memories poisoned by the ever-present "what ifs" and "if onlys" that always attend a relationship breakdown. "Nine years. What a waste of the best years of my life." And then Paula broke down, only comforted by Matthew's tree-trunk arm after an awkward delay.

Barnwell watched him closely throughout Paula's performance, and he did think it a performance. He looked for signs of anger or jealousy in the man but saw none. Matthew did seem to be as thick as a log.

In between sobs, Paula made a muffled sound. "I'm sorry, did you say something?" Graham asked.

"Molly was a problem," she said, sniffing. "I shouldn't be saying this, but you're investigating what happened, and you should know everything." Staring at her even as his pen moved across his notebook's page, Paula had the detective inspector's undivided attention. "She was very flirtatious. Jamie's a good-looking guy, it wasn't unusual. I was alright with it. Well, at first, anyway," she said. "If I did say anything, he would laugh it off. Said they were just workmates, colleagues, you know, just two people having fun, there was nothing to it. But I'm quite sure she didn't see it that way."

"Molly came between you," Graham commented. "That can't have made things easy."

"No, and that's another thing. He was really into Molly for a while. When he and I were on a break. At least that's what I heard. But he stopped it, thank goodness, when we got back together. Before we went on another break. A permanent one. After that, I don't know. It was none of my business."

"Stopped it?" Graham blinked. "Stopped what?"

CHAPTER SEVENTEEN

"**M**OLLY," PAULA EXPLAINED. "The other kind. Not the girl he worked with. Ecstasy. MDMA. You know," she said, embarrassed. "Pretty stupid to be telling the police, I suppose, but you should know everything."

The couple watched Graham pinch the bridge of his nose and almost laugh to himself, while Barnwell sat up very straight and typed into his iPad as fast as he could.

"So, you don't think Jamie continued taking drugs after you split up?" Barnwell said.

"I just said I don't know, Constable. It was none of my business."

"Did he ever mention selling anything, making any money?"

"No, no, that's not how it was. It was just for his own use, recreational," she replied. Then, more determined, "Selling? No, never."

Graham leant in. "It's very important that you're honest with us, Paula. You won't get into any trouble . . ."

"To my knowledge, he was never involved in the dealing of drugs."

"When was the last time you saw Mr. Reeves, Paula?" Graham asked her.

"When I saw him in his hospital bed."

"And before that?"

"A year ago, when I left. I haven't seen him since."

"So, no contact at all? No phone calls, texts?"

"We exchanged a few texts, but that's all."

"Anything recent?"

Paula eyed Graham warily but held his gaze. "No."

"Are you sure?"

"She said 'no,'" Matthew reminded the two officers. "More than once. That okay for you?"

"We prefer it when people speak for themselves, Matthew. Maybe we should interview you separately?" Barnwell's temperature had risen with the big man's intervention.

"Perhaps later," Graham said, closing his notebook, "but that'll do for now. Thank you for your time."

The pair couldn't exit the station fast enough, leaving Barnwell to consider events with Graham in his office.

"Turf war?" Graham surmised. "I mean, it's possible. Makes as much sense as anything. But there's no evidence. It's a big leap from knowing he took the odd molly to him dealing."

"Except for the fact he's now lying in a hospital bed in critical condition."

"Hmm. What did you make of Mr. Walker? Molly at Sanderson's said he'd been inside."

"Matthew? He's a big lad," Barnwell said. "Gives a bloke confidence to do certain things."

"Like what things?"

"Like defending his girlfriend during a police interview or against an old boyfriend."

"Very manly of him. But I'll tell you this," Graham announced. "There's more courage still in telling the truth. And I'm not sure if either of them have yet been guilty of *that*."

Graham began pacing between his desk and the office door, as he often did. "For two people who spent yesterday evening together, their versions of events varied a little too much for my liking. A young couple hitting a roadblock when alibiing each other should always be subject to more investigation. It bothers me that they didn't agree when they went to bed."

"It was just that one detail, sir," said Barnwell. "Easily done."

"No, Constable, they also disagreed about who won the *MasterChef* semi."

"Well, Matthew said he couldn't remember . . ."

"Answer me this, Barnwell. What kind of person watches an exciting hour of televised cooking and then completely forgets who finished first?"

Barnwell pulled a face. "Someone who can down four pints in that same hour?"

"Even if he'd been completely felled by drink, he can't have missed the soufflé. I mean, God knows how she did it."

As Graham started another slow, thoughtful perambulation about his office, Barnwell stared at him as he mentally weighed up whether to ask the question that was on the tip of his tongue. "You, erm, you managed to catch that one then, sir? The semifinal?" The very idea of Graham avidly watching a cooking show stretched credulity.

Graham stopped pacing. "Laura likes it. What's the problem?"

"Nothing," Barnwell said quickly. "Nothing at all."

"So, what's your theory, Constable?"

"I can see three possibilities, sir, all involving that goon as the perp." Barnwell's cognitive reflexes had smartened up in the time DI Graham had been his senior officer. He'd anticipated Graham's question and already considered the options.

"Okay, what are they?"

"Paula gets Matthew all riled up about Jamie and how awful he was . . . And then," Barnwell said, "in a moment of weakness, when his defences were lowered and his brains hobbled by drink, he takes it upon himself to defend her honour by bashing her ex-boyfriend over the head with a heavy object."

"Okay, next."

"She tells him to do it, sir. And he obliges because he's as thick as pig—"

"Yep, okay, got it. And the last one?"

"There's still something going on between the girlfriend and our victim, or Mighty Matthew thinks there is, and he decides to put his rival out of the picture." The two men fell silent as they considered the feasibility of these three theories.

Graham spoke first. "What do you reckon?"

"Bit much?"

"I can see it, just about. Neither of them are towering intellects, but he seemed like he had a gap where his brain should be. She seemed petty and chippy. Certainly unpleasant enough to wind him up, set the bomb off, then stand back and watch the chaos. Her mum's house is only five minutes from where Reeves was attacked."

"But are they capable of such a serious assault?"

"They could have overplayed their hand." Graham drummed his fingers on one of his old filing cabinets. He had a set of two that reached up to his chest. They predated the war and were made of solid oak. When laden with files, the drawers were heavy. Janice, Roach, and Barnwell complained every time they had to retrieve a document from one. The inevitable procrastination surrounding filing case documents would have risen to critical proportions had Janice not implemented a strict rota that, because they were his filing cabinets, even included Graham.

Filing was well below his pay grade, but the detective inspector shouldered the chore because he loved the cabinets, how they looked, and the sense of history they offered. He liked to think that they survived the war because they were hidden out of the Nazi's sight and had played a part in the resistance, storing important documents perhaps. It gratified him to think he still found a use for them.

"So, she's manipulative and resentful. He's a heavy, vulnerable to suggestion or jealousy, and there are inconsistencies in their stories," Barnwell summed up.

"Don't forget that she's lying."

"Lying, sir?"

"Yes, or at least not being entirely honest. Ms. Lascelles said she and Jamie had had no contact recently. Said so twice, decisively. Walker warned us off." Graham picked up an evidence bag from his desk. It contained Jamie Reeves's phone. "This phone, via Jack, says otherwise. Ms. Paula Lascelles has been texting Jamie Reeves in recent days, trying to set up a meeting. I wonder if she mentioned *that* to Mighty Matthew."

"Did Reeves reply?"

"No, and that might constitute a motive."

CHAPTER EIGHTEEN

IT WAS AS picturesque as anywhere on the island. A broad bay swept inland to the south and then curved outward to form impressive bluffs. There at the top, where the tall, white rock was met by cooling onshore winds, stood a two-storey home, palatial both in construction and setting. Up ahead, Janice saw it first, and like most people, felt immediately impoverished and envious.

"Not bad, eh?" she said to Graham, who was driving the station's unmarked police car with his usual care and precision. "What did you say the Granbys do for a living?"

"No idea what the wife does, but he's some kind of high-end investment manager. Friend to the great and the good and the extremely wealthy. The website's still there on my phone if you want to look at it." He nodded at the phone, stuck as if by magic but in fact by magnet onto his dashboard. Graham had come a long way in his willingness to adopt technology. Technically he was a digital native, having been born during the information age, but he didn't act like one. Encouraged by his younger subordinates, however, he was coming along, persuaded by the opportunities technology provided.

Granby Investments' webpage was smartly designed and reeked of affluence and luxury. Janice said, "I don't think my police salary would be enough for them to even open the door."

"Me neither," Graham replied. "But then we don't need money, Sergeant, just our police IDs. Gets us in places we'd never get in otherwise."

"I hope you're not suggesting what it sounds like you're suggesting," Janice said. She didn't approve of the availing of unofficial benefits that came with being a member of the force. She wanted to get places because of her own hard, exemplary efforts, not because of some favour she'd been offered because she was a copper. Although she had skipped the line in Ethel's a few times.

Graham hesitated. "Of course not. Anyway, Mr. Granby should prove a bit more welcoming in his own home. We'll avoid pouncing on him in his office until we need to turn the screws."

"Not sure we could even if we wanted to, sir. I'm fairly sure that one forty-five Marett Lane is an old stone cottage surrounded by wildflowers. Pretty, but small. Definitely not corporate."

"Hmm, just a business address then. Must do all his work from home. Wealth management is an under-the-table business—who you know, not what you know, special handshakes kind of thing. It'll be interesting to meet him."

They followed the quiet coastal road until it forked. The options were to continue down the coast or turn onto a freshly paved track that led to the Granby residence. Now they were closer, they couldn't see the house from their position. It was set lower down on the bluff and hidden from view. Graham turned, and they trundled down the narrow, tarmacked path.

A large, black security gate blocked their way. Graham stopped the car and found the intercom button on a pillar beside the gate. While he waited for a response, he looked around and noticed the discreet black camera tracking his movements. It emitted a slight buzzing sound.

In the car, Harding read more about Silas Granby and his work. His professional profile was littered with photos from all over the world—business meetings in Singapore, Cape Town, Athens, and London, and that was just the first page. In each of the photos, Silas Granby projected a smart, professional, smiling image whether photographed chairing a meeting or on the golf course. Harding wondered whether he would be as equally relaxed in private while questioned by a pair of police officers about a serious attack on someone who had recently completed work at his house.

"Ready to see how the other half live?" Graham said as he climbed back into the car.

Inside the security gate, in the middle of a bright green patch of closely cut lawn amidst an expanse of rough, a small flag fluttered on a pole. "His putting green has more square footage than the house Jack and I are looking for." Harding growled. "We would be happy with two bedrooms and a little garden. And it'd still be smaller than that piece of grass." She gave a strange, dismissive snort. The electronic gate swung open. They kept driving, and as they drove, the house materialised seemingly from the ground.

Two powerful cars—one black, the other a deep violet—were parked on a broad, gravel area in front of the house. They gleamed in the sunshine. Beyond them, more cars sat visible in a garage, a space which could have comfortably sheltered a light aircraft.

"Oh, wow," Harding said. "They *really* went to town, didn't they?" The house —*compound* might have been more appropriate—was perched on the cliff in a blithe defiance of gravity.

"Guess he's not worried about erosion then," Graham said. "This place is only a couple of bad storms away from ending up in the drink."

"Some people don't think they need to worry about things like that," Janice replied.

"Had to have got it through the surveyors and coastal people though." In response, Janice rubbed her fingertips together. Graham nodded. "Maybe. He might have offered them a cash incentive, but if he's that reckless with his private investments, I'm not sure I'd trust him with mine."

Granby's vision for his home was a pair of contoured, semi-subterranean wings. They emerged from the sloping ground, extending toward the cliff's edge. "Wonder how they managed that," Janice said.

"An architect who commands the highest fees in his profession, I should imagine," Graham responded. The walls at the back of the property were comprised nearly entirely of glass, held in place by only the smallest amount of concrete bonding. Even the ceilings of the rooms were made of massive glass sheets. All the light gave the Granby residence an airy, maritime feel, and surely some of the best views in all the Channel Islands. "Oh, I see how it works. It's nice, isn't it? But I can't figure out if the shape might invite people to jump off the cliff or aliens to attempt a landing."

"Either way, looks like a public safety problem," Janice said, thoroughly hacked off and resentful now. "But yes, sure, it's okay, I suppose." Then, a flash of honesty: "I'm just too jealous to admit it's fab."

They parked on the gravel by the two fancy cars and walked down three steps to the discreet entryway. Graham pressed the bell. As he waited for the door to open, he looked around and noticed more cameras—one above him, another at the corner of the house, and two on an outbuilding. From behind the door came a noisy kerfuffle. A woman was arguing with her dog, which was ready either to bolt for freedom the moment the door opened or savage the new arrivals. Graham couldn't tell which.

"The police!" the woman said, opening the thick, wooden door while still trying to calm her overexcited dog, a ball of fluff out of which poked two black, beady eyes, a button nose, and a pink tongue which, due to all the barking, was clearly visible. The dog was tucked under the woman's arm. "Now, why would they come to see us?" the woman asked her dog.

She looked in her early forties, although it was hard to tell. Janice suspected fillers, a nose job, maybe something around the jaw. She possessed a heavy East European accent and was dressed for comfort and exposure—tight, lilac leggings topped with a stretchy white tank top. There was also more gold about her person than Janice had seen in the jeweller's she'd visited shopping for wedding bands.

Graham waved his ID. "Detective Inspector Graham, ma'am. This is Sergeant Harding. I wonder if we could . . ."

Ceaseless in its yapping, the dog was apparently taking a dislike to these two guests. "Enough, Willow!" The woman patted the dog. It growled a warning but stopped barking. The woman looked at the two officers. "Sorry, he's a prize Pomeranian."

Graham ignored the suggestion that he follow up on this statement. He was not at all interested in the dog. "Are you Mrs. Katerina Granby?"

"Katya, please."

"We would like to ask you and your husband a few questions. We called earlier." Graham eyed the dog, which eyed him back as though Graham might suddenly spring at his owner's throat. "It concerns someone who worked on your landscaping."

"Landscaping?" Mrs. Granby said as though the word were new to her. "Ah, you mean the garden?"

"That'd be one way of putting it," Janice muttered before speaking more loudly. "This is quite a home you have, Mrs. Granby." The sergeant had not been quite able to adopt a professional detachment with respect to the interviewee's circumstances, and it showed in her tone. Graham shot her a "do better" look. Harding took the hint. She lifted her chin and lowered her shoulders.

Katya rolled her eyes. "All of this?" she said. "This is all Silas. All his idea. I would have been happy with a cottage, you know? But he says it's for his clients. But of course, please forgive me. You must come inside and sit down. I will tell my husband you're here." As Katya turned, she pressed one of a series of buttons on a pad mounted on the wall by the door.

Graham bid Janice go ahead of him through the marble entryway and into a remarkably spacious, bright living room. Once again, he noted the cameras. They were more discreet inside the house, smaller and recessed into the ceilings. Only someone hell-bent on security would have configured it into the very structure of the building. Far more usually, security measures were tacked on afterward. "Heavens," he breathed, momentarily gobsmacked by what he saw. "The *view*." Beyond the curve of a bespoke, off-white, semicircular couch, through the floor-to-ceiling windows, the English Channel glittered brightly, as calm as a daydream.

"My husband, he likes the ocean," Katya explained, setting down her dog and ushering the officers to the couch. Willow took a few paces then stopped, eyeing the guests from the middle of the room. "His parents had a place on the coast in Norfolk." She pronounced it *Nor-fork*, apparently certain this was correct. "He grew up by the sea." She gestured outside. "It makes him happy. Please, sit."

"Now I know," Janice said quietly to Graham, looking around, "what I want in our living room when Jack and I get our house." She followed Mrs. Granby's direction and sat, experiencing her very first, and probably her last, £30,000 sofa.

Graham did the same while Katya sat opposite on a high-backed chair. Willow sniffed around, still suspicious of Graham but content not to do him violence just yet.

"Now, you said the landscaping?" Katya prompted.

"Yes, I'm afraid one of the young men who worked on your project has been badly beaten."

Katya stared at him. "You mean beating someone at a game? Like, tennis?"

Janice took care of this. "I'm sorry, no. We mean that he was attacked. He was badly injured."

"Attacked?" Katya gasped. "But why?"

On his phone, Graham pulled up the good-quality photo of Jamie his parents had provided Roach earlier. "Do you remember seeing this man around your property? His name is Jamie Reeves." Graham tilted the screen and watched carefully as she took in the picture.

"Tall, yes?" Katya ran her hand from side to side above her head. "A tall man. And strong. They *all* were strong. There were three of them, and sometimes their manager guy, but I think I remember the man you talk about."

"How long did they work on your property?" Graham asked.

"It was . . . three weeks, nearly. Silas, he had so many ideas. You saw the golf place and the garage and everything? There was *so much* work to do. The young man . . . James?"

"Jamie," Janice said.

"He worked very, very hard. Super strong."

With Katya's memories of Jamie apparently firm, Graham pressed further. "Did you ever speak to him?"

"Yes, a little. I went out with the cups of tea on a tray. Like you English do. Chatted a little."

"What was your impression of him?"

"He seemed a nice man. We didn't speak much. Hallo, how are you? That sort of thing. He seemed a little more, how do you say . . . important than the others." She smiled quickly as she found the right words. "In charge." She shifted in her seat slightly. "Except for the manager guy, of course. He was the most important."

"Did you ever see him speaking to his boss, Adrian Sanderson?"

Blinking quickly, Katya searched her memory, but before she could answer, she was cut off by the bounding arrival of her husband. "I'm sorry to keep you waiting," Silas Granby said as he paced down a connecting hallway. He came from a darkened part of the house that was built inside the cliff top into the light, open-plan living area. "The different time zones, important phone calls, you understand. Ah, I see you've met my wife." Graham and Janice stood as Granby entered. They shook hands. Granby walked to stand next to his wife and took her hand as he leant against the tall back of her chair.

CHAPTER NINETEEN

GRAHAM ESTIMATED SILAS Granby was his wife's senior by about a decade. Looking more trim and fit than most men his age, Silas was good-looking in a silver fox kind of way, like he'd stepped off an aftershave advert. He had quick, curious, piercing blue eyes and wore a crisp, white, open-necked shirt pinned at the wrists by silver cufflinks. He had on navy trousers and tan leather shoes. Business clothes even when working from home. "What can I do for you?"

Janice succinctly explained the case. "Jamie Reeves, one of the landscapers who worked here until a week or so ago, was attacked last night in Gorey. He's in a coma. It's touch and go."

"Just awful," Granby said. "But what does that have to do with us?"

"We're here to find out a little more about him," Graham said. Granby dropped his wife's hand and moved to sit in a matching high-backed armchair. "Please, ask away. Happy to do whatever we can to help."

"Were you happy with the landscaper's work?"

"Yes, yes, I thought they did an excellent job."

"There were no disagreements?"

"Not with us. I have happily recommended them to my friends, and I don't do that with just anyone."

"What about relations between the landscaping team? Did you notice any resentments or arguments between them? Your wife said Jamie was in charge."

"Not between the team, but I did notice him and Sanderson having words once toward the end of the project. They stopped as soon as they noticed me watching them from a window. There was a lot of gesticulating and red faces." Granby paused. "There was even a bit of pushing. They were not happy with each other at all."

"Any idea what it was about? The argument?" Graham said.

"It was about the hours," Granby said confidently. "Jamie was a fast worker; still good, but quick. I've heard that Sanderson likes his workers to take their time, make sure to do a good job so the story goes, but I think it's more likely that he likes to stretch things out so he can justify their charges, which I can assure you are not the lowest."

As before, his wife addressed her question to the dog. "Silas always thinks someone is trying to cheat him, doesn't he, Willow?"

"That's because they *do* cheat me," Granby complained. "I don't hide that I've been successful. Some people try to take advantage."

"But you were happy with the work?" Graham asked. "The grounds certainly look first-rate to me." He looked out of the window at the pool and the sea that met the horizon beyond it.

"They were excellent," Katya trilled.

"Quite adequate," said Granby. "Like I said, I happily recommend them to my friends. A mainland firm might have done better, but I always try to use local businesses to help the economy, jobs, and so on. If they charge me a bit over the odds, so be it. I can afford it, and it keeps the wheels greased. I made an exception for the security though. I ended up inviting bids on that. I wanted a state-of-the-art system, the very best. Ended up with a Swiss company. Panic buttons in every room linked up to a private security firm. Even out here, they patrol every few minutes."

"We noticed the cameras outside." And inside, Graham thought but didn't add. From multiple angles. For a private residence, it was intense.

"Like I say, some people like to take advantage, but I'm not gambling with our safety."

"Sensible precautions," Graham agreed. "As a matter of routine, we're asking all of Jamie's friends and professional connections to account for their whereabouts last night."

Granby replied without hesitation. "I was coming back from Italy. A flying visit—literally. I was looking at a jet, but honestly, the yachts were more enticing." He turned to his wife. "Got back in the small hours, didn't I, darling?"

A little slowly, Katya caught up and recognised she was being asked to alibi her husband. "He is always flying. Up to London, then to Europe or China or . . . Timbuktu maybe!" she joked. "Meetings everywhere, money everywhere, never stops. Like a rubber baron, no? I told him once, 'Maybe buy your own plane!' It would be easier. Now he's doing that!"

Granby admitted, "It's tempting, honestly. But mostly my clients have their own jets that they send for me."

"Sometimes," Katya continued, "he spends so much time in the air, I think he's maybe a mix of a man and a bird."

"And you, Mrs. Granby?" Janice asked, politely steering her back on topic.

"I don't like to fly. Boat is nicer. The Med is my favourite."

"Your whereabouts, I meant," the sergeant persisted. "Last night?"

"Oh, I was here, at home, making some phone calls. Charity, you know." Graham's curious eyes indicated that he might not. "For the dogs," she said. Graham's expression didn't change. "The Champions Fund." Katya turned to her husband for help.

"My remarkable wife has a lifelong passion for show dogs. She bred Pomeranians in Hungary . . ."

"The north," Katya said. "Near Austria. Our dogs, they are *so* smart, so quick to learn! My family is amazing at the breeding."

Granby chuckled. "But seriously, Katya's had three national champions in five years."

"Oh, my Rufus, my perfect Rufus . . . I miss him so much." Katya sighed dramatically with the anguish of loss, one hand clasped to her chest, the other around Rufus's replacement, the obstreperous Willow. Katya lamented for a moment in Hungarian, as though praying over the animal's grave. "The *best*. Maybe the best *forever*." Janice eyed the puffball Katya was carrying. *Good thing dogs don't understand human.*

"Rufus was the origin of a powerful, new bloodline. A crossbreed which is . . . unique, only from Jersey," Katya announced proudly. "Nowhere else. I've been raising money to mem . . . mem . . ." Katya looked over at her husband again.

"Memorialise."

"Yes, memorialise Rufus," Katya said, still botching the pronunciation. "We lost him two years ago."

Graham ground his teeth in silence for a moment. "A memorial, you say."

"Yes."

"In what form?" Katya frowned at the detective inspector, not understanding his question or the subtext underlying it. "What kind of memorial?" Graham tried again.

Katya pondered his meaning. "Ah! We are having fundraising activities to produce more champion dogs and fund some prizes each year with Rufus's name on the cups. And a big dinner. Will be fun!"

"Thank goodness," Graham said. "I thought you meant you were going to stuff him!"

"Stuff him? What is this st— Hah! Ah, no. We already have plan for that." Katya pointed to a shelf behind Graham, where eight cedarwood urns stood in a row. "Each one of them is my dog. Here, I show." Katya stood up and brought one of the urns to the detective inspector. Engraved on the front was "Rufus, 2008 – 2020." "You might think this silly, but they are amazing animals. Difficult to train and keep. And others do not take them seriously."

"I'll allow," Granby said, "that it's a little bit daft, but Katya plans to take on some schoolchildren to teach them the ins and outs of the breeding process."

"We have a building we call 'Rufus's Kennel.' Would you like to see it?"

"Maybe later, Mrs. Granby."

"Okay," Katya said, carefully replacing the urn on the shelf and sitting back down. She pulled Willow onto her lap. "Maybe on your way out. Is nice."

Graham turned to her husband. "So, you were returning from Italy?"

"Yes, my assistant Cynthia can confirm."

"And you, Mrs. Granby, were home alone until your husband arrived. What time was that?"

"Uh, really, I have no idea. I was asleep."

"It was around one thirty," Granby confirmed.

"And despite seeing Jamie arguing with his boss, you had no disagreements with him directly?"

"No, absolutely not. Besides, if I had been unhappy, I would have spoken to Adrian Sanderson directly."

"Were you aware of any drug taking at all?"

"No, should I?" Graham raised his eyebrows. "Well, you should really ask Katya. I was away mostly and only communicated with Sanderson."

Everyone looked at Katya. "Drugs? Oh no, no. I see no drugs. Just good men. Hard workers. They do their job well."

On their way out, Granby and Katya led Graham and Harding to an outbuilding. It had a beautiful view of the northern coastline and was strewn with dog toys and an obstacle course. "Willow is in training," Katya said. The outbuilding was larger than Graham's old room at the White House Inn, despite him having had the largest, best-appointed room there. Graham suspected Willow's gourmet canine feasts might even hold a candle to Mrs. Taylor's full English breakfasts and Sunday roasts.

"Well, we appreciate your time. Good luck with your . . . memorial," Graham said, entirely unconvinced of its value. "If you think of anything else . . ."

"Of course, of course. Anything we can do," Granby told him, guiding the two officers to their car. "A terrible thing to happen."

"How might we contact your assistant to confirm your flight details, Mr. Granby?" Janice said.

"Here's my card," he replied. "Call that number and speak to Cynthia. She's in charge of all that sort of thing. I just show up and board the plane when and where she tells me."

"One last thing, Mr. Granby," Graham said. "Do you have surveillance footage of the incident between Mr. Sanderson and Jamie Reeves? You said it was recent."

"Oh no, I keep only a few days' worth of footage. I wiped it long ago. It has all gone."

"Ah, shame. Well, goodbye, Mr. Granby. If you think of anything, please let us know." Graham gave Katya a nod. "Mrs. Granby," he acknowledged.

The standard police Vauxhall looked comically graceless juxtaposed next to Granby's two shiny machines of a horsepower and sensuality the Vauxhall couldn't match, even if it was souped up for high-speed chases. Graham and Harding climbed in. "No wonder he went all in on the security system." Graham counted five cameras trained on them. He'd be overjoyed to have that number spread along the length of Gorey's high street. "You know what these are, Janice?"

"They're cars, sir." He could equally have asked about specialty golf clubs, fine wines, or any of the dozen 'one-percent' hobbies of which Janice knew next to nothing and cared about even less. "The four wheels give them away."

"Maserati," Graham announced. "The coupe, a model from about fifteen years ago. It's got a four-point-two litre engine, drives up to a hundred and eighty miles an hour." Even Janice had to be impressed with that, Graham reasoned. But her expression didn't flicker. "And this little weekend runabout is a Ferrari four-eight-eight. Goes all the way to two hundred if you tell it to."

"I hope he doesn't. In case you haven't noticed, sir, that's well over the speed limit." Janice tutted and shook her head. "Boys and their toys," she muttered.

"Point is, no insurer would have looked at him twice without a world-class surveillance suite."

"The added stress that comes with riches. My heart bleeds." Janice shrugged. "Makes me wonder why they bother making all that money in the first place, poor dears."

The display of such ostentatious wealth made Graham thoughtful about his career choices. A mind like his could readily have found lucrative work in the corporate field; equally, he could have joined the military and risen through the ranks. The latter would have earned him far less money, but he would have benefitted from a decent pension and a second career based on the first that was far more handsomely rewarded. But he knew nothing would give him the challenges and responsibility that came from a serious police investigation. And he'd made his peace with the trade-offs long ago. He wasn't sure Harding had quite done the same.

CHAPTER TWENTY

JANICE KNOCKED ON the door of 145 Marett Lane, Gorey. She'd dropped Jack off at the farmer's market and decided to follow up on Silas Granby's alibi. The address was the one stated on the Granby Investments website. Cynthia Moorcroft, Granby's assistant, lived there.

The address was as picturesque as any on Jersey. Terraced stone cottages lined one side of the quiet lane. High stone walls that hid large, whitewashed houses from public view lined the other. The lane was so narrow, Janice had parked her car tight against a wall to avoid blocking the road. This particular lane led to the beach, and Janice waited to cross as families carrying towels and other beach paraphernalia, walkers with poles, and cyclists passed her on their way to and from it.

The row of cottages she was aiming for was set back from the lane by front gardens that frothed with late spring blooms. Those at number 145 were especially unrestrained. Janice practically had to fight her way through them to reach the front door as she picked her way down the crazy-paved garden path. This was no conventional office, particularly one touted as the corporate home of a business with the name Granby Investments.

The door opened. Janice found herself looking at a woman's chest and immediately adjusted her gaze upward. The woman was easily over six feet tall in her bare feet. She was aged about sixty with grey, wavy, short hair. She wore a striped shirt waister with an apron over the top. She held her hands high. They were covered in flour.

"Ms. Moorcroft?" Janice said, flashing her police ID. "Did I catch you at a bad time?" The sergeant smiled.

Cynthia Moorcroft smiled back. "Not the best, I admit, but not to worry. I'm not at a critical point. My scones can wait. Please come in. I assume you're here about Silas's alibi. He said you might drop by."

Janice went inside. The rooms were small, the ceilings low, the windows few. It was dark until she wandered into the large kitchen, a modern addition at the back. Light flooded in through a skylight and French doors. The kitchen led onto a patio and walled garden that, like the front, fizzed with flowers, many of them, like the woman who lived there, tall and rangy. In the middle of the room, on a wooden table, lay the reason for Cynthia Moorcroft's floury hands. On a board lay a mound of dough and a rolling pin. A recipe book lay open at a page entitled "Soulful Scones."

"I can't offer you a scone, but I can make you a cup of tea. Would you like one?"

"That's very kind of you, thank you," Janice said. Cynthia pointed to a sofa next to the French doors before reaching for the kettle. Janice took a seat. For a quick moment, she relaxed into the squishy cushions, enjoying the sight of the garden through the windows, the sun on her face.

"So, how can I help you?" the older woman said as she clattered about making the tea. The kettle clicked off, followed by a gurgle as she poured boiling water into a pot.

"I'm just making enquiries. Mr. Granby said you could confirm where he was on Friday night. A young man who had recently been landscaping his gard—"— Janice fumbled for the right word—"estate has been attacked. He's hanging on by a thread."

"Yes, Silas told me."

"Did you meet Jamie Reeves, Ms. Moorcroft?"

"Please, call me Cynthia." Janice would do nothing of the sort. It was unprofessional. "I did not. But I heard they did a good job." Cynthia poured Janice a cup of tea and handed it to her. She brought over a hard chair from the kitchen table to sit on.

"What do you do for Mr. Granby exactly?"

"I'm his assistant. He does all the client facing stuff, but I deal with everything else. I take care of all his admin, his calendar. I schedule his meetings. I also handle many of his and Mrs. Granby's personal arrangements."

"Would that have included dealing with the landscapers?"

"No, Silas handled that himself mostly. He was deeply involved in the whole custom build. He worked with the architects, builders, and landscapers directly. It was pretty extreme. The house is his 'place on the water,' and he wanted to get it right. I didn't have much to do with it at all."

"And what about this cottage? It's listed as the corporate office for Granby Investments." Janice looked around her. "It hardly strikes me as that."

Cynthia blushed. She looked at Janice coyly. "A little convenience. Tax, you know. Perfectly legal. I work from here, and it forms part of my benefits package. Mr. Granby is a very generous employer."

"How did you get the job? It seems a cushy number."

Cynthia smiled, not in the least offended. "It is. A contact of mine knew I was looking for a job and introduced us. I had no experience in the wealth management world, but I'm a fast learner. I had no idea what I was letting myself in for, though. No idea who Silas was or what he did. But it all worked out."

"So, tell me about his movements for the last week."

Cynthia moved over to a desk against the wall and unplugged her laptop. Picking it up, she sat next to Janice on the sofa and placed a pair of half-moon glasses on her nose. She turned the laptop so that Janice could see the screen. The sergeant leant over to see April's calendar. Most of the days were filled with appointments. "He came back from Singapore on Wednesday and flew out to Italy, Turin, the next day. He flew back on Friday evening, arriving around six p.m."

Janice's mind whirred. Granby had told them he hadn't arrived back until one thirty the next morning. "Do you have a flight number and times for the Turin flight?"

Cynthia eyed her over her half-moon glasses. "Oh, no. There's no flight number. There are no schedules. This was a private jet, a private arrangement. I don't even know the name of the client. Silas often uses code names."

"Don't worry, I'll be able to get records."

"I doubt it. These are not the kind of flights you and I catch to Marbella for our holidays. These are discreet, personal arrangements. The planes are often sent by clients for Silas. Private jets are like cars to these people. They very much fly under the radar. Literally."

Cynthia closed her laptop with a click and put it aside. "You have to understand, Silas deals with people who possess astounding, unbelievable wealth. He knows their demons, their Achilles' heels, their secrets, and their scandals. He also knows where the bodies are buried. His is complex, delicate, highly confidential work that goes far beyond managing money."

Janice's eyes widened. "Like what, exactly?"

"He might have to manage the child who has been arrested or organise rehab for the one with a drug problem, deal with the ex-wife who's demanding more maintenance, or pay off the mistress threatening to tell. He's often asked to resolve family disputes and do the dirty work. More than once he has had to communicate to one child that they have been disinherited, while another receives it all. Much of his work is to do with protecting the image of the client to emphasise the stability of their businesses to the stock market or simply to protect their standing in society, but it often strikes at the heart of intimate and family relationships.

"High net worth individuals are not immune to tragedy, heartbreak, or chaos. Quite the opposite. Invariably, Silas is the person the client trusts most in the world before spouses and family members, sometimes especially them. He has less to gain. Normal rules, the ones you and I follow, simply don't apply. Rules are bent, ignored, or encouraged out of existence." Like Janice had at the Granby house, Cynthia rubbed her fingertips with her thumb.

Janice considered this for a moment. To her, a member of the police force, the idea that rules weren't followed was unfathomable and simply plain wrong. It upended her heightened sense of justice. She thought about the sacrifices she and Jack were making to save up for a home—the nights spent in, the value packs Jack bought at the grocery store, and the cheaper-priced, oddly shaped vegetables he scavenged at the farmer's market. They both put in so much overtime that they, a couple soon to be married, barely saw each other.

Cynthia closed her laptop and returned to her seat. She leant forward confidentially. "Between you and me, he barely needs a passport. Sometimes he doesn't even get off the plane. There's a whole world out there that is inaccessible to you and me. We can't gain access to it because we lack the wealth, class, and status. Almost nothing is handed out on merit, you know. Moving up in life is simply down to who you know and who your parents were." She sat back. "It's just the way it is."

"But how does Mr. Granby get these clients in the first place?" Janice knew there were people with a lot of money on Jersey, but unless they made their way into custody, the reality of them didn't touch her life. Sure, she saw the boats in the harbour, the big houses, the fancy cars, the odd helicopter, but to her it was just part of the Jersey scene. She felt sure there was still room for her on the island, especially if she ignored the house prices. But perhaps she'd got it all wrong. She had spent her early twenties working on boats owned by the rich, for the rich, and having seen them up close, she did not hold them in especially high esteem. But what Cynthia was describing was a world beyond that. No passports? No rules? A world where money meant no checks, no accountability.

"Most of it is done on the hush-hush. Personal contacts, recommendation by a friend of a friend, that kind of thing. The über-wealthy want people like them, people they can relate to and who can relate to them. It's very much a people business. And the most important currency is trust. These people tell Silas their deepest, darkest secrets. And he's expected to keep them."

Janice wondered if these secrets stretched to crimes. She was almost sure they did. "So, there's no tracking, nothing to prove Mr. Granby was where he says he was. What about the pilot? Aircrew?"

"Huh, good luck with that. They are sworn to secrecy and often don't know who their passengers even are. Many travel with just a pilot. Like I said, it is all done softly, softly; hush-hush. Shadowy figures climb aboard and, at the end of the flight, silently disembark to disappear into the countryside."

Janice frowned. This wasn't at all like her trips to Ibiza with her sister.

CHAPTER TWENTY-ONE

"I THINK SILAS Granby might be lying, sir. His alibi doesn't completely check out." Janice was back at the station, congregating with Graham in his office.

"How do you mean, Sergeant?"

"His assistant says he got back at six p.m., yet he says he didn't get back home until one thirty the next morning."

"Can you check with the airline? He probably flew Turin to Paris and Paris to St. Helier."

"That's the thing, sir. There is no record. He was flying on a private jet. Apparently, for people like him, it's all done on the down-low."

Graham straightened. The inconsistent application of laws, especially when it hinged on whether one was rich or not, offended him. He was aware of the fondness for "ghost flights" among certain elements of the Jersey population, and when he first arrived on the island, the chief officer had explained in fulsome detail why he should overlook them, but it didn't make their existence any easier to bear. And now they were interfering in the rigour of his investigation.

"Okay, let's make a note and bear it in mind."

Confused as to Graham's lack of concern over this seemingly important piece of evidence, Janice steeled herself to ask a question that had been playing on her mind. "We still on for dinner next Friday? I mean, if we still find ourselves in the middle of a serious enquiry and all."

"Yes." Graham was certain. "I hope we'll have it all cleared up by then, but if not, we'll make it a working dinner. We can discuss the case." Janice's face showed clearly what she thought of this idea. "I know, I know, but otherwise we'll have to cancel, and Laura's been looking forward to it. If we discuss the case, not the whole evening obviously, it'll assuage our guilty feelings, and you never know, we might have a breakthrough."

Satisfied, Janice returned to the main office. "Whassup, Bazza? That's some face you're pulling." Over the top of his screen, Janice stared at Barnwell's contorted expression as he battered his keyboard.

"I'm searching the databases for info on Matthew Walker. There's something not right there, I'm sure of it. We've heard that he was inside at some point, but I'm not finding anything on him. Will you have a go? You're the expert."

Barnwell stepped aside to let Janice do her magic. Her fingers flew across the keyboard as she cross-examined the database with the digital incisiveness of a top-flight barrister. After several minutes, she paused, then resumed her interrogation of the PNC. Finally, she let out a breath. "Nope, nothing. He doesn't appear, not even a mention of him. Never picked up, never fingerprinted. Not crossed our paths at all."

"I just don't believe it. He must be known to us. I can feel it in my water."

Janice sat back and folded her arms. "You know, only ninety-eight percent of the criminal records are on the database. If it was a while back, or the station that nicked him used an out-of-date process, it's possible there's a record of him somewhere that never made it onto the central system. You could see if that's the case. It'd be a long shot though."

"Hmm, okay, I'll think about it. It's just a hunch." Janice moved from the computer. "Has Jim said anything more to you about the Met? Did he do anything?" Barnwell was pensive.

Janice shook her head. "Not said a word."

"Do you think he's going to leave us?"

"Probably. I mean he has to at some point, doesn't he? He can't stay here forever. It would be a waste. And we can't really support two sergeants in a station this size."

"Hmm, I'll be sorry to see him go though. I thought he was a right ponce at first, but he's grown on me." Carmen, sensing Barnwell's mood, trotted up and put her chin on his knee. He rubbed her head absentmindedly.

"It'll be for the best, you'll see," Janice said. There was a bang.

"Anybody home?" Roach called out from the back.

"And he hasn't gone yet," she whispered.

In his office, Graham's phone rang. It was Tomlinson. "Alright, Marcus. You know what I want to hear."

"Yes, I do," the pathologist answered.

"So, Reeves is awake? Is he talking?" Graham asked excitedly. "Did he say anything about the—"

"No, David. I'm sorry." Marcus's tone carried the worst possible news.

His shoulders sagging, Graham slumped into his seat with leaden despair. "When?"

"Half an hour ago," Marcus told him. "The damage to his brain stem was unexpectedly severe. They did their very best to keep his breathing going, but too many other systems shut down. His family was with him."

"Damn it," Graham swore quietly. "*Damn* it." There was little else to say. "Thanks, Marcus." He pressed a button on his internal phone.

"Sir?" Janice said, walking up.

It took many seconds, but Graham realised he was gripping his desk as though preparing to tip it over. It never, ever got any easier. "Sergeant, we're going to have that working dinner no matter what, but I'm sorry to say that the Reeves case just became a murder enquiry."

CHAPTER TWENTY-TWO

The Gorey Gossip
Saturday, April 16th, Second Edition

Let's say I have a friend who's thinking about moving to Gorey.

On any other day, I'd be full of encouragement. I'd tell them: "House prices won't attract first-time buyers, they are insane, but the standard of living is exceptionally high. There's good weather year-round, the high street is terrific, so is the castle, and there's a new vibe to the historic, working port. The people are wonderful, and you won't find a prettier place to live in the whole world."

But then, I worry that my friend might ask a question that's much more difficult to answer: *Is it safe?*

This week, I'd have to equivocate, and that makes me desperately low. Small towns thrive on trust and generosity but fall apart amidst fear and suspicion. This week, we're left with a lot of questions, a grieving family, and a new headstone at St. Andrew's Cemetery. After battling bravely, Jamie Reeves succumbed to his injuries overnight, less than twenty-four hours after being attacked on Hautville Road, just down from the Fo'c'sle and Ferret. That he was able to provide no assistance whatsoever to detectives only compounds the tragedy.

My police sources have conceded they are no closer to

identifying anyone with a reason to attack Mr. Reeves. It seems the twenty-eight-year-old was savagely ambushed; the weapon has not been found. Sudden, unprovoked, violent assaults like these often point to robbery, but this was not the case here. So, do we have a mugging gone wrong or a personal attack? The lines of enquiry appear confused, and there is a worrying lack of evidence. The police are reluctant to discuss specifics.

I know that I speak for everyone in Gorey when I say our citizens deserve to feel safe, and that if we're to witness the next dizzying chapter in DI Graham's increasingly crowded career, we trust this investigation will be brief, successfully concluded, and result in the incarceration of the person or persons responsible for a very long time.

My repeated questions to the constabulary on this subject received no reply; DI Graham, if you read this column, please prepare your team to explain to Gorey's public just what happened on that not-particularly-dark road leading to the pub where Jamie was attacked. Was he simply unlucky? Or was something else going on?

If I told my friend that Gorey is a safe place to be, would the DI and his team make a liar of me? Because the simple act of being about Jersey at whatever time of night one might choose should never come with a penalty. We should be free to walk around at will without fear of our safety being compromised. This is as much a human right as breathing the Jersey air, browsing our shops, or taking tea on the waterfront. It's sad, but sometimes the actions of a tiny minority seem to threaten those rights and make us think twice about doing the most normal of things. Our constabulary is there to restore that peace of mind. The ball is now very much in their court.

CHAPTER TWENTY-THREE

WITHOUT A HINT of enthusiasm, Graham parked once more outside the converted suburban home from where Adrian Sanderson ran his business. They'd called ahead and found Sanderson returned from his meeting and Molly still there. He and Janice had just come from the hospital, having interviewed Reeves's distressed parents. It had been a draining experience but had not elicited any information that felt pertinent to their son's murder.

"So, are we going to confront Sanderson about the arguing, sir?" Janice said.

"I think we should ask, see what he has to say for himself. Bashing someone's head in just for expressing an opinion about the business's fee structure seems a bit extreme though."

"Money does the strangest things to people," Janice said.

"Did you follow up on their alibis?"

"Molly was at her friend's dinner party as she told you. She was there all night and didn't leave until the early hours. And Sanderson didn't really give us one, did he? Just his wife. She's not going to say different."

"Okay, I'll push him on that." Graham readied himself to tell Sanderson and Molly that a young man they'd liked, respected, even loved was dead.

"Come in," Sanderson began. His top lip shined. His face was flushed. Anxiety dilated his pupils. "Has there been any change?" Molly was beside him, anticipating news, her hands clasped.

Graham's face did much to convey the reason for his visit. "Could we sit down? I'm afraid I have some very bad news." Molly whimpered, and Sanderson led her to the sofa. "Jamie's injuries were not survivable. He died two hours ago."

Sanderson sat down in a rush. Molly cried out and brought her hands to her face, sobbing. Graham went to boil the kettle as Janice provided comfort and solace. When they'd coaxed the pair to take at least a few sips of sugary tea, Graham explained that some questions in the case were still pressing. Janice led Molly away so that Graham could talk to Sanderson privately.

"I'd like to ask you again about drug use," Graham said. "Did you ever see signs of Jamie using? Probably nothing heavy. Just party pills, that kind of thing."

Sanderson rejected the idea. "Impossible."

"Mr. Sanderson, everyone likes to cut loose a bit . . ."

"No, I mean, Sanderson Landscaping has a strict drug testing policy. Alcohol levels too. Random tests, the whole lot. My cousin overdosed. Wrecked the family. I'm very strict on that sort of thing. Jamie was perfectly fine with it and always clean."

Graham made a note. *Drugs. Different stories. Sanderson. Lascelles.* "Now I'm going to ask about arguments you might have had with Jamie."

Sanderson shifted in his seat. "Disagreements," he said. "Not really arguments. And certainly never violent ones."

"Okay, sir," Graham said, "but we've got eyewitnesses that told—"

"Told?" Sanderson said, suddenly furious. "Told by who?"

"I can't reveal that. Sorry."

"Well, what did they tell?" Sanderson demanded.

"That there were arguments—disagreements—between you and Mr. Reeves, even a physical altercation."

"A *fight?*"

Graham pursed his lips. "I wouldn't call it a fight exactly."

"Me and Jamie? He's off his rocker, whoever he is!" Sanderson appealed to Graham, his hands aloft in confusion. "I bet it was Granby, wasn't it?" Graham's expression remained impassive, revealing none of his thoughts. Sanderson was in full flow, however. "How did he see this, then? From his glass house? That huge greenhouse of his?" Sanderson snorted.

"Why would you think it was Mr. Granby?" Graham said calmly.

"Maybe he wanted to get me in trouble for his own sadistic enjoyment," Sanderson said. "Who knows with these rich, clueless idiots? They're never happy unless they can manipulate others, force them into subjugation! This is the struggle of the worker," he cried, "and it is his responsibility to *resist,* Detective Inspector. Listen, I never touched Jamie, not once."

Sanderson ran a hand through his sandy hair and stared at the floor as he clasped the back of his neck. After a pause, he glanced up at Graham. "Look, I might have the arms of a pro wrestler, but I bloody hate fighting. Gave it up when I was a boy. Never the right way to solve problems. Besides, if I had fisticuffs with one of my own employees on a client's property, they'd have cancelled the job and chucked us all off. Word would get out, and the business would collapse inside a month. I'd have enraged landscapers coming at me with gardening tools . . ." His face dropped. "One fewer now, I suppose." Sanderson rallied and sat up straight.

"Are you sure you never had words with Jamie? It's best to tell me, Mr. Sanderson. We can deal with it if it has nothing to do with the case."

Sanderson paused, then sighed. His shoulders slumped. "Alright, we did argue. Once, at the Granby's." His eyes flashed. "But there was nothing physical."

"When was that, Mr. Sanderson?" Graham asked him smoothly. Now he was getting somewhere.

"Three weeks ago. A few days before the job finished. There were rumours Jamie was getting too friendly with Mrs. G. Nothing serious, but they were flirty. Good-looking guy like Jamie, it wasn't unusual. Granby asked me to remove him from the job. I'm sure there was nothing to it, but I did it. It was for the protection of everyone involved. Felt bad though."

"And what was Jamie's response."

"He reacted badly. Told me it was nothing and berated me for believing Granby over him." Sanderson wiped his face with his hand. "Listen, it was awkward and embarrassing, but it wasn't violent, and it definitely wasn't something to kill over. We each said our piece and moved on like the adults we are . . . were. We never spoke of it again."

"There was nothing physical at all about it, not even minor, like poking or pushing?"

"No! And if that posh twit says otherwise, he's lying. Wish I'd never listened to him now. I might have wagged a finger at Jamie, but that was the extent of it."

"Alright, thanks, Mr. Sanderson. That's helpful. I've also heard that you and Jamie sometimes disagreed about the business's pricing structure."

Sanderson sat back, glancing away and batting a hand in the air, dismissing the suggestion behind Graham's words. "Nah, that's also nothing. We just had different points of view on the subject. We were fine. We went out drinking on occasion. He came to my wife's birthday barbecue last weekend. There's absolutely no truth to the idea that we were on bad terms."

"Can you confirm again for me what you were you doing yesterday evening?"

"Now, just hold on a minute," said Sanderson. "You asked me that earlier. You've come in here, I hope you remember, to tell us that Jamie has *died*. Molly's in pieces, I can hardly think straight, and you're asking where I was after already asking me once?"

"Just routine, sir," said Graham. "We do realise how it looks." Sanderson stared out of the window at a postman emptying a red postbox. "So . . . Mr. Sanderson?" Graham said, his eyebrows aloft. The business owner looked at him. "Friday night?"

"Like I said, I was at home with my wife. It was the *MasterChef* semifinal."

"And you were in all evening?"

"Yeah, erm, except when I went to the off-licence."

"And what time was that?"

'Bout ten."

"How long were you out?"

Sanderson pursed his lips. "'Half an hour? My local shop didn't have what I wanted, so I had to go to the one further down the high street—MacAdams."

"So back at ten thirty?"

"Yeah, *MasterChef* was still on. I mean, that soufflé. How did she do it?" He shrugged. "Look, I'll come down to the station right now if you like. Take a lie detector test. Give my DNA for analysis. Anything you want. But I had nothing to do with what happened to Jamie. You think my wife wouldn't have noticed if I'd come back having just clobbered one of my own employees?"

Graham kept it cool. "We appreciate your cooperation, thank you. If we need you further, we'll let you know. Now I would like to talk to Molly."

"Yeah, well, you be careful. She liked him. Don't know how much, but she'll be in a bad way."

Graham found Molly in the back room. She was staring out of the window. Janice was with her. The sergeant shook her head when Graham came in and warned him, her eyes active and concerned, not to press too hard. She left the room at Graham's nod.

The detective inspector quietly took a seat. "When we talked before," he said, his tone one of mild curiosity, "you mentioned that Jamie and Adrian argued from time to—"

"He didn't do this to Jamie," Molly interrupted firmly. It seemed the only thing she was sure about. "I don't believe that at all. Yes, they got a little cross with each other now and again, but it wasn't hate-fuelled rage likely to lead to murder. They would be laughing and joking ten minutes later. They were more like brothers, not mortal enemies. And . . . Adrian isn't like that. He's a pussycat. Takes care of his mum in the old people's home, charity work, you name it; he does a lot for the local community." Graham didn't tell her that just about every murderer he arrested had defenders like her.

Molly had turned to look out of the window at the yard behind the office. It was full of plants, gardening tools, and building supplies. "Whoever it was who did this," she said, her anger building, "will he go to prison forever?"

This wasn't the moment to explain the various forms of murder charges available under British law and the penalties that ensued from them, but there was no easy, accurate answer. "Probably. Maybe. A long time, certainly."

Molly turned away from the window to look at Graham. "I want to help. But I can't think of anything else I can tell you that might be useful."

Molly was struggling to manage the hot flame of her grief-fuelled anger. Graham knew that over the coming days she would experience a powder keg of competing, conflicting emotions. As far as he could tell, she was both entirely honest and deeply upset. The rest of her weekend would be spent in tears, grieving for someone she'd called her friend. A man she might have liked to have called something more had fate not intervened so cruelly. But there would be frustration, too, at the inevitable slow pace of the investigation, and plenty of that red, unfading anger known only to those who have no way of directing it. Those who have no one—as yet—to *blame*.

Waiting patiently in the reception area, Janice completed her notes. She'd confirmed with Sanderson what he had said to Graham and, having elicited no new information, she wrapped up his statement.

"What did Molly have to say?" she said as she and Graham walked outside.

"Not much. I've wondered if she might have orchestrated something, got someone to do the dirty for her, but on my reckoning, she's either a supremely talented actress or she was genuinely in love with Jamie and can't believe he's dead."

"She has a concrete alibi too, remember? What about Sanderson? He's changed his story with the visit to the off-licence."

"Yes, he has. Please check it when we get back. Technically, he could have done it, but I think he's telling the truth. Could all be a play, but I don't get the sense that his and Jamie's problems went beyond workplace disagreements."

"But what about the thing with Mrs. Granby? Employee fraternising with the client. Could have put his business at risk."

Graham closed the driver's door and sat behind the wheel for a quiet moment. He looked up at the landscaper's premises. Baskets overflowing with pink, white, and blue flowers hung on either side of the door. Tubs with yet more flowers sat on the ground. Nothing else distinguished it as a gardening, or even a creative business. "Yeah, but would you really kill someone over that?"

"He might not have, but what about Mr. Granby?"

CHAPTER TWENTY-FOUR

BARNWELL AND HIS brother were back at their table, sitting in the same wooden seats as Friday evening. It was lunchtime, and the pub was filling with diners looking for a hearty Sunday roast.

"Alright, let's try this again," Barnwell said, "but without the sudden head trauma and pouring blood."

"This is what I wanted you to see," Steve said. He had the family photo album in front of him again, turning the pages. "Look, photo after photo, every few months, no interruption for years. Pictures of you, me, us, all of us. Then"—Steve turned another page—"we skip a whole year. Look, we're much older in this photo. I remember that bike; it was yours, then it got handed down to me and you got a new one." He growled. "You always got the new kit. I had to make do." Steve took a swig of his pint. "In this picture, I could barely reach the pedals." He pointed to a photo three over. "But here, look, I was too big for it. And there are no family photos for two more pages."

The pages were filled with classic family childhood shots attached to the album with neat, white photo corners. Birthdays, Christmases, family holiday shots. One showed Barnwell in costume as a police officer. He looked about six, maybe seven. "Even then, you were determined to arrest people for a living," Steve said.

"Can't really remember wanting to be a copper," Barnwell said honestly, "until I spoke to a bloke at a school careers fair in my teens. I signed some things, went for an interview, and then everything happened at once. Look, what's the point you're trying to make?"

"Don't you think that's odd? That there's a big jump in the photos and none of the family for two whole pages after loads of them in quick succession?"

"Not really. I mean, so what? A few photos fell out."

"But then there'd be empty slots."

"The camera broke then? Lord knows we weren't flush enough to make buying a new one easy. Perhaps they had to save up."

"But cataloguing family memories with photos is a basic parental duty. It was a priority for Mum. After she died, I went through all their things, remember? Took me ages. There were boxes and boxes of photos from our childhood. You know what Mum was like, so organised. Date and place on the back of every photo. Our ages. What we were doing. She left nothing to chance. And yet for the years 1993 to 1994, there are some photos of us, a few of her, but none of Dad or all of us together."

"Maybe Dad just got tired of being in them, or he was behind the camera. Hey, don't look at me like that. It's possible. Selfies weren't a thing then." Barnwell turned to the album, flicking back and forth between the pages. The Barnwells had been a tight unit, their dad a stern, uncompromising man and their mum acting as the perfect foil. She had given Barnwell and his brother the hugs and love they needed, and despite often straitened circumstances, magicked birthday parties, Christmas presents, and holiday fun seemingly out of nowhere. Barnwell had adored her. "What about Uncle Pete and Auntie Elaine? Remember their study? All those little mementos of this and that? Perhaps they know something if you're looking to fill in some gaps."

"Uncle Pete didn't know who I was when I called," Steve said. "He's not well, mate."

"Poor sod. What is he now, eighty?"

Steve puzzled it out. "Four years older than Dad, so eighty-three."

"Was Auntie Elaine more helpful?"

"Not really. Kept talking about her knees."

"Shame. It's a pity we can't get her to take to technology. It would really help with keeping in contact. It annoyed me that Mum and Dad were so reluctant to use it."

"I could have taught Dad to type and use the internet on his own. But you know what he was like . . ." Steve said.

"And Mum told you not to," Barnwell remembered. Basically, once Mrs. Barnwell realised the internet was a pipeline for pornography and gambling, she put as many roadblocks in her husband's way as possible. Their retirement was spent almost entirely together, mostly in the kind of content-to-rub-along happiness people work all their lives to finally enjoy.

"She told me," Steve recalled, summoning an exaggerated but hilarious impression of their mother's voice, "'I won't spend our twilight years bothering an old man to get off the internet or stop playing a game. I'll take a sledgehammer to the thing before . . .'" He broke into laughter, which was mostly Barnwell's fault; he'd always loved Steve's impression of their mother.

They were brought back to earth by a curious and unexpected presence at the bar. "Oh, you're kidding," Barnwell muttered. "Look what the cat dragged in."

"Cat?" Steve asked, reluctant to turn away from his reminiscences. He glanced over to see who his brother was talking about. "Mr. Muscles there?" Steve was thrilled. "Am I gonna get to see you *arrest* someone finally?"

"I'll arrest *you* if you don't pipe down. Give me a second, alright?" Barnwell rose. "Just want to check in with him." Steve raised a glass to salute his brother's diligence and turned back to the album.

The constable covered the distance between him and his quarry before Walker had time to react. "Now then," Barnwell said cordially, inserting himself into a small, conveniently open stretch of bar next to the man.

"Eh?" Matthew looked tired and a bit unsteady. "Oh, it's you."

Barnwell assessed the amber dregs of the pint in front of him. Matthew's eyes were rimmed in a similar colour. "Stinky Bay IPA, if my eyes don't lie." Barnwell estimated that Matthew was on his fifth or sixth pint. He signalled to Lewis that his latest should be Matthew's last. "Rather sophisticated, isn't it? I'd have wagered you were more of a lager man."

"Doesn't really bother me," said Matthew. "Gets the job done, dunnit? You 'avin' one?"

"Not right now," Barnwell said. "First, I wanted a little chat if that's alright with you."

Matthew wobbled; to Barnwell, the collapse of such a mighty frame spelled certain disaster. There was no telling where he might land, or what—or who—he might take with him.

"Wotcha wanna know?" Matthew's face was flushed and fleshy with booze. Barnwell could smell fish and chips on his breath. "Something about the poor bloke what got himself beat up? Then kicked the bucket. Paula's"—he swayed—"*ex*."

"Yeah. Can you help us a little bit more, mate?"

"Am I a 'person of interest'?" Matthew seemed buoyed at the thought.

"That's what the Americans call it, Matthew. To us, you're just someone we want to speak to 'in connection with a case.'"

Matthew nearly spat out a mouthful of beer. "You need to get something a bit snappier than that."

"Alright," Barnwell said, a little more steel in his tone. "Let's just call you a 'person helping us with our enquiries.'"

"That's hardly any better." Matthew wiped his mouth angrily with his hand.

"Until we prove you aren't one."

"And 'ow do I—?"

"Can you assure me," Barnwell said, pausing to make sure he had Matthew's undivided attention, "that you were with Paula all evening?"

"Yeah!" he blurted. "We told you, we watched the—"

"Yeah, yeah, *MasterChef* semi. But convince me. Tell me you didn't go out and whack Jamie because Paula asked you to."

Continuing to sway slightly but saying nothing, Matthew paused to process the question. "Me, like?" he asked quietly. "Wallop some posh girl's ex-boyfriend? *My* posh girl's ex-boyfriend? Because she told me to?"

Barnwell's worst expectations were of a violent reaction, but Matthew seemed more offended by the accusation. "Am I under arrest?" he asked a little too loudly. Watching yards away, Steve Barnwell set down his pint in hopeful expectation of seeing his brother swoop into action.

"No, you pillock," Barnwell said. "Keep your voice down."

"Where I grew up," Matthew said at only a very slightly lower volume, "people didn't make friends by throwing acc-acc . . . things around."

Barnwell raised his hands. "We're just having a friendly chat." His eyes hardened, and he leant forward. "Aren't we?"

Matthew recoiled and glared at him. His corpulent, aggrieved expression reminded Barnwell of a baby who was seconds from bursting into tears.

"What can you tell me that will force us to eliminate you and Paula? So we won't need to think about your connection to the case anymore."

"We ain't got no bleedin' connection," Matthew promised. "Only that Paula used to go out with this digger bloke . . ."

"Landscape architect," Barnwell said.

"He sticks trees in the ground," Matthew argued, "'cos a computer told him to. That ain't *architecting*, mate." He grinned with satisfaction that he'd got his words out right this time. "Look, I never even met him, alright? Not when he was alive," Matthew continued, keen to clear things up. "Not until he was laying there in 'ospital, looking as sick as a dog. Paula said he loved livin' in this out-of-the-way place in the middle of the sea for whatever reason. I don't get it. Do you? Why'd you want to be stuck out 'ere? Miles away from civ-civ . . ." Matthew screwed his eyes up with effort. "*Civilisation*."

Never slow to stand up for his adopted home and seeing a chance to take some of the drunken aggression out of the atmosphere, Barnwell turned to the windows which faced the marina. "Look at that. Sunset on the water, fishing boats. Paradise. Anyway," Barnwell said, turning back, "what else did Paula say?"

CHAPTER TWENTY-FIVE

"REMEMBER WHEN YOU told me, like, us big lads, we're always gettin' into trouble 'cos people think we've been fighting?" Matthew belched with commendable discretion. The pub would have been at risk of destruction by the sonic wave otherwise.

The remains of Matthew's drink had somehow disappeared in the few seconds Barnwell's back was turned. *All the signs of a competitive drinker.* Barnwell had lurched in the same direction himself long ago, to his cost. But in Gorey, since working with Detective Inspector Graham, Barnwell had lived a life so different that he might have believed he was carrying around someone else's memories.

"Yeah," Barnwell said.

"Opposite with little blokes like Jamie, innit?" Matthew said. "The ones that look like . . . what do they call them? Metrosexuals, that's it. No one ever thinks they'd be up to bad fings."

"But you think Jamie was?" Barnwell asked. "Did Paula say that?"

"She just kept saying he could be difficult, hard to be around, you know?"

Barnwell most certainly didn't. Thus far, Jamie Reeves's character references had confirmed only that he was thoughtful and decent, and that he appealed to the ladies. "What do you think she meant?"

Matthew shrugged his shoulders. "I dunno. She says a lot of things. I don't listen to half of it. She was always going on about him. Jamie this, Jamie that. Sometimes she'd be nice about 'im. Other times . . . She never said he hit her or nothin', just that she couldn't stand him. If she wasn't my girlfriend," he said, bashful for a second, "I'd be a bit susp—" Matthew gave up trying to express himself with long words. "Ugh, you know what I mean."

Barnwell blinked a few times. "Mate, men don't normally incriminate their girlfriends in serious crimes."

"It's just the things she's said. I'm sure she didn't do nuffin'." Matthew picked up his glass before seeing it was empty. "But she does go on. Bears a . . . what is it?"

Barnwell waited. He didn't want to be putting words in Matthew's mouth. The heavyset man searched his brain and finally found what he was looking for. "A grudge, that's it. Yeah. But then she couldn't say enough nice things about 'im in the 'ospital. Said he was charmin'. And very good-lookin'. Usually."

"Tends to happen when a person's at death's door." Barnwell stuck his hands in his pockets and rocked back on his heels. "Alright, you're done here. Stay out of trouble and get yourself home."

"Righto, ta." Matthew pushed himself away from the counter. He wobbled again but remembered to pick up his jacket. Barnwell watched him walk precariously to the door, half expecting to need to leap forward to catch him if he fell. Matthew successfully crossed the room to the heavy wooden door. He even negotiated the process of grasping the handle, opening the door, and manoeuvring himself outside in the right order.

Satisfied that Walker would make it home, Barnwell returned to his table. "Sorry about that," he said to his brother.

"Were you laying down the law," Steve asked, "or lending him a tenner? Seemed a bit chummy."

"He's just someone on the periphery of a murder enquiry. Probably just a well-meaning, average bloke," Barnwell said, starting to relax. "Well, perhaps a bit below average, but someone who's got himself caught up in something beyond his comprehension."

"Through no fault of his own?" Steve probed.

"I wouldn't go that far. Guys like him are mostly unlucky. Or hanging out with the wrong crowd. Some are complete idiots, granted." Barnwell thought again of the rumour that Matthew had been jailed for an offence that he couldn't find any record of. "Anyway, enough of that. Where were we?"

Steve tapped the photo album. It took a second for Barnwell to adjust his focus. "What?"

"These photos." Steve leafed through the album again.

Barnwell watched snapshots of his childhood parade across his vision in a tiny evocation of what had been surely a full and complex life thus far. "It's just a few missing photos, bruv."

Steve shook his head, still staring at the photo album. He looked up with dark, serious eyes. "I don't think so, Bazz. He was away."

Barnwell searched for a memory, but nothing bubbled up. "Away?"

"When we were little," Steve said.

"How long? When?"

"For about eighteen months. When you were nine and I was five." Steve added some other family details to accelerate Barnwell's train of thought. "We were in that flat above the chippy, remember? Before we moved to the house on Palmerstone Street."

The wheels of Barnwell's mind were moving, but accumulated rust was slowing things down. "I've got almost nothing, you know, from before that move." Barnwell tapped his temple in disappointment. "I do remember the smell though. Who knew living above a chippy would follow you around for the rest of your days?"

Steve kept trying. "Mum worked at that building supplies place, the one with the big yard out back."

Wait. "The place with the shed where we used to play on Saturday mornings?"

"Remember the manager would tell us off for playing tag around the concrete slabs?"

"Yeah, well, I don't blame him. One slip and it'd be all over for us. It was a dangerous place for kids, especially as young and feral as we were." Piled-high bags of cement and stacks of bricks had provided the perfect cover for their childish games.

"But don't you see? We were there because Mum had no one to look after us. Dad *wasn't* there. Just like he wasn't in the photos."

It took longer than Steve had expected, but then Barnwell said, "Hang on . . ."

Steve gripped the table as though threatened with being whisked away against his will. "It's coming, I can tell! We're off down Memory Lane!"

"The North Sea!" Barnwell exclaimed.

"Finally, mate. How's that Sherlock Holmes detecting thing coming along, eh?"

"He was on the rigs."

"That's what they told us, yes."

"Highly skilled work, good money." Barnwell pursed his lips. "Pity we never saw any of it."

"Right. How long do you reckon he was gone?" Steve said.

"Well, if this gap in the photos is anything to go by, about eighteen months I reckon. Look, there's a photo of us all under the Christmas tree. Tough work on the rigs," Barnwell said. "Stuck out there in the North Sea. Living in confined quarters with other blokes. Limited entertainment. They didn't have phones or the internet back then."

"But," Steve said, closing the album, "doesn't it strike you as funny that he did that?"

Barnwell shrugged. "No."

"Really? You're telling me that Dad took off for months to go hundreds of miles away to live and work the middle of the North Sea, leaving his missus with two small kids, to do something he'd never done before or since? For what?"

"Money," Barnwell said simply. That was the history he'd always understood. "Can't have been fun. Perhaps they had money problems and this was a way to fix it. Or maybe it was a short-term stint to build up savings for a deposit, buy a house, get a leg up." Barnwell was warming up now. "They always were good with money. Remember when Mum would mash up end bits of soap into a pocket she'd cut in the side of a sponge? Makes perfect sense. Thrifty. Waste not, want not; that's what Mum always said." Steve looked at his brother like he'd gone mad.

"But money was *tighter* when Dad came back from wherever he was, not easier, Barry. Don't you remember? He had a steady job before, he worked at the factory, the one at Box End before he went away to the rigs. When he came back, he was out of work, hanging around the home for ages. We were particularly skint as I remember it."

"You were only five, you can't trust your memories at that age."

"Oh yes, I can. I remember we had to keep moving and we'd do it late at night. Mum'd make it into a game, but I distinctly remember being fed up about it because one day I'd be at a school with my favourite teachers and friends, the next I'd be somewhere new, knowing no one. I'd have to make friends all over again at the new school, then it would happen again. And remember when those men came? They took the TV, the microwave, even the iron. I heard Mum crying to Grandma. They thought I was playing in the other room, but I heard them talking. They called them a word I'd never heard before—'bailiffs'. Why would they be coming around if we were flush with oil rig money, eh?"

"I can't remember any of that."

"You were always out with your mates. I was too young. I was with Mum."

"Look, what are you trying to say, Steve? That something was going on? That things weren't all that they seemed? That he didn't go on the rigs?" Steve didn't say anything. "D'you think Dad left Mum or something? Had a fancy woman and ran off with her and spent all his money until, seeing the error of his ways, he came back, and nothing was ever said about it? And they made up the story about the rigs as a cover?"

"That wasn't exactly what I was thinking, no."

"Then what?" There was a disturbance behind them. Barnwell took his eyes off his brother and turned to see what was going on. "Ergh, it's them again."

Steve turned. "Who?"

"Duncan Rayner, Kevin Croft, and Neil Lightfoot, otherwise known as DKN, otherwise known as a trio of oiks." Duncan, Kevin, and Neil had rolled in, laughing and pushing as they came through the door, disturbing the quiet, convivial hubbub of the pub.

"Like a handful of bad pennies, they are," Barnwell said. "They take up far more oxygen than they deserve."

Disturbed for the second time that lunchtime, the look in Barnwell's eye was one of determination mixed with barely restrained aggression. He stood to engage the unruly group. His brother grinned and rubbed his hands. "Watching you do your thing, bruv, is life. Have at it."

CHAPTER TWENTY-SIX

"EASY FELLAS," BARNWELL said, arriving at the bar where the three young men gathered. "No need for us to be rushed or uncivilised, is there? Not in a place like this."

"It's a *pub*," Kevin Croft sneered. His tracksuit was as sloppy and low-slung as it had been the day before.

"In Jersey's history, pubs have always been known as centres of discussion and moral improvement," Barnwell said, repeating something he'd heard Graham say. He'd committed it to memory, suspecting it might one day come in useful. "And today, the Fo'c'sle will be a place of honest recollection and unstinting public service." It was not an invitation but an instruction. Barnwell was in no mood for any messing around.

"Oh, bloody 'ell. Does that mean I have to clean out the bins at the marina again?" Neil moaned.

"*Public* service, not community service, you plonker," said Duncan Raynor, who seemed almost as tired of his friend's plodding manner as Barnwell. Bazza noted that Raynor's poorly judged haircut didn't look so bad today. It didn't accentuate his unattractive features quite so much.

"I trust you've all had your ears wide open like I asked?" Barnwell said.

"Wider than a mile," Kevin confirmed. "Ain't heard nothin'."

"A man is brutally attacked, yards from one of the busiest parts of town," Barnwell marvelled, "and people who literally spend their entire lives in just that same area, they're . . ." He chuckled as if he found it funny just how *unlikely* it seemed. "They're telling me they've heard *nothing whatsoever* about the case?"

Duncan set down his pint and made one of his more cogent points. "Look, mate, I have to ask you this. What is it about the three of us that makes you so sure we're best friends with all of Jersey's finest muggers?"

"Reputation," Barnwell said honestly. "Past encounters with the constabulary," he added, leaning heavily toward Neil Lightfoot, Roach's second arrest. "Dress sense. Daytime schedule. A few other things."

"That's like us asking you if you know Sherlock Holmes just 'cos you're a copper," Neil countered.

"That's not a real person, dimwit," Duncan said, not smart enough to understand that Neil's analogy was spot-on.

"Oh, I don't know," Barnwell said. "We actually have a Sherlock Holmes type back at the station. He's very keen to meet the three of you."

"I'm not going back to the police station," Neil stated firmly, "unless you slap me about, zap me with a taser, and put me in 'andcuffs."

"And I won't go," Duncan said, equally sure, "until I've taken a nice close-up video of you zapping Neil. After that, I promise I'll cooperate. Right after I've loaded it onto my socials."

"Calm down. No one's zapping anybody," Barnwell said. "Focus. What about drugs?"

"No, thanks. I'm trying to give them up." It was Duncan who couldn't resist.

"Should you really be encouraging that kind of thing?" Kevin wondered.

"Shut it, all of you," Barnwell said. "I'm here bothering you lot because some poor guy is dead. We've got a public who's scared witless and a tourism industry that relies on low crime and high cleanup rates. Work with me, fellas. It's in all our favours. Less banter, more intel. Give me something useful."

Thoughtful and quiet, the three went into a huddle. There were hisses of disagreement, mutters of concern, an "oooh" of appreciation. The three parted once more. "My learned colleagues and I," Duncan announced, pompously, "have concluded that it's in your best interests, in this particular circumstance, to speak with Beetle."

Seventy-three percent sure he was about to hear a cartload of rose fertiliser, Barnwell managed to say, "Beetle. Really. Do say more."

"He's plugged in," Duncan promised.

"To the matrix," added Neil for some reason.

"*Connected*," Kevin said. "Like, you know, to the *network*."

"You mean he's a seasoned and accomplished drug dealer," Barnwell said, his patience near breaking point, "or that he's just had new Wi-Fi installed in his house? I've never heard of him."

"The first one," Neil said. "No. Yeah."

Barnwell rolled his eyes. "And how would one communicate with this Beetle?"

"I'll give you his digits," Duncan said. Barnwell gave him a card. After scratching around, Lewis Hurd found him a pen. Duncan laboriously transcribed a number from his phone, curling his arm around it like a six-year-old answering a math problem.

"Too kind."

"But he can't know it came from us."

"Don't worry, fellas. This isn't my first rodeo." Barnwell gave the bemused trio a quick salute. "Stay out of trouble. If," he added before turning back to Steve, "that's possible."

🌀

"This is on our trip to Pembrokeshire." Steve showed his brother a stretch of pristine beach on which they were the only two walking. He moved to another photo, a group of people in front of a fireplace. "Mum, you, me, Uncle Oliver and Auntie Catherine, but no Dad."

Barnwell's mind was being hauled by a team of horses, laboriously and painfully, over rough terrain, in the direction of an unknown destination. He folded his arms and glared at his brother. "Yeah. Look, I'm bored of this. Do you want another drink?" He half rose from his seat.

"Sit down." Steve paused, sighed, and closed the album. "You're not getting it."

"Getting what?" Barnwell threw his hands up in the air. "You're right. I've no idea what you're on about. Spit it out or give it a rest and forever hold your peace, for crying out loud."

An acidic ache rumbled in Steve's gut. "I'd hoped to not have to spell it out, but it seems I'm going to have to. There's one other thing I want to show you." Steve reached into the back of the photo album and slipped out a folded, creased piece of paper. He slid it across the table to his brother.

"What's this?" Barnwell eyed his brother nervously.

"Open it."

"But..."

"Just open it will ya?"

With the tip of one finger, Barnwell flipped the paper open and stared at it. After a few seconds he quietly flipped it closed again. "It's a charge sheet."

"Yes, from 1993. I found it as I was going through Dad's things."

"Okay..."

"I don't think he went anywhere near the oil-rigs. I think he was inside. I want to know why."

Barnwell looked at the folded piece of paper again. It was creased like someone had scrunched it into a ball, then carefully smoothed it out. "I think we should let sleeping dogs lie, Steve."

His brother's eyes sparked with anger. "Well, I don't!"

Their eyes locked, the younger's gleaming with passion and fury, the elder's searching and doleful. "You're going to ask me to do something I shouldn't, aren't you?" Barnwell said.

"I'd be an idiot," Steve replied, "if I didn't at least ask. I've done an internet search but it's too old."

"Look, I'd help if I could, but..."

"It's just once..." Steve argued. "And it does affect you."

"Mate, we're not *allowed* to . . ."

". . . and it would clear everything up, wouldn't it?"

"It *might* make everything a lot worse," Barnwell cautioned. "Have you thought about that?"

As if to emphasise the point, Steve allowed some silence. "Yeah, I have," he said. "A thousand times."

"And?" his brother said.

"Even if you don't, Bazza, I remember Dad going away and coming back a bit different. I want to know what happened."

"Why? How would it help?"

Hands aloft, Steve admitted defeat. "This won't leave me alone, Bazz. I want to know what he did."

Too mired in weighing the problem to answer at once, Barnwell pursed his lips. "We might regret it, mate."

"I know. I feel the same way," Steve said. "But it's worth the risk."

CHAPTER TWENTY-SEVEN

BEETLE, AKA JONNY Hughe-Gordon, couldn't have looked less like an insect. He was in his twenties, tanned, blond, and athletic. He wore an emerald-green polo shirt, shorts, and deck shoes that were worn just enough to prove to Barnwell that he sailed the yacht the constable found him on.

"Afternoon," Barnwell said.

"Hey there, er, Officer." Hughe-Gordon raised his eyebrows. If Barnwell hadn't already formed an impression of the man from his name and appearance, the message these few words conveyed and the accent with which they were spoken would have fed his imagination. As it was, they sealed the deal. To Barnwell, a working-class lad from the East End of London, Hughe-Gordon was a "moneyed, upper-class twit." His precisely enunciated consonants and elongated vowels told Barnwell so.

"I called earlier."

"Indeed you did. How can I help you?" Hughe-Gordon had been polishing the deck when Barnwell walked up. He wiped his hands with a cloth. The white decking and hull gleamed in the bright sunlight, making Barnwell squint. Aware that this put him at a disadvantage, Barnwell pulled out his sunglasses and self-consciously put them on, trying very hard not to look like an American cop off the TV, but also not like a prat either.

"I wanted to have a little chat with you. About the murder of a local man, James Reeves. I was told you might know something."

Hughe-Gordon held his gaze. He had sparkling blue eyes. Barnwell suspected he was a babe magnet. He could just imagine it.

Hughe-Gordon turned down the corners of his mouth and shook his head. "Ah, no. Can't say I know anything about that. Ah, should I?"

"I was told that you are well connected. That you know things, people. Perhaps in your line of work?"

"What line of work would that be, Officer?" Hughe-Gordon flashed a huge smile, revealing uniform, brilliant-white, straight teeth. They were a testament to advanced and expensive dental care that had nothing to do with the barbaric medieval practices that passed for dentistry in Barnwell's youth.

Barnwell decided to lob a missile and see where it got him. "Drugs, mate."

"Drugs? Moi?" Hughe-Gordon widened his blue eyes and opened his mouth in mock astonishment. When Barnwell's stony expression didn't change, he said, "I don't know anything about drugs. Never touch the stuff."

"I never said you did." Barnwell got out his phone and flashed a photo of Jamie Reeves in front of Hughe-Gordon. "Have you ever seen this man among the circles you move in?"

Hughe-Gordon glanced quickly at the photo. "No, can't say that I have."

"You sure? Look again. Longer this time." The younger man took the phone and looked at the photo carefully. "Well, maybe he looks a bit familiar. I think I've seen him at the yacht club."

"Does he sail?" Nothing like that had turned up in Jamie Reeves's profile.

"No, I don't think so."

"I thought you had to be a member to drink there."

"You do, but he might have been a guest if he knew the right people. Might he have?"

Barnwell ignored the question. "Did you see who he was talking to?"

"Hmm, I'm not sure. I didn't pay too much attention, to be honest. He was just another guy in sailing circles. It's not like he stood out. Now, can—?"

Once again, Barnwell stonewalled what he considered Hughe-Gordon's efforts to derail the conversation. "And? What else can you tell me?"

"Nothing really." Hughe-Gordon beamed as though he were offering a substantial piece of information. "Look, what has this got to do with me? I don't know the guy, never spoke to him, barely even noticed him. I'm terribly sorry he's been murdered, but that has nothing to do with me."

Barnwell walked slowly down the side of the yacht, examining it carefully. He picked up a rope and regarded it like it was a precious artefact he was considering buying for a huge sum of money. Hughe-Gordon waited, his jaw working.

"Is this yours?" Barnwell said eventually.

"No, it's my father's. We hire her out. I manage her." Barnwell nodded. "Got a group coming for a few hours sailing shortly; the team taking them out will be here any minute. So if you don't mind . . ."

Barnwell grunted. He did mind. He minded a lot. Anything could happen on the open seas. Anything at all. And it would all go unseen and unnoticed.

"Mind if I take a look? Onboard, I mean."

"Er, yeah, sure." Barnwell climbed aboard, something he'd never have spontaneously dared a while back. But he was a lot nimbler and sure-footed than he had been forty pounds ago.

Barnwell walked about the deck, then poked his head into the cabin. He levered himself down the steps and glanced around. On the floor stood two crates of champagne. Platters of food lay on the work surface. Barnwell suspected that the fridge would be full of more of the same. Hughe-Gordon's boat was merely a vehicle, the open sea a backdrop. The purpose of the yacht's outing was to facilitate relationships and negotiations, deals for those for whom sailing meant hot and cold running attention, not tacking, jibing, and seasickness. It was a world Barnwell had no experience of or interest in. He climbed back on deck.

"How do DKN know you? They don't seem to be your sort."

Hughe-Gordon blushed. Two pink spots flushed his cheeks. He pressed his lips together and squinted, lines fanning out at the outer edges of his bright-blue eyes. He seemed uncomfortable, but nevertheless, beamed that toothpaste ad smile.

"They've done a bit of work for me."

"What kind of work?"

"Bit of this, bit of that. Odd jobs, casual. They clean up the old girl, you know, from time to time." The cloth he waved over his shoulder indicated he meant the yacht. "I hardly know them really."

"How long have you lived on Jersey, Mr. Hughe-Gordon?"

"All my life. Born here."

"For someone who's lived on this island all your life, you seem to have only a passing acquaintance with more people than I would expect for someone who is supposedly *connected*." Barnwell, after a rough start, was quite enjoying the disconcerting effect his sunglasses were having. "Why do they call you 'Beetle'?"

"Ah, I really have no idea. You'll have to ask them."

Barnwell surveyed the young man, tanned and taut from hours on the water. "Right, well, I'll leave you to it. Keep your nose clean."

Hughe-Gordon beamed again. If the sun hadn't already been high in the sky, he'd have lit the harbour up. "Certainly, Officer. Have a great day." The clean-cut, preppy young man climbed back on board, the soles of his deck shoes squeaking on the dry, laminated surface of the deck. He leant on the rails leading to the cabin.

As he was about to leap down, Hughe-Gordon paused and turned to Barnwell, who was still watching him. "I might have seen that Reeves chap talking to a woman at the yacht club. They were leaning in close, laughing. Looked like they were having a whale of a time."

"Oh, yeah? And who might that have been then?"

"I can't remember her name, but she's been out with us on occasion. She was recently a guest of a big-time money guy with some fabulously wealthy clients. He's chartered the boat a few times."

"And? What's his name?"

"Hold on." Hughe-Gordon disappeared below deck and came out shortly afterward, flicking through a large appointment book. "These are details of our bookings. Yeah, here we are. Last time was a couple of weeks ago. A party of eight. Granby, Silas Granby and Katya Granby." He ran his name down the list of names. "There was only one other woman on board. A Molly Duckworth."

If Hughe-Gordon could have seen inside Barnwell's brain, he would have spied sparks as brain cells crackled like lightening. Barnwell wrote the details down and put his notebook and pencil back in his pocket.

"Can I go now?" Jonny Hughe-Gordon said.

"Yes, you can," Barnwell replied.

"Good show. I need to get ready for our guests. They're expecting a good time."

"Cocktails, sunbathing, and being waited on hand and foot, no doubt," Barnwell grumbled as he watched the man disappear below deck. "But as sure as I'm a copper, I bet there's also alcohol, cocaine . . ." He thought for a second. "And orgies. Yeah, I bet that's what they do on them yachts out at sea. Far from prying eyes. Drugs, drunkenness, and debauchery."

CHAPTER TWENTY-EIGHT

"THANKS FOR COMING in, Ms. Lascelles." Graham regarded the surly, unkempt woman in front of him. Her hair was lank and dirty, her face bare of makeup. She wore grey sweats and scruffy trainers. She looked nothing like the Audrey Hepburn-esque figure that had pouted and fussed in Graham's interview room the day before.

"I don't see why I should have to, especially by myself." Paula swept her lap with her hand, brushing off some imaginary fluff to communicate her disapproval of the situation she found herself in.

"I want to talk to you alone about something you said in your last interview." Paula's expression didn't change. "I thought you might prefer it this way."

"Oh? Why's that?"

"It's about some texts we found on Jamie Reeves's phone. You said you'd had no communication with him recently."

"That's right. None in months."

"And technically that might be correct, but we found unanswered texts from you to him on his phone dating back just to the last week or two. I want to talk to you about them, honestly, without anyone present."

Paula's mouth twitched. Her eyes filled with tears. Haltingly she spoke, her voice wavering. "What I said was true. I'd had no contact with Jamie in months."

"But you tried to contact him. These texts prove it."

Paula lifted her chin, attempting to reclaim some of her dignity despite the circumstances. "Yes, but he didn't want to speak to me, did he? He never replied."

"But you wanted to speak to him?"

"Obviously."

"What about?"

Paula stared at him incredulously. "About getting back together of course! What else would I contact him for?"

Graham pressed his lips together and his hands opened reflexively. He gently shook his head. "I find it best not to guess."

"Do you really think I want that thick mammoth of a boyfriend? Matthew 'Muscles' Walker. Darlin' this and darlin' that. Spare me. He's not a patch on Jamie. He's embarrassing." Paula passed a hand over her face.

It crossed Graham's mind to wonder why she kept Matthew around if she thought so little of him. "So, when Jamie didn't reply, what did you do?"

"What do you think I did? I cried, beat my chest, and then I did absolutely nothing, Detective Inspector. Jamie ghosted me. He was telling me something without telling me anything."

"And did you tell Matthew about these texts?"

"Of course not!" Paula was almost spitting.

"Did he know you were still in love with Jamie?"

Paula leant forward, clearly believing Graham to be a simpleton. "Do you really think I would tell my six-foot-four, meathead boyfriend that?" She sat back, throwing her hands in the air. "Who knows what he might have done?"

"So, you sent texts to Jamie hoping to reconcile, and when you didn't receive a reply, you carried on as normal?"

"Yes, Detective Inspector, that's exactly what I did. I like having a man around. Matthew is a plonker, but he's better than nothing. He doesn't hold a candle to Jamie, who was kind, good-looking, intelligent, and a good laugh, but he's all I've got now. That might sound callous . . . but that's how I am. Besides, Matthew gets something out of our relationship too."

"How's that, Ms. Lascelles?"

"Me, of course! He couldn't do better. To him, I'm a prize, however imperfect." Graham regarded the woman in front of him and marvelled, not for the first time, at the human capacity for delusion.

"And Matthew has no idea that you were still in love with Jamie Reeves?"

"No, I'm certain of it. He isn't that bright, Inspector. It's not difficult to pull the wool over his eyes."

"And he didn't leave your side on that Friday night? Didn't pop out anywhere?"

"No, the only place he went was outside for a smoke. My mum doesn't allow smoking in the house."

"And how long was he gone when he did that?"

"About a quarter of an hour I suppose."

Graham mentally calculated whether fifteen minutes was long enough for Matthew to have travelled to Hautville Road from Paula's mum's house, whacked Jamie over the head, and got back in the time it took to reasonably smoke a cigarette. It was possible, just about. He roused himself with a deep breath. "Okay, that's all for now, Ms. Lascelles. Thanks for coming in and being honest. You can go home now and . . . do what you do."

Paula placed a hand on the table, halfway between her and Graham. She tapped the surface with her forefinger. "You know, Jamie was a decent guy. He didn't deserve what happened to him. I hope you catch whoever did this. And you put him, or her, away for a very long time."

※

"Yes, I went on the yacht with the Granbys for the day. It was just a bit of fun. I went to even out the numbers a bit." Janice had been assigned to interview Molly Duckworth at the Sanderson Landscaping office following Barnwell's report of his meeting with Beetle. "All the clients were Japanese businessmen, so Mr. Granby asked me if I'd keep his wife company. It was a nice day. Nothing improper went on. Why?"

"I'm simply interested in the relationship between you and the Granbys. I didn't know you had one."

"Really, it was nothing. I had spoken to Mr. Granby on the phone a couple of times when Adrian was out, and one day he came into the showroom. As he was leaving, Mr. Granby invited me on the yacht, and I said yes. I'm not averse to a little luxury. Goodness knows, I don't have much of it in my life."

"But why didn't you mention this earlier?"

"No, well, I didn't think it was relevant." Janice waited. Molly clasped her hands tightly in her lap. "And I didn't want Adrian to know, you see. He doesn't like us fraternising with the clients. I don't think he'd sack me, but he wouldn't like it. He'd give me a warning and tell me not to do it again." She looked up at the ceiling.

Janice waited. "Is there something else you'd like to tell me?"

"I . . . I said something I shouldn't while I was there."

"While you were on the boat?"

"Yes, I'd probably had a little bit too much champagne."

"What was it, Molly? What was it that you shouldn't have said?"

"I . . . er . . . shouldn't have said that Mr. Sanderson sometimes raises his prices for . . . certain clients."

"Ah, so Mr. Granby knew about that." Molly nodded. She bit her lip. "Probably. I said it to Mrs. Granby, but he might have overheard or she might have told him about it later. I don't know, but either way, I shouldn't have said it."

"Okay, and what did you do on the yacht?"

"Just hung out, chatted to the clients, but mostly to Mrs. Granby. We got on rather well. It was a lovely day, so nice to get out of the office. And there was as much to eat and drink as I wanted. I didn't have to lift a finger."

"What about later? You were seen with Jamie Reeves at the yacht club."

Molly sighed. Her eyes filled with tears. "Yes, it was a lovely evening. When we got back to shore, I went straight there. It's members only, you see, but Mr. Granby saw to it for me. I don't get that kind of opportunity every day. I wanted to enjoy it. I could take a guest, and I asked Jamie to join me. We had a great time eating, drinking, and dancing. And I"—Molly took a deep breath—"I hoped it might lead to more." She sighed. "But no. We went home separately at the end of the evening."

"Do you know if Jamie had been there before?"

"Er, no, I don't think so. I'm sorry I can't help you, Sergeant. I shouldn't have gone on the yacht, but it was all innocent really. A bit boring to be honest. I can see why Mrs. Granby needed a bit of moral support. I think she's lonely, perhaps sad. All that money and all she's got is that fluffy dog for company."

"What was your impression of Mr. Granby?"

"He's nice, kind. Made sure my drink was continuously topped up and I had enough to eat. And it was nice of him to get me into the yacht club. I could get used to that life. It was a bit of a bump to come back to Earth. Especially without Jamie."

CHAPTER TWENTY-NINE

JACK STARED AT Janice in amazement, a tote bag in each of his hands. They stood just by the big wall which ran down the side of the churchyard. "Romantic?" he said quizzically. Above him was the tower of St. Andrew's, the charming parish church which gave the quiet street its name.

"Yeah," Janice said. "Ask anyone. Classically romantic."

"A graveyard," Jack said, some way short of convinced. "Romantic."

"Alright, it's a shortcut," Janice admitted.

"How many steps have you . . ." Janice had borrowed Jack's Fitbit two months ago. She'd wanted to walk herself into her wedding dress. It was a size smaller than she normally wore.

"Mind your own steps," she said, pulling down her sleeve to cover the device. "I've made my goal for today. And, well, I suppose I wanted to see where they buried that poor lad, Jamie Reeves." The few days surrounding Jamie's funeral had been gloomy and marked by a frustrating lack of progress in the case.

"Oh, great. That'll cheer us right up," said Jack. "We've gone from romantic to morbid in less than ten seconds. That'll put us in the right mood for the evening."

Jack was looking forward to dinner at Laura's, but Janice was tetchy. It was their first time socialising with the other couple on their own, and she wasn't sure how she felt about it.

"Oh, sorry. I feel a bit peculiar about tonight. I mean, what am I supposed to call him outside the station? Detective Inspector? Sir?"

"How about David? That is his name," Jack said.

Janice shivered. "Hell, no. That just sounds weird."

Jack rolled his eyes and shook his head. Janice was being irrational. "Come on. Let's go. Don't you normally go to the funeral when there's an investigation connected? Fly the flag. See who shows up, who's crying and who's not."

"The DI went with Roach," Janice reported. "He said it rained, and it was very sad."

"Not much of a poet, David Graham, is he?"

"It was a funeral, not a Highland sunset." Janice rolled her eyes. "Besides, you're expecting an elegy from the wrong man."

"I think you mean eulogy."

"No, I mean elegy. *'Tis better to have loved and lost, than never to have loved at all.'* And all that. Laments for the dead. I learned about them when I was choosing readings for the wedding."

"Good grief. Better not get mixed up or the vicar'll be sending us off into the afterlife for all eternity instead of asking us to forsake all others for as long as we both shall live."

"Alright, alright, clever clogs, come on, let's go. We'll never get there at this rate, shortcut or no."

This premarital sparring on Janice's part had been increasing. Jack wisely put it down to pre-wedding nerves. He put an arm around her shoulders and pulled her into him, determined to not let their exchange disintegrate further. "So, what are we here for exactly?"

Janice looked around at the rows of headstones, some dating back three hundred years. "I'm looking for Jamie Reeves's plot. But this business of *dying*," she said, scanning the graveyard that wound around the church, "seems to be all the rage. Have you got an app for finding recently buried corpses in graveyards?"

"I haven't." Jack's eyes found someone—or a pair of someones—who might be instructive. "But those two guys over there might." Jack strode over to a bench under an ancient poplar on the periphery of the graveyard. Two men sat there eating their tea. A modest, yellow mechanical digger stood nearby. "'Scuse me, do you dig the graves?" Jack asked.

One of the men brushed off his hands. He was short and stockily built. He squinted as though he'd never seen a young man in a freshly ironed button-down shirt and clean pressed trousers in a graveyard before. He frowned, looking Jack up and down before he pointed to his mate and said, "That's Clip. *He* works for the church. I just stand and watch."

"Nah, Fred stirs himself sometimes to press the red button," Clip replied. "And I press the green one. We're for equal opportunities here. What can we do you for, young fella?" Clip had glasses on and a flat cap despite the warmth of the early evening.

Janice caught up with Jack and quickly introduced herself without mentioning her police connection. She asked about Jamie's funeral. "The local news said it was well attended."

"Aye, well enough, I suppose. Varies a lot. Sometimes you'll get an old granny who had relations from here to Khartoum, and there's a big to-do. Sometimes it's just us and the vicar," Fred told her.

"I remember that one because there were that journalist fella hanging around, asking questions when he thought no one was looking. We stood around the back of the church. We wait for everyone to leave before filling the plot in. He didn't see us, thank goodness."

"You'd have given him what for if he had, wouldn't yer, Clip?"

"Was anyone especially upset?" Janice was equally interested in the opposite but had no way to ask without revealing more about herself.

"People," Clip said simply, "go through *a lot* at funerals."

"Some show up, then turn away because they can't bear it," his mate said. "Some folks, they stay at the grave, sobbin' or prayin' or whatever until someone drags them away. We've seen all manner of screamin' and carryin' on. Others," he continued as though talking about fascinating local birds he'd recently seen, "come and go in complete silence, like they're going through the motions, but you know they're all cut up inside. Others prefer to leave it all on the field." Standing and rubbing his fingers together as though fine-tuning something, Fred searched his memory. "Hang on, Clip. Weren't that the funeral with the mob wife?"

"The one who came late, after everybody had gone?" Clip stroked his chin. "You might be right there, Fred. The one with the fancy black car. After they left, we did old Mrs. Hitchins from the nursing home."

"Mrs. Hitchins . . . They all run into one another after a time," Fred said, thinking hard. His face relaxed, his eyebrows popping up to where his hairline used to be. "I remember now. A Maserati, I thought it were, but Clip here, he reckoned it was a Jaguar."

"Ain't neither of us ever gonna afford one, Fred, so who bleedin' well cares which it were?"

"Anyway, we get all types around here," Fred said. "Shell-shocked investment banker husbands, trust fund kids, mobster wives . . ."

"Second wives who stand there blubbering and first wives who grit their teeth. . ."

"'Desperate housewives', he calls them," said Fred. "Every time he tries to get me to bet with him."

"On what?" Jack asked.

"How long it'll be before they're on some new bloke's arm," Clip replied. "We choose a date, note it in our notebook." He pulled out a small, grubby pad, the corners curled over. "Then ask around. I was right to within a week one time. Felt I'd scored a hole in one."

"And I remember telling you," Fred said firmly, more aware of the sensitivities of the situation than his colleague, "that the game were in extremely poor taste."

"Didn't stop you playin' though, did it? Anyway, young Jamie had a visitor who arrived after everyone else had gone," Clip said. "She didn't arrive until even that pretty young lass with the red hair left, and she were the last of the mourners to leave."

"He always remembers them. The pretty, upset ones," Fred said.

"He must have been one for the ladies, that Jamie. There was the petite blonde one with the neckerchief," Cliff said.

"The one with the boyfriend who was built like a brick 'ouse?" Fred replied.

"Yeah, she were crying her eyes out. Bit embarrassing for the boyfriend, I should imagine. There were the one left at the end . . ."

"The one with the red hair?" Janice sought to confirm.

Clip took a big bite out of his sandwich and spoke through his food, his cheek bulging. "That's right."

"And the mobster's moll," Fred finished.

"The poor fella must've had the gift of the gab to string those three along," Clip said, swallowing loudly. "Impressive."

"P'raps one of them did it. Jealousy," Fred summed up. He sat back and folded his arms, quite sure of himself.

"Mrs. Mobster didn't stay long."

"Why call her that?" Janice asked.

"Well, she were like a woman from a film. She were all dark hair, big hat, high heels, sunglasses. Dressed all proper she were, too, in polka dots, but only arrived after everyone had left. Perhaps she got the time wrong."

"We would never strive to overhear human suffering . . ." Fred explained, as if reciting a poem. *Perhaps an elegy.*

". . . But we happen upon a good deal of it purely by accident," finished Clip. Almost unnervingly comfortable, the two gravediggers were clearly aficionados of human behaviour *in extremis*.

"The woman, the one who lingered after the funeral, the one with the red hair, what was she like?" Janice asked.

"Oh, she were completely different, poor lass. She were more upset than most of the mourners. Properly let it all out, she did." Clip spread his arms outward like he was introducing an act at the circus.

"Can you describe her?"

"Er, yeah. Why do you want to know all this?"

"Just curious," Janice said.

"Huh. She were slight, ponytail, red hair like I said, proper upset she was."

"Interesting. Seems like you get to see all sorts in your line of work."

"We sure do, don't we Fred?"

"Yep, we sure do." The two old men sat back. When there were no more questions, they tore bites from their sandwiches and stared at Janice and Jack like silent hamsters, big bulges in their cheeks as they chewed. Clip swigged from a bottle of water.

Janice thanked them and left them to their tea. Her mind was churning, Jack could see, but she was content to walk silently onward through the northern part of the churchyard and to the main road beyond. Five minutes on was Campbell Street, Laura's, and the promise of dinner.

CHAPTER THIRTY

"READY TO TRY Detective Inspector Graham's cooking for the first time?" Jack said when they arrived at the address they had been given.

"What? Oh, yeah," Janice said, distracted.

"Sergeant Harding, are you alright?" Jack bent over and waved a hand in front of her face.

"Just . . . well, thinking, I suppose."

"I try to do as little of that as I can. Gives my brain wrinkles. Especially during my time off."

Janice gave Jack an apologetic squeeze around the waist. "Love, if dinner with Laura and the DI happens to go a bit, um, *operational* tonight . . ."

"I should just go with the flow?" Jack suggested. "Yeah, okay. I mean, once you coppers get going, there's no stopping you. Isn't that right?"

"It's this case, Jamie Reeves. He wasn't exceptional, just a regular bloke who seemed to live a perfectly normal life—no priors, no nothing really. He'd worked on Tomlinson's garden, Barnwell had seen him at the Foc's'le, Roachie had played against him at five-a-side . . ."

"I fixed his computer."

"Yes, just normal stuff in a small place like this. It seems such an ordinary crime, a bash over the head, but someone lost their life, someone who was intertwined intimately with this community, and we can't find out who did it or why."

Jack held Janice at arm's length, waiting until her frustration died down a little. "The tyranny of incompleteness," he said, reaching for the philosophical. "No case is closed until it's *closed*. Halfway doesn't count, and 'nearly' is no good. I understand that frustration."

"We should make you a constable and be done with it," Janice said, giving him a lingering kiss. Which, of course, was exactly when Laura opened the door to welcome her guests.

"The thing about engaged couples," Laura tutted, "is that they can't keep their hands off each other."

Sergeant Harding straightened her jacket. "I make no apologies," she said. "It's Jack's fault for being the best-looking man in the Channel Islands." Behind Laura, Graham walked up. "Present company excepted, of course," Janice added hastily, then wished she hadn't.

"Good evening. Welcome to our small and humble abode," Graham said, smiling. He hadn't been entirely comfortable with the idea of having Jack and Janice to dinner when Laura had suggested it, blurring the lines between the personal and professional as it did, but now the evening was here, he was quite looking forward to it. The couple were good company, and if he were honest, he knew he needed to loosen up. It was all part of "the project."

Jack grinned and handed over the pair of bags he'd been carrying. "Starter and dessert, as instructed."

"Thanks." Laura smiled as Graham turned back to the kitchen, weighed down by bags. "I knew he'd be alright making the main course in our tiny kitchen," she confided to them, "but I didn't want to push it." She ended on a whisper and grinned. She too was looking forward to the evening. It was the first time she and David had been "coupley" with another pair. It felt like the milestone it was.

The living room of Laura's cottage was slowly transforming into a place which represented them both. Graham hadn't given up his house yet, but more and more he gravitated to Laura's. It was more homely, comfortable. His own place, while bigger, was rather sparse, clinical.

Laura's books dominated the living room in a large set of bookshelves which occupied half the available wall space. Two small paintings of the countryside near Graham's parents' favourite holiday place, a cottage on an island in the Outer Hebrides, hung on another wall over the top of a tall, blue vase. A telescope stood in the corner on its tripod, pointing skyward in expectation. There was a guitar, too, though whether it belonged to Laura or Graham wasn't clear. Two boxes of CDs were stacked by Laura's tiny media unit as if trying not to get in anyone's way.

"Has he read Freddie's latest?" Janice asked Laura in an equally hushed tone. "I don't want him forgetting the oregano or boiling the pasta sauce down to a sticky mess."

"He's read it, but said he had 'better things to do.'"

"I wanted to try faggotini," Graham called through, "but there were some tricky challenges." From the doorway, he held his hands up, his fingers splayed wide. "Very 'hands-on.'"

It was Jack who opened the conversational door. "How did you get into making pasta?" From the doorway—the kitchen was far too small for them all—the trio were treated to a display of David Graham's ability to unconsciously juggle several things at once. While his hands found the saltshaker, then the red chilli flakes, Graham launched into a slimmed-down version of one of his favourite stories. "Little *trattoria* in Herculaneum just a few streets from the ruins. Not far from Naples, on the Italian coast," he said. "Perfect place, small and family run. Incredible mussels, simmered with cherry tomatoes and *so much garlic*." He grinned. "Lots of good local wine, of course. And then"—Graham stirred the thickening, deep-red pasta sauce with a wooden spoon—"the owner brings out this plate of faggotini."

"The little parcel things?" Janice said. She'd never heard of faggotini, but not wanting to appear as unsophisticated as she felt, she had quickly looked them up on her phone while hiding behind Jack.

"Normally, they're made from thin pasta rolled out like pastry. Kind of chewy," Graham said. "But in this case, the pasta surrounding the filling was paper thin. So delicate, I couldn't imagine how they'd stayed intact in the boiling water. You just slid a whole one onto your spoon and . . . I'm serious, it was like eating a garlic and cheese infused cloud," he said, reminiscing happily. The occasion had been his honeymoon with his ex-wife, though only Laura knew that.

"How long were you there? In Italy, I mean," Janice asked. She was testing the waters. How far could she probe?

"Ten days, but I'd have stayed there to become an apprentice pasta maker if they'd let me."

"Think of the crime we'd have!" Laura exclaimed. "The world would have better pasta but more unsolved murders."

"Sounds like a reasonable trade," Jack said. Not bound by Janice's sensitivities, he'd squeezed around Graham and rummaged in the kitchen drawers to find a corkscrew. He set to work on a bottle of Chianti.

"One of our citizens would have conniptions," Graham commented. "The crime rate is high enough. Or so he keeps saying on his blog." His tone was one of disdain and concern; Freddie Solomon provided Graham with most of his public relations problems while, in the detective inspector's opinion, repeatedly threatening the integrity of his investigations. "Or maybe he'd prefer it if I *was* a pasta maker. Seems I'm not doing nearly enough."

Janice got there first. "He's full of it, boss."

"Meh, Freddie's entitled to his opinion," Graham said. "No laws were broken in the writing. Well," he added, "not exactly."

Laura exchanged places with Jack and began grating Parmesan. She stood shoulder to shoulder with Graham as he stirred the sauce. "'Not exactly'?" she said.

"Kind of."

"Freddie's *kind of* fallen afoul of the law?" Laura wanted clarity. It wasn't like Graham to equivocate on things like this.

Janice took over. "It's illegal to tamper with a jury. Influence people, coerce them, threaten them, that kind of thing. By writing about cases in the way he does, Freddie is potentially influencing the pool from which a jury will be pulled.

It's been the case with previous investigations, and it will be the same way with Jamie Reeves."

"But you haven't charged anyone," Jack said. "We can't know who the jury will be."

"Not yet, but when we do arrest someone and the case comes to trial, they'll be citizens of Gorey and the surrounding area," Graham told him. "Which is precisely the intended audience of Mr. Solomon's diabolical screed. If I were a lawyer, I'd have no trouble putting together a case which proves Freddie's writings prejudice potential jurors. But his readership is so wide, we would be in danger of not having any jurors if we excluded them."

"How so?" Laura wondered. "Even if they worshiped Freddie, they'd never be silly enough to ignore the clear facts of the prosecution's case."

"If they're worshiping Freddie, they're silly enough to do pretty well anything. And I do wish he'd stop putting himself at the centre of things. He's not qualified. He's never done so much as a ride along with us, let alone been trained in evidentiary procedure."

"Perhaps we should try it, sir, I mean, David, er, boss." Janice suppressed a wince.

"How do you mean?"

"I mean perhaps we should invite him to come out with us, shadow us, see what we do, what we deal with on a daily basis. He might be more understanding, less confrontational. Hell, just some appreciation of what we're up against would be something."

"Hmm, perhaps so, but I suspect that he understands that negative stories sell, positive stories not so much, just like any tabloid. I mean, it's not the criticism I object to so much as the uncalled-for undermining of the trust the public have in us..."

"Wine anyone?" Jack said loudly.

"I'll get the glasses!" Laura said, almost as loudly.

Graham stopped short. "Right." He turned back to stir his pasta sauce, which was almost thick enough. "Going to drain the pasta in a moment. Why don't you all sit down and try Jack's antipasti?"

Jack quickly laid out a selection of pastrami, Italian cheeses, and spiced, pickled vegetables along with a baguette. He'd picked them up from the farmer's market. "I skipped lunch," he explained to Laura as she set about slicing the baguette. "I'm starving."

"Yeah, me too," Laura said. "Some days, the distribution desk is more like reception at A&E, and sometimes equally as life-threatening." She laughed. "I just never know what I might be faced with."

"Really?" Jack said. "I didn't know being a librarian was quite so exciting."

"You'd be surprised. The other day, old Mr. Hetherington showed up looking pale and very out of sorts. I thought I was going to have to call an ambulance for him. Turned out he'd just had a slice of the pizza we lay on for the 'book of the month' group. He'd never had pizza before. It didn't agree with him."

"Aha, his digestion was more used to overcooked greens and grey meat, no doubt."

In the kitchen, Graham tasted the sauce for a final time. "A fraction more sweetness," he said, quickly finding the sugar container. "Thanks for bringing the antipasti," he told Janice, who was standing in the doorway watching him. "I tend to get a bit overambitious with my cooking. Laura's always telling me to scale things back. She's right." He smiled. "She's always right."

CHAPTER THIRTY-ONE

JANICE WATCHED GRAHAM check his sauce, the clock, his pasta, and clear his work surface. She noticed the same precise, considered movements she'd have recognised anywhere. The hard surface of the fridge door felt cold against her skin as she moved to lean against it. Something caught her eye. A photo of Graham with his arms around a young girl sat in a frame on the kitchen windowsill.

"Hey, you two, come and get some antipasti before Jack and I eat it all," Laura called out.

"I was asking him about the case," Janice responded. "Was that alright, or . . ."

"It's fine," Laura said, walking over. "If I objected to David discussing work out of hours, we wouldn't have got very far. He puts things aside when I tell him to though, don't you?" She leant over to give Graham a peck on the cheek. "But I'm pretty sure his mind is never still under that calm surface."

"Wish I could leave it all at the station sometimes," said Graham, turning away from some intensive chopping to grab a hunk of black truffle Pecorino cheese. "Most of my time is spent *thinking*. Pinning down details that we've missed, trying to make connections. It mostly goes on in the background. I try not to let it affect things," he told them all, but his eyes were only on Laura. He popped the cheese into his mouth.

"*Mostly*." Laura chuckled. "There was that time you put yogurt in my coffee."

Graham returned to his chopping. "And what's wrong with that?" he called over. "The Vietnamese have added yogurt to coffee for generations." Another glance at Laura, then a smile meant just for her, one she understood.

"So, sir, I'm learning a lot here, but, um, can I ask about the Reeves case? What are your most recent thoughts?"

"I'm considering the possibility that Paula Lascelles' boyfriend might have done it. She did say that he was outside for fifteen minutes having a smoke. Do you think that would have been long enough to do the deed?"

Janice turned down the corners of her mouth. "I mean, maybe, if he ran. Does he look like a runner?"

"That's not the sport I'd have in mind for him, no."

"What about the boss, Adrian Sanderson? He has a shaky alibi too."

"Hmm, I still think his motivation is rather weak."

"What about Granby? His alibi's questionable. And, you see, on the way here I—"

"Excuse me, Janice. Can I get by?" Graham squeezed past her, holding his chopping board covered in chives above her head. "It's just the damnedest case. No one saw anything of the attack until Jamie staggered into the pub. Nothing on camera," he added heavily, rolling his eyes at this continued hindrance to effective and efficient Gorey policing. He scraped the chives into a pan on the stove. "The gift that keeps on giving us bugger-all when we most need it."

"But sir..."

"And Marcus could provide only the most basic details. Not his fault," Graham conceded. "We were unlucky with the evidence."

"Rain," Jack said, walking up, "can *really* muck things up. Couldn't it have been a run-of-the-mill robbery? One that went sideways?"

"It could," Graham said, dipping his head to accept a pitted green olive from Jack's antipasti tray that Laura popped into his mouth. "But if it was, they failed spectacularly. Not only did they not get anything from him, they killed him to boot. In a moment they went from an opportunistic common crime to the prospect of a life term."

"Maybe he was seen as a rival. He was a good-looking guy. Maybe one of his paramours has a jealous boyfriend, and he flirted with someone who was a little too flirty back," Laura speculated.

"Which, in a manner of speaking, brings us back to Matthew Walker," said Graham.

"And Silas Granby, sir," Janice added.

"Let's not be hasty," Graham replied.

"When I spoke to him, Bazza reckoned Matthew wrestles bison for a living," Jack said.

"Doesn't make him a murderer," Graham countered. "Constable Barnwell is also a man of considerable... Well, he's *considerable*, but I'd never think of him as a killer. In fact, I'd trust him to babysit a child in a heartbeat. And he's pretty soppy over that dog of his. No, size has very little relevance."

"Walker has to be among the field of suspects though, surely," Jack reiterated. "Top of the list, maybe. Perhaps the girlfriend incited him."

Graham thought back to the woman who'd sat across the table from him a few days ago. "Hmm, I don't know that she did that."

"But what about Silas Granby, sir?" Janice was becoming breathless. "I mean,

Adrian Sanderson denies Granby's story about having a physical confrontation with Reeves, and if he's telling the truth, why is Granby lying?"

Her boss appeared to not hear her. "Right now," Graham said, setting down his knife by a neat pile of chopped garlic, "our field of suspects includes almost the *whole of Gorey*. All because, basically, we don't have any good ones."

By general consent and to everyone's relief, dinner party talk veered toward Janice and Jack's upcoming nuptials. With the remains of crumbly Italian cheese and smoked meats now scattered around the antipasti plate, Graham was in the kitchen preparing to serve the faggotini into bowls, though he promised to lend an ear to the discussion.

"People talk about wedding nerves, you know," Jack was saying, "but it's not really *us* that's anxious. It's the other people who are getting hot and bothered, causing us secondhand stress in the process."

"My mother," Janice summed up in a tone of heavy foreboding.

"She's decided to . . ." A year ago, even less, Jack would never have risked a negative comment about Janice's family. Even now, his impulse was to avoid offence, but he and Janice were a team, and both knew it was best to face the inevitable awkwardness of family occasions by sticking together. "Actually, she's trying to decide pretty much *everything*."

"Everything except the husband. She's happy with him." Janice started listing the issues. "She's got opinions on the venue, the service . . ."

". . . the flower arrangements, the bridesmaids' dresses . . ."

". . . even the date. She actually phoned me a couple of weeks ago," Janice said, nudging Jack, who only vaguely remembered this singular conversation but who nodded in agreement, or possibly sympathy, "and asked if we could bring the wedding forward by two weeks. Just like that!" she exclaimed. "And all because she found a great deal on a package holiday to Greece and needed to book it before it was sold out!"

"What's her problem with the venue?" Laura wondered.

Eyes closed, sighing, Janice couldn't even find the words. Jack stepped in. "Our proposed venue 'suffered from an absence of Holy Spirit.'"

"We said no initially to a church wedding," Janice explained. "Got nothing against the idea, not really . . . But as soon as we looked into it, the complexities doubled, then doubled again. I mean, some of my family are atheists. There are hymns to choose, the processional and recessional music. Readings to be selected and approved. Banns posted. But Mum was so insistent."

"I'd just as soon scrap all that, have a ten-minute wedding right on the beach, and then repair to the Foc's'le for a slap-up lunch," Jack said.

"Make it the Bangkok Palace," Graham added, ferrying through four bowls of faggotini from the kitchen, "and I'll be your best man, no charge."

"And *this*," Laura said, admiring Graham's professional presentation of his culinary efforts, "looks amazing." The faggotini was topped with grated Parmesan and a sprinkling of fresh parsley.

"Well done, sir. Could be on the cover of a food magazine," Janice said warmly, forgetting again to drop the "sir" for one night.

"Just keeping things simple," Graham said. "Sorry about the kitchen though. Looks like a toddler tried baking for the first time."

"The mess is worth it," Laura said. She leant over to give him another kiss on the cheek. Jack and Janice exchanged a glance, mutually aware that they were seeing something rare and special: David Graham putting aside his responsibilities and stresses just long enough to be *human*.

Graham popped one of his faggotini into his mouth, making a point of enjoying it before delivering his verdict. "You know, I'm not transported into ecstasy, and my dough could be a hairbreadth's thinner, but these are pretty bloody good for a first try."

"Well done, Dave," Jack said.

While the DI enjoyed his pasta, Janice silently mouthed to Jack, "*Dave?*"

"Remember, it's your wedding day," Graham said. "It's all about you two. Others will have their views, but they don't matter. I recommend you sit down, agree what you want, veto almost everything other people suggest, and have a fantastic time."

"'Almost everything'?" Jack asked.

How was it possible, Graham found himself asking himself later that night, for him to delve back into those memories so easily? His wedding, his honeymoon in Italy. Those gold-flecked days—dozens upon dozens if one is lucky—which sweep by when a new marriage is just *perfect*. Eight years together, as happy as any man could expect, until that one moment when everything fell apart.

"The car," Graham said. "Get a nice car. You and your bride must leave for your new lives together in something *showstopping*. And I don't mean a paddy wagon waiting outside the church with its lights on."

Janice laughed. "I can just imagine me, dress every which way and furious, having to clamber into a vehicle that recently transported our most recent murderer. I would not be impressed. Are you listening, Jack?"

"Yes, ma'am. Got it, loud and clear. No paddy wagon."

"An Aston Martin would be a good choice."

"Or one of Silas Granby's motors," Janice added. She sighed wistfully.

Graham didn't answer. He was working on his final faggotini, admiring its proportions. "I'm not going to be competing in *MasterChef* any time soon, but these are gratifyingly edible."

"Like eating at a restaurant," Jack said. "Do I detect a dash of fish sauce?"

Eyes closed, absorbed in his faggotini, Graham failed to reply, so Laura stepped in. "A tablespoon. Just isn't the same without it." She watched Graham for a moment. The others worried briefly that they'd overstepped but were not sure how. Before the conversational momentum could dip, Laura did the sensible thing and steered things back to the wedding. "And the flowers? What are you choosing for the flowers?"

CHAPTER THIRTY-TWO

ONCE EVERYONE HAD eaten and retired to the living room, Graham brought through a steaming cafetière of coffee and, of course, a pot of tea. "Now, where were we?"

"Means, motives, and opportunity," Janice reminded him. "Matthew Walker, Adrian Sanderson, Silas Granby, or some unnamed individual we have no idea about."

"Matthew might not be the brightest," said Graham, "but Barnwell maintains that Walker denies everything. Was genuinely offended at being accused. He even tried to inform against his girlfriend. I don't completely trust either of them, but she was still in love with Reeves, and his opportunity was slight."

"Perhaps they are double bluffing," Jack suggested.

"That would require coordination and brains the likes of which I simply don't think they possess."

"Adrian Sanderson, then," Janice said. "You met him twice, didn't you?"

Graham nodded "And both times he was angry about what had happened to Jamie. Even considered him a protégé. Maybe someone whom he might give the business to when he calls it quits."

"But if Jamie threatened the stability or future of his business . . ."

"Yes, I agree it's possible, and he did have that small window of opportunity when he went to the office, but again, it's hardly conclusive."

"Then what about Silas Granby, sir? His story differs from Sanderson's. Granby says there was pushing between Jamie and his boss. Sanderson denies it. Granby said the argument was about the cost of the job. Sanderson said it was about flirting with Mrs. Granby. One of them is lying."

"Yes, that is problematic, I agree. Did you get anywhere looking for the murder weapon?"

"No, sir. Unfortunately not." Refusing to be deterred again, Janice pressed her point home. "Suppose Sanderson is telling the truth. Maybe Granby felt threatened by Jamie. Maybe he decided to do something about it, coshed Jamie over the head when he was supposed to be in Turin, and made up the story about the costs and the pushing to put Sanderson in the frame."

"Hmm. Maybe. I can't see it, can you? I mean, why would he? He has far too much to lose."

"It might be nothing, but on our way here, we were talking to two gravediggers. I spoke to them about Jamie Reeves's funeral."

"Oh?" Graham poured Janice another cup of coffee.

"Apparently after everyone had left, another woman arrived. They said she was distressed."

"Did they say who she was?"

"No, but they said she had dark hair, a big hat, high heels, and sunglasses."

"She wore polka dots," Jack added helpfully.

"Katya Granby, sir."

"How can you be sure?"

"She arrived in a black Maserati. It must have been her. Maybe she was closer to Jamie Reeves than we thought. I'm sorry, Laura." Janice found her host's arm with an apologetic touch. "We've turned dinner into a briefing."

"Not a bit of it!" Laura replied. "I want to catch the attacker as much as you do. Besides," she said, "I find it rather thrilling. I can enjoy the mostly peaceful life of a librarian while living vicariously through you lot. It's fascinating to me how you develop theories and go about interpreting people and their behaviours."

"People are quite predictable. I mean, most of the time, we can take basic information, make some simple deductions, and then just depend on people to be *themselves*," Graham said.

"They'll surprise you sometimes, though, given enough provocation," Jack pointed out. "I mean, I'm basically a very quiet person, and I've got most of the characteristics for an introvert. But," he added, "I also managed to ask a beautiful woman to marry me when I didn't know what she was going to say."

"Yes, you did," Janice argued, quite certain.

"*You* knew, but *I* didn't. It was like walking over hot coals," Jack recalled.

"You sweet little lamb," Janice said. She squeezed his waist.

"And while we're talking about people surprising us," Laura added, "Barnwell dangled from a helicopter."

"And someone got me to jump out of a plane," Graham said. "More than twenty times, but that doesn't change my basic, cautious self."

"When on earth did you . . . ?" Jack was surprised.

"Back when I was younger and had too much energy. I used to skydive. I found it relaxing," was all Graham said. "But you're right, given sufficient provocation, people will act out of character. I still think Granby's a poor fit for the attacker though, and he'll stay that way unless something significant crops up. Walker? Not so sure."

"And what about Sanderson? What would it take for you to change your mind about him?" Janice wondered.

"Corroboration of Granby's story about Sanderson physically struggling with Jamie. Them having words is not enough. Or some proof that he was lying about the content of their argument."

"I think the Granbys are definitely worth another chat," Janice said. "I thought they were a strange couple. The dog thing is just weird."

"I know about the dog memorial thing," Laura said. "Mrs. Granby asked to put up some posters in the library inviting donations. There was an article in last week's local paper about it too."

Laura saw Jack was confused. "We've still got it, haven't we?" she asked Graham, getting up from her seat. "The paper."

"I think it's in the recycling," he said.

"Yeah," Laura soon called from the corner of the kitchen, "here it is. They're building a memorial to their top dog, and they're establishing a fund to help build a new one for each fallen champion." She stopped, puzzled by something, but soon handed the paper to Jack. "Here, next to the article about the exhibition we went to last week. Everyone finds their contentment *somewhere*, I suppose."

Jack read from the article, which was accompanied by a photo of Silas, Katya, and the prancing Willow playing in their sunlit living room.

"For those who love dog shows and the breeding of champion dogs, the Granby and Padalka-Lyons families are a guiding light. Determined both to encourage participation in dog trials and to memorialise the great prize-winning pooches of the past, a small group of women have found a calling in a cause which is often overlooked."

"Overlooked," Graham grunted, "because it's a complete waste of . . ."

"Everyone has their hobbies," Laura reminded him. "You might not agree, but then I can't imagine any of those ladies enjoying early twentieth-century classical music or researching British prime ministers from the century before that." Graham had developed a fascination with the life and times of George Canning, who until recently possessed the distinction of holding the shortest period in office of any British prime minister. His sole term lasted one hundred and nineteen days, from April 1827 until his death in August 1827.

"And then there's this." Laura gestured at the telescope setup—a stout, black cylinder atop a tripod. "Birthday present," she said.

"Wait, he has *birthdays*?" Janice exclaimed.

Jack leant forward, interested. "What are you seeing out there?"

The night sky wasn't yet dark enough for a practical demonstration, so Graham launched into an explanation instead. As he gave them a rundown on the Messier objects—distant, faint nebulae and galaxies—Laura found her attention wandering. It didn't normally; she'd learned a lot about bird migrations and magnetism the other day, and just last week, she received an upbeat, savagely comical critique of the Police Act of 1964. There was no dissuading Graham from these mini-lectures it seemed, and so Laura resolved merely to steer him toward greater conciseness. It worked for them both.

But something was bothering her, and it wasn't Graham regaling Jack and Janice about the "rapid," many million-year cooling of ancient gases around failed stars hundreds of light-years away. Laura poured more coffee, served little dessert mints, and laughed along with Graham's overly enthusiastic hand gestures as he depicted a distant supernova. But she wasn't with them, not really, and for the rest of the evening, she found herself quietly distracted by a thought. At first, it refused to properly form, and it took most of the rest of the evening, but an idea began to percolate through the fog.

Later that evening, after Janice and Jack left and Graham had insisted on cleaning up, he walked out of the bathroom, wiping his face on a towel. He'd just cleaned his teeth and smelled minty and fresh. Laura sat on the bed. "All yours," he said. She didn't move and stared pensively at the light from the lamp across the road. He sat next to her. "What is it? Did you not enjoy yourself this evening?"

"What? Oh no, no. I really had a good time. I was thinking about something else." Laura shifted to face him. "You know that night you refereed the under-fourteens?"

Graham rolled his eyes. "How could I forget?"

"Janice and Jack and I went to the exhibition at the council offices, remember?"

"Hmm."

"On the way out, a man bumped into an elderly couple on the steps so hard they fell into Jack. The man was in a huge rush and didn't stop; he just kept on going. It was exceptionally rude."

"Okay."

"Well, that man, I recognised him from the paper."

"Love, you're not making much sense."

"Oh, sorry." Laura shook her head. "The man who ran out of the exhibition. I'm sure of it. His picture was in the paper. It was Silas Granby."

CHAPTER THIRTY-THREE

ONLY ABOUT A third of the council building's employees were at their desks when DI Graham strode in and made the strangest of requests with respect to the paintings exhibited there earlier that month. "The exhibition's finished, Detective Inspector," the office manager, a well-turned-out woman in her early fifties told him. "We replaced it last week with a selection of computer-aided drawings of the—."

"I know that. I just walked past it." Heartfelt and commendable, however amateurish they may have been, the local artists' paintings from the Wordsworth retreat had all too quickly been replaced for Graham's liking. As far as he could tell, the lobby now hosted an exciting debut exhibition by R2D2. In fact, it was a collection of blueprints depicting the council office's renovations. "Here's what I want to know," Graham said. Since Laura had told him about Silas Granby rushing out of the exhibition, he had been anxiously waiting for the offices to open on Monday morning. "What happened to them, the paintings?"

Some of them were gone for good, he soon found, deliberately destroyed by one of the artists as part of an "Activist-Performative Gathering." "I think her name was Belinda. A young girl with weird ideas. Really got her head in the clouds," the office manager said. Graham was strangely and hypnotically drawn to the woman's bright, glossy peach lips that stood out in her otherwise unadorned face, spouting words he didn't want to hear.

"Destroyed? How?" Graham asked. His notebook opened in his hand almost unbidden.

"'Ritualistic purging,' I think she called it. She put it on YouTube. You might find it there."

"What does ritualistic purging consist of? Did you watch it?"

"A bunch of teenagers stood in a field, staring in different directions, while a small pile of terrible paintings got what was best for them, if you ask me. A good, hot barbecue."

Graham fired off an expletive fractionally too loud. "Sorry. It's just . . . I need to get hold of as many of them as possible." He handed her his card and began looking around. "Is there a list of the artists somewhere or promotional stuff for the . . ."

"I'm not sure, I wasn't involved in the planning or take apart. But I know where the remainder of the paintings are now. Shall I take you to them?"

Graham's heart jumped. "That would be most kind."

The woman led him through the warren of cubicles, odd corners, and converted rooms which formed the main body of the council building. The public facing part was bright, clean, and new. The rest was a depressing collection of rooms that owed nothing to the best architecture and even less to interior design.

Councillor Zara Hyde, still only days into her role, was on the phone in her office, a large but still undecorated space at the end of the broad hallway. "All those windows," Graham wondered aloud, looking at the huge sheets of glass held in place by old steel frames, the yellowed white paint peeling off them. "How does she cope when she needs to jump up and down in a searing rage?"

"Oh, I don't think she's that kind of a person," the office manager told Graham. "Very into"—she paused, searching for the right word—"'esoteric' practices, I think she called them. She wants us to begin meditating. Can you imagine? She even brought in a design company to assess the 'flow' of our offices! Now she's considering expensive changes." The office manager tutted. Profligacy, her expression said, was a vice not to be entertained at Gorey Council. Her peach lips pouted.

"Can we please just get the rest of the new cameras first before we throw money at other things?" Graham said. "I've a local man murdered just round the corner from here, and the only thing to witness it was the pavement he landed on."

"Terrible," the woman agreed, leading Graham into a suite of dingy rooms which reminded him of the sets of a Scandi noir crime drama he sometimes watched. "Here we've got some expansion space for when new projects come in," she said as though describing a modern, slick multi-use office rather than an unused, windowless room that hadn't seen a mop or a cloth in quite some time. "And back there is the storage. That's where you'll find the paintings. We've given the artists three months to pick them up." Her expression and crossed arms told Graham that she thought that was being far too generous. "And then we'll throw them out."

"Magnificent," Graham said, heading straight for the stacks of frames he could see propped against boxes. Some were placed neat and vertical, but others had been left higgledy-piggledy, as though certain of their imminent disposal. "These works are going to have a surprise second exhibition," Graham announced. "But could I trouble you for some help? Do you have any photos of the assembled exhibition?"

"Freddie Solomon took a huge number of photos at the—"

"I'd prefer the council's official shots, if you don't mind," Graham said, making a note all the same. "And can I borrow one or two of your people?"

The office manager stared at him, her mouth open slightly, her peach-slicked lips catching the light. Suddenly, she smiled as she chose to convey some of the town's respect toward their lead police officer. "To help out Gorey Constabulary and the famed Inspector Graham? In a murder case, no less?" She reached for a white, internal phone. "I think we can manage that."

The artists arrived at odd intervals, called from their homes by the enthusiastic efforts of the assistants the woman with the peach lips had seconded to the job of helping Graham out. Fergus, the agitated Scot prone to hissy fits, walked into the room with a perplexed but curious look on his face. He seemed to be hoping for a spectacle, or at least something to justify the hassle of being suddenly called down to the council offices. He'd not been particularly happy with his paintings in the first place, and now they would begin a second life as . . . evidence?

Argumentative on the phone, Belinda refused to attend until Graham threatened to compel her through legal means. "What do you want from me?" the young woman kept asking from the moment of her arrival. "Burning *The Crescent Bay Quartet* was always the plan. It completed the cycle. That was how it *had* to be." Her passion rose quickly to the surface, leaving her ruffled but unapologetic about her art and its demise. "It's a concept I'm drawn to. You probably wouldn't understand," she pronounced, clearly conveying she thought Graham far too old, conventional, and uncool. "You don't feel about them like I do. The immolation was a sign of *hope*."

"Well, right now," Graham told her, "my hope is that you're the only artist who's burned evidence before I could see it."

"Evidence?"

It was the most common question from the artists, all of whom had gathered by midmorning. Philomena Courthould-Bryant arrived second from last, despite living eighty yards from the council building. She was accompanied by her husband, all-round art snob Percival Courthould-Bryant, whose presence was unnecessary but the result of being in possession of an overactive curiosity and having nothing better to do. Mrs. Courthould-Bryant clutched four of her canvases. "Can you believe it, Percy? My little paintings being significant in a police enquiry," she said proudly.

"That's good," her husband muttered, "because they were never going to be significant in art history."

"Stop being rude about my art," his wife snapped. "Look at it; really look." She held one of the canvases up.

"Oh, right. I see!" her husband said, standing back to look at what she was holding up. "I get it. Sorry, Philomena. I was being slow." Courthould-Bryant had no idea what he was looking at but hadn't stayed married to his wife for fifty-five years without understanding when he needed to smooth things over now and again.

"See? Just because I'm not one of your classical artists doesn't mean I have nothing to offer." Philomena stalked off to talk to a more sympathetic soul, Dr. Ramachandran.

Abandoned, Courthould-Bryant looked around. "Detective Inspector, good day to you."

"Mr. Courthould-Bryant," Graham exclaimed. "A very good day to you too."

"A very *strange* day, I'd say it is," the elderly man continued. He'd lost none of the sergeant-major vigour he'd shown at the review of a historical miscarriage of justice months earlier. He still had the air of a man who always wanted to be in charge of any situation, his lack of comprehension with respect to its nuances notwithstanding. "Are you investigating forgers, then?" Courthould-Bryant asked. "Is that it?"

"Is what what, Mr. Courthould-Bryant?"

"Forgeries. You reckon one of these students is knocking out fakes? Selling them on the what's-it-web. You know, on the FreeBay." Courthould-Bryant leant in close. "You can tell me," he said, tapping his nose. "I'm a super confidant."

CHAPTER THIRTY-FOUR

GRAHAM SUPPRESSED A laugh only with effort. Courthould-Bryant was a super confidant for Freddie Solomon, more like. "No, we're not chasing forgers. Was your wife able to find all her paintings from the exhibition?" he asked.

"Yes." Courthould-Bryant leant in conspiratorially. "Unfortunately. One might rather she'd joined that young gel in a purifying immolation ceremony, or whatever she called it." Graham raised an eyebrow.

"Alright, alright." The elderly man raised his hands. "I'll be nothing but polite about Philomena's splashes of colour. Beauty in the eye of the beholder and all that."

"You could try being her *muse* from now on. Talent should be nurtured," Graham told him. "And especially later in life, we should all seize opportunities to bring pleasure to others and ourselves." Before the stunned septuagenarian could respond, Graham reiterated his main point: "Be nice to your wife. It'll do you good."

As Graham walked away, the elderly man decided to follow the detective's advice and headed off to help Philomena with her paintings. Graham had arranged for a conference room to be made available, and the artists were busy selecting their artwork and arranging it around the room.

Graham found his way to a small, pleasantly plump woman with thick-rimmed, round glasses who wore an elegantly draped saree in a bright-yellow batik print. "You must be Dr. Ramachandran," Graham said. He extended a hand. "Thank you so much for coming over."

"Please call me Dr. Hiruni. Everyone else does." Dr. Hiruni was affable and gracious, and though bemused by the situation, intrigued as to where it might lead. "When they told us the paintings might be useful to the police," she said, "I assumed they meant an artistic crime had been committed, not a violent one." Like the other artists, she had propped up her paintings against an uncluttered wall. Fergus banged nails into it so they could be hung.

"One never knows," said Graham, "where vital evidence is going to come from. And we have to try everything. Are your paintings in the same order as before?"

"Yes, but I can't see how they'll be of any help. They're just landscapes, and not especially good ones, I confess."

"They're very attractive," Graham said. "And as for whether they are evidence, leave that to me."

Rumours had spread quickly, and by the time the last artist from the retreat, Magda Padalka-Lyons, finally showed up with Pom-Pom the Pomeranian trotting along behind her, the five-person artists' collective understood the seriousness of the case and their role in it, even if they didn't understand how their paintings mattered.

"Mine were here and here." Philomena was pointing as the exhibition took shape once more. "And over there." Graham helped her hang the pictures while her husband held his wife's handbag.

"I suppose," Belinda said, considering the space, "that my pictures occupied these four gaps. But they're not here now."

"Of course they aren't here now," Fergus said. "You burned them, remember?"

"I mean," she said, "that their *resonance* isn't here anymore. There can't be *harmony* now."

"Ah," Fergus said, and left it at that.

Sheets of card were fixed to the walls to represent Belinda's pieces, and she eventually consented to providing rough sketches of them, quickly done in pencil. They became ghostly in their incompleteness, as though the artist had tired of the work and given up or met with some terrible fate.

"Thank you, Belinda," Graham said, mindful of her prickly character as he sought to sustain her cooperation. The others were largely bemused by the whole thing except Fergus, who was enjoying himself, this second exhibition, and the inevitable attention *far* too much, all the while muttering about the inconvenience.

"Don't be daft, lass," Fergus was saying to the stupefied Dr. Hiruni. "Yours were *here*, and mine were next to these other ones *here*."

"That's not how I remember it," Dr. Hiruni objected. Clearing up their conflicting memories took only five minutes using the council's promotional photos, at which point Fergus offered a grudging apology.

"What does it matter, the order?" Fergus asked as Graham paced steadily around the room, fixated on the L-shaped row of pictures that spread across one wall and part of another. "I mean, why do we have to recreate it exactly as it—"

"Because exactitude is a virtue, Mr. Barr," Graham answered, unwilling to share his thought process with the artists. "Whatever Peregrine Wordsworth believes." Graham had seen Wordsworth's show on TV once and only once, vowing never again to spend his time in such a manner. He had been relieved to hear that the leader of the retreat had disappeared off the island immediately after the public viewing of the paintings was over. Wordsworth was currently somewhere in South Asia.

Once Belinda's reconstructions were complete and Dr. Hiruni was content as to the arrangement of the pieces, Graham labelled each painting with the date and the artist's name. He began his 'survey.' "I hope you won't mind me asking for complete quiet," he said, his back to the artists. "I'll call on you if I need to, alright?"

※

Roach pulled his pole out of the back of the patrol car and grabbed Carmen's lead as she jumped down. He'd parked the car at one end of Hautville Road, and now he stared down the row of houses to the Foc's'le at the other. He knew Janice had already searched the front gardens of these houses, but she'd encouraged him to have another go at finding the murder weapon.

"Right, Carmen, old girl. Let's give you a good old sniff."

A car pulled up and Janice got out. As she walked across the road to Roach, she took a call. "Hi, Laura . . . Uh-huh . . . Council offices, okay, I'll look him up. . . I will, take care." She hung up. "What have you got there, Roachie?" In his hand, Roach held a bloodstained shirt. Janice recoiled at the sight.

"It's Jamie Reeves's from the other night. I'm going to let Carmen sniff it and then see where she takes us."

"Is that even allowed?"

"I don't see why not. I considered using Bazza's shirt—he had a load of blood all over him—but I thought his scent *and* Jamie's would confuse her. Let's see what she can do, eh? If it doesn't work, we'll resort to the sticks." He raised the pole in his hand.

Roach crouched and held out the shirt for Carmen. She gave a little bark but seemed uninterested in it. "Come on, girl. Take some notice, will ya?"

"She's too young and untrained, Jim."

Roach tried again, but Carmen turned in a circle, unsure of what was expected of her. He sighed. "Okay, it was worth a try. Poles it is then—whoa!" Carmen took off. She ran to a spot in the pavement two houses up.

"That's where the trail of blood started. It's where we think he was hit," Janice said. "He then staggered or crawled his way up the road to the pub." As if to confirm what Janice was saying, Carmen started to pull on her lead in the direction of the Foc's'le.

Roach let her follow the trail as he and Janice jogged behind her. When Carmen reached the pub doors, Roach gave her a treat. "Good girl, Carmen, *good* girl. Alright, what shall we do n—" Carmen strained on her lead, but this time in a new direction. She led him down the side of the pub. "She's heading for the bins, Janice!"

"Could be nothing, but let's see." Carmen ran up to a green industrial skip and stood on her hind legs, whining and pawing at it.

"I'll grab that pallet," Roach said, leaving Carmen with Janice as he manhandled a crate over to the side of the skip. Janice climbed up to peer over the top into the pile of bottles, pizza boxes, and other detritus generated by a lively pub one day away from collection day.

"Give me your pole." Roach handed it over and watched Janice carefully as she poked and prodded. Her eyes lit up. Carmen was still whining. "Shush, girl, shush. I think she's got something."

From her pocket, Janice pulled out a pair of gloves and reached into the skip. "Aha!" she said, holding up her find for Roach to see, her eyes shining.

"What is it?" Roach cried.

"This, Sergeant Roach, is a bloodstained chunk of pebbled concrete of the exact kind one will find to excess at the Granby house."

CHAPTER THIRTY-FIVE

THEY HAD PRODUCED sixteen exhibit-worthy paintings in all, but Graham immediately eliminated seven of them: all four of Belinda's, two of Dr. Hiruni's three, and one of Magda's. He politely asked each artist to retrieve their works. "Very good," he said of them. "Please don't be discouraged. They simply don't possess the relevant evidentiary features."

The muttering began, encouraged by an overly excited Fergus. "We should be filming this, you know. It'd make a great documentary."

"Shh," advised Dr. Hiruni. "He's thinking."

"He's barking mad," Fergus hissed. "Are you sure he's a real detective and not just a local crank who's, like, a 'consultant,' or whatever?"

Ten yards and many worlds away, David Graham was assessing . . . But then the rude distraction of Freddie Solomon's particularly annoying voice wrecked his concentration. As certain as the sunrise, Freddie Solomon had somehow arrived in the conference room. "Upsetting to see your art utilised in this way, isn't it?" he began sympathetically to the group. "Who feels like sharing?"

"Solomon!" Graham cried. "Who let you in? Are you *trying* to get arrested for interfering with witnesses? Is that what's going on?"

The artists all took three steps back as though Freddie were radioactive. "Let me guess. You're planning a special article called 'Inside Gorey Constabulary,'" Graham continued, "where you blog from one of the cells. I can imagine it now. 'The conditions are appalling, but my fight is just. Please send donations to . . .'"

"I have every right to speak to members of the public."

"Blog on down the road, Freddie. Steer clear of this one."

"This is intimidation of the press!" Freddie cried. "The latest in a long history!" He turned to appeal to the artists, but there was no sign of them. They'd disappeared like mist over water at sunrise. "It's like being a journalist in a police state!"

Freddie stalked off, leaving Graham alone. Once he'd gone, the confused gaggle of artists showed their faces again. "I apologise for the interruption," Graham said. "Now, where were we? I have questions about the paintings."

"We weren't really supposed to be exact about everything," Dr. Hiruni explained.

Graham summed up what he understood of Wordsworth's philosophy and process: "You were instructed to produce gusty, colourful gestures to celebrate one's joy in the creation of art, yes? Precise details of people and things half a mile away, not so much."

The lack of detail bothered Graham acutely, and this worsened as his study of the exhibition reached its conclusion. "This," he muttered to himself, "is going to be tricky. Did you make anything up? Paint things that weren't there?"

There were a lot of furrowed brows. "I think the scenes were pretty much as I painted them, certainly as I interpreted them," Philomena Courthould-Bryant said.

"I don't have enough imagination to put things in that aren't real," Magna simpered. "If I did, there'd be dragons and shapeshifters everywhere."

"For me, Peregrine helped make a good container for my practice," Fergus said, finding such buzzwords irresistible despite his dislike of them when uttered by anyone else. "But I didn't need all his advice. The stuff about letting the details go and what have you. 'Breathe through the painting,' he said once." Fergus shook his head. "Anyway, what did you want to know about my work?"

Graham kept his questions direct. "Did you paint this one on Friday?" He tapped the frame of a particularly vibrant pastiche of swirls and loops. Over these, Fergus had painted in contrasting colours a series of dots.

"They signify details. I thought the precise colour coding provided an evocative contrast with the surrealism of the background. Sort of like life—a series of adventures imprinted over a lifetime."

"Er, right. So . . . Friday?"

"Yes, I think so."

"In the morning or afternoon?"

"After lunch. Does that matter?" Fergus asked.

Graham ignored his question and continued to stare at the paintings, pondering the many elements—the depictions of the water, the small strip of beach at the foot of the cliffs, the grey complex of low clouds which signalled another incoming rainstorm. Instead, Graham brought his full attention to the right-hand side of each picture, where the cliff face swept upward and out as though sculpted by the wind, leaving a plateau of land which jutted into the Channel.

Janice appeared at his elbow. "Boss? Everything alright? Laura said I might find you here." What Laura had actually said was "David might be on red alert today. You might want to keep an eye on him."

Thus far, Janice found, Graham had succeeded mostly in confusing everyone, including the staff at the council offices, several of whom kept peeking into the conference room to see what was going on. They saw only a man dressed in a dark grey suit standing thoughtfully in front of the paintings. "Boss?" she asked again.

"Good day, Janice," Graham said without turning round.

"You, um, think you've found something, sir?" Janice watched him for a reaction, but his face was impassive and focused. "In the paintings?"

"Maybe." Graham stepped right, becoming absorbed again in Fergus's painting from the Friday lunchtime.

"I've got some news, boss."

"Okay." Graham didn't look up from peering closely at Fergus's dotty composition. Janice blew out her cheeks. She looked around. She'd save Carmen's find until she had the DI's full attention.

"You'd have thought," Fergus whispered to Belinda, a few yards away, "he'd seen enough the first time around."

Unconcerned with plaudits but fascinated by the inspector and his process, Belinda shrugged and watched the detective work. He moved steadily through the space, always aware of everything, his eyes constantly in motion. "What's he *doing*?" she whispered.

Dr. Hiruni had depicted the Granby home almost like a kind of mushroom exploding upward out of the rock. Graham stared at it, his nose almost touching the canvas. *Friday morning, purple van and one black vehicle.*

Graham moved along to the next painting. *Friday, early afternoon, no van, no black vehicle . . .*

One after another . . . *Friday late afternoon, man and woman beside pool, purple shirt, bikini, no van, black vehicle.*

Next . . . *Saturday morning, man, woman sunbathing. Black vehicle only.*

The paintings were of varying quality, and some were mere compilations of splodges of colour on canvas, but viewing the paintings side by side multiple times, Graham layered the pictures in his mind. He built a composite image of what they conveyed even though when viewed individually, their meaning was near impossible to determine. It was almost like flicking through an old-fashioned flip-book. They only made sense when viewed together, comprising an uncommon witness to events otherwise unseen. He closed his eyes, encoding the images into his memory.

There were more questions, highly specific and direct. "Magda, come and look at your third painting with me," he said. "Can you remember how many people you saw around the house?" As Magda ransacked her memory, Graham also brought Fergus forward. "Cast your mind back and convince me you painted *exactly* what was there."

His cheeks puffed out; Fergus was nervous at this challenge to his accuracy. Would his work be sufficient to help the police? Might he be partly responsible for catching a violent criminal?

Belinda remained silent. She sat on the floor, leaning against a pillar sketching the scene. Harding glanced down to see a hastily sketched row of people pointing at the artwork, a taller, imposing man at the centre. He appeared to be directing them, organising their work. "I don't think the DI's been commemorated in art before."

"I'm just trying something out," Belinda said, barely restraining her first impulse to shield her sketchbook from view.

"It's great," Harding said, smiling. "I just hope you don't feel the need to burn it this time, that's all."

"Fantastic." Belinda snorted. "I'm typecast. Am I to be forever 'The Girl Who Burns Her Work'?" She sighed, still young but already weary of the world.

"Alright, love. As you were," Harding muttered. She moved on and eyed Freddie. He had scuttled in again when she'd arrived. "Takes all kinds to make a world, doesn't it, Freddie?"

For once, the blogger was fascinated by DI Graham and didn't care who knew it. "This is his process! Right here in front of us!" he whispered to the others excitedly. "I *wish* I could interview him right now."

"Don't you dare," Janice advised. "He'll likely make sure you end up in a Category-A prison, sharing a cell with a terrorist."

"Best not then," Freddie said, crestfallen. "Still, I might be able to press Laura for a few details later."

"Come on, Sergeant," Graham called over. There was a note of urgency in his voice, a quickness to his stride like he'd suddenly plugged into an energy source.

"Where are we going?" Janice said, trying to catch up as they travelled along a dark corridor. Graham hadn't even said goodbye to the artists.

"The Granby place," Graham replied. "I enjoyed their topiary. Fancy myself another look."

CHAPTER THIRTY-SIX

"TOPIARY?" JANICE SAID, diving into the passenger seat before she was left behind. They were soon driving at a speed which would have left Graham liable to arrest were he a regular person. "You've got a theory then, boss?" she asked, holding on tight and hoping Graham hadn't lost his mind.

"A theory? We'll see," said Graham.

"Care to share it? Something? Anything?"

"When Mozart was nearing the end of a composition, did people barge into his studio and ask to see the incomplete manuscript?"

"Probably not," Harding admitted. "But, sir, I mean, comparing yourself to . . ."

"My manuscript is ninety-six percent finished, Sergeant. With a little bit of luck, you'll be witness to its completion." He turned right onto the newly laid, single-lane track. When they reached the security gate, Graham stayed behind the wheel while Janice gained them access. The moment she shut her car door, Graham raced around the edge of the Granby's putting green and past the two superb sports cars resplendent in the sunshine.

The car stopped. Graham was in a hurry to get out and speak to the Granbys. "What was that news you mentioned?" He was already tripping down the front steps. The deep *bong* of the doorbell could be heard within, followed by hysterical barking.

"Oh, God, not again," Graham muttered. "Give me a golden retriever any day."

"Jim and I had another poke around for the murder weapon. And we think we found it."

Graham's eyes widened. "What? Where?"

"In the bins behind the Foc's'le. Carmen found it."

"Well, what was it?" Graham could hear footsteps getting louder behind the door.

"A bloodstained lump of concrete . . . of a particular type that matches that holding up this precise residence. Jim's testing it as we speak."

"Well, hello again!" Katya Granby looked shiny and radiant. Janice suspected an intense multistep skincare routine involving products that cost the equivalent of her monthly salary. "Look who it is!" Mrs. Granby said to the dog under her arm. Willow had the suspicious, aggressive eyes of an animal prepared to square up to anyone. "It's the police again. What do they want this time, hmm?" she asked her dog. Willow licked her fragrant, sticky face appreciatively.

"Might we come in please, Mrs. Granby?" Graham said. "We have a few more questions. Won't take long." Invited in, he walked past Katya, who continued uttering childish nonsense to her dog. Once he reached the living room, Graham rather brazenly took a seat in the middle of the living room couch.

"Make yourself comfortable," Katya said, setting down her dog. It patrolled around her feet, hoping either for scraps of food or, Graham suspected, an excuse to finally bite someone. "The news," she said, abruptly changing her tone, "about Jamie. Very, very sad. So young. So *tragic*."

Graham supposed he'd gone through the usual motions of bringing out his notebook and pen but couldn't remember doing so; they were simply in his hand, ready. "I'm afraid I have to disagree with you there, Mrs. Granby."

"I'm sorry?" she said. "You know, English is my second language. Maybe I make many mistakes."

"About it being a tragedy. Do you know the origin of the word?"

Katya looked at her dog, then at Harding, then at Graham. "Is it an English test?" She laughed. "I didn't prepare."

"The Greeks," explained Graham, "would call a story a 'tragedy' when our main character is headed for disaster, but one which is inevitable, one that cannot be forestalled."

Katya struggled to catch up. "Cannot be . . . what? Like, cannot be stopped?"

"That's right. A person is walking into disaster—another Greek word, by the way—and can do nothing about it."

"But . . . it's *tragic*, no? Jamie. Bad news. The worst, the most terrible!"

"But not inevitable," Graham reiterated. "Actions could have been taken to avoid such an outcome."

Harding was no help, despite Katya's pleading eyes. "I really don't understand. Maybe you should talk to my husband."

"That sounds like a good idea," Graham said.

"But . . . I need to tell you, he's very upset today." Katya's slick face fell. "Very angry."

"Why's that, Katya?" Janice asked gently. She might as well play good cop. Graham was clearly doing his damnedest to be obtuse.

"A problem," Katya said, heading down the hallway to her husband's study, "at the airport. Very big trouble. Was a . . . how do you say? A *fiasco*."

Silas Granby answered the knock on his study door with a gruff expletive but was soon persuaded by his wife to greet their guests. "'Fiasco' is right," he said, coming through to shake the officers' hands. "First time it's ever happened to me. They behaved as though they'd never seen a British passport before. Problems with my visa. Highly unusual."

Graham took in every detail, as usual, from the man's tousled hair to his comfortable, expensive carpet slippers. "Where were you heading, sir?"

"New York," Granby answered. "Three days of meetings, then onward to Beijing. Honestly, some years I reckon I do more air-miles than a migrating bird. Makes it even harder to understand the problem this morning. I mean, I've been through immigration about a million times. They even gave me two different reasons, and they couldn't both be true!" He threw up his hands. "Typical government idiocy. I've had to delay my trip."

"Terrible," Janice trolled. Granby looked at her sharply. She gazed back and smiled sympathetically.

Graham motioned to the couches, a strange gesture perhaps in someone else's home but symbolic of what would come next: this was now his show. Part of him craved a more generous crowd, but he knew the moment had come, and he could not delay.

"Sergeant, let's begin with what we know," he said, standing now while the others sat, experiencing varying degrees of concern.

"Before you launch into something, can we please talk about why you're here?" Granby said, unwilling to relinquish control of the situation in his own home.

To Graham's surprise, Katya rolled her eyes at him. "Darling, the Jamie Reeves situation? Remember? They're investigating."

"Still?" Granby said.

"We've been developing some lines of enquiry," said Graham, "and they took time to bear fruit."

"Splendid," said Granby. "I hope you catch the monster. But how can we help?"

"Sergeant Harding, why don't you tell Mr. and Mrs. Granby what you told me?" he said to her. "About the graveyard."

🌎

"Jan told me that some records aren't always in the database. That some get 'lost' in the process of digitising." Barnwell was in the office talking to Jack, who'd popped in at Janice's behest.

"Yeah, they're not 'lost' as such, they just aren't in a compatible format. It takes time to convert them, and some never make it. They're somewhere, but not always available on the main system." Jack stood behind Barnwell, who sat in front of his computer screen, a mug of tea warming his hands.

"See, is there any way to find them?" Barnwell twisted his head to look at Janice's fiancé. "I've got a feeling about this Walker guy. He has 'ex-con' written all over him. But I can't find him in the system. And he's not saying nuthin'. I'd like to go a step further to see if we can winkle him out."

"If you get me the records, I can see what I can do. I might be able to rip them and even roll them into the system so they are there for the joy of every police officer in the land."

"That would be fantastic. But to get them, who would I talk to? I've no idea. Walker's from London, so most likely someone in the Met."

"I know someone," Jim piped up from behind his screen. He was typing up a report on the forensic findings on the lump of concrete found in the skip next to the Foc's'le. "I met him when I was there. Let me give him a call."

CHAPTER THIRTY-SEVEN

"THERE WAS A sighting of one of your cars, Mr. Granby," Janice said.

"A 'sighting'?" he said. "How do you mean?"

"Someone drove your Maserati, Mr. Granby. It was seen. And the driver wasn't you."

"Impossible," he said brusquely. "Only I'm insured, and I never let friends borrow . . . Oh," he said, with a look of concern. "Oh, wait." He turned to his wife. "You mean . . ."

"Mrs. Granby," Janice said, "could you please tell us about the visit you made to the graveyard at St. Andrews church?"

Blinking, Katya forgot about her dog, which ran sniffing around the edge of the room. Eventually it toddled away down one of the hallways. "She means the cemetery, yes?" Katya said. "The place for the dead peoples?"

"One dead person in particular," Graham said. "Could you tell us why you chose to visit Jamie Reeves's grave?"

Three pairs of eyes observed her every movement as she struggled to retain her composure and simultaneously answer a question which was difficult emotionally and linguistically. "It is normal, no? To say goodbye to someone. At home, it is like this. You have it here too."

"We do," Janice said. "The thing is people who quietly visit gravesites alone are usually loved ones."

Katya's face reddened. "*Love?*" She glanced around the room. "Please, you misunderstand. Was not 'love.' How could it be?" She reached for her husband's hand, finding it cold. "I am married lady, after all. Just, I was . . ." She made several false starts before saying, "You know, just sad for the young man, sad for his family. Is normal, no?" she asserted again. "I was passing and thought I would pay my respects."

"But you chose not to join the other mourners at the funeral," Graham pointed out. "His parents, his colleagues, his friends."

"Of course, of course." No further explanation was forthcoming.

"You didn't want to be seen there," Janice said. It wasn't a question. "One might wonder if coming late, alone, was a good way to remain unobserved."

Through all of this, Granby kept absolutely quiet. He sat back on the couch, his legs crossed, his fingers interlocked over his knee as though watching a solemn scene at the theatre.

"The family would be so sad, no? Was a tragedy, even if the Greeks don't agree." Katya smiled politely at Graham. "I got the time wrong. Was late was all."

"Very considerate," Graham said. He held Katya's gaze for a moment before dragging it away to look at her husband. "Now, if I could ask you, Mr. Granby, about one thing you told us?"

"By all means," he said. He smiled briefly, spreading his hands.

"You claimed that you witnessed an argument between Mr. Adrian Sanderson and his employee, Jamie Reeves. Do you still make that claim today?"

With a little shrug, Granby asked, "Why would I want to change what I said? I remember it distinctly. They disagreed about the fee they would charge me."

Graham let the bitterness slide. "It was Sanderson who wanted to charge you a higher price?"

"Certainly. Everyone who's worked on this place has done their share of price gouging. I'd have taken half of them to court except . . ." He raised his hands before letting them drop in his lap. "Eh, I can afford it. I see it as a way to contribute to the local economy in the wider sense."

"And you maintain there was pushing."

"I do."

Abruptly rising and striding to the front door, Graham took them all by surprise. "I want to conduct a little experiment. Ears open, ladies and gentlemen. Please be ready to repeat back to me everything I say when I'm outside."

"He's leaving?" Katya stood, perplexed. Willow sensed the same. The Pomeranian suddenly appeared and chased Graham to the door.

"Bugger off," he hissed.

Katya retrieved Willow from Graham's ankles and he headed outside, closing the Granby's heavy patio doors behind him. The transition from the cool, air-conditioned interior to an unseasonably warm, spring outdoors made Graham sweat. Deciding quickly how to proceed, he stood in the centre of the paved area three steps down from the doors, adopted a heroic, theatrical stance, and went for it.

"'Friends, Romans, countrymen,'" he cried, his voice huge and stentorian. "Lend me your ears; I come to bury Caesar, not to praise him. The evil that men do lives after them," he warned with a raised finger. "The good is oft interred with their bones; so let it be with Caesar.'" Graham straightened his jacket, gave a small cough, and threw open the door as fast and as far as its mechanism would allow. "Any notes? Marks out of ten?" he asked his audience of three.

"You are back?" Katya cried, entirely confused. Granby stared up at Graham from his unchanged position on the sofa.

The expression on Janice's face said it all. She sat poised with her notebook, ready to dictate, but apparently hadn't heard a thing.

"Oh, for heaven's sake," Graham complained. "I know it's been twenty years since I won the school Shakespeare prize, but please tell me I've still *got it*."

Fascinated but now entirely lost, Janice could only watch, wondering what on earth William Shakespeare might have to do with the Reeves case.

"What about you, Mr. Granby? Did you catch the performance?" asked Graham.

"I'm afraid not," he said, still relaxed on the couch despite Graham's unexpected theatrics.

"I gave it my all," Graham said, deflated. "Well, it's as good a reason as any, I suppose."

"What is?" Janice replied.

"My performance."

"To do what?" Harding said.

"To arrest Mr. Granby."

Katya shrieked, which set off the dog. Above the din, Janice couldn't stop herself from exclaiming, "Arrest him? Because he doesn't like Shakespeare?"

"No, because he didn't *hear* it. I was projecting fit to fill the Albert Hall and not a word came through." Graham turned to Granby, who was sitting forward watching the detective with narrowed eyes and a clenched jaw, his mind working as he tried to anticipate what the detective might say next. "I've got to say," Graham continued, "that's one heck of a glazier you hired, Mr. Granby. These windows are absolutely first-rate."

Predictably, Katya's comprehension was fixated on one word. "*Arrest?*" she asked again and again. "*Arrest* my Silas?" Harding gestured for her to be calm, but it did little to help. "For *what?*"

Annoyed it had taken so long, Harding was, however, finally able to latch onto Graham's floating, cross-field pass and run with the ball. "If DI Graham's Shakespeare was inaudible, you'd have been unable to hear a conversation between Jamie and Mr. Sanderson as you state."

"Perhaps," Granby said, still quite relaxed. "If they were closed. But one of the back windows was open. It's been so warm for April."

"I realise that you have money to burn, Mr. Granby," Graham said, "but only a fool runs their air-conditioning *and* opens the windows."

"You wouldn't be the first to call me a fool," Granby said. "Although I'm not sure failing to admire your Shakespeare is grounds for arrest."

"No, it's true," Graham said, putting away his notebook and pen. "They don't let us arrest people for those things."

"Well, there's a happy state of affairs," Granby summed up. "Isn't it wonderful to live in a democracy?"

"But," Graham added, "they do let us arrest people on suspicion of murder."

CHAPTER THIRTY-EIGHT

"YOU'RE OFF YOUR bleedin' rocker!"

"Please be quiet and go inside, sir."

The answer was another noisy complaint. "Ge'roff me, you big twit! I'm already in handcuffs. What more do you want?"

"Sergeant Harding, I present to you Mr. Matthew Walker," Barnwell said to Janice as he succeeded in manhandling Matthew into the reception area. Janice was entering the details of Silas Granby's arrest into the computer. "He has been detained on suspicion of the murder of Jamie Reeves."

Harding watched the two men struggle briefly. It was at times like these that she wished she had a taser on her, something she could call upon easily without needing to complete a bunch of paperwork. She decided to threaten instead. "Mr. Walker?" she said loudly to the enormous, angry man. "Are we going dancing down Electric Avenue, or are you going to behave yourself?" Carmen came running into reception, her nails clicking on the hard floor. Excited by the commotion, she ran between Walker and Barnwell until the constable put his hand on her head to calm her. "Sit! Good girl." He pulled a treat from his pocket. Carmen snuffled it down in a second.

"He's only gone and bleedin' nabbed me!" Matthew howled. "Read me me rights and everything! Been 'elping 'im all week, telling 'im the truth, answering all 'is questions. 'E's got it in for me, 'e 'as!" Walker's London roots were showing.

"Don't be bloody daft," Barnwell rasped.

"Well, I dunno what else to fink." Matthew slumped into one of the plastic chairs set out in reception. The chair was dwarfed by his bulk, the fight suddenly leaving him.

"Afternoon, Janice," Barnwell said brightly. "It turns out that Mr. Walker has a colourful and fascinating past, previously unknown to the Gorey

Constabulary, one he didn't care to share with us. Initial searches of the Police National Computer revealed no criminal record for the name, but some sleuthing and a stroke of luck changed the sitch. He's done some *very* bad things."

"That ain't me," the furious man complained loudly. "I'll plead mistaken identity!"

"Plead? You couldn't bloody well *spell* it," Barnwell growled. He turned to Harding, his tone all sweetness and light once more. "Sergeant Harding, I ask you," he said, feeling very pleased with himself, "is there anything that our fabulous computer forensic consultant can't do?"

"How do you mean?" she asked, too conflicted and lost to even begin the arrest paperwork. If Matthew was the killer, he certainly wasn't ready to confess. The anger evaporated off him as he rhythmically knocked his handcuffs against the underside of the chair he was sitting on.

"Police forces throughout the whole country," Barnwell explained, "have been digitising their criminal records. Takes ages, really tricky. Some of the records slot right in, others take longer, and some just never quite make it into the main file. They get stuck in a desk drawer . . ."

"Or shredded by mistake," Harding added, something she'd learned from conferences.

"Or, in this case, left on a form of media that none of our machines can read."

"Ah-hah," Janice said, making the connection. "Couldn't read until a certain technical wizard entered our midst?"

"He's a wizard, alright. Only had sixty records on the disc. London didn't know what to do with it, but they found an 'M. Walker' on the index, and we thought it worth a try."

"Unlucky, Matthew," Harding said. She looked over. "Lying about previous offences won't help your defence, man."

"I didn't lie. I ain't saying nothin' more without a lawyer," Matthew declared, quietly pleased that he'd thought of it. "Never had anyone pin a murder on me. Bloody ridiculous!"

"Oh, come on, lad, there's no need to sell yourself short. You were convicted of beating a man almost to death." Barnwell looked at Janice and paused for dramatic effect. "With a snooker cue."

Matthew was sulking now, beaten. "That bloke was a bloody liar. Exaggerated 'is injuries. Told the police a bunch of absolute rubbish."

"Medical records prove otherwise. And while you were banged up for five years, you got into a fight with a Scottish hard nut who put *you* in hospital for a fortnight. Sound familiar?"

"No."

"Want to show me your back, on the left side, where you were stabbed?"

"No."

"Must have been some fight over something at least one of you thought important."

"Self-defence on my part." Matthew was surly now. "What are you arrestin' me for anyway?"

"Suspicion of murder. Obstruction. A few more we can lay at your door if we have to."

Harding reiterated Matthew's rights under the law. "You do not have to say anything, Matthew, but remember that 'it may harm your defence if you fail to mention something you later rely on in court.' Them's the rules for you, just now."

"Yeah, he told me all that already."

The door to the interview room opened. Graham emerged. "What's going on?"

"Matthew's got previous for GBH, sir. Never mentioned it. Tried to hide his past from us."

"No, I didn't!" Matthew protested. "Was all on that disc thingy in London, you said! And," he yelled at Graham, "no one even *asked* about that!"

Graham was tired. It had been a long day already, and it wasn't even close to being over. Now, he felt pulled in two directions at once. He pinched the bridge of his nose.

"He did it, sir. I'm sure of it. Ten minutes in there with you," Barnwell said, pointing to the interview room, "and he'll sing like Ella Fitzgerald."

"I can't sing, I won't sing, and you lot are off your bleedin' rockers!" Matthew repeated. "I didn't kill anyone!"

"Funny, I've got a chap sitting in there right now," Graham replied, "who's saying the same thing."

"Two of us? What, now?" Matthew sneered. "Are you just arrestin' anyone you feel like?" He shook his head like a dog with a flea in his ear. "That's what you lot all do, innit? Make it up as you go along."

Determined to let silence reign for a few seconds, Graham gave the atmosphere time to settle. "Finish off booking him in and put him in a cell. Barnwell, step into my office. And Janice, could I borrow you too when you're done with that? We'll leave the door open to keep an eye on reception."

Five minutes later, Graham used dividing gestures to organise his office like a court room. "I'm the judge. Barnwell, you're the prosecution, and Harding, you're defending Walker. Alright?"

"I'll give it a try," said Harding.

"Bring it," Barnwell added.

"Barnwell," Graham began, "set out for me why and how Matthew attacked Jamie Reeves."

The constable listed the sequence of reasons on his fingers. "A violent past, uncontrollable jealousy, rising anger, plenty of lies and deception, and a ton of alcohol. Insanely jealous of Reeves still having command over his girlfriend's affections, he goes out on the night in question and hits Reeves over the head to take him out of the picture."

"Right. Thanks. Harding?" Graham nodded at Janice. "Over to you."

"Do you have a confession from Mr. Walker?" Harding asked.

"Quite the opposite. But . . ."

"Right, so how exactly do you think Mr. Walker committed the offence?"

"He left the house he was sharing with his girlfriend on the Friday night, followed Mr. Reeves, or encouraged him from his house somehow. Either an argument took place, or he simply took a pop at the victim."

"Mr. Walker says he was at home all evening."

"Walker is alibied only by his girlfriend, who has said he was outside for fifteen minutes. He couldn't tell us who had won *MasterChef*. The house he's staying at is only five minutes from where the attack took place. He slipped out to batter Reeves and got back within fifteen minutes."

"Witnesses?" Janice asked Barnwell simply.

"None."

"Corroborating forensic evidence?"

"Unavailable." A gnawing feeling formed in the pit of Barnwell's stomach.

"Certainty about his motivation? That Matthew knew Paula wanted to get back together with Jamie?"

"Not established," Barnwell said, losing traction by the second.

"Did you know that earlier we found a bloodstained lump of concrete matching that found at the Granby house in a skip next to the Foc's'le?"

"I did not. Drat."

"But you had a *feeling*," Graham said. "Didn't you? Something in your gut told you, *insisted* to you: 'This is the only thing that makes sense. This *must* be the answer.' A confidence that you've *definitely* got your man, even though the evidence isn't quite there yet. Right?"

"Something like that, sir." It was best to be honest, Barnwell thought as his theory shed its wings and tumbled into a terminal descent.

"You were premature, Constable. But I like that you're listening to your instincts."

"Sounds like you know the feeling, sir."

"I do. I'm experiencing it right now, as it happens." Graham rose to put the kettle on.

"Sir?"

"Silas Granby. He's in the interview room," Janice said.

"The snooty chap with the expensive cars, the brunette mail-order wife, and the ridiculous house?" Graham raised an eyebrow. "Sergeant Harding told me, sir." Janice looked at her black police boots.

"That'd be the same man, yes," said Graham. "You see, I've got a feeling. A feeling in my chest telling me that Granby is the only suspect who makes sense. A feeling that he *must* be the murderer. A certainty that I've . . ."

"Definitely got your man," Barnwell said, "even if all the evidence doesn't line up yet."

Graham poured boiling water into his new teapot. It had a Dutch windmill scene on the side, the handle of his old one with the willow pattern having finally become too fragile to be serviceable. He took a few seconds to enjoy the sinuous curls of steam emanating from the waterfall of concentrated heat, the rising of a grassy, optimistic aroma. Every single time it brought him joy and lit up his brain. Especially right now. "That's the thing, though," he said to Barnwell, delighting in the delicate oolong scent coming from the pot. "My evidence *does*."

Janice's phone pinged. "It's Roach, sir. He's got a blood match on that lump of concrete."

"For whom?"

"Jamie Reeves, sir. We've got a conclusive connection between the victim and Granby."

CHAPTER THIRTY-NINE

JEFFREY LANGHAM ARRIVED just as Graham and Barnwell finished their planning for the interview with Silas Granby. There was no need for him to introduce himself; the pin-stripe suit, expensive briefcase, highly polished shoes, and superior air marked him as a high-powered lawyer. Graham ushered him into the interview room where Granby sat in front of a cold cup of tea.

"Mr. Shiny Shoes is going to tell Granby to shut up and hope for the best," Barnwell guessed. "Isn't he?"

Graham handed Barnwell a mug of tea, a hot one, and then laid out the standard *modus operandi* for such lawyers in these circumstances. "Find irregularities in the arrest or charging, pick holes in our arguments and evidence, then demand release on bail, at the very least."

"Can't see you going for that, boss," said Barnwell.

"Not in a month of Sundays. Granby's a flight risk."

"Want to keep him downstairs overnight?"

"Maybe."

Barnwell blew out his cheeks. "This case, I tell you, it's as twisty as a snake."

"Good thing then that Gorey Constabulary is staffed by sharp-eyed birds of prey," Graham said, his notebook out and ready.

"You seem very sure Granby is your man, boss." Barnwell was reluctant to let go of his idea that Matthew was the killer. But he had yet to hear the full story about the wealth manager, and he knew that Graham would have solid reasons for arresting him. "No doubts about him at all?"

"We'll see. Got a couple of things to fall into place yet. We've got the wife too. She's not being straight with us either."

Just then, Janice escorted a woman with flowing brown hair perfectly coloured with red highlights into Graham's office. The woman wore large, anonymising sunglasses and heels which were perhaps three inches too high for the occasion. No one was surprised to find that Mrs. Katerina Granby was absolutely furious. Barnwell left to man reception.

"She," Katya said of Harding, "is nice. Is a nice lady. But *you*, Inspector"—she pointed accusingly—"are a devil!"

"I've been called worse," Graham said.

"Where is my husband?" she demanded.

"He's with his representative on the other side of that wall." He pointed. Katya bolted for the door, but Harding caught her forearm. "We'll be speaking to you separately, and due to evidentiary constraints, you may *not* speak with him alone." Graham's hard eyes held Katya's, and some of the steel in hers faded. She yanked her arm away from Harding. "Would you like some water? Tea?"

"*Tea?*" Katya sang in amazement. "How can you think about *tea*, you crazy man? I swear to heaven," she said, perhaps hoping Granby would hear through the wall, "the *second* we leave this horrible little place, we'll make complainings about all of you! *Official* complainings!"

Behind her, Harding wasn't impressed with these threats. "I can hand you details of our complaints procedure when you leave," she said.

Katya ignored her, focusing squarely on Graham. "We begin, yes?" she said, gathering her resolve.

"Faster we're in, faster we're out," Graham assured her. "All you need to do is to tell the truth."

"Truth?" Katya scoffed. "Truth is created by men and by money. That is the only truth."

"Smash the patriarchy, eh?" Harding muttered under her breath.

"Fascinating notion, but I haven't time for it right now." Graham clicked his pen. "Ready?" Katya nodded gravely. "Please sit down." Katya sat in the chair across the desk from Graham, crossing her legs and clasping her linked fingers around her knee. "Mrs. Granby, I wonder if you'd characterise your marriage to Mr. Granby for us?"

"Character . . . Oh, you mean what kind of marriage? Is nice!" she said. "Is love and happiness."

"The marriage hasn't hit any trouble recently?" Graham asked. "Any extra-marital issues? Infidelity?"

Katya glanced at Graham, whose expression was hard to read. "Every couple has troubles. But we are good, thank you."

"Mrs. Granby, lying to investigators is a criminal offence. You could go to prison."

"What?"

"Let me ask you again . . ."

"No!" Katya insisted. "No troubles. I don't know why you ask this!"

"Calm down, love," Harding said to her. "Just answer the question truthfully." This did nothing but ignite Katya's anger further until she was bouncing in her seat.

"You think . . . you think I'm a criminal!" she shrieked. "What have I done? Did I break a crime . . . I mean break the law?"

"That depends," Graham said, "on whether or not you know that your husband killed your *lover*."

Katya's face tightened into such a rictus of scorn and anger she couldn't speak. Graham waited for some response to his trial balloon. When none was forthcoming, he asked her another question. "Did anyone from Sanderson's come back to check on their work after the project was finished? After sales service, that kind of thing?"

"I can't remember a visit," Katya said.

"You can't remember, or you don't want to tell us about it?" Graham pressed.

"Is a new house. Is a . . . ah, *complicated* place. People come and go all the time," she said. "Maybe Mr. Sanderson, maybe not."

Graham paused for a few seconds, just to be sure in his own mind. "One more time, Mrs. Granby. Did Jamie Reeves attend your house after the landscaping was finished?"

Katya was silent, then shook her head. "For the benefit of the tape, Mrs. Granby has indicated in the negative," Graham said. She trembled slightly.

Graham leaned on his forearms, facing Katya squarely. "Look, Mrs. Granby, we can prove that you are not speaking honestly about your relationship with Jamie Reeves. If you continue to do so, I will have to arrest you on suspicion of conspiring to pervert the course of justice. Now, would you like another try?"

Katya's eyelashes fluttered as her eyes flitted around the room. Her hands twisted in her lap as her mouth opened and closed several times. But no words came out.

"Mrs. Granby, what do you seek that money can't buy?" Graham asked when Katya had settled down. She was impassive now and, with her lithe body and long neck, strangely insect-like.

"Something that money can't buy?" She pulled her sunglasses from her hair. Thick, lustrous tresses now unbound fell around her face. "A dog masseuse who really *gets* Willow. One who makes dogs their life, their *calling*, you know? Who puts dogs before *everything*."

"I'm not sure I . . ."

"I have no idea what you are talking about!" Katya cried. "I don't understand these questions, so many questions, all in English. It's like a terrible river!" she said, miming a torrent overwhelming her. "All English, English, never a word of Hungarian. And *he*," she said, standing now and pointing at Graham as though unmasking a traitor, "is a crazy, *crazy* man! He is the most English of all! It's like he has teas"—she mimed—"coming out of his ears!"

Graham's voice cut across the interview room. "Almost, Mrs. Granby, but not quite." Except he said it in Hungarian. "*Majdnem*, Mrs. Granby, *de nem egészen*."

Pulled in three directions at once—raging anger, sudden amazement, and delight at the sound of familiar words—Katya was speechless again. Graham, his objective accomplished, saw that Katya was back in her shell, hermetic and silent. She was near motionless.

Graham took the tablet that laid on his desk and turned it so that Katya could see the enlarged image of one of the paintings from the exhibition. "Please look at this, Mrs. Granby. Do you see anything familiar?"

Katya gazed at the painting but shook her head. "I don't understand" was all she would say.

"Let's try another one." Fergus Barr's painting was the most detailed of them all. "The pool, once more. What do you see?"

Katya leant over to look. Her hand faltered as she spread her thumb and forefinger to expand the image. She began to cry, her sob subtle, almost silent. Harding, even from behind, heard it and, showing a sharp degree of sensitivity, sent what felt like a telepathic wave in Graham's direction. A tear rolled down Katya's face. The detective inspector wrote in his notebook.

When he looked up again, Katya was still staring at the image. Something about it had grasped her attention, and she picked up the tablet. She held it close to her face as though perhaps wanting to dive into the painting, into a simpler reality, and be rid of this chaos she now found herself amidst.

"Who is that? In the painting, Mrs. Granby."

"It's me." Fergus had painted her lustrous brunette hair, white skin, and the little black dots on her red bikini. "And Jamie. Sweet, sweet Jamie." Abruptly, Katya pushed the tablet away, more tears streaming down her face. "It was scandalous. What I did. What *we* did." She flicked a hand in the direction of the tablet. "I cleared the cameras, but I did not know about *this*."

CHAPTER FORTY

"I WELCOME THE opportunity to defend myself," Granby said in a strikingly mild tone. He was in the interview room with his lawyer. Graham and Barnwell sat across from him. "If you have evidence, sir, I hope it's more convincing than your Shakespeare charade."

"You only failed to enjoy it," Graham argued, "because you were deprived of my finely crafted oratory. And yes, it will convince twelve members of the public. It's a perfectly valid piece of evidence. A reconstruction should do it."

Barnwell glared at Granby, pained that his own theory was crumbling. He already felt the urge to slip next door, apologise to poor Matthew, and let him go home.

"Lying to us about hearing that argument," Graham said, "badly damages your defence. I suggest that you wanted to incriminate Sanderson in Jamie's murder by convincing me that they were at each other's throats."

Granby smiled, a snake taunting its prey. "Now, why might I do that?"

Graham leant forward, his elbows on the table. "Revenge, Mr. Granby, for one. Payback for being exploited. And deflection for two. I put it to you that after you returned home from your trip to Turin, you confronted Jamie Reeves and attacked him, injuring him so severely that he later died." As the detective inspector waited for a response to his accusation, the atmosphere in the room became thick, noxious, almost solid, like a knife wouldn't cut through it and they'd need a hammer and chisel.

"Listen, I did not kill Jamie Reeves. Okay, so I wanted to cause trouble for Sanderson. So what? He deserved it. But I did not, I repeat, did not kill Jamie Reeves."

"Mr. Granby, you are a man of considerable means. In the last week or so, I've tried to put myself in your shoes. To see the world from the perspective of someone with fabulous wealth, money to burn. I thought to myself, 'If I were filthy rich and I could already buy anything I desired, what *else* would I want in my life?' Which of those special, elusive things that money can't buy would I covet?" Graham turned to Barnwell like they were running a seminar. "Constable?"

"Erm." Barnwell thought quickly. "Partnership? You know, love, that kind of thing?"

"Mr. Granby is a happily married man though. As far as we've established, anyway."

Barnwell twirled the pen he used for his tablet between his fingers. "It can't be travel that he's short of. How about career satisfaction?"

"Mr. Granby appears very satisfied. He's at the top of his profession by all accounts. Why don't you tell us, Mr. Granby. What might *you* be looking for that money can't buy?"

"Faith? Is that it? Now I'm rich, am I supposed to get religion?" Granby said sarcastically.

"What about stability?" Graham said. "Predictable patterns of life. Markets are volatile, and the people you work with doubly so. But a contented domestic life, well, that's priceless! A welcoming kitchen, dogs to fuss over," he said with a glance at Barnwell. "A beautiful, charming, *accommodating* wife at your side. A wife you can depend on, trust to be there for you. Your career is built around managing risk, but you must want a counterbalance at home. Yet recently, perhaps you saw signs in your wife's behaviour that posed a genuine threat to that stability and peace of mind."

Granby folded his arms and sat back. "You have a modest flair for psychoanalysis," he said, "but nothing you're saying makes sense to me."

"Well then, let's leave Freud behind and talk about Peregrine Wordsworth instead. What did you make of the art exhibition? Must have been quite a thing seeing your own home rendered a dozen different ways." He watched Granby with pixel-sharp intensity.

"Amateurish, but yes, enjoyable," Granby said.

"Unflattering in places?"

"How do you mean?"

"You left the exhibition early, sir," Graham spelled out, "and by all accounts, in a fury. In fact, you barged into an elderly couple standing near some other visitors on the steps as you left. I have witnesses. Strong ones." When Laura had told him that she recognised Granby from his photograph in the local paper as the man who had bumped into Jack at the exhibition, Graham's synapses had lit up like fireworks on Bonfire Night.

Granby laughed off Graham's suggestion. "Maybe their depictions of my house left something to be desired. They were hardly flattering, often unrecognisable. But I lay that at the door of their artistic abilities, not my architects. I wasn't angry." Granby glanced over to his lawyer, who remained stone-faced.

"Let's take one more gander around the exhibit, shall we?"

"If we must," Granby said, "but I have to say, this is all rather—"

"Friday morning," Graham said, producing from a file a photograph of one of the paintings from the retreat. "This was created on the first day of the workshop. What can we see at the Granby house?"

Granby pulled a face. "God alone knows," he said. "I suppose it could be my place, but it's a very confused representation."

"I've learned a lot about art interpretation recently," Graham said. "Look at this." He pointed to an uneven black splotch the approximate breadth of a thumbnail. "You know what that is?"

"Creative licence?" Granby guessed. "I saw a BBC thing about Peregrine Wordsworth once. He sounded like he'd lost his marbles. This only proves it."

"Looks to be a vehicle, doesn't it?"

"Perhaps, but I wouldn't recognise it," Granby said.

"And look at this?" Next to the black splodge was another one around a similar size, purple this time. Four dark shapes under a rhombus of purple could have been tyres.

"Constable, please describe Sanderson Landscaping's livery to Mr. Granby?"

Barnwell jumped. "Eh?"

"The colour of his vans."

"Purple," Barnwell replied. "And gold. Looks very smart."

"It's distinctive," Graham agreed.

Now as perplexed as he was angry, Granby said, "The firm was doing some work for me. They have a purple van. I have a black car. So what?"

"The landscaping was finished over a week before these canvases were painted." Graham showed him a second painting.

"Same day the black splodge is still there, but the purple one has disappeared. And there is another series of splodges over here by the pool. What do you see, Mr. Granby?"

Granby rubbed his eyes and shook his head before answering. "Scrawled, basic approximations," he said, dismissing the images. "Could have been painted by a child. Quite worthless."

"Then let's try something else. Later on Friday afternoon. Quite late, about five p.m. the artist said." Graham showed Granby a third image. The photos were now lined up next to each other on the table. "Here, this artist is more traditional. Less, oh, I don't know, impressionist. It's clear what's in this painting; it isn't just a series of swirls, swoops, and curlicues."

"You're certain they weren't drunk? I could do better, honestly."

"The artist is a seventy-four-year-old woman without the least shred of humour, and a complete teetotaller."

"Seventies, eh? Eyes like a hawk then," Granby scoffed.

"Actually," Graham said, "you're righter than you know. Look more closely."

"What am I looking at?" Granby asked, frustrated.

"Do you see the swimming pool at the front there?" prompted Graham.

"Yes. I know where it is. I helped design the damn thing."

"And do you see anything next to the pool?"

Granby peered. "Birds?" he guessed. "Or something created from the artist's imagination?"

Graham quickly slipped Fergus's less impressionistic, most representative painting, the one he had shown Katya, in front of Granby. "The pool, once more. What do you see?" Graham said.

"I see some people, like stick figures," Granby said. "Probably to make the painting more realistic. Or something. There is no telling with these types of people."

Graham raised an eyebrow. "Are you sure, Mr. Granby? Look again. There's meaning in those depictions."

CHAPTER FORTY-ONE

"SO WHAT?" GRANBY shouted. "This is a whole cartload of nonsense, and nothing more. You've got yourself all frustrated at not catching anyone, and so you've invented this flight of fancy. What am I seeing? I don't know! What am I meant to be seeing? I don't know!"

"What we're looking at is your wife lying by the pool on Friday afternoon with a man. A man that isn't you. A man in a purple shirt who drives a purple van."

Granby was aghast. He laid both hands flat on the table as though ready to stand up and take someone on. "What . . .?" He looked at the picture. "She . . .?"

"Oh, come on, Mr. Granby. How long are you going to spend imagining that we're a bunch of idiots? I put it to you that at the time you walked into that exhibition, you already suspected your wife had a history of cheating on you with Jamie Reeves. Perhaps you'd noticed them being over-friendly, or you'd heard rumours. But we know that you were concerned because you asked Adrian Sanderson to take him off the job."

"You are making things up. Jamie was becoming too familiar with my wife? *My wife* asked for him to be removed. Really, you people." Granby folded his arms again and looked away.

"I suggest you went to the exhibition and found that you'd been duped. The artist made it easy, didn't he? Purple van. Purple shirt. Tall, distinctive young man by the pool. Your wife in a bikini. Where were you when this was painted? On a business trip, no doubt."

"Sydney . . . I . . . I was in Sydney." Granby couldn't seem to drag his eyes away; they were drilling furious holes into the painting, at the representation of his home and the poolside as depicted by the brushes of Fergus Barr.

Graham pressed his point home. "When you attended the exhibition, I suggest you saw what was happening and realised that your wife was cheating on you. You subsequently lost your temper and stormed out. As you did so, you bumped into the elderly couple and caught the attention of a witness."

Granby broke his focus and sat back, folding his arms. "So, you think I killed this Reeves fellow because he was having an affair with my wife? Well, I did nothing of the sort. I left that exhibition in a hurry because I had to take an important phone call. You can check my phone. It was from a client in Manila. This is all news to me." Granby waved his hand at the table.

"A lump of concrete that matches the kind used at your house was found with Jamie's bloodstains on it close to where the attack took place."

Granby shrugged again. "It isn't unique. I'm sure you'll find plenty of it at any builder's yard."

"Constable Barnwell, let's review things. What do we have so far?"

Barnwell checked items off his fingers. "Motive," Barnwell replied. "Revenge for the affair. Means, the bloodstained rock . . ."

"And what else?" Graham watched Granby closely.

"Opportunity, sir. There is no proof that Mr. Granby was where he said he was when Jamie Reeves was attacked."

Granby's eyes flickered left and right as he searched his memory. "What? I was on my way back from Turin." He made a show of calculating the time difference. "I was in Swiss airspace when the attack took place."

"Can you prove that?" Graham said.

"I told you Cynthia, my assistant, has all the details about . . ."

"But where's the proof?" Granby was silent. "Ghost flights, Mr. Granby. Isn't that what they call them?" Graham leant forward. "Your assistant was very helpful. Turns out that few of your flights are trackable. Isn't that correct? And therefore, no one really knows where you were on that Friday night."

Granby's pale cheeks flushed. "It is not uncommon in my line of business."

"Say nothing, Silas," interjected Granby's lawyer. He'd been silent this whole time. "They're guessing. There's nothing there. They just want a quick collar. And all the more satisfying to take down a 'one-percenter,' eh, Detective?"

Graham pushed away his notebook and stood. "Mr. Langham, is it? We have procedures for lodging complaints. You are free to make use of them. In the meantime," he said, glaring at Granby, "I suggest Mr. Granby think long and hard about telling us the truth."

🌍

"What the . . ." Graham came out of his office. He'd been preparing to go home for the night when he heard shouting. Janice had taken Katya Granby home. Barnwell was releasing Matthew Walker. Roach was en route to the cells with Silas Granby.

"This is a travesty! Are you on someone's payroll? Dirty cops? Don't you understand? Money isn't enough for some people," Granby railed. The reality of his situation seemed to have suddenly hit him. "They need to deceive you, to get one over on you, to watch you fall. In the end, everyone wants their pound of flesh!" Roach manhandled him just enough to persuade Granby that he was the stronger of the two and waved away Barnwell's offered assistance.

Dazed but genuinely entertained by the spectacle, Matthew was leaning on the reception desk as though he were about to ask Barnwell to pour him a pint. "So, is this, like, a regular day for you lot, then?"

"What's that, Matthew?" Barnwell said, still enjoying the memory of Roach's strong hand on Granby's shoulder; there was something authoritative about it, even if Granby had ruined the moment with fearful complaining.

"Arrestin' people for murder and such like. Bangin' people up. Regular sort of day?"

Barnwell slowly swivelled his gaze from his computer screen to regard the big lad; he looked tired and sweaty, but there was the sense that after five pints and a couple of packets of barbecue-flavoured crisps, all would be well. "It happens from time to time," Barnwell said. "You should know, though, that we generally don't cause the murders, so we can't predict when they'll happen or the subsequent arrests."

Nodding, Matthew said, "Yeah, suppose that's right. Anyway, is that it?"

"Is that what?"

"*It*?" asked Matthew. "This whole thing with the dead boyfriend and the expensive wife and the rich idiot? 'Coz I'm off down the pub, if that's alright." Barnwell appeared at his shoulder. "And if you see me there, you won't ask me any more questions, will you? You could buy me a pint, though. Wouldn't want a complaint on your record, eh? For wrongful arrest or whatever they call it," Matthew said, wagging a finger.

"Get outta here, lad. Stay out of trouble."

Matthew laughed and bashed open the double doors with his hefty body. "I'm not the one chasin' thieves and murderers!" He had a thought and turned. "I could apply, though, right? To be a fuzz. I'm not too old or nothin', and there's a limit on my convic—"

The reception's lights went out. "'Night, Matthew."

🌍

The next morning, Graham whistled to himself as he bounded up the steps to the station. He had come in early, eager to press on with questioning Silas Granby. "Morning, Barnwell!"

"There you are, sir." Barnwell came around from behind the reception desk. He flapped a notebook against the palm of his hand.

"How did things go overnight?" Graham nipped around the desks on his way to his office.

Barnwell ignored his question. "I'm waiting for a call from Sergeant Roach, sir." The constable looked weary. He had completed an eighteen-hour shift, some of it spent on a camp bed in the break-room.

"Good stuff. Off you get home. You must be exhausted." Graham was light-footed and looking forward to his second cup of tea of the morning. He'd already enjoyed a perfect cup of Oolong with his breakfast, and now he planned an equally perfect cup of Assam. It would get him in just the right mood to verbally spar with Silas Granby and hopefully nail down his confession. Graham was in such a good mood he was almost skipping.

"He's been called out to the Granby house."

"Who has?"

"Roach, sir. I've been trying to call you. The cleaner was hysterical." Graham came to a halt. He took two steps backward, bringing Barnwell into his field of vision.

"Hysterical?"

"Roach's on his way there now. To the Granby home."

"Oh?" A cold hand clutched at Graham's heart. "Why?"

"Katya Granby, sir. She's dead."

CHAPTER FORTY-TWO

"CLEANER FOUND HER, sir," Roach informed Graham as he put on paper bootees. SOCOs were beginning to arrive. "At about seven thirty this morning. Called it in as soon as she saw her." Roach consulted his notebook. "Which was about half an hour after she entered the house."

"Didn't find her straightaway, eh?"

"No, sir. You'll see why."

"Alright, Sergeant, lead the way."

Roach led Graham through the house, past the sofa on which he'd interviewed Katya the day before, and across the patio where he'd delivered his Shakespearean speech.

It was a cool day, but Katya was wearing a bikini, a red one with little black polka dots. Graham recognised it as the one from Fergus Barr's painting. She was lying on her back on an inflatable, sunglasses covering her eyes. She looked like she was enjoying the morning sun.

"What's she got in her arms?"

"Looks like an urn."

"Jesus Christ, her dog's ashes." Graham looked around. "Where is her dog, anyway?"

"In the urn, sir."

"Not that one, the other one. The live one."

"Not sure, sir. No sign of it in the house."

Graham stared at the slim but pale body floating across the pool, the inflatable swaying slightly in the breeze. Katya's leg dangled over the side, her foot bobbing in the water. She looked like a memorial to the rich, wasteful, and utterly pointless. "So, what are we thinking?"

"No sign of any injuries. We found pills and a bottle of wine on the kitchen countertop, so I'm thinking overdose."

There was a noise behind them, and Marcus Tomlinson appeared around the side of the house. "Morning, lads. What have we got?"

Graham looked from Tomlinson to the figure in the pool. The three men stood mournfully on the side gazing at it for some moments. Roach broke the silence first. "Overdose we think. Pills and wine in the kitchen. I've taken photos."

Tomlinson pursed his lips. "Right, then. Who's going to get her?"

Graham and the pathologist both looked at Roach. The sergeant blinked before straightening his shoulders and casting around for tools that might help him. Propped up against a wall was a wide pool brush. Roach used it to prod the inflatable to the shallow end. Rolling up his uniform trousers, he waded in to bring Katya ashore.

Tomlinson looked her over. "Help me lift her." Graham and Roach moved to tilt Katya on her side. "Okay, you can let her down."

Tomlinson kneeled. "Ah, my creaking joints." He took Katya's body temperature. "Roach, take some more pictures, will you? Get some close-ups." The sergeant moved around the body, taking photographs from various angles, his trousers still rolled up around his knees.

"What can you tell me, Marcus?" Graham asked him carefully. Tomlinson was notoriously stingy with his information until he had done a full examination, but today he was more magnanimous. "Death around fourteen to fifteen hours ago I suspect. She's been here overnight."

"That's not long after Janice dropped her home." Graham's head swam. Had he, by pressing for an admission about the affair, contributed to her death? He closed his eyes.

"And she didn't overdose." Tomlinson sniffed. "I smell Rohypnol. There's some faint bruising around her arm here, but no obvious signs of injury except for . . ." Tomlinson leant over and looked closely at the bruising. "That looks like a puncture wound." Graham stared.

"You mean she was drugged, killed, and then staged like this?" Roach said, horror creeping into his voice.

"Maybe, young man. The urn's interesting. Who's Rufus?"

"Her dog, former dog. A champion apparently." Graham was as stunned as Roach.

"But this means . . ." Roach said.

"Her husband can't have done it," Graham finished for him.

"And if he didn't kill her, who did?"

They stepped back as the ambulance crew arrived to collect Katya's body. "I'll let you have the report as soon as I have it. By the way, I was impressed with your ingenuity earlier, Sergeant Roach. I felt sure you'd show us your aquatic skills." Tomlinson closed his doctor's bag of instruments.

"My what?"

"Your lifesaving skills. Except, of course, there was no life to be saved here. Swimming."

"If I'd tried that, you'd have had another body on your hands," Roach replied. Tomlinson frowned, puzzled. "I can't, sir. Swim."

Tomlinson's eyebrows rose. "Ah. Well, you'd better get that sorted out. You might have to save someone from drowning in the Thames when you get to the Met." He winked at Graham. "Goodbye, Inspector. Speak to you later." Graham continued to study the pool as though he might find the answer to his thoughts at the bottom of it.

"So, what do you think, sir? Are we back to square one?"

"No, not square one. But we've definitely got a conundrum on our hands. Who killed Katya and why?" He didn't say the next part out loud. *And did they kill Jamie Reeves as well?*

Screams sounded from the front of the house, followed by yapping, barking, and shouts. Katya's best friend and artist from Peregrine Wordsworth's retreat, Magda Padalka-Lyons, had arrived along with her dog, Pom-Pom, and Katya's dog, Willow. "Katya left Willow with me. She said she pick him up this morning. She not arrive. Someone say she's dead! Killed herself!" The short woman stood in front of Graham, her hand at her throat, her mouth twisted with grief. "Tell me it is not so, Inspector."

"I'm very sorry to confirm that Mrs. Granby is dead, Mrs. Padalka-Lyons."

Magda staggered back into a patio chair. "Oh my God, I can't believe it." She waved her hand in front of her face, taking huge, deep gasps.

"Did Mrs. Granby tell you what she was planning to do? Was she going anywhere, meeting anyone? Why did she need you to look after Willow? Mrs. Padalka-Lyons?" Graham pressed after a pause.

"Hmm? Oh, she didn't go anywhere without Willow, but she said he needed better company than she could give him, so could I look after him. I did that sometimes when, well, you know, she needed to be discreet. I never asked her what she was doing. I don't know who she was meeting or where she was going or if she was doing anything. I thought she maybe wanted to be by herself."

"How did she seem?"

"Well, she was upset. Her husband had just been arrested for the murder of her . . . her landscaper. But I didn't think she was going to do a suicide. I would have stopped her!"

At his owner's wailing, Pom-Pom started yapping, followed shortly by Willow, their chorus ear-splitting. "Thank you, Mrs. Padalka-Lyons. I'm sorry for your loss." Graham stalked off. "Roach!" he barked. "Come with me." Roach trotted after his superior. "Let's get out of here. And Tomlinson's right. It's not a requirement, but you need to learn to swim. It's a basic life skill. You never know when you might need it."

CHAPTER FORTY-THREE

The Gorey Gossip
Tuesday, April 26th

It is with consternation and not a little trepidation that I have to announce the death of Mrs. Katya Granby, wife of Silas Granby, CEO of Granby Investments. Mrs. Granby was found floating in her pool earlier today, clutching the ashes of her beloved dog, Rufus. Her husband was not available for comment, detained as he currently is at Her Majesty's Pleasure under arrest for the murder of Jamie Reeves, a landscaper who recently worked on the Granby property and who was battered to death just a few days ago.

Initial reports suggested suicide as the poor woman, her husband cast as a murderer, had been devastated by news of his detention. However, rumours have reached me that Mrs. Granby's death is now being considered suspicious. If so, this is a most worrying development.

For, should it turn out that Mrs. Granby was indeed murdered, there are two major issues that our local police force needs to resolve as soon as possible. First, whether Mrs. Granby's killer and that of Jamie Reeves is one and the same person, rendering Mr. Granby's arrest a terrible error that gave an unknown person licence to kill. Or, possibly worse, we have TWO killers in our community, one of whom is still at large. This further development in the case undermines considerably the community's confidence in our boys (and one girl) in blue.

Can we trust them to investigate this case to a successful conclusion and restore our feeling of safety? Remember, Mrs. Granby was killed in her own home.

Where are you, Inspector Graham? Another life has been tragically lost. The public needs answers. And our patience is running out.

Correction: April 26th

A previous version of this article mischaracterised Jamie Reeves as Mr. and Mrs. Granby's gardener. He was their landscaping project lead.

CHAPTER FORTY-FOUR

GRAHAM AND ROACH bundled through the station doors. Janice was at reception. Barnwell sat behind her at his desk, sipping a coffee. "Barnwell, you still here?" Graham said.

"Yes, sir. Couldn't leave until I knew what was going on."

"Well, you might be here for quite a while in that case. Janice, call Granby's lawyer. I want him here when I tell Granby about his wife. Then everyone come to my office. Got it?"

"Yes, sir," they cried.

Five minutes later, Graham was pacing. He hadn't even been able to calm himself to make a cup of tea. He took a deep breath and walked up to the whiteboard. "Right, let's go through what we've got. I want to assume that Tomlinson is right and Katya Granby was murdered. We've got a big problem, and I want to get a jump on it."

"A second murderer, sir?" Barnwell said.

"Or Granby isn't our man, and we've got a double murderer on the loose," Janice added. Graham wrote the two options on the whiteboard, placing question marks after each of them. Neither of them gave him any comfort at all.

Graham posed the question they had all been asking themselves. "Why would someone kill Katya? What motive would they have?"

"Lust, loathing, or loot," Roach said. "That's what the textbooks say."

"Let's examine loot first."

"Someone wanted money from her, a robbery that went wrong?"

"Possibly. Argue for or against."

"Maybe it was a house burglary that went wrong . . . or . . . or . . . a kidnapping attempt. They were going to hold her to ransom and demand money from her husband," Janice said.

"Who's currently in a cell under suspicion of murdering his wife's lover?" Barnwell countered.

"Maybe the murderer didn't know that."

"Alright, alright. No squabbling," Graham said.

Roach piped up. "Hmm, I can't see it. She was killed without violence and carefully posed. That suggests a cold, calculating killer."

"What else? Lust. Give me the textbook definition, Roach."

"The motive for someone murdering a romantic rival. Jealousy."

"Who might that be? Someone who's in love with Granby and wanted Katya out of the way?"

"Surely not. We've seen no evidence of that in our investigation."

"Someone who's in love with Katya and thinks if he, or she, can't have her, no one can?"

"Again, wouldn't that be her husband? Or has Katya been playing the field and there's another lover out there?"

"Blimey, I can't keep up."

"Let's move on to loathing."

"Someone hated her."

"What about Molly Duckworth?" Janice said. "She was in love with Jamie Reeves. Perhaps she knew about the affair. Paula Lascelles for the same reason."

"Reeves's mother if she indirectly blamed Katya for his death."

"Someone else who simply didn't like her?" Barnwell shrugged. It was all he had.

"Was there any sign of forced entry?"

"No, sir."

"So, it was probably someone known to her, then."

"Molly knew Katya from her day on the boat."

"Tomlinson has confirmed cause of death, sir." Roach scrolled his phone. "Cardiac arrest. Puncture wound in her right arm. Suspected administration of an unknown drug. Blood samples sent to toxicology."

Graham tapped his pen against the large filing cabinet. "Hmm. Alright, folks, this is what we're going to do. I think Ms. Lascelles and Mrs. Reeves are long shots. They didn't know Katya or about her relationship with Jamie. Let's put them aside for now. Janice, I want you to speak to Molly Duckworth. Check her alibi. If it's weak, look into her background for something relevant—nursing, access to drugs, that kind of thing. Roach, get down the lab. Oversee the forensics. I'm looking for anything that connects Katya to someone linked to this investigation. Barnwell, come with me. We have to tell a man his wife is dead. Lucky us."

"Hello?" Janice called out. She stepped further inside the Sanderson Landscaping office. The place was as silent as the *Marie Celeste*. Nothing stirred.

Janice walked through the office. "Hello!" She peered through the glass patio doors that led out to the yard behind. Sitting on a bench surrounded by young saplings in wooden pots was Molly Duckworth. She leant on her knees, talking furiously into her phone, her free hand gesticulating wildly.

Janice watched her for a few seconds. Molly glanced up and caught sight of her. Her body tensed and she wound up her call. Janice opened the doors and stepped out into the sunshine. "Good morning, Molly."

Molly stood, smoothing down her skirt. "Hi. Are you here about Katya Granby? I read about it in the *Gorey Gossip*."

"Yes."

"I'm very sorry to hear that she died. She was a nice lady."

"Can we go inside, Molly?"

"Yes, yes of course. Would you like a cup of tea?"

"No, thank you. Let's just sit and chat." They walked over to the white sofa. "How well did you know Katya Granby?"

"Not at all, really. A couple of times, I'd run over to the Granby house to take a few supplies that the lads needed. I saw her then, but we didn't speak. My interactions were mostly with Mr. Granby, and then it was only when I answered Adrian's phone to pass on a message. He did come in here once, and that's when he invited me on the boat, like I told you earlier. Before that day, I hadn't spent any time in Mrs. Granby's company at all."

"I understand you thought that Mrs. Granby was lonely, is that right?"

"Yes. She was quiet when she came on board but perked up as we chatted. And I'm sure the constant champagne refills helped. She was quite charming. Talked about her dog a lot. I like dogs so I didn't mind."

"Were you aware of the rumours about her and Jamie?"

Molly's face fell. Colour flushed her cheeks, and she looked down at her lap. "Yes, I'd heard the rumours. She's—was—a very attractive woman. Bit old for him, but some men like that, don't they?"

"What was your reaction to the rumours?" Janice inclined her head to insist Molly make eye contact with her.

"I thought he was a bit mad, to be honest with you. Seemed unlike him too. He wasn't normally reckless. He was risking everything—his job, his reputation—for what? A bit of fun. And look where it got him."

"And what was your personal reaction? How did it make you feel?"

Molly sighed. Her shoulders rose and fell. "It made me sad. Like why couldn't he go for a girl his own age? Someone without . . . baggage. Perhaps he was entranced by her glamour and wealth. He obviously didn't deserve what was coming to him, but what an idiot. He was playing with fire."

"Did you see Mrs. Granby after your day on the boat?"

"No, she said we should get together again, but I'm sure she was just being nice. I went to the yacht club and invited Jamie to join me, and that was the end of it. It was back to Earth with a bump for me."

"Did you know that Silas Granby has been charged with Jamie's murder?"

"I read about it at the same time I heard about Katya's death—in the *Gossip*.

Do you think the two deaths are connected? I mean, they must be, mustn't they? But it must have been someone else who killed Mrs. Granby if Mr. Granby was in jail." Molly put her hands up to her face. "Oh, what a mess."

"What's a mess, Molly?"

"This whole situation: Jamie, Mrs. Granby, Mr. Granby. The drama. Being involved in this kind of thing isn't me. I like a quiet, normal kind of life. Friends, family, a bit of fun. Adrian hates all this too. We simply want the person or persons who did this to go away for a long time and for this to be over."

"Okay, Molly, one more thing. Where were you yesterday evening?"

Molly's eyes widened. Janice intervened quickly. "It's just routine."

"I was in France with Adrian. We'd gone on a buying trip. He needed to negotiate with a new supplier. It always looks better if there are the two of us. You can check with him, or even the supplier. I can give you their details. We came back on the late ferry. Got back in around ten p.m."

"It wasn't Molly, sir. She was with Sanderson in France. Didn't get back until late last night. It all checks out. She was on the ferry manifest, as was he."

"So, we have to rule out Sanderson too, eh? Not that I could see why he might wish to do Mrs. Granby harm."

"How did he take the news, sir?"

"Hmm?"

"Mr. Granby."

Graham replaced his cup in his saucer. It had been a gruelling morning. For all his poise and sophistication, Silas Granby had been broken by the news of his wife's death. His lawyer had made a swift exit after the announcement, and Graham and Barnwell had been left to comfort the new widower as he alternately lashed out and clung to them.

"He's back in the cell, but I don't know how long I can keep him. He's in no fit state to talk, but I can't let him go either. We might never see him again."

"What would you like me to do, sir?"

"Go take a break. Be prepared to interview him this afternoon. We can try tackling him together. Let me know when we hear from Tomlinson. I want to know the drug that caused Katya Granby to go into cardiac arrest."

Janice left, and Graham turned to the view outside his window. Katya Granby's demise had thrown a wrench into his expectations for the Jamie Reeves's case. He needed to keep an open mind. Maybe Granby wasn't involved after all and there was another killer out there who had murdered both Reeves and Katya. Or maybe Granby had killed Reeves and like that idiot Solomon suggested, there was a second murderer on the loose.

Graham squinted. A super yacht made its slow way across the horizon, the sun bouncing off its gleaming white surface. It cost more than he would earn in a lifetime. He admired the sleek curves of the streamlined hull, the three decks at the back, one a helipad. He knew that below deck, the interior would be opulent, all polished walnut and deep, squishy sofas. He was at one moment envious of those like the Granbys whose lives involved such a reality and simultaneously relieved that his did not. No one coveted him or tried to cheat him; his friends were genuine. He could place his feet on the ground and know that it would be solid beneath him.

And yet there was no denying the pull of the lifestyle, the yachts, the private jets. Could he genuinely say he wouldn't want it if it were offered? The tension between the two worlds—that of the superrich and the perfectly ordinary—had collided with this case. It was his job to clear up the mess. And as he stared at the hugely expensive yacht set against the perfectly free sun and sea, he was buggered if he knew how.

CHAPTER FORTY-FIVE

"**D**ID YOU HEAR the latest?" Barnwell walked into the break room to fill Carmen's water bowl.

"No, what?" Janice didn't look up from her screen.

"Roach and the boss are with Tomlinson. Roachie says Rohypnol rendered Katya Granby unconscious, and then she was plied with massive doses of an epilepsy drug which caused a heart attack."

"So she *was* murdered." Janice sat back in her chair. "But who, Bazz? Who could have done it?"

"Beats me. Feels like we're back to square one, and if not, we're only up to square two. Wotcha up to?"

"Wedding research," Janice mumbled, resuming her scrolling. "Taking a break before the boss wants me in with him and Granby. Can't say I'm looking forward to it." Her elbow was propped on the break room table, her head in her hand. "I need to find some shoes. Not too expensive but not so cheap they're uncomfortable. I need to stand in them for hours."

"You could go barefoot if you had a wedding on the beach."

"Tell me about it. But I'd never hear the end of it from my mother. What are you doing?"

"Just covering reception, but if you get a chance, could you spell me so I can take Carmen for a walk? She hasn't been out since this morning."

"Okay, I'll be there in a sec." Barnwell left her searching "satin wedding shoes comfortable jersey uk."

Barnwell returned to reception and placed Carmen's water bowl on the floor underneath the counter. No one could see her down there. When he was manning the desk, she liked to lay across his feet. It was sweet but restricting. He found himself getting cramps from not moving, but he hated to disturb the lady in his life. He bent down to scratch between Carmen's ears. She'd been a great help earlier in the year when he was coming to terms with both of his parents' deaths. He'd had to take some compassionate leave to attend their funerals and, after his mother's passing, to clear out the family home and put it up for sale. While he was gone, the Gorey police team had each taken it in turns to care for Carmen, and Barnwell had been grateful. Roach had even moved into Barnwell's flat to avoid disrupting Carmen more than necessary.

Barnwell's mind wandered to his brother. Steve's time on Jersey was coming to a close. He had just a couple of days left. The constable looked at the clock. He had a few minutes before Janice returned from her lunch break. He took a deep breath and prepared to run a search of his own.

A few minutes later, a door slammed. Barnwell hastily shut down his screen, but there was no need. Janice ran from the break room and grabbed her uniform jacket. As she tapped keys on one of the office computers, she said, "What was the name of that epilepsy drug? The one that killed Katya Granby?" The printer warmed up and spit out a sheet of paper.

"Eh? Erm . . ." Barnwell scrolled Roach's texts on his phone. "Dexa . . . meth . . . amine. Brand name Elli . . . Ellip . . ." He found the text he was looking for. "Ellipsis, yeah that's it. Ellipsis."

"Bloody hell." Janice hesitated for a second, just one, then came to a decision. "I gotta go, Bazz. Sorry."

※

Again, Janice parked her car so tight against the stone wall on Marett Lane that if she'd had a passenger they would have been trapped. Before crossing the road, she waited for a couple to walk by on their way to the beach. The pair held hands as they strolled, beach towels under her arm, deck chairs under his. They were chatting quietly. As they passed Janice, the woman threw back her head with a peal of laughter. The sergeant noticed the woman's clerical collar. *A female vicar. Unusual. Wonder what my mother would make of that.* They were followed by three louts in tracksuits, the bottoms of which hung virtually to their knees.

Janice rapped on the door of the cottage a bit louder than she meant to. The door opened, and Cynthia Moorcroft stood in the doorway. She was less poised than before, her hair mussed. She wore no makeup. Dark circles under her eyes aged her. There was a stain on her shirt. "Oh, hello. I wasn't expecting to hear from you again. Come in."

Inside the cottage, Janice looked around. Nothing seemed awry. "Are you alright? After Mr. Granby's arrest?" she said to Cynthia.

"And Katya's death." Cynthia clicked the kettle's on button. "I can't believe it. I would never have thought that Silas would kill anyone, nor that Katya would be next. There's a rumour that someone murdered her too!" Cynthia placed a mug of tea in front of Janice and dropped two teaspoons of sugar into her own. The older woman wiped her pale face and let the kitchen table take her weight as she levered herself into a chair.

"Everything has changed since we last spoke, hasn't it? What will happen to the business, do you think?" Janice said.

Cynthia looked at Janice with only half-seeing eyes before realising what the sergeant was saying. "Oh, I don't know." Cynthia shrugged. She waved her hand in the air slowly. "It's over for Silas. Trust in him is lost, and his business is all about trust."

"But doesn't he know where all the bodies are buried?"

"Yes, and some of these people are gangsters in Savile Row suits. They won't want the whiff of a police enquiry anywhere near them. A lot of the rest will fall away. They won't want to associate with someone on the edge of a double murder enquiry either, even if he is exonerated. They're probably digging up those bodies as we speak, helped by other wealth managers who'll step in like the vultures they are."

"What about you being that person, Cynthia? Can't you take the business over?"

Cynthia laughed. "Me? No chance. I want to get away from these greasy people." She tapped her finger against her lips.

"The thing is, Cynthia . . . can I call you Cynthia?" The older woman nodded. Janice thought how to phrase her next question. She took a sip of her tea. "You told me that you got the job with Granby through a mutual contact and that it was your first experience with the world of wealth management."

"Yes, that's right."

"And that you'd never heard of Silas Granby before that."

"Yes. I had been just a lowly secretary in a firm of accountants."

Janice unfolded the piece of paper that she'd printed out earlier. On it, a copy of a newspaper article was headed:

> "Distraught Mother Loses Her High Court Battle with Pharmaceutical Company."

It continued:

> "Frances Macintyre, whose daughter lost her life one day before she married her childhood sweetheart, defeated in her legal fight to bring company she blames for her daughter's death to justice."

Alongside the article was a picture of a woman holding up a pair of satin wedding shoes and a framed photograph. The article had been written nearly twenty years ago, but Janice saw clearly that Frances Macintyre was a younger version of the woman who sat across the table from her.

"But isn't this you?"

Cynthia peered at the picture. "No."

"She looks just like you."

"Well, it's not. You are mistaken. Look, it's not even my name." Cynthia held Janice's gaze.

"Okay, then tell me this. This woman who looks just like you. Who has a dead daughter. Who, according to this article, blames her daughter's death on the lack of a drug that might have saved her. Who believes that if the company that manufactured the drug hadn't made it so prohibitively expensive, her daughter might still be alive. Tell me, why does this woman now work for the man who was the CEO of the pharmaceutical company at the time? A pharmaceutical company that made a drug found twenty years later in the body of that former CEO's wife who died while he was held in custody for the murder of her lover?"

Cynthia stood. She smiled. "Let me show you something." She walked over to a dresser that stood against the wall. She picked up a photograph. "See? *That* is the woman in the photo. My sister, Frances. It was her daughter, my niece, Holly, who died. Frances killed herself on the first anniversary of Holly's death."

Cynthia leant down to show Janice the photo. Janice took another sip of her tea. In the photo, a woman in her early forties hugged a very attractive younger woman. They beamed for the camera. In her hands, behind the older woman's neck, the younger woman held a pair of wedding shoes. As Janice looked, the shoes went in and out of focus. She squinted and forced herself to concentrate on the delicate beading down the back of the heels. "So not you, but yes, you," Janice said, except it came out garbled.

Cynthia's face swam into view. She was grinning maniacally, and there were three of her. Janice opened her mouth again, but it felt like it was stuffed with cotton wool. She reached out to push Cynthia away. And then, everything went black.

"Janice here?" Graham said, looking around reception.

"No, sir. She went out."

"Huh, I was expecting her to interview Granby with me. Never mind; you'll do, Constable. Roach can man the desk."

"Righto, sir. Give me a moment if you will. My brother's coming down to take Carmen out for a walk. He should be here any minute."

CHAPTER FORTY-SIX

HER CHEEKS JUDDERED. Darkness enveloped her. Her neck cracked with every shake. A sharp pain pierced her skull, immediately followed by a dull ache. Janice shivered. She blacked out again.

Slowly, she realised she was in the boot of a car. Her nostrils stung. Musty carpet overlaid with the smell of petrol. The car's engine revved and came to a stop.

The small amount of light that seeped through her blindfold brightened. Restraints around her ankles snapped and loosened. Those around her wrists remained. "Get up!" Janice recognised Cynthia's voice.

Feeling around, Janice stuck her feet out of the car. She made a noise through the cloth between her teeth. A breath of warm air hit her cheek, then a hand grabbed her armpit and roughly pulled her from the car. She stood, wobbling. Distracting herself from the nausea that rose from her feet and the weakness that threatened to drop her to the ground, she strained to hear seagulls . . . and waves.

Another surge of nausea rolled over her. A shove in the back forced her onward. Stumbling, she nearly fell. Uneven ground gave way to the crunchy, spongy texture of wet sand, the tiny, weathered particles of rocks and minerals slipping away beneath her with every step. She staggered again. The woman beside her silently took her weight.

The air was cool. Was it morning? Evening? Nighttime? Janice had no idea. She peered through her blindfold, but it was hopeless. After a few more feet, the ground rose.

The air temperature dropped further. Her skin tingled. Staccato plops of water seeped through her hair to her scalp, a cold creep. A sharp, sudden pressure on her shoulder and she tumbled to the ground. Once again, a wave of panic washed over her as her ankles were tied again. Whimpering, Janice lashed out, her boot connecting with nothing but air.

A curse and the tie around Janice's ankles tightened, her bones rubbing together painfully. She sagged and brought up her knees, curling into a foetal position. Her shoulders ached.

"What's your boyfriend's name, hmm?" Cynthia's voice was hard, cruel. Janice remained silent. A pain shot through her leg.

"Ah-eh-or."

"What?" The gag in Janice's mouth loosened. She spat it out.

"What the hell?" she cried. "What are you doing with me?"

Cynthia laughed. "I'm putting you somewhere you can't cause any trouble. By the time they find you, I'll be long gone. You too, probably. Tide'll rise tomorrow morning."

"What? Where am I? You're leaving me here to drown?" Janice wriggled like a maggot, and just as helpless. Cynthia laughed.

"Now, tell me your boyfriend's name."

"I don't have a boyfriend."

"Course you do. You've got wedding to-do lists in your Notes app. Are you going for the gluten-free almond flour cake or the one with the pâte à bombe icing? Name."

"No." Janice squealed with pain as Cynthia pressed down on her ankle.

"Want to rethink that?"

"What have you done?"

Cynthia squatted and reached behind Janice's head. She pulled off the scarf that covered her eyes. Light from Cynthia's phone assaulted Janice despite the gloom, and it took a moment before she placed herself. She was in . . . a cave? Janice glanced over Cynthia's shoulder. Nazi markings defaced the rock walls. An old war tunnel!

Cynthia wrapped the blindfold around her fingers. She pondered the scarf's striped pattern, brooding. "My niece died because of Silas. He effectively killed her. And he as good as killed my sister, inflicting unbearable cruelty on her." Cynthia looked up at the Nazi emblems. "My niece was ill, very ill. She had been for two years. She'd fought and fought but had exhausted her options except for this one drug. Her mum, my sister, found out about it, but Holly's doctors wouldn't prescribe it. In Holly's case, it was an off-label use for a disease that the drug wasn't intended to treat, but in a few cases had been found to be helpful.

"The doctors said it was experimental, unproven. It was also wildly expensive. Thousands of pounds for one vial, and Holly needed lots of them. Frances thought that if the company that manufactured it would give it to her for free, or just a small amount as a compassionate gesture, Holly's doctors would agree to administer it. Of course, there was no guarantee it would help, but Franny would have done anything, *anything* to save her daughter, her only child. Franny personally appealed to Silas to donate the drug. And he . . ." Cynthia pulled the scarf tight in her hands. "Refused."

Cynthia sighed, closing her eyes momentarily. "Holly died the day before her wedding. Franny was heartbroken and took the company to court. When her civil case failed, it was like Holly had died all over again. The next day, she simply walked into the sea."

"But what has that to do with anything?"

"It has everything to do with your case."

"What? How? Are you saying *you* killed Jamie Reeves? What did he have to do with what happened?"

"Nothing. He was merely a stick to beat Silas with. I wanted Silas to pay for what he did to my niece and sister, but I bided my time. Silas's reputation in pharma was mostly destroyed by the case, and he moved into wealth management. He has no idea the woman who took him to court was my sister. I quietly networked my way into his circles and persuaded him to take me on. I got to know the ins and outs of his business while I plotted my revenge for him hurting my sister so. I thought about bringing his company down. I could have done it easily. A well-timed rumour would have been enough, but I wanted more. I wanted recompense for my pain and, more than anything, justice for Holly and Franny."

"But he didn't recognise you? You look just like your sister."

"Oh no. Posh blokes like him don't notice the little people. I dyed my hair, changed my name. I'm older. It's been twenty years. That was more than enough to hide my real identity. The Silases of the world don't see people like you and me."

"So, what was your plan?"

"I went to the exhibition at the council offices and saw that Katya had been fooling around with the landscaper. There had been rumours. I realised this was my chance. I thought an affair the perfect cover for a double murder, framing Silas in the process and causing him emotional pain. Despite everything, he really loved Katya. He had to, to put up with that stupid dog memorial idea of hers . . ." Cynthia trailed off for a moment before snapping to attention. "So, I took a lump of concrete from a pile when I was at their house the day after the exhibition and killed the guy when he returned home the next evening."

"Cold."

"Icy. Frigid. When I left him, I thought he'd bleed out, but he hung on for a while. The damage was done though."

"Granby said he was in the air on the way back from Turin."

"He was, but there are no records, see? I could say anything I liked. I changed his calendar to show that he was at home to make you think he was lying. He wasn't. And you bought it."

"And you killed Katya too?"

"Yes. I didn't want to, but Silas had to go away for a long time, the rest of his life. I was worried that the Reeves murder wouldn't be enough for that. Shame, really. Katya wasn't too bad, but her death served my purposes perfectly. Not only would being found guilty of two murders put Silas away for good, just as importantly, the pain of losing someone he loved would floor him. I wanted him to suffer like I and my sister had."

"So how did you do it?"

"I went over to the house, spiked Katya's drink, like I did with your tea, then injected her with Ellipsis. Like with Reeves, I planned to make it look like Silas had done it. I had arranged his calendar to make it seem like he was at home, but in reality he should have been on another of his business trips. Unfortunately for me, it seems border force were doing their jobs for once. They stopped him from leaving without the proper paperwork. I didn't know your boss had arrested him. I thought he was in New York."

"And the Ellipsis?"

"The drug that could have saved Holly. Silas had boxes of the stuff lying around. Talk about adding insult to injury. He said he had it in case anyone in his circles needed a favour or there was a chance of a bit of cash in it. I knew a colossal overdose would bring on a heart attack, and so it did. Katya never came around from the Rohypnol. I thought the urn a nice touch. I put her in a bikini too. My little joke. Now, tell me again, what's your boyfriend's name?"

Janice glared at her. "What are you going to do?"

"Wouldn't you like to know? Maybe I'm going to tell him where to find you."

Janice considered this. "Jack."

"Jack," Cynthia repeated as she scrolled.

"Right, sweetheart. I need to go. Dubai calls. Maybe Panama. A private jet and riches await me. Being Silas's assistant affords me certain benefits, don't you know? My just desserts." Cynthia looked at her watch. She unwound the scarf from her hands and reached to tie it around Janice's eyes. Janice pounced, biting Cynthia's hand hard. In response, a sharp sting and the clap of a slap stunned her.

"Tomorrow morning, this tunnel will be full of water. You'll be whisked out to sea. And I'll be whisked away on a private jet to live the life of Riley. Or maybe Jack will find you. Either way, sorry not sorry." Cynthia turned and headed to the beach.

In for four, hold for four, out for four, hold for four. Janice focused on her breathing. The sound of Cynthia's footsteps cracking and shooshing across the sand receded. Drops kept on plopping.

"Hellooo!"

Ten miles away, Jack opened the door to the house he shared with Janice. It was in darkness. His greeting was met with silence. He'd been working late and had popped into the supermarket on his way home. His phone pinged and he put the bags on the kitchen counter to check it.

```
"Hi, sweetheart. It's an all-hands tonight on the case.
Don't wait up. Going to be a long one. See you tomorrow.
XXX"
```

Huh. Janice didn't normally call him sweetheart, but he quite liked it. Jack put his phone away and unpacked the bags. He'd been planning to cook salmon, but it looked like he'd be eating a frozen microwave curry on his own instead.

◈

In Laura's kitchen, Graham stared at the picture of him and Katie on the windowsill. He cradled a mug of camomile tea in his hand. Outside, the night was quiet except for an owl's mating call, persistent in the darkness. Graham's mind wandered to the case. Granby was still denying murdering Jamie Reeves. Tomorrow, without further evidence, the inspector would have to let him go.

Thoughtfully, Graham took a sip of his tea. He'd racked his brain to create new angles with which to break Granby's story. He simply couldn't fathom who else Reeves's murderer might be. Nor did they have any leads as to Katya's killer. He'd even had Tomlinson revisit the idea that she killed herself.

Above him, floorboards creaked. Laura was finished in the bathroom. Graham emptied his mug, and running it under the tap, he left it on the draining board. With one last hoot ringing in his ears, he turned off the kitchen light and went upstairs.

CHAPTER FORTY-SEVEN

"HEY, JIM!" JACK bundled through the front doors of the police station.
Roach looked up from his computer and quickly ran over to help Jack before he dropped the tray of coffees he was balancing onto the floor. "For us?"

"Yeah, you must be exhausted. Thought I'd bring you some breakfast." Jack dropped a brown paper bag onto the counter. "Four bacon butties and four coffees. Where's Jan?"

"I don't know. Don't you?"

"She sent me a text last night saying she was working late. I assumed you were pulling an all-nighter to wrap up this case."

"Not that I know of, mate. I'm the only one here. Got in half an hour ago." The double doors banged and in walked Barnwell, Carmen trotting at his heels. "Mornin', Bazz. Do you know where Janice is? She told Jack here she was working late last night, but there's no sign of her."

Barnwell stopped in the middle of the lobby. He threw his arms wide. "She went out after lunch yesterday, and that was the last I saw of her. She was going to spell me on reception when she said she had to go out. She was in quite the tizzy. Didn't hear from her again. I assumed she'd clocked off at the end of her shift and gone home."

Another bang. Graham walked through the doors. Three pale faces brought him up short. "What is it?"

"Janice is missing."

Janice arched her spine. Cold burned her nostrils and cheeks. Sleep had eluded her, and overnight, she'd dozed only fitfully in between shuffles designed to propel her inch by inch further into the tunnel. But she existed inside a black hole lacking any sense of time or distance. She shuddered. Her body seemed to weigh four times more than normal, her thoughts slow and dull like a particularly heavy blanket she lacked the strength to throw off. She had, she thought, slowly pushed herself further up the tunnel away from the rising tide, but she couldn't be sure.

Reaching deep into the dark cavern of her despair, Janice once again lifted her knees and pushed off with her feet, the hard rock under her shoulder grazing her skin despite her uniform jacket. Ahead of her, tiny shafts of light penetrated her blindfold. Was there a way out from this hellhole? Or did the tide and certain death await her?

"What were her last movements?" There had been no time for tea. Graham and the three men were at the whiteboard.

"She left here just after two p.m. She was going to cover me on reception so I could take Carmen out for a walk, but then she said she had to go out. I've no idea where she was going or why," Barnwell said.

"And what was she doing just before that?"

"She was in the break room having her lunch. She said she was looking for shoes on the internet." Barnwell was answering Graham's questions as he asked, but he couldn't shake the feeling that he'd failed in some way. Nothing he said appeared to be of any help whatsoever.

A picture swarmed Graham's memory. He was in the Fo'c'sle and Ferret. An undercover officer had told him her cover was blown. He hadn't reacted swiftly enough that time. He wasn't going to make the same mistake again.

"Alright, listen to me. Barnwell, raise the coastguard. I want the helicopter out and all boats patrolling the coastline. Alert the airport and ferry terminal."

"Sir."

Graham took two steps forward. He pointed his pen at his sergeant. "Roach, contact St. Helier. Tell them we've got an officer missing. They need to activate all units. I'll call the chief officer."

"Yes, sir!"

Graham reached for Jack and put a hand on his shoulder. "Trace her phone," he said, quietly.

"Where can she be? Where *can* she be?" Roach drove. In the passenger seat, Barnwell combed the crowds of tourists and schoolchildren enjoying the good weather. They had been driving for twenty minutes. An air/sea/land operation had been launched involving every coastguard and police patrol available. In an hour, resources from other islands would be mobilised. The ports were shut down. Jack was frantically working to determine the location from which the previous evening's text had come.

"Stop!" Roach slammed on his brakes. Barnwell opened the car door and sprinted down a causeway to a gaggle of lads in tracksuits hanging out at the water's edge. "Have you seen a policewoman, probably in uniform, about this high, mousey hair, sergeant's stripes?"

Neil Lightfoot smirked. "Lost 'er, 'have yer? Careless."

Barnwell grabbed him by the collar of his tracksuit. "None of your lip. This is serious," he fumed.

"Okay, okay. When?" Duncan Rayner asked, forcing an arm between them and pushing Barnwell off his friend.

"Anytime after two p.m. yesterday." Rayner turned down the corners of his mouth and shook his head. Barnwell huffed and made to run back up the causeway. Kevin Croft placed a hand on his arm.

"I think I saw her," he said quietly. "Marett Lane. We were going to the beach. She was getting out of her car. That was just after two yesterday. Yeah, I'm sure of it. I remember thinking she was pretty fit for a fuzz."

Barnwell ignored the reference. His heart leapt. "Good lad." He patted Kevin on the shoulder, and as he ran back to the car, he radioed the news to Graham, who was coordinating the search from the station. "Sighting: Marett Lane yesterday afternoon."

"Confirmed, Constable. I've just had a second sighting. Copper from the mainland heard about the search and phoned it in. Saw her park her car and cross to a cottage." Surging with optimism, Barnwell gave Roach a thumbs-up as he streaked up the causeway.

"Marett Lane, Roachie. Fast!"

Barnwell's radio crackled. Graham's voice floated through the air. "One forty-five Marett Lane, business address of Granby Investments. Also, home of Silas Granby's assistant, Cynthia Moorcroft. Janice interviewed her about Granby's alibi for the Jamie Reeves murder."

Roach spun the car like he was in a TV cop drama. Barnwell turned on the blue lights and sirens. It was only the third time he'd used both at the same time in his entire Gorey police career.

Janice's car sat forlornly across the road from Cynthia's cottage. Leaves from the tree above scattered across its roof like autumnal confetti. Roach shielded his eyes and peered through the front windows of the cottage. It was empty. Around the back, Barnwell was less restrained. He shouldered the rear door open and walked through the house to let Roach in. "There's no one here."

In the kitchen, mugs of tea still sat on the kitchen table. A fluffy, brown cat eyed the visitors curiously before deciding they were of no consequence and padding off up the narrow stone stairs.

Barnwell bent to pick up a piece of paper. "This looks like a printout from our printer." He showed it to Roach.

"That's Granby," Roach said.

"Who are the women? Frances Macintyre. Holly Macintyre."

From the table, Roach picked up the framed photo of the two women that Cynthia had showed Janice. "No idea, but these are the same people. Relative? Sister perhaps?"

"Says here Holly died because she didn't get the drug she needed from Granby's company. Frances, her mother, took him to court. She lost."

"Uh-oh. That can't be a coincidence. Maybe Janice worked out the connection."

"And came to confront her."

"And now she's been missing for hours."

"Why didn't she ask me to come with her?" Barnwell said, exasperated.

"You know what this means, don't you, Bazz?"

"Yeah." Barnwell looked around. "We need a photo, Jim. We can circulate it. Granby can identify this Moorcroft woman when we get back to the station."

"You do downstairs, I'll go up." Roach ran for the stairs the cat had just climbed.

Barnwell looked about. He heard a shout. "Found one!" Roach scrambled back down the steps. "At least I think this is her." He showed Barnwell a picture of three women as he picked up the framed photo from the kitchen table and compared them. "Look, these women are Frances and Holly Macintyre. I bet this one is Cynthia."

"Good enough for me! I'll circulate it on the way back. We need to find her."

The lapping water had got louder. It slapped against rock with every push of the tide. Janice rubbed the back of her head against a hard surface. The blindfold loosened, then slipped. Trapping it, she tilted her chin upward. The scarf fell away. A thrill passed through her like an easy, flowing stream.

Relief quickly gave way to despair, however. Sight was infinitely preferable to blindness but only confirmed her peril. The tide was most definitely rising.

With all units and ports alerted for signs of Cynthia Moorcroft, Barnwell quietly spoke to Graham. "How're you getting on, sir?" It had been fifty-five minutes since Jack had arrived with breakfast. It felt like fifty-five years.

Graham had given his office over to Jack and sat in reception, alert to notifications coming in from search patrols. He blew out his cheeks. "Jack's not had any luck locating the phone. She could be out at sea or in a dead zone, anywhere really. Besides, we'll only find out her last location. She could be long gone from that spot by n—"

"I know!" Jack shouted from Graham's office. The other three rushed in. Jack banged Graham's desktop with his hands. The slap must have hurt, but Janice's fiancé paid no mind to his stinging palms. "Her Fitbit. She's always wearing it. She goes a bit mad if she doesn't get her ten thousand steps in. For the wedding. She wanted—wants—to be in good sh-shape." Jack's voice cracked. He spent a second or two wrestling his emotions. "I might be able to get a signal from it if it's still charged."

"What do you need, Jack? Anything we can get you?" Graham asked.

"No, just peace. It's a long shot. I need to download an app . . . yes, here we are. Come on, come on. Okay, here we go." Jack stared at his phone's screen. "It's my Fitbit, really. If she's close by, it will sync to my phone." They all waited. After nearly a minute, Jack's shoulders dropped. "It's not syncing."

"What does that mean?" Barnwell whispered to Roach.

"She's not nearby, I think," Roach replied.

They looked at Jack. He was surrounded by screens, phones, cables, and headphones.

"Can we drive around trying to find her? If we are close to X marks the spot, won't the Fitbit tell us?" Roach asked him.

"Yes, but we need to narrow things down first."

A message flashed up on one of the phones strewn across Graham's desk. Jack pounced on it. "Wait . . . The text! It was sent from . . ." He reached over to punch some coordinates into his computer. A map flashed up on the screen. It showed a remote part of the island to the north. "What's there? Just woodland, right?"

"And a lot of rocks. I know where it is," Roach said. "I used to go crabbing there as a kid."

"Well, what are we waiting for?" Barnwell said, grabbing a backpack and Carmen's lead.

"Follow me. I'll take my bike!" Roach was already running to the break room and his leathers.

"I'll drive!" Graham cried, grabbing his jacket, for once prepared to break the speed limit.

"What about Granby?" Barnwell said. The wealth manager was still in the cells.

"Leave him. I'll get someone here from HQ." Barnwell winced. Leaving a prisoner locked in the cells while alone in the building was totally against the rules. But this was an emergency, and Graham didn't think twice. "We've got more important things to worry about! He won't even know we've gone if we don't tell him!"

CHAPTER FORTY-EIGHT

"JANICE!" THE FOUR men shouted themselves hoarse. They had spread out, working their way across woodland. Officers from all over the island were en route to join the search.

"She could have been moved by now. I mean, we don't even know if she was with the person who sent it," Jack said doubtfully. Initially elated at locating where the text had been sent from, he was struggling to remain calm and optimistic. "And it doesn't mean she's still here. That text was sent hours ago now."

"I'm confident we'll find her, Jack. It's the best lead we've got. Let's each take a lane. Stay in touch, everyone," Graham said.

For the next fifteen minutes, the four men crossed the wood, widening their search when they turned up nothing. Carmen pulled at her lead, sniffing her way through the undergrowth and once attempting to chase a squirrel. "Hold on, girl," Barnwell muttered, as he pulled her on. "Perhaps I should have left you with someone."

Yards to his left, Roach swished a pole through the undergrowth. To Barnwell's right, Jack nervously stepped forward, his eyes on the ground, desperately hoping to find something but, at the same time, worried about what that might be. They were quiet now, alert to any sound. Up ahead, Graham led the charge. Every so often, he stopped and shouted, "Janice!"

They stopped and listened but could hear nothing but the cries of seagulls and the rustling of bushes as a forest animal ferreted around. They resumed their march through the brush, silently repressing their fears and focusing on the job at hand.

"Arrgghhh!" Barnwell and Roach turned to Jack in panic. He screamed at the woodland canopy, his face contorted, his fists clenched. In different circumstances, Barnwell might have expected him to turn green and explode out of his shirt. "This is hopeless! We're never going to find her!"

Barnwell walked over. He hesitated, but then wrapped Jack in a hug. "It's alright, mate. Jan's a tough cookie. Keep the faith, hmm? Why don't you go back to the car?"

Jack leant into Barnwell, taking comfort from the bulk of the big man. After a few moments, his equilibrium mostly restored, he pulled away. "No, no. I'll carry on." He looked across the woodland. There was a shout.

"Where's the boss?" Roach called out. Up ahead of them, Graham had disappeared. Jack, Barnwell, and Roach stood still, turning their heads in arcs over a hundred and eighty degrees.

"Bloody hell," Barnwell said. "Is this day going to get any better?"

Graham had gone ahead primarily to lead his men but also to clear his head. With each passing minute, his anxiety built. Ice filled the marrow of his bones. His muscles wound as tight as a boa constrictor; his mind fizzed. He did not want to convey his worries to his officers, and especially not to Jack.

Janice had been missing for hours. Jack was right; she could be anywhere by now, in any condition. He stamped the ground as he marched along, casting his eyes in a wide semicircle. They could be miles off target or right on top of her.

That last thought struck him as he fell. Darkness engulfed him, and his stomach churned as he flew through the air. Sharp pain assailed him as he banged his head, his limbs scraping rocks. He shut his eyes tight as he braced for impact. In those moments, he thought of Katie. Then Laura.

"Radio him, text him," Barnwell shouted across to Roach. He pulled out his own phone. "Where are the backup units from St Helier?" He blew out his cheeks. "Time to call reinforcements," he muttered as he began tapping his phone.

"Perhaps he's just out of sight, gone further ahead," Jack said.

"He's not replying," Roach shouted.

Jack's phone pinged. He punched the air, his worries about Graham forgotten. "The Fitbit's synced. She's close!"

Graham's eyelids fluttered. His skin tickled with damp and cold. Pain sliced through his shoulder. Another stab of pain carved down his leg. He moaned as it —first sharp, then dull— receded. Where was he? And why was he there? Then he remembered. There was a shuffling noise, a grunt. Someone or something—he wasn't sure it was human—was alongside him.

Janice! Her eyes, huge in her deathly pale face, bore into him. She made a small noise. Her lips were blue. Painfully, Graham lifted his hands to untie her gag.

As the scarf fell away, Janice sighed. "Thank you." She closed her eyes. "I managed to get my blindfold off, but the gag defeated me."

"Where are we?"

"You fell down a chute. We're in a war tunnel." Above them, a smidgen of daylight peeked between undergrowth that covered the entrance to the hole Graham had fallen into.

"And I hate to tell you this, but the tide is coming in. I've been shuffling away from it for ages, but I'm tired and very"—Janice let out another sigh, summoning some of the last reserves of her energy to finish her sentence—"very cold." She lifted her eyes to Graham's face. He noticed her long, wet eyelashes stuck together. "Sir, I'm frightened." Her voice was husky.

"The boys are up top. They'll find us. Don't worry. We'll be out in a jiffy." Graham made to sit up. Another shot of pain ran up his leg to his neck. "Arghhhh. My leg."

Janice wriggled around. "Looks broken, sir. Well, we're a right pair, aren't we? Not a full set of working limbs between us.

"What about I untie you?"

"Zip-tied, so unless you . . ." Janice couldn't finish her sentence. She pressed her lips together so tightly they went from blue to white.

"Perhaps my phone . . ."

"Smashed. Over there. Nothing doing. I already checked." Janice nodded in a direction Graham couldn't see. He'd have to take her word for it. Feet away, a trickle of seawater crept around a rock.

"Hey! Down here!" A pulse of adrenaline stabbed him. His voice wasn't carrying up the chute. Graham tried again. "Barnwell! Roach!" He turned to Janice. "Let's try together. Just make some noise. On three. One, two, three!"

Janice did her best. Her throat and lips were parched. She'd had no water since the day before. The irony of being surrounded by it, in great peril, wasn't lost on her. She yelled in time with Graham, but her voice was tremulous and weak. "It's just echoing around this chamber. They aren't going to hear us, are they?" Graham silently agreed with her. Janice shuddered.

"Here, squish up against me." Janice wriggled closer, and Graham lifted his good arm to pull her into him. They lay side by side like a pair of lovers, Janice's head on Graham's shoulder. He wrapped his arms around her. Hypothermia might take her before the tide.

🜨

"She can't be far. This thing doesn't have a long range. We're close!" Jack's energy had returned, making him hyper. His voice shook. "Janice!" Barnwell and Roach joined him.

"Graham!"

"Alright, let's keep doing what we're doing but keep in this local area. She has to be here somewhere," Roach said.

Carmen pulled hard on her lead, and Barnwell staggered, nearly falling into a bush. "Hold on, girl." The three men redoubled their efforts, searching the same ground from a different angle. Nothing. They congregated in a huddle.

"Any news from the boss?" Barnwell said.

Roach checked his phone. "Nope, he's well and truly gone."

Barnwell thought back to what Graham had told him over a week ago. "Is there a war tunnel running under here? Jack, can you see? Some of the tunnels reached to the coast so the Nazis could move supplies, men, and contraband in and out of the island without anyone knowing." Carmen pulled on her lead, and this time Barnwell let go, unwilling to spend more of his energy restraining her. She'd come back.

Jack interrogated his phone, swiping, tapping, scrolling, and finally, expanding. "Yes! Yes, there is one." Staring at his phone, he started to walk. "This way." Roach and Barnwell fell in behind him. After ten yards, he stopped. "It runs here." He waved his hand right to left. "The tunnel runs from the beach and heads toward St. Lawrence."

"That's where the war tunnel centre is. Is the Fitbit still syncing?"

"Yup. She's here, beneath us!"

"Then let's go!" Roach started running to the edge of the wood and the beach. Jack followed. Barnwell heard Carmen barking. He hesitated.

CHAPTER FORTY-NINE

WATER RUSHED INTO the tunnel. The strength of the tide was building. It soaked Graham's back, freezing-cold water filled his ears. "Janice, there's a ledge. It will lift us another two feet if we can get onto it. Do you think you can make it?"

Janice murmured. Graham, unsure if she really understood what was happening, took his arms from around her and forced himself into a seated position. He grabbed Janice around her waist and as he helped her, she roused herself into a sitting position. "Use your legs to push yourself to the ledge," Graham told her. "Like this . . ." White-hot pain shot up his broken leg. "Arghhhh." Graham closed his eyes and forced the stars he saw there to stop spinning. "You go. I'll think of something else."

"Wait, in my hands," Janice said. Behind her back, she held onto the scarf that had acted as her blindfold. "Strap your bad leg to your good one. It'll stabilise it. Use your arms to pull yourself along." Graham did as she suggested, and then, like crustaceans, they used their limbs to push and pull themselves across the rocks to the ledge.

"You go first," Graham said when they reached it. "Put your back against it and push yourself up with your legs until you can roll onto it."

Janice wriggled around and positioned her feet to manoeuvre herself onto the ledge. She paused. "I'm not sure I can. I don't have the energy."

"Yes, you do. Think of your wedding, Jack, your future, whatever you want it to hold. Go on."

Janice gritted her teeth and, her face twisted with effort, she shakily forced her body up onto the step that lay two feet above water level. She rolled away to give Graham the space to do the same.

With a broken leg, Graham's task was even harder. Grimacing, he pushed himself upright using his good leg, the broken one tied to it, having no choice but to follow. His thigh muscles trembled with exertion, the pain almost making him pass out. He thought of his past, Katie, of his future, Laura, and the colourful possibilities that might follow. When his chest cleared the ledge, he twisted to face it. Leaning on his hands, he stood up.

His last manoeuvre would be the toughest. He sat on the ledge, galvanising his resolve. Gritting his teeth and roaring in pain, he raised his legs and swung them around. Janice shifted over more, and he rolled in beside her. "We made it, Janice. We're good here," he whispered in her ear, panting, tears stinging.

Janice shook uncontrollably. Graham held her tight against his chest, although the warmth they were now able to share was negligible. Time was running out. "Stay with me, Janice. You've got to hang on. Jack is waiting up there for you."

She murmured. She was so sleepy. Her mind drifted. Somewhere, though, in the swirling fog that was left, she understood she should talk, say something.

"Sir, have you ever regretted joining the force?"

Graham's mouth twitched. "Well, I'm not loving it right at this moment, I can tell you that." He couldn't see, but Janice, her eyelids closed, gave a small smile at his answer. "But no, not really. I've been in some tricky spots, but I wanted to be a policeman ever since our local village bobby returned my toy dump truck that someone else had taken when I was a little boy. After that, I got a uniform, and my mum said I would wear it to bed sometimes. I even had one of the old-style helmets, the ones with the chin straps. I would wear it to the shops, anywhere."

He reached for Janice's frozen hands and rubbed them. "Justice has always appealed to me. I want everything to be squared away, balanced, just so. Of course, it's a pie-in-the-sky endeavour, but I enjoy the challenge. It drives me on."

"Did you like cop shows? That's what enticed me. *Prime Suspect*, *Juliet Bravo* . . . Way before my time, but I loved watching them. I got given box sets for my birthday. Now, there are more female detectives on the telly."

"I was into *Morse*, although the plots got ridiculous towards the end."

"It's funny, isn't it, how we end up in the force . . . When I was younger, I was a free spirit. Travelled the world a bit . . . somehow got into cooking for rich people on yachts for cash . . . and I ended up here. Didn't want to leave. I went to bail out an idiot boyfriend who'd got done for being drunk on a night out in St. Helier . . . and ended up answering an ad I saw on their noticeboard. The job looked kind of interesting." Janice exhaled. That had taken a lot of effort.

"My route was less colourful. University, police recruitment scheme, Met, then I applied to come here." There was a long pause. Graham jiggled her. "Janice?"

"I've always wondered about that, sir. Why such a change? Fast, hard-charging career and then you swerve to this idyllic backwater." Janice's words were slurred. She was speaking slower with each breath. Each sentence cost her more of her rapidly depleting energy.

Graham cast a glance across the tunnel. The water was continuing to rise.

Like Janice, he was starting to shake uncontrollably. His fingers had gone numb long ago.

"I was married. We broke up. I needed a change, a complete change. I thought Jersey sounded appealing, away from it all, about as different from working in London as could be."

"Do you think you'll get married again?" Janice mumbled.

"I hope so. I liked being married. Life is a bit grey without someone to enjoy it with."

"I worry about it sometimes . . . I love Jack to pieces, but the thought of being with the same person for the rest of my life is . . ." Graham jiggled her again. ". . . Daunting."

"Lots of people think of marriage the wrong way. They see it as limiting. But it isn't; it's freeing. If you've chosen the right one, and you have, you can be confident your person will be there for you. They provide you with a solid base from which to kick off. You can take risks and have adventures the likes of which we rarely experience on our own."

"When are you going to ask Laura to marry you then?"

Graham smiled. "I don't know. Do you think she'll have me?"

"Definitely. I think she's just waiting for you to ask. You make a good couple. Not many women . . . um, never mind . . ."

There was a long pause. Graham tried rocking Janice. Her eyes stayed closed. "Janice," he said sharply. He attempted to pat her face, but his numb fingers refused to cooperate, and he had to settle for rubbing her cheek. The water level was still rising. It would cover the ledge soon.

Janice stirred. She wriggled around and turned to face him. Her eyes still closed, she lifted her head like a sleeping baby before laying it down on Graham's chest. "Last thing, sir. Who's the little girl in the photo on your windowsill? I saw it the other night."

"Ah, that's my daughter Katie."

"You've never mentioned her. Is she with her mother? Do you see her?"

Graham closed his eyes briefly. Behind his eyelids, he saw Katie laughing, squealing as he chased her around the garden with a spray hose. "She died in a car accident a few years ago. She was five."

"I'm sorry. Tell me about her." Janice snuggled in closer to Graham, and he squeezed her waist.

"Well, she was funny and happy and giggly. She loved platypuses and dogs. She'd have loved Carmen. When she was a toddler, if she ever had a tantrum, I'd plop her in the bath, and she'd calm right down."

"When I was little, I loved dressing up in my Disney princess dresses. Did she do that?"

"She loved her Disney princesses, but we did a lot of Lego too. Just before she died, her favourite thing was bedtime. I'd read her a story, then roll her back and forth on the bed super-fast. When she was out of breath, I'd give her Eskimo kisses and she'd give me butterfly kisses, then it would be lights out." Graham smiled in the dark. "I miss that bedtime routine."

Janice sighed. "Do you think you'll have children with Jack?" Graham asked her. There was no answer. He looked down. "Janice? Janice!"

Searching for a way into the tunnel, Roach and Jack streaked to the edge of the woodland. It ended in a cliff across the top of which was a hiking trail worn into the grass. A small fence four feet away from the edge warned hikers not to get close. Jack ignored it. He peeked over the edge. His face, flushed with excitement and exertion, paled. "The tide's in." Roach joined him. "Look down there. The entrance to the tunnel is flooded." Jack's stricken face turned to Roach. "Oh my God. If she's in there, she's dead, Jim, dead!"

Feeling almost as panic-stricken as Jack, Roach gripped his arms. "Let's not give up now, lad. She might be making her way to St. Lawrence for all we know. She's a smart girl." A shout went up. "Come on, that was Bazza. Maybe he's got something."

They found Barnwell standing in a clearing with Carmen by his side. She was still barking. Roach and Jack rushed up. "I've found them. Or Carmen did. Shush, girl." Barnwell bent down and she licked his hands. "They're down there." Jack and Roach peered as Barnwell parted the bushes. Graham's white face looked up at them, his eyes a bright blue in the gloom. He held Janice in his arms, her eyes closed like she was a sleeping child. The tide was rising. Deep water surrounded them. Graham was submerged up to his shoulders as he fought to keep Janice's head above the surface.

A shout. Barnwell turned. "About *bloody* time." Running toward them were twelve men, headed up by their leader, former SAS major, Bash Bingham. Members of Fortytude, the early morning running group Barnwell ran with, had arrived in response to Barnwell's SOS. Bash carried survival gear. Behind them, marching at a slower pace, were paramedics Sue Armitage and Alan Pritchard, Melanie Howes, the Gorey fire crew manager, and half a dozen firefighters. Marcus Tomlinson brought up the rear. All of them carried equipment that Barnwell, confronted with the rescue operation that faced them, felt quite sure would be essential.

"Step back! Cavalry's here!" Bash cried out. He walked up to the hole in the ground and looked over. The members of Fortytude stood back, as did the paramedics. The firefighter captain joined Bash at the opening.

"I hope they get a move on. They don't have much time," Barnwell murmured to Roach. Roach bit his nails, a habit he'd broken with effort as a teenager. Catching himself, he grabbed hold of Jack and held him in a tight embrace.

"Harness! Rope!" the firefighter captain shouted. Bash took the equipment and threw it down to Graham. He knelt on the ground. "Put the harness around her!" the fire captain instructed as Bash and another firefighter fitted a contraption that looked like an instrument of torture across the top of the chute.

Graham had his hand under Janice's chin, lifting her face out of the water so she could breathe. She was unconscious. He lifted the harness over her head and brought her arms through it. Feeling around in the water, he was able to bring the lower strap under her body and lock it to her front. It had to hold her in place. Barnwell, Roach, and Jack joined eight other men around the chute to hold the winch in place while two others readied to operate a mechanism that would pull Janice to safety. Two more stood by to bring her to ground when she emerged.

It was a job of brute force. Straining, the eleven men exerted all their strength to pin the winch down as Janice was slowly lifted to safety. "Unconventional, but effective," Bash muttered as an unconscious Janice cleared the chute and was gently levered onto a stretcher.

Paramedics Sue and Alan immediately got to work. Sue cut off Janice's wet clothes and wrapped her in blankets, tucking hot packs in between the layers while Alan took her vitals and fed her oxygen. Tomlinson hooked up an IV through which he delivered warmed salt water into her veins. His voice shaking uncharacteristically, the pathologist kept up a constant stream of chatter, and after a few minutes, Janice's eyelids trembled before opening. She blinked rapidly as her eyes adjusted to the sunlight. After wrapping her in another layer of thermal blankets, they moved her away from the rescue theatre as Jack hovered.

Down in the tunnel, matters had become even more urgent. Cold, exhaustion, and pain had rendered Graham barely conscious. "We're just over sixty seconds away from submersion," Bash said. "He's exhausted, in shock, hypothermic, and injured. A lamb to the water."

"We need to get him out! He'll be swept away, or he'll drown in place!" Barnwell cried. "We need to get someone down there to help him."

"Out of the way!"

"Hey!" Bash yelled.

Roach curled into a ball, tucking his arms in as he dropped into the chute. The water broke his fall. There was a splash, and he bobbed up beside Graham in the tunnel.

"Throw me the harness!" he shouted, spluttering.

🌐

Twenty minutes later, Graham and Janice loaded into the ambulance, Barnwell turned to Roach, who clutched a thermal pack. He was pale and shivering. Barnwell wrapped him in a shiny emergency blanket.

"Tomlinson told me you couldn't swim."

"Yeah, no, I can't. But I wasn't letting you get *another* medal."

CHAPTER FIFTY

OF COURSE, THE rain that had been promised stayed away now that Barnwell had remembered his jacket. He'd walked from the station to the Foc's'le and Ferret up on the hill. Its reassuring presence gave him confidence, somehow, that despite the day's torrid events, the world would continue to rotate on its axis as it should.

"And they found her!" he heard a voice at the bar cry. "Took eleven men to bring her up." His brother leant into the ear of a pretty young woman next to him. Barnwell stood for a second, admiring his brother's unerring ability to make new friends. He caught his eye. "The man of the hour! Lewis! Lewis, lad, it's an emergency." Steve waved an empty pint glass at the barman. The woman sidled off. "Lewis, I demand that you pour this man a double of your finest scotch."

"They're *all* fine," the barman insisted. "Wouldn't pour them otherwise."

"Then it's dealer's choice," Barnwell said. "And it's just a tonic water for me, thanks."

"Wha—?" his brother cried in mock astonishment. "Well, not for me. I'll have a single."

"You've just got yourself a new pint," his brother pointed out.

"And I shall have a whisky chaser. Don't worry. That'll be my limit."

Lewis hauled a box from the shelf, wiped dust off the top, and brought out a slender bottle with a simple, white label. "Ever tried a twenty-one-year-old Bruichladdich?"

"Since you've gone to the effort of pronouncing it, it'd be rude not to," Steve said.

Once served, the men found their usual table and settled in. Barnwell spotted Matthew Walker at the end of the bar, talking amicably with a couple of lads his age. He gave Barnwell the tiniest hint of a salute.

"There I was," Steve said, "hoping that the highlight of my visit this week would be the sight of you hauling that big old barrel down to the station in handcuffs."

Barnwell sipped his tonic, finding it refreshing. "Actually, I did, but we released him after an hour or so."

"You don't say!" Steve exclaimed.

"He ended up being just another poor fella who found himself caught up in something." He took a sip of Steve's whisky. It tasted peaty and medicinal. He found it lowered his stress levels. Just focusing on the flavour profile—a robust earthy eruption tempered by meltwater from a woodland glen—gave him valuable moments of calm and quiet, but he wouldn't have any more. He wanted to take Carmen out for a run later.

"Well?" Steve said. "You going to leave me hanging or what? What happened with your case? Everyone's talking about the rescue."

"The age-old tale," Barnwell replied. "Girl meets boy, but girl is already married to a fabulously wealthy banker-type. Then someone paints a portrait of boy and girl swimming together and everything falls apart. Someone with a historical beef settles some scores, necessitating some heroics from people other than yours truly, and the mystery is solved. Straightforward, really. Just humans being exactly as they are. Flawed. Extremely so in some cases. We haven't actually caught the perp yet—she's on her way to Honduras—but she'll have a surprise when she arrives."

Steve wrinkled his nose, puzzled. "I guess I'll follow when it comes to trial. Well done, by the way," he said. "Must feel pretty good."

"It's a relief more than anything. Started to do my head in not knowing what had happened, or why."

"Speaking of not knowing, did you have any success getting the you-know-what from the you-know-where?"

The envelope was in Barnwell's jacket pocket. "I printed the whole thing. Fairly standard file for the time. I had to get some help it was so old, but it'll be fine." Barnwell hadn't fully explained to Jack what he wanted or why, but there'd been an unspoken understanding between them that they'd never speak of it.

"Did you read it?" asked Steve, his pint held in midair.

"Yes."

Steve set down his glass. "Am I in for a shock?"

"I suspect not, Steve. Seems to me that you always knew."

"Maybe. Not for certain. Just little bits and pieces down the years." Steve looked down at the envelope Barnwell held in his hand. "Can I read it?"

"Yes, but then I'm going to eat it. I could get sacked for this, and Dad never wanted us to know. After you've read it, we're going to forget all about it, okay?"

Steve nodded. Barnwell gave him the envelope. His younger brother tore open the flap and took a deep breath. "Wow, you've got a photo too."

"From his arrest," Barnwell explained.

Steve read, and as he did, he was almost overcome. How many times had he guessed what this report would say? Now everything was clear. "He hit someone with a pint glass?" Steve wondered quietly. "Our dad? He glassed someone?"

"Look at the details," Barnwell said. "It was 'last orders.' You know how things got before the laws changed."

"People pouring drink down their necks at top speed before the barman chucked them out," Steve said.

"And the guy he attacked, I looked him up." Barnwell leafed to one of the final pages in the report, a simple biographical data sheet for one Anthony Hood, later Councillor Hood, Anthony Hood MP, and then Baron Hood, member of the House of Lords. The man was their father's age. "They were at school together. He nearly lost an eye in the attack."

"So, what happened?" Steve wanted to know. "I mean, Dad didn't just go around *hitting* people. He never raised a hand to us."

Barnwell explained the quiet effort he'd put in to get to the bottom of his father's eighteen-month absence. "I called the old barman at the Queen's Arms, where it all happened."

"Hellfire, Bazz. How old's he?"

"Eighty-nine. His hips were a bit rickety, but his mind was as clear as a bell. He remembered the incident."

"What did he say?"

"That Hood wound Dad up. Started talking about their school days, how he'd been more popular than Dad, had more girlfriends, all the usual childish stuff. Barman said Hood was upright but pretty drunk."

"Dad hit him because of *that*?"

"He made a comment," Barnwell explained carefully, "about Mum. Something about her, umm, *behaviour*."

"He didn't!" Steve said.

"Yeah, in front of the whole pub. Dad got two years, ended up serving eighteen months."

"Eighteen months. Otherwise known as a stint on the oil rigs." They were both quiet as they digested this revision of their family history.

"Makes more sense now, doesn't it?" Steve said. "How he'd not want to see his son a copper. They were the enemy to him."

"Mebbe, or maybe he just didn't want his secret getting out. I'm amazed it hasn't before now to be fair."

The news was a shock, but also it wasn't. There had been signs—whispered conversations, adult tears quickly wiped away, their father's moodiness. That there had only been one incident and with mitigating factors was an enormous relief. To Barnwell, that he might discover that his father was a repeat offender, a violent thief, or something worse had been terrifying.

"Anyone," Steve said, "*anyone* can get themselves into something. Don't care who you are. When there's booze and emotions, it doesn't take much."

"No, but he shouldn't have done it. No wonder he never drunk a drop again." Barnwell fingered the report. "I hadn't the first *clue* he'd been through this," he said. "Me applying to the force must have been shocking, him thinking his secret was going to get out. What I can't understand is how I got here."

"What do you mean?"

"I'm a police officer. A background check on me, standard procedure during the recruitment process, would have turned up this information. I would have been questioned about it. They would have to make sure I wasn't open to bribery or blackmail because of it."

"Wow, they must have thought you were worth taking a chance on. Perhaps they saw you were no threat—it had been a one-off—and decided to let things slide."

"I can't remember really, it was too long ago, but I would have answered negatively when they'd asked about convictions in the family. They must have concluded that I genuinely didn't know about Dad's record, decided it didn't affect my application, and let me through to the next round. Amazing really when you think about it."

"Dad must have been in ribbons, though, thinking his secret was about to be exposed. He was a proud man. Reputation stood for something back then. He wanted to be our dad. He would never have wanted us to see him as a criminal. The shame of it."

"But he kept it in all those years! I just didn't know. Me prancing around in my uniform must have been excruciating for him. No wonder he tried to persuade me to do something else. I thought it was because it was embarrassing. The police weren't the most popular round our way, were they?"

"I don't think he saw it like that," said Steve. "Actually, I can prove it." He pulled a frame from a plastic bag he'd been carrying.

It was an image Barnwell recognised immediately. Taken from above, the green-black night vision image showed a man suspended under a helicopter, gesturing to someone. Beneath him was a tiny, storm-tossed boat, and beyond that, the blackness of the English Channel at night. Tucked into the frame was a wallet-sized photo of Barnwell's visit to Buckingham Palace to collect his Queen's Gallantry medal, his mother standing next to him, smiling proudly.

"Dad had this on the mantel above the fireplace in the living room. Said he couldn't believe you'd ever do anything so stupid." Steve laughed.

"He didn't know me that well then."

"But you know what else?" Steve said. "He mentioned it every time I saw him. Every *single* time, he told me how much he admired you."

"Ah well, guess I made him proud in the end. Better late than never." Barnwell picked up Steve's scotch glass. "To Dad," he said.

"To Dad," replied his brother.

CHAPTER FIFTY-ONE

"SLOWLY, JACK. SLOWLY!" Jack manoeuvred Janice's wheelchair down the corridor. She still looked pale, and there were purple half-moons under her eyes, but a sparkle had returned to them when her nurse said she could visit her boss. They were making their way to Graham's room now. A bunch of yellow roses lay across her lap.

As Jack wheeled her through the door to Graham's room, Janice's eyes widened. Laura, Barnwell, Roach, and Tomlinson turned to look at her.

"Here she is!" someone cried.

In their midst lay Graham, his arm in a sling, a blanket hiding the metal frame that pinned the bones of his leg together.

"Good to see you looking so well, Sergeant," Graham said.

"You too, sir," Janice replied. Awkwardly, she put the flowers on his bed. "I, um, brought you these."

"They're beautiful, Janice," Laura said. "I'll put them in water." She wandered off, her eyes beckoning Jack to accompany her.

"So how are you both doing?" Marcus Tomlinson said. "That's a fearsome Ilizarov frame you've got there, David. Your leg was badly broken. I took the liberty of looking at your X-rays."

"Yeah, there was a long surgery to straighten everything out and fix them into place. Just got to wait for the bones to knit back together now."

"How long before you're back on your feet, sir?" Janice asked.

"Hmm, some months to fully recover they tell me. I'll go stark staring mad before that, so I'll be back in the office way before then, even if Barnwell has to carry me around. How about you?"

"Oh, I'll be fine. Nothing a few days rest and some decent food won't fix."

"It's good to see you looking so well, Janice," Tomlinson said, putting his hand on her shoulder. "I was so glad to be able to help when you were pulled out. You had me very worried."

Tears welled at his kindness. Janice's throat tightened and her chin wobbled. Graham noticed, and he smiled at her. That just made it worse, and Janice looked down at her hands in her lap.

"Hey, I have an announcement," Roach said. He'd also noticed Janice's distress.

"Oh? What's that?" Graham responded.

"I'm not sure. I haven't opened the letter yet. It's from the Met. About a . . . a job application I put in a few weeks ago." He pulled a white envelope from his inside jacket pocket. It had the Metropolitan Police insignia stamped in the corner.

"You bugger, you did put in for a transfer," Barnwell said. "We wondered if you would. But you didn't breathe a word."

"No, I wasn't sure if I'd get it, or if I'd take it if I did. I'm still not sure if I'm honest." Roach took in a deep breath and dropped his shoulders on the exhale.

"Well, go on then, Roachie, don't keep us in suspenders," Barnwell said. "Open it."

Roach turned over the envelope and tore at the flap. Pulling out the letter, he unfolded it and began to read. His eyes gleamed. A smile fluttered across his lips.

Unable to wait, Barnwell looked over his shoulder. "Congratulations, mate!" Barnwell wrapped his arm around Roach as the younger man continued to stare at the letter that told him his application to join Homicide and Major Crime Command based at Scotland Yard had been accepted.

Tomlinson reached over to shake his protégée's hand. "Well done, young man. I'll be sorry to see you go, but our loss is the Met's gain. Don't forget the little people." Roach laughed.

While the three men huddled over Roach's letter, Janice wheeled herself over to Graham. "Good for Roachie. About time."

"It is. Time for him to fly. He'll do well." Graham settled his gaze on Janice, searching her face. "And how are you? Really, I mean."

"I'm okay. Still shocked if I'm honest. Might take some time off."

"Take as much time as you need, Sergeant. And avail yourself of the force's counselling services. That was a scary situation you found yourself in."

"It was my own fault, sir. I should never have gone to Cynthia Moorcroft's alone. When I realised she'd been lying to me, I was livid. I let my personal feelings get the better of me. It was unprofessional."

"Well, I got it wrong about Granby, and perhaps if I'd paid more attention to your contributions, you might not have had such a visceral reaction. I think that means we're quits. And thankfully everything turned out alright."

"Thanks to you, sir. If you hadn't found me, I'd have drowned."

"I'm glad I was able to help, Sergeant."

"And thank you for entrusting me with your story about your daughter. It can't have been easy. You must miss her a lot."

"Yes, I do, but I'm glad it's finally out in the open. I don't want people to feel awkward or like they have to say anything. It is what it is. Katie's part of the story of my life that makes me who I am, just like this incident will mould you."

"You know, I was thinking about the people in this case. No one was really the person they claimed to be. They all lived behind some kind of front."

"Don't we all, Sergeant? One way or another to a greater or lesser extent? None of us present a completely authentic picture of who we are. We're all painting a portrait of a person we'd like others to see."

"Yes!" Barnwell's fist shot into the air like a firework. Graham, Janice, Tomlinson, and Roach turned to look. Barnwell was staring at a text on his phone. "She failed!" He looked at them, his eyes shining much like Roach's had a moment ago. "Carmen's new handler took her for a physical. She failed!" Barnwell looked around at his stunned, silent audience. "Don't you see? Carmen can't move forward to sniffer dog training! She can stay with me. She has a stigmatism. Might make her squirrel hunts a bit pointless, but hey, I'll take it."

Everyone relaxed, smiles on their faces at the thought of Carmen staying with them. Graham quietly spoke again to Janice. "Of course, dogs are the exception to that rule. They are the very definition of authenticity."

"Even Pomeranians, sir?"

"*Especially* Pomeranians, Sergeant.

EPILOGUE

Cynthia Moorcroft was met on her arrival in Honduras by government secret police who committed to returning her to Jersey despite there not existing an extradition treaty between the country and the United Kingdom. Rumours abound of a swap with a Honduran drug lord living in Kent, but this has been neither confirmed nor denied by the British government. On her return, Cynthia can expect to be charged with double murder and sentenced to a whole life tariff—life imprisonment without any possibility of parole or conditional release.

After it was revealed that his assistant had killed his wife and her lover, **Silas Granby** returned to the Granby house, where he lives alone quietly. The house was recently listed for sale, and both the Ferrari and Maserati have disappeared. Granby Investments is no longer registered at Companies House, and it is assumed that Silas Granby is between enterprises or retired. Willow was given to Katya's friend, **Magda Padalka-Lyons**. Willow and Pom-Pom live in mutual conflict.

Molly Duckworth gave her notice at Sanderson Landscaping and travelled Australia and New Zealand, supporting herself as a cattle drover and camp cook. She spends her days on horseback and her mornings and evenings preparing food for hungry cattlemen and women.

. . .

Adrian Sanderson was deeply affected by Jamie Reeves's death. In a frank and moving interview with Freddie Solomon, he spoke of the plans he'd quietly made for he and Jamie to run the business together as an equal partnership. Sanderson Landscaping continues to operate on Jersey, and Adrian hopes that one of his sons will eventually take over the business.

Paula Lascelles broke up with **Matthew Walker** immediately on her return to London. Shortly thereafter, she made a splashy engagement announcement in *The Times*, sharing that she was to marry the deputy assistant head of corporate accounts at the company she works for, only to rescind and cancel everything four days later. She's currently dating her ex-fiancé's boss, described by his own sister as "nice, but dim." Matthew half completed an application to join the police force, but he soon forgot the idea and returned to his life in London.

Sir Peregrine Wordsworth FRSA MPhil (Oxon) recently announced on his website that his twice-annual "Wordsworth of Seascapes" workshops were fully booked for the foreseeable future. He recently appeared in a web-TV show entitled *To Catch a Murderer*, where he joined experts to discuss "the intersection of art and justice." He claims to have made his "first and final" attempt to make a lake vibrate using only a paintbrush.

Three weeks after the rescue, **Detective Inspector Graham** was discharged from hospital and embarked on a rigorous program of rest and rehabilitation. He was occasionally seen in a wheelchair around Gorey, accompanied by one of the members of his police team. After a further month, he progressed to crutches and began appearing at the station, professing a need to return to work. To the relief of many, he has no plans to return to refereeing.

Following a period of panic over leaving Jersey for his new posting and ultimately an intervention led by Dr. Tomlinson and his mum, **Sergeant Jim Roach** set off for the Met. A tankard bearing the words "Shipshape and Bristol Fashion" was a gift from his fellow Gorey officers. Over seventy people attended his leaving do in the Foc's'le. The latest word is that he is settling into London ways nicely but is a "little Jersey homesick." He has joined a gym with a pool.

Janice and Jack cancelled their wedding plans in favour of a rethink. They are now organising something smaller and more spontaneous, possibly a surprise. They have been coy about their thoughts and will only say that "time will tell," although they plan on keeping the cake with the Swiss chocolate French buttercream pâte à bombe icing. Janice's mother took the opportunity to accept a great deal on a package holiday to Greece and had a wonderful time.

Barry Barnwell couldn't be happier with **Carmen's** failure to pass through to the next stage of police dog training, and they continue to be seen running around Gorey together. His "Dog and Doughnut" stories have proved to be extremely popular with the Year Ones, and to avoid further tears, he now has a monthly standing order with Ethel's for an entire box of iced doughnuts, all of them with sprinkles.

ALISON GOLDEN
Grace Dagnall

USA Today Bestselling Author

AN INSPECTOR DAVID GRAHAM MYSTERY

The Case of the Body in the Block

The characters and events portrayed in this book are fictitious. Any similarity to real persons, living or dead is coincidental and not intended by the author.
Text copyright © 2024 Alison Golden
All rights reserved.

No part of this book may be reproduced, stored in a retrieval system, or transmitted in any form or by any means, electronic, mechanical, photocopying, recording, or otherwise, without express written permission of the publisher.

Cover Illustration: Richard Eijkenbroek

Published by Mesa Verde Publishing
P.O. Box 1002
San Carlos, CA 94070

ISBN: 979-8340203168

CHAPTER ONE

MELANIE HOWES CAREFULLY positioned a ladder against the outside wall of the White House Inn and, without pausing, climbed it. The back stairs would have been easier, but overnight storm damage made the ladder the only safe approach to what hotel proprietor Mrs. Taylor called the grand attic. At the top, Melanie levered herself through a skylight into the darkness beyond, and when she stood upright, wooden floorboards creaked beneath the soles of her heavy, fireproof work boots. A strong draft and the mustiness of damp wood wafted around her.

The Gorey fire crew manager stood in a corridor that ran from the front of the hotel to the back. The walls, once painted white, were now a murky grey, dust and dirt gathering on the rough surface of the interior stucco. "Uh-oh," Melanie muttered. The upper hallway was a muddied ruin, its roof partially caved in.

Leaning through the skylight, she waved at the ground. Her two companions waved back. "All clear!" she shouted. When firefighter Phil Bevis and Constable Barry Barnwell joined her on the landing two minutes later, their eyes tracked the surroundings, constantly alert to falling debris that might at any moment decide to rain down upon them from the damaged roof above.

Running the entire length of the White House Inn, the giant attic was now cordoned off. And while the Jersey Fire Service inspected, Mrs. Taylor fretted. Having to close the hotel at the insistence of three different local authorities had been a terrible blow. Melanie raised her hand and called out to the two men following her. "I've got smashed tiles and splintered wood. Mind your feet!"

Using Mrs. Taylor's skeleton key, Melanie swiftly unlocked the door midway down the passage. Although invited to witness the inspection firsthand, Mrs. Taylor had thought better of it. How she would navigate the ladder had been one thing. Her distress at what she might find was quite another. "Constable Barnwell has kindly offered to go in my place," she had told Melanie. "But you'll let me know what you find, won't you?"

Once in the attic, Melanie turned to find her firefighting colleague. "Where's Bazza?" she asked him. "Phil, you dozy sod, you didn't forget about him, did you?"

"Right here, matey," called a voice from the landing. "Just taking some photos."

"This isn't a crime scene, you know," Melanie called out to her guest. Taking Barnwell with them on this exploratory mission wasn't in the fire service manual, but she'd accepted the constable's presence as a favour for Mrs. Taylor. "There's no criminal evidence to gather up here. It was the fury of the gods that did this, plain and simple."

Barnwell appeared in the doorway, ducking slightly and dusting off his hands. "Blimey, I've never seen Gorey from this perspective before. Thought I'd take some snaps while I'm up here. Amazing view over the water."

The constable's eyes widened as he took in the state of the attic. An enormous hole blown between the old beams and clay tiles, the gnarly sky starkly visible through it, projected light into the gloomy space. Through it, thunderous clouds shone brighter than the surrounding sky. Elsewhere, tunnels of light protruded through smaller points of damage, like satellite planets around the moon. "Oh, wow."

Barnwell switched his phone's camera to black-and-white mode. Without hesitating, he quickly snapped a shot of Melanie standing beneath the wind-torn roof with its odd-shaped holes, looking up at the desecration of a much-loved Gorey landmark rendered so by a constant foe, the unpredictable British weather. It was a picture that couldn't go wrong—the contrast of dark and light, the moody, debris-strewed foreground, and the single, curious firefighter trying to make sense of it all.

Barnwell was there to catalogue the scene for Mrs. Taylor, but he couldn't pass up the opportunity for some photojournalism. He looked again at his image, pleased with the shot. "You might even call it art," he murmured to no one in particular.

"You'd think we were surveying bomb damage in the Blitz, wouldn't you?" Barnwell showed his picture to the young fireman next to him. "If it weren't for the modern uniforms."

"May as well have been a bomb," Melanie said ruefully.

"Poor old place. It's just not fair what's happened to it." Phil, a born and bred Jerseyman, sounded almost personally offended by the attic's condition, aggrieved on behalf of Mrs. Taylor and her hotel.

What had begun as a sudden squall out in the Bay of Biscay had soon gathered terrifying strength and muscled its way eastwards, causing damage and despair in some of Normandy's traditional coastal villages. But it appeared to the Jersey locals that the storm's actual target had been the island, which it approached from the southwest, preparing to deliver a right-fisted haymaker.

Similar to a storm a few years ago, the island had been in virtual lockdown by midafternoon the previous day. At sunset, Gorey's public was dealing with numerous power outages, no water, and several injuries, all while pummelled by winds that could knock a man flat. The White House Inn, standing alone and proud on a clifftop, had borne the brunt of it.

The following morning should, by rights, have brought a healing spell of bright sunshine, but the weather remained stonily overcast. "At least it's stopped raining," Melanie said. "We can get a sense of what's going on up here without getting drenched in the process."

"Bleedin' chaos," Phil moaned. "May as well tell Mrs. T. right now she'll need a new roof, minimum."

"Only once we're done," Melanie cautioned, taking her own photos. "It's a real mess though. The fabric has taken an almighty whack. You don't need any training to see that. Alright, let's get to it. They've lost about . . . what, forty percent of the roof tiles?"

"Something like that," Phil agreed, peering out through one of the holes. On the tarmac in the car park at the front of the inn, and on the roof of the sunroom, countless angry, star-shaped spatters of terracotta punctuated the surfaces, each the remains of an ancient roof tile swept earthward by relentless winds. It was as though leprechauns had spent the night smashing plates in some kind of gratuitous frenzy.

"And there's structural damage." Melanie pointed to a thick, century-old beam cracked in two as if it had been a length of old, dry firewood. "That'll need to be replaced." She tapped a bevy of words into her tablet, beginning her report of the reconstruction that would be necessary.

Melanie worked carefully, applying nearly twenty years of experience to her review, followed by the ever-curious Constable Barnwell with his camera. "Having fun?" she asked him between phases of the assessment. Melanie and Barnwell knew each other well. They often walked their dogs together—his beagle, her pit bull—at the weekends. Theirs was a friendly, platonic relationship, full of banter and gentle ribbing. "Didn't think you lot would be interested in this. Just the result of wind, rain, and age, really," she said. "Too much of it over too long a period of time."

"I'm here to keep Mrs. Taylor calm. She asked me to accompany you, be her 'man about the house,' if you know what I mean." Melanie frowned. Barnwell, for once alert to the fact that this preference of Mrs. Taylor's might suggest a lack of confidence in the fire service, or in Melanie in particular, patted his buttons and added quickly, "It's the uniform. Comforting." Melanie stared at him, her expression vaguely reminding Barnwell of her dog, Vixen, before nodding curtly and resuming her inspection.

The grand attic was now something to behold. Locally, it was believed that during the war, it had housed young Nazi soldiers, a rumour Mrs. Taylor had been at pains to play down. Later, when the inn returned to its original purpose, it had acted as a dormitory for young men needing cheap accommodation. Now, though, it was full of the flotsam and jetsam of a long-running enterprise that dealt in the business of travelling humans. All kinds of detritus were strewn about, much of it from long ago.

"Flotsam" perfectly described the items scattered mostly against one wall. They literally appeared as though debris from a shipwreck. Wooden chairs tumbled over each other. Overflowing cardboard boxes, wet and ripped, spilled their contents across the floorboards. Furniture had fallen, their heavy weight proving no defence against the forces hurled at them overnight, and some had travelled significant distances before coming to rest in a higgledy-piggledy pile of dark, varnished oak.

"Blimey, it must have been some wind to do that," Barnwell said. "I'm impressed. Everything's been blown over. Even this . . ." He slapped a large dresser that pinned an upholstered winged armchair to the wall. The dresser had flattened the chair, leaving the wings flapping, broken at the joints.

The effect of the wind's force had been to mostly clear the main thoroughfare, pushing everything to one side of the attic. The two firefighters and one police officer walked around the space freely, assessing, cataloguing, and photographing the damage.

As he strolled, Barnwell picked a faded red velvet cushion from the floor. Bedraggled, stringy, frayed tassels hung from each corner. He tossed it on a similarly upholstered banquette that lay in the corner on its own, far from the piles of bric-a-brac and paraphernalia.

Barnwell regarded the banquette curiously, then sat down on it with a hard bump. "Flippin' heck, this is the most uncomfortable sofa I've ever sat on. No wonder Mrs. T. put it up here."

"Probably why it's still in the corner and didn't make its way over there with all the rest," Phil said, lightly testing a beam with his hand. "Solid as a rock."

"You're right. It's as hard as concrete." Barnwell knocked on the velvet covering. Beneath the fabric, his knuckles met a hard, unrelenting surface. "You know what . . ." Barnwell worried at a tear in the cover's seam and poked his finger through. His fingertip came away dusted with white powder. "I think this *is* concrete. What's a block of concrete doing up here covered in red velvet?"

"Well, that's why it didn't move. Surprised it didn't go through the floor," Melanie said. "C'mon, it's nothing. We're done here. Let's see if we can get down the stairs this time."

But Barnwell didn't hear her. Intrigued by what he was sitting on, he ripped the velvet along the seam. The concrete sat in a mould of red brick. As he opened it to the air, a section crumbled along an edge. He froze.

"C'mon, Bazza. Let's go and get a coffee." Barnwell dragged his eyes upwards to look at Melanie, his mouth open. He remained silent. The fire crew manager smiled. "Alright, see you down there, then."

Barnwell watched her and Phil disappear through the door and waited until he could no longer hear their footsteps as they descended the stairs. He pulled out his phone. Scrolling his contacts list, he tapped a number.

"Sir?" His voice came out croaky. He tried again, stronger this time. "Boss, it's

Barnwell. I'm at the White House Inn. Listen, I think you'd better get down here."

A minute later, after describing what he'd found, Barnwell ended the call. His eyes widened again as he regarded the reason he had made it. He blinked several times, his heart beating as fast as it did on one of his runs through the streets of Gorey with Carmen. He squinted, focused, and blinked again.

It was the most extraordinary thing. But there it was, as plain as the Rich Tea biscuit he had dunked in his tea earlier that morning. His mind ran wild as he processed what he was seeing. For if Barnwell's eyes weren't deceiving him, and he fervently hoped they were not now that he had called in his superior, there appeared to be in the corner of Mrs. Taylor's attic, poking an inch out of a concrete banquette, a human fingernail on the end of a decidedly human finger.

CHAPTER TWO

DETECTIVE INSPECTOR DAVID Graham trotted up the steps to the front entrance of the White House Inn. Barnwell was waiting for him. "You know, it's funny. I spent a few months here when I first came to Jersey. I wandered around the hotel a fair amount, but I never made it to the grand attic," Graham said.

"And if you had, you'd hardly have suspected you were sharing the space with a, well, whatever it is, would you, sir?"

"Hardly, Constable."

Half an hour earlier, Barnwell had quietly followed the firefighters down to the ground floor and found a corner in which to discreetly kill time until the inspector arrived. He hadn't breathed a word of what he'd discovered to anyone, not even Melanie. Now he huddled with Graham in a corner of the White House Inn lobby as they discussed the situation.

"Good job on keeping things quiet, Constable. The force that is Mrs. Taylor might be a lot to bear if this is what you think it is."

"We can't keep it from her forever, sir."

"No, but we can keep it from her for *now*. Just until we know more. Who knows, it might not be what it looks like."

"No, possibly not. But it did look like a human finger, sir. I wouldn't have called you if it didn't."

"And you were absolutely right to. Why don't you lead the way, and we'll take a look together? Where is the redoubtable Mrs. Taylor at this precise moment?"

"Talking to that oik, Solomon, about the damage to the hotel." Graham rolled his eyes. A few feet away at the reception desk, Mrs. Taylor was speaking to Freddie Solomon, "citizen journalist," about the previous night's horrors. The blogger's expression alternated between "compassionate concern" and "unexpected Christmas."

"You know, I had a vision!" Mrs. Taylor wrung her hands. Freddie's thumbs flew in a flurry of typing. "A vision of being swept up by the storm, like Dorothy in *The Wizard of Oz*! I thought the whole inn"—Mrs. Taylor gestured to the elegant crown moulding—"would be picked up and thrown into the sea! I'd have believed it, Mr. Solomon!" Marjorie Taylor was desperate for someone to understand. "*Never* been so scared, not in *all* my life."

Mrs. Taylor was, quite plainly, at sixes and sevens. She would take three steps in one direction and stop to glance worriedly at the reception ceiling as though it might decide to collapse out of malicious caprice. Distracted, she would turn and walk six steps in the opposite direction, closing her eyes and gripping her hands together as if in fervent, desperate prayer. Freddie swung between comforting a distressed woman and eliciting from her the most dramatic version of her story.

"Did it feel," he asked her, leaning in close like the trusted confidant he wished to be, "like the hotel was doing *battle* with the wind?"

Graham grimaced. "She doesn't need that tiresome idiot pestering her today. Perhaps you should escort Freddie out so I don't do it myself and risk losing my temper with the little weevil." Dozens of interfering, speculative articles in Freddie's local crime blog had already put him on Graham's radar, and the blogger was building a history of narrowly avoiding arrest on charges of obstruction, even perverting the course of justice. "And maybe get Janice down here. She could have a word with Mrs. Taylor."

"What kind of a 'word,' sir?"

"A kind one. Janice is good at that."

"I think that would be good coming from you, sir. I mean, a good part of Mrs. T.'s roof just got scattered all over Gorey, the council has designated her business a hazard, and she might be about to learn there's a body encased in concrete in her attic. Lord knows how long it'll take her to recover from all that. I think she'd appreciate a kind word from you as the senior person. And expecting Janice to do it, isn't that a bit . . . what does she call it? Patronising. Expecting her to do 'women's work.'" It was a big, risky speech from Barnwell, but he was correct. Chastened, Graham coughed and stood a little taller.

Among them, only he had the ability to truly imagine the ferocity with which Mrs. Taylor was likely to respond to such news. The fabric, history, and ownership of the building were all part of the same indivisible whole. To injure the White House Inn was to injure Mrs. Taylor. Body and soul of both were inextricably linked.

"Yes, yes. Of course, you're right." Graham opened his mouth to say more, but Barnwell wasn't finished. "And do we really want to put that on Janice? I mean, like, *now?*"

Graham's expression transformed from stern to stricken. "Oh, hell, I hadn't thought of *that*," he said, angry at himself. "The wedding . . ."

"Jan had a block booking here for her out-of-town guests. Mrs. T. gave her a good deal. What's Janice gonna do now? Reckon she won't want their twenty-odd guests staying in a hotel where the wind's whistling 'Here Comes the Bride' at all times of the day and night." Barnwell sighed as he prepared to shoulder the responsibility Graham had delegated to him. "But it's alright. I'll tell Janice. See if she wants to come on down. She's off today."

"On second thoughts, let's leave Mrs. Taylor to Freddie. He'll keep her busy while we slip past."

"What are we going to tell the fire service?"

"The who?"

"The firefighters. I went up with them. They only let me join them because Mrs. Taylor asked specially. They'll want to know why we want to go up there again." Graham huffed.

"Just tell them there's something you want to show me. Keep it vague. But hurry. I don't want anyone to suspect anything." Barnwell lumbered off in the direction of Melanie Howes, who was sitting outside in her vehicle writing a report. Five minutes later, she led Graham and Barnwell into the attic.

They went up the back stairs, now cleared and declared safe, so avoiding Mrs. Taylor and Freddie and the climb up the outside of the building that had proved necessary earlier. "Mind the step," Melanie said. She had insisted on accompanying them. As he entered the attic, Graham, like Barnwell before him, stared at the sky through the huge "porthole" in the roof. "Not so 'grand' now, is it?" Melanie said. "I hope the insurance company is feeling generous because the restoration is going to need a *serious* budget. What is it you want to look at again?"

"Just something that Constable Barnwell was a bit concerned about. It's probably nothing, and we don't want to worry Mrs. Taylor unnecessarily." This seemed to satisfy Melanie, who shrugged and turned down the corners of her mouth but said nothing.

"It's over here, sir," Barnwell said as he walked to the far corner. Graham gazed at the banquette covered in faded red velvet, now ripped and sagging, the grey concrete block and surrounding red brick partially exposed. He followed Barnwell and squatted next to him. "There, sir." Barnwell pointed to a crumbled section of the cement. The grey tip of what was unmistakably a human finger protruded from it.

With his phone in hand, Graham switched on the magnifier. He placed it over the digit and stared for some seconds. Barnwell held his breath, glancing at his boss's face, waiting for a signal that calling Graham had been the right thing to do. At the other end of the room, Melanie stood with her arms folded, oblivious to the men's concern. She stared through a hole in the roof, gazing out at the still-tumultuous sky.

Finally, Barnwell could contain himself no longer. His voice was low. "What do you think, sir? Is it . . . you know?"

Graham turned his phone to examine the fingertip from a different angle. He didn't answer Barnwell but stood and ripped the velvet to reveal the entire block, sweeping his eyes along its length. He might have been examining a work of art or a precious antique.

He knocked on the block's surface and rubbed it, examining the dust left on his palm. With the ball of one foot, he pressed the floorboards next to it. Only then did he suggest that he'd heard Barnwell. He took a few steps to his right and leant into his constable. He murmured, "Seal the room, Barnwell. And call Bob the Builder. We'll be needing tools. I'll call Tomlinson."

CHAPTER THREE

GRAHAM TOOK PHOTOS and, leaving Barnwell to secure the area, headed downstairs to wait for Dr. Marcus Tomlinson. He expected to find Mrs. Taylor in the lobby, and in a terrible state. Both hunches were correct.

"Like the wrath of God!" Marjorie was still exclaiming to Freddie Solomon in an otherwise deserted lobby. "The whole place was shaking, rattling. It was *awful*. You could hear the tiles coming down in twos and threes, hitting the ground like bombs going off. One-half of the hotel had to be evacuated at three a.m., guests in their pyjamas huddling under umbrellas in the car park!" Mrs. Taylor trembled at the memory. They hadn't noticed him, and Graham, shaking his head, quietly made his way to the tearoom.

The tearoom was offering a skeleton service, not least to provide refreshments to the workers who were coming and going, although Graham doubted the finer points of tea-making would be exercised on their behalf. "Builder's tea" would be offered—strong, black, a dash of milk, and two sugars, take it or leave it. No one would leave it, not even Graham. But after the discovery in the attic, he fancied something fresh, uplifting—a dragon pearl jasmine, or a fruity citrus, perhaps even a green tea. Laura would be impressed.

"What can I get you, Inspector?" Polly, a favourite of his, asked him. She knew just how he liked his tea.

"Let's go for the champagne of teas this morning please, Polly."

"A Silver Needle White it is then, sir. No milk and sugar, correct?"

"The milk is unnecessary, the sugar redundant, so no thank you."

Five minutes later, Polly returned carrying a tray. As she placed the tea set on the table in front of him, Graham sat in his chair, his elbows resting on the arms, his hands clasped in front of him.

"Would you like me to pour? The timer is about to go off," she said.

"I'll do it, thanks." Polly left him to it, and when the final grain of sand had dropped into the bottom sectional of the classic egg timer, Graham leaned over to pour himself a cup of the pale-yellow tea. He sniffed it and closed his eyes as the fragrance of freshly cut hay warmed his cheeks, then took a sip of the hot, slightly acidic yet smoky blend, its warmth bathing him in a seductive, heady, musky blanket. He shut his eyes, exhaled, and relaxed his shoulders.

Just as Graham was draining his second cup, Marcus Tomlinson surged into reception like a caped avenger. He resembled a thunderstorm of his own. He shook rain from his hat and brushed the shoulders of his jacket. "Goodness, Mrs. Taylor, this is a carry-on!"

Mrs. Taylor turned to him without blinking and replied, "Miss Howes from the fire service told me the rainwater has only just stopped coming down the upstairs walls! It's a calamity!" She paused, then squinted. "But what are you doing here, Dr. Tomlinson?"

Inspector Graham swarmed in, intercepting Tomlinson before he could say anything that Mrs. Taylor or Freddie, who was still hanging around, might latch onto. "He's here to meet me for a chat, that's all." Suppressing a wince at his misrepresentation, Graham quickly guided Tomlinson by the elbow up the back stairs. Freddie watched them go, the heavy lids of his green eyes lowering slightly, although Mrs. Taylor seemed too wrapped up in the prospect of her failing hotel to disbelieve the inspector or consider that anything questionable was occurring within it.

"How are things?" Dr. Tomlinson whispered as they passed through the door to the back stairs. "I hear the storm has delivered the hotel a hammer blow. That guests are cancelling to stay elsewhere or fleeing the island altogether. Are things as bad as they sound?"

"Hard to say. The staff are dealing with simultaneous storms on different fronts." What Graham didn't give voice to, not yet anyway, was that the discovery of a body on the premises would likely cause an earthquake capable of upending the other meteorological challenges, thereby ending life as Mrs. Taylor knew it.

He led the pathologist up the three flights to the attic, briefing him as they went. When they reached the top, Tomlinson paused.

"Hold on a second, man. Let me get my breath back." He blew out his cheeks. "It's times like these that I realise I'm not as young as I was." Graham waited patiently, silently berating himself for his eagerness to begin the next part of the investigation into what he was now calling "the body in the block."

Above them, they heard shouts as roofers wrestled with a tarpaulin. Barnwell had followed Graham's instructions explicitly. Crime scene tape crisscrossed the doorway to the attic, and the massive hole in the roof had been covered. Inside, Barnwell stood on a stepladder sealing the smaller holes.

When Dr. Tomlinson had regained his breath, Graham led him to the corner where the banquette sat. The velvet cover had been put back in place, the concrete block now resembling his grandmother's sofa. Graham pulled the fabric aside to reveal the concrete-filled brick mould, the incongruity of a finger poking out at one corner stark and obvious.

"Do your worst, Marcus. Is this a prank or some unfortunate person's resting place? Tell me, I need to know."

Tomlinson carefully kneeled while Graham peered over his shoulder. Like the inspector earlier, the pathologist lightly touched the fingertip before reaching into his bag for a tiny brush. With a couple of quick flicks, he wicked away particles of dust before inserting a round, black magnifying eyepiece into his eye socket. Peering intensely at the finger's almost black, wrinkled pad, he sighed.

"If this is a shop dummy, it's a very good one. That is most definitely a fingerprint."

"We have Bob the Builder on standby."

"Bob, eh? He's a good lad. He'll keep his mouth shut too. But before we do anything, I'd like to consult with a friend of mine, Professor Alexander Papadopoulos. He's an archaeologist based on the mainland, but he's on Jersey right now on holiday. He popped in to see me just yesterday. Perhaps he wouldn't mind interrupting his relaxing break to help us with this rather unusual situation." Marcus looked at Graham hopefully. The inspector hesitated.

"We can't just crack on?"

"Honestly, I feel a little out of my depth here, David, but between me, Alex, and Bob, we'll have the best chance of extracting whoever is in here without too much damage. It'll make things a lot easier down the road."

Graham rocked back on his heels. He couldn't risk losing evidence in the name of speed, especially after what was obviously some time. "Of course, whatever you say. It's been here a while, so a few more minutes won't matter. If he's happy to help us, that would be fantastic."

"Jolly good. And David?"

"Yes?"

"We need to proceed on the basis that this *is* a body. We're essentially exhuming it. Respect must be conferred. Just me, you, Alex, and Bob. No . . ." Tomlinson pointed a finger to the ceiling where the stomping of the roofers' boots was punctuated by shouts and laughter.

"Understood. I'll have them down tools. How long will it take, do you think?"

Tomlinson pursed his lips. His eyes lingered over the block. "Who knows? Might be as slow as an archaeological dig, or the concrete might crumble at the first sign of pressure."

"Sir?" Barnwell interrupted.

"Hmm?"

"Sir!"

"What is it, Barnwell?" Graham sounded irritated.

"You, um, might want to come here to see this, boss."

"Excuse me, Marcus. It seems I'm needed elsewhere. You'll call your friend?"

"Will do."

"What is it?" Graham asked Barnwell again, reluctantly turning to walk the length of the attic. As he got close, his eyes landed on what Barnwell was bringing to his attention. It was a very familiar shape, but important parts of Graham's brain were yelling that it absolutely did not belong. "What on earth is that doing up here?"

"That's what I was wondering. And does it have something to do with . . ." Barnwell nodded in Tomlinson's direction. "You know . . ."

"Indeed, Constable, indeed. What make is it, can you tell?"

"Smith and Wesson, sir. It says so right here on the barrel."

CHAPTER FOUR

"HELL'S TEETH." GRAHAM inspected the gun. It lay on the floor next to a chest of drawers.

"Am I calling the firearms guys, sir?"

"Hang on. Let's see what we've got." Graham stepped forward. He retrieved some forensic gloves, a fresh pair of which lived permanently in his inside jacket pocket, and handed them to Barnwell. "Off you go. Pick it up and place it on the top there." He pointed to a table, still upright and undamaged. Barnwell wriggled his meaty hands into the gloves. "And when you pick it up, tell me if it feels *regular* heavy or *extra* heavy."

"Why do you ask?"

"I need to know if it's loaded." Barnwell blinked but lifted the gun delicately by the butt and barrel with his thumbs and forefingers. He gingerly placed it on top of the table. "Doesn't seem particularly heavy, sir."

"Excellent. How did you come to find it?" Graham fixated on the weapon. He donned his own gloves and bent down so that he was at eye level with the gun. He twisted and turned to view it from every angle.

"I was just clambering around fixing holes. These drawers must've been hit by some debris. It looks as though there was a small, red suitcase in one of them. The case must've fell out and burst open. I noticed the gun laying on the floor next to it. My guess is it was forced out of the suitcase when it was damaged."

On the floor was a tomato-red, hard-shell suitcase. Alongside the chrome handle was a label: Tourister. The interior was lined with cream satin. Two elasticised pockets were sewn onto the inside. Graham poked his fingertips inside first one, then the other.

"Aha, here we are." He pulled his hand away and opened it for Barnwell to see. Three bullets lay in his hand.

"These look like thirty-eight wadcutters," Graham said. "What else was in the suitcase?"

"Just some fella's belongings," reported Barnwell. "Stuff from a while back, I reckon. They look a bit dated. Seventies, eighties, d'you think? There's some clothes, books, bits and pieces . . . Look." Barnwell picked up a small item from the floor. "I had one of these. A Walkman. That's definitely eighties. And this." Barnwell picked up the book in his gloved hands. "*The Hitchhiker's Guide to the Galaxy.* That was the eighties too, wasn't it?"

"Douglas Adams wrote the first book in 1979," Graham said from memory. Barnwell glanced at him as the inspector took the book from him and flicked through it, his eyebrows raised. "I was something of an Adams aficionado in my day, devouring the books, radio shows, TV shows, films, anything he wrote," Graham added. He scanned the other items. "All this and a large-calibre handgun stuffed in the bottom drawer of an old chest of drawers, eh?"

Putting the book aside, Graham, still fixed on the weapon, turned it over carefully, keeping its barrel pointed at the wall. "Stay this side of me, please," he said. "I don't think it's dangerous, but . . ." He tested its weight. "Alright, it's either unloaded or there's only one round, maybe two, in the cylinder. Revolvers don't expend their bullet casings like rifles and pistols. If someone fired it, the spent round might still be in there."

Graham clicked the release switch to disengage the lock, and the cylinder swung out easily. He gave it a quick sniff. "Hasn't been used recently. And no rounds in the chambers, spent or otherwise." He laid it down again and peered at it. "Do you know what this is?"

Barnwell coughed. "Thought we'd decided it was a gun, sir."

"Indeed, a Smith and Wesson," Graham said before patiently adding from his considerable storehouse of knowledge. "The model twenty-eight, late fifties. Unpolished steel, pretty simple. It was a low-cost revolver called the 'Highway Patrolman.' Very popular with cops in the US back in its day." Even with gloves on, Graham handled the weapon as little as possible. "But no experienced criminal would be caught dead with a relic like this these days. Lord knows what'd happen if we tried to fire it."

Barnwell regarded the gun quizzically. "Big old thing, isn't it?"

"Bit risky to bring this on a job, even back in the eighties, if that's when this is from. I mean, when the model twenty-eight was first manufactured, our grandparents were still spending shillings and sixpences."

"It's a bit rough, I'll give you that, but I bet it gets the job done. Maybe it was all whoever owned it could manage to protect themselves with."

"Possibly, Constable, but the good people of Gorey aren't generally fans of guns." It was pleasingly rare for a firearm to be connected to a crime on Jersey. Graham hadn't come across one yet.

"Well, someone was, as you say, back in the day," Barnwell concluded with a shrug. "They didn't have this big old thing for nuthin'. Do you think this has something to do with . . . ?" He nodded over to the corner where Marcus was talking quietly into his phone. "You know. . ."

"I don't know. Possibly. It'll be our job to find out."

CHAPTER FIVE

IN THE BACK office, Mrs. Taylor hung up. She had just finished pleading with someone about something, successfully it would appear, and like an apparition, when Graham and Barnwell reached the lobby, she suddenly materialised behind the reception desk. She erupted in an explosion of noise when she saw them. "What *now*? What on *earth* is it *now*?" she demanded, seemingly not of the police officers who stood in front of her but of the Almighty as she waved her hands and raised her eyes to the ceiling before noticing that Barnwell held an evidence bag with a gun inside.

"A gun? You found . . . a gun? In *my hotel*?" It was too much. Her eyes welled with tears. "Oh, Inspector Graham, what must you think of us?"

"Please, take it easy, Mrs. Taylor," Graham began.

But Mrs. Taylor was distraught, assailed from too many sides at once on a single, awful day. She began pacing again. "What *will* I tell people? Another big carry-on with the police. Imagine the rumours . . . Oh, the *rumours,* Inspector," she said, clutching her chest. "They'll be the death of me."

Graham attempted to calm her. "It's just an antique gun, Mrs. Taylor. I mean, look, it's virtually a museum piece. Quite harmless." *Unless someone loads and fires it, of course.*

Mrs. Taylor's mutterings continued. "There's that big, new hotel in St. Helier, the LeisureLodge, or whatever they're calling it. Half my prices! I don't know what I'm going to do, I really don't . . ." She wandered back into her office.

Graham turned to Barnwell and leant in. "I've changed my mind. I'm completely serious about getting Janice down here. And as soon as possible. We need reinforcements. All hell's going to break loose when Mrs. Taylor finds out about"—he jabbed a thumb upwards—"*upstairs*. More than anything, she'll need an injection of kindness and calm."

Barnwell conjured up a more extreme solution. "Maybe Dr. Tomlinson injecting her with a sedative would be more helpful."

"No, we need Janice," Graham pressed again. "Tell her things are probably not as bad as they seem if she appears reluctant."

"But what if they are?" Barnwell asked darkly as he dialled Janice's number and waited for her to pick up. "So, we're all up with the patriarchy, then?"

"Wha— Er, yes for now. I'll make it up to her."

"Ah, hey, Janice? What are you up to, love? Fancy an extra half shift?" Barnwell turned away from Graham to focus on his conversation, pressing one finger to his unoccupied ear to drown out the noise of the workmen clearing debris from Mrs. Taylor's tearoom.

Inwardly, Graham cringed. He knew Mrs. Taylor was right to be worried. People no longer stayed in old grand hotels just for the fun of it. Spiffy, modern places were threatening to take over, but the White House Inn remained special, a genuine landmark, much loved in Gorey, with an unbeatable view. It needed some work—nobody would argue that—but as Mrs. Taylor liked to remind her guests, its imperfections were its charms.

Still, charm didn't come cheap. And reputation was everything. But as he stared at the firearm recently discovered in her ruined attic, Graham realised that now was undoubtedly not the time to remind Mrs. Taylor of the fact.

He focused on the bright side. Maybe insurance-funded renovations would be the boost (and the potential amnesiac) necessary to counter the horror he was about to unleash. Mrs. Taylor would surely need them if the White House Inn were to reopen and compete for tourist's travel budgets.

A continuous stream of people arrived, called on to respond to the storm and its aftermath. These included grey-suited chartered surveyors tasked with drawing up estimates for the repair work. Their presence—and the bowel-roiling expense the repairs would entail—elevated Mrs. Taylor's blood pressure further. It was hard to decide which was worse: the costly and unsightly damage to the inn's century-old roof or the tremulous prospect of closing down the hotel until repairs could be finished. "This'll be the *death* of me," she promised them again, coming out of her office and pacing anxiously, uncertain which crisis to worry about next.

"Do you really think Mrs. T. doesn't know anything?" Barnwell quietly asked Graham once he finished his call. He nodded at the gun. "Jan promises to come down. She seemed quite keen, to be fair. She's showing her mother around St. Andrew's at the moment."

"Judging by her performance, I doubt it, but we'll ask her directly. Once she's scraped herself off the ceiling."

For a minute, they watched a perpetually moving Mrs. Taylor direct her staff, shoo away gawkers, and dispatch a pair of hard-hatted engineers to the basement. Graham hesitated to add more complexity to her day, but the gun was an unusual find.

"I know absolutely *nothing*," answered Mrs. Taylor with total confidence.

"Never seen it before, and neither have my staff, I'm quite certain. I'd not have allowed it in the hotel if I'd known. I've no idea how it got there. It's a terrible liberty for a guest to take," she said, disappointed with whoever had been thoughtless enough to leave a *gun* lying around. "Quite against the White House Inn's policies. I mean, it looks old, and if I think about it, it must have been left there well before my time. Yes, yes, that must be it. I haven't been up in the attic in years."

CHAPTER SIX

AN HOUR AFTER Barnwell called her, Sergeant Janice Harding strode into the White House Inn lobby. From the stairs, Barnwell spotted her and trotted down. "Did you manage to agree on the hymns?"

"Not exactly," she answered glumly. "This would all be a lot simpler if we could just have a small beach wedding and be done with it. Is it too late to elope to Tahiti?" She looked around. "Oh, hell. What's all this bloomin' palaver?"

Barnwell looked skyward, aware he was about to deliver bad news. "It's the roof."

"I know about the roof, Bazz. It's all over the car park. It looks like a bomb site out there. I had to park in the public car park." Janice tutted as if the five-hundred-yard walk to the hotel had been a personal insult. "Half the place is closed according to Freddie's blog. My wedding guests are going to be bedding down on yoga mats in our back room at this rate."

"*Temporarily* closed," Barnwell said, doing his best to instil optimism into his voice.

"Right, well, here I am. In uniform, as you asked. What do you need me for? I don't know the first thing about roofs."

"Yeah, so, some other things have happened."

"Oh?"

Barnwell, faced with Janice in an obviously pugnacious mood, hesitated. "I was poking around upstairs, see . . ."

"Yeah, and?"

"I found a gun." Barnwell castigated himself. He'd bottled it; gone for the lesser bombshell first. But at least Janice's reaction wasn't too bad.

"Oooooooh," Janice said, her eyes gleaming. "Was it big and shiny?"

"Six-shot revolver. A classic, actually. The DI gave me a lecture on the different variants of the model twenty-eight, just in case I ever come across one again. Which I almost certainly won't."

"Was it loaded?"

"Empty. But there were bullets. The interesting bit is where it was found."

"Oooooooh." Janice was thrilled again. This was a lot more exciting than reminding her mother that most people can't hit the top (or even the middle) notes of "Morning Has Broken." Or that Rosemary Harding needed to mend the tiff with her brother—Janice's Uncle Timmy, a Welsh choir mainstay and baritone—if the fifty members of her wedding congregation were to pull off "Jerusalem" as Janice's mum wished. "If he doesn't come, it'll be a lot of people mumbling and mouthing the words with no sound coming out. Your choice," Janice had told her pouting mother as she left her at the church half an hour earlier. "Did you find it in the roof? The gun, I mean."

"We certainly did, Sergeant." DI Graham walked up behind them. "Looks like it was in a suitcase stuffed in a drawer. Fell out when the dresser was karate-chopped by a falling beam. I just overheard Mrs. Taylor on the phone calling someone a 'greedy little so-and-so,' so she might be a while. Once she's done though..."

"I should calm her down enough so I can ask her about this gun?" Janice guessed.

Barnwell saw a way in. "Er, yeah. And there's something else."

Graham turned to Barnwell. "You haven't told her?"

"Told me what?" Janice's eyebrows shot up. "What?" she said again, her wide eyes flicking between the faces of the two men.

"I found something else up there. Something different but perhaps related to the gun."

"Really?" Again, Barnwell hesitated. Janice frowned. "Well?"

"Mrs. Taylor's not gonna like it."

"Well, she can't run from it. Come on, tell me."

"There's also a concrete block up in the roof."

Janice frowned and tucked her chin in. "Concrete? Up there?" Her eyes narrowed as she sucked on her lower lip.

"And I noticed that where the concrete had worn away..."

"Yes?"

"A fingertip was poking out. Tomlinson's up there now waiting for an archaeologist to advise him on how to excavate it without disturbing too much. Keep it, you know... *intact*." Barnwell's words came out in a rush.

Janice's head shot forward, her eyes growing even bigger, her jaw slack. "Wha..."

"It might have been there for forty years," Barnwell added.

"For..."

"Shush, Jan, quiet," Barnwell pleaded, looking around. "We haven't told Mrs. T. yet. She's gonna go ballistic."

Graham chuckled. "Punny, Constable." Barnwell frowned. "Ballistic? Oh, never mind."

"How do you know it's been there for forty years? The body," Janice whispered.

"There are some things with the gun that look like they're that old. Mrs. Taylor says she hasn't been up there in years. If everything's connected, they could have been in the attic all this time."

"And we were wandering about down here, oblivious. Blimey." Janice was dumbstruck as she thought about the possibilities.

In the distance, they heard Mrs. Taylor clucking as she ordered workmen about before she appeared in one of the doorways that led off the lobby. The three police officers who had been huddling in an alcove under the stairs, immediately sprang apart and assumed casual poses, Barnwell even feigning complete and exhaustive interest in an enormous rubber plant.

"Sergeant Harding, how nice of you to come up here to see us! So good of you. Please pardon the mess. You've no need to worry. We'll have everything sorted out in time for your wedding guests." Thankfully, Mrs. Taylor didn't stop but passed through the lobby, walking outside to look skywards at the roof for the fifteenth time that day.

"I get the distinct impression everyone's avoiding the truth," Janice said. "We're hiding the aggro in the attic from her, and she's not being truthful about the state of this place. There's no way she's going to be open in just over a week."

"Do you fancy a quick jaunt up there? They haven't started drilling yet. We need to collect evidence before they do. You'll need a hard hat and some hi-vis," Graham said.

"Can't wait," Janice said. "Jack reckons I look my most alluring in hi-vis gear."

Barnwell squeezed his eyes tight shut. He didn't want to think of the dependable, motherly, more senior Janice as "alluring." "Enough, enough. Let's go," he said.

CHAPTER SEVEN

BY THE TIME they reached the top of the stairs, yellow jackets and headgear in place, Janice could track some classic smells—dust and mould, the odour of things covered up and forgotten—and once inside the attic, she saw why. "You know that secret government storage room?" she said, struck by the comparison. "Right at the end of *Raiders of the Lost Ark*?"

Barnwell laughed. "Well, this is mostly just old furniture that didn't get thrown away when it should have long ago. Plus, a possible body encased in concrete, of course. It's there in the corner." Janice wandered over. Dr. Tomlinson sat on an old, metal fold-up chair, scrolling on his phone, his legs crossed.

"Hello, Janice."

"Bit of a turnup for the books, eh?"

"I'll say."

"You look like you're waiting for a bus, sitting there like that."

Tomlinson smiled. "I'm waiting for some expert input from an archaeologist friend of mine. He's on his way." Janice regarded the pathologist. The lines on his face appeared deeper than normal, his pallor a little grey.

"Bazza says you think you've got a body in there. Must have been well sealed not to have been noticed."

"Yes, but if the concrete was thick and dense enough, it would do the trick."

"What's the plan?"

"With a bit of luck, I'm hoping the tomb will have dispelled its secrets by the end of the day. With some good advice and the help of Bob the Builder, we should be able to extract as much of the remains as possible and I can take them to the mortuary for examination and testing."

"Rather you than me, Marcus. Fingers crossed?" Janice smiled and, patting

Tomlinson on the shoulder, left him to his phone. She suddenly felt in need of a drink. Or at least most of a bar of good chocolate.

She returned to Barnwell, who stood in the attic's opposite corner. "What've you done with Carmen while you've been doing all this?"

"Uh, me 'n' Melanie left her and Vixen with the hotel's groundsmen until we're done here. They were gonna give them a runaround." He looked at his watch. "Right about now, she's probably snoozing on top of a pile of compost in their big, warm shed. Sounds good to me."

Janice laughed. "Yeah, it does. And I'll have to remember that. Perhaps that pile of compost will be a good resting place for my guests if the hotel isn't back up and running by the time they're due to arrive." She clapped her hands. "Right, then. Show me what's what."

"I'll give you the tour." Barnwell spent the next few minutes showing Janice where the roof's support beams had come crashing down, hurling tiles everywhere and permitting a nightlong deluge of rain to flood the attic. "Melanie reckoned there was a weak spot in the roof that had been holding for a while, but the winds worried at it, and the heavy rain was the final straw."

"It was a downpour to be sure." Janice marvelled at the destruction around her. A full quarter of the White House Inn roof had opened to welcome the elements.

"Yep. Melanie said—"

"Did she now? You're quite chatty with this Melanie, aren't you? Melanie this, Melanie that."

Barnwell held Janice's gaze. "Yeah, so?"

Janice smirked. "Nothing, nothing. Where'd you find the gun, then? Did it get a cold dousing like the rest of the attic?" Yards from the tarped hole, wind-blown rain still collected in puddles on top of storage boxes and soaked old sofas.

"Actually, no. We think it was in this suitcase which opened when a chest of drawers got poleaxed. I found the gun next to it but not damaged, along with some other stuff which is mostly fine. There's the suitcase. All the stuff around it fell out. But the boss found bullets in the inside pockets. Everything needs collecting, logging, and bagging."

"Okey doke," Janice said. "I'll handle it. Poor Mrs. T. must be out of her mind." She rubbed her hands. "Brrr, it's cold and damp up here." She sheltered between a large upright beam and an upturned old bed frame that stood under a part of the roof that remained intact. While the storm had died down, the inn's exposure on the cliff meant the wind still whistled around it. They had to raise their voices to be heard. "Going to need major repairs before this place is watertight again. I wonder what the insurers are going to think of that?"

"From the expression on Mrs. Taylor's face, I'd worry for my life if I was them. I heard her claiming that the insurers were suggesting that there might have been 'pre-existing structural weaknesses' in the roof. That went down about as well as you might imagine."

The sound of footsteps behind them signalled Graham had arrived. "As one of my early sergeants used to say, 'A copper can always recognise a cop-out.' Sounds like Mrs. T. can too. Barnwell, would you go and chat to the staff while Janice does the bagging? See if you can find out anything about what it was like here forty, fifty years ago. You never know, there might have been rumours passed down. Be discreet. *Don't* mention the . . ." He nodded towards the banquette. "Worth a try at least. Janice can join you when she's done here."

"I'll see you downstairs, Bazza."

As Janice watched Barnwell's retreating back, she sighed. She tried to keep her thoughts at bay, but the White House Inn was central to her wedding plans, and from the looks of the place, it would not be able to perform the role she intended for it.

"Bit of a mess, eh?" Graham seemingly read her mind.

"I'll say so, sir. I've got my nan and step-grandad booked in here along with eighteen or so others. And, to make things easier for Nan—she's eighty-two, the trip over will be quite something for her—we also booked the hotel restaurant for the rehearsal dinner. At this rate, we'll be in the youth hostel and down the chippy."

Janice frowned at the sodden conditions and stepped away to text Jack:

> WHI attic looks like a bomb went off. Hotel closed. Go to Plan B for Accommodation Group Charlie. Repeat, Plan B. 😔

She had time to reach for her forensic gloves and an evidence bag, but her fiancé's reply was near instant and reassuring:

> On it. Got six hotels I can try. It'll all be fine! 😊

CHAPTER EIGHT

TO BARNWELL'S IMMENSE annoyance, Freddie Solomon quickly read the changed atmosphere in the White House Inn. As word circulated through the staff that something more than the weather was up, he hovered among them, a watching, listening drone, noting exclamations of shock or a curled lip of disgust. Barnwell had made a list of every staff member and was hunting them down as they helped with the cleanup. All of them were too young to have been at the White House Inn forty or so years ago, but had they heard "any old stories or rumours about criminal activity or a gun, perhaps, anything handed down by previous staff members?"

As Barnwell roamed the hotel and Janice bagged evidence upstairs, Graham sat in the tearoom again, mulling over what he knew, reconstructing what might have happened, and tweaking one variable after another. Following two big discoveries, his senses were sharper, his pulse just a little elevated.

From where he was sitting, he could see Mrs. Taylor behind the desk, dealing now with a crippling one-two punch—the vengeful storm plus this new embarrassment. She had poured herself a large Bristol Cream sherry from the hotel's bar and, for now, sat sipping as she watched the chaos unfold before her in a post-traumatic daze. She noticed Graham watching her and picked up her glass.

Walking over, she said, "You don't partake, do you?" and dabbed the rim of her sherry glass. She sat in the high-backed rattan wicker chair next to him.

"No, thank you," Graham said. "I can hardly blame you, though, under the circumstances." It was barely lunchtime.

"Is there anything I can help you with? Anything to do with this . . . *gun*." Marjorie Taylor spoke as though the Smith and Wesson Model 28 was a nasty infectious disease they were all in danger of catching.

"Well, the main thing now is to confirm when it might have been left where it was found. I'm having a bit of trouble working out how we might do that. We'll have to take it to the lab. Run some forensics. See if that yields anything." Privately, Graham thought the concrete block would yield far more evidence, but he didn't want to alarm Mrs. Taylor any more than necessary until it was either prudent to tell her about the body or it became unavoidable.

Before she could take another sip of her drink, Mrs. Taylor had to answer the phone and tackle yet another storm-related problem. In her absence, Freddie sidled up, his target clearly the detective inspector. But Graham, spotting Solomon making directly for him, raised his hand as though he were stopping traffic. Freddie took the hint and, choosing not to test Graham's patience further, slunk in the direction of the front door.

Graham's eye then caught Barnwell, who had just finished his interviews with the staff. "Anything? You've not taken long."

"Was no need. They're mostly kids, really," Barnwell said. "For them, 'a long time ago' was the week before last."

"Not surprising, I suppose. They'd have to be in their late fifties or sixties to have worked here during the period we're looking at."

"And they were all spooked at the idea that there'd been a gun here. Gawd knows what they're going to think about someone dying and lying for decades directly above 'em."

Graham sighed. "Humanity experiences a one-point-five percent turnover every year. Each of those hundred-odd million people has to die *somewhere*."

"Yeah, I s'pose that's true, but this is the second suspicious death here in recent memory, and there was that monkey business after the last big storm. One of the kids called this place the 'Fright House Inn.'" Graham cracked a smile. It had been a long morning.

More workmen were arriving, vying for Mrs. Taylor's attention at the crowded reception desk. "We're here about the windows, love. Lost a few in the storm, did you?" one asked.

Janice appeared, running down the stairs, passing a couple of smirking builders. "It was *horrible* up there!" she said with a frustrated cry. Ruffling her hair and flexing her shoulders as if to shake off a mat of cobwebs and dust, she shuddered. "There's wildlife 'n' all."

"How wild?" Graham asked her.

"Spiders and stuff. Birds. I disturbed a nest!"

"Of what?"

"I have no idea. That was the worst part. If being a hotelier doesn't work out, Mrs. Taylor can always open a petting zoo for really weird teenagers." Janice handed over the battered red suitcase and two big, clear, plastic evidence bags, one containing the suitcase contents, the other a blue tweed jacket. "Not much, is it?"

"Some people travel light," Graham said. "He probably wasn't planning on staying long. Not with that gun." The inspector focused on the bag of clothes. He could see a thin sweater, a T-shirt, a white vest, a pair of underpants, and a pair of socks, as well as a bulky, midpriced electronic watch, the type that could do calculations.

Just out of earshot but doing his best to overhear anyway, Freddie Solomon continued to lurk, ready to ensnare anyone who might know anything. Having ferreted out the discovery of the gun after Mrs. Taylor's histrionics had given the game away, more intel was clearly of paramount interest, and he was making notes on everything he observed.

"Quite a find, eh?" Freddie began cordially as Graham walked past him on the way to his car. The detective inspector was having none of it.

"Just somebody's belongings, Freddie." Graham was keen to be rid of the man with his twitching thumbs. He wanted word from Tomlinson, who was still standing vigil over the body in the block. He wanted to know the status of Tomlinson's friend, the archaeologist. He wanted to unleash someone on the forensic evidence. And he wanted more tea. Probably in that order, unless the need for tea became preeminent. He most certainly did *not* want to deal with Freddie Solomon.

"A revolver though?" Freddie said, trotting alongside Graham as he seemed so often to do. "Loaded, was it?"

"Be off, you foul creature," growled Graham.

"Then it *was!*" Freddie resumed making notes, still trotting, head down.

Graham stopped and spun around so fast that Freddie ran headfirst into his chest.

"Wow, blinkin' heck," Freddie said, staggering back, his hand reflexively reaching for his forehead. "It's like walking into a *wall.*"

Graham brushed imaginary crumbs of Freddie from his jacket. "That'll teach you to bother an officer while he's executing his duties. Now, look, *Freddie,*" he said as though unconvinced of the blogger's prerogative to possess a name, "I've warned you about this before."

"It's a very unusual weapon, I understand," Freddie said, keen to press his chance. "The calibre of it, I mean, and . . ."

Graham grasped Freddie's arm with more conviction than Freddie expected. Or, it has to be said, was strictly warranted. "If you print a word about that gun or any other evidence, I'll . . ."

Freddie opened his mouth, ready to protest vociferously against whatever DI Graham had in mind for him, when both men were interrupted by Mrs. Taylor's call from the entryway of the White House Inn. "Detective Inspector! Would you like another cup of tea?"

CHAPTER NINE

"I THINK THIS is him," Barnwell said into his phone. He was standing in the White House Inn's temporary car park, some yards from the regular one that was adjacent to the hotel. The new parking area, a section of the inn's formerly manicured lawn but now a roil of mud and grass, had been so consigned both for the protection of guests' cars from the ongoing danger of falling debris and because the permanent car park was full of fire trucks, pickup trucks, all kinds of workers' trucks.

"All clear" was the reply from Graham in the lobby. "Intercept him and we'll bring him up the back stairs. Mrs. Taylor is in the kitchen."

A few moments later, Barnwell, Graham, and Dr. Alexander Papadopoulos entered the attic, the archaeologist unaware of the clandestine nature of his visit.

"Alex!" Dr. Tomlinson strode across the floorboards, his arms outstretched, evidently relieved to see his old friend. "Twice in two days. That's some kind of record."

"Marcus, it's good to see you again, and so soon. But these appear to be strange circumstances, no?" Dr. Papadopoulos spoke in lightly accented English as quietly and calmly as he might if he were the narrator of a particularly reassuring children's bedtime story. He was a short, stocky man who wore an ill-fitting brown suit and a brown and yellow paisley-patterned tie. It was strange attire for someone on holiday, but later Barnwell speculated that perhaps Papadopoulos travelled "ready for anything—and, in these circumstances, just as well."

Spectacles with thick lenses were propped on Papadopoulos's pudgy nose, and his eyes appeared unnaturally small when viewed through the prism of the glass. They gave him the appearance of a shortsighted mole. "Your message was intriguing. What do you have here?" Dr. Papadopoulos cast his tiny, glass-obscured eyes around until they alighted on the concrete box in the corner.

"Forgive me for interrupting your holiday, but we've got an unusual case on our hands. We believe we may have a body buried in concrete, and I'd like your advice. I'm not quite sure how to proceed with the exhumation, or perhaps that's *excavation*, without damaging the remains."

"Is that it over there?" Papadopoulos said, not taking his eyes off the corner.

"Indeed," Marcus replied.

Dr. Papadopoulos lumbered over and peered at the concrete through his bottle-thick spectacles. He knocked the brick surrounding it and placed the flat of his hand on top as though testing the temperature. "How old do we think the remains might be?" Papadopoulos raised his head and looked at Marcus, blinking as if he'd just breached the earth's surface after many years in darkness.

"From other items found which we think might be associated with the body, we estimate forty, maybe fifty years."

"Do you have any thought as to the condition?"

"Not exactly, but we have this fingertip." Marcus pointed it out. "Given that it's intact, it's possible the remains might be in a decent state, don't you think? But the concrete's thickness and composition present a problem accessing them."

Papadopoulos reached deep into his trouser pocket to pull out a metal tape measure. Briskly, he measured the length, width, and depth of the block and, tapping his lips with his forefinger, murmured to himself as he contemplated the problem faced by Tomlinson and his team.

"Adipocere appears to have formed which will help, but you'll certainly need to be cautious. Have you considered employing any imaging techniques to get a clearer picture before excavation?"

"Ah, yes, that's a good idea." Dr. Tomlinson rolled back on his heels. "But the Gorey forensic budget doesn't stretch to concrete-penetrating radar, I'm afraid. We don't come across this kind of thing too often, you see."

"Alright, let's make some reasonable deductions. Whoever created this tomb, which is effectively what this is, built a brick exterior around the body and then filled it with concrete. They placed it across the joists for support. If we consider the position of this exposed digit, we might reasonably conclude that the end next to the wall is where we will find the feet. I suggest we start there."

"Right, you are. Anything else?"

"Once we've found the feet, we'll have a better understanding of the body's position, and we can proceed with selective excavation. I recommend using hand tools at first, then we can follow up with a pneumatic saw."

Papadopoulos leaned over and knocked the side of the brick mould several times along its length before continuing with his assessment. "I would endeavour to take the concrete from the top, thereby exposing the body while still supporting it via the concrete underneath. Having it lie on a bed as it were. That will protect the integrity of the remains and help further your study in situ. When you've completed your examination here as far as it can proceed, we can attempt to lift the body for transportation to your lab."

"But surely the body will be in good nick, won't it?" Barnwell whispered to Graham.

They stood a few feet away from the two doctors, along with Bob the Builder. Bob was a stocky lad, a local in his late fifties, a bricklayer since before he left school. Everyone knew him as "Bob the Builder," so much so that only his family knew his real name.

Bob's work took him all over the Channel Islands and sometimes to the French mainland. Having spent most of his life on a building site of one kind or another, he took over his father's construction contracts with local authorities when he retired, and this now comprised most of his work.

Bob had built everything from brand-new houses and barn conversions to shoring up historical stately homes. He was the person everyone turned to for building jobs, although now it was the younger men he hired who did most of the backbreaking work. On Graham's orders, Barnwell had called him in to help, giving Bob strict instructions to tell no one about the details of this "urgent, small job at the White House Inn." Chewing his lip, a bag of tools in one hand, an electric saw at his feet, he looked on nervously.

"I mean, won't the concrete have protected the body from turning to mush?" Barnwell added.

"Not necessarily," Graham said, wincing at his constable's choice of words. "Even if the concrete created an airtight space, the bacteria in and on the body at the point of death will have done their worst."

"Also, how well the concrete was made will have had an impact," whispered Bob, overhearing and leaning in. "Can't imagine anyone making their best mix under these circumstances. They were probably in a right panic. They must have lugged bags of cement, sand, and gravel up here without anyone seeing. And that's if there's a water source up here. If not, they'd have had to have lugged that up an' all."

"How's it going?" Janice said softly, sidling up. She'd been in her car strategising with Jack about the new accommodation arrangements for the bridesmaids and groomsmen. The conversation had been fraught. "I don't think that's a good idea, Jack. Having Suranne and Ava and Toby and Dexter all under the same roof is asking for . . . shenanigans," she'd said. Jack had eventually conceded the point, and they'd agreed to have a rethink.

"I think they're making progress. Just discussing what to do," Barnwell whispered back. "All done downstairs? Thought you'd have gone back to your day off."

"Wasn't going to miss this, was I? The Gorey equivalent of discovering Tutankhamun's tomb, the Mrs. T. factor notwithstanding. And dealing with my mother was the alternative."

Tomlinson looked over at them. "Okay then, let's get started. Alex will supervise and tell you what to do, Bob."

Straightening his shoulders, Bob picked up his electric saw and wandered with his tools to the corner. Despite working on large, sometimes grand building projects, Bob had never refused a job, no matter how unusual or small. He would lay patios and build outdoor kitchens. He would rebuild low pub walls demolished by patrons who shouldn't be driving. He had even built pigsties around pigs. But uncovering a body in a block of concrete was the smallest, most delicate, unusual job ever asked of him.

"Target this corner here, by hand, bit by bit, please, sir. When you find something, stop, okay?" Dr. Papadopoulos said.

Bob grunted and moved in. With his bolster and sledgehammer, he broke the brick at one end, then chipped away at the concrete half inch by half inch, watched intently by the four other men and Janice.

Barnwell had silenced the roofers on top. The only thing the three police officers, two doctors, and one builder could hear was the *tap-tap-tap* of metal on metal and occasional gusts of wind as the last vestiges of the storm receded. Clumps of concrete fell to the floor as they waited for a sight or a change in sound that would signal Bob had found what they were looking for.

"Stop!" Papadopoulos cried. Barnwell jumped, startled.

Bob straightened and stood back, wiping his upper lip with the back of his hand, his face puce from effort.

Papadopoulos beckoned Graham and Tomlinson over. At the end of the block, surrounded by near-white concrete, they could see the tip of a leather sole.

"A shoe. Keep going," Graham said. Bob chipped away a little more of the concrete. The tip widened and lengthened to expose a hand-stitched sole of a low-heeled shoe.

"Well, we now know their shoe size. Nine and a half," Tomlinson said, reading the number clearly visible on the leather sole.

Papadopoulos turned to Bob. "Do you have a small rotating saw?"

"I certainly do."

"Then let's move on to the next stage. We'll now attempt to reveal the body as cleanly as possible. We must shield the area from view and work in silence behind the screen. It is important for the integrity of the burial site and to offer dignity to the deceased," Papadopoulos said solemnly.

"We'll see to it," Graham said. "And leave you to your work."

CHAPTER TEN

"ALL THAT I was told," Mrs. Taylor explained, more composed now that Graham had accepted her offer of tea and was sharing a pot with her, "was that the grand attic was once a dormitory room. I think for unmarried lads back when this place was private apartments, before it was a hotel. In the twenties, thirties."

"Imagine having a whole stretch of this place to yourself," Graham said, admiring the slightly faded grandeur.

"Then the Germans turned it into a military outpost during the occupation," she continued. "You know, Hitler and his lot. Once we kicked them out, nobody paid much attention to the old place. It sat up here on the clifftop empty for a decade or so, then was bought by someone with plans for a retirement home. But they went bankrupt before the idea got off the ground and it was turned into a cheap hotel. Run by a Miss Lovell." Marjorie sniffed and took a sip of her tea. "She was as old as I am now when she took the building over and ran the hotel for twenty years before she eventually died. God rest her soul."

Mrs. Taylor crossed herself and paused respectfully for a second before enthusiastically returning to her subject. "As a girl, I'd watched this place for years, you see, wondering about it, dreaming. I could see the possibilities, the potential. When it eventually came up for auction, I had just enough money to snatch it up." She sat, her back stiff and straight, puffing out her chest.

"September 1982. I was very young, in my early twenties. Newly married I was. Back then, with a hotel to my name, I suppose I got a bit full of myself. Had some grand ideas, maybe *too* grand. Went around telling everyone I'd be converting the grand attic into a restaurant with an ocean view or some such, I seem to remember. The surveyors and assessors and bean counter people, well, they said not to take the risk, and I didn't. But perhaps I should've. In those days, they doubted a woman could run a place like this and made their views known as plain as day. I was happy to prove them wrong," she said primly, the hotel's decades of success more than enough proof that she was right. "But I did forgo the idea of that restaurant. It would have been difficult with the kitchen on the ground floor.

"Of course, Mr. Taylor helped. In those days, it was different. A woman was often not taken seriously. I could be very stern. I had a confidence beyond my years, but sometimes a man's touch was required. Mr. Taylor was very good. He was usually merely a presence in the background, but there was one time when a guest, a Mr. Madingley I seem to remember, would not accept that he hadn't made a reservation and that we didn't have a room for him. Was causing quite a ruckus in reception, he was. I was about to call you lot, but my Timothy got it sorted. A few quiet words were all that it needed. He was good like that—a help, but he never took over." She gazed into the distance. "I miss him."

After a brief experiment with twenty-first-century tools, Graham had returned to the policeman's traditional notebook and pencil as the means by which he recorded his conversations. As he listened to Mrs. Taylor recite the history of the White House Inn, he created page after page of odd, interconnected symbols. Silent next to him, Barnwell lost track of what Mrs. Taylor was saying as he watched his boss doodle.

Despite their appearance, the scribbles were not meaningless. Graham's pencil made familiar motions, but some strokes were forced into a tight compression, while others were truncated into a complex little graphical suffix. Some marks resembled mini pictograms, as though Graham were borrowing from the Chinese language. Only through context could one even be certain it was English. It was a form of shorthand Graham had devised for himself and appeared to serve as a form of meditation as the detective inspector focused solely on transposing the words to which he was listening. Watching the pencil move up and down and from side to side creating this indecipherable code mesmerised Barnwell.

"In the end, I ran out of money, and I never got around to it," Mrs. Taylor lamented, returning to the subject of the seafront restaurant. "Too much competition, and then the package holidays started. My margins were crunched. We survived all that, several recessions, changes in government. But now? Now I'll be lucky to drum up any business at all." Her voice rose almost to a wail. She began to tear up and dabbed at her eyes with the scrunched-up tissue she held in her hand. "I mean, who wants to stay in an old wreck with only half a roof!"

Graham second-guessed himself half a dozen times but finally put his pencil down and placed a comforting arm around Mrs. Taylor's shoulders. "It's been a rotten day, Mrs. Taylor, but remember something: the White House Inn is a Gorey institution. We can't imagine the place without you." Seeking reasons for optimism was a trick Laura had shown him. "Besides, the surveyors and assessors are working up plans to fix the roof right now. The insurance will prioritise it, and in a couple of weeks, they'll give you the green light. You'll be back in action in no time, you'll see."

"They know your back's against the wall and they'll nip it in the bud," Barnwell added, "if that's not mixing metaphysics or whatever."

"Metaphors, Constable."

"Yeah, them."

Their chivvying seemed to help Mrs. Taylor a little. Sighing, hands clasped, fingertips endlessly clutching at her opposing knuckles while her thumbs tucked the shredded tissue into her palms, Mrs. Taylor thanked the officers, and after draining her teacup, she stoically headed to her office. "That's the body language of someone who has passed through the early stages of grief," Graham told Barnwell, "and is inexorably approaching some kind of acceptance."

"But won't she get thrown right back into the thick of it when we tell her . . . what we've got to tell her?"

"Yes. And that's why we need Janice." Graham looked around. "Where is she?"

"Last I saw, she was talking to Melanie. Having a good chinwag, they were. Had a lot to talk about it seemed. Women in a man's world, I suppose."

"Mrs. Taylor will be alright. At least, I think she will. The carpet still looks good, if a little trodden on by the firefighters, and the old place could never lose its sense of grandeur. People'll soon forget, I'm sure. Don't you think?"

"Yeah, 'course they will. It's a Gorey icon. The place wouldn't be the same without it. Soon it'll be as good as new 'n' life will carry on as before." The two men looked at each other, unsure as to whether they were being genuine. Secretly, they were jollying themselves along, intent on convincing each other that once word got out that a body had been buried in the White House Inn attic for *decades*, nothing would change for Mrs. Taylor, and she would go on exactly as before. They both knew that was highly unlikely.

"You know, Barnwell, when I first arrived, I wasn't too sure about staying here, but the quality of the tea service persuaded me. I thought I'd stay for a week at most, but then the atmosphere dug into my soul. Did you know I met Laura here?" Graham nodded over to the reception desk, a large, Victorian, oak-panelled affair. "In the lobby, and I like to think especially in this sunlit tearoom, one can hear a faint call from an era when a hotel could be restrained, a true cathedral to travel. A mini palace that one could miraculously call one's own, if just for a week, in the quest for rest, relaxation, and an escape from the trials of everyday life. A place where anything might happen, anything at all—conversations, characters, circumstances, all novel to the traveller. I found it set my Spidey senses alive."

"Blimey, sir, you'll be invoking that annoying little Belgian fella any minute. The one off the telly."

"Hercule Poirot? He would have loved this place, Constable. His essence embodies it. One might imagine seeing him patrol the corridors at night if one believed in that kind of thing."

Barnwell regarded his boss quizzically, then drained his tea with a slurp. "Er, right, sir. Shall we be getting on, then?"

CHAPTER ELEVEN

FOR THE NEXT four hours, under Dr. Papadopoulos's careful guidance, and behind sheets provided by the White House Inn's housekeeping department and hastily erected by Barnwell and Janice, Bob the Builder painstakingly sawed chunks from the block of cement. Dust flew and settled in a field of microscopic particles around him.

Marcus Tomlinson sat quietly on the far side of the attic, away from the dust. Occasionally, Dr. Papadopoulos would request his assistance, and he would disappear behind the curtain, resurfacing a few minutes later. As time dragged on, Graham joined the pathologist, bringing over a chair. They sat in silence as the constant, shrill whirring of the saw filled the air.

Eventually, the saw stopped, the silence ringing in their ears, and the tiny particles of cement that had hung in the air for hours slowly sank to the floor. They settled on the dusty wooden boards already marked with footprints. Papadopoulos swept aside the sheet and peered around it. He was covered from head to toe. A paper suit, booties, gloves, a face shield, a mask over his mouth and nose, and, of course, his glasses, shielded him completely. It might have been impossible to identify him but for his distinctive bottle-glass thick lenses.

"Gentlemen, it is time to show you what we have uncovered. Please come this way."

Eager after so much waiting, Graham and Tomlinson did not hesitate. Similarly suited and booted, they slipped behind the curtain, their eyes widening instinctively as they absorbed the scene.

On a concrete bed lay the body of a man, almost perfectly preserved. He had thin, translucent hair; a short, wide nose; and a pointed chin. Skin around his mouth stretched across his jaws, revealing a set of large teeth perfectly aligned except for a gap between the front two. His eyes were closed, weighed down by large metal washers, and one arm lay across his chest, under which was pinned a bloomless, twisted, thorny stem. The other arm was propped in the air by a crude wire construction as it crossed his body, one finger pointed like he was hailing a taxi. The extended forefinger was clearly the one that had alerted Barnwell to the body's presence.

The man wore a green polo shirt, muddy and faded now, which lay unnaturally over his bony rib cage. An embroidered crocodile motif adorned the left breast. A gold crucifix had settled into the crease of his neck, and jeans, the stain of which was still a pale blue, ended in a pair of black, laced shoes.

"What can you tell us, Alex?" Tomlinson asked.

Dr. Papadopoulos adjusted his glasses before speaking. "Marcus, Inspector, it is quite a rare scene we have here. As you mentioned, we think the body we've unearthed has been encased in this concrete possibly for over forty years. The concrete has acted as a preservative, albeit a grim one. The body is in excellent condition. However, there are telltale signs of decomposition. The concrete slowed the process but couldn't stop it entirely. You'll see that the torso structure has collapsed due to the decay of internal organs, and the legs are wizened to almost nothing. The spongy ball and socket joints have deteriorated. But I believe we have a man who was in his prime when he was struck down. You'll be able to estimate his age from dental records and carbon dating his bones, but a quick assessment tells me that he is a fully developed adult male."

"What about the wire?" Graham asked.

"A rough support we made to preserve the position the body was found in. I suspect rigor mortis had set in when they buried him, which would explain the unnatural pose. When we removed the concrete, the arm was precariously suspended in midair and liable to collapse." Papadopoulos turned to Tomlinson. "I thought it might give clues as to the cause of death."

"Do you have any thoughts about what killed him?" Graham wondered. "I was expecting bullet wounds, but I don't see any."

"That's where things get tricky. The concrete and decomposition have made it difficult to identify his injuries. But I agree, I see no sign of bullet wounds. Hopefully, forensic analysis and perhaps even historical records will help you piece together what happened."

"When we get him back to the mortuary, we'll be able to say more," Tomlinson reassured Graham. "There's a lot I can do."

"I'm assuming his death was intentional. Someone went to great lengths to hide the body. They had to have had a good reason," Graham said.

"It's certainly a possibility," Dr. Papadopoulos replied. "But I wouldn't say it's a certainty."

"No, it's not, but it is curious. Encasing a body in concrete isn't something done on a whim. It suggests at a minimum a deliberate effort to conceal evidence."

"What are you thinking, David?" Dr. Tomlinson asked him.

"My working theory is that he was killed deliberately, and the murderer chose to move the body here for some unknown reason or, more likely, killed him in the attic."

"Or there's another possibility: the man died of natural causes, and someone chose to conceal his body for another reason entirely. But that's more your field than mine," Papadopoulos said, pushing his glasses higher up his nose. He smiled.

"Exactly so." Graham exhaled. "Right, well, thank you for the insight, Dr. Papadopoulos. You've been a great help. Looks like we've got our work cut out for us." Graham turned to Tomlinson and smiled ruefully. "Over to you, Marcus."

CHAPTER TWELVE

JANICE TRIED HER best, but in the end, it wasn't enough. It was likely that nothing would have been sufficient to prevent Mrs. Taylor's bloodcurdling scream when she learned there was a body in her attic. The sergeant bravely tried to talk her down, but it was Dr. Tomlinson with a sedative who saved the day. "I'll sit with her for a bit in case she wakes up," Janice promised Graham.

"Good of you, Sergeant." Graham pocketed his notebook and checked his watch. "Right, if no one here has any ideas about who this guy is, I'm off." He glanced at his car, finding in the early evening light an unwelcome presence hovering next to it like a feverish poltergeist. "Oh, for the love . . ."

"You want me to see to him?" Barnwell offered.

"I've got it. I'll see you tomorrow." Graham strode towards the car and turned his attention to the shivering apparition beside it. "Now, Freddie, where were we?"

"Erm, as I remember, you were threatening me."

"Oh, yes, now I remember. If any of what went on today goes into print"—Graham opened his car door—"I'll make you write a retraction along with an apology from your jail cell."

"Impinging on the freedom of the media!" Freddie immediately announced to the parking lot like a crier in a market square. "Detective Inspector Graham's oppressing me!" he continued, full-throated. "And denying my readership the—"

"Will you *cool it* this instant?" Graham growled, keeping his voice low.

"Police cover-up!" Freddie shouted. Hearing this, Barnwell came rushing over, Carmen, newly awoken from her peaty potting soil bed, bounding alongside him.

"Trouble, sir?" Graham nodded ever so slightly.

"Free—" Freddie continued to yell.

"Shut," Barnwell said, grabbing Freddie's wrists, "your bleedin' cake-'ole." Somewhere at the edges of the febrile firmament that was Freddie's brain, he felt a cold, metallic handcuff against his wrist, then heard a click as Barnwell locked it.

"Hey, wait just a minute!" Freddie cried. Graham moved to stand squarely in front of him.

"We're in the middle of a serious police inquiry, Solomon. My officers *rely* on evidence, you thoughtless little weasel, and if the guilty party or someone close to them knows what we've found, they can disrupt, pervert, or otherwise counter our investigation. We do not need you helping them do that."

"But there's a *pattern*!" Freddie insisted. Horrified, he glanced down as Barnwell cuffed his other wrist.

"The only pattern around here"—Barnwell gave the chain between the handcuffs a quick tug—"is one of you jeopardising police investigations when you were specifically told not to."

"But..."

"Get in the car, Freddie," said Graham, "or I'll clip you to the door handle and make you run all the way." It was just over a mile and a half to the police station, and the thought pleased Graham immensely, even if he had no intention of fulfilling his threat. "Then I'll roast you over an open fire until you understand that investigations require *integrity*."

Freddie continued to protest as Barnwell placed a hand over his head and guided him into the back seat of the car, the door silencing Freddie's protestations as Barnwell slammed it shut.

"I never intended to interfere in any..."

By now, a crowd of perhaps eight passers-by were watching the unedifying scene, so Graham climbed in to continue his telling off. "I don't give a monkey's about your intentions. You're constantly messing up the juror pool, directing public opinion, and muddying goodness knows what else with your brainless ramblings."

"But, the gun, Inspector. It's part of a pattern I'm researching for my book." News of the remains in the concrete hadn't appeared to have reached Freddie. Yet. He was still on about the gun. "It's what I've been waiting for!" Freddie wailed. "I was just at HMP Holbrooke interviewing two old guys. Hard lads from the East End who had connections to Jersey..." The rear door of the car slammed as Barnwell shut Carmen in. She leaned over the back seats, excited to greet the stranger sitting there. Freddie closed his eyes and cringed as her moist breath warmed his neck. He wasn't a dog lover.

"It's a nice spot for a relaxing break, Jersey. Loads of people do it, haven't you noticed?" Barnwell climbed in next to Freddie.

"Hard lads from the East End who had connections to Jersey *before the law caught up with them*," Freddie finished.

"We usually do."

"I think they came to settle old scores and transfer money. I think in addition to Jersey being a tax shelter, it was a bastion for money laundering and a gangster hideout back in the day. Before Spain became the favourite spot for expats wanting to lay low."

"You're taking a couple of random data points, a fanciful imagination, and an ability to write fiction and combining them to create a cockeyed theory that you'll never be able to prove," Graham said from the driver's seat.

"I'm working on it," Freddie said. "Good journalism takes time."

"How would you know?" Barnwell added, earning a silent acknowledgement from Graham for some sharp wit. Graham texted Laura before starting the motor.

"You know, this is typical of you, Freddie. You've never met a conclusion you didn't want to jump to," the inspector added after pressing "send."

"But you've seen it yourself," Freddie pleaded. "You looked back through those old case files I mentioned to Laura. I know you did. You wouldn't have been able to resist. It's all going in my book, you know."

"What are you talking about?" Barnwell said.

Graham eyed Freddie in his rearview mirror. "Mr. Solomon here is researching historical unsolved Jersey cases for a book he's writing."

"Working title: *Murder Island*," Freddie said proudly.

Barnwell rolled his eyes. "That's gonna go down well with the tourist board."

"Listen, there were isolated incidents that don't add up to much, but you've gone and raced ahead yet again, coming to conclusions without *any* proof." Graham shook his head. "Have you learned nothing from wasting my time these past few years?"

Glum and defeated, though never entirely hopeless—it wasn't part of his makeup—Freddie sat in the back seat quietly while Graham drove to the police station. "Um, can I ask a question?" Freddie said when they pulled up outside.

"Hmm?" Graham's eyes flicked to the rearview mirror and caught Freddie looking at him in it.

"I haven't been arrested, have I?"

"Thus far," Graham told him, "you're merely helping us with our enquiries."

"Into what?"

"Into just how much of a bleedin' pillock you are," Barnwell grunted next to him. He had been looking forward to a run with Carmen after a long day. He had hoped to follow that with a nice piece of mackerel gifted to him by one of the local fishermen as he'd patrolled the storm-beaten island before being called to inspect the White House Inn's roof. That seemed a long time ago now.

Resigned to an evening of unpleasantness, Freddie remained determined to defend himself. "Well, according to you, that'd take weeks."

"It's alright," Graham said, bringing the car to a halt. "I've called in reinforcements."

CHAPTER THIRTEEN

"FREDDIE! WHAT DID you do?" Laura stood in reception, her arms folded, with a frown so fierce it threatened to crack a pane of glass in the station's window. Barnwell removed a cuff from Freddie's wrist and guided him onto a chair, clicking the empty handcuff around the back support. Carmen ran past them and settled herself in her favourite spot under Barnwell's desk. Graham headed to his office, leaving Barnwell and Laura to keep an eye on the meddlesome blogger for a few minutes.

The constable moved quickly to the reception counter to enter Freddie's details should Graham decide to charge him with anything. Privately, Barnwell hoped to avoid the paperwork that accompanied an arrest but looked forward to a lengthy excoriation of Freddie courtesy of Graham or Laura. He didn't mind which.

"This is all just ridiculous. I haven't done anything . . ." Despite her furious expression, the sight of Laura buoyed Freddie. Although not technically a member of the Gorey Constabulary, Laura's proximity to Graham meant that within their ranks she was the closest thing to a supporter that Freddie had. It was kind of her to come out for him, especially considering that running interference on his behalf put her in an awkward position. This time, though, she seemed angrier than usual. "You know what he's like," Freddie said to her, hopeful for an intervention, or at least a soothing word.

"As a matter of fact, I do," Laura said. "And he generally has his reasons."

"It's preemptive censorship," Freddie said haughtily. He turned to Barnwell. "We live in a democracy, you know. You should be ashamed of yourselves."

"Steady on," Graham called from his office.

"Only totalitarian monsters imprison their journalists!" Freddie cried out.

"You've not been banged up yet," Barnwell told him. "But it can easily be arranged." He jostled the keys on his belt to illustrate his point.

"I haven't corrupted any investigation," Freddie insisted.

"No, but it's your habit to do things that make my life complicated, and for that reason, I'm here telling you now: cease and desist before you do." Graham came out of his office and walked towards him.

Freddie answered as though his was the only possible response. "Absolutely not. It's the public's right to know what's going on."

"If you publish details of the evidence found at that hotel," Graham said, "you'll be in trouble. This is an active inquiry, and to ensure its success, *we*"—Graham pointed his thumb at his chest—"decide when to release information, not"—he pointed his forefinger at Freddie—"*you*."

At this, Freddie's indignant, righteous fury evaporated like water in the desert. His shoulders slumped. "Okay, I understand," he mumbled.

"Alright, then." Graham headed back to his office.

"This is important," Freddie said in a low voice to Laura. "It's about press freedoms. One of these days, he's going to arrest me properly, and there'll be no justification at all."

"Knowing that, as you do," Laura said, "you shouldn't upset him. It's your own fault."

"I didn't *do* anything!" Freddie insisted again. "He's just overzealous."

"He's a professional."

"So am I!" A splutter of amusement from behind the desk told Freddie what Barnwell thought of *that*.

"Oh, yeah, Bazza? Got something to say?" Freddie said, suddenly confrontational again.

"Constable Barnwell to you, Sonny Jim."

"I wouldn't get on the wrong side of the constable either, you know," Laura said. "Look at him, built like a brick house with a mood to match after a long day." Barnwell cackled like an evil super-genius and stroked an imaginary cat lying on his shoulder.

Freddie gulped. "I thought you were my friend, Laura." Freddie's eyes darted around. He was still cuffed to the chair.

"Can I leave now?" he asked Barnwell plaintively.

"No," came Graham's voice from his office. "Sit there and think about what you've done and still might do if you're not careful."

"But I didn't even . . ."

"Constable?" Graham bellowed. "Isn't it about time we recertified the taser equipment?"

"That date's coming up here quick, sir. Yes." Barnwell regarded Freddie with the *schadenfreude* of happy expectation. "What say we make it a live test, sir?"

"Stop it," Laura said, surprised by their immaturity and cruelty but unaware of the stress of the police officers' day. Though even if she had known, she wouldn't have approved.

THE CASE OF THE BODY IN THE BLOCK   515

Silent while Graham wrapped up his day and Barnwell closed down the station's computers for the night, Freddie's glum, put-upon demeanour returned as he slumped in his chair. But within moments, his affect changed again. He leaned down and, with his free hand, brought out his slender laptop from his satchel. Industriously, his blues forgotten, he balanced the computer on his lap, opened it, and started tapping with one hand.

Laura was worried. "Wait, you're not . . ."

"I'm writing my next piece for the *Gossip*, as you'd expect."

"If there's anything Inspector Graham doesn't like in there . . ."

"I don't write it for him!" Freddie retorted. "I have responsibilities to my readers." He paused. "Do you think I should describe Mrs. Taylor as 'freaked out' or 'losing her mind'?"

"Won't matter," replied Laura. "She'll beat you to death with a rolling pin either way."

"And the inspector's off his rocker," Freddie added, continuing to type, "if he thinks I'm asking permission from the *police* before publishing."

"On this occasion, you can ask first," Barnwell said, "or be told later. And that wouldn't actually be your biggest problem. Let me introduce you to the Criminal Law Act of 1967, particularly section five, subsection two," he said invitingly.

"Eh?"

"'Where,'" Barnwell quoted from his computer screen, "'if a person causes any wasteful employment of the police by knowingly making a false report . . .'"

"I'm doing no such thing!" Freddie protested.

"'. . . tending to give rise to apprehension for the safety of persons or property . . .'"

"Nobody's feeling apprehensive!" Freddie insisted. "I haven't even . . ."

"'. . . he shall be liable on summary conviction to imprisonment for not more than six months, or to a fine of not more than . . .'" Barnwell had to think for a second. "Boss, is it two thousand five hundred for wasting police time?"

"Yep," Graham called back. "Also," he added, "don't forget embracery."

"Last thing I want is a hug, sir," Barnwell quipped. "Especially from him. Or did you mean something else?"

Graham appeared in his office doorway and folded his arms, a sure sign that he had knowledge to dispense. "The offence of 'embracery' involves tampering with a jury to achieve a favourable result. Freddie's obsession with dispensing information in the name of the public's 'right to know' arguably causes him to interfere with potential jurors. Which is," he reminded them, "almost every adult on Jersey."

"It's not like that," Freddie complained.

"Come to think of it," Graham added, mulling over what he knew of this particular law, "I could probably nab you for embracery right now, Freddie."

"I've never heard of it," Laura said.

Graham coughed. "Well, it is a fourteenth-century statute."

"Bang up-to-date, then," Freddie muttered.

"Also," Graham admitted, "the offence was abolished a few years ago."

"So now I'm being arrested for ancient, obsolete crimes?" Freddie sat up straight in his chair, still cuffed to it, and assumed as much authority and dignity as someone could in his position. "DI Graham, you're either going to lock me up for the night on a public order offence or lecture me. But I don't think you'll waste time doing both."

"Rule nothing out," Graham said. "I can be remarkably thorough."

Freddie stood awkwardly, his cuffed hand forcing him to stoop. He was proud of his defiance. Especially in front of Laura, who sat, her arms folded and legs crossed, watching this unseemly drama unfold. Freddie wondered if she found him courageous. Or amusing, at least.

"Are we arresting him, boss?" Barnwell said. "Or should I turf him out so that Miss Beecham and you can get some dinner?"

Graham regarded their prisoner. "Well, Freddie, what do you think? Should we lock you up for the night, bed and breakfast courtesy of His Majesty, or shall we let you go and risk you spilling Crown secrets?"

"I'm not . . ." Freddie caught Laura's eye as she glanced sideways at him. He coughed and sat up straight. "As I have been neither arrested nor charged, I believe I am free to go." Laura raised her eyebrows. Freddie shifted in his seat and lowered his voice. "I think you should let me go . . . sir."

Graham glanced at Laura. She winked at him. He silently counted to five. "Okay, Constable Barnwell, let him go." He glanced at his watch. "I'm hungry. It's been a long day." Barnwell walked around the desk and freed Freddie from his chair. "But Freddie? Listen. This is a warning, and I want you to take it seriously."

Laura leaned in. "Freddie, look, this obsession you've got with 'mobsters' and 'criminal elements' from London—"

"It's not an obsession! You, of all people, know *exactly* what I'm talking about!" Freddie erupted again. "One of them followed you down here and tried to kill you!"

"That wasn't the same thing as organised crime on Jersey's shores, and you know it."

"Alright, that's enough," Graham said, intervening. "I've had enough for one day."

"My research will prove everything!" Freddie cried. "You'll see. And then you'll owe me an apology." With that, he turned and stalked out of the station, his chin high, his eyes shining. Once outside and out of view of the police station, he blew out his cheeks and began the long trudge to collect his car. It was still parked outside the White House Inn, where he had left it earlier before . . . everything.

CHAPTER FOURTEEN

LAURA FOLLOWED GRAHAM to his office as he finished packing up. "Freddie's not genuinely a danger to anyone, is he?"

"Yes, he is," Graham said pointedly. "And he's the kind of danger one underestimates at one's peril."

"What on earth do you mean? It's a harmless . . . well, *mostly* harmless blog."

Graham was more than ready to think about literally anything else. "Freddie's a complication," he summed up, guiding Laura out and closing his office door behind him. They headed through the reception area. "What are you doing tonight, Barnwell?"

"I planned to go for a run with Carmen." Barnwell looked outside at the now dark evening. "It's not raining, so I'll probably still do that. I have fresh mackerel in the fridge, but I might pick up a Chinese on the way home instead." He rubbed his hands together. "Choices, choices."

"Have you heard from Jim at all?"

"He's busy, I know that, sir. And enjoying it up there in London. He's coming back for Janice's wedding though."

Graham's eyes brightened at this news. "Is he? Top lad."

"We'll have a right old chinwag then."

The inspector smiled. "We will that. Righto, 'night."

Graham had the patrol car for the evening. He was on call, but he and Laura hadn't yet agreed what to do. "I thought we'd hit the Bangkok Palace. It's been a while," he said. "Khun Thongsong said that if I can manage his spicy shrimp *gaeng som*, he'll induct me into the Order of the Perfumed Jewel."

"What's that?" Laura laughed. "Like joining the Freemasons, but for chilli fiends?"

"It's for people who survive food challenges. The ones that are normally fatal. You know, poisonous fish . . ."

"Deadly mushrooms . . ." Laura guessed.

"Psychoactive fruit, that kind of thing."

Laura frowned. "You weren't really going to lock Freddie up, were you?"

Pausing as he was about to start the engine, Graham said. "Maybe, maybe not. Whether it happens in the future, well, that's up to him. I've given him plenty of warning."

"Promise me," Laura said as he got the car going, "you'll talk to me before you do that?"

"If the situation allows it," Graham said, "but I've got to protect our investigations."

"I understand, love," she said. "But there are different methods of getting through to people, and bullying Freddie at the station might not—"

"Bullying?"

"It didn't look that way to you? It did to me."

Uncomfortable at Laura's admonishment, Graham was quiet on the way to the restaurant. As he pulled into the car park, determined not to spoil a night out, he conceded. "I'll find a way forward with Freddie. No one will get charged as long as we can agree on some simple rules."

Laura wasn't sure Graham was seeing the main point. "He's not going to let you censor his writing. And if you insist, then Freddie won't be the only one who's upset about it."

"Come on," said Graham, exasperated. "You know I wouldn't do anything overly vindictive. I've said I'll work it out with him. And I'll only take redress if he steps over the legal line which, to be honest, he's already stepped over multiple times. I'm well within my—"

Laura remained in her seat, expectant but still. "I need you to promise."

"Promise what?"

"That you won't kick off some great big stink and get Gorey Constabulary on the evening news . . ."

"Me?"

" . . . because one of the coppers lost his mind and arrested a journalist who'd written unfavourably about him. Because that's how it will look whether it's strictly true or not. You're in danger of becoming your own worst enemy."

"Look, I'm not going to get a hammer and smash his laptop. Back in the day, illegal publishers had their presses broken by the—"

"Promise you won't stop him publishing."

"Other responsibilities notwithstanding, I so promise."

"And you won't lock him up."

Now Graham was laughing. "Laura, I couldn't even promise not to lock *you* up. That decision depends on what people *do*."

"Not true!" she argued, flipping off her seat belt and opening the door.

Apparently, they were finished with the in-car part of the discussion, which suited Graham perfectly; since breakfast, he'd only eaten a bag of crisps he had snatched from behind the bar at the White House Inn. The *gaeng som* offered itself invitingly. "Really?" he said, climbing out of the car.

"You were all set to arrest Freddie just for talking to others about the case. He could have scared up some useful witnesses..."

"Highly unlikely," Graham said. "Oh, good evening." He handed his jacket, and then Laura's coat, to Nan, one of the Bangkok Palace's traditionally attired servers.

"Sir, if I may ask, is it true you intend to order the special *gaeng som*?" Nan asked.

"It is," Graham announced. He licked his lips.

Nan's expression darkened with concern for the condemned man. "And you'd like table seventeen, as usual?"

"If it's free," Graham said. He could already see it was set for two.

The server nodded to a male colleague, who then nodded to another, and together they headed into the kitchen. When they barged back through the swing door, each carried a full-sized fire extinguisher. They set them next to table seventeen on either side of the chair Graham normally sat in. One of the canisters, Graham noticed, had a yellow label.

"Wait, is that a wet chemical extinguisher?" he asked, frowning.

"Khun Thongsong ordered us to be prepared for all eventualities," the server said politely.

Graham couldn't help laughing for a moment, then explained to Laura. "It contains water and various types of potassium powder used for high-temperature fires."

"Sounds like a sensible precaution," she said, taking a photo of this improvised safety setup. Two other couples, waiting for their starters, glanced over, amused. Graham ordered a pot of restorative jasmine tea, while Laura had a Thai beer poured for her. "Put it this way," she said, jumping back into their discussion about Freddie without preamble, "if you arrest him, he'll become your archnemesis." Graham's mouth twisted, and he raised his hands to wave away her idea. But Laura was having none of it. "No, I'm serious. When he's onto something, Freddie's the veritable 'dog with a bone.'"

"More like a gerbil with an especially annoying face."

"David..." Laura warned.

"And no writing talent."

"He's *helped* you in the past." Graham raised an eyebrow. "Well, sort of, and probably will again if you two can work things out. I thought after the successful review of the Sampson's Leap case, things would get better. He's not all bad, not really. He's annoying and inappropriate, but he could become an ally."

"Look, it's really up to him," Graham said. "I won't make things any worse. How about that?"

At least partly mollified, Laura nodded. The double kitchen doors opened to reveal a waiter in a beekeeper's outfit, carefully carrying a tray.

"You alright in there?" Graham asked, grinning.

"No money for hazmat suit," the waiter said as he set the tray down gingerly. "Nearest thing."

"Any advice before I start?"

The waiter reached into his jacket for a slip of paper. "Owner Khun Thongsong says, 'The explosion will be bad, but the resulting black hole will be much worse. Farewell and enjoy.'" The server stared at the note, then looked at Graham through a layer of mesh. "What's it meaning?"

"I suppose we'll see." Graham reached for his fork, the cue for the waiter to scuttle away. "By the way, we found a body today."

"Oh?"

"In the attic of the White House Inn. Freddie doesn't know. But Mrs. Taylor does. I'm surprised he didn't hear her scream. It's been lying there for years."

Laura banged down her beer. "And you didn't think to tell me this earlier?"

"Strictly speaking, I shouldn't be telling you *now*. We think it's been there for about forty years. Marcus called in an archaeologist. It was buried in a block of concrete." Aromatic beyond belief, the curry was a rich yellow broth swimming with large shrimp and chunks of Thai aubergine.

"Well, who is it?"

"No idea. Some guy. Probably related to the gun we found in a drawer."

"A gun?"

"Uh-huh. That's what all the fuss was about with Freddie. He heard about the gun and was fishing for more. Marcus is doing some urgent prelims. He'll try to get the remains to the lab tonight. They'll start decomposing rapidly now that they're exposed to the air." As Graham leaned down to inhale, the chilli fumes hovering above the plate seared his nostrils. By the time he'd swallowed his first forkful, tears had begun; five minutes later, pounding water but undefeated, Graham hoarsely offered Laura a bite.

"I think I'd rather sit on the grass at Chornobyl and have a sandwich."

"It's very tasty," he croaked.

"It's wildly unsafe. They should keep only a tiny sample and lock it away in a lab somewhere. Perhaps Marcus could oblige."

"Where's your sense of adv . . ." Graham started, but the need to draw cool air over his tongue took precedence.

"Adventure? I'm with *you*, aren't I?" Laura laughed. "That's adventure aplenty, thank you very much." She returned to a subject more pressing. "But this body, what are you going to do?"

"We have to wait for Marcus to complete his investigations. I'm a bit worried about him, to be honest. He's looking tired. I think he's feeling the loss of Roach a bit. He says he wants to keep going for a while yet. To give his favourite pinot vines a year or two more to mature in the Napa Valley before he visits, he says, but I think he's feeling his age a little."

The waiter returned with more water, asking anxiously for the fourth time, "Ambulance?"

"I told you, it's delicious," Graham insisted, pushing away his empty plate.

Blinking in disbelief, the waiter withdrew and returned with the bill. Next to the mints lay a small, clear crystal alongside an improvised "Get Well Soon" card. The crystal sat atop a small, red-velvet drawstring pouch, the fabric reminding Graham of that used to disguise the concrete block in Mrs. Taylor's attic. "From Khun Thongsong," the waiter explained. "To welcome you to the Order of the Perfumed Jewel." He bowed courteously, a foot removed from the table, apparently afraid to stand any closer. "He is on holiday in Ireland, but he texted every five minutes to see if you were still alive."

"A very thoughtful host." Graham paid the bill and rose with Laura. "Would you thank him for me?"

"I wish you good fortune in the black hole!" the waiter said as the couple left arm in arm, unaware that the entire cooking crew of the Bangkok Palace had left the sanctuary of their kitchen. Shaking their heads in disbelief, the crew congregated at the restaurant window to peek through the bamboo blinds and watch the mad Englishman and his pretty girlfriend saunter to their car.

CHAPTER FIFTEEN

STRIDING DOWN THE rain-soaked path from the church to the meeting hall, flanked on one side by ivy and old stone, Reverend Bright reviewed his must-do list. Once this upcoming meeting concluded and the details of the Harding-Wentworth wedding were finalised, he had two calls to make. One to a parishioner, recently widowed, and the other to his tax accountant, ceaselessly scrupulous. After completing both tasks, he had some free time until he had to drive the choir to their concert in St. Helier at six.

"Free" didn't really mean free. It just meant he had time to attend to the myriad of items on his "not-necessarily-today" to-do list that included sermon prep, fundraising, and choosing the dates for next year's church events. Never a dull day, Vicar.

Wait, had he brought the wedding insurance and legal paperwork with him? He stopped by a headstone—lichen-spattered and green-wreathed—to find the papers in his folio. "Okay, good," he told himself. "I'm still with it after all."

"Good morning! You must be Reverend Bright!" called out a middle-aged woman in a striped, cotton dress and straw hat as he approached the church hall.

"Yes, that's right. Joshua Bright," he replied, holding out his hand. "And you are . . . ?"

"Rosemary Harding, mother of the bride and mother-in-law-to-be," the woman said.

"Ah." It wasn't the first time Reverend Bright had discussed wedding arrangements with the parents of the happy couple in attendance, especially if they were paying for it, but he did find it set a tone, one that required a certain deftness on his part.

"Now, I know I'm not late, which means you're mad keen to get them married, aren't you?" he said with a smile, bringing out a big iron key.

"Can't *wait*!" Rosemary blurted out, beaming. "Been looking forward to this for a very long time. Ah, here they are."

Janice and Jack swung open the church lychgate and slowly walked up the path to the church entrance. They glanced around them, confused, until they saw Rosemary and the reverend, who waited while they caught up with them.

"And the young couple too, I hope?" Reverend Bright chuckled, his eyes searching them both. "Excited?"

If anything, the couple seemed slightly worn out. "Definitely," Janice said, more with determination than dewy-eyed anticipation.

"Super stoked. Just hoping things go nice and smoothly," said Jack, putting his arm around Janice.

"Of course they will!" Rosemary pronounced. "I'm sure Reverend Bright has done a million of these, haven't you?"

"Maybe only *half* a million," the reverend allowed. "I've been doing this for over thirty years, and that's sufficiently long for plenty of Jersey folk to fall in love. Let's go to my office."

Reverend Bright walked them to a side door, and soon they found themselves in a sunny, comfortable room. Floral soft furnishings and dark oak dominated the décor, making the room warm and inviting. Bright caught sight of himself in the mirror he used to check his garments before a service. He suppressed a wince. The sun shone unrelentingly, cruelly casting shadows across his face, deepening his lines and making him craggy. The vicar gestured to a deeply cushioned, comfortable armchair. "Please, Mrs. Harding."

"Thank you, Vicar." Rosemary swept her skirt behind her legs and sat down, her handbag upright in her lap, her bottom crushed into the crease between the seat of the chair and its back.

Reverend Bright gestured to a sofa from the same set as the chair. "The happy couple . . ." Janice and Jack sat also, bobbing a little as the springs accommodated their joint weight.

"I simply *love* weddings," Rosemary said. "I've seen our old VHS tape of the Royal Weddings compilation I don't know how many times—"

"Nobody can count that high, Mum," said Janice.

"—so I know *exactly* what to do."

Bright raised a finger. "And so do I. Let's run through my list."

"Yeah, and Mum, remember?" Janice said. "All the ways the royal couples are *different* from Jack and me?"

Jack piped up. "Like, our preference for keeping things . . ."

"Small," Janice said, "with maybe . . ."

"Just us and some friends . . ."

"A few dozen people . . ."

"And not a lot of fuss."

"Oh, it's no fuss, dear!" Rosemary said, proud of her self-declared confidence in matters matrimonial.

Before Reverend Bright could even speak a word, Rosemary was listing the bold, even ambitious elements which comprised, in her view, "the perfect wedding." Janice and her husband-to-be looked on with silent, practiced patience; nothing of Rosemary's performance was unexpected, but all of it was unwelcome, a festival of second-guessing and interference that couldn't end quickly enough.

Rosemary Harding had insisted on coming early to Jersey to supervise the wedding plans personally. "I'll even get on a plane to visit you. And you know how I hate planes!" she had cried. Janice and Jack had simply been unable to shake her off.

"I mean, at the last royal wedding, there were six *hundred* guests!" she exclaimed, turning to Reverend Bright. "As befit such a grand occasion."

"Exactly," Janice said, hoping to press home the point. "Let the extent of the arrangements match the proportions of the event. In our case . . ."

"Small is beautiful," Jack said, returning to one of their themes.

"Not everyone can manage six hundred invitations, of course," said Rosemary, speaking as though she hadn't heard them. "Or even a couple of dozen," she added glumly. Janice's mum had been as disappointed at her eldest daughter's lack of ambition concerning the scope of her wedding and the number of guests as she might have been if Janice had told her she'd opted to study cosmetology instead of neuroscience. It had quite taken the imperiousness out of her for a few days.

"Forty-five," Janice corrected. "Small enough to get married on the beach even."

"The *beach*?" Rosemary shrieked, appalled. "Surrounded by . . . litter? Rotting fish? Seagulls pecking at the ladies' hats? I think not," she said, leaning into the vicar in hope of support. He sensibly kept out of it, happy to have a solid booking, the requisite fee, and of course, the chance to marry a delightful couple.

"Mum," Janice said, a tiny growl creeping into her tone, "these details are decided. They cannot be changed. The invitations were sent out weeks ago. Can we move on?"

"Yes, but to what?" Rosemary said next. Reverend Bright suppressed an eye roll. "Happy-clappy music and guitars? Some folk nonsense about overcoming oppression and smoking whacky-backy?"

"There are no guitars. And they're singing classical, Mum, for heaven's sake."

"Bach," Jack underlined. "Traditional, remember? You know how you like that."

"Very beautiful," Janice said.

"And nearly inaudible," Rosemary shot back. "*Four* choristers? Ridiculous." She suddenly clutched her handbag to her chest as though she suspected that Jack, or the vicar, maybe even Janice herself, might steal it.

Reverend Bright felt it prudent to interject before relations deteriorated further. "I sense that you're a big fan of the royal family, Mrs. Harding?"

"Of their *weddings*," Rosemary specified. "I'll admit I was *captivated* by

Charles and Diana in eighty-one. Sad how it all worked out, but the ceremony was unforgettable! I thought Kate's dress rather plain though." She turned down the corners of her mouth. "And as for—"

"Right, Vicar, let's move on, shall we?" Even Jack was getting testy.

"Well, I hope you'll forgive our particular venue its modesty," Reverend Bright joked. "We can't compete with Westminster Abbey, but St. Andrew's can seat around a hundred and twenty in the church, so the planned forty-five guests will be no problem at all."

"Forty-five," Rosemary muttered again, still disappointed.

"Good. Plenty of room to spread out," said Janice, determined to rise above her mother's negativity. Having conceded to Rosemary's wishes for a church wedding, Janice was insistent that it would henceforth follow *her* plan, long considered and carefully tailored to her and Jack's wishes. "So, we've decided on music and readings. Here's a list of . . ."

"The 'Widor Toccata'!" Rosemary exclaimed. She raised her hands and wiggled her fingers, comically emulating the skills necessary to play the famously busy, celebratory piece. "You *have* to!"

Sensibly soothing her temper, Janice proceeded to remind her mother about the wedding details for what felt like the twentieth time. "We haven't hired an organist, Mum. Remember? We said it would feel too formal."

"But the *spectacle!*" insisted Rosemary. "The tingle down the spine!"

Jack jumped in with a smile. "Well, we're getting married, finally. I'm already pretty tingly about that."

"Me too," agreed Janice. "Plenty of tingles to go around."

Reverend Bright was always ready to throw some work his organist's way, but he saw in the eyes and set jaws of this family group that his main role was to ease the tension and lower everyone's stress levels. He would, in the final analysis, most certainly side with the young couple, but he would attempt to do so while not alienating this overly invested mother of the bride.

"No one could hope to make up a bride's mind for her," the vicar said, somehow avoiding criticism of Rosemary's graceless insisting, "but I was at a performance in Chichester Cathedral just the other week, and all the music was *a capella*. You know, without instruments. Just natural human voices in that remarkable space. It was exceptionally beautiful. Talk about tingles,'" he said encouragingly. The story was only partly true—a rapper had been involved—but as a veteran of such things, Bright knew that bridging a widening gulf between mother and daughter was worth a white lie.

"But the 'choir' only has four singers!" Rosemary complained. "And please don't tell me you've forgotten the trumpeter for the processional?"

Janice went through the setup again as patiently as she could. "Look, Mum, no organist, no trumpeter. Just a straightforward choral piece arranged and sung by our friend, supported by four choristers."

"But what about music? You're not going to have recorded music, are you?

That awkward pause while the congregation waits for someone to press the right button then gets the wrong one, and instead of Bach's 'Jesu, Joy of Man's Desiring,' we get Kylie Minogue singing 'I should be so lucky, lucky, lucky.'" Rosemary shuddered. "Sherenice had that at her wedding, and you know how that turned out."

CHAPTER SIXTEEN

"NO, MUM, NOTHING like that. We have a string quartet. They're reuniting for us specially as a sort of thank you to Gorey police for rescuing them. Well, Roachie and Bazza found them. They were trapped under the castle a few years ago."

Janice's words seemed to have no effect. Rosemary's arguments continued unabated. "But you only get married once!" she said. "And the church is huge. Have you seen that vaulted ceiling? It's the most special day of your life! And that deserves pomp! Circumstance! A volley of rifles! Isn't that right, Reverend?"

"Er, well, a volley salute is usually performed at funerals, but I take your point. However—"

Jack interrupted. He sensed that if Janice had had three older sisters, her mother would by now have purged herself of the Royal Wedding bug. As it was, all Rosemary's unrealistic, intrusive expectations fell on his fiancée as the first daughter to be wed, and whose plans and protestations at her mother's objections had over the past months fallen on deaf ears. Jack's sympathies lay firmly with his future wife, and he would support her as he should. "For us, Rosemary," he said, "'special' means 'the way we'd like it to be.'"

"But . . ."

"A wedding is a family event," Jack stated firmly, "and it's a simple fact, a power law, that families will argue in inverse proportion to the number of weddings, funerals, and divorces they experience. This is our first," he reminded Rosemary. "And for Janice and me, it will be our last. We will have our wedding the way we wish it." Rosemary, unused to being confronted by anyone, not least her beloved future son-in-law, was momentarily stunned.

"Very nice choices of readings," Reverend Bright said, quickly exploiting Rosemary's breathlessness and shock. "Especially the reading you've chosen,

'Song of Solomon.'" He cleared his throat and quoted with relish. "'Thy cheeks are comely with rows of jewels, thy neck with chains of gold.' Just beautiful, isn't it?"

"At least it's traditional," Rosemary offered, recovering her voice, albeit sulkily. "There's people quoting science fiction, the Teletubbies, and all sorts at weddings these days."

"No one's quoting the Teletubbies at our wedding, Mum. Don't exaggerate," Janice said gently, kindlier than she felt, and, in Reverend Bright's opinion, more patiently than her mother deserved. Janice placed a hand on Rosemary's arm and smiled at her. Her mother sniffed. A hint of a smile fluttered on her lips.

By now, Jack looked mostly poleaxed by the whole exchange, so the vicar blurted out, "I had someone quote a stretch of Michael Jackson the other week. Someone else performed Tina Turner. 'Simply the Best' it was, I seem to remember. And a couple of years ago, we had a funeral at the crematorium, an older fella," he continued, turning to black humour to ease the tension further. "And when they were sliding him in, do you know what music they requested?"

Snapping his fingers, Jack was frustrated that it wouldn't come. "Janice?"

"Nothing yet."

Grinning, the vicar sang softly, "Smoke gets in your eyes . . ."

It was a bad joke, a dad joke at best, but they all laughed. Even Rosemary. The tension dispelled, and with the mother of the bride subdued, if only temporarily, Reverend Bright signed his paperwork, and within moments, the formal part was done.

"I suppose you'll be off to sample cakes or some such?" Bright said, rising. The Harding-Wentworths were pleasant enough people, but the calls to the widower and the accountant were pressing. Taking his cue, his visitors rose also and allowed themselves to be escorted out to the church path.

"There's an idea!" Rosemary exclaimed, appealing to the sky. "A traditional three-tiered wedding cake! With dried fruit! Not the strangest of expectations, now, is it?"

"I told you, Rosemary, my father is allergic to raisins," Jack teased her. "And my mother's gluten-free." He and Janice had decided on the cake ages ago but had chosen to keep its nontraditional details to themselves. They suspected, rightly, that Rosemary wouldn't approve of the layers of chocolate sponge, homemade fudge, and strawberry compôte that would be liberally covered in Swiss chocolate French buttercream pâte à bombe icing.

"There'll be a healthy vibe to the dessert," Janice added.

"It's a selection of fruit," Jack said. Both of them kept a straight face.

"Fruit!" Rosemary cried. Reverend Bright backed away, disappearing into the church as this new potential for disagreement raised itself. Jack and Janice exchanged looks, wry smiles on their faces. "Slices of orange!" Rosemary exclaimed. "Like it's a hundred years ago or halftime at the football!"

Jack pulled Janice to him and whispered in her ear, "When are we going to tell her?"

"Let's give it a little longer, eh?" Janice kissed Jack on the cheek, and holding hands, they walked down the church path, her mother following them as she continued to exclaim about the aberration of a lack of wedding cake.

"As we've said several times, Mum," Janice called out, "fruit at a wedding is considered auspicious in many parts of the world."

"Like where?"

"India, for one."

"*India*?! But people will be expecting..."

"There's a reason for it," Jack said.

"For fruit? What exactly would that be then?"

"It's good for blood flow."

"What?"

"For blood flow, Mum. You know..." Janice raised her eyebrows and pursed her lips, a sly smile dancing across them. There was a pause before Rosemary gathered her daughter's meaning. She gasped and clutched her handbag to her.

"Well, really!" Rosemary huffed. "Fruit!" She opened her mouth to say more, but a firm, female hand grasped her wrist.

"People will be expecting me to bring you down the station on a charge of interfering in a wedding if you don't hold your noise soon, Mum. I *promise*!"

Rosemary merely shrugged. "You've been promising to take me there ever since they made you a sergeant."

"The other day, I watched Jan arrest three people for affray," Jack said. "Super impressive."

"Of course she is! This is my Janice!" The wedding was forgotten for a second. Janice relinquished her mother's wrist, and Rosemary put an arm around her daughter's shoulder. "Who did she arrest, anyway?" Janice's mother sensed a story that might just bear repeating to her gardening circle. "And why didn't you help her?" she added, glaring at Jack, suddenly protective. Rosemary believed in the traditional roles of men and women. She didn't hold with "women's lib." It was yet another point of contention between her and her eldest daughter.

"I would have if there was any requirement for it, but Jan is perfectly capable. She didn't need my help. Three lads were fighting outside the pub," explained Jack. "Barnwell hadn't even left the station yet, but Jan's there, wading in to break things up on her evening off. I tell you, she's got a commanding vocal presence."

"They started free, they ended up arrested, that's all. Anyone with powers of detention can do that," Janice said.

"Yeah, but they were punching each other when you arrived," Jack reminded her.

"Leaping into the middle of... a *punch-up*? On Jersey? You could have been hurt, you silly girl! Very unladylike." Rosemary had always regarded Janice's choice of career with some distaste, but living on the mainland, she had mostly been able to ignore it. That hadn't stopped her, though, from regaling her friends about her sergeant daughter who was a whizz on the computers, searching out criminal masterminds and bringing them down with her forensic policing skills and a Bluetooth mouse.

Every word from her mother raised Janice's temperature—*silly* was bad, but *girl* was worse. "I wasn't about to fight anyone, Mum. Just shouted a lot and then hauled the three of them away."

"*And* gave first aid to the unlucky one who got the brunt of it all," said Jack.

Rosemary shuddered again, the frames of her glasses shaking slightly. "Drunkards and fighting and dressing wounds . . . You know, I never understood . . ." she said, beginning what Janice knew would be act one, scene one of her mother's ongoing, one-woman play, *My Daughter and Other Needless Tragedies*.

"Jack, I'm off back to work."

"Yep, me too. You alright, Rosemary, or would you like me to accompany you to your B&B?"

"I can find it, dear, thank you," Rosemary said, unusually perceptive for once. "See you for dinner like we said?" She kissed them both, stretching on tiptoes to reach Jack's cheek. She waved goodbye, leaving Janice and Jack watching her toddling down the sleepy, tree-lined lane towards the beach, holding her handbag in the crook of her arm.

"How does she do it?" Janice said.

"Do what?"

"How does she suck the energy out of me and seemingly plug it into her veins? Look at her go! Full of vim and vigour while I feel in need of a long nap."

"Perhaps it's a mother-daughter wedding thing."

"Perhaps."

After leaving the Harding-Wentworths, Reverend Bright found a moment of peace in the church's sanctuary. Meeting the mother of the bride was always an experience, although not all were as overbearing and needy as Mrs. Rosemary Harding. The sunlit late morning and the tall, centuries-old stained glass casting hazy spectra on the pews reminded him to slow down, to take a moment. Sometimes he mused for a while, but today, there just wasn't time to tarry.

For his brief moment of peace, Reverend Bright allowed himself just to be present there in the familiar, glowing space, watching dust motes suspended in the sun's rays. But then he let himself imagine the silliest thing he'd heard in a long time and managed a little chuckle as he headed through to the office. "People quoting the Teletubbies in their marriage vows . . . Whatever next?"

CHAPTER SEVENTEEN

DR. TOMLINSON GLANCED at his watch and then at the arrivals board. Good. The flight from Gatwick was on time. Since Jim Roach had left for the Met, Tomlinson had worked alone in the forensic lab while also fulfilling his regular pathologist duties. He quickly realised that it was too much. "Age catches up with one eventually," he had told Francine.

Francine was his girlfriend. He wasn't too old to call her that. And he made sure they enjoyed life. "At our age, we need to make the most of our time, and I don't have any at the moment."

Acknowledging he was feeling his age was a big admission. Marcus prided himself on his athletic abilities and being more active than men half his age. But he had a professional respect for the inevitable effects of aging, even if he was reluctant to accept them for himself.

Realising he needed help, Tomlinson made a few calls and now found himself awaiting the person he hoped would give him more opportunities to enjoy life—life with Francine, with wine. Heck, even a nap in the afternoon would be nice. Yesterday was long, with more work ahead, and he eagerly looked forward to sharing his responsibilities.

Jersey Airport wasn't large. The flow of crowds came in waves as planes landed and the passengers disembarked. The pathologist had arrived amidst a lull, and after checking the state of play concerning flight EJ203, Marcus ordered himself a coffee and sat down to wait. As he sipped his drink, he scrolled through his phone, looking at the photographs of the remains they had unearthed the day before.

He had spent the previous evening taking samples and measurements, then overseen the extraction of the body from its bed of concrete prior to its transport to his mortuary. There, the remains could be protected from further degradation by the sterile, climate-controlled environment and with the liberal use of chemicals. With Dr. Papadopoulos's help, the extraction had gone well, and the body had been moved almost entirely intact.

Marcus had never had such a case in his nearly fifty-year career. Despite examining countless bodies in that time, he had never encountered one squirrelled away in concrete. For the person he was meeting, he was certain the same was true. For them, the case they were about to embark upon might prove career-defining.

Exhumations of any kind were extremely rare. Marcus had only been involved in two. In one instance, a family accused a care home of the misidentification of a deceased relative, suspecting that the burial of the wrong person had taken place. Marcus was able to prove the accusers wrong, and no further action was taken. In the second instance, where a family sought to repatriate remains to the deceased's home country, he attended the exhumation and confirmed the identification of the remains before release. In each case, there had been coffins and the exhumations performed within months of death. The extent of Tomlinson's work had been to take DNA samples and report the findings.

It was more common for bodies to be referred to him following some period of decomposition. It was not unusual for someone to die alone and remain undiscovered for a while. Marcus would be required to determine the cause of death in those cases. The identity of the person was almost always known or suspected.

Drowning victims weren't rare during his long career either. On occasion, he was tasked with identifying bodies of fishermen or swimmers washed ashore. He would use either dental records or other DNA evidence in these cases.

The remains found in the concrete at the White House Inn were a different proposition altogether. He needed to perform tests and procedures to determine the cause of death, extract DNA for help in identifying the man, perform ballistics on the gun, and examine the body and belongings for any other evidence that might help Inspector Graham and his team solve this very cold case.

Alexander Papadopoulos, accustomed to centuries-old remains, had been ecstatic to find the body in such good condition, especially how it had held up after being moved. Marcus, his experience confined to working with recently expired corpses, was more challenged. But it was a case he was pleased to pursue with the help of the young person whose plane, according to the announcement to which he was now listening, had just landed.

Marcus looked out of the window at the aircraft cruising into view. He watched it park, waved into place by a marshal, their gender extinguished by an excess of hi-vis gear. The door behind the cockpit opened. Steps were wheeled and secured into place.

Passengers hauling children, backpacks, and carry-on luggage, much of which seemed to be in excess of the cabin's weight restriction, exited the plane as Marcus attempted to identify his new helpmate. He had interviewed her via video and checked out her social media, so he knew what she looked like. But his eyes weren't so good at this distance, and there were a lot of potentials. He watched as the first passengers reached the terminal, then headed to the gate.

As they walked through the terminal door, it was obvious from their attire that the vast majority of passengers were tourists. Marcus could see no one he recognised, his heart beating faster with every person who passed him, citing no recognition. After the last straggler drifted away, Marcus glanced at his watch and the arrivals board. Maybe she hadn't made it. Sighing, he pulled out his phone.

"Dr. Tomlinson!" Walking towards him, a tall woman—slim, brunette—rolled a large suitcase behind her. She was wearing a T-shirt and jeans. On her feet were deep blue ballerina flats. At this distance, she looked like Laura's younger, darker sister. The woman strode up the tunnel as Tomlinson waited. Three feet from him, she stuck out her hand.

"Good morning, Dr. Tomlinson. I'm so happy to be here."

"And I'm very happy to see *you*, Fiona."

CHAPTER EIGHTEEN

"SO SORRY IF I worried you. My luggage was too big for the overhead. It was stored in the back of the cabin so I had to wait for everyone to get off before I could retrieve it."

Marcus laughed. "You did worry me a bit. But you're here now, and that's the main thing." He took the handle of her rolling case. "Here, let's go to the car and I'll take you to your digs. I hope you've come ready to work because I've got something special for you. Just popped up yesterday. Literally."

The automatic glass doors opened with a shush in front of them, and they stepped out into the bright, warm sunshine. Fiona gazed at the cloudless sky. "As we flew in, the island looked beautiful, but I can't wait to get to work."

They found Tomlinson's old silver Mercedes at the furthestmost point of the car park. "It's good for me to stretch my legs," Marcus said as he lifted Fiona's bag into the boot of his car. "Jump in, and I'll take you to your flat." He checked his watch again. "We've got plenty of time before the tide goes out."

Fiona looked at him askew. "What's that?"

Marcus chuckled. "You'll see."

A few minutes later, he smoothly spun the car's steering wheel as he expertly navigated Jersey's winding, narrow roads. Fiona sat beside him looking out of the window, drinking in the view. He had purposefully taken her the coastal route, doing everything he could as a good host and a hopeful mentor to imprint the delights of the island in Fiona's mind.

"When you're settled in, you'll have to come for dinner. Francine, my girlfriend, is a wonderful cook."

"Sounds fab," Fiona said. "I'm delighted to be working with you, you know. When I heard from Bert you were looking for someone, I jumped at the chance.

Did you know I worked with him and Inspector Graham on the "screaming beauty" case?"

"Of course I did, Fiona." Marcus took his eyes off the road for a second and winked at her. "I did my homework. Bert Hatfield is an old, trusted colleague, and because he'd worked with David in the past, I gave him a call to see if he knew of anyone. He mentioned you immediately. He told me you'd kept in touch throughout university and medical school, said you were interested in becoming a pathologist, and here we are."

"And here we are," Fiona repeated, turning her face to the warm sun. "Where are we going, anyway?"

"Ah-ha! I heard from Bert you were up for an adventure, so I thought I might give you one of the best." When they reached St. Helier, Marcus pulled into a parking space on the cobblestone seafront. "We'll leave the car here." He placed his "doctor on call" card on the dashboard.

Fiona giggled. "Should you be doing that?"

"Not really, but it's technically true. Plus, I know an inspector who'll help us out if I get dragged across the carpet." He led Fiona a few yards down a concrete ramp to a bus stop. Fiona frowned. Marcus smiled at her confusion. "It'll be a bit of a squeeze with your luggage, but there's no better way to travel. Ah, here she is."

Fiona turned to look out to sea. A brightly coloured blue ferry was coming in, but as soon as it left the water, she saw it had wheels. It covered the ground like a bus.

"This is the amphibious ferry. It'll take us over the water to your digs."

"What? Over there?" Fiona pointed to the ruins in the distance.

"Elizabeth Castle, yes. There's an apartment there. I thought you might like to stay in it for a while. You can walk along the causeway when the tide's out or take the ferry at any time. Francine was a bit worried it might be too remote. You're welcome to say no, and we'll find something else, but I snagged the flat while I could because it's very popular."

Fiona's eyes gleamed with excitement. "I'm going to stay there? On an island? In my very own castle? Looking out to sea?"

"That's right. It's rather cool, isn't it?"

"I'll say!"

"I can drop you off, let you get settled in, and come back when you're ready if you like."

"Oh no, I can explore later. I'd like to see the lab if I may and be briefed on this very interesting case you mentioned."

Marcus exhaled. Relief flooded his body. He hadn't realised how much he had enjoyed having a young, curious, hardworking mentee until Roach left. Fortunately, Fiona's enthusiasm appeared to match her predecessor's. Which was just as well. They had their work cut out for them.

"Alright, if you're sure, we can go straight to the lab, and I'll introduce you to Mr. X."

Fiona raised her eyebrows. "Mr. X, eh? Sounds intriguing."
"Oh, he's intriguing alright."

CHAPTER NINETEEN

GRAHAM HUMMED SOMETHING operatic and triumphal as he pushed open the doors to the Gorey police station. "A palace," he said to no one in particular as he breezed in, "dedicated to the pursuit of truth and justice." He hung up his coat and greeted Janice and Barnwell, who were already at work. He glanced at his watch. It had just gone eleven. "Morning, all." Carmen trotted up to him, her lead in her mouth. Her big, brown eyes looked up at Graham hopefully.

"Not just yet, Carmen." Graham bent down to give her a series of pats and scrubs. "I'll take you later." Carmen must have understood because she good-naturedly wandered off and curled up under Barnwell's desk for a snooze.

Barnwell manned reception while Janice, already exhausted by the meeting at the church, attempted to ignore texts from her mother by attending to the following month's shift roster. She would be on honeymoon for part of it, and the Gorey team would need backup from headquarters.

"Morning, sir," they chorused in unison.

"You're in a very chirpy mood this morning, sir," Barnwell said.

"And so I should be. I have a great team, and we've got this knotty cold case to get our teeth into. My office, five minutes." It wasn't a question.

But then the inspector's phone rang. His hands full with his briefcase, jacket, and keys, Graham could either open his office door or answer the phone. He decided on the former, so the call had to wait. "Hang on, hang on," he said, dropping his stuff on his desk. *Click.* "DI Graham here."

"David!" came a familiar voice.

"Ah, Marcus." Graham flipped on the kettle and flopped into his seat. "How're things going?"

"With Mr. X?"

"Is that what we're calling him?"

"That's what I'm calling him for now. I need the go-ahead for some lab work," Tomlinson said. "We'll have to forward some of this stuff to Dr. Weiss in Southampton, and you know how the bean counters make us justify every *minute* on the UV spectroscope."

"Go ahead," said Graham. "I'll keep things straight with Finance. How are you doing without Roach?"

"I miss him, of course. He was a fine young man." There was a pause as Tomlinson remembered his former protégé, now living the high life policing the mean streets of London.

"He was," Graham said. "Still is. Thanks for looking after him while he was here. You were a great fount of knowledge and a fine mentor to him. He wouldn't be where he is now if it weren't for you. You know how much I appreciate that."

"Will you get a replacement, do you think?"

Graham pursed his lips. "Hmm, not sure. I'd like to see how we do, just the three of us, for a while. It'll save a bit of money that I can put towards training or some new equipment. But probably not for long. We need some resilience in the team, and with just us three, it leaves us a bit thin. We'd be underwater in no time if anyone was put out of action or wanted a change of scenery."

"Have there been any rumbles? Anyone wanting a transfer?"

"I don't think Barnwell's thinking of going anywhere, but with Janice's wedding coming up, she might feel like a change, and then we'll have to take action PDQ."

"Hmm, Roach taught me a valuable new skill."

"Really?" Graham asked, surprised.

"*Delegation*, dear chap! *Del-e-gation*! I've recruited a new assistant, someone to replace young Roach. She's just looking around her new flat. Her name's Fiona Henson. She worked with you on the "screaming beauty" case. I tracked her down via Bert Hatfield. Do you remember her?"

It didn't take more than a few nanoseconds for Graham to pluck Fiona's name and her contribution to the case from his memory. "Rather. She was the reason we cracked it. She made the connection to the lottery ticket."

"That's the lass."

"Fabulous. I'll meet her when I come down for the postmortem. What time will you start?"

"Four p.m. on the dot. Come earlier if you want a cup of tea beforehand. It'll be a curious one. Not sure how the body will react, but we'll do our best."

"See you then."

CHAPTER TWENTY

JANICE AND BARNWELL waited for Graham's call with Tomlinson to end and then assembled in Graham's office as instructed. Steam rose from Graham's teacup.

"Right, team, so what do we think happened at the White House Inn? We have a body concealed in cement and abandoned in the attic for some unspecified amount of time. We have a gun and some items that presumably belonged to the body. What can we deduce?"

"Well, sir, we can definitely date the scene to sometime after 1979 because, like you said, that's when *The Hitchhikers Guide to the Galaxy* came out *and* that particular book had a publish date of 12 October 1979 on the copyright page. It is a first edition. I took a look before it went off with the forensics guys," Barnwell said, proud of his initiative.

"Good work, Constable. So, we can set an outer boundary at the end of 1979."

"But that still gives us decades to play with," Janice said.

"Right, but we know that Mrs. T. took over the hotel in September 1982. She denies any knowledge of the body. She told me she hadn't been in the attic for years. I think we can assume that this happened before her time."

"So, we're looking at the period from October 1979 to September 1982," Janice summed up.

"A period when the hotel was owned and run by a Miss Lovell, deceased," Graham added.

Barnwell piped up. "Could it be, sir, that someone killed him, decided to bury him on the spot, shoved the belongings in the drawer, and scarpered?"

"That's one theory, Constable."

"But how would they do that without being seen? I mean, that was a lot of cement they had to mix," Janice said.

"And all the way up those stairs 'n' all. Would need to be strong."

"And determined," Janice added.

"Well, if you've just killed someone, I suppose you would be." Barnwell was thoughtful. He stared at the floor as he imagined the scene.

"They'd need to have time, sir. To do the work I mean. How long would it take?" Janice asked Graham.

"They could bury him during a night, I should imagine. The cement would take a while to dry, but if no one was going up there, it would work out with a bit of luck."

"But why were his belongings, and the gun, shoved in a drawer?" Janice waggled her head from side to side. "Seems a big oversight if you've just spent the night going to the effort of burying the body."

Barnwell had an idea. "Perhaps the murderer forgot them when they scarpered." He paused as he thought some more, and then raised his eyebrows as another idea came to him. "Maybe they thought if they shoved the belongings in the drawer, they'd be long gone before the items were found. I mean, maybe they just wanted to delay the body being discovered until they were far enough away that we couldn't catch them. Maybe the burying was just a delaying tactic, and it was dumb luck the body wasn't found until now."

Graham wasn't so sure. "Hmm, maybe. The effort they went to suggests to me that they didn't want it to be found for a very long time. I mean, burying a body in the attic is a bit like burying a body under the patio . . ."

"While you carry on living there," Janice said.

"Exactly, Sergeant. But let's keep an open mind on that. Both theories are valid."

"One thing that's bothering me, sir."

"Yes, Barnwell, out with it."

"It might be nothing, but . . ."

"Yes?"

"Well, that velvet covering. The thing that made it look like a sofa. It was sewn to fit. Someone must have made it special-like."

Graham's eyebrows shot up. "You're right, Barnwell. The person who buried him had to be a man given the physical effort required. But maybe a woman was involved somehow."

"I know! While the murderer was doing the heavy work, she was running up a little number with her Singer sewing machine!" Janice exclaimed.

"Isn't that a bit sexist?" Barnwell was disappointed in Janice. "Could easily have been a man. Even I've been known to do a bit of sewing here and there." Graham and Janice stared at him for a moment, processing this unanticipated piece of Barnwell knowledge.

"Right, Bazz, but we're talking 1982. It was different then. It's unlikely."

"He's right, though, Sergeant. It could have been a man, an enlightened one, perhaps."

"Yeah," Barnwell said. He pursed his lips, pleased to be supported. "Anyhow, we should follow the evidence, sir. That's what you always say, right?"

"Yes, Constable Barnwell. Let's focus on that timeline until Marcus gets back to us with some results. He successfully moved Mr. X to the mortuary last night and will be performing a postmortem this afternoon. He's also hired a new assistant from the mainland to help him." Janice and Barnwell exchanged looks. "She'll be taking over the responsibilities previously fulfilled by Sergeant Roach, so I'm hoping for some quick progress. But we need to do our bit while we're waiting. Any guesses as to what that might be?"

"Something to do with mispers, sir?" Janice ventured.

"Exactly, Sergeant. What can we do to push that along, eh?" Graham looked meaningfully over the rim of his teacup as he brought it to his lips.

Barnwell stiffened. "No," he said, the whites of his eyes showing.

"Yes, lad."

Barnwell shivered. "You're not really sending me down there again, are you?" He remembered past forays into the basement filing room. Remaining to be digitised were twenty-five large boxes of old police records, many of them unopened and unexplored.

Moving to calm the officer's nerves, Graham said, "It's a specific search this time."

"Last time was 'specific,'" Barnwell recalled, "and I was down there for eight hours."

"It's all terribly inefficient, I understand, but I can't think of another way. You look for files on missing persons registered with Jersey police over the past, oh I don't know, let's start with thirty years, fifteen years before and after the period we're looking at."

"*Thirty?*" Barnwell almost screeched before clearing his throat. "Ahem, thirty years, sir?" Graham stared back at him, unblinking. "I mean, it's a lot. A very lot."

"Yes, it is, Constable, but you're up to the challenge, aren't you? Or would you rather I do the searching, and you go to the postmortem in my place?"

Barnwell most definitely would not prefer that. He took a deep breath, straightened, and pushed his shoulders back. "No, sir. Yes, sir. I understand, sir."

"There can't be that many people who've gone missing on Jersey. It's a small place."

This didn't alleviate Barnwell's desire not to spend his day amid clouds of dust, looming darkness, poorly labelled files, and possibly the odd small rodent, but he considered the alternative. "Have we spoken to Mrs. Taylor some more, sir? Can she help?"

"She might, and we could. But that won't get you out of going down to the basement, Constable. Nice try though." Graham turned to his sergeant. "Sergeant Harding, cross-reference anything Barnwell might find with the PNC database."

"Yes, sir."

"Excellent. Off you go, then."

"Sir, so you're going to the postmortem?" Janice asked.

"I was planning to. Why, are you volunteering?"

"Thought I might, sir." Janice was standing very upright and staring straight ahead. "Not every day you get to observe one on a body so ancient." Graham paused as he considered this. "Okay, why not? Good experience for you. It's at four p.m. Full report on your observations by—"

"I'll get them to you today."

"Alright, Sergeant, if you're sure."

"I am, sir."

When they left Graham's office, the gloomy expression on Barnwell's face gave Janice a dark laugh. "Let's hope you find something, Bazz."

"Bet you a tenner it'll be a wild-goose chase."

"Yeah, maybe, but the boss wants it done. Might as well get it over with."

"Alright." Barnwell groaned, low and long, as though anticipating a twelve-hour patrol in the rain. "'If I die,'" he said dramatically, "'think only this of me . . .'"

"'That there's some corner of a police filing room that is forever England'? I daresay you'll survive. It is a post-war building, after all," Janice reminded him. As she shepherded Barnwell down the hallway to the door, rarely opened, that led to the basement, she awkwardly attempted to put her arm around his burly shoulder before giving up. Her arm simply wasn't long enough. "The electric lights might even be working again down there."

Another groan and Barnwell opened the door. Darkness loomed ahead of him.

"But, Jan, why do you want to go to a poxy postmortem? You don't normally do them."

"Stop yer stallin'. Get on down those stairs." Janice patted him on the shoulder, and Bazza reluctantly pushed off, descending the steps to begin his task.

CHAPTER TWENTY-ONE

"WE'VE MOVED THE REMAINS to the mortuary, but I want you to get a feel for the case." Marcus had driven Fiona to the White House Inn and, deciding not to trouble the front desk, led her up the back stairs to the attic. "This is where Mr. X was found."

Fiona looked around her at the attic, still tarped and draughty. She took in the motley collection of furniture and bric-a-brac that congregated in one corner. "We found a gun amongst all that lot," Tomlinson said. "An old one, along with some items that we think date from the eighties. There was a 1979 copy of *The Hitchhikers Guide to the Galaxy* amongst the things. It'll be part of our job to date the body. We don't know his name or how he died."

"Huh," was all Fiona said.

"Our man was over there." All that was left in the corner where Barnwell had stumbled upon the concrete grave were chunks of cement, broken bricks, and a pile of crumpled, faded velvet. "A chance find. They were examining the storm damage when a police officer got curious. The cement was well-made and dense. It protected the body from decay. It's in remarkable shape—you'll see when we get to the mortuary."

"How was he not found earlier? Did no one report him missing? Did no one wonder why this immovable object sat here for so long?"

Tomlinson shrugged. "Your guess is as good as mine. Out of sight, out of mind? Mrs. Taylor, the present hotel owner, claims she hasn't been up here in years. I guess no one else came up here much either."

"And due to minimal bacterial activity and the composition of the cement, any odour would be brief and faint."

"That's right."

"You mentioned Mrs. Taylor is the present owner. What about the former?"

"Long dead, so no help there."

"Curiouser and curiouser," Fiona said. She grinned at Tomlinson. "Let's go and see the main man, shall we?"

"Beautiful, isn't it?" Tomlinson said. Fiona stared out the side window as they drove to the mortuary, taking in the sights: the pretty, brightly painted buildings that bordered Gorey harbour, the wide open green fields, and clear, sandy beaches.

Fiona was a naturally pretty woman, with small features and straight, dark hair that she pinned off her face with a sparkly clip. Her plainspoken manner and unadorned appearance transmitted a no-nonsense approach that Marcus suspected would go down well, especially with Janice and Laura. Francine would appreciate her enthusiasm and energy. Graham would enjoy her intelligence. And he, Marcus Tomlinson, looked forward to benefitting from her willingness to get stuck in, literally and figuratively.

"It certainly is," Fiona replied. "How far is it? The mortuary."

Tomlinson smiled. "A few minutes, that's all.

When they got there, Marcus pushed open the doors for her and introduced Fiona to his mortuary assistant, Aidan, a big, bearded bear of a man with a plethora of tattoos. Aidan nodded a curt welcome and continued with his work cataloguing lab samples.

"A man of few words, Aidan. Great worker though. And a gentle giant. Perfect for what we do here," Tomlinson whispered. Raising his voice to a normal volume, Marcus added, "First, let's get you suited and booted. I'll show you where the gear's kept."

Once they had donned their paper suits, Marcus directed Fiona to the bank of drawers that lined one wall. "We'll have to get you put into the system," he murmured as he used his fingertip to unlock one of the drawers. A sound—a "clunk"—could be heard from deep inside the drawer as the mechanism unlocked and it opened. Fiona's eyes widened as the body slid into view in front of her. "Have a good look and tell me what you think."

"Wow, you were right. He *is* in good condition. Almost mummified." Fiona's eyes scanned the body.

"Already air exposure and movement have caused some deterioration. The rib cage is more concave, his facial features less distinct."

Fiona's eyes raked the body from top to bottom, taking in the arrangement of his limbs, facial features, height, and clothing. "Was he discovered in this position, with one arm raised and the other across his chest?"

"Yes. What does it suggest to you?"

"Hmm, either that he was buried in that position or rigor mortis had set in beforehand and there was no alternative."

"Agreed. Any preference for either theory?"

"I favour the latter."

"Why's that?"

"Because of this. Was it a rose at some point?" Fiona delicately pointed at the thorny stem that had been threaded beneath the man's palm lying across his chest.

"Yes," Tomlinson confirmed. "It certainly looks like it. The petals had disintegrated. But why does that make you believe rigor mortis had already set in?"

"Because unless he died clutching the rose like that, whoever buried him took care to put the rose there. That suggests consideration. If the body was still malleable, given that level of care, I would have expected them to lay this suspended arm across his chest if they could."

"You think the person burying him in concrete in an attic was being thoughtful?"

"Yes, but for what reason? Concern, respect, or . . ."

"Some diabolical purpose?" Tomlinson processed this new theory. It was unsettling.

Fiona moved on. "Hmm, the clothes aren't very helpful. This is a brand-name T-shirt. They've been around for years and still going strong. Quality brand. The jeans are jeans and the shoes are shoes. Can't see that they can tell us anything at the moment. Can we get DNA?"

"Yes, I'm hoping he's on the database. If not, it'll be like looking for a needle in a haystack. If we can't identify him, the police will have to search old missing persons records going back decades, following up on many lines of enquiry."

"What about the cause of death?"

"Well, that's also interesting. As I said, we found a gun among some effects in the attic. Maybe related, maybe not. But there's no sign of a bullet wound. The cause of death isn't immediately obvious to me. So that's our other challenge. I'm hoping the postmortem we're going to spend this afternoon performing might turn something up. The police certainly hope so."

"Well, you were right when you said you have an intriguing case. Shall we get to work?"

Marcus smiled. "I was hoping you'd say that."

"I'll make a start on his belongings."

"I think that would be excellent. We have an appointment with the ballistics centre in a couple of days, but for now, take a look at what the police found in his suitcase. It's over there." Tomlinson pointed to a metal counter on which lay several bags of items collected by Janice the day before. Next to them was a small, bright red suitcase.

"That was his case? Bit feminine for a man."

"It also looks older than the period we're considering. You might want to look it up. I'll leave you to it. Aidan will get you a password so you can access the computer systems."

"Leave it with me." Fiona donned a new pair of forensic gloves as Tomlinson returned to his office. He watched her through the glass as she carefully opened the bags and laid the items in them on the counter. But soon, Marcus's eyelids flickered, and his breathing slowed. Yesterday was catching up with him. In moments, he was quietly snoring.

The lab was almost silent as Fiona carefully catalogued all the items. Tapping their details into her tablet, she handled them as though they were delicate, precious, laying them side by side on the sterile metal counter as she processed them.

They didn't amount to much: a blue jacket, thin sweater, T-shirt, white vest, underpants, and socks. Fiona peered inside a tan leather wallet, but it was empty. Toiletries were limited to a disposable razor and a toothbrush, along with a flannel. She put those to one side. Picking up the large, chrome electronic watch with its digital clock face and calculator buttons, Fiona stared at it for some seconds. She had never seen anything like it.

The Walkman was new to her too. She pressed a button on the side of the black plastic case and a drawer popped open. Inside was a cassette tape, "Dire Straits" printed on the side.

Next, she flicked through the pages of *The Hitchhikers Guide to the Galaxy*, checking to make sure nothing was tucked inside the pages. She noticed an address written in blue ballpoint at the bottom of the inside back cover: 4 St. Julian's Road.

After noting the address on her log sheet, Fiona turned her attention to the suitcase. It had already been dusted for fingerprints, and the talcum-based white powder coated the red exterior unevenly. It reminded Fiona of the big, fluffy powder puff her grandmother used on her face and neck before going out.

The fine powder had turned up nothing useful. Fingerprints last indefinitely, but temperature, humidity, and exposure to the elements can erase them. Fiona popped the clasp and looked inside. The satin lining was smooth, silky, and cool as she ran her gloved hand over it. She slipped her fingertips inside the elasticated pockets sewn into the sides. They were empty, the bullets Inspector Graham had found having been removed and bagged with the gun.

But as she examined the lid, Fiona noticed the lining stitches had frayed. The satin had detached from the hard shell of the case. The corner of something flat poked out. Using tweezers she inserted into the gap in the lining, she teased it out, careful not to damage or crease it. It was a card, still in its cellophane wrapper.

Fiona turned it over. On the front, two cartoon bees were surrounded by red hearts. Above them was printed "Bee my valentine!" Fiona studied it for a moment before making a note and placing the card next to the other items on the counter.

Looking through the glass into Tomlinson's office, she saw that he was asleep.

They still had an hour before they were due to start the postmortem. A movement in her peripheral vision alerted her to Aidan's presence. He lumbered into view. Fiona exhaled, lifted then relaxed her shoulders, releasing the tension in them. "Fancy a cup of tea, Aidan?"

CHAPTER TWENTY-TWO

The Gorey Gossip
Saturday

Let's just be honest, squelch our natural reserve, and say it out loud: Jersey is a seriously attractive island.

We've got beaches to rival much of Europe. We've got history—no visitor could ignore the splendour of Gorey Castle, the War Tunnels, *or* the haunting Elizabeth Castle. We've got a first-rate zoo too. There are idyllic country lanes to potter down, parks for picnics, and walks for walkers. Our restaurants, everything from posh places to unpretentious pubs (see the *Gossip's* new review section, "The Dine Mine") offer *truly* great fresh, locally caught seafood at fantastic prices prepared to top-notch standards.

But just as a school of fish attracts a variety of predators, occasionally encountering something large and truly dangerous, Jersey can fall prey to undesirable elements. I'm afraid that in the past some of our visitors were *not* here to support the local fine hotels or to catch up with friends in one of our elegant tea rooms.

Sadly, and steadily, alongside its beatific scenery and delightful communities, Jersey of the past accrued a history of violence, and I'm not just talking about the Nazis. Couples fall out, friends come to blows, and idiots throw punches in the pub indeed, but these London-based gangsters came to our island to cause *mayhem and misadventure*.

I'm talking about the Mob, so named due to their enigmatic nature. The mainland police forces tend to see gangs as monolithic, all linked and gathered under a single umbrella. My research is showing that they couldn't be more wrong.

Small gangs, quite separate from any larger organisation, attracted by the remoteness of our beautiful island, its status as a tax haven, and its sunny climes, have used the Channel Islands to make dead drops, deposit money, launder cash, meet with co-conspirators and, yes, to threaten and in some cases inflict violence on one another. In studying Jersey's past, I've uncovered evidence of *at least seven* mob-related murders here since 1950. These killers are professionals. Their crimes are premeditated, not opportunistic.

In yesterday's post (*A Storm, A Gun, and a Thousand Questions*) I laid out evidence relating to the discovery of an ancient gun at the White House Inn. Today I am learning about the unearthing, just a few feet from said gun, of a body encased in concrete, the unfortunate victim likely having lain there for decades. It doesn't take a detective to understand that a powerful handgun and a secreted death do not belong, but it *does* need a detective's acumen to make the connections that reveal the truth.

In these pages, I labour to convey reality along with integrity and sincerity. As loyal readers, you know that accuracy is my priority. That said, I am not bound at the ankles by evidence or beholden to any authority.

These freedoms let me speculate that the man found dead in the White House Inn yesterday didn't meet a natural end. He carried a gun, after all.

We don't know who he is yet, but he had no discernible occupation or business on the island. If he had, his disappearance would have been noted and we would have learned of him earlier. So we ask: Had he been to Jersey before? Was he here to commit an act of violence? Did he succeed? Or did violence arrive at his door first?

The evidence is mounting quickly, and it all points to one thing: mob warfare raging on Jersey in the latter part of the last century. Considering the desirous nature of our wonderful island, it only stands to reason that gangs with their depraved motives duelled and competed and settled scores here. *Maybe they still do.*

CHAPTER TWENTY-THREE

"JUST A PRELIMINARY update. I've got good news . . ." Tomlinson began.

The pathologist had spent twenty minutes taking notes, peering through magnifying instruments, and completing a couple of simple chemical tests.

"Great! Let's have it!"

"If I may finish, David . . ."

"Sorry."

"Good news, bad news, and a question. What would you like first?"

"Start with the bad, move onto the good, and leave the question until last."

"Fair enough. The bad news is that the belongings don't give us much to go on. The wallet is empty, and there isn't much to be said about the rest of his things."

"Capital," Graham moaned. "And what's the good news?"

"I'm sixty percent sure I can recover a usable DNA sample from his effects. His hairbrush is our best bet. We can also try for some from the bones."

"The DNA database wasn't set up until 1995. That won't be much use."

"Ah, but it gives us a base sample in case more evidence appears. Like a match with a family member who *is* on the database. So, it's worth doing. Of course, it's entirely possible these clothes, and the gun, have nothing to do with our Mr. X."

"Yes, it's possible, but I find it hard to believe a gun and a body found within feet of each other are unconnected. What about his clothes?"

"A jacket, sweater, T-shirt, a white undervest, underpants, a pair of socks. That's it. An overnight kit, basically. The suitcase was an older model, popular in the sixties, mass produced, nothing very notable."

"Our guy didn't plan on staying very long, then. A quick in and out."

"Looks like it. Could be a salesman. They move around all the time."

"Sure. Most of them don't carry a model twenty-eight though."

"I was just about to mention that," said Tomlinson as he walked over to Fiona, who was examining the revolver. "We'll do some tests on it, get a ballistics sample for comparison."

Graham winced. There would be a record if the handgun had been involved in a crime. *Provided it had been digitised.*

He had heard stories from veteran detectives recalling the terrible delays to investigations while ballistics samples spent weeks crisscrossing the country; nowadays, the process took mere moments if they had been catalogued in the system.

"We did find something else. It was stuffed between the suitcase shell and the lining. Fiona seems to think it wasn't hidden as such but put there for safekeeping."

"Oh, what was it?"

"A Valentine's card. Just a store-bought one, nothing special."

"Was it written in?"

"No, still in the plastic wrapper. Not sure it means anything but wanted to mention it."

"Huh, perhaps all this happened around Valentine's Day then."

"Yes, remember the rose stem in the man's hands?"

"Hmm. You said you had a question?'"

"Ah, yes."

Graham heard Tomlinson move away from the soft, rhythmic whirring of a laboratory centrifuge and close his office door.

"David, how did Mrs. Taylor come to have this man's belongings?"

"She didn't say much. She was a bit, ah, shocked at the time. But she claims no knowledge of any of it and believes whatever happened must have taken place before she took over the hotel. She says she never went up into the attic, nor did anyone else. I'm leaning towards accepting her explanation. Maybe someone, at some point, innocently or not, cleaned up the room and popped the belongings in a drawer. Then, for some unknown reason, they were forgotten."

"They thought it best to forget about a *firearm* belonging to a man who had died and store it away in the attic?"

"When you consider someone encased a body in concrete and stored it for decades, it doesn't seem so strange. In fact, nothing makes sense in this case. The whole thing seems odd."

Marcus composed a thought carefully. It took a moment. "David, perhaps I could throw an idea into the air?"

"Always."

"Maybe whoever stored the things *didn't know* there was a gun in the suitcase. Just stashed it away."

"Indeed, another possibility. One of many."

"Is there anyone *at all* from the time who's still there? Maybe one of the older staff might remember an incident."

"Not many people work in the same hotel for forty-odd years," Graham replied, "but I'm going there this afternoon. If Mrs. Taylor hasn't gone supernova, I'll have the chance to ask."

"I've been a pathologist since I was twenty-six. There's something to be said for institutional knowledge. I'm a big believer in it. So rare these days though. People move through and on so fast."

"They do. Good record-keeping helps, I find. Let me know as soon as you discover anything, even if it's inconclusive."

"Will do."

"By the way, Sergeant Harding is attending the postmortem in my place."

"Okay, that's unusual."

"Yes, she volunteered. Not sure why. Not her regular beat."

"Well, she can meet Fiona. Oh, and David?"

"Hmm?" The DI was on his feet, already distracted by the next thing on his list.

"It *is* possible this Mr. X is just a regular guy who died of natural causes, you know."

"Of course."

"It's just everyone's heading off in different directions, and someone needs to say the simple, normal thing."

"I'll grant the importance of varied viewpoints," said Graham, "but to me, this case feels neither simple nor normal. Being buried in concrete doesn't suggest either."

CHAPTER TWENTY-FOUR

DISTRACTED BY THE blue tarpaulin still spread across the roof, Graham drove up the drive to the White House Inn. He sighed. It would take weeks for the hotel to recover, and for many visitors—and at least one anxious engaged couple he knew of—the storm had tossed a serious spanner in their works.

At least the car park was cleaned up. Only some faint smudges and the odd nick in the tarmac where roof tiles had succumbed to wind and gravity remained. The car park was, however, almost empty. Not a good sign.

Mrs. Taylor was at the reception desk, holding the old-school phone receiver tight and close. It was clear her stress levels had not dissipated. She tapped a pen against the counter as she listened.

"Right . . . right," she said, then ran her finger down the page of her reservations book, also old-school. Mrs. Taylor wasn't one for using the latest "fandangle thingamabob" when the old methods worked for her just as well and, she was wont to exclaim, added to the hotel's charm. "Three doubles, a single, and then another single with a cot. You're a marvel, Derek. Thanks for taking in some of our displaced guests."

She replaced the receiver and, unaware Graham was steadily approaching, allowed herself a vigorous, unrestrained jiggle, shaking her arms and shoulders until her fingertips tingled. Then, with a deep breath, she looked up. "Oh, Inspector! What a *time* I'm having thanks to this storm! My business and livelihood are under real threat. I'm having to re-home some of our most faithful guests. And then there's your nasty business." Mrs. Taylor closed her eyes and shuddered. "I don't even want to *think* about what you've come for."

Mrs. Taylor's litany of disasters had lengthened: water damage was suspected in several top-floor rooms, the silent, invisible threat of mould not far behind.

"They want to come in here," she said, appalled, "and rip down all the old walls on the second floor!"

"Ghastly state of affairs for you."

"They're going to charge me a king's ransom for some fancy sealant. Did you ever meet anyone with such bad luck?"

"Mrs. Taylor, it's a rotten time for me to ask a favour, but I need some help."

"Oh, don't worry, Inspector! You're about the only person around here I'm not furious with!" It was only half a joke; such a series of crises would give anyone a stern test. "I held a staff meeting, you know. Told them what happened. We're determined to carry on as normal. You've taped off the attic and we will not go up there. Not that we ever did, or we might have found that poor man earlier. I blame myself." Mrs. Taylor's hand fluttered at her throat.

"You mustn't do that, Mrs. Taylor. No one could have susp—" Graham stopped. "Anyhow, we'll keep things discreet. Only disturb what we have to, when we have to. Right now, we're narrowing down the period during which our man in the concrete met his demise. You wouldn't happen to have any records for the period 1980 to 1982, would you?"

"You know me, Inspector Graham. Never throw anything away. I have all the reservation books from the day I took over, but not from before my time, no. There was nothing left for me like that at all. I had to start from scratch. But that wasn't necessarily a bad thing." Mrs. Taylor folded her arms and sniffed.

"Okay then, did you hire any of your predecessor's staff?"

Mrs. Taylor sniffed again. "I don't take kindly to her being referred to as my predecessor, young man."

"Oh?"

"The hotel was a *very* different type of establishment back then."

"How so, Mrs. Taylor?"

"It was more . . ." Marjorie looked skywards as she searched for the words. The quest for an appropriate euphemism ultimately required more energy than Mrs. Taylor could muster, and she found herself defeated. Her shoulders slumped. She whispered, "Downmarket. The hotel had a *reputation*."

Unwilling to let her off the hook, Graham raised his eyebrows. "For what?"

"Oh, Detective Inspector, must you make me spell it out? This place was cheap back then, run down. It attracted, you know, the wrong sorts. There were stories about women of the night visiting. Even plying their trade in the bar!" Mrs. Taylor voiced her feelings about such enterprise with a downturn of her mouth and the employment of stringy neck muscles. "It was why I was able to pick up the old place for a song. Nobody wanted to touch it. I even changed the name to the White House Inn to make a clean break of it. It used to be called The Grange."

"I see. So, you didn't keep anyone on when you took over?"

"Now, I didn't say that." Mrs. Taylor snapped her fingers and pointed. Graham took this to be an excellent sign. "Janet Northrop, the lady who comes three times a week to help with afternoon tea." It didn't take any time at all for

Graham to locate a memory of the slight, efficient, somewhat taciturn, white-haired woman who ran the tearoom. "She's here today, helping out. A real trooper, she is. Mrs. Northrop would know far more about that time than me. Let me get her. She's in the kitchen putting Polly and Raj to work. Wait there a moment."

The two younger staff members claimed they could manage without Mrs. Northrop's oversight for a few minutes, and a petite woman came through to reception to speak to Mrs. Taylor and the detective inspector. Energetic and slender, Janet, bedecked in a red-and-white checkered apron, had only recently turned sixty. She had a schoolteacher's manner, highly organised, and always on the move with sinewy forearms that were marbled with veins so big Graham suspected Barnwell would covet them.

"Has Mrs. Taylor presented you with your Long Service Medal yet?" Graham asked. "Quite a tenure you've had here."

"The people are wonderful. Our staff and the guests both. And at my age, everyone needs *something* to keep them out of trouble," Janet said brightly. She laughed. Graham sucked on his bottom lip. He hadn't heard Mrs. Northrop laugh before, and he had been in the tearoom during her shifts aplenty.

While Mrs. Taylor fretted behind the desk, shuffling invoices and trying not to overhear, Graham asked Mrs. Northrop about her time at the hotel before Mrs. Taylor arrived. "I know you've heard the news. What we found upstairs in the grand attic . . ."

"Not so grand with a great hole in the roof," Mrs. Taylor muttered.

"Well, it's from a while back," he said, taking Mrs. Northrop's arm and steering her out of Mrs. Taylor's earshot, "and we're trying to figure out how it got there. Do you remember anything that might help us? Would have been between late 1979 and October 1982." Janet Northrop's first instinct was to glance at Mrs. Taylor, now studying the reservation book with the fervour of a student up against a deadline. "Mrs. Taylor didn't take over until in September 1982. This was during Miss Lovell's tenure. Do you remember?"

"Do I remember?" Janet Northrop raised an eyebrow. "Marjorie showed up here with the deeds to the place and not two pennies to rub together. And yet she announces that we're reopening 'the grandest hotel on Jersey' in only three weeks!"

CHAPTER TWENTY-FIVE

"IT WAS *MARVELLOUS*," Mrs. Taylor called over, her hearing newly appreciated by Graham for its acuity. Easily nudged into nostalgia, she added, "We begged and stole and . . . well, not *stole*."

"We were very creative," Janet Northrop said, raising her eyebrows at the inspector.

"More like 'extended borrowing,' eh?" Graham suggested.

"That's right."

"So, before Mrs. Taylor bought this place," Graham said, now guiding Mrs. Northrop into the conservatory, "do you remember a guest passing away in one of the upstairs rooms?"

"Freddie Solomon's been writing about him, hasn't he?" Janet said.

Graham's eyelids dropped a fraction of an inch. "Mrs. Northrop, please put out of your mind anything you might have read and simply answer my questions." Graham's words were clipped, his tone hard.

Janet Northrop frowned and looked down at her hands. "And this was 1980 to 1982, you're saying?"

"Yes, there are reasons to think it might have happened in February. Around Valentine's Day."

Mrs. Northrop gave it her best, rapidly tapping the pad of her forefinger against her thumb as memories built themselves. "It's an awfully long time ago," she said. "And in 1982, I wasn't even here. I went to the Scilly Isles. I remember that because my big sister treated me for my eighteenth. First time on a plane for both of us, it was. We went for the weekend. My birthday isn't until June, but she couldn't afford it then, so we went in the low season. We had a lovely time. Even in February, would you believe? Beautiful sunshine. I loved it."

"And you went around Valentine's Day?"

"Yes. I remember because someone from the local flower farm handed us bunches of white narcissi as they met us off the plane—they're famous for those there. Anyhow, we were told the flower was called Scilly Valentine in honour of it being Valentine's Day that weekend." Mrs. Northrop's eyes glazed over before snapping back to the present. "But I remember nothing about anyone dying. Ever."

"Please think carefully," Graham said.

"No, I'm sure of it," Janet replied, pressing her forefinger into her shoulder. "You'd remember something like that, wouldn't you? And I don't remember anything about Valentine's Day in 1980 or '81. In '82, I wasn't back before later in the month. I didn't hear of anything happening while I was away."

"Ah, well," Graham said. "It was worth a try."

"I feel so awful that he died," Janet said. "That man. And under our roof, of all places. Must be quite a test for you, the case I mean. Being so old and such." Janet Northrop continued to deliver a speech that was very familiar to Graham. It was entitled, *Why I Love Police Mysteries on the Telly*. When she paused midspeech to take a breath, he politely thanked her and stepped away to finish his handwritten notes.

"Not very helpful, was she?" Mrs. Taylor said, appearing moments later at his shoulder. "I wish we could help more, not least because the sooner this mystery is solved, the better it will be for all of us."

"You've got enough on your plate, Mrs. Taylor," Graham said, putting away his notebook. "You leave the mysteries to us," he said kindly. He smiled at her.

"I'll be getting on, then," she said, politely returning his smile. From far away, up many flights of stairs, came the distinctive crunch of an old beam being taken down, followed by a burst of hammering. Mrs. Taylor winced, standing still for a pained moment before finding whatever energy was needed to press on.

Graham called Janice. "Mrs. Northrop's reaction was interesting. Her story was quite elaborate and precise. Almost like it was rehearsed."

"Well, she's worked there forever, sir, and the roof has just caved in. She must be a bit upset. Perhaps she's overcompensating."

"I've watched Mrs. Taylor's staff cope with a missing turkey delivery at eleven p.m. on Christmas Eve before now. I've seen Mrs. Northrop face up to a hundred of the most entitled tea drinkers on Jersey without blinking, all in one afternoon. Her prep guy, Raj, once told me that when things get hectic, she can command a kitchen like she's mobilising an infantry battalion."

"So, Mrs. T. and Mrs. Northrop are both forces of nature," Janice replied. "Even institutions are allowed to throw a wobbly now and then. Might be worth talking to her again. Want me to bring some charm to the proceedings?"

"I think I've got it for now, Sergeant, thanks." Graham chuckled. "How was the postmortem?"

"Unpleasant, sir. As you know very well."

"Any findings of interest?"

"Male, midtwenties. The cause of death was a heart attack. Dr. Tomlinson said the heart looked healthy, other than the dead bit, of course. That was a bit unusual. They're doing further tests on the shirt he was wearing, tox screen, et cetera. Other than that, nothing stood out. I ran his fingerprints through the system—nothing."

"Hmm, mundane."

"Precisely. What do you think we're looking at, sir? If it's a heart attack, it's natural causes, surely?"

"Possibly. Bit young though."

"Young men do suddenly drop dead occasionally. There was that lad playing football for St. Helier that time, remember? Fell like a stone on the pitch. I remember Roachie talking about it."

"It does happen, of course, but if it was natural causes, why was the body secreted as it was?"

CHAPTER TWENTY-SIX

"DID IT COME through?" Tomlinson asked Fiona. He sat in an office chair, gently pressing the floor with his foot so that he swung from side to side.

"Yep," Fiona said, sitting at her workstation so that Tomlinson could see her screen. "Doesn't look much like the original object though."

"Ah, yes," Tomlinson said. "Wavelengths of light. It's all about the wavelengths." He raised his voice. "Isn't it, Dr. Weiss?" Dr. Miranda Weiss was head of the forensic science lab in Southampton, to which particularly complex Jersey cases were referred. The lab possessed an array of technology not available on the island, which regularly both challenged and excited Marcus.

Over the speaker, Fiona and Tomlinson heard her chuckle. "Let me know if this gets too *Star Trek* for you, Marcus."

When it came to refuting ageism, Tomlinson's pump was already primed. "I understood every word of the briefing you gave me."

"Even the parts you slept through?"

"My elbow," he explained slowly, "merely slipped off the table. You had my full attention."

"And I assume I still do." Dr. Weiss shared her screen with the Jersey pair, quickly adding layers of colour and detail to the image on it. "There, that's better."

In front of them was a roughly symmetrical shape, not unlike an inkblot test but which resembled nothing in particular. "I have no idea what I'm looking at!" Fiona admitted in a tone similar to one she might use when she couldn't wait to open her Christmas presents.

"You created the image yourself not half an hour ago," Dr. Weiss told her.

"Wait... This is from Mr. X's shirt?" Fiona said. "Wow! I thought it'd be like looking at a close-up photograph."

"You're thinking of an electron microscope, Fiona. These are results," Tomlinson said, "from an ultraviolet spectroscope. A spectroscope interprets a different kind of light. Different animal. Dr. Weiss has even more sophisticated gear up there in the buzzing metropolis of Southampton." He returned to the image on the screen. "And what kind of animal are we looking at right now, Miranda?"

"We're seeing varying levels of reflectivity," said Dr. Weiss. "I know it's your first time with one of these, so I'll go slow." At her end, Dr. Weiss used the mouse to point out a roughly symmetrical pattern at the top of the screen. "If it's a different colour, it's a different chemical. Everything has its unique way of reflecting light. That's where the rainbow comes from," she explained simply. "Ultraviolet light is special because it can show us whole categories of chemistry. Over here," she added, circling a broad, dull area, "is just normal carbon weave. The black stuff is the polyester. No surprises there, but these lighter marks near the buttons of his shirt..."

"They're a different chemical completely," Fiona said. She leaned in and added, "But they're not part of the shirt."

"Why do you say that?" asked Tomlinson.

"The marks are inconsistent, spread out over his shirt in a random pattern."

"You think they're random?" came Dr. Weiss's voice, leading Fiona onward. The young woman appeared stumped, a tiny furrow forming between her eyebrows.

Tomlinson's experience allowed him to race ahead. "Could we say in this case," he asked, not even looking at the image now as he made quick notes in Mr. X's file, "that the majority of the substance is down the centre, below his shirt buttons? And that the rest is divided, so we see about forty percent on his right side and sixty on his left?"

As Dr. Weiss adjusted the view, it emerged that Tomlinson was right about the dispersal ratio.

"Huh, interesting," Fiona said. "So, what does that mean? And what kind of chemical is this, anyway?"

"Ever eaten a Cornish pasty? A really flaky one?" Tomlinson asked her.

"Wouldn't have them any other way."

"Messy, aren't they? Crumbs everywhere."

"Yes," Fiona admitted, "but it's well worth the mess."

"Really? Personally, I'm not much of a fan."

"Madness!" Fiona exclaimed. "They're delicious."

"I have the sense Mr. X would have said the same," Dr. Weiss said.

"Wait..." Fiona gestured to all the machines and screens and accoutrements of modern forensic investigations that lay around them. "Was all of this just to discover he spilled puff pastry on his shirt?"

"Ha-ha, no, but there are two things we can say with reasonable certainty,"

Miranda Weiss said, her low, rumbly voice reverberating through the screen. Reaching for his phone, Tomlinson said, "He's right-handed. I'd bet my wine cellar on it."

"And these marks," Dr. Weiss said, "are a lot more exciting than whatever your Mr. X had for lunch."

"Cocaine?" Graham sat up straight.

"Probably," Tomlinson said. "I'm judging from experience. It's a white amphetamine powder. I'll show Fiona how to do some more chromatography and some mass spectroscopy, then we'll be sure."

"Well," Graham said, "there's a thing."

"The pattern suggests a right-hander, albeit marginally. Small amounts spilled down either side of his shirt buttons."

"That'd explain it," said Graham. "Our victim enjoyed too much Bolivian marching powder and keeled over."

"Or just enough of it," said Tomlinson. "As far as I could tell, his heart looked in decent condition, but it's possible he was a habitual user, or he mixed the cocaine with alcohol. If any of those were the case, he'd have been at risk."

"Wouldn't have to be an overdose, you mean?"

"Not necessarily."

"Curiouser and curiouser. So, we have a young man visiting Jersey between 1980 and 1982 while in possession of a gun who dies of a heart attack while snorting cocaine during his stay at the White House Inn, aka The Grange. Identity and reason for visit and gun still unknown."

"That's about the sum of it so far. Ballistics soon. We'll see what that throws up. How are you getting on trying to find out who he is?"

"Nowhere yet. Barnwell's still in the basement. Janice found nothing in the databases. And Mrs. Taylor doesn't have any record. We're drawing a blank at the moment."

"Fiona's sent off hair samples for DNA analysis. That might help."

"Thanks again, Marcus. Anything else comes up . . ."

Tomlinson assured him, "You're always my first call."

CHAPTER TWENTY-SEVEN

FIONA GRACELESSLY PLONKED Marcus's mug in front of him although she didn't seem too put out by his request for yet another cup of tea. "In a rush to go somewhere?" Tomlinson said.

"Yes. My next task is to verify the quality of the cocaine on Mr. X's shirt. I'll be back shortly." Fiona turned to leave before pausing. "You know, there's some AI software that takes skeletal data to generate an impression of how that person might have looked when alive. Maybe I could try that?"

"Sounds expensive."

"I could log in to the software in my previous office and do it remotely, if you like. There's also a free app that enables you to age a person from a photo so you can see what they look like at different points in their life."

"Hmm, interesting. Let me talk to Inspector Graham. See if he thinks that would be useful."

As Fiona got to work, Marcus quietly sipped his tea—he liked it piping hot—as he listened to the tapping, whirring, and whooshing sounds coming from the lab. The sound of a door opening interrupted him. Fiona appeared in the doorway, flushed and frustrated. She waved a piece of paper and wiped her brow with the back of her wrist. "I need some help. The spectroscopy tests spit out some strange results I've not seen before. Either I haven't done it properly, or Mr. X's coke contained a *lot* of adulterants. The chart shows not only multicolour spikes in the right areas of the chemical spectrum for cocaine, but also others I can't identify. Come and see it on my screen. It's nearly a third of the mass."

By the time they got to Fiona's desk, the software had come back with a solid hit for the variances in the chart. Fiona pointed to her screen. "What's that?"

Tomlinson cleaned his glasses and squinted at the results. After a few seconds, he straightened, peeling his glasses off one ear and then the other. "That, my dear, is a reason for Detective Inspector Graham to stop what he's doing right now and give us his attention."

<hr />

"Poisoning?" Graham exclaimed for the second time that day. Then, in almost the same breath, "*One* cause? There were others?"

"I think whoever did away with Mr. X went a little overboard. If they hadn't, we might not have caught it. You see, the cocaine which drifted down onto his shirt contained traces of two different old-fashioned rat poisons."

Pen already flying, Graham visualised the scene. "Alright, so our killer couldn't make up his mind, or used two poisons just to make sure?"

"Hard to know. The red squill is a cardiotoxin. It works by causing heart attacks, usually in rats. It's a common rodenticide."

"How quickly are we talking?"

"Extremely quick. As far as I can tell in this case, death appears to have been immediate. If he clung on for more than a few moments, there'd be signs of internal bleeding. There were none that I could identify."

"Could they have been hidden by the effects of decomposition?"

"I would have seen some sign even at this late stage. There were simply none. The state of the remains is really rather remarkable."

"What about the second poison?"

"Ah, that's different. If he'd lived longer, we'd have seen the effects of thallium poisoning."

"Flu symptoms," Graham recited from memory, "stomach trouble, tingling in the feet, and hair loss. Kills slowly though. A week or more."

"My opinion is that the heart was stopped by the red squill, and death was instantaneous. The thallium served as backup but became unnecessary. Mr. X was fortunate his ticker gave out as soon as it did."

"One method causes immediate death, the other a lingering agony. Sounds like our murderer was organised or maybe determined enough to give the Grim Reaper some options. Who would choose to poison an enemy in such a way?"

"Indeed," Tomlinson added. "And why."

When Graham put down his phone, he fired up his computer. Pursing his lips, he idly tapped a few words into the search bar and pressed "enter," pausing to read the entries that the internet produced. He typed again, refining his search, and this time, his eyes widened as blood rushed to his cheeks. He sat up straighter in his chair before jotting some notes in his notebook, abandoning his computer, and shrugging on his jacket.

As he walked through the main office, Carmen's head popped up. Hope sprung into her deep brown eyes. Graham paused to scratch her head.

"Sorry, Carmie, not now."

"I'll take her when Jan gets back," Barnwell said. "She just popped out. Something about her mother and flowers, she said."

"Okay, good. I'm going out for a bit."

"See you later, sir."

CHAPTER TWENTY-EIGHT

SINCE THE STORM, the White House Inn had transformed into a building site. People were up on the roof tossing down ragged, smashed pieces of tile and split timbers. Inside the grand attic, the site having been released as a crime scene, a workshop was being set up to install the new beams. All of this generated a near-constant hailstorm of noise.

"It's like having surgery!" Mrs. Taylor said to Graham between the many bouts of drilling. "Like they're replacing my hips without anaesthetic!"

Graham murmured sympathies, but he was there on police business. "I wonder if I could bother Mrs. Northrop again?"

More drilling almost drowned out Mrs. Taylor's reply; it seemed to resonate all the way down, through the walls, to the foundations of the building. "Again? Must be important."

"We're making progress," Graham told her. "So, is Mrs. Northrop here?"

Janet Northrop took a moment's finding, but Mrs. Taylor found her in the walk-in freezer. She meekly followed Mrs. Taylor into the reception area. Her reluctance was obvious from the set of her shoulders and her expression, which was a mixture of resentment and resignation. "It was so very long ago," was the first thing she said, anticipating Graham's questions. "So very long, and—"

"Tell me again about the Scilly Isles," said Graham companionably. "The week you spent there with your sister."

It was a surprising turn, but Mrs. Northrop recounted again the same memories as before—the unseasonably sunny weekend of sand and sea with her sister. "It was lovely. Once we both got married and her first husband landed that job in Copenhagen, I hardly got to see Judy. But we made the best of the time we had before that."

Animated flipping of the pages in the inspector's notebook brought Mrs.

Northrop to a halt, as he'd intended. "Ah, here it is, yes." He read aloud from what sounded like a weather forecast. "Twelfth to the fourteenth of February 1982. Scattered showers on Friday, heavy rain almost continually from Saturday morning to Sunday teatime." He closed his notebook. "Sounds awful. Must've been cold too. The original, authentic 'wet weekend' in all its glory. Isn't that right, Mrs. Northrop?" The woman's gaze faltered, and she broke eye contact with Graham, glancing at the ground, murmuring something he didn't catch.

"Hell's bloomers! That's not for *this* weekend, is it?" Mrs. Taylor asked, wrongly overhearing and horrified that her roof would be open to the elements.

"Second weekend in February, 1982," Graham informed her. "The date of the weekend you say, Mrs. Northrop, you spent with your sister. A happy, *sunny* weekend, you said. 'Thunderous rain' was the weather reported for Cornwall and Devon that weekend, which includes the Scilly Isles, of course. It's amazing what you can find out these days."

Janet Northrop stared at him. Mrs. Taylor stared at her. "Janet?" she asked. "Are you *positive* about those dates?"

Mrs. Northrop immediately crumbled. "I'm not . . . I mean, I didn't . . ."

"Would you like to go into my office for a quiet chat, Inspector?" Mrs. Taylor offered. Unusually for Mrs. Taylor, she sensed the mood. She didn't want yet another public scene.

Inside the office, pulling up the guest chair for her tearoom manager, Mrs. Taylor gestured to her office chair for Graham. As she reached for the door handle to give the pair some privacy, Janet Northrop piped up.

"C-could Marjorie sit with me? We go back a long way. It would help calm my nerves." In a flash, Mrs. Taylor was by Mrs. Northrop's side.

"We do, Inspector. We really do," Mrs. Taylor said. Graham looked up from his notebook and regarded the two women, one eager, the other pleading. "Very well, but please don't intervene, Mrs. Taylor. You're here to support Mrs. Northrop only."

"Yes, of course, Inspector." Mrs. Taylor pulled out another chair and sat next to Mrs. Northrop.

"That means don't say anything, Mrs. Taylor."

Marjorie slowly clasped her hands in her lap and, gazing steadily at the inspector, lowered her head, still holding eye contact with him. "I understand, Inspector. Please, proceed." Feeling he was already at risk of losing control of the situation, Graham continued as smoothly as he could.

"Mrs. Northrop, it would appear that the dates you gave us for your trip were not, in fact, accurate. Was there a reason for that? Did you get the dates mixed up?" Comfortable answering his own question, he added, "Or perhaps it was because you wanted to convince me that you weren't here during the period we're investigating. When, in fact, you were."

"It was *so very* long ago, Inspector."

"So you keep saying, but we don't normally forget our eighteenth birthday celebrations, Mrs. Northrop. Especially when they involve once-in-a-lifetime activities."

"I'm an old woman, you know," Janet Northrop said, her hands curled in her lap. "Things aren't quite as good up here," she said, tapping her temple.

"Poppycock," muttered Mrs. Taylor, defending her friend but also undermining her claims. "You're as sharp as the chef's knives, Janet."

Graham glared at her. Chastened, Mrs. Taylor bit her bottom lip and settled into her chair some more. The inspector resumed his questioning.

"I'll just ask this: What happened after the body was found?"

Now Mrs. Northrop was shaking her head. "You don't understand. It was Miss Lovell. I was too young. I didn't know what to do. She said not to mention him, the man who died. Not to say anything to anyone."

"Why?" asked Graham.

"Our reputation!" Janet said as though it were obvious.

"But people die in hotels all the time without it resulting in disaster."

"No, it's the weather that does that," Mrs. Taylor muttered quietly.

Graham ignored her. "Mrs. Northrop?"

Fear brightened the woman's blue eyes at the inspector's prompt. "Well, I wasn't the boss, was I?" she protested. "I was eighteen, for heaven's sake. And if Miss Lovell said, 'Not a word to *anyone*,' she got silence from me. What right did I have to question her? It's not like there was a lot of employment on the island for someone like me in those days. I wanted to keep my job."

"So, what happened? Tell me," Graham said.

Mrs. Northrop folded her arms and looked away defiantly. "I'm not saying anything."

Graham leaned forward. "I really think you should, Mrs. Northrop. There's a family out there who lost someone. And they don't know what happened." Mrs. Northrop was unmoved.

"And you're implicated in the concealment of a body. Perverting the course of justice. You clearly lied to deflect from your involvement." Still, Mrs. Northrop didn't return his gaze. Graham glanced at Mrs. Taylor.

"Before my time," Marjorie said, quickly distancing herself from the situation. She, too, looked away and folded her arms, pursing her lips. Then she turned back and appealed to her friend. "But, oh, Janet, what on *earth* happened back then?"

At her appeal, deeply uncomfortable at being forced to wade through this historical territory, Mrs. Northrop deflated. She reached out to grasp Mrs. Taylor's hand for comfort, perhaps for fortitude. "I wouldn't go back in there, Marjorie. Not into that room. Oh, it was awful. I found him, you see. 'Natural causes.' That's what Miss Lovell told me. But I knew something was wrong. He was staying in the attic, you see. It was a guestroom back then. After I told Miss Lovell about him, she went into the attic alone, and closed the door so, so quietly."

"How long was she in there for?"

"Ten minutes, maybe less."

"What was she doing?" Graham asked carefully.

"I don't know. Didn't see. And like I said, no way was I going back in there."

"What do you *think* she was doing?" Graham was determined to press Mrs. Northrop, his only true lead.

"I'm not a mind reader," Janet Northrop retorted sharply. But then she felt Mrs. Taylor's hand on her shoulder. Marjorie leaned over to whisper. Noting Graham's frown, Mrs. Northrop said, "Marjorie here wants me to tell you everything I know. She's a good egg, isn't she?"

"An excellent egg," the DI agreed.

"Go on, love," Mrs. Taylor said softly. "It might help the inspector. And with your nerves. You know how they affect you."

Janet Northrop closed her eyes and sighed. "I was so scared I stayed as silent as a mouse. I've never told anyone. Even when Miss Lovell died, I didn't want to rake it all up. I saw her go into the attic and that was the end of it. I don't know what happened, and I never wanted to find out. I assumed that the body was taken away in the dead of night and disposed of. But obviously, that isn't quite what happened."

"Do you remember his name or anything about him that might be relevant? We're still tracking down his identity. You could help a lot with that."

"His name was Mr. Smith. I'll never forget." Janet thought back. "He was in his mid to late twenties. A heavy smoker. We didn't have no-smoking rooms in them days. Drinker too. But he was charming, with a nice, big smile."

"You remember his smile?" Graham frowned.

"He was a flirt. I was young, remember? Bit of a looker I was back then. And it was Valentine's Day 1982. He said he didn't have a date but that seeing hearts everywhere was making *his* heart 'go all aflutter.' He was a bit leery, I thought. Trying it on. Well, he didn't get anywhere. Not with me."

"What nationality was he?"

"He was English. London, I'd say."

"Why didn't you say all this when we spoke before?"

Mrs. Northrop made to apologise, her palms open. "I was told not to, wasn't I? And I didn't want to get involved. I wanted . . . I *want* it all to go away. I don't want to remember what I saw. Or that I was told to look away and say nothing. And I . . . well, I committed a crime, didn't I?"

"Why do you think Miss Lovell didn't declare the body?"

"I should imagine it was because of what it might lead to."

"And what might that be?"

"There were rumours . . ."

"Of what?"

"That she had a side business. That the hotel wasn't her only source of income. Perhaps not even her main one." Mrs. Northrop looked down at her hands. Graham glanced at Mrs. Taylor.

"*Drugs*," she mouthed. Graham's eyebrows shot up.

"You mean Miss Lovell might have supplied him with something that could be traced to her? Something that caused his death?"

Janet Northrop squeezed her eyes tight shut and nodded. "Hmm. Or she simply didn't want the police poking around. She was in her last months, although I didn't know that at the time. Miss Lovell had cancer, you know. She died about six months later."

Graham sat back and paused as he processed this information. He lifted his chin, stretched his neck, and breathed out through his nose.

"Who would have helped her with the concrete? She couldn't possibly have done it by herself."

"I don't know."

"Surely you've some idea. Can you give me a name?"

Mrs. Northrop screwed her eyes up tight again, her lips pinched together. When she relaxed them, she said, "I would try Neville Williams. He was her grandson. He was in the building trade back then. Just a young lad, an apprentice. But I've no idea where he is now. We're talking over forty years ago." Graham flipped his notebook shut with a flick of his wrist. "We'll find him. Thank you, Mrs. Northrop."

"Will I . . .? Will I be charged?"

"Well, technically . . ." Graham caught sight of Mrs. Taylor's expression. It conveyed that her tolerance of his presence in her tearoom was subject to conditions. "Uh, it's unclear at the moment. I do require that you not leave the island, however."

"How did he die, Inspector?" Mrs. Taylor said.

"Heart attack."

"Hardly surprising, I suppose, given his habits."

"Smoking, drinking, even to excess, don't normally lead to heart attacks in otherwise healthy young men, Mrs. Taylor." Graham stood, preparing to leave. "But the two kinds of rat poison he inadvertently snorted up his nose could easily be judged as the *decisive* factor."

CHAPTER TWENTY-NINE

"MURDER? In my hotel. Again!" Three of her staff took Mrs. Taylor to the quietest part of the hotel, providing tea and sympathy and shielding her from new stresses. Before she left, Mrs. Taylor clutched the hotel's reservation book to her as though someone had threatened to steal it, taking small comfort in the hotel's future bookings, unseasonably thin as they now were.

"I'm sorry to have to break it like that," Graham said to Mrs. Northrop when Mrs. Taylor had gone.

"The poor man," she said. Then with lip-curling distaste, "Up his nose, did you say?"

"That's the most common way with cocaine. It's also typical," Graham pointed out, "for innocent people to speak the whole truth first time around when interviewed by a detective. Again, I can't help noticing you chose not to do that." Mrs. Northrop was silent. "I'm trained to regard that as suspicious, madam."

Janet Northrop remained calm for a second before erupting into a fireworks display of apologies. Someone brought tea, for which Graham could have awarded them a medal, and it gave Mrs. Northrop a moment to collect herself.

"When the body was found, I wanted to see if the man's death would be ruled an ordinary one, or if something would turn up about drugs," Janet Northrop explained quietly, keeping her voice level. "I was aware of the rumours about Miss Lovell at the time."

"But why the hesitation? Why wait to see if we found anything? Why did you not simply tell us? You have to admit it looks suspicious and forces us to look at you and what you've told us very carefully. If you're innocent, why put yourself in this position?"

"I didn't know about the rat poison," Janet said firmly. She was trembling.

"Only the drugs. She was a very forceful personality, Miss Lovell was. A bit of a bully, to be honest. And she made me *swear*."

"As she was your boss and the hotel owner, I appreciate Miss Lovell had a great deal of influence. You were young. But, and I know it's not nice to think about, laws were broken. A man died," Graham reminded her. "And the authorities weren't informed. His family hasn't known what happened to him all this time." Mrs. Northrop shrugged and cast her eyes downwards into her lap. "It was decades ago. Miss Lovell is long dead."

Janet Northrop shook her head, unable to explain.

"How old was Miss Lovell?"

"She was nearly eighty. She seemed ancient to me at the time. Tiny thing, she was. If you sneezed, you worried you'd blow her over. And then you wouldn't hear the last of it. My, she had a temper. Lorded it over everyone, she did. We were all terrified of her."

"Hmm, it seems to have been quite the cover-up Miss Lovell was hatching. I know why *she* did it, and honestly, I can understand why you kept things quiet at the time. But you're not eighteen any longer, and you haven't been for a long time. You *stayed* silent. Even when Miss Lovell died, even when you learned the body had been found."

"I don't know. I was scared you would put me in prison, I suppose. For not telling the truth at the time or since." Mrs. Northrop was grey with fatigue. Graham sighed.

"Did you see what Miss Lovell did with his belongings? Especially the gun?"

"I don't know anything about a gun. I didn't see one at the time," Janet said.

"And what about a suitcase?"

Janet shook her head. "I remember him arriving with it. It was red. What happened to it after . . . you know, I have no idea."

"And it was definitely red?"

"Yes. It was very noticeable. Unusual." There was a pause. Janet rubbed her top lip with the tip of her tongue. Graham sensed that she was wrestling with something. He waited until what was lighting up her brain's synapses faded. As they were vanquished, her eyes dulled.

"Perhaps she didn't know it was murder," Mrs. Northrop said. "Miss Lovell. I mean, if there was poison in his mixture, could Miss Lovell have not known about it?"

"Well, we can't know for sure. She might not have been the source of the drugs that killed him. And if she was, was she the one cutting it, or was it cut before it got to her? Either way, she committed several crimes—not reporting a death to the authorities, disposing of a body, and the perversion of the course of justice. And that's just in relation to this case. It's enough to be going on with, but I could continue. I suspect Miss Lovell knew that, and once she'd started down the path of obfuscation and denial, getting off it became almost impossible."

Janet rubbed her face with her hand. "So who exactly *was* he, this 'Mr. Smith'?"

"Well, that's a bit up in the air still. But your evidence has given us some leads to chase."

"Well, that's good. Can I go now, or do you have any more questions for me? Things have been *awful* lately, what with the storm and now this. For Mrs. T., the staff, everyone. I'm not sure how much more I can take."

"No, no more questions. Not today anyway. If I think of some more, I know where to find you. If you wake up at three a.m. with a blinding flash of insight or a memory, call the station. If no one picks up, leave a message and a sleepy constable will call you back. And please, Mrs. Northrop..."

"Yes?"

"Try to be honest from here on out, okay?"

There was a knock at the door. Graham opened it and found Mrs. Taylor gripping an old reservation book bound in green cloth. "I had another look, and I found something, Inspector."

Before she continued, Janet Northrop slipped between the two of them, muttering about "getting back to the tearoom."

When she and the inspector were alone, Mrs Taylor spoke again. "I called in two of my bar staff to help me. You see," she explained sincerely, "I can't have rumours again. You know, like before. The ghost stories and the gossip..."

"I understand," said Graham. "We'll do everything we can to clear this up quickly."

"Exactly." Mrs. Taylor opened the book. "From '82. Before my time." Opening a page marked with a yellow sticky note, she said, "I think this might be him. Mr. John Smith."

Graham snorted. "Of course." The "4" next to his name had been struck out with a red pen.

"What do you think that means?" Graham wondered.

"He was booked in for four nights." Mrs. Taylor added woefully, "I suppose the strike-through means that he didn't complete his stay. On account of him, you know... dying." Graham coughed. "As I said, Inspector, this was *before* my tenure."

"Alright, so, as best you can recall, Miss Lovell never mentioned anything to you about this?"

"Not a word, not a word." Mrs. Taylor looked weary, beset by the most debilitating of challenges: those that arrive *all at once*.

"It's just that there was an unregistered firearm and an unidentified body in your attic, Mrs. Taylor, and that's obviously not the best thing to happen."

"But I didn't know they were there!" Mrs. Taylor replied. "Isn't that obvious?" Her face fell.

"You also didn't mention the rumours about drugs."

"Oh, I'm sorry. I've been so upset about the storm and my business and...

Am I in trouble?" she asked thinly, clasping her hands once more. "Oh, Inspector, if I'd known anything . . . oh, for heaven's sake, I'd have told you in a flash! Back then, I was so busy renovating the hotel and learning the business, getting my first guests . . ." Marjorie shook her head. Her hand-wringing intensified, and she turned away from him, overwhelmed.

"You're not in any trouble, Mrs. Taylor," Graham said. "We don't believe this situation has anything to do with you." Amid this crisis, it was churlish to harangue her, but finding a dead, armed man in her loft *was* a serious situation. "Are you sure you can't tell me anything else about the victim? This Mr. Smith?"

Marjorie saw Graham's frustration in his body language and the angular symbols he made with his pencil in his notebook. "I'm just trying to make sure I don't tell you something that isn't accurate," she said. "I know how important these details are. And, I'm sorry, I can't help you."

"Very well, Mrs. Taylor. I'll take my leave. No need to see me out."

When Graham left the hotel and reached his car, he dialled Marcus Tomlinson's number. "We have a breakthrough, Marcus. A date. February 1982."

CHAPTER THIRTY

"BARNWELL!" GRAHAM HAD barely opened the doors to the police station before he was bellowing for his constable. Barnwell wasn't on reception. No one was.

No one appeared to be in the main office either. But when the door swung closed behind the inspector, Carmen came bounding towards him, her long, floppy ears bouncing around her.

A hand appeared on a desk, and Barnwell appeared red-faced, puffing with effort as he clutched onto the desktop to lever himself upright. Janice appeared a second later, looking awkward and straightening her uniform.

The inspector looked at them curiously, but the urgency of his order superseded his interest in whatever Barnwell and Janice were doing on the floor. "We've got a date and a suspect. My office." Barnwell and Janice clocked his mood immediately and followed him.

"Sounds like you've been busy, sir," Janice said as Graham dumped his keys and notebook on the table before flicking the kettle on.

"Mrs. Northrop spilled the beans. She said she went to the Scilly Isles for her birthday in February 1982. Said the weather had been lovely. Just a hunch, but I looked it up. It's amazing what you can find on the internet these days. Anyhow, her memory and the reality didn't match up, so I went back to question her, and I got quite the story."

"What did she say, sir?" Barnwell had brought a packet of Viennese Whirls with him. He offered it to Graham.

"Oooh, don't mind if I do." With his fingertips, he delicately picked one up, careful not to squeeze it too hard in case the jam and cream filling fell out from between the two soft, sweet, crumbly biscuits they were sandwiched between. Janice declined Barnwell's offer with a shake of her head.

"Mrs. Northrop told me that it was she who found the body. His name was John Smith, but I think we can assume that was fake. Can you check the police database though, Janice? Midtwenties. British, perhaps from London. Smoker, bit of a drinker. Drug user, unless it was forced down him, which I think unlikely."

"Sir." Janice acknowledged his order.

"When Mrs. Northrop found the body and raised the alarm, the owner of the hotel, Miss Lovell, took charge. She forbade Mrs. Northrop from mentioning anything about the death, and that was the last she heard of it. She told me that she had kept schtum all these years. Not told a soul."

"Wow, why would she do that?" Barnwell wondered.

"More recently, Mrs. Northrop thought we might arrest her for not saying anything, rightly as it happens. But back then, it sounds like Miss Lovell ruled the roost with a rod of iron."

"You're mixing metaphysics, sir."

"Wha—oh yes. Anyway, our Miss Lovell, who was a mere eighty years old at the time, had a side hustle. Drugs."

"At the White House Inn? Are you serious?" Barnwell struggled to comprehend the idea.

"Mrs. Taylor said there were rumours at the time. It would have been in Miss Lovell's interest to cover up the death if the rumours were true."

"Blinkin' Nora." Barnwell was still struggling to imagine the graceful, elegant hotel as a drug den.

"But do we think she murdered him, sir? Did she add the rat poison to the drugs?" Janice asked.

"That's for us to find out, Sergeant. We need to follow up on the drug-dealing angle though, and hunt down a lead that Mrs. Northrop offered. Miss Lovell is long gone. She died of cancer about six months after our Mr. X, but she had a grandson who lived on the island. He was in the building trade—an apprentice, and a young lad at the time." Graham consulted his notebook. "A Neville Williams. We need to find him."

"I wonder if Bob the Builder knew him," Barnwell said.

Janice reached for a calculator on Graham's desk and tapped in some numbers. "They'd have been about the same age in 1982. Perhaps even apprentices together, working for Bob's dad."

"Good thoughts. Constable, you follow that up." Graham bounced a pencil in his hand. "Did your exploits in the basement bear fruit?"

Barnwell suppressed a shudder. "Not a sausage. No missing persons from the period we're looking at, at all."

"Nothing on the mispers database either, sir. Nothing that I can tie to Jersey, at least, but now we have more intel and a tighter timeframe, I can run some more checks."

"Someone must have missed him. He can't have just disappeared into a block of concrete without *anyone* noticing."

"What about Dr. Tomlinson, sir?"

"He's still waiting on the DNA results. And there's the ballistics to come. Perhaps if you need a break, Sergeant, you might like to have another cup of tea with Mrs. Taylor. She's still struggling."

"Perhaps I'll send my mum over. They'll get on well."

"Right, off you go, the two of you. Let me know if you turn up anything. I'm going to take Carmen for a walk." Barnwell and Janice turned to leave, but Graham stopped them. "Oh, and . . . what were you two doing on the floor?" Barnwell and Janice glanced at each other. Janice flushed. "Or should I not ask?"

It was Barnwell who spoke. "Just putting Jan through her paces, sir." Graham raised his eyebrows. "A few press-ups, sit-ups, you know." The inspector stared at them, the explanation he so obviously needed hanging unspoken in midair. Janice blinked.

"I've been stress eating, sir. After all these months of dieting and exercise, a few days before the big one, I'm struggling to get in my wedding dress."

🌍

Barnwell raised his head as soon as he heard the doors open. Carmen entered the station first, Graham following, the red lead he held in his hand connected to a similarly coloured harness around the beagle's body.

"Found him, sir! Neville Williams. I was right. Bob the Builder did know him. They were apprentices together until Williams disappeared in, wait for it, 1982. He's not been on the electoral roll on Jersey since. He lived with a Dorothy Williams, presumably his mother, now deceased; she was the daughter of Emily Lovell, owner of The Grange, also deceased; then the trail went cold. No criminal record, but I tracked him down with the help of the DVLA and confirmed with Bob that it's him."

"Where is he?"

"In Bournemouth, sir."

"Excellent work, Constable. Fancy a day trip to the south coast?"

CHAPTER THIRTY-ONE

"YES?" THE DOOR opened only as far as the chain would allow. A man squinted through the opening.
"Neville Williams?" Barnwell raised his police ID so the man could see it. Graham, standing behind him, did the same. The IDs were only partially glanced at. Williams's eyelids flickered. "Can we come in, sir? We'd like to ask you a few questions." The man hesitated, then closed the door. Barnwell braced himself, then heard the chain rattle and the door opened wide.

A skinny man with long limbs, his face ravaged by hard living, stood on the dirty hall carpet. He didn't look at the two police officers but waved them in, his other arm dropping resignedly to his side where it dangled like a forlorn windsock.

Barnwell passed him, followed by Graham. As they walked down the hall, Barnwell peered into the rooms that led off it. "Anyone else here with you?" he called over his shoulder.

"Nope, I live by myself. Always have and always will," Williams said. "Go into the living room. I've been waiting for you. Do you want a cup of tea?" Barnwell looked to Graham for guidance, who gave a minute shake of his head.

"No, thanks. You're fine."

The three of them moved into the front room, cluttered with newspapers, pizza boxes, and takeaway wrappers. Graham walked over to the windows and opened them.

"Please sit down, Mr. Williams," Barnwell said.

"Wha—oh, alright." Neville Williams folded his long legs as he sat on a cracked and peeling synthetic leather chair. He was awkward like a giraffe and nervously picked at his cuticles, giving Graham the impression he was on something, or at least jittery, nervous. "Aren't you going to sit down? You're making me nervous standing like that," Williams said.

Barnwell sat on the sofa. Graham peered at a framed poster on the wall. A man with a huge afro, exotic features, and a long, lanky physique riffed on a guitar. Underneath was printed "Thin Lizzy, Fort Regent, Jersey, UK. 1981."

"Mr. Williams, I'm Constable Barnwell. This is Detective Inspector Graham. We're from Gorey. You grew up there, I understand."

Williams's eyes flicked around the room, unsure on what to alight. Eventually, he nodded. "Yeah, but I haven't lived there in decades. Left when I wasn't even twenty. Too small for the likes of me. I lived with my mum." He didn't continue, so Barnwell prompted him with a turn of his head as he raised his eyebrows. Williams sighed like a teenager being asked to lay the table.

"Left school as soon as I could. Hated it, you see. Got an apprenticeship with a local builder—Bob the Builder. Bob Simms, senior. Good man. He's dead now, but his son carries on, or so I heard through the grapevine." Williams looked out of the window at the narrow, quiet street lined with terraced houses and their owners' cars. With another sigh, he turned back. Graham moved on from the poster, peering at a mess of papers and unopened envelopes on a sideboard.

"So why did you leave?" Barnwell asked Williams.

Williams shrugged. "Wanted something more. I was a young guy. Gorey was much too small for me. Needed the bright lights."

"You just hopped it and left?"

"More or less. I had no ties, nothing to stay for. Nothing much, anyway." Williams stopped and seemed to have come to the end of this branch of his life story, so Barnwell shifted tactics.

"What about your grandmother, Emily Lovell? She ran a hotel in Gorey, so we heard."

Williams shifted in his seat. "Yeah, my nan. My mum was her only child. They're all dead now, long gone. What about her?"

"And she ran the hotel until her death in 1982?"

"She died of lung cancer, yeah. She chain-smoked. Hopeless case. Nothing would stop her. Didn't matter what we said."

"See, there's been suggestions that the hotel was a place you could go to get drugs and that Emily Lovell was in the middle of it. What do you know about that?"

Williams shrugged once more but broke eye contact with Barnwell and looked out at the street again. Two teenage girls walked by in their school uniforms, gossiping, their ties—as bright blue as their blazers—askew against their white blouses. Williams didn't answer Barnwell's question.

"Mr. Williams? Neville?"

When Williams continued to ignore Barnwell, Graham leaned forward and tapped him on his knee. Williams looked vaguely at Graham as if seeing him for the first time.

"The thing is, Mr. Williams, we believe that Emily Lovell was selling drugs out of the hotel."

"The drugs had nothing to do with me," Williams answered quickly. The words came easily, eagerly even. "Yeah, she was on the make, at least that was the rumour, but I never saw anything of it. Nannie Em was always telling me to stay away from the stuff. She was pretty hard, my nan." Williams's eyes cleared.

Seeing he had his attention, Graham pressed on. "While the drugs might not have had anything to do with you, something related did happen in which you got caught up, didn't it?" Williams glanced outside at the street again. They could hear the jingle of an ice-cream van pealing repeatedly.

"Mr. Williams, when you opened the door, you said you had been waiting for us. We gave you no advance notice of our visit, so what did you mean by that?"

Williams dragged his bottom teeth against his top lip and dug in so hard that Graham expected him to draw blood. But Williams pressed his lips together, rolling them between his teeth. "Nothing."

"Nothing? Doesn't seem like it would be nothing to me."

"Look, it was nothing to do with *me*, okay?" Williams glared at Graham. "The drugs, none of it. It was all her."

"What was all her, Neville? What wasn't anything to do with you?" Williams twisted in his seat, lengthening his long legs, and began to rock, his hands on his knees.

"I can't tell you."

"What can't you tell us, Neville?" Graham prodded. Williams continued to rock, his eyes focused on his hands. Slowly and gently, Graham placed his own over Williams's, and gradually the distressed man ceased his rocking.

Suddenly, Williams pulled his hands away. After a series of deep breaths, the words he had been refusing to speak came forth, first in staccato bursts, then in a torrent.

"She asked me for help . . . She was my nan. I was only seventeen. . . What could I do?" Williams sniffed, then began to sob. He grabbed Graham's wrists. Barnwell tensed.

"All my life I've waited for you to find me. I can't believe it's taken you this long. Why did it take you *so* long?" Williams's wild eyes looked into Graham's calm ones. "This could have been over long ago!" He released Graham's wrists and pushed them away, almost in disgust. "You've no idea what my life's been like. Always looking over my shoulder. Never feeling safe. And the nightmares! You can't imagine!"

Williams glanced at Barnwell, his eyes appealing. It occurred to the constable that the distressed man could have confessed at any time. He chose not to.

"What happened, Neville?" Graham asked. "Did your grandmother call you for help?" He leaned against the mantelpiece, seemingly unperturbed by the man's erratic behaviour.

"She said to get down to the hotel. I was due at work, but she said she had a more important job and that I should call in sick."

"When was this, Neville?"

"It was the day after Valentine's in 1982. A Monday. I'll never forget."

CHAPTER THIRTY-TWO

"EIGHT O'CLOCK IN the morning. The cleaning person had found a . . . body in his room. It was awful, it was." Williams sobbed and slapped his palms forcefully across his eyes. Barnwell winced. That had to have hurt. "He was lying on the floor next to the bed. Looked like he'd fallen off it."

"What was your grandmother doing?" Graham was as cool as ice. Calm.

"Not much. She just stared at him, like. Then she told me to 'deal with it.' I said, 'What do you mean?' She said, 'Deal with him. I don't want him found.' Her cancer was terminal, you see. She'd only a few months to live. 'I recognise him. I gave him the drugs that killed him, Nev,' she said. 'I'm not having my last months messed with. No one must find out about this until I'm gone.'"

"What did she mean by that?"

"She had it all worked out. She wanted me to bury him in cement. She told me I had to build a brick frame and mix and pour the concrete into it halfway. When I'd done that, we put the body inside and covered him up."

"Sounds like hard work."

"It was. I had to lug the bricks and mixes up the back stairs and do it without anyone seeing. I laid the bricks, then filled it in like she said. Nannie Em helped me with the guy, but by the time we moved him, he was stiff as a board and hard to handle. Regardless, I got the job done. It wasn't the best. The mortar between the bricks wasn't completely dry when I poured in the cement. I was worried it would fall apart, but I propped the brickwork up with lengths of wood in the hopes that it would hold. And it must have."

"Then what did you do?"

"I tell you what I didn't do. I didn't hang around. I got out of there as soon as I could. I moved away immediately. I couldn't stay there, not on Jersey. Not with the memories and living with what I'd done. I've hated myself ever since. What happened ruined my life. I never married, never had kids, always going job to job, looking over my shoulder. I mean, Nannie Em, she was a mean old bird, always was. You did what she told you, no messin', and you didn't argue if you knew what was good for you. I wanted no part of anything to do with her after that. I left the island, and I haven't been back since."

"And nothing was ever said?"

"Nothing. It was like it never happened. No one came knocking. As far as I know, Nannie Em lived out her last few months with that . . . that . . . thing above her, and everyone was none the wiser. Then she died, lucky old bag. I still can't believe that bloke's laid there all this time without anyone finding him."

"Take me back to when your grandmother called you. What did she say?"

"Oh gosh." Williams put his hand to his head and looked up at the ceiling. "It was a long time ago."

"Broadly, then. What did she say?" Graham sat now in an armchair facing Williams.

"She didn't tell me why until I got there. She showed me to the attic. We went up the back stairs, and she pointed to the man on the floor."

"And what did you see?"

"He was fully dressed, lying next to the bed. There was a glass coffee table beside a sofa, and it was obvious that he'd been snorting cocaine, then perhaps stumbled to the bed and didn't make it or did make it and rolled off. His hand was clutching the bedspread across his body like this." Williams crossed one arm to his opposite shoulder and made his hand into a fist.

"We had to prise the bedspread out of his hand. The other lay on his chest. He was on his back. His eyes . . ." Williams wiped the back of his hand across his top lip. "Oh." He exhaled. "They were open, and they *wouldn't* close. They stayed like that the whole time I was working. I had to put the bedspread over him. Terrible, it was. In the end, I found some washers to weigh down his eyelids."

"And your grandmother didn't want to declare the body because . . ."

"I told you. Because she had supplied him with the cocaine. She said so. He must have overdosed. That's what she said, anyway. 'I'm not having my last days on this earth spent on remand for supplying,' she told me. I knew she was ill, but I didn't know she was definitely dying, so that surprised me. I was in shock. I was just a lad. It was . . . horrific. I've regretted it every day since. I asked her, 'What about me? They'll find him eventually and come after me?' But she didn't seem to care nothing. Just shrugged. Said I was young enough to deal with it. Bloody old hag, she was. Before it happened, I didn't mind her, but afterwards . . . "

"Would your grandmother have cut the cocaine? You know, made it go a little farther, more profit for her?"

Williams's eyes grew wide. "No, I don't think so. But then, what would I know? I was just her wet-behind-the-ears grandson. And I wish it had remained that way."

"Did you see a gun in the room when you were there . . . mixing?"

"A gun? No, nothing like that. I'd have remembered."

"What about a red suitcase?"

Williams screwed up his eyes as he cast his mind back. "Er, yeah, maybe. But Nannie Em dealt with all that. I was just the mug who had to bury the body. Nothing more, nothing less. That was enough."

Graham sat back in his chair and leant his elbow on the arm, thumb under his chin and his forefinger laying on his cheekbone as he regarded the man, only seventeen when this crime was committed but now nearly sixty.

"Mr. Williams, I am sure you'll understand that, while perhaps coerced into this action and only a minor at the time, you have kept this knowledge to yourself for over forty years. That's forty years during which the family of this man has had no idea what happened to him, causing trauma to them. And"—Graham's mind drifted to Mrs. Taylor—"to others who have been affected by the discovery of his body and the knowledge that it lay there as they lived their lives." Williams stared at the floor and nodded.

"As such, it is required that we arrest you in connection with charges that relate to preventing the decent burial of a corpse, disposal of a corpse with intent to obstruct or prevent a coroner's inquest, and the perversion of the course of justice. There may be further charges to follow. Do you understand?" Williams continued to stare at the floor. Again, he nodded.

"Constable Barnwell, would you please . . ."

Barnwell stood and, putting a hand around Williams's arm, lifted him to standing. Williams offered him his wrists, and as Barnwell read him his rights, he locked the handcuffs around them.

"The local police will take you to the station and we'll liaise with them in connection with your case. It will be the local court's decision whether to let you out on bail or place you on remand."

Williams fixed his eyes on the floor before raising them. "I want you to know, I gave him a decent burial . . . in the circumstances. Said a little prayer, I did. And I laid a rose across his chest. It wasn't much—the rose had wilted—but it seemed the right thing to do."

As they left the house an hour later, Barnwell closed the front door behind them quietly. "Poor lad. Getting caught up in that when you're only seventeen."

"He had forty-two years to confess," Graham replied. "He didn't, and now he's reaping what he sowed."

Barnwell straightened his uniform jacket. "Yep, you're right, sir. Should've taken his medicine long ago. Wouldn't have been nearly as nasty."

"No, and if he had, this wouldn't have been our case to clear up. It would have been someone else's. As it is, we've still got a long way to go. Miss Lovell didn't adulterate that cocaine with rat poison. A supplier would know it would kill and their business would go poof. Also, there were no other deaths at that time that would suggest a bad batch. No, that rat poison was placed in Mr. X's cocaine deliberately. Someone wanted to kill him, specifically him."

"But who?"

"Who indeed, Barnwell. Who indeed."

CHAPTER THIRTY-THREE

LAURA BUSIED HERSELF making sure the research desk was in good order before the lecture finished. In a few minutes, thirty-five or so enthusiastic and newly informed amateur genealogists would be hungry for resources. Her role would be to guide them to the icon on the library website for the digitised parish records and then answer questions about a hundred different other things. With the lecture wrapping up, she was pressed for time.

Freddie Solomon hovered. He would take the number of questions she had to answer to a hundred and one. Or a hundred and twenty-five. There was no telling with Freddie.

So far that afternoon, he'd asked her all manner of random questions—about the library's *whole* range of programs, planned renovations to the annexe, meeting room bookings—everything *except* about the case of the unfortunate Mr. X, in which she suspected he was mostly interested.

"There's no point dancing around, Freddie."

"Aww," he complained, "that's a shame. You're quite the dancer. I've been watching you."

It was a tactic of Freddie's that Laura knew well: keep her talking until she either inadvertently revealed something or lost her patience and told him to clear off. "Please, Freddie. I'm about to get slammed. What do you want?"

"Any news on the White House Inn mob case?"

"Crikey, if David hears you calling it that, he'll slap the cuffs on you again."

"I'm a member," Freddie proudly reminded her, "of the Fourth Estate."

"Yes, well," Laura replied, stepping away as the lecture crowd streamed through from the annexe. "The way David is with these things, I wouldn't be surprised if he's already burned down the first three. So, you'll be next whether you like it or not." Laura continued forward and headed off the genealogists at the pass. She sent one group to the computers and the other to a suite of desks flanked by shelves and displays: the library's new Local History Resources Section.

Once the chaos was reduced to a simmer, Freddie sidled over again. "I'm going to sound like a broken record..."

"My grandmother recommended fixing electrical things by giving them a stout slap," Laura said with relish. "If you get stuck, I can perhaps help you out by following her advice."

"These guys did all kinds of things back then, Laura. You know it and I know it."

"Stop inferring." Her eyes still on her patrons, Laura scowled. "You have no idea what I know. We're past the time when men get to speak for women, Freddie."

"I mean you're from that part of the East End," he said.

"I'm from Kent, not Albert Square. I only worked in the East End peripherally and only for a very short time. It just happened to be a momentous one. Thanks, probably, to my friendly and reliable manner that causes people to trust me sometimes"—Laura leaned in close to Freddie and opened her eyes wide—"*prematurely*." Laura had ended up on Jersey having entered a witness protection scheme after overhearing details of a diamond heist while working in a pub.

Characteristically, Freddie didn't respond to her corrections of his assertions. To do so would be to admit that he had been wrong. He simply acted as though he hadn't heard her. "These guys, the ones in HMP Holbrooke that I've interviewed, they *used* people to take down the competition and punish snitches, and yet they've gone down for precisely a single armed robbery apiece despite a career spanning *decades*."

"So? They're in jail, Freddie. And they're in their seventies, aren't they?"

"Seventy-nine," he said. "If we could get another conviction, that would bring closure for somebody, surely." Laura ignored his use of the word "we."

"And plenty of new readers for you." Laura turned away.

"My blog is both a thriving business and service to the public," Freddie said, apparently unaware of how puffed up and ridiculous he sounded.

"I'm quite sure." Laura coughed. "But consider this. Even if you uncover a hidden truth and deliver some 'just desserts' that'll satisfy your readership, how much would the extra life sentence matter?"

Freddie raised his voice just enough to press home the point. "Justice. I believe in punishing criminals."

Laura sighed. "Look, what is it that you *want*, Freddie?"

"I want to help in the Mr. X case!"

"And what is it that you want from *me*? Because I'm sure you're not here to admire my latest 'New Books' display."

Freddie shifted from one foot to another. "I thought maybe you had some intel you could toss my way. Or..."

"Or?"

"Or you know someone who might." Laura had had more than enough of

Freddie for one day. She turned away again. "I thought you believed in justice!" Freddie hissed, mindful of the library's rule on silence.

"I believe," Laura said, heading away, "in providing high-quality local library services. Toodle-pip."

Thwarted in his mission, Freddie didn't leave at once. He continued his systematic search of the Channel Islands press, but as usual, there wasn't any mention of the incidents he was chasing up and nothing that pertained to the identity of Mr. X. "Officialdom, pressurising the media," he muttered, "forcing self-censorship to spare an inevitable panic. That's what this is."

There was nothing for it. He had to return to his source—happily, a pair of sources—who had so far helped him outline his book. *Murderer's Island* (working title) would be a gritty and exciting narrative, his first entry in the true-crime genre.

But it would only work if the two men, Arthur and George Parnaby, a pair of former gangsters who Freddie had befriended, would speak freely. They'd both spent twenty-five years in prison and, for one of them, justice had already come knocking. He was terminal. Freddie hoped that death for one and grief for the other might spare the pair for another few weeks. Just until he could apply for another HMP Holbrooke visitor's pass.

CHAPTER THIRTY-FOUR

"WOW," FIONA EXCLAIMED, lifting off her ear protection. "This thing is a *monster*."

"Even underwater apparently," said Tomlinson. "Let's be grateful it wasn't a high-speed weapon."

"Why's that?"

"The water tank can only slow down a bullet so much. If it starts out too quickly, it'll make it all the way through the glass . . ."

"And ruin the experiment," concluded Fiona.

"And flood the place. And I remember asking for *two* rounds, young lady." Tomlinson peered into the water tank as the waves slowed their sloshing. "But if I can still count, and I believe those capacities are still in place despite my advanced years, that was six."

"Got carried away," Fiona said with a rueful grin, releasing the Smith & Wesson from its mount by the tank and setting it on the table.

"Easily done, I suppose. It's not every day you get to fire one of these." Tomlinson bent over, his hands on his knees. He regarded the firearm suspiciously. "Now we've got our impressions, what does Detective Inspector Graham want done with this fiendish thing?"

"He said to store it in the new 'Ancient Arms Room,' wherever that is." Fiona bagged up the weapon and the pair stepped into the hallway.

"One level down," the on-duty firearms sergeant said, looking up from his screen. "You, er, you like guns, then?" he asked Fiona.

"Ooh, yes. Not in a weird way though," she added quickly.

Tomlinson followed Fiona from the ballistics room, past several other labs and a small open-plan IT hub until they reached a keypad that opened one door, and then another. They eventually arrived at an electronic, heavy metal slider that was operated by a guard once they showed him their passes. Entering a white-painted room, the walls lined with shelving, they glanced around. It would have been a routine storage space except the shelves were crammed with guns.

"Stone the crows!" Tomlinson exclaimed.

"Or," Fiona replied, looking at the vast arsenal, "we could just shoot them." She grinned. Tomlinson rolled his eyes.

"Clever. Half of this stuff is from the Jerries by the looks of it. That's an old MG forty-two." Tomlinson pointed to a machine gun standing on a bipod. "Bloody *lethal*, they were."

"I didn't know you were into that sort of thing." Fiona was toying with a handgun so ancient it was partly rusted. "Perhaps I should have something like this back at the castle. To defend myself in case anyone tries to storm the battlements."

"How are you getting on out there? Not too eerie, is it?"

"Yes, it is. And I love it!"

"Ah. Bert was right then."

"How so?"

"He said you were a game girl, not easily frightened."

"That sounds about right. I like novel, exciting, strange." Fiona opened a velvet-lined drawer and peered at a short-barrelled pistol laying inside.

"That's a Sauer 38H you're looking at. Favourite of the German police during World War II."

"Looks posh." Fiona stared at the gun's ivory grip and gold inlay. There was an engraving on the side.

"They were sometimes presented to Nazi officials to commemorate things."

"You mean like tankards for long service, or gold watches?"

"Something like that. Ah-ha! I knew there'd be one in here." Tomlinson spied a black, stubby weapon and pulled it from the shelf. "Ever seen one of these?"

"Only in documentaries."

Marcus set the Sterling submachine gun on a table near the door. "Got your phone?" he asked her, clapping his hands and rubbing them together.

"Yeah, why?"

"Set the stopwatch."

"Okay, ready."

"Go!" The elderly physician's hands became a studied whir of motion. Pieces were coming off the gun, large and then smaller, until it was set out like a manufacturer's diagram: muzzle, barrel, magazine, stock, firing pin. "Finished!" he said, stepping back and standing neatly to attention. His hand twitched as he almost saluted.

Staring at the pieces as though Marcus had forged them from thin air, Fiona finally said, "You know what? I work with the *strangest* bunch of people."

Marcus laughed and used his handkerchief to clean his hands of gun oil. "Army Medical Corps for three years in the seventies. When patients were few, the other doctors and I got competitive about the *silliest* things. Anyway," he said, a little bashful about his field-stripping ability, "let's find Mr. X's revolver a home."

It went into a padded drawer labelled and electronically tagged. "What do you think it means that Mr. X was carrying this gun?" Fiona wondered as they headed out.

"Could be all manner of things," Tomlinson said. "Difficult to speculate."

"I mean, it could punch a bullet through a brick wall. You could stop an elephant with it. How often are charging bull elephants a genuine risk to the average person?"

"Not often, that's for sure. Let's find out where it's been, shall we?"

The ballistics discovery process, courtesy of the National Ballistics Intelligence Service in Birmingham, was almost entirely digital, but on this occasion, the test's findings required another quick phone call to Miranda Weiss. "The striations are a perfect match. The incident was in the late seventies," she informed Tomlinson.

"What kind of incident was it?" Dr. Weiss hadn't referred to a murder or even a crime.

"Best I can tell, some lunatic got trigger-happy outside a pub and shot up his mate's car."

"Heroic."

"I see you sent six images," Miranda said as she finished downloading the high-definition scans showing microscopic analyses of the bullets. "Did your assistant get trigger-happy too?"

"Something like that. She's new and prone to the odd moment of giddiness."

"Well, tell her never to get giddy around firearms again. And," Miranda added, her tone softening, "that she's welcome to come to Southampton anytime. I've got a pile of stuff waiting to be analysed, and my best technician went into labour two weeks early."

"If Jersey can spare her and we don't find another collection of weird evidence in someone's attic, I dare say she'll accept," Tomlinson said, winking at Fiona next to him. "Will you let her play with the new UV setup, the one with the—"

"View that integrates three wavelengths at once? Maybe, if she's good." When combined, the separate feeds—visible, infrared, and ultraviolet light—revealed *everything*.

"Is it really like having X-ray vision?" Tomlinson said.

"Yes, and half my incoming calls are about borrowing it. I wrote a nineteen-thousand-word proposal to get that thing, Marcus, and it's *mine. All mine.*"

"What kind of evidence would someone need to get some time on it?"

Dr. Weiss thought for a second. "Jack the Ripper's underpants, still with the label on."

Marcus laughed as he brought the call to a close. "I'll see what I can do."

Fiona continued to puzzle over photographs of the gun. "What can we deduce from this?"

"Difficult to speculate. But if he was planning to deprive another human of life, he must have been dangerous. Dangerous people aren't always the smartest. They do stupid things, like carrying a gun already known to the police."

"A galumphing, great *big* gun already known to the police."

"The heavier it is, the less likely that he was an accomplished hit. Pros like them small, fierce, quiet, and efficient."

"I see what you're saying. If our guy was here to target someone, he was setting himself up for difficulty, if not failure. Not being very bright. Suggests inexperience."

Tomlinson turned to Fiona, her eager face full of intelligence and curiosity, her eyes alight. "Exactly so. But perhaps he was here on a suicide mission, literally. Perhaps the drugs and his heart got to him first. We don't know that he intended the bullets for someone else. Maybe he decided to do away with himself on a beach overlooking the ocean." Tomlinson's phone pinged. The DNA results were in. Marcus handed Fiona a mug. "Would you be a dear and make me another cup of tea?"

When she had gone, he quickly switched to his computer screen to open the email. He scanned the report, his temperature rising. Picking up his phone, he sent a text.

> Ballistics and more. Interesting.

Over a hundred miles away, Barnwell was driving to Poole where he and Inspector Graham would catch the ferry back to Jersey. His senior officer focused on his phone. Tired and puzzled after his interview with Neville Williams, Graham tapped the screen as he placed a call.

"Marcus? What have you got? Something good, I hope."

"The bullet striations show that the gun was used in 1978. Man in a car was shot at."

"Got the C/N?"

"Yep, 15635897."

"Great. I'm on my way to catch the ferry back. Could you send the info to Sergeant Harding? She'll look it up. What was the other thing you had to tell me?"

"We got the DNA results from the hairbrush, but our man doesn't appear on any database." Graham scrunched up his nose and pursed his lips. "But there was a strong match with someone who does." Graham sat up a little taller. "Twenty-seven percent—with a certain Angela Dillon."

"Twenty-seven percent? What does that mean?"

"My guess would be a cousin, aunt, maybe a half sister."

"Hmm."

"Fiona told me she could reconstruct our guy's face from the remains and some sorcery using artificial intelligence jiggery-pokery. Would you like her to do that? It wouldn't be perfect, but it could help. It would provide you with a picture of what Mr. X might have looked like when he died."

"Brilliant. That would help a lot. Send everything to the station. I'll take it from there."

"It's simply amazing what they can do these days. If we had a photo of him, she could manipulate it so that we could see what he looked like at any age, she said."

"Well, let's hope we find out who he is soon. Good work, Marcus. Thanks a bunch. And thank Fiona too."

"Angela Margaret Dillon, date of birth March sixth, 1968. Wandsworth. String of arrests for prostitution starting in 1983, last one 2013," Janice told Graham over the phone.

"Long career. Where can we find her?"

"Her last known address was 43 Walking Topham, Leeslake." Graham looked it up.

"Are you sure?" he said, frowning.

"That's what it says. Posh, isn't it?"

"I'll say. What was her last arrest for?"

"Soliciting."

"Nothing about keeping a brothel or anything more lucrative?"

"Nope."

"Okay, see what else you can find out about her. We may need to pay her a visit too. What about the gun?"

"Ah, yes. 1976, Clapham. Tiff between two small-time gangsters. The suspect was Arthur Parnaby. At the time he was known for piddly stuff—laundering, a bit of dealing—but seems to have escalated: protection with menaces, violent assault. Currently well into a twenty-eight-year stretch with his twin brother. They're in HMP Holbrooke for armed robbery."

"Holbrooke?"

"That's right, sir. Security guard killed. No charges were ever brought in connection with the earlier gun incident and no further record of the gun until it turned up in Mrs. Taylor's attic."

Graham squeezed his eyes tight shut as fragments of a memory swooped around his brain, gathering force and substance. Freddie. He mentioned having sources in HMP Holbrooke.

CHAPTER THIRTY-FIVE

The Gorey Gossip
Monday Evening Edition

You already know what some say about me: I'm an irritant, a fly in the constabulary's ointment, a man the police could never trust. I get emails calling me a "crank," a "conspiracy theorist," and a "dull, unenterprising wordsmith." (Of the three, only the last stings.) Detective Inspector Graham and his team dismiss me, most recently as a "thoughtless little weasel."

But I know a thing or two about right and wrong. A man died in his room at the White House Inn on the evening of Sunday 14th February 1982. His body was not disclosed and left to lie undiscovered for over forty years until it was recently unearthed in a roughly hewn concrete tomb. That is wrong.

But here's what is true: Jersey is neither as safe as we hope, nor as it could be. I'm certain that a sequence of mob entanglements has marked the last several decades of our island's history.

It stands to reason, given his inauspicious burial, that the man at the White House Inn did not die from natural causes. And after speaking with my sources deep inside the dangerous world of London's organised crime, I'm certain I'm right to doubt the Gorey police investigation. Given what I know, DI Graham's work so far has been slow and incomplete. Simply put, they are going in the wrong direction.

Because the past has chosen to present itself and because our law enforcement appears to be going down blind alleys, I am compelled to speak out. I am not party to the intimate findings of the investigation, and my suspicions are speculative, but they are grounded in intel gained from insider sources and combined with a good dose of common sense.

I suspect that the dead man was the target of a diabolical, premeditated murder. I believe it is likely that he was on Jersey for nefarious reasons. And that the gun in his suitcase was either to perform a hit or to protect himself as he completed whatever job he was here to perform. I also suspect his death is maybe the tip of an evidentiary iceberg. Are there, in fact, other shoes still to drop?

I hope I'm wrong, but everything so far—including years of reporting on Jersey's criminal community—is telling me that I'm right.

CHAPTER THIRTY-SIX

"WHEN I SAY *immediately*, Freddie, I don't mean whenever it suits you." Detective Inspector Graham was standing in reception when the blogger finally arrived. Graham's plan had been to close out the day and go home, but Freddie's blog post had compelled an explanation. He had been summoned to the station.

"And I don't recall being a member of the constabulary," Freddie shot back, "so I don't have to follow your orders."

"Doing anything *other* than that," Graham argued, "would be considered impeding my duties. Or is that your intention?"

"*Impeding* your . . . ? You work for me, remember?"

"The longer a murder remains unsolved, the more you can write about it in your ridiculous blog. More sensational articles mean more revenue from your advertisers—"

Freddie interrupted the inspector. "They're called commercial partners these days."

"All of whom need their heads examined, if you ask me. I'd sooner partner up with half the cons in Strangeways than with you. So, investigative delays serve your purposes quite well, don't they?"

"What delays?" Freddie demanded.

"I could be working on the case, but I'm here, having to yell at you for imperilling my investigation. *Again*."

"I haven't *imperilled* anything," Freddie insisted passionately. "I'm a private citizen running a successful and legitimate business. A member of the Fourth Estate."

"So you keep saying. I'm going to give you one final chance." The redness in Graham's cheeks receded gradually. "Retract your latest article and issue an apology." Remembering Laura's advice for situations with Freddie—and with everyone else, for that matter—he attempted an incentive. "It won't take a minute. I'll even put some tea on. You can use our Wi-Fi."

"No," Freddie said simply, like a child.

"You're certain?"

"Certain." The two men glared at one another, Freddie doing a creditable job of attempting to intimidate a man six inches taller than him. Thrusting his chin out, he defiantly held eye contact with the inspector. After five seconds, Graham blinked.

"Very well, Freddie. Constable?"

"Boss?"

"Would Mr. Solomon be more miserable in cell one with the air vent that perpetually rattles, or in cell two with that cold draft we can't pin down?"

"Weatherman said it's going to be a chilly night."

"Then get cell two ready, there's a good chap."

Freddie's panicked expression said it all. "You're *not* going to . . ."

"Yes, I am," said Graham. Barnwell jangled his keys and whistled contentedly; he had a new customer.

"Can I speak to Laura first?" Freddie asked brazenly.

Graham stood, his temper fast approaching a red line. "You can speak to a *lawyer* once you're charged."

Freddie sat stock-still. "I'm not retracting, and I'm not apologising."

Graham rubbed his hands together. "Glad to hear it. Now hear this. Frederick Solomon, I'm arresting you on suspicion of perverting the course of justice and for obstructing an officer in the course of his duties. You do not have to say anything unless you wish to do so, but it may harm your defence if you fail to mention something you later rely on in court."

"Are you *serious*?" Freddie followed this up with a highly colourful oath.

"Those cells have got *bars* on them. Isn't that right, Constable Barnwell?"

"Yep! Big, strong, steel ones, sir."

"Sounds serious to me," Graham said. He looked at his prisoner. "Come on, let's take a look at your accommodations for the next day or two."

"But I was being helpful!" Freddie complained, pressed forward by Barnwell's uncompromising knuckles against the knobbles of his spine. "I'm starting to crack the puzzle."

"You're the one who's cracked."

"And if those old guys in HMP Holbrooke open up to me some more, I'll know everything! I might even be able to help you iden—" Freddie tripped over his own feet.

"Mind your step," Graham said. "We don't want any loony theories propagating about how you nearly died in police custody."

"I want to talk to Laura!" Freddie begged fruitlessly.

"No."

"You talk to her then. She'll tell you that I was being helpful!"

"You're being a massive pain, and I'm dealing with enough of those already." With Barnwell ceremoniously holding open the cell door, Graham urged Freddie inside, then shut it with a convincing *clang*.

"Go to Hull!" Freddie cried through the door.

Graham opened the small, eye-level hatch in the cell door. "Same to you. Didn't your mother teach you any manners?"

"Hull, I said! H-U-L-L. Go to HMP Holbrooke. It's near Hull. You know, the big prison there?"

"Know it? I practically populated it to overflowing." Graham smiled through the grill, proud of his record. "I was instrumental in creating a thriving and diverse community at HMP Holbrooke."

"Really?" Freddie said, taken aback. Had he a major source of information on his doorstep this whole time?

"Yeah, it wasn't difficult. I just arrested, charged, and got convictions on a whole range of dodgy people who lived life in the fast lane. Anyhow, I'll be leaving you now. I do hope you enjoy your stay with us." Graham's face in the small slot disappeared, only to be replaced by that of Constable Barnwell.

"Would you like microwave lasagna or microwave butter chicken for dinner?" Barnwell asked him.

Freddie muttered something Barnwell pretended not to hear. "I think you should have something. It's gonna be a long time 'til breakfast."

"Butter chicken." Freddie was sullen.

"I'll be back in a bit. Don't have too much fun in there."

"George and Arthur Parnaby. Talk to them!" Barnwell closed the hatch just in time to see Freddie throw himself on the cell bench and sling his arm across his eyes like a grounded teenager.

His plaintive cries followed them up the stairs, but Barnwell and Graham exchanged smiles and carried on. They were freed for now from the pestilence of amateur news media. The only downside, the one that Graham was attempting to push from his mind, was that Laura wouldn't like what he had done one little bit.

CHAPTER THIRTY-SEVEN

EXHAUSTED AFTER HIS long day, Graham did his best to sneak in quietly, but removing his coat, setting down his briefcase, and levering off one of his shoes made enough noise to wake Laura and then some. She appeared at the top of the stairs. "Are you a burglar?" she asked, shining her phone at him, "or an overzealous policeman?"

"My zeal is legendary," he replied. "And yes, I am returned from the bounteous evidence buffet that was Bournemouth via a small detour to the station on my way back."

"It went well, then."

Graham nearly fell over trying to get his second shoe off. "Better than expected in some ways. Not so great in others. We're no closer to catching our murderer, but it was useful in ascertaining how our Mr. X came to be buried in Mrs. Taylor's attic."

"You still don't know his full name?"

"Nope, still stuck on that. I would have been home earlier but for your friend and mine, Mr. Freddie Solomon."

Laura turned off the light on her phone. "I saw his post."

It came out quickly; Graham's fatigue loosened his tongue. "He's interfered in police business for the last time."

"What do you mean?" Laura said as Graham slowly climbed the stairs. She didn't budge from her position at the top of them. "For the last time?"

"There are proper channels for submitting information about active or even closed cases. His blog is not the place for it. Still, he chooses again and again to press the 'publish' button."

"He has a large readership now, including outside the Channel Islands..."

"That makes things even worse. No one's *forcing* him to reveal sensitive information, love. He chooses to print salacious titbits that compromise our work and rubbish us in the process. It's a one-two punch, one he insists on consistently delivering. I've had enough. Someone has to hold him accountable. I've arrested him and thrown him in a cell for the night while he thinks about his actions."

Laura frowned, her hands on her hips as she stood defiant, sternly guarding the stairway. Only the moon-and-clouds night lamp on her landing dresser provided any light, and she appeared ghostly.

"What have you done?" she said. "What about the freedom of the press?"

Two steps short of Laura's guard post, Graham stopped. "If you'd been there, you'd have seen I had no choice. I don't like the idea of locking up journalists any more than you do."

"Good to hear you're not turning into a dictator." Laura stood her ground, barely contained fury radiating from her.

"Look." Graham wearily set his shoes down on the stairs. "Say for a minute that we'd found solid DNA evidence connected to Mr. X's death—someone who's alive and known to us. If we arrested and charged them, I wouldn't be able to find a single juror who . . ." His words faded in the face of Laura's unyielding but quiet, fierce rage.

"Reach for the black grip underneath," she said, "to pull out the sofa bed."

"Laura, please. That's not very reasonable."

"You denied him his freedom, so now you get denied too. In your case, a comfy bed."

"Look, all I want is a shower and a good night's sleep." Wordlessly but firmly, Laura pointed back the way he had come. "I've only put Freddie Solomon in a nice, warm holding cell for the night. That's all. I should have done it ages ago. I didn't lock him in with anyone who'd beat his lights out. By breakfast, he'll be playing chess with Barnwell, you'll see."

"You forced Barnwell to suffer the consequences of your foolhardy decision?" Laura had the temerity to wag her finger at him. She folded her arms tightly, unimpressed. "You should have talked to me first."

"That's what Freddie said."

"Well, he was right! And he'll be right to publish an excoriating piece about Gorey Constabulary as soon as he gets out. I mean, he'll hang you out to dry, won't he? Investigative overreach, suppression of the media . . ."

"I'm not the KGB, for heaven's sake."

"What do you think the national press will make of it?"

Alarmingly, amidst this crowded, complex case, Graham had entirely forgotten to consider the wider impact of the arrest. "Ah."

"After your brilliant years here, that'll be all you're remembered for: the policeman who lost his mind and started jailing journalists."

"He's only a bl . . ." Graham began but wisely killed the thought. Freddie had already established his credentials with Laura and the community. They didn't amount to anything as far as he was concerned, but that's not how others perceived him. Standing there on the step, feeling like he'd just run a marathon in the wrong direction, Graham sighed.

Only slightly softer, Laura said, "Go and let him out."

"Tomorrow," he offered. He looked at his watch. It was past one o'clock. "Today." He was exhausted.

"*Now*, please," Laura insisted, her tone's bite growing. "He needs to be rested so he can cover Janice's wedding at the weekend, for one thing. And not be threatening a punch-up with you across the aisle while he's at it for another."

"Alright. I'll call Barnwell and . . ."

"You'll go yourself. I won't have you outsourcing the job of solving your self-made problems to your subordinates."

"He's at the station anyway. He has to keep an eye on Freddie."

"Show some leadership and conviction for your decisions. Go."

"It's raining," Graham complained. Twenty hours awake, two ferry journeys, and multiple long drives had dulled him almost to insensibility.

"Just one of the many hassles that could have easily been avoided by talking to me *before* you made a silly decision," Laura said, tall and mighty on the top step.

Graham sighed again loudly. "Okay."

"And an apology to Freddie would be nice too," she said as he slowly turned to go. "But it doesn't have to be in writing."

Graham took two steps down the stairs. "Is the condemned man afforded a last meal before dying of ritual humiliation at Freddie Solomon's feet?"

"No, he is not." Laura wouldn't even let him change his clothes until the wrong was righted.

Allowing his subconscious to handle the seven-minute drive to the police station, Graham worked to set aside his weary frustration with Freddie. But all too soon, he was interrupted by the nagging necessity of apologising to the man. Unprepared, he chose to wing it and keep it short.

"You're a contagious little sewer rat," Graham said to him, accompanying Barnwell as he opened the door to Freddie's cell. Graham handed the blogger his satchel. "And a continuing threat to my work. That said, I defend wholeheartedly your right to publish your opinion, provided you label it as such—an opinion."

"I'm not labelling anything," Freddie said boldly. He was surprisingly bolshie for someone woken from a slumber in the early hours, having fallen asleep on top of a plastic moulded shelf.

"And any established facts . . ."

"We might differ on what constitutes a 'fact.'"

" . . . that you publish must do nothing to prejudice any ongoing police investigations." Graham stopped and appeared to consider throwing Freddie back in the cell before continuing. "No more, Freddie, alright? I mean it. No interference, and no speculation when it comes to ongoing cases. Capiche?"

Instead of the crisp obedience Graham so obviously wished for, Freddie put down his satchel and rubbed his tired eyes.

"Think about it, Freddie. You're attending the wedding on Saturday. How will it look if you've just published a hit piece against the bride's boss and her constabulary?"

But Freddie was done with voicing his objections. "I want to thank you for reconsidering and for coming out so late." He checked inside his satchel to make sure everything was there—laptop, charger, phone, notebook, wallet—then hoisted it onto his shoulder and made for the door. "I have all that I need," he said rather cryptically, shaking hands with the bemused Graham. "Goodnight, Detective Inspector."

After Freddie left, Graham turned to Barnwell. "You go home too. I'm going to stay here to think through a few things."

"Are you sure, sir? Janice has Carmen, and I've still got to type up the statement from Neville Williams. Do you want me to keep you company?"

"Good lord, no. You can write that statement up tomorrow. Go and get some rest. We'll reconvene in the morning. Off you go."

Graham popped the kettle on and went to the kitchen for a cup and saucer. It was part of Barnwell's nightly duties to clean up, and he had left the washing up on the draining board to dry.

As he walked back to his office, Graham heard the kettle click off. The water had reached boiling point. The inspector idly wished he could do likewise. He, too, had reached his limit. He would like to turn himself off.

The Mr. X case with its interminable logic, its gaping holes, and its vintage nature was vexing. The complication that was Freddie Solomon was an unwanted bonus. Attempting to solve the case was akin to fixing some knitting that had gone haywire rows earlier without a pattern and the wrong size needles. They still did not have an identity for the victim!

Graham warmed his pot and spooned some organic yuzu tea leaves into it. They resembled dried grass cuttings but smelled divine—fresh, citrus, sharp. He hoped the tea would revive him. He brought the pot and the cup and saucer to his desk and sat down, setting an alarm on his phone for three minutes.

While he waited for the tea to steep, he sat back in his chair and stared at the ceiling, running through the interview with Neville Williams from earlier that day—correction, yesterday. It was Graham's view that Williams had been a young lad put in an impossible position by an older, malignant relative, one who had abused and exploited him. By enlisting Williams in a process to avoid the ruin of her own life, Emily Lovell proceeded to ruin the rest of his.

Graham shook his head. His mind ran to Laura and her displeasure. She was right. He had been petty, small-minded, and driven by his emotions. His normally sound judgment had left him, and he risked dragging his reputation and, inexcusably, that of his officers, through the crowded harbour of Freddie's complacency.

A ripple of gentle, tinkling notes massaged his inner ear, rousing him from his thoughts. He gripped his teapot and watched as the steaming, dark, honey-brown liquid plunged in a perfect arc into his china cup, tumbling and swirling before settling into a glassy calm. He would drink his tea black.

Desultorily, Graham picked up his phone and checked the home screen. There was nothing new—no texts or email updates. He tossed the phone gently onto his desk and raised his teacup.

Holding it to his face, the steaming tea tickled the fine hairs under Graham's nose. He inhaled, and hints of citrus—lemon, mandarin, possibly grapefruit—assailed his nostrils, captivating him. He closed his eyes and breathed in some more. This was what he so loved about tea, its restorative properties.

As the tea did its work, thoughts began to form. The uptick in transport between his synapses was marked. Abandoning his tea momentarily, Graham opened his computer and logged in. Inputting "Holbrooke" into the police database, he scanned lists of names before switching and logging into the Gorey charge sheets.

He picked up his phone again and checked the time, pursing his lips before coming to a decision. He dialled a number on the screen. The recipient answered immediately.

"Freddie? It's Graham. Let's talk."

CHAPTER THIRTY-EIGHT

"AY, AY, BAZZ. How're you doing?" Janice sped past Barnwell. She was carrying a cardboard tray laden with two coffees. "A decaf almond milk latte for you," she said, placing the cup on his desk. "And an iced caramel macchiato for me."

"Isn't that basically a bag of sugar mixed with cream and caffeine? Stress eating again, are we? I thought you'd had a 'reset.'"

"It's true. But that, Constable Barnwell, was before my mother woke me at five thirty a.m."

"What's she on about now?"

"I can barely remember. But let's just say a girl needs the occasional break. And a bag of sugar mixed with cream and caffeine is *just* what I need."

"That bad, eh? Nothing for the boss?"

"No, I didn't think he'd be in."

"He's not been out!"

"Huh?"

"He arrested Freddie when we got back from Bournemouth and threw him in a cell for the night. I'm guessing Laura gave him an earful because he came back almost immediately and let him go."

"What did he arrest him for?"

"What d'you think? Interfering with an investigation. Put some blog post up that got the boss's goat."

"Nothing new, then."

"Anyhow, I came in this morning, and he was still here! Fast asleep with his head on his desk."

"Do you think Laura threw him out? She likes Freddie. Well, perhaps not *likes* him exactly, but she sticks up for him."

"Dunno, but when he woke up, he was out of sorts. He looked terrible. He asked *me* to make him a cup of tea!"

Janice took a sip of her coffee. It was syrupy, succulent, sublime. "And did you? Make him tea?"

"Course I did, but none of that fancy-pants rubbish you and he drink. Straight up Tetley's, milk, and two sugars. Lovely jubbly."

"He doesn't take sugar. Not anymore anyway. Gave it up when he moved in with Laura."

"Doesn't he? He didn't say anything, and he drank it all up. Looked a lot better after it 'n' all. Set you up for anything, one of my cuppas will."

"Put hairs on yer chest, will it?"

"That it will."

"So where is he now? Has he gone home?" Janice giggled. Her mother had driven her almost to madness in the last twenty-four hours. Anything not associated with Rosemary Harding sounded wildly hysterical to her.

Barnwell's eyes widened. Behind Janice's back, Detective Inspector Graham appeared in the office area, wiping water from his face with a towel. "No, he hasn't. But he is focused and ready to work. I hope you are too, Constable. We have a trip to prepare for."

"Another one?"

"Yep, your turn again. I'm sure Sergeant Harding is tied up with last-minute wedding plans. Flowers, hymns, that kind of thing." Barnwell glanced at Janice worriedly and waited for her response. He had a feeling she wouldn't agree, despite Graham's good intentions.

"Oh, it's no trouble, sir. I'm happy to accompany you. Barnwell has only just come back from a visit and I'm sure he'd like a break. And Carmen missed him when he was gone."

"But don't you have things to do? I thought you'd appreciate staying put with just a couple of days to go."

Janice beamed, her smile unnaturally wide. "No, no. Everything's taken care of. And Jack can step in if there's a last-minute problem. He's very capable and fully involved, so he knows what's what."

"But your mother's—"

"Yes! Yes, I know. But she'll be fine by herself for a day. She's a grown-up. As am I, sir." Janice held eye contact with Graham fractionally longer than was necessary.

Graham hesitated. Barnwell stepped in. "I think you should let her go, sir. It's only fair. You know, *equal opportunities*." Barnwell's eyes widened. Graham raised his chin and lowered his eyebrows.

"Ah yes, alright. If you insist. It'll be a long day, Sergeant. Two interviews interspersed by a long drive, bookended by flights to the mainland."

"Perfect, sir. When do we leave?"

CHAPTER THIRTY-NINE

JANICE DROVE THROUGH the narrow country lanes, tall grasses and hedgerows on either side obscuring her view on tight bends. "Phew, I'd forgotten these lanes were barely wide enough for half a car."

"Worse than Jersey, eh?" Graham replied.

"I'll say."

Graham looked at his phone. "We're nearly there."

"I've never been to this part of the world. Too upmarket for the likes of me. The villages are tiny, barely a few cottages and a shop."

"And a pub."

"Of course, always a pub."

"In fact, these villages are made up of enormous houses at the end of very long drives obscured by ancient trees. You just can't see them."

"You must need a pretty penny to buy one."

"Definitely. This is stockbroker belt. Quite a number of them here."

"Along with a few lords and ladies, the odd celebrity."

"Probably. An oligarch or two as well, I shouldn't wonder."

"A heaven for thieves."

"Occasionally, I'm sure. But these people hire private security. And dogs. Lots of dogs. And you know how the thieving fraternity like them." Graham looked at his phone again. "Turn right here."

Janice drove onto a tiny single-track road and followed it deep into woodland, eventually reaching a gate. Just as Graham had forecast, a man with a dog approached. "Here we go, sir." Janice let down her window and showed her police ID. Graham leaned over and held up his. The man with the dog leaned in and scrutinised them.

"Hang on a minute," he said, holding up a finger. He walked away and put a phone to his ear.

"He's calling ahead. Should we stop him?"

"No, this is a friendly visit. We're here to ask Angela Dillon if she has a missing relative, someone who disappeared forty years ago. If she's going to spend a minute hiding how she's gone from street prostitution to billionaire island in a remarkably short period, we don't need to know about it." The gate opened, and the guard waved them through.

At the top of the drive stood a huge, Georgian, red-brick house draped with purple wisteria. Janice looked up at the skylights as she climbed out of the car. "I always wanted a bedroom up in the roof with a window like that. Like something out of the books I read as a girl. A place where you could get away . . ."

"From your mother?"

"Exactly." Janice pressed the bell. The door opened to reveal a butler dressed in traditional black and whites. "We're here to see Ms. Angela Dillon," Janice said. She and Graham held up their IDs again. The butler glanced at them and, obviously prepared for their visit, stood back to let them in.

"Please follow me." He led them to a sitting room. "Ms. Dillon will be with you shortly."

Janice regarded the room around her, the sage green walls lined with Georgian portraiture. "Am I in a stately home? These carpets are so squishy and thick, they're like trampolines. I can bounce."

"It's the padding underneath that gives you that. But these are undoubtedly high quality." Graham pressed the balls of his feet into the wool pile. A noise behind them interrupted their conversation and in walked Angela Dillon. Immediately Graham revised his estimation of her. Unrealistically, he had been expecting someone younger, a woman whose demeanour and appearance reflected her tough life on the streets and in jail cells. But Ms. Dillon defied this expectation.

An elegant, attractive woman with thick, bobbed brunette hair appeared in a shiny blue, paisley-patterned wrap-over dress, cinched in at the waist by a gold chain belt. She wore no makeup except for red lipstick and mascara that framed eyes so blue they were almost purple. She wore mules, although Graham wouldn't have known they were called that. He knew they weren't slippers though and suspected that the delay at the gate had allowed Ms. Dillon time to upgrade her appearance for her visitors rather than for any dubious reason.

She smiled broadly at them and held out her hand. "Angela Dillon. Pleased to meet you. Won't you sit down?" She gestured at one of two sofas that sat facing each other, separated by a walnut coffee table. "Can I get you some tea?"

Graham, sensing he might be in for a treat, replied. "That would be lovely, thank you."

"Would Darjeeling suit? Assam?" This did suit Graham to no end.

"Darjeeling would be exquisite, thank you." Angela looked at Janice for her answer.

"Same, thanks." Angela pulled a bell rope in the corner of the room and immediately the butler appeared. After a quiet word with his employer, he disappeared again.

Graham and Janice sat on a grey sofa with languorous curves and studded arms. It wasn't terribly comfortable, but it kept them alert. Angela sat on the opposite sofa, which appeared only marginally more agreeable. She smiled at them.

"Now, how can I help you? It's been a long time since I last had a visit from the police." Angela seemed unperturbed by their visit and smiled at them disarmingly as she crossed her legs and clasped her hands around her knee.

"We're from Jersey, ma'am."

"Jersey? The Channel Islands?" Angela pursed her lips and twisted her head to the side before turning to face them again. "I've never been there. What does Jersey have to do with me?" The door opened, and a young woman entered with a tray of tea things. She placed it on the table and quietly left the room, just like the butler.

Angela released her knee and uncrossed her legs. She poured the tea gracefully and with a steady accuracy that perhaps only Graham appreciated. "Milk? Sugar?" Graham declined both, but Janice accepted some milk. Picking up the cup and saucer, Graham took a sip. The Darjeeling was the delight he had suspected it would be. Hot, humid, refreshing.

As he drank, Graham searched for the right words. "We're investigating a case that dates back some forty years. We're wondering if someone related to you went missing around that time?"

The woman stared back at him without blinking before slowly placing her teacup and saucer on the coffee table and interlinking her hands in her lap. "Inspector Graham, I am estranged from many members of my family. Over time, several have disappeared, sometimes reappearing after not being in contact for decades. Others remain missing, their whereabouts or situations unknown. We are that kind of family. Chaotic, messy, dysfunctional. We breed profusely without regard for love, friendship, or even acquaintance beyond a few hours. And we scrap our way through life, living on our wits or the dole, having benefited from very few advantages and even fewer expectations." Graham pointedly glanced around him, but there was no forthcoming explanation for the opulence in which Angela Dillon lived. Instead, she simply said, "I have very little contact with anyone I'm related to."

"Very well. Perhaps I may show you a photograph. I'm sorry to tell you that we recently discovered some remains on Jersey. Testing showed that you share twenty-seven percent of your DNA with this man. This would mean he may be a half brother, a nephew, or a cousin—someone not immediately related to you but only one or two steps removed. We estimate the man to be in his mid-twenties. He died in February 1982. We have prepared an image of what he may have looked like at the time. And I would like to show that to you now."

Seemingly unmoved, Angela said, "Very well. You want me to tell you if I recognise him?"

"Yes, please." Graham slipped out the image that Fiona had prepared for him. Angela took it and sat for several moments, staring at it. She briefly put her finger to her top lip before handing the image back to Graham.

"That's my half brother, one of many I may add. We share a mother. I have no idea who his father is. I doubt he or my mother knew either. I haven't seen him in decades."

"And his name, Ms. Dillon?"

"Dylan. My mother's little joke, I suppose. Dylan Dillon. We called him Dilly." Angela reached for her teacup. "So, he's dead, is he?"

"You didn't wonder what happened to him?"

Angela's nose wrinkled, two short lines appearing on either side. "Can't say I did. I had my own problems, and as I said, family members come and go all the time. I assumed he'd gone abroad, Costa del Sol or somewhere. That was all the rage in the eighties for ne'er-do-wells."

"Would you happen to have a photo of him?" Janice asked.

"Of Dylan?" Angela raised her eyebrows as though the idea that she had a photo of her half brother was a strange one. "I don't think so." Pausing for a second, she continued. "No, no, I'm sure I haven't. It's all so long ago. A different time." She scanned the room—the expensive art, the antiques, the plush furnishings. "I have a different life now."

"He had a suitcase with him when he died. Do you know anything about that?" Graham handed her a photo of the tomato-red Tourister suitcase.

A small smile crossed her lips. "Well, well, well, so that's who took it. I wondered what happened to it. I loved that suitcase. I got it off a secondhand stall on the Portobello Road. It was cute. Vintage. I got in an argument with my boyfriend over it."

"How so?"

"Because when I went to write the Valentine's card I got for him, I found the suitcase in which I'd stashed it was gone. You had to do things like that in my family. Anything worth anything to anyone else, even a stupid Valentine's card, would go missing if you didn't hide it. It was too late to get another, and I got dumped over it." Her face fell, the light on her features changing so that the contours of her cheekbones became apparent, aging her in a second. "I was heartbroken. It was the start of a very dark path for me."

CHAPTER FORTY

"YOU'VE GOT TO hand it to the Victorians," Graham said as he and Janice walked up to HMP Holbrooke's visitor's entrance. "They could certainly build to *intimidate*." As functional as it was unlovely, the prison loomed dark and ominous, a hulking stone and steel warehouse for men who had fallen afoul of the law, often many times.

Janice had only experienced the more modern facilities in St. Helier. "It's like a fortress."

At the front desk—a large, glassed-off office that resembled border control in some European airports Janice had passed through on her holidays—they signed in and were handed passes to attach to their jackets before being shuffled on to the next stage of their journey by a warder assigned to them.

As they walked along the corridors of the prison, Janice calculated their speed to be slower than that of a car during London's rush hour. This was mostly due to the number of doors that required unlocking and relocking as they passed through. She found their passage along the empty, echoing halls thoroughly tedious, the experience depressing her further with every stop and start as they made their way deeper into the bowels of the building. Eventually, they reached the governor's office.

Mike Tenbeigh was in charge of this fortress. He certainly looked the part. His tall, military bearing towered over even Graham, and Janice suspected that his wide, bristling, and greying moustache had seen sights not always savoury or wholesome.

"How many prisoners have you got here?" she asked him.

"Around a thousand or so. Changes every day, of course," Tenbeigh replied. "We're not max-sec. Maximum security," he added in response to Janice's frown. "We mostly take prisoners on remand, but we have a few longtimers—old boys like the Parnabys—the ones with a bad rap but limited energy and impact due to their advanced years. Over time, lower testosterone and poor health tend to age guys like them out of the criminal mainstream and they become less of a threat. I wouldn't have them if I thought they were still criminally active or influential. Too many young ones come through who might turn around with the right input. They're vulnerable, and I don't want them corrupted by old mobsters who think they've still got it, even if they haven't."

Now that they were walking through the admin wing, the painted, scuffed Victorian brick had given way to a refurbished interior that was all glass and chrome, replete with cameras and digital locks, a dizzying contrast to the earlier crumbling patched and austere stonework. "We've not had a serious incident in eight months," Tenbeigh added.

"Serious incident" meant that none of the inmates had succeeded in murdering one of the others. Or attempted to do so. "Congratulations on that, Governor. Long may it continue," Graham said.

"Thank you. I pray every night that it will. I'm very proud of what we've achieved here. We're showing the world how to run a modern jail. Even if, from the outside, it looks like a legacy from the Dickensian era. We have a few bad lads here, but we keep them under control."

"You've got some 'whole-lifers,' I think?" Janice said. "Whole-lifers" were offenders with no prospect of release.

"Currently, we have seventy in the UK, with some housed here. Whole-lifers get moved around more than anyone else. Does nothing for their temper, I can assure you. And these lads know they're never getting out. This means they have nothing to lose if a situation flares. With no hope of release, they already exist in a floating state somewhere between life and death."

"But how does that square with your lower security designation? Do you keep your whole-lifers in solitary, away from the general population?" Janice wondered.

Tenbeigh showed them to the control room. It was bright and modern, with a bank of screens across one wall showing feeds from dozens of cameras.

"For a couple of years, whole-lifers are certainly kept apart. It's not ideal, but it's for their safety. We have to assess their mental state. Understanding you're never getting out, never having a normal life again, no hope of redemption or purpose in life is a challenge for the mind to contemplate and accept." Janice nodded. "And they often need protecting from other inmates. People naturally order themselves into a society, and inside a prison, it's no different. Aggravated murder or serial killing is the usual crime for whole-life orders, and people charged with heinous crimes like that are not appreciated. But we don't have new whole-lifers here, just ones that are deep into their sentences. We're talking about evil people often unable to reflect on their crimes or show any remorse."

Thus far, Graham had felt relatively mellow inside the prison, but he was becoming uncomfortable. Perhaps it was the tedious layers of security or some residual discomfort about the necessity of coming to an agreement with Freddie that had led to this visit. More likely, he decided, it was the thought of being surrounded by men he had put away, and the deeds that caused him to do so. The speech would have come out, regardless.

"'Evil' connotes something unchangeable, intrinsic to the self," he said to Tenbeigh, who immediately understood he'd walked into a philosophy lecture by accident. "Do you have children?"

"Megan's three," Tenbeigh answered, puzzled. His eyes narrowed. As the governor of a large prison, he didn't normally host visiting detective inspectors. He left that to his subordinates. However, he had heard about Graham and been curious. Tenbeigh now understood why Graham's reputation preceded him. He was no ordinary blokey DI.

"Is Megan capable of despicable criminal acts?"

"Of course not."

"Agreed. Now, imagine offering a girl access to only a failing school, and with parents who either can't read or just won't. Place her somewhere she's forced to choose between fighting bullies or teaming up with them to survive. Or maybe she decides her best bet is to hide inside a gang, hoping she's not chosen as a honeytrap charged with luring a rival gang member into an ambush." Janice opened her mouth to speak. "I realise, Sergeant, that some are not unwilling participants and play their parts with gusto and a lack of conscience, but hear me out." Graham kept his tone steady even as his temper rose.

"Then, *then*, when she makes a mistake or enough of them, slap a custodial sentence on her. Henceforth, the path to decent work will be shut off, but that's alright because she knows about crime now. She has something to fall back on. And so it continues. Limited options lead to even fewer options until there are barely any at her disposal."

The assumptive inference of his daughter notwithstanding, Tenbeigh was enjoying this tirade from a slight remove. Once he realised Graham was finished, he said, "Ah yes, the 'criminals are made and not born' speech. I see they weren't wrong about you."

"Who wasn't?"

"I spoke to a few people when I heard you were coming. Nigel Needham, for one."

"You did?" Graham wished that Tenbeigh hadn't bothered his old mentor. "He's not well, you know."

"Yes, it's sad," Tenbeigh said soberly. They moved from the control room to another part of the admin complex where a new suite of offices and interview rooms were in busy use judging by the number of people toing and froing from them. "He mentioned your performance at the Harrogate conference. Around nine or ten years ago, was it? Nigel said you tore a DCI to shreds for even *suggesting* compulsory lie detector tests for violent criminals."

Graham recalled the incident with crystal clarity. "It was a dangerously stupid idea. Got short shrift, thank goodness."

"It was only an informal brainstorm-and-biscuits session, he told me!"

Tenbeigh laughed at the thought of the scene: a younger, angrier Graham ascending the moral high ground at a gallop while his older superiors hid behind their teacups, their cheeks reddening, speechless. Tenbeigh had been to plenty of similar meetings; they were tedious and rarely resulted in any positive action. "I'm sure you livened up the proceedings no end. Anyway, Needham says you wrote the book on interrogation techniques."

"Only one of the chapters," Graham said just modestly enough.

"So, I'm looking forward to seeing how you handle these two."

The crimes of George and Arthur Parnaby were serious: two armed robberies, the latter ending in the killing of a security guard by another of their gang. The Parnabys were convicted of manslaughter. They had been on the Met's "most wanted" list for years.

Evading capture, and consequently punishment, they had had the luck of cats with nine lives each, but the law finally caught up with them. While their cases had been difficult to prove, the judiciary had made certain that the sentencing for those charges that stuck compensated for the earlier difficulties by being the maximum allowed.

"Have they been behaving themselves?" Graham asked.

"They haven't stuck up any more armoured cars, that's for certain," Tenbeigh remarked. "In all seriousness, we've had no complaints lately. They've been on their best behaviour. We even let them do a couple of interviews for a book someone's doing. They were each given twenty-eight years, required to serve twenty-five, and are hoping to get out as soon as they do."

"Will they?"

"George, maybe. But Arthur will be here longer." They navigated a hallway that ended in three glass-walled meeting rooms. "A couple of years ago, he stabbed another inmate in a dispute over a pot of yogurt. The ones with the fruit in the corner."

"To death?"

"Almost. They're good, those yogurts, and they take on additional currency on the inside. I thought the stabbing a bit excessive though. The victim recovered, but Arthur got three more mandatory years. Since then, he's been good as gold. Almost helpful, you could say. The brothers support us in policing the younger ones. A bit of seasoned experience in the inmate ranks can be useful to us. Both men are nearly eighty and realise their stick-up days are over.

"George has been diagnosed with congestive heart failure so he's simply trying to hang on long enough to see the sun again. You might find them keen to strike a deal. They've got a parole board hearing coming up."

They had finally arrived at the interview suite—a dark room that Mike Tenbeigh had clearly passed over when allocating the facility's modernisation budget. Graham completed some quick paperwork, and then the guard radioed for the Parnaby brothers to be escorted to the room. "What's brought you up here, then? To speak to them?" Tenbeigh wondered. "Something from the eighties, I heard."

Janice briefly explained the discovery of the body in the attic and the powerful handgun. "We have evidence that our man was perhaps an associate of the Parnabys. There's a connection between them that we're following up."

"Oh?"

"The gun found with the body was used in a crime in which Arthur Parnaby was a suspect."

Just then, two elderly men with nothing but wisps of hair on their heads were led into the room by a pair of watchful warders. One of the old men rode a motorised scooter. They looked sallow and poorly fed but also strangely optimistic. Graham wondered if they thought this meeting might somehow be their ticket home. Or maybe it was just the break in their monotonous routine that had captured their mood.

Tenbeigh took his leave. "Well, have fun. If you need anything, you can call this number." He handed them a business card. "I have a meeting with the minister for prisons in five." Tenbeigh smiled and stuck out his hand. "Nice to have met you both. I do hope your journey will prove fruitful. Perhaps see you later at lunch."

"Thanks, Mike. Hope I didn't bend your ear off. I can get passionate at times." Graham shook his hand. Janice did likewise.

"Not at all. It was good to finally meet the man behind the stories, Detective Inspector Graham of Jersey, formerly Scotland Yard. Watch out for these two. They're wily fellas."

CHAPTER FORTY-ONE

"ARTHUR PARNABY," ANNOUNCED the elderly man who walked without assistance. It was just as well that he identified himself; the brothers were identical twins. Bald, stooped, and reed thin except for bellies that resembled footballs under their prison shirts. "At your service, sir!" He was mocking Graham, but there was an underlying truth to what he said.

Arthur and George Parnaby had agreed to this interview, not for the attention or for any service to humanity but for the "bennies"—advantages that were currency in prison and which they were keen to accrue. The Parnaby twins were there to do a deal.

Arthur pointed a thumb at the man next to him. "This is George." George's rounded shoulders suddenly straightened.

"'ow do." His voice was a ruined whisper, and he breathed with difficulty. A cannula connected to an oxygen cylinder on wheels that trailed behind him hung beneath his nose. He seemed confused, unsure why he was in this dark, windowless room with his brother and not watching prison life pass by in front of him, which was how he usually spent his hours. "'Oo are you, then?" he said, eyeing Graham and then Janice.

"I'm Detective Inspector Graham, and this is Sergeant Harding. We're from the Gorey police force. We're here to ask you a few questions."

"They're following up after that little fella, George. The journalist," Arthur said loudly. "Remember? Might be somethin' or nuthin.'" He raised his chin defiantly, then dropped it before winking at his brother. "They might be able to help with your art project."

George raised his head. "Yeah?"

"And more time in the garden for me."

Graham had handled this kind of sparring before. Brief feints to lay out their opening gambits. The Parnabys were in this for themselves. Freddie had warned him...

"Nothing is guaranteed. But if you're helpful, I'll make sure the authorities here know that."

"Sounds like a plan." Arthur grinned as his brother wrestled a chair out from the table and, supporting himself with one hand on the back, the other flat on the table, lowered himself into the seat. Arthur did the same, although considerably quicker. "Whatcha wanting to know about?"

Graham could have laid out the folder of evidence and walked the two inmates through what he'd learned, but he decided to keep things simple. "I'm writing the biography of a revolver," he said. "A three-fifty-seven, a ferocious piece. Goes missing for many years, then turns up in someone's attic on Jersey."

Arthur's old man's eye, its corner creasing ever so slightly in reaction to Graham's mention of the island, caught the inspector's attention. Hundreds of tiny muscles govern human facial movements. Children, adults, and the elderly use those muscles in different ways, and the nuances of these two identical craggy faces as the men processed 'Jersey' told Graham much. The island resonated with them in a way that they were keen not to parse. And if the word elicited such a response, there would be others. Graham watched for them while listening with a blazing intensity.

"Jersey's where they had all the Nazis and stuff. Superman lives there, the nerdy one."

"Uh, yes." It wasn't how Graham would have characterised the island. He would have described its beautiful scenery, beaches, and history. Not mentioned the bedevilment of the Nazi occupation during WWII or that it was the home of the local-boy-cum-Hollywood-actor best known for playing Clark Kent. Graham hadn't even understood the last reference. Janice filled him in later.

"The Smith and Wesson model twenty-eight. A rare firearm, and an unusual find, I think you'll agree. We did some comparisons, some testing . . ."

Arthur's face darkened, and he leaned over to his brother, whispering.

"Hey, hey!" Janice said urgently, her arm outstretched, her palm facing down. But it was too late. The message had been transmitted. Arthur, the healthier, fitter brother, stood up. "We didn't come here for this! It's a setup job, George. Careful what you say, alright?"

"Yeah," George answered. Graham, unsure if they were bluffing to force an advantage, stayed impassive.

"No one's setting anyone up. Look, we're being straight with you here. We're just trying to understand who owned the gun. Running it through our system provided a link with your good selves." Seeing his brother remain at the table, Arthur slowly sat down again.

Through the bubbling marsh of his lungs, George said, "I've never used a gun personally. They make the most bloody awful noise."

"Ah, yes, it was your *accomplice* who fired the shot during the robbery that left a man dead, wasn't it? Nevertheless, it led to your arrest and incarceration here," Janice responded pointedly. She cast her eyes around the bleak room. She had read the Parnabys' case file on the flight over, and then again while waiting in the visitors' centre. The lives of the two brothers would make for an intriguing film.

George, despite his breathing apparatus, age, and dire prognosis, still possessed the confidence, some might say self-delusion, of a man far younger and healthier. He put one hand on his hip and leaned an elbow on the table, resting his chin casually on his thumb as he faced Janice. "Look, love, I wasn't told anything about guns. We just drove the van."

Graham also knew the case well. It was encapsulated in Metropolitan Police lore and his own untrammelled recollections of stories passed down to him from veteran officers. "Of course you did. You 'drove the van,' but you also scoped out the security company and tracked their armoured cars for days so you could plan the robbery in minute detail. You devised the plan, hired the team, and doled out the loot. Dumb getaway drivers you were not."

Laughing hard, an awful sound that conjured the image of air forcing its way through thick, black paint, George eventually found the breath and clarity to speak. "I'd never call it a 'plan.' We were a bunch of idiots trying to rob a van and screwing everything up. Your mate, that Freddie fella, wants to paint us as the mob, some kind of organised crime gang. Ha! Organised? We were more like Laurel and 'ardy."

"A man died," Janice reminded them. "It was more than a botched job."

Arthur shrugged. "Not our fault some numpty gets trigger-happy on his first job."

"That 'numpty' cost you nearly thirty years in the slammer, and he was a numpty you hired, but hear me out," Graham said. "You've spent your final years inside, and you may well spend whatever time you have left in here as well. But if you answer everything we put to you today, you can redeem yourself in part . . ."

Arthur snorted. "Redeem? Who cares?"

Janice leaned forward. "No one. You could spend more time with your roses though. Imagine that? You'll get more time outside in the sunshine, pruning, clipping, and mixing in fertiliser. The colours of the blooms you grow could really sing. You could pull carrots and potatoes from the ground and cover your raspberries with netting so the snails don't get them. It's annoying when the bugs destroy everything after all the hard work you've put in, isn't it?"

Janice peered into Arthur's blue eyes. They glazed over as he pictured what she described. "Maybe you could even win a few bets with the other men who work their gardens, build your status that way."

Seeing an opening, Graham followed this up with a metaphorical rapid right hook. "We've got a victim, someone who died a nasty, painful death. And it's not impossible you know who he is."

George laughed again, though everyone in the room wished he had not. Janice especially. His gurgling, phlegmy wheeze made her feel ill. "What, and you need our help? We've never been to Jersey. Either of us. Honestly, you'll be reaching for the divine next. Bleedin' miracles now, is it?"

"Look." Graham pulled out two sheets of paper from his folder. "Here's a slug fired from the gun by our ballistics expert just the other day. And here," he said, putting the two printed images side-by-side, "is one fired in 1976." The images looked roughly the same, small chunks of cylindrical metal, badly malformed and compressed by impacts.

"Miracles, I tell ya!" George repeated. "You two weren't even *born* in seventy-six."

Janice folded her arms. He was irritating her. He wasn't helping his brother get any closer to spending more time with his beloved roses either. At this rate, she was hard-pressed to believe Arthur would even lay any atop George's coffin when the time came. Which, judging by his cough, wouldn't be long now.

Arthur made a dismissive noise. "Two bullets fired from the same gun, years apart. So what?" He tipped his head to one side and languidly glanced around the bare, peeling, plastered walls.

"Remember this chap?" Graham slipped out another image from his folder, turning the mugshot photo so Arthur could see it.

"Bloody hell, we really are off on a jaunt down memory lane, aren't we?" Arthur leaned over to study the image, then he sat back as George reached over to pick it up, the flimsy paper shaking as he tremulously studied it before lapsing into a long chuckle that sounded like a traction engine suffering an oil leak.

"Well? What do you say?" Graham said.

Arthur Parnaby flicked a speck off his trousers before replying. "Yes, for cryin' out loud, I recognise him. It's Potty Patty. Right loon, 'e was."

"Also known as Patrick Havers."

"What's he got to do with this?" Arthur added. His eyes lit up. "Is he dead?"

"Oh, he's been dead for years," said Graham. "But sometime in October 1976, he was seen by two friends of yours in the car park of the Angel and Greyhound in Clapham, enjoying overly friendly relations with your then-wife."

There was no restraining his guffaw, so George let it all out. "Overly friendly . . . relations . . ." Janice shut her eyes and wished she could shut her ears as George coughed into a white handkerchief and then heaved once again with laughter. "That's . . . a good one . . . " he wheezed.

"Shut it," his brother said, his cheeks blooming as his anger grew. Arthur snatched the photo from his brother's hands and looked at it again. "Ask what you're here to ask and be done with it. Did I have him killed? Is that what you want to know?"

CHAPTER FORTY-TWO

"WELL, YOU CAN see why I might think that, but no, he died of natural causes. And a few years before he did, you chased him, threatened his life, and fired several rounds at his car as he tried to flee."

"Maybe, maybe, but I missed the bugger completely," said Arthur. "'E was alive and kickin' when I last saw him."

"Hit his car three times though. Which was later impounded following Mr. Havers's arrest two days later for dangerous driving."

"He always was a dozy sod. He should have dumped the old thing. Would've saved us all a ton of bovver." Arthur growled and pushed his chair away from the table, folded his arms, and looked down at the floor.

"The bullet fragments found in the car were logged," Graham continued, "and carefully photographed. Comparisons with the gun we uncovered on Jersey were possible. The testing proved that it was the same one that fired at Patrick Havers's car, the person who was having an affair with your wife, Arthur. At the time, it was suspected that you fired that gun, but the case was dropped for insufficient evidence and probably a host of other reasons that law enforcement often employ in relation to rolling up serial offenders like yourself."

The two old cons were sufficiently experienced to understand when silence was golden, especially their own. They let this snooty, overeducated detective inspector say his piece, hoping it would soon be over and there wouldn't be too many long, fancy words.

"So this gun, the one you used, Arthur, was on Jersey in early 1982," Graham told them. A subtle fluttering of recognition crossed the men's faces, but they said nothing. "What I want to know is—who did you give it to after you shot up Patrick Havers's car?"

Within moments, the two men were huddling to discuss the question.

"Oi," Janice objected, "none of your secret conspiracies in here, thank you. Just tell the detective inspector what he wants to know."

It took time and more assurances. "One hour *every afternoon* on the allotment," Arthur clarified. "And I get to have the rain days roll over."

"I'll see what I can do. No promises though," Graham said.

"And George Van Goff here can have as much paint as he likes to throw at the art room wall provided he cleans it all up after."

"I don't *throw* it," George rasped, offended. "I *liberate* it."

They had a deal. Graham would do his best. Arthur swung into gear. "I gave the item in question to a man who I employed now and then. I'd used him as an odd jobs man and labourer."

"Why? Why would you give an odd jobs man a gun?"

"As payment in kind."

"You paid a bloke for some odd jobs with a firearm?"

Arthur nodded solemnly. "At his request, yes."

"A firearm which had been used, in public, to attempt some rough justice." Arthur pressed his lips together. When it was clear he wouldn't answer, Graham continued. "So, Arthur, to whom did you give the gun? Give me a name."

"Dylan Dillon," came the reply. "'Dilly' for short. It got too complicated otherwise. Stupid the things some parents do to their kids. Practically grew up together, we did. We were a bit older though."

"A lot older, bruv. Ten years. Always had his nose in a book, did Dilly."

"And what became of Dilly?"

Arthur cracked a smile. "Nah, mate. I've given you what you wanted—a name. If you want more, you have to pay. What's he say in that flick? The one with the bloke who's chained up in a glass cell?"

His brother helped him out. "*Silence of the Lambs*. 'Annibal Lecter."

"Yeah, yeah," Arthur said. "When he's working things out with the FBI girl, right, he says . . . you know . . . if there's something for me, then there'll be something for you."

"A *quid pro quo*," Janice said. "Is that what you're reaching for?"

"Yeah, exactly. Squid provo. You want more? What's in it for us, eh?"

Outwardly, Graham's expression remained inscrutable, but his mind, which had been huffing along with the efficiency and velocity of a high-speed train, hit a speed bump. Efficient negotiating was hard when his opponents had absolutely nothing to lose or in their calendar.

"Now," Arthur explained, "the currency is *time*."

"If either of you tells me something that leads to a conviction . . ."

"An *arrest*," Arthur countered. "Not a conviction. That'll take way too long. No good to me nor 'im."

"If you tell me something that leads to a *conviction*, then I'll make a case and remind the parole board that twenty-six years is not that much different from twenty-eight." The old men glared at their opposite number across the table.

"And the extra thing?" Arthur asked eventually, a little less confrontational. "I'm seventy-nine. Shaving a year or two off my stretch doesn't mean much when I've got another six to go."

"You mean the violent assault which put an inmate in hospital?" Janice said.

"Lost my temper, didn't I?" Arthur Parnaby grumbled. "Paid the price in solitary, day after day, for *three* months."

But Graham wouldn't be drawn. "These decisions depend on people higher up the chain. I can't promise what I can't deliver. It's not down to me."

"No promises from you, no insider intel from us." George lifted his chin as he spoke before dropping it low and looking out from under his eyebrows. "We're putting ourselves on the line here. We could be looked at as grasses. That won't make our lives easy in this place."

Graham highly doubted that the brothers telling him about a case that occurred over forty years ago would dent their inmate reputation in any way. "I can't make promises," he said, "and you're not well placed to demand any, but I'll ask them to consider releasing you as a pair."

"Alright, but no new charges, okay?" said George. "Immunity from self-immolation."

"I think you mean incrimination."

"Yeah, incrimin . . . Yeah, that."

"It depends on what your role was."

"Then we're not saying anyfin'."

Graham had already ascertained that the brothers could not possibly have had anything to do with the death of Dylan Dillon. In February 1982, they had been under surveillance by Met officers for a bank job. On February 14th, undercover cops observed the Parnabys meeting two men in a park at eleven o'clock at night. They hadn't been there to play on the swings, but neither had they been involved in a killing on Jersey. But Graham wanted to hear from the Parnabys' own mouths what they knew about what had happened to Dillon.

"Alright, you give me everything you know about Dillon, including names and dates, and there'll be no charges with respect to the case we're investigating. *If* I get an arrest that leads to charges and a conviction, I'll ask them to release you as a pair at George's next parole board meeting. How about that?"

The two brothers turned to one another. Some silent twin language must have passed between them, because when they looked back at the two officers, Arthur said, "Squid provo. You ask us the stuff. We'll do our best for you."

Finally.

"So, let's start again," Janice said. "When did you last see Mr. Dylan Dillon?"

"Dilly?" George said. "Phew, ages. He's long gone, isn't he?"

"I'm afraid so," Janice said. "On Valentine's Day, 1982, he was found dead on Jersey."

Graham saw it again: those tiny flickers of movement around the eyes. They were never entirely meaningless, but their hidden nuances required interpretation.

"His body, along with his belongings, was discovered in his hotel room."

The Parnaby twins furrowed their brows and turned down the corners of their mouths but remained silent.

"Forensics found traces of average-purity powdered cocaine on his shirt," Janice continued.

Neither man suppressed a guffaw, and after coughing extensively, George added a phlegmy bark of congratulation: "Good old Dilly!"

"Died as he lived" was Arthur's assessment. "He always was a rascal. Way to go, man! Fair play to the lad. Bit young though. I'd raise a glass if they'd ever let us have one in here."

"We found something else on his shirt too."

"Chicken tikka?" Arthur guessed.

"Spilled scotch? Ash from his B&H?" George chuckled.

"When did you last see him?"

"Hmm, let's see," Arthur said. "Early 1982. We told that other fella. 'E went to Jersey and never came back. Last we saw of 'im."

"Do you know of anyone who might have wished Mr. Dillon harm?"

It was a key question, and Graham's focus grew more intense. It was their eyes again. Arthur seemed to look down and away, blinking; George's eyes narrowed a smidgen.

"I suppose you wouldn't bother coming up here if he'd just keeled over from a drug overdose," Arthur said.

"Someone did him in, then?" George added.

"You haven't answered my question."

"About what?"

"Who might have wanted to spike Mr. Dillon's cocaine with rat poison?"

Graham watched them carefully. There was a pause as the two men stared straight ahead, their faces a carbon copy of the other, blank and unreadable. He noticed a minuscule twitch of a muscle. Were they processing this information and what it might mean? Did they actually know anything worth knowing?

"You're talking about forty years ago," Arthur said eventually. "We're not young men anymore. Things slip away, you know?" He raised his hand to touch his temple before letting it drop in a broad arc, mimicking the journey of a memory leaving his mind, becoming forever lost.

Graham tried a different approach. "Do you know why he was on Jersey, then?"

"For his holidays?" Arthur replied. "To read a few books on the beach, drink a couple of afternoon pints. Sounds alright to me."

Graham wrote in his notebook with his custom shorthand and soon saw that neither brother cared for this. They both watched him silently. Arthur shifted in his seat and passed a hand across his face. "Did he regularly take breaks on his own? Disappear for the weekend?"

"We were his mates," said Arthur. "Not his wife."

"No," George said simply.

"When he travelled was it typical for him to bring a handgun? *Your handgun*, I should say?"

"How should we know?" Arthur said. "I figured he'd sell the gun. I didn't want it no more. Bloody great thing was too heavy anyway. Good for nuthin'."

A phone's jingle sounded. The prison officer stationed in the room, who had been quiet up until now, stirred. With the tension broken, Graham pushed himself away from the table. Arthur Parnaby smacked his lips. George coughed. Janice watched the two men intensely.

"Lunchtime!" Arthur stood, straightening slowly. "Oof," he moaned, his hand pressing the small of his back.

"It's fettuccine alfredo or meatloaf if I remember correctly," George said. He shifted to his motorised scooter but was soon wracked with coughing again. He followed Arthur out, his oxygen tank trailing while his older brother wore a knowing, high-handed smirk that bothered Graham intensely.

CHAPTER FORTY-THREE

W HEN THE BROTHERS left, Graham stretched his arms to the ceiling. He squeezed his eyes tight and made fists with his hands. Janice walked over to the tiny, reinforced glass-and-barred gap in the wall that barely deserved the title of window. She looked outside. In the distance, she could see men in the exercise yard.

"They're hard work, aren't they, Arthur and George? Slippery characters. All matey to your face, but you know underneath they are for no one but themselves. Wouldn't even stand up for each other if push came to shove, I shouldn't wonder. Their mere presence exhausts me. There's simply no part of them that is likeable or that isn't self-serving," she said. "And they're people who you would think would share everything they knew in case all they have to look forward to is the privilege of dying in one of the best-run all-male prisons in England. I mean, it's a very amenable facility Governor Tenbeigh has here, but it is, let's not mess about, a *jail*."

"We need to be on high alert with them. If I don't watch it," Graham said, "I'll end up agreeing to support their release just because I added some interesting case notes to the file. We need to understand *why* Dillon was on Jersey. Without knowing that, we can't move forward."

"Do you think that they know? Apart from the gun connection, we don't have anything else to connect them. Not to Dillon's trip to Jersey anyway."

"No, but they told Freddie that two members of their gang disappeared after they visited the island. Never saw or heard of either of them again. They gave him no names though. Clammed up, he said, when he pushed them."

"You don't think they're stringing Freddie along, do you? Making up stuff in exchange for painting supplies and seeds?"

Graham rolled his eyes. "I sincerely hope not."

A prison warder appeared at the doorway. "Governor Tenbeigh asked me to tell you that lunch is this way."

"Smashing," Graham said to him before following Janice out of the dreary room. He was looking forward to a cup of tea. Any kind would do. He wasn't, at this point, fussy. "They'll try to make a little look like a lot, that's for sure. They'll offer details which seem helpful but lead nowhere, or tell us things we already know, like the name of the guy whose car Arthur shot up in seventy-six. Like," he pointed out, "them telling us Dillon enjoyed reading. All of those small elements *seem* significant, somehow, but none of them take us closer to solving the case or an arrest. At least Arthur admitted giving the gun to Dillon, but even that isn't game-changing."

When they got to Governor Tenbeigh's office, they found lunch laid out for them. Nothing fancy, just a few sandwiches, crisps, and biscuits. There was a pot of tea though. "We heard you liked a good cuppa, Detective Inspector," Tenbeigh said, suddenly appearing. The tea was a bog-standard brew, but to Graham, at that moment, it was like the elixir of life, immortality, and eternal youth all rolled into one. He closed his eyes as the piping-hot, brown liquid grazed the soft flesh at the back of his throat, warming it and soothing him.

With nothing helpful to add, and with Graham's tone and body language signalling he was ready for a "big think," Tenbeigh wordlessly invited Janice to leave the inspector to it. When the governor pulled the office door closed, Graham was muttering to himself and scribbling in his notebook.

"Why don't we get our lunch in the senior prison officer's section of our newly refurbished staff canteen?" Tenbeigh said. "I imagine you've earned it this morning. Must've been an early start for you."

"Very early," Janice replied. "Four a.m. to be exact." She stifled a yawn. "That seems a long time ago now."

"I believe salmon en croute and Eton mess are on the menu today."

"Sounds lovely. Reviving."

Back in the governor's office, his eyes closed, Graham sighed and set his notebook on Tenbeigh's desk. At first, the lunch break had felt like an imposition, but he needed time to consider his game plan.

The cautious sparring with the Parnabys would endure until Graham played a weak card. Then they'd see his notebook held nothing to boast about. There were worrying limits to his inquiry. The passing of time meant he needed to build an ironclad case. A confession backed up by forensic findings, ideally. He was a long way from achieving that.

Graham had a victim but no witnesses. He had a means but no motive. He lacked both a suspect and any discernible reason why anyone might risk poisoning Dillon. He didn't even know why Dillon was on Jersey and why he had taken a weapon with him.

"Someone got into his hotel room," Graham muttered at the office walls, "and switched out a portion of his cocaine for rat poison. Two types for good measure. It wasn't elegant, but it was near certain to succeed provided Dillon had dependable, consistent cocaine habits. Like, you know he's going to roll up a tenner and break out his stash. That would require intimate knowledge, someone who knew him well."

Graham couldn't pace properly in Tenbeigh's office, so he strode out into the hallway, smiling briefly at the handful of staff he encountered. They stared at him curiously before their eyes glazed over and they lost interest in him, returning to their work or their phones.

"The chosen murder method was highly personal," he said to himself in a low whisper. "A substance the victim rammed up his nose, entered his bloodstream, and travelled to his brain and then, fatally, his heart. Something that was *supposed* to make him feel *great*. But because the poison was self-administered, the method was one step removed. It required intimate knowledge but no direct hand." He turned around and returned to Tenbeigh's office, where he stood looking out of the window with his hands clasped behind his back until Janice found him some minutes later.

"Enjoy your lunch, sir?" Janice looked at the table. Nothing had been eaten. Even the tea was cold.

"Our killer was the victim's buddy, someone he knew quite well," Graham told her.

"Huh? Wait, how did you get there?"

"The drugs. Dillon was poisoned. There's something *intimate* about it."

"Not just a cold mob hit, you mean. Not just business."

"No, it was too messy for that. A mob hit would have made certain—a gun preferably, or strangulation, a beating. They wouldn't leave until they knew he was dead. This is less certain. It was less efficient. And it wasn't foolproof by any means. Have you managed to get anything on him yet? This Dylan Dillon." On the way up to Holbrooke, Janice had liaised with her opposite number at police headquarters in St. Helier.

"Yes." Janice pulled out her tablet. "He doesn't have a record surprisingly, given his associates, but he was known to the law as a teenager. Petty stuff, nothing significant. But one thing stands out. He had his tonsils removed at nineteen."

"Why is that interesting, Sergeant? So do around thirty-seven thousand other people each year."

"He listed his next of kin as one Charles Cross from Mile End. I guess they might have been school friends, but strange, no? You'd put your mother or a family member down, especially at that age. Who do you think Charlie Cross might be?"

"I'm not sure. These Parnaby guys were never my patch. I don't know them or their mates," Graham admitted. "They've been in jail since I was in middle school. I don't know their accomplices, their methods . . . but I have an idea whom we might ask." He pulled out his phone. "My only worry is that he won't remember any of it."

Janice continued to read the report from St. Helier. Her voice rose in volume and register. "Listen to this, sir. A Dylan Dillon left Jersey on February *fifteenth*, 1982. He reentered Jersey in *October* 1982. And since then, according to records, he's never left."

CHAPTER FORTY-FOUR

AFTER WHAT FELT like an entire morning of pedalling through Jersey's rural areas, Barnwell pulled his bicycle over to the lane's grass verge to catch his breath. He was almost certain he'd already searched this section. It was easy to recognise—again—the big, almost unruly copse which sprang out of the farmland, surrounded in part by a centuries-old stone wall.

As he took a breather, Barnwell once more brought out the note he had made of the address he was hunting down: 4 St. Julian's Road. Fiona had alerted them to the scrawl in blue ballpoint on the inside back cover of the paperback copy of *The Hitchhikers Guide to the Galaxy* found in Mrs. Taylor's attic, and Barnwell had taken it upon himself to undertake some sleuthing. Originally a BBC Radio 4 comedy science fiction series, the novel the radio show spawned was unfamiliar to Barnwell, but he had occasionally watched popular old repeats of the TV show of the same name and knew of its cult-like status.

Barnwell had called Graham as he drove north on his way to interview the Parnabys to tell him of his lack of success in locating the address. The sun's rays beat down, and even Carmen, normally as energetic as a hummingbird, dragged a little.

"Keep trying, Constable. I know it's just a note on the back of a book, but however unconnected to the case, we must find that address, if only to eliminate it. It's a discrete, straightforward piece of evidence, and as such, a rarity. And you're at St. Julian's Wood, aren't you? It must be there somewhere."

"Doesn't explain why no one's even *heard* of it," Barnwell grumbled when he got off the phone. He wiped beads of sweat from his brow and untucked his white police shirt from his trousers. The internet was almost no help, pointing him only to a collection of trees, a two-acre stand of hawthorns which offered no help or comfort.

Barnwell pulled out a collapsible dog bowl from a pannier on his bike and popped it out with his fist. He filled it from his water bottle, and as Carmen drank, he pulled up a map of the area on his phone, spreading his second and third fingers across the screen to magnify the destination to which he was being guided. Looking up, he raised his head and surveyed the surrounding countryside, trees to one side, open fields to the other.

Once Carmen had drunk her fill, Barnwell threw the remains of the water into the hedgerow. He swung his bike around and, laboriously pushing off, got going again. He headed into the trees, more relieved than ever to have changed his diet and slimmed down.

"Imagine pedalling along like this," he said to himself as he heaved the bicycle back up to speed, "while weighing twenty percent more." Each time he stood on the bathroom scales, a shiver of achievement rippled through him. Briefly, it would be tempered by regret—*why did I wait so long*—before he would be buoyed further by newfound confidence. For one thing, he looked *a great deal* better in his uniform. And for another, he could keep up with Carmen who, lithe, young, and always game, galloped along beside him.

"But more importantly," he muttered through gritted teeth, "where the blinkin' heck *is* this house?" Emerging from the canopy of trees into green fields on the other side of the wood, he put his foot down and once more turned his bike around to retrace his route. This time, he found a rough turnoff excavated by tire tracks but partially covered by brush. It led deeper into the woods in a different direction.

With no better ideas, Barnwell headed down the track, navigating channels of dried mud and leaves through the brush and trees, disturbing nothing but the odd bird and perhaps other wildlife. As he travelled along, he thought he heard voices, but the path ended in a silent, open, dry, flat stretch flanked by vegetable allotments. Beyond them was a row of neat hedging. "Can't make head nor tail of this place," he complained to Carmen, bringing out his phone. "Will we even have reception? We're miles from anywhere civilised."

A year ago, Carmen's astigmatism caused her to be rejected from police dog training. The eye disorder was inconvenient but nothing more. The diagnosis hadn't affected Carmen any, but the threat to the local squirrel population diminished substantially. She couldn't catch anything, but she had a happy time trying.

Now she was Barnwell's—and by extension the Gorey constabulary's—pet, living a life of canine indulgence: regular walks with Barnwell on his beat, plenty of treats, and snoozes in the station. In return, she accompanied him to his "Dog and Doughnut" sessions at the local primary school. Sitting quietly, acting as a therapy dog, Carmen showed remarkable tolerance as young children took turns to cuddle her while Barnwell gave road and child safety talks to classes of twenty.

"Are you stuck in the maze?"

Barnwell turned to see a woman in her thirties smiling curiously at him. She wore a loose red dress, her hair braided in a halo around her head. Under one arm was a basket full of what looked like leaves, and a sleeping baby lay swaddled against her chest.

"Ah, well, I'm not exactly sure," he said. "Looking for St. Julian's Wood. Is this it?"

The woman rolled her eyes good-naturedly. "It certainly is, Detective!"

"Just a constable, ma'am."

"Well, Constable, we call it Julian's Wood these days."

"We?"

"There are a few of us living here. Five families, no pollution, no problems."

"All recycled and what have you?" Barnwell asked, interested. "Low carbon footprint and all that?"

"Zero, if we can."

"Great. Well, I'm looking for number four St. Julian's Road. Do you know where that is?" He peered behind her, only now noticing a row of semicylindrical steel huts. Painted a shade of light green, they blended perfectly with the surroundings. Barnwell eyed them curiously.

"They're Nissen huts," the woman informed him, noticing his interest. "We've restored them. They look good, don't they?"

"Yeah, yeah, they do. Must've taken a bit of work." The cylindrical corrugated metal huts lined up in military formation, their entrances facing out across fields.

"We've completely rebuilt them but kept the original footprint and shape. We used environmentally friendly materials and installed solar energy for power. There's even underfloor heating and a wood burner."

"Blimey, you've got better facilities than I have in town."

"We love it out here," the woman said, smiling and gazing at her sleeping baby. "So, you're looking for number four? We don't really go by addresses out here. Do you mean the fourth one to be built?"

"No, I mean house number four. Like on a residential street. And back in the early eighties." The woman frowned and turned down the corners of her mouth. "Oh, never mind." He knew he sounded delirious.

Strewn around, Barnwell could see strollers, potted ferns, barbecues, and bikes. A few yards away, a pile of logs, neatly stacked, fenced off a children's play area, and beyond that, half a dozen goats grazed quietly.

As he spoke to the woman, Barnwell noticed the intrigue and curiosity his arrival incited. First out of the huts appeared a young child around the age of two, three fingers in her mouth. She stared at the dog and the stranger, who wore an even stranger costume. A tall, stringy man dressed in faded jeans and a work shirt followed the child. More people emerged from the huts, gazing intently at Barnwell, around twenty-five in all—men, women, and children of all ages and sizes.

They didn't seem threatening, just curious. It was weird. Barnwell wondered if he had somehow stepped into another world.

A slight sheen appeared on his upper lip. Suddenly acutely aware of his push bike and lack of backup, he searched for something to say as he glanced around.

Each vegetable patch was well-tended; some families kept chickens. It seemed idyllic, especially with the children running around.

"Are you a commune?"

The woman smiled again, and a chuckle rose from deep within her throat. "Some would say so."

"I thought a commune would be a bunch of sticks and a tarpaulin strung between branches," Barnwell admitted, "or, you know, people living in broken-down caravans. But you've got a nice little thing going on here."

"We got permission, gave it a go, and made it work," the young woman explained, making soothing sounds as her baby fussed. "I'll get Rory. He might know about number four."

CHAPTER FORTY-FIVE

WARY AT FIRST, Rory wiped his hands on dirty jeans as he walked up to Barnwell and looked through dark hair that needed a trim. "What's all this, then? Trouble with the law, is it? We're all legal, like."

"No trouble," Barnwell promised, and briefly explained his afternoon assignment.

"Ain't got numbers, only names," Rory replied. "The two newest ones are *Bluebell* and *Foxglove*."

"How do you support yourselves out here?"

"I'll do anything, but I learned as a carpenter. Some of us work locally in the community. The others digitally, software engineers and the like, working for all sorts. All remote now. Good broadband service. We've got good throughput out here."

"So, you're only slightly off-grid, then. I mean just a bit, falling off the edge kind of thing." He smiled but the man looked at Barnwell uncomprehendingly. "Never mind," he said again. "How did you come to choose this site?"

Rory hitched up his jeans and looked around him. "Ah, well. Scouts used to camp here and such. I was one of them. We used to call it Fort Feathers 'cause of how soft the pine needles are around here. There's some buildings through the trees. All run-down like. They were put up for sale, what, ten year 'go? Nobody besides us made an offer. We just wanted the land and these huts. We left the buildings for the animals, did up the huts, and moved in. Thankfully"—he laughed, exposing a couple of missing teeth—"several other families had the same idea, and here we are."

Barnwell scribbled words in his notebook. He was glad to have left his iPad back at the station. It would have appeared out of place in this idyllic, eco-friendly paradise. "Buildings? You mean"—Barnwell looked at the curved huts—"bricks and stuff?"

Rory nodded. "Like I say, the scouts had them before. We never bothered with them."

"And before that?"

The carpenter puffed out his cheeks. "Before? Well . . . it'd have been . . ." He scratched his sandpaper beard. "Just . . . a *wood*, I expect!"

Others in the community were able to offer more help, or at least hearsay. As the men had been talking, adults and children, like timid wild creatures, had slowly crept closer to within earshot. "My nan used to say it was, you know, um, they used the buildings for, like, seminars," said one of the younger women. She was perhaps of upper school age, although Barnwell suspected she hadn't seen the inside of a school of any kind in some time.

"Meetings, conferences, that kind of thing?" Barnwell thought the idea strange in such a remote location.

"Dunno, really. She said, like, they ran out of money or something and, like, closed everything down."

No one else knew anything about house numbers. "Did they do wrong, then? Someone?" one elderly man wanted to know. It was a reasonable suspicion given Barnwell's uniform. "Late on their taxes, is it? Or they not got the proper permits?"

"Permits?" Barnwell asked. "What kind of permits?"

"To be here in the woods living our lives this way 'n all that. Needs permits, permissions from the council."

"Why?" Barnwell asked. He thought it best to keep the questions short.

"'Cos they have to come and have a look every now and again, make sure we're not growing anything we shouldn't or selling the kids into slavery."

The young woman from earlier piped up while breastfeeding just yards away. "I tried that already with this one, but they told me to come back when he's old enough to wash dishes." Everyone got a chuckle except Barnwell, who still didn't understand why an address from forty years ago had yielded a community created only recently and a rather unexpected one at that. Still, no laws were being broken that he could see, and the place had a pleasant balance of the relaxed and industrious. It was a little bit glorious in fact.

One of the oldest members of the community, "Grandma Pam," told Barnwell, "We like to live our lives at a slower pace than most. Folks come to take photos of us sometimes, as though we're eco-warriors or something." She cackled, showing off yellowing teeth and old, dark fillings. "But we're just here to find ways of living sustainably, giving our kids a better childhood and chance at life."

Barnwell thought that *did* make them eco-warriors, but he thanked her for her input. Feeling he had got as much as he could from this visit, he made his way back out to the path he had come in on. As he went, he reassured the crowd that followed him, apparently unwilling to let their novel visitor go. "Just trying to chase down an address for an enquiry."

"Someone who lived here before, eh?"

"Not sure. All we've got is the address."

"Did something awful, did they?" Rory's concern grew again. The crowd was still following. "Are you lot going to be out here with mechanical diggers and what have you, tearing up the place looking for bodies?"

"Almost certainly not."

"'*Almost* certainly not.' I like that," Rory said, unimpressed.

"We're investigating a case, and the address might relate to it. It also may be absolutely nothing."

The carpenter laughed again, saying as he stepped away, "Hard for it to relate to much of anything if it ain't real!"

Privately, Barnwell was forced to agree. Then Grandma Pam caught his elbow. "Did they show you the ruins?"

Images of sacred standing stones and cavorting druids troubled Barnwell immediately, but as Pam took him a hundred yards through the woods, he made out some unnaturally straight lines ahead.

As they drew up, Pam pointed. "It was a cottage, someone said, but a man passing through once told me it used to be a chapel."

"Looks like it caught fire," Barnwell said. Only ruined blackened beams and tumbledown walls remained, half grown over with vines dotted with white flowers.

"Probably kids mucking about one night, letting things get out of hand. But not since we've been here. It was like that when we arrived."

"What are those over there?" Barnwell wondered. To the right of the burned building and through the trees were more broken-down walls of brick.

"A few more cottages, old and dangerous to my mind. We don't let the children go anywhere near this place."

Barnwell left her to tramp through the brush and nettles, focused only on the piles of brick ahead of him. Almost completely buried beneath weeds, more vines, and undergrowth, he found a row of semi-detached cottages and some outbuildings, not burned but partially fallen down and certainly derelict. He counted them before walking back to Pam, Carmen, as ever, by his side. "Well, I think I've found number four."

CHAPTER FORTY-SIX

"I KNOW MIKE Tenbeigh was in touch recently, and I'm sorry if he . . ." His brow furrowed, Graham brought every ounce of courtesy he possessed to his request. Veronica Needham was taking her duties as the wife of a retired superintendent suffering from early dementia with the intensity (and potential bite) of a guard dog. "I'm sorry Nigel was so tired afterwards, and I promise I won't take more than two minutes of his time." Graham listened patiently as Veronica laid down the ground rules for his conversation with her husband and reflected that for the second time that day, he had to accept someone else's terms of engagement.

A few seconds later, a different voice sounded on the line, at first gruff and impatient, then cordial. "David?" Nigel Needham sounded in fine fettle at least.

"Good afternoon, sir. Sorry to bother you."

"Not a bit of it. Happy to hear from you. Veronica makes a fuss over every last little thing, but she means well. What can I do for you?" Graham could hear Needham shuffling into his study and closing the door on his maddened and maddening spouse.

"George and Arthur Parnaby," Graham said.

"Bad boys!" Needham said immediately. "We nicked them for that armoured car job in Shoreditch in . . . ninety-nine I think it was. The guard shot in the back. Only a lad. Didn't make it through surgery." Needham sighed. "That's the curse of this bloody disease. You forget the good stuff and remember the upsetting bits."

"Who are these guys, sir? They act like they were nothing but a couple of minor players." Graham knew the brothers' criminal careers amounted to much more than that but wanted to hear Needham's telling of their story.

"Bloody *menace*, they were. Four of them, originally going right back to the seventies. We put people in there, got close a couple of times, but the more dominant one—Arthur, if I recall . . ."

"That's right."

"He got suspicious, and we had to close the operation down both times. He was an all-round nasty piece of business. We wanted him for a string of other serious crimes but couldn't pin things down."

"What was their setup?"

"Originally in their twenties and thirties, the brothers ran a builder's merchant with the help of a couple of younger lads. It looked legit on the outside, but there was some 'import-export,' pills, dodgy paperwork, this and that. The other two moved on in the early eighties and the brothers went solo, bringing in people for different jobs as and when. They did everything from beating up a grass or two and running a protection racket right up to armed robberies. Did a few bank jobs and all. No one killed though, until the Shoreditch fiasco. A thoroughly unpleasant pair whom everyone knew and steered clear of if they had the chance."

"Who were the other two?" Graham asked. He wished now that he had contacted Needham earlier, despite the awkwardness of depending on an exhausted mind. Graham imagined Needham's rheumy eyes unfocused, his mouth gaping slightly.

"Eh?"

"Who made up the band of four? The younger two?"

"Dillon and Cross," Needham said without pause, as though naming his own dogs. "Suspects in a couple of post office jobs, and I fancied them for an odd, rural burglary in Northamptonshire."

Gears turned for a couple of seconds, then the file popped up in Graham's brain. "Planned a hostage-taking . . . affluent young couple?"

"That's the one. Then the dozy buggers realised they'd forgotten the rope and tape. Ended up running off with whatever they could carry."

"Sound like amateurs to me."

"Oh, they were appalling, incompetent criminals. Should have gone straight while they had the chance. But they were influenced, led astray by older, harder men looking for patsies. And they were lucky they never got caught." Needham rattled off a list of the Parnaby jobs he could remember.

"Arthur and George gave genuine mobsters a bad name. They did what a lot do when they don't have the intelligence. They compensated with menaces and ultimately violence. And as time went on, their crimes depended on it. But Dillon and Cross were involved fairly early. By the time of the Shoreditch job that sent the Parnabys down, those two lads were long gone."

"What happened to them?"

"Vanished, as far as I can remember. They never crossed my path again, that's for sure."

"Well, I can solve one-half of that mystery. Mr. Dillon's just turned up dead on Jersey."

The assumption was instant. "Murdered?"

"Looks that way. In 1982. We found his body bunged in a block of concrete in a hotel attic—the White House Inn where you stayed when you came over for that conference a few years ago." Graham waited for some murmur of recognition from his former boss, but none was forthcoming.

"Some bright spark cut his cocaine with rat poison. The owner of the hotel was running a drugs racket while dying of cancer and wanted to avoid a scene. So instead of raising the alarm, she blocked him up. His remains were found by accident some days ago." Graham hoped his words would spark something in Needham's memory.

After a pause, the former DCI said, "You like rock'n'roll, don't you, Dave?"

"Who doesn't?" Graham responded tentatively, afraid the *non sequitur* signalled an abrupt and unwelcome change of topic.

"Think of your classic rock band. Usually," Needham said, "one band member lives hard and checks out early. Overdose, suicide, that kind of thing. Two of the others keep on rocking as a duo, reliving their heyday until age catches up with them. And the fourth one, often the brainiest of them all, what does he do?"

"Well, if he's smart, he makes his millions while he can and goes off to live on a farm in the Wiltshire countryside."

"Exactly."

With thanks for his help and good wishes to his wife, Graham ended the call with Needham and immediately placed another.

"Freddie? I have a question for you."

CHAPTER FORTY-SEVEN

JANICE AND GRAHAM were huddling, talking quietly, when the two Parnaby brothers returned to the interview room.

"Dylan Dillon went to Jersey to murder Charlie Cross, didn't he?" Graham said as soon as they resumed the interview.

Arthur blinked at him. "Afternoon to you 'n' all. How was your food? I thought the meatloaf was a bit dry."

George rubbed his stomach and licked his lips, grinning widely to reveal a couple of missing canines that seemed to have gone AWOL during lunch. His volcanic lungs rumbled into action. "I had the pasta with the creamy sauce. Very nice, it was."

Graham ignored these comments. "Did the two of you order him to do it? Or was it Dillon's idea to go to Jersey? I mean," he said, turning to Janice as if to explain, "he must have been incensed at the way Cross ripped you all off."

Janice blinked in amazement. "East End, low-end, dead-end mob lackeys ripping each other off?" She gasped. "Whatever next?"

"Shove it where the sun don't shine, lady," George rasped.

"Cool it, George. She's only trying to understand what the good detective inspector is saying. And frankly"—Arthur turned to Graham—"so am I."

"In 1981, I put it to you that Mr. Cross decided, on reflection, not to pursue a career as an aimless hoodlum any further. He felt his talents might extend beyond nicking bikes, threatening village postal workers, and jemmying back windows. As law enforcement officials, we normally welcome this kind of revelation, don't we, Sergeant?"

"With open arms," Janice agreed.

Graham paused. He was extemporising. He pulled together everything he had learned, made some educated guesses, and lobbed a theory to test the brothers' reaction. "But this new convert's erstwhile brethren, during their grief and anguish at their friend's abrupt departure, made a highly incriminating discovery."

Hand under his chin as though thoroughly engaged in story time, Arthur said, "Eh? Oh, no, please don't stop. It's great, this. Quality entertainment."

"Nothing like watching coppers try to prove a crime they just made up," his brother said. "Go on, don't let us stop you. Is there any popcorn?" George turned to Janice, whose mild, almost disinterested expression gave him no satisfaction.

Graham stood. After hours in a car, then more hours trying to lever information out of this miserable pair, he'd lost all feeling below his left knee. "Carry on, Sergeant," he said, flexing his ankle.

"This discovery was an unpleasant one," Janice said. "Mr. Cross likely fancied setting himself up for a life of luxury . . . Well, a few years of it anyway. Whatever third-hand safe, or space beneath a squeaky floorboard, or back bedroom mattress had become the resting place of your loot, Mr. Cross found it."

"Sounds like it must have been annoying," Graham added, "to find that your former mate has summarily slinked off with most of the takings from your post office jobs."

"I mean," Janice added, "it must have wound you up something terrible."

"If I'd known you were going to waste my time with fiction, I'd have gone to the library after lunch. They have better stories." Arthur sniffed.

"I'd have hung out in the canteen a bit longer, maybe blagged an extra pudding," said George. "There's always someone with a fresh face you can snatch one off of."

Graham took over again. "Was it on your orders that Dylan Dillon went to Jersey to find Charlie Cross?"

"Orders?" Arthur scoffed. "It wasn't the bleedin' army or anyfin'. We worked together in the building trade is all."

"'The building trade'," parroted a sceptical Janice. "Threatening shop owners for protection money." She checked off a list on her fingers. "Collecting on payday loans from young single mums, intimidating a local councilman to—"

The two brothers interrupted her with a synchronised routine so smooth she suspected they had rehearsed it. "No charges were ever brought," Arthur intoned.

"And we have nothing to add to our earlier statements."

"Okay, fine. Thanks for all your help," Graham said, his hands on his hips. "Sergeant Harding, if we hurry, we can grab that earlier flight." He made a note with a final flourish and folded away his notebook. "And it seems I won't have to make any phone calls in support of these two after all. They've decided to wither in HMP Holbrooke in one final gesture of defiance. Will they deem it worth it in the final analysis? Ah well, not our concern. You know what they say about old dogs, new tricks? Defying the police is a lifelong pursuit for these two. Seems they can't change even when it's in their best interest."

Graham took a moment to glare at the brothers as he spoke, regarding them like decrepit museum pieces, destined for dust. Graham found George's eyes, and they were those of a sick man, veined and yellow. "You've got months at best, I'd wager, not years. Why spend them in here miserably?" He opened the door for Janice.

The pain of confusion involuntarily curled George's fists into tight balls. "Stop him," he growled to his brother. "We ain't finished here yet."

CHAPTER FORTY-EIGHT

IN THE CAR on the way to the airport, Janice helped Graham note down every last detail the Parnaby brothers had eventually told them, and then on the flight back to Jersey, she played devil's advocate as they reconstructed events as best they understood them. By the time the inspector was done, they were on the final approach, the journey passing in a flash amid the blur of work, fuelled by an overpriced but gloriously caffeinated double-tea-bag cuppa.

"So, now we have Cross's life story," said Graham. "An everyday one, really. Bloke grows up surrounded by stubborn, middle-aged men who never taught him to control his impulsivity and anger. He gets in with the wrong crowd and ends up among the Parnabys and their lot, thieving and threatening. But he sees the way the wind's blowing—the Parnabys, his older brothers and cousins, other associates—and decides he won't end up like them."

"It takes time, but he plucks up the courage," Janice guessed, "gets himself set, and absconds with all their loot in the middle of the night. More options that way. Gave him a head start, the means to disappear."

"But Dillon tracked him down to Jersey." Graham paused, jutting out his chin. "Dillon arrives on the island full of fury at being double-crossed, whipped up by the Parnabys. He ferrets out his prey. But before he can take action, someone, maybe his target, gets to him first. Kills him."

"But, sir, the timeline. According to passport records, Dillon travelled from Jersey to France immediately after his death, then returned in October 1982. After that, we lose him. He, or someone posing as him, must still be on Jersey." They had landed and were taxiing down the runway when Graham's phone picked up a cell tower and delivered an avalanche of texts.

"Not necessarily, Sergeant. Dillon was a British citizen. Did we need our passports for our jaunt to the mainland?"

"Ah, no. So, Dillon wouldn't use his passport if he's traveling to and from the British mainland. Only if he's crossing a country border."

"That's right. He could have reentered Jersey from France, then gone back to mainland UK and we wouldn't have known. I assume the flight and ferry manifests are long gone?"

"Yes, I checked. So, Dillon could be anywhere in the UK?"

"Yes."

"But he was dead, sir."

Graham blew out his cheeks. "Yes. I'm thinking that he must have had his passport with him when he arrived on Jersey, perhaps because he had plans to go to Europe and hide out for a bit. Then someone, perhaps his murderer, used it, and that's who we're seeing travel to France and back."

"Charlie Cross, do you think?"

"Maybe. Did you get anything back on him?"

"Yes and no. There's another puzzling thing. There are no records for Cross at all after 1981 when the Parnabys said he disappeared . . . And that means . . ."

"Yes, Sergeant?"

"He could also be anywhere in the UK."

"Or he too is dead." It was Janice's turn to blow out her cheeks. Graham looked at his phone again. Barnwell was calling.

"Phew, I'm already wishing we were back in the air, uncontactable for a bit longer." Graham pressed the "accept" button. "Yes, Barnwell?" Chatter and laughter filled the background.

"Hope you had a fruitful day, sir. Just wanted to let you know that I had another go at finding that address in Julian's Wood, and I think I found it. Four cottages, some outbuildings, and another building, perhaps a chapel. The story, ah, let's say the folklore, is that someone ran courses there, seminars. Can't imagine in what—bushcraft? When that stopped, the scouts took over. At some point, a fire came along and burned part of it down. The buildings were abandoned. But now the area's a thriving eco-warrior commune with gardens and such. It was all a bit strange, to be fair. But that's all I got. Doesn't seem like it had anything to do with our case. Dead end if you ask me."

"Hmm, okay. Thanks for doing that. Pity it wasn't more informative."

"No problem, sir. Me 'n' Carmen are having a rest in the Foc'sle. Good crowd tonight. Beer's off though. Bad barrel. I'm drinking tonic water."

"Good man. We need your clear head first thing, Barnwell. Have a good rest of your evening. We'll see you tomorrow." The seat belt sign turned off, and Graham helped Janice bring her laptop bag down from the overhead compartment. "Here, let me. You need to look after yourself. After all, you've got that small thing in a couple of days."

"Hallelujah," she muttered.

"Hmm?"

"Nothing."

"Jitters are natural, you know. My wife was like a cat on a hot tin roof just before our wedding."

"Oh?" Janice arched her eyebrows. Graham caught himself and stared straight ahead. Sensing his discomfort at this slip of personal information, Janice said, "I can't wait to marry Jack."

"Glad to hear it."

"It's my mother."

"She doesn't like him?"

"No, no, she'd marry him herself if she could. She'd just do it her way."

Even without years of detective work, Graham would quickly have made the deduction. "You came on this trip to get away from her, didn't you?"

"Something like that."

"Janice," he said. "Tenbeigh runs an efficient joint, but . . . it's Holbrooke. Not exactly Saint-Tropez. As far as jollies go, it was hardly worth it."

"Oh, you'd be surprised. Holbrooke had at least one feature that made it an attractive destination," she said as they walked past the baggage carousels and looked for a cab.

"The thrill of the case?" he said.

"Great title for your autobiography." Janice smirked.

"Or just a getaway from your mother."

"How about a little of each? Like pie and ice cream for pudding."

A taxi pulled up. "Don't forget, Laura and I are here if you need us."

The heavens burst as Graham opened the car door for his sergeant. "My only advice is to remember to turn off your phone during the ceremony," he reminded her, "because your "Stayin' Alive" ringtone isn't going to do justice to the acoustics at St. Andrew's."

"Don't worry, it's on my 'List of Things to Do Before Getting Married.'"

"What else is on it? Your list," he said. The rain was coming down harder now.

"Exile my mother to the Outer Hebrides!" she shouted before the door slammed shut.

CHAPTER FORTY-NINE

CARMEN'S EARS TWITCHED. She trotted out from under Barnwell's desk as the doors to the station opened.
"Mornin', all."
In unison, Barnwell's and Janice's heads popped up. Delighted smiles spread across their faces, their eyes shining.
"Roachie!" Janice cried. She hurried around the reception desk, her arms outstretched, ready to give a big hug to tall, lanky Detective Sergeant Roach, formerly of Gorey Constabulary, now a member of Homicide and Major Crime Command based at Scotland Yard.
After they hugged, Janice stepped back, clutching Roach's arms and scrutinising him, just like his mother had done an hour earlier. "Look at you. I swear you've grown two inches since we last saw you." Janice punched him on the bicep. "And so muscly. Bet all the London girls are after you!" Yeah, exactly like his mother.
"Ah, not really. At least not at the moment. We'll see." Roach raised his eyebrows. "How's Jack? All ready for tomorrow?"
Janice smiled. "He's well. And we're as ready as we'll ever be."
Behind Janice, Barnwell stirred. "Hiya, mate," he said shyly.
"Wotcha, Bazza." Roach smiled. They shook hands.
"Aw, c'me 'ere," Barnwell said after a tiny pause, and he too pulled Roach in for a hug, a manly one, their hands clasped between their chests and accompanied by a hard, rough mutual pat on the back.
When they separated, Roach looked across and saw Graham standing in his office doorway, leaning against the frame. He was smiling. "Hello, sir." Graham pushed himself off.
"Detective Sergeant Roach, good to see you." They vigorously shook hands,

but there was no hug in the offing this time. Telepathically or by osmosis, they both understood that simply wouldn't do. "How's it going up there in London?"

Jim Roach had certainly matured in the ten months he had been away. It showed in his chiselled cheekbones and square jaw, both more angled since he was last on Jersey. In his eyes, a confidence, an assuredness that reminded Graham of his younger self, bloomed. Stubble and an up-to-the-minute haircut, replete with gel, completed the makeover. Roach had never been a slouch, but now there was a slight air of danger about him, an edge.

"Great, sir. I'm enjoying it. Bit of a culture shock at first but getting an arrest or two under my belt helped a lot."

Hearing this, Graham's heart swelled. His cheeks reddened and his heart kicked up a beat or two. "Good man." He looked at his watch. "Well, I think it's time for an early lunch, don't you? Why don't the three of you go and have yours? I'll man the fort here. I'll call you if I need you."

Janice and Barnwell didn't need telling twice. Immediately, they grabbed their jackets, shut down their computers, and marched out into the sunlight. Janice grabbed Roach's arm and, linking his with hers, chattered away, updating him on all the news, clearly delighted to have him home as she bounced along next to him. Barnwell trailed behind, Carmen trotting alongside him, a familiar sight.

Alone in the office, Graham's phone chimed. It was Laura. "Yes, love. How's your day going?"

"Not bad. Bit quiet for a Thursday, but the old boys are asleep with the *Racing Post* and *Daily Mail*. St. Helier has just delivered a huge pile of requested books. And I have an enormous backlog of returns to shelve. You?"

"Ah, just mulling the Dillon case, not getting very far. Jim Roach has just arrived for Janice's wedding. I've sent the three of them off for lunch, so I'm here by myself."

"Aw, poor you. I'd keep you company if I didn't have all these books to shelve. I was ringing to tell you the amount of work I have to do this afternoon is all down to you."

"Me?"

"Yes, I've spent this morning doing some research on your behalf."

Graham paused. "Research?" Graham was relieved that it wasn't something serious, something perhaps to do with Freddie Solomon and his involvement-slash-interference in the Dillon case.

"Julian's Wood. What you told me last night. Barnwell was almost right about the seminars."

"Almost?"

"Back in the day, the place was a seminary, a small one. As far as I can tell, just a dozen or so theological students. Its funding dried up, and it fizzled out, eventually closing." At the other end of the phone, Laura smiled, pleased with her sleuthing.

Graham pushed his lips out as he considered this. "Hmm. And when did it close exactly?"

"The mid-eighties—1983 to be exact. Is that helpful?"

"Not sure. Seems odd."

As Graham ended their call, loneliness and disappointment swept across him. He had no idea how the address of a long-closed seminary written on the back cover of a novel found at a crime scene was relevant to his investigation. He tossed his pencil on his desk as he sat down, leaning forward and rubbing his face with his hand.

The case reminded him of a mug of tepid, weak, milky tea. When making tea with a tea bag, if you add the milk first, before the tea, the hot water cannot extract the flavour from the leaves. It doesn't matter how much you stir, the tea will not steep. The fundamentals are wrong.

Graham couldn't escape the idea that he was missing something fundamental about the case of Dylan Dillon. It didn't seem to matter how much evidence they gathered; none of it added up.

Graham deliberately cleared his mind and reviewed what he knew, rhythmically tapping his pencil on his desk, hoping that a flash of insight would pop into his head. But nothing struck him. The inspector leaned back and sighed, resting his hands, fingers interlinked, on his head.

He had hit a wall. And with Janice's wedding tomorrow, he had to put the case aside. Laura would expect it of him, and she would be right. He stood to make another cup of tea. Perhaps that would help. He would make sure to put the tea bag in first.

CHAPTER FIFTY

GRAHAM STRAIGHTENED HIS narrow, black tie before shrugging on his uniform jacket and buttoning it. He stood back from the mirror, tugging at the jacket's hem. He checked everything was in order: the two pips on his epaulettes, silver now (they had been gold when he was in the Met); his three medals for bravery and honourable conduct; the position and arc of his whistle chain that stretched from between his first and second buttons to his breast pocket. Upside down on the bed, a pair of new white gloves sitting inside, lay his uniform cap, the black band on the peak denoting his status as a detective inspector.

"How do I look?" he asked Laura as he pulled on his cuffs. She looked him up and down.

"Devastatingly handsome, I'd say." She leaned forward on tiptoes, her lips puckered for a quick kiss. A notification came through on Graham's phone, and it pinged. "I'm glad you resolved your differences with Freddie in time for today. I'd been anxious about the two of you bumping into each other. I thought it might overshadow the occasion and spoil Janice's wedding."

"Her mother's doing her best to achieve that. And resolving our differences is going a bit far, I think. A temporary truce is more like it. And he better not write anything else about the case. That was our agreement. We're making progress, albeit slowly, and I don't want him prejudicing any court proceedings that might occur in the future. He can have his day in the sun later."

"Well, whatever you want to call it, I'm pleased. And today is a good day, a happy day. Finally, Janice and Jack are getting married, despite her mother's efforts, and we get the chance to dress up to celebrate it." Laura leaned toward the mirror to smear her lips with gloss. Still in her dressing gown, her fair, shoulder-length hair piled high on her head, she looked like a model posing for an impressionist painting. *Woman in Mirror* or some such.

"I'm disappointed the case is still hanging over our heads, though. I had hoped to have it resolved by the wedding. It is such a baffling case." Graham sighed. "Are you coming with me? I have to leave now." Graham, along with Roach and Barnwell, were ushers. His phone pinged again, and he picked it up.

"I hope that's nothing important," Laura said.

"No, not a number I recognise. So, are you coming?"

"I'm not quite ready yet. You go, and I'll catch you at the church."

Graham picked up his hat and gloves. He breathed in deeply through his nose and out through his mouth, relaxing his shoulders. "I'm going to do my absolute level best to forget about work and enjoy today."

"Woo-hoo! You mean like a normal person?"

"Yes, like a normal person." He pecked her jauntily on the cheeks and smiled. "See you later!"

Laura watched him stride down the short path through her cottage garden to the car parked outside. She looked at her watch. A frisson of panic shot through her. "Oh, my gosh! I'd better get going!" Bounding up the stairs to the bedroom, she plugged in her hairdryer and started wielding it like a weapon, rolling her hair into big curls with a thick, round brush. Eight minutes later, she turned off the dryer, and as she leaned over to stuff it in a drawer, she glanced out of the window.

She straightened slowly. Something was wrong. David should be at the church by now, but his car idled at the curb.

Inside it, the detective inspector sat in the driver's seat, frowning. He was staring at his phone.

In the photo, the two boys looked like brothers. Same light brown hair, short wide noses, and pointed chins. Their eyes crinkled at the outside corners as they posed, their arms around each other's shoulders, the faded black-and-white colours and long, pointed shirt collars hinting at the photo's age. It had been sent to Graham by Angela Dillon.

> Found this. Dylan is the one on the left. Don't know the other boy. Taken early 70s.

Graham guessed the boys were around fifteen. Dillon grinned broadly, revealing familiar metal tramlines that were the bane of pubescent teenagers the world over and which almost completely obscured his teeth. The unidentified boy next to him grinned a gappy-toothed smile, his lips stretched thin and wide as he cheekily raised a two-fingered peace sign. Graham thoughtfully tapped his phone with a fingernail before sending a text of his own.

> Thanks for this. Your brother had braces?

Graham knew of the organisation, time, and effort required for this type of dental treatment, and it didn't jive with what Angela Dillon had told him about her family. Almost immediately, he received a text back.

> We all had them. Free on the NHS. It was out of character for our mother, but she had terrible teeth herself and insisted. She was a huge fan of the Osmonds.

Graham glanced at the clock on the dashboard and sprung into action. He scrolled through his contacts and, finding the pathology lab's main number, he placed a call. Then, switching his phone to vibrate, he quickly fired up the engine. He was running late. Dylan Dillon and his braces would have to wait.

"Yes, yes, I can do that," Fiona said. She paused as she listened to Graham on the other end of the line. "Um, ten minutes?" She paused again. "'Kay, I'll send it straight away." The call ended, but almost immediately her phone's screen flashed, accompanied by a familiar peal of notes.

"Take a break, Fiona, it's the weekend." It was Tomlinson. He was on his way to the church too. Francine, resplendent as always, today in purple, sat next to him. She was driving.

"I know, but I'm waiting on the bone DNA results. In respect to the Dillon case. I still haven't received them."

"But they won't tell you much more than we already know. Go home and relax."

"Oh, alright. I'm not very good at relaxing, but since you insist. Inspector Graham just called and asked for another aged photo, but after I've done that, I'll leave."

"Are you on your own there?"

"Yes, Aidan left a little while ago."

"Do you know if he called the funeral directors? About Dylan Dillon. The body will be released to his next of kin soon now that we've finished our tests and know who he is. He needs to be moved and prepared for his service."

"He said he'd do it on his way home."

"Okay, thanks. Are you going to Janice and Jack's evening do?"

"Yes. It was nice of them to ask me. I can meet the rest of the team. I'm looking forward to it. I'll see you then. Have a lovely time. Bye, Marcus."

Fiona hung up. Comfortable among drawers of dead bodies, five currently, she opened the software she needed to complete the task Inspector Graham had asked of her. Taking the photo of the two teenage boys he had sent, she isolated Dillon on the left and set about aging his face fifty years as he had asked.

When it was done, she texted the image to Graham and prepared to leave.

Looping her bag over her shoulder, Fiona walked to the bank of light switches and turned them all off. Darkness descended, and she paused for a moment, appreciating the peacefulness of the mortuary, the only sound the buzzing of the refrigeration system.

Shutting the door as she walked out, her phone began a steady, rhythmic tinkle that repeated twice before she answered it, listening carefully. Seconds later, Fiona rushed through the mortuary door, rapidly switching on the lights, the room suddenly ablaze as she powered her computer back on.

CHAPTER FIFTY-ONE

JACK WENTWORTH, HIS younger brother Toby, and his best man Dexter arrived first, all roguishly handsome thirty-somethings in their grey morning suits and top hats.

"Cool," whispered Toby, looking around him at the ancient stonework, the soaring arched ceiling, and the dramatic flower arrangements at the end of every pew. He spoke as though the church were half-full, not empty. It was still early, an hour to go.

Dexter's contribution was a loud clap, hands above his head, followed by a graceful C-major arpeggio in his light-opera baritone. "I have to hand it to you, Jack, mate, it's a fine venue," he said in his broad Geordie accent. Jack and Dexter had been at university together.

"We searched for an acoustic that would make your voice soar while me and Jan sign the register," Jack said. "First order of business, that was. Promise." Dexter wandered off to the front of the church. There, the four members of the string quartet that would accompany him were setting up underneath the large, colourful stained glass window of a mournful St. Andrew holding a cross and surrounded by fish.

A year before, Jack and Janice had almost everything planned for their wedding when Janice was kidnapped and nearly drowned. They postponed the wedding until things had settled and they could think again.

When they were ready to proceed, they had slightly different priorities. They had wanted something smaller, personal, intimate. Something that reflected their wishes whilst also meeting the needs of their family members—salt-of-the-earth types, steeped in tradition, who held strong views on the milestones of life being taken in the "right" order. No babies before marriage for Janice and Jack! Living together had been as far as they had pushed it. Even that had been met with tight lips and stiff backs, both eventually relaxing once the older generation realised that the effort required to maintain the tension wore them out and was utterly ineffective.

St. Andrew's, though, was a keeper from the original plans. Jack's priorities had been to find a church that didn't feel too big, wouldn't insist on a huge fee, and would satisfy Janice's mother. On the sunlit morning Janice and Jack attended a service, they had felt warmth emanate from within its stones. Perhaps it had come from hours of bathing in the sun's heat—it had been a hot day, even at the 11 a.m. Sunday worship service—but they'd felt comfortable committing to a date.

Tipping the scales for Jack had been its spaciousness, despite it being a relatively small church. He had appreciated the unique way the church wrapped him in a timeless calm each time he walked in. He thought his future mother-in-law might like it.

Jack was a simple guy, easygoing with respect to most things. At one point, he and Janice had considered a beach wedding somewhere nice and warm. But the explosion of fury that would have emanated from Mrs. Harding if they had chosen the heat of sand beneath their feet instead of that radiating off the sixteenth-century church stone filled him with horror.

As he reassured his fiancée many times during the preparations, the most important consideration was that they be married. The details of how and where were unimportant to Jack. They could wed in a cow barn and he would be happy.

The same couldn't be said for Janice. And certainly not her mother. Jack anticipated trouble and resolved to be the bulwark, a commitment that had tested him many times over the previous months.

"And what did Mrs. Harding think of the church?" asked Toby.

Jack savoured a fleeting moment of calm, sure that the day would later be full of opportunities to be otherwise. "She thought this was an annexe to the main building," Jack recalled, his eyes closing in discomfort. Rosemary's comportment during her tour of the church had been one of poorly restrained disappointment. As she'd expected, Janice later received a fulsome chronicle of her mother's objections in the form of six very long and detailed voicemails.

"I feel guilty," Janice had said to Jack after finally pressing "delete." "I want you to know that. But, sweetheart, this is self-preservation."

"From the way she talked up your wedding last night at dinner," Dexter said, returning from his chat with the musicians, "I'm expecting nothing less than a Royal Air Force flypast." He turned to the brothers; one was a shorter, stockier version of the other. Jack cringed.

"That's Rosemary for you. This is a significant moment in her life. Maybe the most significant. I suppose it is for all mothers of a bride. Rosemary is . . ." Jack tried to explain, "really enthusiastic about this wedding." For a moment, he and Toby privately appreciated their sisterless existence in silence.

"Will she have you waving at the crowd from the balcony like the royals?" wondered Dexter. "So nice of you to come." The best man partnered a royal wave with the accent of landed gentry, his voice falsetto, feminine, and ludicrous. "Paupers and the other unwashed may watch in silence from the back," he added, dropping his voice and mocking the prim, high-handed elocution of the privileged.

"Leave her alone. She's not that bad," Jack said, regretting not shutting down the subject of his soon-to-be mother-in-law the moment it had arisen.

He allowed himself a laugh. If he could manage not to take Rosemary Harding too seriously, not to let her meddling bother him, there was a decent chance he might enjoy his own wedding day. "Alright. I'm going to find Reverend Bright. You two stay here and wait for the ushers to arrive. They should be here any minute."

"No problem, mate. It's your wedding day. Your wish is my command," Dexter said, saluting.

"Thanks, pal. That's what I need today." Jack left them and headed through to the vestry.

Reverend Bright was there, but he wasn't alone. Jack slowed his pace and prepared to wait. Bright had so many responsibilities in the community, from arranging funerals to scheduling bake sales, that he could have been doing anything. As Jack got closer, Bright ushered someone to the door.

It was Rosemary, here at the church much earlier than planned. Why wasn't she at the house with the bridesmaids? Perhaps Janice had got shot of her.

"I really wish you'd speak to them again," she was saying. "It's short notice, but there must be several organists on Jersey."

"I've long since learned," Bright said, his patience still intact but beginning to drain, "that musical choices are very personal. It would be wrong of me to intervene."

"It's just . . . the spectacle of it. I think they're losing out on so much." It was then, as the reverend closed the vestry door behind them and they emerged into the sunshine, that Rosemary noticed Jack. Far from embarrassed, she tried once again to recruit him to her cause. "That huge sound, Jack! It'll fill the place! Let's get the organist to play "Widor's Toccata" as you walk out together and really lift the roof! What do you say?"

CHAPTER FIFTY-TWO

JACK'S BRAIN CLENCHED like a vice. His expression said, "We've been over this a million times." His mouth said, "Morning, Rosemary! Great day for it." He nodded to Bright. "How are you, Reverend?"

"Jack, you lucky lad! Best day of your life, this is!"

"It's highly promising, that's for sure." Jack smiled. "Are you, um, with the bridesmaids, Rosemary?"

Before she could answer, the reverend's mobile phone rang—always jarring and tricky to find given it had to be retrieved from within his cassock. "Joshua Bright," he answered affably. He turned away from them but not before his face darkened and his mouth fell open.

Jack caught the vicar's reaction and tracked Bright's responses to the caller, searching for clues, worrying they might be related to the wedding. "Yes, of course, but . . ." Bright said.

Janice's mother seemed unconcerned about the call and the vicar's reaction. She watched the groomsmen's tails flutter in the breeze as Toby and Dexter approached. "I trust your best man has the ring?" Rosemary said. "He didn't seem completely with it during the rehearsal dinner. Are you sure he is up to his responsibilities?"

Jack defended his best man. "Dexter was vice-chairman of the Durham University Debating Society and he's been my friend for nearly fifteen years. He's on the case, don't worry."

Not in the least reassured, Rosemary caught Jack's gaze and joined him in watching the now-pacing vicar. She tried to lip-read but had to settle for interpreting his body language. "Now he's distracted," she said. "Humph."

"Everything all right, chaps?" Dexter said as he and Toby reached them.

"Bigger churches assign you a liaison," Rosemary claimed, "because they're dedicated to making sure the . . ."

Jack whirled around to look at her. "Rosemary!" he said through clenched teeth. "Will you—"

"Of course!" said Reverend Bright cheerily, turning back to them as he ended the call. He smiled at the wedding party and waved at them, telegraphing all was well and narrowly preventing Jack from losing the temper he had so carefully kept in check for so long.

"Is there a problem?" Rosemary inquired.

"Not at all." Bright beamed and clapped his hands. "How's everyone feeling?" he asked, smiling broadly, injecting into the group the warmth and energy for which he was generally admired by his congregation, small and elderly as it often was. "Jack, when did you last see the blushing bride?"

"Not today, obviously!" interjected Rosemary. "Worst kind of luck to see her before the organ strikes up."

"I saw her last night at the end of the dinner," Jack replied calmly. "And speaking of lifting the roof off, four choristers plus Dexter and a string quartet are going to perform during the processional and at the end of the service, Rosemary. They'll do us proud. They may well lift the roof off. Perhaps you'll consider paying for the repairs, eh?"

Rosemary's body language was tortured and dissatisfied, like a child offered jelly when she craved ice cream. With thirty minutes to go, she seemed to be finally accepting that things were not going her way. "Singing. Yes, you said."

Rosemary flounced off to await the arrival of the bridesmaids whom she'd left at Janice's home. They had been giggling with the bride, glasses of champagne in their hands, and Rosemary had been unable to bear their gaiety and complete unwillingness to listen to her remonstrations. Bright took her departure as his cue to leave and also vanished, although rather more elegantly, his cassock skirts flowing.

In the distance, Rosemary noticed Marjorie Taylor walking down the lane to the church, her forefinger and thumb delicately holding in place a spaceship-size pink hat wrapped in mesh. She was early, but finally, here was a mature, sensible woman with whom Rosemary could hold a decent conversation. She raised her hand and called out to attract Marjorie's attention.

Toby turned to Jack, a hand on his arm. "And you, lucky boy, get to call her 'Mum' for all eternity."

"Yeah, but Jan's got her number. There's a reason she lives on a small island hundreds of miles and a large stretch of water away." Rosemary may be proving to be the most irritating mother-in-law in history, but Jack was keeping his eye on the prize. "Shortly," he told his friends, "I get to marry the single most amazing woman I've ever met."

"And someone who can arrest your neighbours if they're noisy in the small hours," Dexter said. "Win, win."

"It'll be Rosemary getting arrested if she's not careful," warned Jack. "Jan won't stand for it. Tampering with a police officer's sanity on her wedding day sounds criminal to me."

Arriving alone at the lychgate, Graham stopped to hear the curious mix of words floating across the green, sunlit churchyard: sanity . . . police officer . . . criminal . . . "Uh-oh," he laughed as he opened the creaking gate. "Don't tell me I'm needed!"

"Only if you think slinging Rosemary in a holding cell for three hours while I marry her daughter would help," Jack said, then saw the attraction. "Actually, is that a real crime? 'Tampering with a police officer's sanity'?"

"Just one in a long list of offences still awaiting their place in the statute book," Graham replied. "Jack, my lad, you look fantastic. And these two ruffians must be Dexter and Toby," he said, quickly introducing himself. Graham rubbed his hands together. He felt his phone vibrate in his pocket.

"Morning, all." The lychgate creaked again, and Graham quickly glanced at his phone as he turned to see Roach and Barnwell, also in full dress uniform, walking towards them. As usual, at Barnwell's heel trotted Carmen, a spray of baby pink roses to match the groomsmen's buttonholes attached to her collar. "Here's the rest of the gang. Are we all set? Tell us what to do and we'll do it."

"Yep, you're to be stationed at the door," Toby said. Dexter groaned and rolled his eyes. "What?"

"Stationed, geddit?"

It was Toby's turn to roll his eyes. "Yeah, yeah, wagster. Come with me, guys. I'll show you where to stand."

Inside the church, the warm, musty air elicited comforting childhood memories for Graham, and the three officers looked in awe at the enormous stained glass at the opposite end of the church as they listened to their instructions.

"Welcome the guests as they arrive. Hand them an order of service. Ask them if they're with the bride or the groom, and then lead them to a pew on the appropriate side."

"The what side?" Barnwell whispered to Roach.

"If their connection is to the bride, they sit on the right side as the vicar looks from the front. They're on the left side if they're with the groom," Roach whispered back.

"The first two rows are for family," Toby added. "Now, where are those orders of service? They should be on that table." He looked around him. "Hmm, wait there and I'll find the vicar. He'll know where they are."

Dexter walked up and spoke in Toby's ear. "Your parents have arrived. I think you should speak to them. They're by the war memorial."

"But Dex, we don't have the order—"

"Don't worry, you see to your parents. I'll find the vicar," Graham said, taking charge. "It's no problem."

Dexter clicked his heels. "Excuse me while I attend to the potential natural disaster that is Mrs. Harding, as tasked to me to prevent the fraying of the groom's already shredded nerves. She needs constant management such that we avoid a meltdown of nuclear proportions. I'm sure you understand. The vestry's that way." He pointed to a side door at the front of the church.

"Understood," Graham said. He turned to his officers. "Right, lads, I'll be back in a minute."

As he walked up the side aisle, his phone vibrated again. He pulled it out and glanced at it. It was Fiona. She had sent him a text and copied Tomlinson. As he read it, his heart turned over.

> Massive development. Bone DNA just in. Does not match with hair. I repeat, DNA from bones does not match hair DNA. Mr. X is not Dylan Dillon. 🌍

Graham paced the back hallways of the church, still attempting to track Reverend Bright down. The place was immaculately neat, its offices bright and clean, the hallways spotless. According to the poster on the noticeboard exhorting sign-ups, there was a "Godly Play" after-school program on Thursday afternoons. Graham could imagine the tumble of schoolchildren filling the ancient space with fun and noise, and his mind briefly wandered to Katie.

At other times, so the noticeboard told him, the church held coffee and cake mornings, popular with the elderly in Graham's experience, and baby yoga classes. Then, three evenings a week, support groups created a more sombre atmosphere. Focused as they were on bereavement, addiction, and mental health, they provided for those who attended an indispensable service. Reverend Bright had certainly created in St. Andrew's a busy, thriving cornerstone that underpinned the Gorey community.

Graham was about to go outside to explore the cemetery when he checked the vestry for a third time. He discovered Bright standing in the middle of the small room, the door ajar. His back faced the door, his head bent.

"Ah, just the man," Graham said, knocking on the door to announce his presence.

Quickly burying his mobile phone among his cassock folds, Bright turned to greet the detective inspector. He eyed the inspector's uniform and waved him in. "Come in, come in." With a dramatic flourish, Bright lifted his wrist to check his watch. "Can I help you? I haven't much time. I'm about to . . ."

"I'm here about the orders of service, Reverend. We're missing them at the door." Graham smiled. "I'm one of the ushers. And the bride's boss."

"Ah, of course. Hold on, they're around here somewhere." Bright walked over to a small table by the wall and opened a drawer. "Yes, here they are. Sorry, they should have been waiting for you."

"No problem. Thank you." Graham waved the pamphlets in salute. Bright smiled broadly.

Graham turned to leave, shutting the door behind him. The first guests who had been milling around outside chatting entered the church. It would be a race as to whom would reach the ushers first—Graham or the guests. The inspector briskly strode through the church to reach Barnwell and Roach anxiously waiting for him by the door. And then his stride faltered.

Avalanches of information converged in Graham's mind. At first, they were barely more than wisps of ideas nudged by memories, but they gained momentum and stature to form a roiling torrent, eventually converging into a wild, powerful river of ideas and theories into which the inspector, his investigative intellect overwhelming his instincts for decorum and tradition, now plunged.

Barnwell and Roach watched as Graham drew to a halt midway down the aisle.

"What's he doing, Roachie?"

"I'm not sure, Bazza."

"He's got the orders of service in his hand."

"I can see that, but he's turning around. Where's he going?"

"I dunno, but those guests are going to get here in around ten seconds, and we'll not have the orders of service to hand them."

"Stall them with Carmen. I'll go get them off him." But Graham had disappeared, and Roach, like his former boss earlier, began traversing the back hallways of the church looking for him.

CHAPTER FIFTY-THREE

"REVEREND BRIGHT?" GRAHAM had knocked on the vestry door and tried the handle. Inside, he found the reverend sitting in an armchair, his hands clasped in his lap around his phone. He looked mildly at the detective inspector. "May I come in?" Graham said.

Bright gestured with his hand, inviting him. "There isn't much time, Inspector."

Graham closed the vestry door. "I know, but I have a few questions I thought you might know the answer to. Now seems as good a time as any. Won't take long."

Bright sat up in his chair. "Okay, fire away."

"St. Julian's Wood. There's a small commune there now, but they tell me it used to be a seminary. Does that ring any bells with you?"

Reverend Bright paused, a thumbnail to his teeth, considering it. "St. Julian's." He said the name as if drawing the memory from a deep well. "Yes, yes. Back in the day, it was a small theological seminary. Just a handful of people."

"And it closed in, what, the mid-eighties?"

"Something like that. It ran out of money, as these things often do. I think some local people have set up in the woods as some sort of eco-friendly community now." The vicar blinked quickly and smiled. "Hard even to remember the way it used to be. But why would the police be interested in St. Julian's? Trouble with the people there? Surely not."

"We're investigating a murder," Graham said, reluctant to bring gravity to a such joyous day.

"Oh, I see," Bright said, quickly catching onto the seriousness of Graham's enquiry. "Is this about the man discovered at the White House Inn? With the gun? How awful for the poor soul to have been up in the attic all those years."

"I see you've been perusing Freddie Solomon's latest."

"Of course. As a local vicar, it's always a good idea to keep an eye on the community's comings and goings. Even if they are, er, at times, a bit extreme. But I'm still not following you."

Graham glanced at the large antique wall clock; there were only minutes until Janice's wedding ceremony was to start, maybe a few more if she was late. He could hear the hubbub in the sanctuary building as the wedding guests arrived, and their low but animated chatter burbled through the cavernous space. "The seminary's address was among the physical evidence."

"The poor soul's belongings?"

Graham saw no reason to avoid sharing. "Written on the cover of a novel."

"Well, who was he?" Bright added quickly, "You'll forgive some professional concern when a seminary, even a long-closed one, finds itself embroiled in a murder enquiry. And as it happens, I've just been asked by our local funeral directors if I would conduct a service for him. I understand his remains will be released to his next of kin soon."

"We believe a man named Dylan Dillon came to Jersey to carry out a hit. Freddie Solomon has theories about East End skull-breakers coming to Jersey to do dirty work, and honestly, I still consider them to be mostly fantasy, but I do think he's right here. Dylan Dillon was a small-time crook who was either ordered or incited to murder his former friend and accomplice by his criminal bosses."

"And was the planned killing carried out?"

"Doubtful. Certainly no gun-related death was recorded on the island at the time."

"I see, Inspector." Bright stood. "That's all very interesting, but, well, I'm sorry, don't you have a wedding to attend? I certainly do."

"Why would Dylan Dillon have that address written down, do you think, unless he was following a lead on the whereabouts of his target?"

"Well, I . . . You think he was looking to kill someone at the seminary? But it was just a group of young men devoting themselves to a godly life! The idea that they were involved in any criminal activity is ludicrous."

"But it would be the perfect place to hide out, wouldn't you say? Especially if you had been part of a criminal gang engaged in activities that brought you in contact and relationship with people you'd now rather not know or be associated with."

Bright blinked and raised his eyebrows. "Maybe, but I—"

"At the risk of derailing my sergeant's wedding, I'm hoping you can shed some light on the matter so that we can get things over with and back on track without delay. It would be enormously helpful if you could. Because you see, we followed the trail to the Parnaby twins. They're a couple of hard nuts currently serving twenty-eight years for an armed robbery. They told us about a lad called Charlie Cross. Dillon and Cross were childhood friends, inseparable until one day in the early eighties when Cross did a runner with a pile of loot. The Parnabys' loot. They weren't best pleased. They still aren't."

THE CASE OF THE BODY IN THE BLOCK   687

"I can imagine. But I'm sorry, Inspector. What does that have to do with me?" Bright made for the door, but Graham swiftly moved to place himself in front of it. Bright attempted to go around him. Graham stood firm. Bright huffed. "Inspector, look, we really should be going. It's not good form for the vicar to arrive *after* the bride." Graham cast his eye over the desk in the middle of the room.

"There's no computer in here. You don't use technology?"

"Not too much. There's little need for it except for admin, and my secretary does that from home. And I find it gets in the way of God's work. Puts up barriers. It's rather unhelpful."

"In police work, we use it a lot. And technology has moved on since the eighties. It's amazing what you can find out." Bright stared mutely at Graham, his eyes fierce, penetrating. "We can trace DNA from the tiniest of samples, old ones too. We can track down relatives of our victims even if we don't know their identity. We can dredge up images from long ago. And we can age the people in those images too. Fascinating stuff."

"I see."

"I wonder, Reverend Bright, if you would look at a photo for me?"

"Why?"

"To tell me if you recognise anyone in it."

The vicar shrugged. "Okay."

Graham pulled up a photo on his phone. He turned it to Bright. "These boys. Recognise either of them?" Bright looked at the old, faded black-and-white photo booth picture of the two fair-haired teenagers with cheeky grins, short, stubby noses, and pointed chins. Bright regarded the boys impassively and then said, "No, sorry. Can't say I do. But that looks like an old photo. How am I supposed to know them?"

Graham didn't reply but scrolled to another photograph. It was the image he had shown Angela Dillon, the one Fiona had modelled from the facial remains of Mr. X. "This is one of those boys as a twenty-five-year-old man. Perhaps you recognise him now?" Bright shook his head.

"No, Inspector. Are you sure you don't want to return to the wedding? The groom will be wondering where you are. And I really should be preparing."

"Just one more." Graham scrolled to another photograph. "How about this one?" This time, he showed the vicar a photo of an elderly man. It was the image that Fiona had sent him earlier. Bright sighed. He hesitated before speaking. "No. I have never seen any of these people."

"Really? Are you sure? Because, to me, the man in that photo looks exactly like you."

Bright looked over Graham's shoulder at the picture of Christ on the wall. He muttered silently.

"What's that, Reverend?"

The vicar cleared his throat. "I said that's impossible."

"What is?"

Bright nodded at the phone. "That that's me."

Graham turned the phone around and looked at the photo. "Looks like you to me." Bright gazed past Graham's shoulder again.

"We need to go. The bride will be here soon."

"It's too late for that, I'm afraid."

"What?" Bright's eyes darted between Graham and the door and back again. His cheeks bloomed. His chest rose and abruptly dropped. "Look, I have a lot of things to do. I need to get the readings ready. Set my sermon out. Oversee . . . everything. I need to get things back on track. Now, please!"

"If you think I'm going to let you go out there and marry my sergeant only for the full story to come out later and sully the memory of her wedding day, you can think again. Now tell me, is this you?" Graham showed him the picture of the schoolboys, then swiped left to the image of the elderly man.

Bright sat down, and trapping his soft, fleshy inner cheeks between his teeth, he pursed his lips in a mew before closing his eyes, his lips moving in silent prayer. As he muttered, his body seemed to diminish, shrivelling as Graham watched.

Eventually, Bright opened his eyes. His pupils dilated, appearing as deep, black holes. "Very well, Inspector. I'll tell you."

"Good." Graham pulled up a chair and sat down facing him. "Now, tell me, who are you, exactly?"

Reverend Bright crossed his legs and brushed his cassock skirts, smoothing them. He took a deep breath. "I'm Dylan Dillon."

CHAPTER FIFTY-FOUR

"THEN WHO IS the man in the mortuary?"
"I suppose it must be my old friend, Charlie Cross."
"Arthur and George Parnaby, two lowlifes I interviewed recently, said that one of their crew absconded with over a hundred thousand pounds' of loot. Tore their gang apart overnight. Nothing was the same again, they reckoned."

"They were right about that last part," Bright said simply.

"So, you admit to knowing the Parnabys?"

"I do. I did."

"They say Dylan Dillon, you, came here to locate the absconder and recover the money. You checked into the White House Inn, formerly known as The Grange, under the name of John Smith on the thirteenth of February 1982. Records show that you entered France two days later. You returned to Jersey in October of that year."

"You've done your homework, Inspector. That's right, although a small quibble. I was *compelled* to come here to track down Charlie, believing he had stolen money, money that I thought, in part, I was owed. I had been given an address: 4 St. Julian's Road."

Graham closed the door to the vestry. The noise from the sanctuary was getting louder as the wedding guests got restless. But he couldn't afford to be distracted. For the first time in this case, two plus two suddenly made four without any irregular, inelegant remainder. As he listened, Graham graduated to higher-level maths: the cold calculus of conspiracy, and the convoluted algebra of death.

"It is the most terrible weight being party to a violent death," Bright said, resplendent in his vestments, minutes shy of a much-anticipated wedding ceremony. "But I felt that I had to bear it, that there was simply no other way."

"You killed Charlie Cross?" Bright shifted in his seat.

"Not exactly. Do you think I killed him?"

"It did cross my mind. But if you didn't, what happened?"

"It's important that you understand. You see, it was him or me. Brutally simple." Joshua Bright/Dylan Dillon uncrossed and recrossed his legs and rearranged his cassock skirts so they fell evenly over his knee, the wedding forgotten, forty-year-old memories taking its place in the vicar's mind.

The calculations changed again, and Graham found he could complete all three sides of the investigator's classic, triangular geometry: method, motive, opportunity.

"Robbed blind by one of their own," he said. "The Parnabys exploded."

"Charlie didn't rob anyone, blind or otherwise. That was just the story the Parnabys bandied to discredit him, cover their backs, and incite me to murder. They hadn't lost any money. But they had lost Charlie. And he knew too much."

Graham drew back like a shrewd, patient, investigative bird of prey gaining altitude for a clearer view. "So, what did he do? Charlie. Left the gang, the family, the life?"

"You never leave people like the Parnabys," said Bright. "You can't even take holidays."

"But Cross tried. And the Parnabys couldn't allow that. They couldn't just . . ."

"Leave him floating around, a potential witness to dozens of crimes? Never. That's why they set me onto him. They gave me a gun and told me to deal with him."

Bright sat back. The clock ticked onward. Graham was acutely aware of the growing clamour in the church. The guests were getting fidgety.

"I don't suppose you'd still let me . . . ?"

"Not in two months of Sundays," Graham said. "I won't have Janice and Jack joined in matrimony by someone I'm about to arrest. Just tell your story and be quick about it so we can sort all this out without too many tears." Privately, he thought they were way past that point. He glanced at his watch. There was no time for a long expository. Janice would arrive any minute.

"Very well, Inspector." Bright began his story. "In 1981, Charlie was at a loose end, let's say. He'd always daydreamed about joining the clergy. Strange, I know, given his earlier life, but thieving and criming were never him, not really. It was more my kind of thing. He just came along for the ride. When he arrived on Jersey to get away from all that, he hid inside the seminary, passing himself off as a theology student."

Graham had a quiet respect for the humble toil of the priestly life. "Some people have a calling. I've watched some turnarounds in my time."

"You're a brilliant detective, Inspector Graham. Gorey is lucky to have you."

Graham frowned. "Just tell me what happened."

"I came to Jersey planning to shoot Charlie. He had reinvented himself as a do-gooder, a theology student. He was thinking of becoming a vicar. We met up. He told me he lived under a false name, Joshua Bright, because he didn't want his past catching up with him. I thought I'd be able to get him to tell me what he'd done with the money, but he convinced me he hadn't stolen anything. We ended up doing some coke together in my hotel room just for old time's sake, as you do . . ."

"Quite."

". . . when he suddenly keeled over." Graham squinted. "I panicked. Left the hotel immediately, abandoned my stuff, and walked around all night. I got myself on the early morning ferry to Calais first thing."

Graham spent a moment piecing together the timeline of events. "So, the body found in your room was Charlie Cross."

"Must've been."

"And the people who found him believed him to be you."

Bright shrugged. "We looked very similar. We were always being mistaken for brothers. The only difference was a gap between Charlie's front teeth. I had the same gap as a child, but my mother insisted on braces."

The clock was ticking; perhaps two-thirds of the guests were now seated in the wooden pews, an odd few mingling in the aisle, catching up with friends not seen in a while. Graham opened the vestry door and peered out.

He spotted Mrs. Taylor taking a seat, leaning forward, pinching the bridge of her nose in a moment of quiet prayer. Of Rosemary Harding there was no sign. It occurred to Graham that perhaps her absence wasn't necessarily the mercy it seemed; if she wasn't causing trouble that he could see, she was probably causing it for Janice.

"So, you left in a panic and went to Calais. What did you do then?"

"I hid out on the continent for six months or so. I kept checking the papers expecting to see something about Charlie's death, but there was nothing. It was confusing. I didn't know what to do."

"So, in October 1982, you returned here? To Jersey?"

"Yes. I wanted to find out what had happened. And, like Charlie, I didn't want to go back, not to the Parnabys. I thought they would kill me."

"But you never left the island?"

"Yes, I stayed here. In my efforts to understand what happened to Charlie after I left him on that bedroom floor, I went to the seminary and knocked on the door. When they opened it, they welcomed me in like a long-lost friend. It was bizarre until I realised they thought I was Charlie. I was bewildered at first, but I quickly saw my opportunity."

"Stuck between a rock and a hard place, you assumed his identity."

"As Joshua Bright, yes. I got to escape my past and the Parnabys. Dylan Dillon effectively disappeared in that moment."

"And no one suspected? Really?"

"One person at the seminary appeared suspicious. But I just said I'd had some dental treatment while I'd been away."

"And how do you think Charlie died?"

"I assumed he overdosed, although he didn't use much that night. He brought two bags of coke with him, small ones. He had one, I had one."

Graham tapped his phone against his mouth, thinking. "And if I told you his coke was cut with rat poison?"

Bright's eyes grew big. "No!"

"Yes." Graham leaned forward. "And why should I not believe that you did that?"

Bright tucked in his chin. When he spoke, he sounded affronted. "Because I planned to shoot him. Why would I risk bringing a gun to the island if I was going to kill him with rat poison?"

Graham sat back, considering this answer. "And what did you think all these years? Years that you assumed the identity previously assumed by Charlie Cross, who you left for dead on the floor of your hotel room for other people to find?"

"I didn't know what to think. After a while, I just got on with life." Bright regarded Graham coolly, his legs still crossed, his cassock skirts smooth, his hands placed one on top of the other in his lap.

There was a knock at the door. Roach appeared around it. He was red-faced. And breathless. "There you are, sir. Um, we're in dire need of the orders of service." Graham stared at him. "The wedding, sir?" Roach hesitated before plunging on. "Janice's . . . wedding?"

Graham shook himself and swatted away an imaginary fly. "Roach, get Barnwell, then arrest this man and take him to the station."

CHAPTER FIFTY-FIVE

LAURA LOOKED AMAZING as she walked up the church path, past the war memorial, in a silky, shiny, emerald satin wraparound dress—tall, just a little shy, and the only woman at St. Andrew's who was in danger of upstaging the bride. As she approached though, she slowed a little as Graham's knitted eyebrows conveyed a distinct warning. "Problems, dearest?" she asked quietly when she reached him.

Graham didn't answer at first. His hand found hers, and with the other, he leaned for a second against the wall of the church. It appeared to offer support, and after a moment more, a trickle of energy.

"Laura, would you honour me with a peculiar favour?" he said, his tone amenable but his brow terraced like a rice paddy. "Stroll on into the sanctuary and oblige the groom in the direction of the front entrance, would you?"

Laura did some pointing and figuring out of things. She glanced at her watch, then at the lychgate. "That's where . . . the . . . um, bride is going to be very shortly, isn't it?"

"Yes, the bride and the groom need to talk. And we need to be there when they do."

"You mean, now?

"Yes. And, um, one more thing," Graham said, coming closer. "This is going to be the strangest day you and I have spent in a while."

Hands on hips, Laura retorted, "David Graham, you took me on a hot date in London three months ago . . ."

"I remember it well."

". . . where we both attended the London Ambulance Blood Spatter Conference for six hours."

"That's not what it was called."

"No, but that's what it *was*. Today can't be stranger than that!"

"You were unlucky. The second day was compelling. Anyway, aren't you friends with Councillor Jenkins? She was the one who invited me."

"I know her. She helped us out, gave a talk at the library to open the . . . She's the wife of a bishop, you know."

"Great! Give her a ring, would you? We might need her help," Graham said as abruptly as the moment demanded. "We'll be needing some paperwork expedited."

Laura blinked, half affronted by his tone, half curious as to the reason for it. "What's going on, David? Is it anything to do with Rosemary?"

Graham's eyes closed at the mention of Janice's mother's name. "Not yet. But brace yourself." He was away, pointing for Laura to head back into the church as he walked to the lychgate to await Janice's wedding car.

Inside the church, Laura elegantly sashayed up to the front and, as discreetly as she could, she parted the confused groom from his groomsmen and began guiding him down the aisle to the doors. "Just doing some photos," she said, beaming at those in the aisle seats as she and Jack zipped past. At the door, fresh from traumatising a flower girl, they encountered Rosemary Harding.

"What's *he* doing back here?" she demanded. "He should be at the front."

"There's been a change of plans," Laura told her, confident that this was the case but unsure as to what they might be and certainly unsure of the reason for them.

"But Janice will be here at any moment!" Rosemary's voice was increasing in volume and register in line with her alarm.

"Yes . . ." Laura sensed an emotional outburst incoming. She put her palm up. "Wait there."

Laura left Jack and Rosemary staring at one another in the south porch while she nipped back inside the church, returning a few seconds later with Marjorie Taylor still resplendent in dusty pink and mesh. "Mrs. Harding, Mrs. Taylor will keep you company while we sort this out. Jack, you come with me." Laura grabbed Jack's upper arm and pulled him down the gravel path to the lychgate.

"She is coming, isn't she? Janice?" Jack said.

"She's in the car, and you are getting married today. I'm just not sure under what circumstances."

Panicked, Jack looked back at the church. "Is the place on fire?" Just as they reached Graham and he made to explain, Janice's black limousine rounded the corner. The door opened, and Janice's father helped the bride gather her skirts.

The lychgate creaked, and as Graham opened it ahead of her, he said, "Janice, you look absolutely beautiful."

"Inspector, thank you! It's lovely to see you." Janice glanced over his shoulder. Jack opened his hands and shook his head, his lips turned down in confusion. "But what are you doing here?"

Dragging her eyes from the huddle under the lychgate canopy, Rosemary Harding turned to Marjorie Taylor. "Now's the time when organ music would have been so very wonderful. And . . . what's that Mr. Graham doing?" she complained.

In the distance, but within earshot of Rosemary's piercing voice, Laura turned. Her eyes and those of Mrs. Taylor met. Laura winked. Marjorie acknowledged her signal with a minute dip of her head. Cluelessly, Rosemary continued her ranting.

"I knew it! This is very bad luck, and quite extraordinary, and I can't imagine for a moment why—Ow!" Pulled sharply by the elbow from behind, Mrs. Harding deflated like a sandcastle meeting seawater.

"If Michelangelo is in the middle of painting the Sistine Chapel, you don't scale his ladder and witter at him," Mrs. Taylor said through gritted teeth as she all but heel-dragged Rosemary around the back of the church.

"How dare you . . ."

"Mrs. Harding, Rosemary," Mrs. Taylor said, pulling up, her eyes flinty, her cheeks unusually red. "People sometimes underestimate the detective inspector, but I've learned to trust him, whatever he's doing."

"Even if he's in the middle of ruining the . . ."

Mrs. Taylor's eyes flashed. They burned. Her voice, full of controlled rage, trembled. "Mrs. Harding, you have a beautiful daughter who is about to marry a wonderful, charming man. Their union will be blissful, and in time, you will have equally beautiful, wonderful grandchildren running around your ankles. Do you know how lucky you are? Now stop your moaning, stand down, and enjoy your good fortune in whatever form it takes!"

Rosemary Harding's eyes grew larger than her gaping mouth. "Wha—H-How dare—Wha—!" Taking advantage of her disarray and knowing that she had only moments to act, Mrs. Taylor grabbed Mrs. Harding by the wrist and bundled her into the vestry through the back door, proceeding to lean her entire body weight against it, so trapping Mrs. Harding inside.

Rosemary banged furiously on the ancient oak until it dawned on her that her efforts were fruitless and quite possibly blasphemous. On the other side, Mrs. Taylor folded her arms and settled in to wait, pressing her back against the door. It was in this position that Graham, Laura, Janice, and Jack found her five minutes later.

"She's in there, Detective Inspector. She's quietened down now. Would you like me to step away?"

"I would, Mrs. Taylor. Thank you very much."

"Mother, cool it!" Janice shouted through the door, her wedding dress skirts gathered in her arms. She reached out to open the door as carefully as one might when releasing a feral feline from a cat carrier. "You can come out now," Janice said more quietly.

Rosemary appeared, ruffled and out of sorts. She glared at Marjorie Taylor in the sunshine. "Mum, there's an excellent reason why we're breaking with wedding protocol established across millennia. Right, boss?"

"Yes, indeed," said Graham. He straightened his jacket and smoothed his brown hair into an unusually formal side parting. For the first time, he missed his cap. He couldn't remember where he left it. "And that means I've got good news and bad news."

"Is he already married?" Rosemary said, glaring at Jack. He suppressed an eye roll that would have had him viewing his brain stem. He opted instead to beam at Rosemary with a smile that even she considered to be conceivably sarcastic.

"The good news," Graham said, cutting across her, "is that Janice and Jack are getting married."

"Hooray!" said Janice, her voice conveying no confidence at all.

"The bad news is the vicar has vacated the vestry."

Rosemary sputtered into life again. "Well, I know that. I've just been in there for goodness knows how long and he wasn't with me."

"What I mean is that we've identified the man involved in the death of Mr. X in 1982. And since, in the circumstances, it would be inappropriate for him to conduct the ceremony . . ."

"The vicar murdered Mr. X?" Jack cried.

Janice smirked. She looked around. "Where's Freddie when you need him?"

Laura walked up, pulling the phone from her ear. "She can't do it," she said simply. "Councillor Jenkins."

"What?" Graham said. "But I . . ."

"She's not on the island, and she's the only person with the authority to extend your wedding officiant licence to the Bailiwick of Jersey. The wedding wouldn't be legal if you did it."

There was silence from Jack, a hysterical giggle from Janice, and an "I knew it!" from Rosemary, words quickly stifled when she caught Mrs. Taylor's ferocious eye.

"What are we going to do?" Janice said to Jack. "We have guests in their finery, you in your posh togs, me in me posh dress, flowers up the wazoo, oranges galore . . ."

Laura continued. "So, there's been a change of plan. Councillor Jenkins spoke to her husband, the bishop, and he's sending a new vicar. Someone who's here on holiday celebrating their wedding anniversary."

"Excuse me, excuse me! Yoo-hoo!" They all turned. A woman in a T-shirt and shorts opened the lychgate and walked up to the wedding party with confidence and purpose. Behind, a man accompanying her stayed outside the gate, looking slightly less confident and with a lot less purpose. He looked vaguely familiar to Graham, and the detective inspector searched his memory banks for some recollection.

"You're looking absolutely divine, my dear," the woman said to Janice, taking in the bride's full-skirted ivory dress with ruched bodice and lace, three-quarter length sleeves. "Now, I hear you're in a spot of bother over a vanishing vicar. But you're not to worry." The woman stuck out her hand. "Reverend Annabelle Dixon. Perhaps I can help?"

CHAPTER FIFTY-SIX

"PHEW, THAT WAS close." Jim Roach wrestled his way through the crowd, narrowly avoiding spilling the beer in the glasses he clutched tight above his head as he made his way over to Barry Barnwell. His erstwhile colleague, who sat by himself quietly feeding Carmen scraps from the buffet, lit up when Roach came into view.

"Ah, lovely jubbly, mate. Thanks." Barnwell sipped the foam off his drink, then took a good swig and smacked his lips. "Just the ticket. All the wine and champers is nice 'n' all, but you can't beat a good pint of Jersey ale."

"That you can't," Roach agreed, following Barnwell's lead. "I miss it."

"What, the beer?"

"Yep, and all the rest. The people, community, my mum. You, Jan, even the boss."

"Feeling a bit homesick, eh?"

"A bit. I mean, I'm as busy as heck, and I'm learning loads. It's just fast-paced. So very different from here. It's a nice change to come back."

"Must be dangerous, is it? All that knife crime and drugs."

"There's more opportunity for it there than here, for sure. But, you know, there's lots of backup. You're trained for it. I wake up every morning and have no idea what the day's going to throw at me. One minute I could be called to a suspected trafficking, another an armed raid. It's exciting. Right now, I'm trying to decide if I should specialise. They're always looking for people in the different units. We even have one dedicated to cold cases."

"Feel like I could apply for that one after this case. It's been like pulling teeth." Barnwell gazed across the dance floor. "Would you look at that? Rosemary Harding enjoying herself."

"Who's that dancing with her?"

"That's the archaeologist Tomlinson brought in to help us extract the body from the concrete. Papadopoulos. Greek. Top man."

"Must have been a bit of a shock finding a finger poking out like that."

"Gawd, I'll say. Shook me right up, it did. But, as you say, all in a day's work."

"Thank you so much for stepping in, Vicar." A few feet away, Marjorie Taylor chatted with Reverend Annabelle and Laura. "You quite saved the day."

"You did a wonderful job at such short notice," Laura added.

"Oh, I was delighted to be asked. I got to spend my first wedding anniversary on the island where we honeymooned marrying someone else. What could be more fun than that? Heavenly. And they seem such a lovely couple."

Janice was laughing with one of her bridesmaids, while next to her, Jack put an orange quarter in his mouth. The look of surprise on his mother-in-law's face when he opened his orange-filled mouth to smile hideously at her from the edge of the dance floor was almost worth all the earlier kerfuffle.

When, in response, Rosemary threw back her head and laughed while jigging around to the music opposite an equally jiggy Dr. Papadopoulos, Jack knew everything would be alright.

Outside, Graham and Fiona sat across from one another on a pub bench, both grateful to be away from the flashing lights, darkness, and loud music inside. "Do you still keep in touch with Bert Hatfield? He was a fine pathologist."

"I do! He's still doing the same old thing and still loves it."

"And is he still having his heart broken on the regular by Charlton Athletic?"

"He still is."

"Thanks so much for putting in the extra time today. It changed everything."

"No problem. The DNA results were confounding, weren't they?"

"They truly were. And I couldn't believe it when I looked at Reverend Bright and saw the man in that aged photo of Dylan Dillon staring back at me."

"That must have been some surprise. Changed the trajectory of the day, that's for sure."

"You can say that again."

"When did you know you were barking up the wrong tree?"

"The first sign was the photo of the boys. It showed Dillon with braces, but our body in the block had imperfect teeth, so I knew there was a possibility that things weren't as they seemed."

"There *was* a gap between the two front teeth!" Fiona exclaimed. "I remember now."

"That's right. Then you sent through the DNA results and confirmed my thoughts."

"You know, I took another look at the DNA." Graham glanced at her quickly. "I compared the DNA from the hairbrush, which we know was Dillon's because of the match with his half sister, and compared it to the bone DNA. There was a match there too."

Graham leaned forward. "Oh? Was it strong?"

"Pretty strong. It was as strong between Dillon and Cross as that between

Dillon and his half sister. It's perhaps why they so closely resembled one another."

"You mean they were half brothers?"

"Or maybe cousins. It's also perhaps why they gravitated to one another. They shared a close relative and maybe personality traits."

"They lived on the same estate. And Dillon's sister said family members were promiscuous to a fault." Graham leaned back. "Wow, blood relatives, perhaps brothers, intent on killing one another. That doesn't happen very often."

"Do you think the boys knew they were related?"

"I didn't get that impression." The pair sat in silence as they comprehended this new information.

"So, it was death by misadventure, you think? Cross administered the poisoned drugs to himself?"

"Looks like it, by mistake. At least that's Dillon's story. At this distance, it'll be difficult to prove otherwise. Everyone's dead or long gone. But there were enough crimes surrounding this case to keep us busy for a month of Sundays." Fiona stirred her gin and tonic.

"Do you like it here?" she said.

"On Jersey? Yes, I love it."

"You don't miss the hustle and bustle of London, the strategic, far-reaching cases that involve networks of criminals all over the country, sometimes the world?" Fiona grinned.

"Not at the moment. I appreciate the discreet containment of individual crimes. It's very satisfying. In many ways, I've had a broader experience here than in London. I get involved in all aspects of the policing. And I enjoy working closely with my team. I get a lot of pleasure out of their development. It's made me a more rounded person. Balanced." Fiona nodded. "What are your plans?"

"Well, I've had great fun working on this case. It's given me the chance to try lots of new things. Have more responsibility, you know?"

"This was an unusual case. They're not all like that."

"No, I get it, but as you said, I've the chance to get involved in aspects of forensic pathology that I wouldn't normally. And Dr. Weiss has offered me the opportunity to cover for people on her team from time to time. It's all grist for the mill. I can see myself staying here for a while. Plus, I get to live in my very own castle!"

Graham glanced at Fiona quizzically. "Dr. Tomlinson rented me a flat in Elizabeth Castle. It's just about the best commute I can think of. And it's eerie at night. So many spooky noises and weird lights." Fiona's eyes gleamed as she raised her hands and contracted her fingers like claws.

Graham smiled uncertainly and took a sip of his drink. "Not your average experience, that's for sure."

They glanced over to see Tomlinson sitting in an armchair on the terrace, animatedly talking to Freddie Solomon.

"Freddie looks pale. Perhaps it's the light," Graham said.

"Nah, Marcus is probably educating him on the finer details of postmortems and the assist, if complicating factor, corpse wax can provide."

"Corpse wax?"

"Another word for it is 'adipocere.' It forms when fat on a body turns into a hard insoluble substance under conditions of high moisture and an absence of oxygen, like wet ground or mud or . . ."

"Newly mixed concrete."

"Precisely. It's what helped our Mr. X stay in as good a condition as he did."

"Interesting."

"I've had so much fun on this case, Inspector. The spectrometry, DNA tracing, ballistics, using software and AI to build the man's face from the remains. It was all new to me. It was an experience I couldn't have anywhere else. In bigger labs, I would get stuck with photographing and weighing brains and such. Every day. It quickly gets boring."

"Boring? I hope you're not talking about my lab, young lady." Tomlinson walked over.

"I was saying the exact opposite," Fiona replied. "Are you finished talking to Freddie?"

"Yes, it took some time, but I think I finally managed to utterly repulse him. He was looking quite green by the time we were done. I invited him to drop by the lab, told him he could view my collection of anatomical oddities that I've saved over the years, but I don't think he was interested. I doubt we'll be seeing him anytime soon. He told me you'd granted him an exclusive on the case for his book, David."

"Yes, I promised him, as long as it doesn't go out before sentencing. He helped me, I helped him. Squid provo." Graham grinned ruefully.

"But how was he helpful? I thought he was a lightweight, meddling troublemaker with nothing useful to add," Fiona said.

"The Parnaby brothers told him two of their gang had gone to Jersey and disappeared. I think Freddie thought, hoped maybe, that they'd been murdered on gangland business. That turned out to be wrong, but it gave me a wedge I could use to get information out of them. Do you want to sit down, Marcus?"

"On one of those hard benches? No thanks. I'd never get up again. I came to tell you they want us inside. I think the bride and groom are doing something. Going away on honeymoon perhaps."

They traipsed in to find the wedding guests outside the front of the venue. From deep inside the grounds came the sound of tins being dragged along the tarmac. An Aston Martin rolled into view. It seemed almost entirely filled with Janice's ivory dress, the bride squeezed into the middle of it, white silk and net petticoats puffed up all around her like a marshmallow.

Next to her, Jack beamed in the driver's seat. A cheer went up, and Janice waved, shaking her bouquet high in the air above her head. Barnwell whistled while Roach whooped, both delighted to see their sergeant making this personal milestone, one she had longed for in what seemed like forever.

With Francine by his side, Dr. Tomlinson clapped as Fiona stood next to him, the old pathologist and his new assistant standing next to one another. Graham found himself across from Freddie, and as the car drove between them, they caught each other's eye, a small nod passing between them, an acknowledgement that despite their differing opinions and objectives, tonight there was a truce, some element of mutual respect and a "squid provo."

The Aston Martin drew up alongside Graham, and Janice, her happiness and joy radiating from her so forcefully it was catching, waved furiously at him and then tossed her bouquet into the air. As was Janice's intention, Laura had no choice but to catch it.

Janice laughed, waved, and leaned in to kiss her new husband's cheek. The car drove onward into the Jersey darkness, the tin cans dangling from the bumper continuing to rattle even after the car had long disappeared into the night.

CHAPTER FIFTY-SEVEN

Extract: *Murder Island: The Mob on Jersey* by F. J. Solomon

If you talk with Gorey's vibrant community of senior citizens, you'll know the greatest gift of retirement is more time with family. Two acquaintances of mine, Arthur and George, had the same expectations—to play with the grandchildren, maybe enjoy a bit of sunshine, and indulge in some hobbies. Greying and, in George's case, ill, they kept their big dates firmly in mind, determined to get there and enjoy the fruits of their patience.

Except these two men weren't about to draw their first pensions. Arthur and George Parnaby, convicted armed robbers, each received a twenty-eight-year prison sentence in 1999. When I first met them in the visiting suite at Holbrooke prison, they were just completing their twenty-fourth year. I interviewed them several times for my forthcoming book, *Murder Island: The Mob on Jersey*.

During those interviews, I gained information that I handed over to the States of Jersey police as they processed an inquiry into the death of a man whose body lay undiscovered for over forty years in the attic of Gorey's White House Inn. As we now know, it was an investigation with a remarkable outcome.

Through interviews with the lead investigator, the proprietor of the hotel where the body was discovered, the person arrested in connection with the death, and anonymous but dependable elders who were in Gorey at the time, I have successfully reconstructed the events of February 1982 and their lead-up like never before.

Charles Cross was a little different from those around him. Growing up on a sink estate in London, unemployment, poverty, and that scourge of the underclass—drugs—surrounded him daily. His environment offered little in the way of a stable upbringing, and being a sensitive boy, the bullies made Charlie suffer. Being the "wussy kid," it was hard for him to make friends, and Charlie cherished those he had: a cluster of dropouts without a grain of ambition between them.

But when one of them left a corner shop without paying (again), Charlie and his best friend, Dylan, were suddenly "in" with two older boys, and Charlie's life of exclusion and ignominy ended.

These two older boys had a reputation already, but to Charlie and Dylan, the Parnaby brothers became instant family. From them, the younger boys learned to drink and smoke and do drugs. They coveted the latest gadgets, technology we now consider "quaint" but which were transformative at the time.

Those pastimes required money, and gaining it became an ongoing challenge. While his friends had few qualms, Charlie found dishonesty discomforting. And he hated violence. Lashing out at victims in the street, outside the pub, or at each other after consuming too much drink disgusted Charlie. But he seemed unable to loosen the gang's grip on his life.

As time went on, the violence grew. A menace growled at someone in the street. A brawl in the pub. A knife an inch from a commuter's face. They all figured in Charlie's life, even if his role was a passive, observant one. These offences could be but one of a string on the same evening. Eventually, inevitably, blood would be drawn, the older, drunken Parnaby brothers pivotal in the act and unquestionably to blame.

But a shroud of silence between the four held strong, and understanding grew. Charlie remained quiet but low-key participatory in the group's endeavours. He wouldn't turn his back. Nor, as time went on, could he.

"I was under the Parnabys' spell from start to finish," recalled Dylan Dillon the first time I interviewed him in La Moye prison, St. Helier. Dillon is better known to Jersey residents as Reverend Joshua Bright, vicar of St. Andrew's Church, Gorey. "Charlie, less so. He did everything he could to fit in, to make sure he was available and willing, but his reluctance was noticeable."

Charlie read books, including the Bible, often in secret. "I didn't understand, and I'm sure his family didn't," Dillon says. "My half sisters and half brothers and I grew up in a chaotic, disorganised fashion. Our parents, who were a bewildering array of people, floated in and out of our lives regularly. The churn was extraordinary. There was no structure, no expectation, no education.

"Charlie's family was more normal, poor but decent. He gravitated to anything that provided stability. He couldn't afford Boy Scouts. The youth centre closed. So, he mostly went to church. It was his way of sitting out the experience of the chaotic estate life around us. Can you imagine? I suppose it gave him belonging.

"The Parnabys already had me down as a foot-soldier type, someone who'd jump up and do any mundane job he's told to—passing a message, leaving a dead drop, or making a collection. They wanted Charlie to do the same. But Charlie was quieter than me, less impulsive, with no stomach for the rough stuff. The Parnabys found him frustrating but kept him on. He was useful. You'd never look at him and think gang member. He was good cover.

"But one day in 1981, he had enough. He went to church and then witnessed another awful beating outside a pub. Charlie and me fell out. I was into partying, all the club drugs. I was using a lot. It puffed me up, had me thinking I'm a king-pin, a stud.

"I fancied myself as a criminal mastermind, running my own patch, raking in the money. I was a regular drug user, cocaine being my preference. It was the eighties, and it was everywhere. I had illusions of grandeur; that I could achieve anything. But all cocaine does is make you sound like an idiot.

"Charlie was no angel though. He was right alongside me, using, petty thieving, occasionally menacing. It was just that it was an act with him. One he put on but didn't really live into. He wanted to go straight. He had ambition. And he needed to find some peace."

Eventually, Charlie made his choice: he packed his things and fled. We can judge the Parnaby brothers' reaction from their interviews with Detective Inspector Graham of Gorey police and the senior officer in charge of the case.

"They were black with fury when I raised Cross's disappearance with them," the DI said. "They told the world that they were 'well shot,' implying his disappearance was the end for them. But it was far from it."

Caught between the Parnabys and his friend, Dillon attempted to tread the line between them. "I knew everything the Parnabys had done. Ten years of petty crimes, big crimes, and stupid, nonsense, pointless crimes. They had done them all, sometimes just because they were bored. They became paranoid. I tried not to get involved, but eventually it ate them up, and they executed a plan for which I was the fall guy."

Arthur, George, and Dylan would face lengthy stretches in prison if Charlie grassed them up. "They saw only one course of action open to them," DI Graham told me. "Charlie Cross had to be hunted down and the threat he posed eliminated."

But there was a problem they had to overcome. The Parnabys were menaces and meat-headed thugs, but they weren't about to put themselves on the line. Dylan Dillon would need to do the job.

But Dillon was Cross's oldest friend. How would Dylan be persuaded to kill Charlie? They convinced Dylan that Cross had ripped them off.

"They sold me this story about their haul being raided by Charlie," Dillon told me. "That a hundred thou had gone missing. They implied that a significant part of that money was mine, although, with hindsight, it's unlikely that they would have shared it with me. That just wasn't their style. They weren't honourable gangsters."

Dillon, abandoned by his friend, was confused, then furious. He came to believe that Charlie had betrayed them and needed to be taught a lesson. "The

Parnabys manipulated me like a pawn, a useful idiot, to get rid of Charlie and remove the threat he posed to them. All while keeping their hands clean. They modelled themselves on London gangsters—the Krays, the Richardsons—but really they were small-time and pathetic."

"Small-time and pathetic" the Parnabys may have been, but they were successful in turning Dillon. It seems the young man had made up his mind—he would do the job.

Over to Inspector Graham: "The Parnabys gave Dillon the gun and the address. When I interviewed them, the brothers maintained their story of the stolen money. Later, they told me it was Dylan who visited Charlie's sister, roughing her up and demanding information."

Dillon countered this version of the story. "No! That wasn't me. I wouldn't do such a thing. I'd known Lou since we were kids. It was Arthur Parnaby who threatened and beat her. He broke her wrist, blacked her eye. He deserves every second of his sentence, however long it is, just for that." Louise Cross, who died in 2001, never brought charges, and the true nature of the incident remains a mystery.

DI Graham commented, "This is endgame stuff for dysfunctional gangs on the verge of breakdown—they accuse one another."

At first, while on the run from the gang, Charlie Cross found exactly what he most needed: peace, quiet, and a clean slate. "When we met, he told me he wanted to help other people. To find his place in the world. And after everything," Dillon added heavily, "he felt the need to atone."

But all that changed in February 1982. For months after his arrival on Jersey, the quiet seclusion he had found at St. Julian's seminary gave Charlie Cross the life he was looking for. But then, he made a devastating choice.

"Everything told Cross that his life was on the line," said DI Graham. "His sister was begging him to be careful, warning him the gang wanted his blood. Meanwhile, Dillon was raging, egged on by the Parnabys, who made up the story of Charlie as a 'Judas,' a 'grass.'

"Remember, Dylan had been with the Parnabys for ten years, since he was fifteen, an impressionable teenager. These people he trusted completely were warning him of an existential risk—his childhood friend. They permitted him to act on the gang's behalf and empowered him by handing him a gun."

Dillon now says, "I was completely mad with anger and fear. I was determined to kill Charlie. It was how I planned to become a truly 'made man' in the Parnabys' small, ad hoc, but demanding organisation."

"The Parnabys treated Dillon like a chess piece. One who could be manipulated," continued Graham. "They showered him with responsibility, comradeship, and cocaine, then sent him into battle."

Dillon: "I think Charlie knew I was coming. His sister probably alerted him.

He told me he staked out the ferry terminal, meeting the boat from Poole and Portsmouth daily. He knew I hated flying and would be unlikely to arrive that way." As it was, Charlie spotted Dylan Dillon the minute he stepped off the big, blue car ferry from Portsmouth.

"He walked right up to me. Imagine it, me thinking I was on a secret mission to kill an enemy turncoat, and he greets me like a long-lost brother. He suggested we meet up the next day and I agreed, unsure what to do. I wasn't an experienced killer."

But Charlie Cross had not yet completed his transition to Joshua Bright, theologian and man of the cloth, not entirely. The plucky East End scamp who had struggled through school bullies and jaded, disinterested teachers, who had pulled free of a gang culture that would have seen him jailed in the end, now faced the possibility of a fate so terrible it was absurd.

To those who know him, "Reverend Bright" is a generous and decent man, and so the next part is difficult to relate.

"The second I saw Charlie, my plans to kill him, such as they were, fell into disarray. I couldn't take the chance of sitting down with him in public," Dillon said. "So I invited him to my hotel room. I intended to learn more about his life so that I could plan the hit in a way that I wouldn't be caught. I could hardly take the risk of splattering him all over some nice Gorey tearoom.

"I suggested we do some lines. I wasn't sure he'd be up for it, not now he was living clean. But he surprised me. He was hopped up, spurred on. Seemed really into it. From what I know now though, I realise he fully intended to kill me before I killed him. It was a dog-eat-dog situation.

"He came to my room with a bottle of whisky that night. We downed it all and then another. It was like old times."

Inside the room, Cross pulled out two small bags of cocaine and gave one of them to Dillon. "There wasn't much, just enough for a few lines. It was all over quickly. I had barely laid mine out before he keeled over. I couldn't believe it. There I was, on Jersey, tasked with a quick kill, and before I'd even the chance to use my gun, my target had died. I didn't know what to do. I could barely think. My only thought was to get out of there. I took my passport and the cash I'd brought with me, and I ran.

"I must be the most hapless criminal ever. I don't know what I was thinking, really. The whole plan was nuts. And my friend died."

Inspector Graham concludes this part of the story. "We suspect Cross adulterated one packet of cocaine with rat poison at the seminary, intending to supply Dillon with it, killing him. Perhaps he was nervous, or disorganised, but in his drunken state, he got the packets mixed up and took the compromised batch himself. It was a murder plan that went awry."

Dillon continues: "What I didn't realise, obviously, is that there would be a cover-up. Lady Luck was protecting me. After travelling through France and spending months in Spain, not knowing what happened was driving me mad. There was nothing in the papers, so I took a risk and returned to Jersey. I went to the seminary where, to my astonishment, one of the students mistook me for Charlie. He took me inside, and they genuinely believed I was him. That was when I realised something odd and unusual had happened.

"I saw their acceptance of me as a sign, one telling me to leave my old life behind. Over the next days, I mingled, observed, and followed the others' lead. It wasn't hard. They lived a simple life, far less complicated than the one I was used to.

"I did my chores and learned my Scripture, ate and slept, and let the world turn. I didn't talk too much. I was terrified I'd be exposed, but it never happened.

"Eventually, the seminary closed. By then, I had successfully created an identity as Joshua Bright. I could barely remember the old me. I spoke differently, walked differently, and most importantly, I believed differently. I didn't want to go back to being Dylan Dillon. For the first time in my life, I felt safe, weird as it might seem, and I wanted to do good.

"And so I stayed here, blocking out memories and questions that I didn't want to confront. If ever my mind wandered to what happened that night, I would busy myself with my parish work and my thoughts would go away. I could say that I felt troubled, that I experienced nightmares or panic attacks, but that would be a lie. Conducting my life as a local vicar is, I hope, some atonement for my sins in the eyes of God.

"The actions of the hotel owner helped me enormously. I see that now. Throughout the years, I wondered why I heard nothing about Charlie's death, but I pushed my questions away. For me, it was dumb luck that he was buried in concrete and lay undiscovered for over forty years. The downside is that I've been waiting that long for the authorities to arrive.

"Charlie Cross was my oldest friend. What happened to him was tragic, outrageous. I hold the mendacious, rapacious Parnabys responsible. I rue the day we ever met them."

The science of Charlie Cross's death is best explained by Dr. Marcus Tomlinson, Jersey's senior forensic pathologist. He agreed to discuss the case with me.

"The three substances—the cocaine and the two poisons—were almost the same colour," said Tomlinson, showing me side-by-side analyses derived from a sophisticated UV spectroscope. "The two adulterants are used in commercial brands of rat poison. Probably purloined from a garden shed, perhaps at the seminary.

"Adulterants are highly dangerous," Tomlinson told me. "'Spiking' someone's drug supply like this is a rare and risky method of murder, not at all foolproof. It's possible Cross knew this and so made extra sure by adding two different poisons to the cocaine. Unfortunately, he signed his own death warrant in the process. His death would have been quick, near instantaneous, the poison inciting a massive heart attack."

🌐

"Once we found Charlie Cross's body," Inspector Graham told me, "we faced the challenging task of identifying him." Tomlinson and his assistant Fiona Henson were herculean in their efforts to examine and identify the remains. "It was like completing a very complex jigsaw puzzle—each piece leading us to the next one until we built up a picture of who our guy was and what happened to him. For the longest time, we thought Dylan Dillon was the murdered man."

The men looked remarkably similar, and an image generated from the remains confused both the inspector and Dillon's half sister. However, persistence eventually paid off and uncovered two pieces of vital information. Ultimately, it was this evidence on which the case turned.

"First, we received a photo of Charlie Cross and Dylan Dillon as teenagers. Dillon wore braces, yet the man in the concrete had a gap between his two front teeth. If the body had been Dillon, I'd have expected his teeth to be perfect.

"I began to suspect that the remains were not those of Dillon. I tasked Fiona in our forensic pathology lab with taking the photo of the teenage Dillon and aging it so that I could see what he would look like today. The confirmation of my suspicion came when the DNA samples taken from the body and the effects found with it didn't match. We knew for certain that the DNA from the effects was that of Dillon because it matched with his half sister."

This, then, begged the question: Who was the body in the block? And then, as it is wont to do, luck intervened.

Inspector Graham again: "Imagine my surprise when, a few minutes after receiving this information, I met Joshua Bright and found myself looking at the face in that aged image of present-day Dylan Dillon. My questioning of Reverend Bright led to him revealing his true identity.

"Eventually, we were able to match Cross's DNA with family members and confirm the remains were his beyond a reasonable doubt. Extraordinarily, we found that Cross and Dillon, although they didn't know it, shared a close relative, which may account for their similarities in physical appearance and personality."

🌐

In 1982, when Mr. Cross's body was originally discovered, Miss Emily Lovell and her grandson, Neville Williams, prevented the crime scene from being secured. According to DI Graham, "Nearly everything needed for a conviction—fingerprints on the bag of cocaine, powder left sprinkled on a coffee table or the floor, footprints, the exact position of the body—all would have been available to the police at the time. I'm sure they would have established the situation quickly."

"The scene was likely to be rich with toxicology evidence," Tomlinson agreed. "Right up until the hotel proprietor involved herself."

Police interviews with hotel staff revealed a disturbing truth. Long before Mrs. Marjorie Taylor took over the hotel, its previous owner, who, let me be clear, was neither a business partner of, nor any relation to, the present proprietor, sought to shield herself from justice. It has been claimed that Miss Lovell ran a drug-dealing operation out of the hotel. She dealt in small amounts of drugs for the casual user. According to interviews, Miss Lovell, who had been diagnosed with terminal lung cancer and had only a few months to live, attempted to conceal the death of her guest to avoid being implicated in it. She wanted to avoid spending her last months under investigation.

DI Graham is slightly less generous. "She opened the door on a crime scene, worked diligently to destroy the evidence, including the concealment of a body, contaminated the rest, and left it in a dusty attic for forty-odd years, telling no one."

He added, "She did not want her last weeks and months on earth spent embroiled in a police investigation, her reputation tarnished, and her liberty jeopardised. So, she sought to hide not just the circumstantial evidence but the body, with the help of her grandson Neville, only a young lad at the time.

"This was another case of an older person who should know better preying upon and manipulating a younger person to do their bidding at significant risk to themselves. Neville was a builder's apprentice on the island and, as part of this investigation, eventually faced charges relating to his involvement back when he was seventeen.

"At Miss Lovell's behest, he lugged the materials to mix concrete up the back stairs and built a brick coffin, filling it with concrete." Neville Williams disappeared to the mainland soon after the incident. Miss Lovell also departed Jersey soil a few weeks later.

The gravity of Miss Lovell's actions was not lost on DI Graham. "If Miss Lovell had been caught disposing of a body in this way, she would have been convicted and jailed until at least 1988. As it was, Charlie Cross was only discovered when the storm that lashed the Jersey coastline also damaged the attic in which he had been buried."

DI Graham understandably takes a very dim view of this action, not least because of the long-term consequences of the behaviour exhibited by those involved in this case. "Charlie Cross, Dylan Dillon, Emily Lovell, and Neville Williams all sought to evade justice. But in so doing, they provided cover for perhaps the most heinous people of all—the Parnabys. The brothers continued their activities, which, as is the nature of crime that is allowed to go unchecked, escalated in severity. Perhaps if any of the aforementioned had done the right thing at the time, a young security guard killed in a Parnaby-led armed robbery seventeen years later would still be alive."

Even now, many of us who live in Gorey find it hard to believe that our beloved, longtime local vicar once sought to end the life of another, harbouring so many secrets for so long. The question I was left with was: did he, Joshua Bright/Dylan Dillon, truly believe in the Word of God, or was it all an act to escape justice?

There was no outright confession. At least, not to this author. "I confessed before the court, just as I confess every day, in my own way, before my Maker. His Word transcends laws or prisons and frees every sinner," was his enigmatic reply.

Dylan Dillon received an early draft of this book and approved it without changes, except for saying one thing: "DI Graham coming to see me like that was God's gift. He offered me the chance to be honest, almost by luck, and thank God, I seized it. I accept my punishment and will repay my debt to society and God." Dillon faced a criminal trial, with his confession to DI Graham the crux of the case for conspiracy to murder Charlie Cross.

The future for Dillon is uncertain, but his forty-year investment in religious life gives Detective Inspector Graham some hope, and for Dillon, a chance at redemption. "Dillon has received a custodial sentence, and I've requested that his skills and experience be put to good use at whichever prisons he finds himself incarcerated. Most prison sentences are a complete waste. I hope that isn't the case here."

"He planned to take a man's life, then covered up his death—there can't be a 'but' after that," said Graham at the end of our interview. "He must pay the price. While he's doing that, he has the chance to help those who need it."

Dylan Dillon should see the sun outside that of a prison yard again in his lifetime. The two men who betrayed him and Charlie Cross, though, will never see it again. "Their prior cases and their involvement were revisited. With Dillon's help, additional evidence came to light, and Arthur and George Parnaby were reinterviewed."

With a small lift from my research and Dillon's recollections, a team of Metropolitan Police detectives, many of them former colleagues of Detective Inspector Graham, made progress on a dozen cases. Twenty-four arrests were made, and sixty-eight charges were submitted to the Crown Prosecution Service in London and Eastbourne as a result.

Inspector Graham had an interesting take. "Despite his apparent insignificance, Charlie Cross acted as the moral centre of the Parnabys' little gang. They didn't realise it, but Cross's reticence for violence and more serious crimes had prevented the gang from radicalising further. Without him, the Parnaby brothers, Dillon, and whoever else they initiated into their gang spiralled quickly into increasingly violent crimes and, eventually, the chaotic, deadly robbery in Shoreditch.

"The Parnabys cooperated well enough to avoid curtailment of their privileges inside prison and earn themselves some points with the powers that be in Holbrooke," Graham said. "But when convicted, their sentences were extended. In court, we showed they ordered the murder of Charlie Cross to protect their own hides. They incited Dylan Dillon to perform the hit. The Parnabys must share responsibility for conspiracy to murder." Dylan Dillon testified against the Parnabys in respect of charges related to this case and many others.

☯

Two elderly men, longing for freedom and family time, were denied both. And another, someone who served Gorey's Christian community and brought new life to St. Andrew's Church, will have to continue his work from within the ugly confines of a British prison.

And where does this leave Gorey as it recovers from a major investigation?

Proud of the constabulary, for certain.

Proud also of the unsung heroes, including the tireless Laura Beecham, whose research connected Dylan Dillon to St. Julian's seminary, where the guilty, terrified "Joshua Bright" found refuge.

Proud of Detective Inspector Graham, who I interviewed exclusively for this book and who put ego aside and spoke to me about what I knew to bring two old gangsters to justice.

Proud of my friends in the senior community, who are both a trove and a treasure.

Proud of Doctor Tomlinson and his assistant, Fiona Henson, who took no time at all to prove her worth. They undertook technological wizardry under what were sometimes the most unpleasant conditions.

Proud of Mrs. Taylor, owner of the White House Inn where the body of Charlie Cross lay undiscovered for so long, and who gave the police every assistance, all while her hotel seemed in danger of collapse.

Proud of Gorey for coming together in a spirit of light and honesty, for facing an awkward past, and never flinching from the truth.

☯

As a journalist, I am proud to have helped the investigation identify the "body in the block" and have a small hand in bringing to justice those who did harm.

I first interviewed the Parnaby brothers when I was merely doing research for this book, and they told me something I shared with the constabulary as soon as I was able. Little did I know at that interview that those words would later set off an investigation the likes of which Gorey has never known. From the lips of Arthur Parnaby and endorsed by his brother George: "You're from Jersey. We did a bit of work on Jersey. Sent one of our boys there in the early eighties looking for another one who'd done a runner with some loot. Dunno what happened. Never heard from either of them again. Good riddance. Useless eejits."

This is an edited extract from *Murder Island: The Mob on Jersey* by F. J. Solomon, to be published by Smithson Collingwood on 13 April.

EPILOGUE

Arthur and George Parnaby were convicted of conspiracy to murder and asked for nineteen other charges to be taken into consideration. Each had seven years added to his sentence. George's condition worsened, and he passed peacefully a month later. Arthur moved to a lower security prison where he grew prize runner beans and supplied the prison kitchen with potatoes. His penchant for yogurts with the fruit "in the corner" has not waned.

Dylan Dillon was sentenced to seven years in prison for conspiracy to murder, failing to report a body, and the perversion of the course of justice. While incarcerated in prison, he serves as a mentor and counsellor to the neighbouring young offenders' institution. He hopes to one day return to the clergy in some capacity.

Further DNA testing confirmed the familial relationship between **Charles Cross** and Dylan Dillon, although the exact nature of the connection is unclear. Charlie's remains were cremated and eventually claimed by his family. The Parnabys continue to maintain that Charlie Cross stole £100,000 from them. Yet, despite a forensic bank audit, no money was ever found.

Angela Dillon disappeared from the village of Leeslake. A man of Middle Eastern appearance now lives in the house with his teenage daughter. Ms. Dillon's half brother tried to contact her from prison, but his efforts were not reciprocated, and her whereabouts are not known.

. . .

In light of his age at the time, the influence of his grandmother, and his lack of a police record in the time since the offence, **Neville Williams** avoided prison and was given a two-year suspended sentence. He was required to work in the community with "at-risk" teenagers. He enjoyed the work so much that he studied for a degree in social work and was eventually employed full-time in the field.

Janet Northrop retired from her long-time position at the White House Inn but still visits often. It was determined that it was not in the public interest to bring charges against her, but she has arranged for a monthly subscription of Scilly Isles narcissi to be delivered to the White House Inn as a form of apology for bringing unwanted attention to the hotel.

Freddie Solomon's book, *Murder Island: The Mob on Jersey*, was serialised in the *Daily Mail* and hit the *Sunday Times* bestseller list in the United Kingdom. His publisher sent him on a promotional book tour, the pinnacle of which was being interviewed on the BBC's *The One Show*. Freddie was last seen in the Orkneys talking to a crowd of around twenty-five in the local library.

Jack whisked **Janice** off on honeymoon to a private island, where they relaxed on their own white sandy beach and slept in a luxury villa serviced by a dedicated butler. They kept the destination a secret until their return to avoid the possibility of an ambush by her mother.

Graham and Laura returned to the Bangkok Palace on several occasions, but Graham decided that one entry into the Order of the Perfumed Jewel was enough. At Laura's behest, he restricted his menu choices to pad Thai, tom yum soup, and other "cooler" dishes for the next several visits. The Palace staff were relieved to be able to leave the fire and chemical extinguishers in their usual spots.

Barnwell and Carmen continue their regular runs around the streets of Gorey and Sunday walks with **Melanie Howes and Vixen**. After a stilted, awkward conversation, Barnwell and Melanie agreed to leave the dogs at home one evening and go to the pictures together.

. . .

THE CASE OF THE BODY IN THE BLOCK

Marjorie Taylor was delighted when, on the Monday after the Wentworth's wedding, repairs to the roof of the White House Inn began. The hotel eventually reopened after six weeks of almost total closure, the repairs assisted by a vigorous, local GoFundMe campaign. Business is brisk, and the hotel is booked to near capacity for the next two months.

Fiona Henson continued to stay in the apartment on Elizabeth Island, although she found the crossing a bit choppy in bad weather. Much to **Marcus Tomlinson**'s chagrin, **Miranda Weiss** offered Fiona a job in Southampton, but she decided to stay on Jersey for at least another year.

Rosemary Harding returned to the mainland after her daughter's wedding, exhausted but satisfied. She wasted no time regaling at length the unfortunate members of her local Ramblers club with tales from the wedding. This ultimately spawned a rebellion by a few of her fellows who, on one weekend, met at a different car park from usual and did not tell her.

After their experience travelling to Jersey for Janice's wedding, her nan and step-grandad became members of the Youth Hostels Association. They became avid budget travellers, visiting countries across Europe and beyond. They harbour particularly happy memories of Jersey fish and chips.

Thank you for reading *The Case of the Body in the Block*! I will have a new case for Inspector Graham and his gang soon. To find out about new books, sign up for my newsletter: https://www.alisongolden.com.

If you love the Inspector Graham books, you'll also love the sweet, funny, *USA Today* bestselling Reverend Annabelle Dixon series featuring a madcap, lovable lady vicar whose passion for cake is matched only by her desire for justice. This omnibus edition contains the first four books in the series and is available for purchase from Amazon here. Like all my books, the omnibus is FREE in Kindle Unlimited.

And don't miss the Roxy Reinhardt mysteries. Will Roxy triumph after her life falls apart? She's sacked from her job, her boyfriend dumps her, she's out of money.

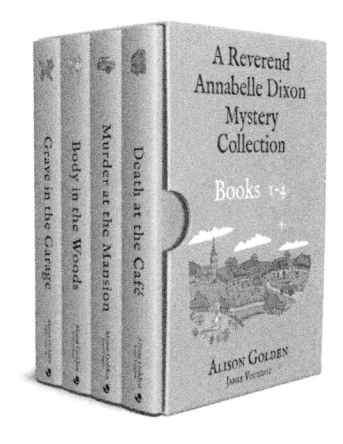

So, on a whim, she goes on the trip of a lifetime to New Orleans, There, she gets mixed up in a Mardi Gras murder. *Things were going to be fine. They were, weren't they?* Get your copy of the Roxy Reinhardt trilogy here. Also FREE in Kindle Unlimited.

If you're looking for something edgy and dangerous, root for Diana Hunter as she seeks justice after a devastating crime destroys her family. Follow her journey in this non-stop story of suspense and action by purchasing the omnibus edition featuring the first three books in the series. This omnibus is FREE in Kindle Unlimited.

Turn the page to read an excerpt from the first book in the Reverend Annabelle Dixon series, *Death at the Cafe* . . .

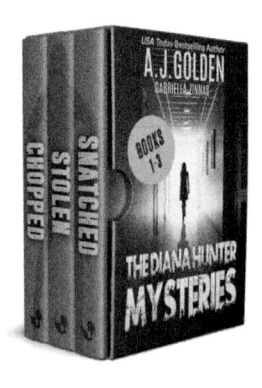

A Reverend Annabelle Dixon Mystery

death at the café

Alison Golden
Jamie Vougeot

DEATH AT THE CAFE
CHAPTER ONE

NOTHING BROUGHT REVEREND Annabelle closer to blasphemy than using the London public transport system during rush hour. Since being ordained and sent to St. Clement's church, an impressive, centuries-old building among the tower blocks and new builds of London's East End, Annabelle had been tested many times. She had come across virtually every sin known to man, counselled wayward youths, presided over family disputes, heard astonishingly sad tales from the homeless, and still retained her solid, optimistic dependability through it all. None of these challenges made her blood boil, and her round, soft face curl up into a mixture of disgust, frustration, and exasperation. Yet sitting on the number forty-three bus to Islington, as it moved along at a snail's pace, was almost enough to make her take her beloved Lord's name in vain.

On this occasion, she had nabbed her favourite seat: top deck, front left. It gave her a perfect view of the unique streets London offered and the even more varied types of people. Today, however, her viewpoint afforded her only a teeth-clenchingly irritating perspective of a traffic jam that extended as far as the eye could see down Upper Street.

"I know I shouldn't," she muttered on the relatively empty bus, "but if this doesn't deserve a cherry-topped cupcake, then I don't know what does."

The thought of rewarding her patience with what she loved almost as much as her vocation—cake—settled Annabelle's nerves for a full twenty minutes, during which the bus trundled in fits and starts along another half-mile stretch.

Assigning Annabelle, fresh from her days studying theology at Cambridge University, to the tough, inner-city borough of Hackney had presented her with what had been an almost literal baptism of fire. She had arrived in the summer, during a few weeks when the British sun combined with the squelching heat of a city constantly bustling and moving. It was a time of drinking and frivolity for some, heightened tension for others. A spell during which bored youths found their idle hands easily occupied with the devil's work. An interval when the good relax and the bad run riot.

Annabelle had grown up in East London, but for her first appointment as a vicar, her preference had been for a peaceful, rural village somewhere. A place in which she could indulge her love of nature, and conduct her Holy business in the gentle, caring manner she preferred. "Gentle" and "caring," however, were two words rarely used to describe London. Annabelle had mildly protested her city assignment. But after a long talk to the archbishop who explained the extreme shortage of candidates both capable and willing to take on the challenge of an inner-city church, she agreed to take up the position and set about her task with enthusiasm.

Father John Wilkins of neighbouring St. Leonard's church had been charged with easing Annabelle into the complex role. He had been a priest for over thirty years, and for the vast majority of that time had worked in London's poorest, toughest neighbourhoods. The Anglican Church was far less popular in London than it was in rural England, largely due to the city's disparate mix of peoples and creeds. Father John's congregation was mostly made up of especially devout immigrants from Africa and South America, many of whom were not even Anglican but simply lived nearby. The only time St. Leonard's had ever been full was on a particularly mild Christmas Eve.

But despite low attendance at services, London's churches played pivotal roles in their local communities. With plenty of people in need, they were hubs of charity and community support. Fundraising events, providing food and shelter for London's large homeless population, caring for the elderly, and engaging troubled youths were the churches' stock in trade, not to mention they provided both spiritual and emotional support for the many deaths and family tragedies that occurred.

The stress of it all had turned Father John's wiry beard a speckled grey, and though he knew his work was important and worthwhile, he had been pushed to breaking point on more than one occasion. Upon her arrival, he had taken one look at Annabelle's breezy manner and fresh-faced, open smile and assumed that her appointment was a case of negligence, desperation, or a sick prank.

"She's utterly delightful," Father John sighed on the phone to the archbishop, "and extremely nice. But 'delightful' and 'nice' are not what's required in a London church. This is a part of the world where faith is stretched to its very limits, where strong leadership goes further than gentle guidance. We struggle to capture people's attention, Archbishop, let alone their hearts. Our drug rehabilitation programs have more members than our congregations."

"Give her a chance, Father," the archbishop replied softly. "Don't underestimate her. She grew up in East London, you know."

"Well, I grew up in Westminster, but that doesn't mean I've had tea with the Queen!"

Merely a week into Annabelle's assignment, however, Father John's misgivings proved unfounded. Annabelle's bumbling, naïve manner was just that—a manner. Father John observed closely as Annabelle's strength, faith, and intelligence were consistently tested by the urban issues of her flock. He noted that she passed with flying colours.

Whether she was dealing with a hardened criminal fresh out of prison and already succumbing to old temptations, or a single mother of three struggling to find some composure and faith in the face of her daily troubles, Annabelle was always there to help. With good humour and optimism, she never turned down a request for assistance, no matter how large or small it was.

When Father John visited Annabelle a month after the start of her placement to check on a highly successful gardening project she had started for troubled youth, he shook his head in amazement "Is that Denton? By the rose bushes? I've been trying to get him to visit me for a year now, and all he does is ignore me. You should hear what he says when his parole officer suggests it," he said.

"Oh, Denton is wonderful!" Annabelle cried. "Fantastic with his hands. He has a devilish sense of humour—when it's properly directed. Did you know that he plays drums?"

"No, I didn't know that. He never told me," Father John said, giving Annabelle an appreciative smile. "I must say, Reverend, I seem to have misjudged you dreadfully. And I apologise."

"Oh, Father," Annabelle chuckled, "it's perfectly understandable. You have only the best interests of the community at heart. Let's leave judgement for Him and Him alone. The only thing we're meant to judge is cake contests, in my opinion. Mind those thorns, Denton! Roses tend to fight back if you treat them roughly!"

To get your copy of *Death at the Cafe* visit the link below:

https://www.alisongolden.com/death-at-the-cafe

"Your emails seem to come on days when I need to read them because they are so upbeat."
- Linda W -

For a limited time, you can get the prequels for each of my series - *Chaos in Cambridge, Buckeye Breakout, Hunted* (exclusively for subscribers - not available anywhere else), and *The Case of the Screaming Beauty* - plus updates about new releases, promotions, and other Insider exclusives, by signing up for my mailing list at:

https://www.alisongolden.com/graham

TAKE MY QUIZ

What kind of mystery reader are you? Take my thirty second quiz to find out!

https://www.alisongolden.com/quiz

BOOKS IN THE INSPECTOR DAVID GRAHAM MYSTERY SERIES

The Case of the Screaming Beauty (Prequel)
The Case of the Hidden Flame
The Case of the Fallen Hero
The Case of the Broken Doll
The Case of the Missing Letter
The Case of the Pretty Lady
The Case of the Forsaken Child
The Case of Sampson's Leap
The Case of the Uncommon Witness
The Case of the Body in the Block

COLLECTIONS

Books 1-4
The Case of the Screaming Beauty
The Case of the Hidden Flame
The Case of the Fallen Hero
The Case of the Broken Doll

Books 5-7
The Case of the Missing Letter
The Case of the Pretty Lady
The Case of the Forsaken Child

Books 8-10
The Case of the Missing Letter
The Case of the Pretty Lady
The Case of the Forsaken Child

ALSO BY ALISON GOLDEN

FEATURING REVEREND ANNABELLE DIXON
Chaos in Cambridge (Prequel)
Death at the Café
Murder at the Mansion
Body in the Woods
Grave in the Garage
Horror in the Highlands
Killer at the Cult
Fireworks in France
Witches at the Wedding

FEATURING ROXY REINHARDT
Buckeye Breakout (Prequel)
Mardi Gras Madness
New Orleans Nightmare
Louisiana Lies
Cajun Catastrophe

As A. J. Golden
FEATURING DIANA HUNTER
Hunted (Prequel)
Snatched
Stolen
Chopped
Exposed

All prequels are available as ebooks for free in my

Starter Library. Sign-up here: www.alisongolden.com.

ABOUT THE AUTHOR

Alison Golden is the *USA Today* bestselling author of the Inspector David Graham mysteries, a traditional British detective series, and two cozy mystery series featuring main characters Reverend Annabelle Dixon and Roxy Reinhardt. As A. J. Golden, she writes the Diana Hunter thriller series.

Alison was raised in Bedfordshire, England. Her aim is to write stories that are designed to entertain, amuse, and calm. Her approach is to combine creative ideas with excellent writing and edit, edit, edit. Alison's mission is simple: To write excellent books that have readers clamouring for more.

Alison is based in the San Francisco Bay Area with her husband and twin sons. She splits her time between London and San Francisco.

For up-to-date promotions and release dates of upcoming books, sign up for the latest news here: https://www.alisongolden.com/graham.

For more information:
www.alisongolden.com
alison@alisongolden.com

facebook.com/alisongolden.books

THANK YOU

Thank you for taking the time to read books 5 through 7 in the Inspector Graham series. If you enjoyed them, please consider telling your friends or posting a short review. Word of mouth is an author's best friend and very much appreciated.

Thank you,

Printed in Great Britain
by Amazon